SOMETHING MORE SINISTER

by

BEN GEER

United Kingdom

This first edition published in 1998
by Access Marketing & Publishing.

Typeset by Typerite SA.

Printed and bound by Cox & Wyman Ltd., Reading, United Kingdom.

ISBN 0 9531568 0 X

A CIP catalogue record for this book
is available from the British Library.

This novel is dedicated to Hermann.

Southern Africa 1972

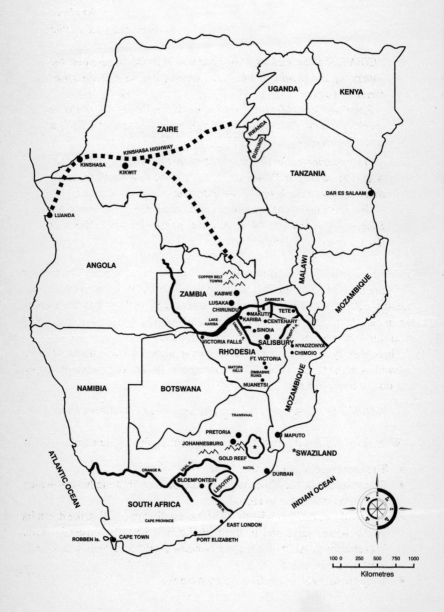

INTRODUCTION

The Daily Echo
England
Friday 26 May 1995

SCIENTISTS are making slow progress in trying to pinpoint the source of the deadly Ebola virus among animals in the rain-forest of Zaire.

They are considering asking the US military for help in tracking down the cause of the epidemic which has killed at least 108 people.

'The animal collection has not been that successful so far,' Nigerian virologist Professor .... said in Kikwit, the town that has borne the brunt of the outbreak.

'We are looking at bringing a team from the US Centres for Diseases Control (CDC) in Atlanta, possibly with soldiers of the US army, to collect animals.'

You might well ask what is remarkable about this news report. The answer is frightening in its simplicity. It is not exceptional. Reports like these are coming out of Africa with alarming frequency. Something has been going on in Southern Africa since the 1960s and what is even more disturbing than this—the reports are not confined to *Ebola.*

Three deadly viruses are currently laying waste to large tracts of land. Devoid of humans, the villages are now empty, the entire inhabitants wiped out due to these viruses:

MARBURG – EBOLA – HIV (the Human Immunodeficiency Virus).

What does this deadly triad have in common? In fact, quite a lot!

- They emerged about the same time.
- Scientists are baffled because they cannot even find the hosts—which all viruses must have to reproduce.
- They kill—and kill efficiently. Whereas the first two will strike down its victim within days and in the most horrific way, *HIV* usually leads irreversibly to AIDS—*Acquired Immune Deficiency Syndrome*—and, most certainly, death.
- They are all fatal—there is no known cure!

Like all viruses *HIV* is a parasite—requiring a host cell to replicate itself. But whereas the outside protein coating of a virus tends to change every so often producing a new strain, such as the *influenza* virus—*HIV* is different. It is very unstable in that it alters rapidly, so much so that hundreds of variations are found within the same person. The problem lies with the fact that every time the 'coating' changes, a new antibody must be generated in the blood in order to identify the new 'coating' and fight it.

If that is not bad enough, *HIV* is immune to all human antibodies. Therefore it is more difficult, if not impossible, to cure the related illnesses caused by *HIV*. This ability to mutate so quickly has given rise to speculation that its genetic structure has been in some way altered.

Since this killer emerged, the question remains: is it something which was hitherto unknown in humans, or a harmless virus that was manipulated by man?

Genetics has raced ahead rapidly, superseding even space exploration—making those efforts seem not far removed from Galileo's. Engineered plants, animals and even medicine affect our daily lives and there can be little doubt, that in the future, our descendants will be the results of gene manipulation. Today, do we really have to ask if the production or manipulation of a few viruses is possible?

Is it enough to speculate whether AIDS could occur due to natural possibilities, or should we speculate further and consider the predisposing factors that would have to have been present, if we wish to know how, when and why AIDS may have been created?

Something had to be happening out there. Research that was not in the public domain; combined with necessary medical expertise and resources. There would have to be a plausible biological pathway for the development of *HIV*, and establish what purpose these 'engineered' viruses might serve.

They may well be an array of perfect invisible and invincible weapons!

While today many nations could develop germ warfare weapons, at the time AIDS first appeared, relatively few had this capability. To contemplate such a weapon in itself is such madness, that it must be linked to a strong case of 'justification'. However warped the thinking, it must be then deployed without fear of retaliation. This seems to exclude the likelihood of involvement by one of the major powers. And by their exclusion—this would point to the possibility of some other likely candidate.

Immediately questions arise. What conditions prevailed that would have induced anyone to deploy these weapons? When considering the psychological profile of such people, it is necessary to ask who, if anyone, had such a perverse sense of 'justice' that, given the opportunity, they would be so heinous as to resort to these extremely violent measures to uphold their fanatical aims?

Finally, who, if anyone, was responsible for AIDS?

- Who would have had some kind of involvement in associated medical or genetic research, at the time of the sudden emergence of AIDS in the mid-nineteen sixties?
- Who would have had the resources and the biological expertise to create these terrible viruses?
- Who would have had sufficient motive to use biological weapons, and against whom?
- Who would have been so totally devoid of moral conscience to have used such a weapon?
- Where could it have been deployed—taking the emergence of the AIDS time-scale into account?

Whoever engineered these viruses clearly would not want to publicise the fact; instead it would remain one of their darkest secrets. Therefore, the use of biological weapons must be seen, at best, against any supportable evidence, circumstantial or otherwise.

For instance, it has been suggested that AIDS may have been developed by the Americans, Russians or Chinese. Here, an immediate dilemma is apparent. Who could any of them have used it against? Given the need for a selective target, its isolation for fear of self-contamination, and the potential risk of spreading disease—this seems unlikely. In addition, the perpetrator would have to be under some dire threat, prepared to run the risk of media exposure and way beyond the pale of acceptable behaviour or rational thought.

This work of fiction is set against this background.

Those sections of the novel based on documented facts in the public record, or historical and political events, are indicated throughout by * asterisks. These are shown at the end of the relevant passages, to include the preceding indented text or (in the absence of an indent) preceding paragraph. These are for the reader who may wish to know where fact and fiction meet.

Apart from the heads of state and other political figures referred to in this novel, the characters are entirely fictitious and are not based on real persons, living or dead. However, many events which have a factual basis are utilised. At the beginning and the end of part two, a brief section on the political history of Southern Africa appears (under the heading African Affairs). This should provide the reader with a clearer picture of what really happened, give a subjective idea of the mood of the people, and aid understanding as to how and why these events may have come about.

The contents herein do not, in any way, demonstrate that the various viruses and pathogens mentioned originated in the manner described, or that the views expressed by named politicians are historically accurate.

Most pertinent in the context of this novel, which is about RACISM and merely speculates about AIDS, it is a condemnation of the terrible misuse of power by White regimes in Southern Africa. It considers what might have happened or what may indeed lie behind certain public announcements and certain actions undertaken by those in authority.

The reader is left to deliberate over these possibilities.

oOo

Please note that a list of acronyms, glossary of terms and the hypothetical biological pathways mentioned in this novel are included as appendices.

The quotations that appear at the beginning of the chapters are included merely to indicate the leanings of, and provide an insight into, several political figures of that time.

THE RESEARCH

Cape Town, South Africa

1971

CHAPTER 1

Addressing the OAU: "...our situation [Afro-Americans] is as much a violation of the Nations Human rights Charter as the situation in South Africa or Angola."

Malcolm X
Black Nationalist-Muslim leader, 1964
Assassinated in 1965

Terrified, Carla clung desperately to the rock-face, helpless; her wide-eyed stare riveted on the bodies of her two climbing companions cartwheeling into the abyss. Surging winds off the Atlantic, now channelled through the breach at False Bay, tugged fiercely at her clothes. With enormous force the gale had enveloped the Cape Peninsula mountains, and a clawing, violent gust had torn them away from the sandstone cliffs, snatching away their screams of terror. Then suddenly they were gone.

An inquest returned a verdict of accidental death—the latest victims on the rugged heights of Table Mountain, the uppermost point in the range.

o0o

At the base of Table Mountain lies Cape Town, home to the Groote Schuur Hospital which became assured of a place in history when, in December 1967, the South African surgeon, Dr Christiaan Barnard astounded the world by pioneering human heart transplant surgery. Fifty-three-year old Louis Washkansky's diseased heart was replaced with that of twenty-five-year old road accident victim Denise Darvall. Washkansky survived with his new heart for eighteen days before his body's natural defence system finally rejected it. The associated problems of donor tissue rejection, due to the body's immune system, had yet to be overcome. Four years after the first heart transplant, Christiaan Barnard's profile was still flying high as he drove flamboyantly in his golden Mercedes from transplants to press conferences. The successful operations thwarted only by the omnipresent rejection problem.*

o0o

20 January 1971

Sometime before the tragic incident on Table Mountain, one mile away from the Groote Schuur Hospital at the nearby Mueller Research Laboratories, Professor Tinus Mueller stood at the window gazing out at a spectacular view. Clouds had spread neatly over the mountain's distinctive flat summit before cascading over the edge, then caught in a down draught they met the warmer air below and disappeared, creating a phenomenon known as the 'tablecloth'.

The southeaster, laden with moisture from the sea, was sweeping through the region again with such intensity that pollutants were being swept away, leaving behind one of the healthiest and cleanest environments of any city in the world. The wind, like the cloud, acquired its name over the years from the locals to become known as 'The Cape Doctor'. Professor Mueller smiled, remembering that because of his reputation for sweeping change and innovative ideas in microbiology, he also had acquired the nickname 'Cape Doctor'. It did not concern him that he had heard, more than once, less adventurous peers in his field maintain it was necessary to be more prudent than the Cape Doctor in their line of work.

His aim was to build a small team of the most brilliant graduates from South Africa's universities, gathering the finest into his fold with the promise of worldwide recognition such as that bestowed on Professor Barnard. That acclaim was not the only carrot the five selected graduates were offered. The added attractions of working for the most prestigious private laboratories in Cape Town, a better salary than could be afforded elsewhere and an opportunity to advance, almost guaranteed their services.

Tinus Mueller had allowed his new employees into the laboratories to familiarise themselves with their new environment. It was widely assumed—not least because Tinus hinted at it—that the forthcoming projects were concerned with the problem of transplanted organ rejection. The team, after a few days, had become restless, eager to get on with the work in prospect. Finally, Tinus had called them together and now he waited for their arrival in the conference room to apprise them of the aims of his laboratories.

Tinus, still taking in the view, nevertheless grew impatient and turned his gaze from the mountain to look at his watch just as the door opened.

He glanced fleetingly over his shoulder, observing his protégés as they entered. All of whom were enthusiastic and capable—they would not have been there otherwise—but every group produces its leaders and in the coming weeks he would need to know on whom he could rely, and trust with responsibility, and more importantly, whom he could not.

He waited until they were seated. Then he moved from the window to face his new team—one seat remained empty!

At that moment, Michael Bernstein was putting his aged metallic-grey MGA through its paces. It had been a brilliant weekend but as he negotiated a corner and pulled the steering-wheel hard right, his shoulder ached dully; he was unsure whether it had been from the 'friendly' rugby match that Saturday, or a result of the rowdy drinking binge after the game. He had spent a quiet Sunday tanning on Muizenberg beach, trying to survive the day. Still, this morning he had overslept and was running late.

Michael had a zest for life and enjoyed living on the edge. The traffic-lights ahead changed to red. 'Damn,' he cursed, applying the brakes and glancing at the clock. He could still make it in time for the meeting—if he hurried.

The traffic-lights remained red. 'Come on, come on.' He checked twice. There was no crossing traffic so he spiritedly engaged first gear and shot forward to the blare of a horn from the stationary vehicle behind. As the open sports car pulled away—his dark-brown hair swept back giving him a boyish, if not a rakish look—he smiled generously into the rear-view mirror at the other driver.

This was only his second week in the job and he needed to give a good impression. He put his foot down further on the accelerator. Inwardly he was content, the future looked bright and he had every reason to be pleased. Michael had achieved his first goal and was pursuing his objectives with great purpose. He had everything to live for.

'Good morning, ladies and gentlemen...' The rasping South African accent was slightly tinged in places with guttural German pronunciations so that it seemed at odds with the genial words. Introductions over, Tinus dealt first with mundane matters of administration, then fire evacuation procedures. The team turned to look where he was pointing '...in emergencies you will leave by these exits...'

The door burst open and Michael rushed in.

'Morning Professor. Sorry, I was caught in traffic.'

'Spare us the details, Bernstein, and quietly take a seat.' He appeared irritated, as the others laughed, watching Michael head for the vacant chair.

Michael, mildly embarrassed, his eyes bright with the carefree attitude he normally approached life with, glanced at the colleague next to him and smiled engagingly—he had spoken fleetingly to Carla in the past few days.

'Nice!' she thought, noticing his prominent eyebrows and sharp nose. 'But his clothes!' Where everybody else wore suits he had arrived attired in an open-necked shirt and casual trousers. Dressed like that he wasn't going to endear himself to the professor, or for that matter to her, she decided, and turned away.

'Settle down. Now if I can proceed...' Tinus reached the point they were waiting for.

'So! Why have I assembled, in these laboratories, some of the best young minds that South Africa has to offer? Because we have important work to do here. I expect you all to go on and attain your PhDs and these laboratories will assist you greatly in this respect.' He spoke as an actor delivering a monologue, punctuating his delivery, looking at each of them in turn, continuing only when certain that he had their undivided attention.

'We are all aware of the body's capacity to look after itself—at least I hope we are.' He waited.

His audience fidgeted, unsure if this was meant to be humorous or whether they should acknowledge his statement, or it might have been another of his characteristic pauses.

He continued unabashed. 'All transplanted tissue is attacked by the immune system in order to destroy the foreign material and then graft rejection takes place. So much for basic immunology, but this is most unsatisfactory, of course, from the point of view of the recipient.'

He judged his timing correctly.

'What I am talking about, as you all know, ladies and gentlemen—is heart transplants.'

At last! They were getting down to the nuts and bolts, Michael thought.

Tinus disclosed his plans. 'There are two ways in which we can enhance survival for the heart transplant patient. Firstly, with improved immuno-suppressants to block this rejection mechanism. Secondly, by finding new drugs that will cause a reduction in the opportunistic infections that prove to be life threatening post-operatively.'

Professor Tinus Mueller scanned the faces before him and was not disappointed to see them elated at the prospect of involvement in this exciting new area of research, brought to the attention of the world so recently as a result of successful heart transplants.

Pleased with their enthusiasm, he continued. 'While another group will work on more conventional research in immunology and genetics, initially you five will undertake, shall we say, more innovative tasks. I have some interesting concepts concerning some experimental immunosuppressant drugs,' he went on, 'and someone will be working in that area. Another, will carry out transplants and study the body's defences firsthand. A few of you will deal specifically with the rapidly growing problem: the emergence of drug-resistant micro-organisms to known antibiotics. Or, if you prefer, the study of pathogens developing resistance to antibiotics and other chemical agents, used successfully in the past to treat these infections. I think you will agree that there is plenty of variety here for us to get our teeth into, ja?'

There were quiet sounds of agreement from his audience.

Tinus speculated on the future, attempting to emphasise the importance of their research. 'Imagine if one day we could achieve compatibility between the recipient's body and the donor organ by simply integrating some DNA—the coded message of life—from a recipient's cells into the DNA of the donor's cells. And in so doing, this would mean that when the transplanted organ is introduced, the recipient's defence system would recognise the organ as non-invasive and therefore would not attack and reject it.' He looked around calculatingly. The work to be undertaken was contracted by the transplant team at Groote Schuur, and gratified, he saw in this group a willingness to do whatever was necessary for a share of the glory. 'In effect, we would have deceived the immune system. That is the theory and, like most theories, it sounds simple and straightforward. In practice, these processes take time and effort, all of it painstaking...'

Considering the published work of US scientists, one of the researchers, only half concentrating as his mind raced to meet the challenge, voiced a concern. He interrupted the Professor in mid-flow.

'Yes, but how can this benefit heart transplant patients? Organs are found at such short notice—surely Chris Barnard's group would need to achieve compatibility immediately?'

Professor Mueller gave him a withering look over the top of his glasses. They were all young and inexperienced. He had wanted PhD graduates, but his financial backer had been insistent he make do on the budget provided, and much to his irritation one of the backer's offspring had been foisted upon him as part of the deal. And because of the particular association with his backer, although far from happy, he had been unable to refuse.

'Ach...Bernstein!' Though his voice was outwardly pleasant, his steel grey eyes seemed to pierce right through his new researcher as they stared unblinkingly at him. He had been warned about Michael's outbursts, but his abilities were essential for the project. An enquiring mind it might be, but already Michael was becoming over-confident. This one he would have to hold on a very tight leash, he thought with certainty.

'Er...yes, sir.' Michael Bernstein suddenly felt uncomfortable as his throat tightened. During the past few days he had become familiar with the Professor's intellectual achievements, but it had not been long before he discovered they had little in common on a personal level. Already he had felt a tension between them. The fifty-six-year old Professor was of German extraction and a conservative of the old school. Michael on the other hand had youth, a liberal attitude to daily life, politics—and he was Jewish. It would have been more surprising if they had hit it off.

'Well, Bernstein. You and I will discuss the possibilities at greater length when we are finished here,' he said sharply.

'Yes, Professor, sorry,' Michael apologised. The Professor had used few words, yet his expression conveyed the message—Michael felt he had been put in his place.

Without further interruptions from the assembly, Professor Mueller continued, 'It was merely an analogy that I gave,' he continued to stare at Michael, 'I could name several reasons why this could not work, but mainly because it would be impossible to target every relevant gene.'

He felt Michael had got the message, and he pressed on.

'The implications of our research will have profound effects on humanity in the future. I am sure you are all aware that certain religious groups, until recently, believed the heart was the seat of the human soul. Well, Professor Barnard has demonstrated what we scientists always knew—that it is simply a very efficient pump. Genetics and transplants are the wave of a new and exciting future in which I believe anything will be possible.' He stunned his audience with examples of the infinite theoretical possibilities of genetic mutations that he visualised in the years ahead.

In the office Michael stood uneasily before the seated Professor, feeling that maybe he had spoken out of turn. He had always done so: at school and university, whether it concerned his politics or a shouted retort to a player who had fumbled a ball on the rugby field, his mouth had often landed him in trouble. The Professor was reading the top page of a file on his desk and looked, at first glance, a little effeminate. He was short with a compact body, and his habit of peering over gold-rimmed half-moon spectacles on the end of his nose forced him to carry his head down, displaying a shiny pink pate surrounded by closely cropped, greying hair. Then Tinus stared up at him with expressionless eyes and all thoughts of effeminacy were quickly dispelled.

'Now, Mr Bernstein,' the Professor began, his tone cool, 'I see from these university reports that you have achieved outstanding successes in everything you have set your mind to.' Although the impudence of this young man's outburst had annoyed him at the time, the interruption to the momentum and flow of his address had indicated that this employee was ahead of his colleagues and he respected him for that. Michael's achievements were not limited to his academic abilities; while microbiology remained his forte, his accomplishments included the captaincy of both the rugby and cricket teams and a successful term as a free-style swimmer.

Tinus did not wait for a response. 'It is healthy for an inquisitive young mind to question new ideas. But I want you to understand that in these laboratories I expect all my researchers to adhere to the protocols and work hard at the tasks to which they are assigned. I will expect you to provide the results I know can be achieved.'

The 'without question' was left unsaid. Michael knew that it was implied.

18

Tinus had picked the group's natural leader and was outlining the régime. 'There is a permanent place for you here if you want it. Do you want it, Mr Bernstein?'

The Mueller Laboratories were the finest private laboratories in Cape Town, probably in the whole of Africa. It would be folly to turn down an opportunity here. The mere inclusion of the name on his résumé would be enough to open doors, and even if his stay was only temporary it would still be worth it. He would try to get on with Tinus Mueller. The nature of the research was such that they would probably see one another infrequently anyway.

'Yes, sir, I want it.'

'Good. Now let me remove a popular misconception. While some of the work we do here is under contract to both Groote Berg, and Groote Schuur Hospitals—Chris' group as you put it—by no means is all of it confined to Professor Barnard's research. Our efforts may well prove beneficial to him, if he had time to notice,' Tinus hesitated, 'but this is not the only reason for the research, though I don't intend to trouble you with the politics of the business. It's results that I want. It may surprise you to know that I have chosen you to lead the project from the antibiotic-resistance point of view. I firmly believe it is in this area of research that these laboratories will produce the biggest impact.'

In view of the personal tension between them, Michael was dumbfounded that he had been singled out to lead this project. All he managed to get out was a simple 'Thank you.'

'You may have the assistance of others if you need it, but otherwise they will be engaged in more orthodox approaches to these problems. I expect all areas of research will overlap from time to time, so you will work together on occasions. Take this.'

Professor Mueller pushed a large ring-binder across the desk. 'Here is a summary of my requirements, together with the results of some work I have already done. It is by no means complete. You have much to do, and—consult with me on these issues when you need to.'

A quick flick through the file showed that everything was meticulously set out in indexed sections. Tinus Mueller had been very thorough.

'Thank you, Professor. I appreciate your confidence in me.' Realising it was time to quit while he was ahead, he started for the door. 'I'll get onto it immediately,' he said over his shoulder.

'Not so fast.' Tinus held up his finger staying Michael's exit. 'I have organised some events for this weekend before you all get down to work.'

Michael stared at him questioningly.

'The arrangement is for us all to share some outdoor pursuits in order to bond our new group together—at the Laboratories expense, of course,' he smiled wryly. 'Copy this and pass it to the others.'

He handed Michael a schedule detailing various adventure activities for the forthcoming weekend in the countryside with the express purpose of 'getting away from it all' before 'getting stuck in on your return.' Michael had the impression that there was no choice in the matter and was beginning to wonder what sort of man he was working for.

On his way out, Professor Mueller cloaked him in the warmest of fatherly smiles so that Michael inwardly apologised for the poor impression he must have given earlier. He had let himself down. 'For Christ's sake we haven't even started yet and already I'm up before the beak,' he thought. Michael made a note to be more circumspect in judging people so quickly in future.

During their adventure break Professor Tinus Mueller hoped to surprise his young assistants with a display of strength, stamina and agility belying his appearance. He was especially keen to demonstrate these attributes on the sheer cliffs of Table Mountain.

'It is over a thousand metres high,' Tinus told them as their four-wheel drive bounced over the foothills, 'and scalable by near on three hundred separate routes to the summit. I have chosen an interesting climb that you amateurs should find testing. It is not particularly dangerous but neither is it a stroll in the park, so treat it with respect.'

There was nervous laughter in response. He was clearly passionate about the sport, despite his age.

Shortly after setting out from their vehicle, they followed the path to the start of their chosen route, each contemplating the climb, when Michael suddenly broke the silence.

'Blast!' he cursed, after stumbling heavily on a boulder. 'That bloody hurt...I think I've twisted it,' looking dispiritedly at his ankle.

Tinus was concerned and decided that his intended climbing partner, Carla Boshoff, escort Michael back to the vehicle with their gear. She was displeased to be denied the climb and made certain he knew how she felt. With bad grace, Carla drove them to the cable-car station at Kloof Nek.

While the climbers were bonding as a team on the cliff face, Michael and Carla were left to make their acquaintance on the saddle of land between Signal Hill and Table Mountain, where the cable-car would return with their companions much later in the afternoon.

Sensing her mood, Michael struck up a cautious conversation. In and around the laboratories Carla had appeared serious and aloof in her white lab-coat and spectacles, her blonde hair swept up into a loose bun. He had barely paid any attention to her until now. Her clear green eyes which, without her glasses, were large and bright, interested him. Away from the confines of the workplace she had let her hair down to hang over her shoulders and the sun caught and illuminated it like thousands of strands of gold thread. Despite her mood, she smiled easily, a radiant smile of even white teeth and soft full lips with a slight dimple on her left cheek. Her skin was smooth and lightly tanned, her figure petite.

With time to kill, they sat chatting affably until it became too hot in the vehicle and they climbed out to sit in the shade of the trees.

At length, Michael stood to stretch his legs. 'Would you like to stroll about the foothills...something for us to do?' he asked and was surprised when she readily agreed. Testing his foot, he hobbled behind her, chivalrous as African tribesmen who walk behind their womenfolk in the bush to protect them from a stalking attack by a predator. Watching her hips sway and her shorts strain, his preoccupation was a gratifying experience if a little precarious, causing him to swear occasionally as he stumbled on unnoticed rocks. Despite her displeasure of losing out on the climb, he received sympathetic glances from Carla for his injured ankle.

During the next few hours, Michael discovered that Carla was twenty-two years old—an Afrikaans-speaking graduate from Stellenbosch University. Yet there was no trace of any guttural inflection in her accent, so common among Afrikaners. Instead it was softer and more rounded. To his ear, her second language—English—was without blemish.

'I'm proud of my ancestry. My papa,' she told him, 'is a descendant of the first Dutch settlers who landed here with Jan van Riebeeck and colonised the Cape Peninsula way back in 1652....' She revealed her father, Andries Boshoff was one of a long line of Boshoffs to head the family's multi-million rand wine-grower's business from the famous Boshoff estate in the Groote Drakenstein Valley, east of Stellenbosch. Her ancestors had stayed behind to consolidate their fortunes while others, rebelling against their new British masters, had distanced themselves from the Cape of Good Hope by undertaking the Great Trek north and east to colonise the vast interior of Southern Africa.

Michael reciprocated, telling her of his upbringing by his Black nanny. 'Sophie looked after us after my mother died giving birth to me....'

By the way he broke off direct eye contact to stare at the ground as he spoke, she sensed he carried the guilt of her death. He told her of his father, who subsequently passed away, and of the family business he left to his two sons, which Michael preferred to leave in the hands of his elder brother, Aaron, so he could pursue his chosen profession.

They were at ease with one another and, time passed surprisingly quickly while they talked. Michael told her of his sporting days, hoping to impress her with stories of his achievements, but as they negotiated an outcrop of rocks, moving from one to another in a series of small hops, it suddenly dawned on Carla that there was nothing at all wrong with Michael's ankle.

21

She felt intensely irritated. Had he invented his sprain simply to part her from the rest of the team?

She stopped abruptly and rounded on her unsuspecting colleague. 'There isn't anything wrong with your damn foot!'

'Yes there is,' he said wincing.

She continued to glare at him, annoyed, causing him to glance at his boot.

'Okay, okay,' he said, holding up his hands in mock surrender. 'You win.' He paused briefly, tipping his head back slowly, his eyes following the cliff face from its foot to the summit and he swallowed hard. 'I can't climb that. I'd rather take on the Springboks than that mountain.'

Carla merely cocked her head slightly, her expression unchanged.

'I can't explain it and I'm sorry, but...'

Still she didn't respond.

'I get vertigo—and then some!' He stole another glance at the sheer rock face. 'If I find myself anywhere I can fall from,' his throat was beginning to dry at the mere thought of it, 'I freeze. There's no way I could get ten metres up that mountain.' He worked some moisture into his mouth. 'I'm sorry if I spoiled it for you.' The confession over, he looked directly into Carla's eyes, holding his breath while he waited for a torrent of abuse he was sure would follow.

She looked him up and down as if seeing him for the first time. He was at least six feet tall and put together as solidly as the boulder on which he stood. His exposed limbs were bronzed by the African sun and his suede desert boots were well-worn and dusty from frequent outdoor use. Wide shoulders stretched the short-sleeved shirt across his chest. She thought he was actually rather handsome. Her eyes lingered on his face a little longer as she considered his disclosure, finally deciding he had an honest look about him. 'Fear is not reserved for the weak and feeble,' she thought and her expression softened.

'You poor sod,' she said at last with genuine sympathy.

Michael exhaled gratefully and sat down.

She came back to sit beside him on the boulder. 'I don't have such a fear, as far as I know, but I do have an idea of what it's like. My little sis' has a dread of spiders,' she laughed as she recalled an incident in her childhood. 'Louise only has to see a picture of a spider and she jumps back as if she's had an electric shock.'

They sat for a while in silence eating their packed lunches, enjoying the splendour of the view. From their vantage point they could see the old town in the foreground, contrasting dramatically with the backdrop of skyscrapers built on the foreshore reclaimed from the sea. Carla tried to identify the building where her father had a suite of offices, while Michael's attention focused on a speck out to sea—Robben Island.

He speculated idly on the penal colony's inhabitants, incarcerated for their political beliefs, having dared to challenge the Government. Then, not wanting to spoil the moment, he pushed thoughts of Nelson Mandela, Walter Sisulu and the other political prisoners from his mind, as he focused on Signal Hill—Robben Island now forgotten in the shimmering haze of the distant seascape. Fleetingly, he considered asking Carla if she would like to take the scenic drive to the top, but it was a renowned spot for courting couples so he dismissed the idea.

They talked until the daylight began to fade, taking with it the fierce heat.

Carla broke the spell she was unintentionally casting on him. 'Time we were making a move,' she said.

'Sounds like fun. What did you have in mind?'

'Come on, tough guy, better get back to the cable-car station. It strikes me the Cape Doctor isn't the type of man to be kept waiting.'

'Got you calling him that now, has he?' Michael looked at his watch and reluctantly agreed. The mood was gone and they walked slowly to the meeting point without further conversation.

The cable-car docked as they approached—the passengers alighted. Tinus, having changed from his climbing boots into socks and sandals once more, emerged leading a weary team.

'Better put on a show,' Carla said as their colleagues came towards them. Michael gave her a blank look. 'Your ankle,' she reminded him. 'You're supposed to be an invalid!'

'Hell, I forgot!' he exclaimed, suddenly developing an exaggerated limp.

She raised her eyes skywards. 'God help us,' her voice conveyed despair. 'Your other leg.'

Research into antibiotic-resistance was exacting and Michael threw himself into his first task, reading the reports of the Professor's work. In doing so he gained further respect for Tinus Mueller—it was truly pioneering, his style exciting and his ideas revolutionary. If the project led to the results outlined under 'Purpose' in his report, Michael would certainly find himself receiving worldwide acclaim as a leading member of the research team.

He began by honing the Professor's theories, using as his starting point the recent emergence of this latest medical phenomenon—where pathogens had become resistant to the drugs previously used successfully against them—was precisely the problem he sought to resolve: to knock out the opportunistic infections which presented a major secondary risk to heart transplant patients post-operatively.

Recent research from abroad indicated that, within the membrane wall of a *pathogen*, apart from its chromosome, there were other independent structures—plasmids. They had developed an antibiotic-resistant gene, capable of transferring this undesirable characteristic from one *pathogen* to another of the same species and then, at times, between different species. Michael's excitement for the project was derived from the lack of previous research in this area. Professor Mueller had recently reminded them that each cell in the human body has forty-six chromosomes, each one of which has, on average, two thousand genes.*

Michael's strategy was straightforward. He would find antibiotics and chemical agents that would combat the errant gene. Having discussed his proposal in detail, he walked out of Tinus' office with the consent he sort for tests, and with the feeling that he had won the respect of his employer.

Following Tinus Mueller's example, he made thorough notes, documenting and indexing the details in the same manner. The months passed and he built on the original report until it overflowed into two, then three, large meticulously maintained ring-binders. The work was exacting but he was quick and persevered with enthusiasm, usually working more than twelve hours a day.

He made excuses periodically to seek Carla's collaboration.

Since returning to the laboratory environment from their outdoor encounter at the foot of Table Mountain, she had resumed an air of detachment from her colleagues. Back had come the spectacles and her hair was swept up once more. The white laboratory coat, a fraction too large for her small frame, hung shapelessly from her shoulders and the long sleeves were rolled up at the cuffs. She pursued her own researches diligently, this consuming most of her time.

Now that Michael knew something of the girl beneath that exterior, he felt she had softened a little towards him. She was more than willing to assist him, more so than she was with any of the others, he thought. There were other things he noticed too and was pleasantly surprised when she not only accepted, but appeared to enjoy his advances.

Carla was examining a slide under the microscope. 'Take a look at this and see if it confirms my findings,' she invited.

He deliberately crowded her, enjoying the closeness and the discreet scent of her perfume. He fully expected a rebuff for such blatant behaviour. Standing up to let him take the seat, she confused him by barely giving him enough room. He had felt her body beneath the loose coat against his arm and lingered as long as he dared, before sitting and pressing his eye to the lens.

'Yes, I'd go along with this...' seeing nothing of the slide beneath.

For her part, Carla viewed Michael's forwardness with amusement, although admittedly she was pleased by the attention. She stared at his broad shoulders while he was bent, peering into the microscope.

Women would kill for his thick lustrous hair, she decided, finding pleasurable the almost voyeuristic sight, at such close quarters, of his hair neatly cut short at the nape of his neck. Her eyes travelled over his tanned muscular arms in stark contrast to the white coat which she found strangely enticing. He smelt clean, and faintly of cologne...

He turned suddenly from the microscope to face her and she smiled mischievously. At that moment they knew their relationship had changed. Thereafter they regularly made time for one another for lunch in the canteen, or assisting in the other's research and dated after hours.

On reflection it surprised him for, as a Jew, he would not normally be accepted so easily by an Afrikaner. He knew that during the war the sympathies of many Afrikaners had lain with the Axis powers and particularly the Nazi's anti-Semitic policies.

Michael found that Carla took a different view of politics from most Afrikaners, and their relationship flourished. Rather, she was rebelling against the strict lifestyle and Nationalist viewpoint her father had tried to impose on her. Michael, sensitive to her stance, was concerned that she might be nurturing their friendship simply to use him as a symbol of that rebellion. However, as time went by he became more sure of her, finding that he was worrying needlessly. Carla's affection was genuine.

Carla's job was just as demanding as Michael's. Her research revolved around the experimental immunosuppressants.

Approaching the rejection problem from another angle, namely, the body's natural defence mechanism, she was frustrated by what she found. While the immune system beneficially staved off infection, at the same time it produced antibodies in order to destroy invasive heart tissue. Then the administration of immunosuppressants, necessary to stop organ rejection, created other problems, by allowing opportunistic infections, such as pneumonia, to invade, hence contributing to a general decline in the patient's health. Furthermore, the side-effects from the drugs used to ward off infection were more pronounced because of the patient's debilitated condition. Then to top it all, the situation was exacerbated as the surviving pathogens sometimes developed antibiotic-resistance.

Like Michael, she immersed herself completely in her work.

After achieving encouraging results with in-vitro tests, those undertaken outside the living body, Carla prepared the way for in-vivo tests, within the body, on two vervet monkeys. The test subjects had been deliberately infected with antibiotic-resistant pathogens. They were becoming increasingly prevalent, and it was necessary to test immunosuppressants under these adverse conditions as well. The theory had been worked out well enough—now it had to be proven in the laboratory.

Her colleague Paul, who had performed the transplants on the test animals, was in attendance. Following the operation he was keen to see the outcome and offered to stay on and help, besides he was infatuated with Carla, despite knowing it was a whimsical notion that anything might develop while Michael was around.

'Thanks Paul, but there's little to do, unless you're prepared to put the kettle on?'

Happily he provided a seemingly unending supply of sweetened coffee, while she tended the 'patients', adjusted flow meters and read the cardiographs regularly throughout the day. Almost immediately after the experimental immunosuppressant was administered, the condition of one vervet began to deteriorate.

By the following day Carla and Paul were struggling desperately to keep the second one alive. After all the effort, Carla had expected the tests to confirm her theories but now they seemed disproved. The anticipated outcome became a certainty and by late afternoon it was over. The resistant pathogens and toxic drug had killed the test animals but far too soon to allow for accurate evaluation of the immunosuppressant's performance. Carla's feeling of disappointment was worsened by her depth of feeling for the animals which, try as she might, she had never managed to suppress.

Paul sensed her mood. 'Call it a day, Carla. Go home. I'll see to this,' he said, offering to clean up the laboratory for her.

'That's sweet of you,' she gave him a rueful smile, accepting the offer gratefully. She left the laboratories, looking forward to a long, hot bath and an early night.

Michael completed his research for the day and then looked for Carla. He was not surprised to find she had already left as he had worked late trying to overcome a particularly difficult problem. It had taken only a moment's thought at the exit to decide which way to turn: right for home, or left to Carla's. Recently their relationship had become closer and whenever they had the chance they would eat out or see a show together. Other than that, he had made no further advances—Carla was too special. He turned left heading for the 'sought-after' suburb of Rondebosch where she lived.

Carla opened the door, dressed in a short bathrobe and a towel wrapped around her head. Even as the door closed behind him, Michael began to tell her of his disappointments, explaining the poor results his tests had achieved. He seemed not to notice her lack of attire.

'Hi! You wouldn't believe it, but the plasmids are still messing me around. My new cultures are as antibiotic-resistant as ever...'

'Is that all you have to say?' Carla responded, her voice heavy with sarcasm. 'Oh! I suppose you might as well make yourself comfortable, but I trust you're going to be more cheerful.'

He was quick to heed the rebuke. 'Sorry. It's just that I've had a hell of a time. I've been so caught up with this thing lately.'

'Never mind. If it's any consolation, I know how you feel.' As she headed down the passage to the kitchen she called over her shoulder while he made his way to the lounge. 'Would you like a glass of wine? I've just opened a bottle of Papa's best.'

'I'd love a glass of 'Papa's best'. What is it?' He tossed his jacket over a chair, then settled on the sofa, stretching his legs and throwing his arms across the backrest. He began to relax. Carla returned with two glasses of chilled wine. Handing one to Michael, 'Try this—it's a Semillon.'

He took a deep draught of the sweet white dessert wine.

'Semillon, you say? I wouldn't know about that, but I know what I like and this is pretty darn good. Just what I need after such a lousy day.'

'So you think you've had an awful day? Ha! Wait until you hear about mine. If you had arrived five minutes sooner, by the way, you wouldn't have got an answer.' She indicated her robe, 'I've only just got out of the bath.'

They sat for a while in conversation, commiserating with one another, before Carla excused herself to remove the towel from her head and dry her hair. Michael took his glass and gingerly stepped out onto the sixth floor balcony, keeping well away from the rail, to listen to the wind and to watch the distant lights dancing in the residual heat haze hanging over the city.

Though much of the day's oppressive heat—generated by the uncommonly hot wind rushing down over the desert far from the north—had dissipated, the air was still dry, so dry that Michael's nose and throat had become parched. The ice-cold wine went down like nectar. Carla towelled her hair and changed her bathrobe in favour of a loose-fitting kaftan. She joined Michael on the balcony, refilling their empty glasses. She turned towards the unusually warm breeze, reaching for the rail, closed her eyes and tilted her head back to let the air finish drying her hair, which flew gently behind her revealing a slender neck. Michael wanted to go to her but held back as he looked down over the balcony.

They spent almost an hour savouring the evening and the wine, talking about their country and its peculiarities, before going inside.

The topic drifted back to business, as always, and they recapped on progress; Michael outlined his understanding of her research and she filled in the blanks. She stared ahead intently pondering the problem, while Michael gazed at her perfect profile, softened by the warm glow from the table lamp. Her lustrous golden hair framed her face and fell loosely about her shoulders, and for a moment he forgot everything as his eyes caressed her loveliness.

'Right,' she said abruptly, pulling him back to the matter in hand. 'If I suppress the immune system to stop rejection, in order to help the new organ—as I attempted this morning—then I assist the invading pathogens which rapidly multiply.' She sipped her wine speculatively. 'It's a Catch-22 situation, but maybe the problem can be tackled differently?'

She glanced at Michael and, judging by his expression, was unsure if he was listening at all. She continued unperturbed. 'For instance, if it were at all possible to block the activity of antibiotic-resistant pathogens in some way—then I could still test the efficacy of the immunosuppressants without infection masking my results. What do you think?'

'Mmm,' he sighed deeply, 'And you were complaining about me talking shop when I arrived. Tell you what, when I crack my overriding problem with the plasmids I will have resolved yours as well.' At that moment, looking at her in the subdued light and relaxed by the effects of the wine, he had other things on his mind.

'You haven't been listening, have you?' She recognised his expression now and her own softened to match it.

Michael stared dreamily into her eyes.

She reached out her hand to lay it softly on his cheek, studying his strong jaw-line down to the shadowed chin. 'I suppose this was inevitable,' she murmured, leaning towards him and they embraced, a long kiss, revelling in the warm glow of the wine and each other. She nuzzled his ear with soft moist lips while her fingers found the buttons on his shirt and she whispered, 'We can discuss your plasmids later.'

Back in the laboratory Michael tried to push loving thoughts of Carla out of his mind and concentrated on his work. With the latest tests he was initially excited at the prospect of an improvement on his earlier conclusions, but as the days and weeks rolled by it became apparent that the results showed only marginal success. The answer still eluded him. He was discussing the lack of progress with Carla when Professor Mueller walked in on them.

'Carla, sorry to take you away from this important work, but I need you to do something for me. It'll mean you won't have much time to spend over here. Would you mind?' It was a rhetorical question. 'Come, and I will explain what I'd like you to do, ja?'

Michael was put out. He enjoyed having Carla near him and used every excuse to arrange it. Now Tinus Mueller was taking her away and, by the sound of it, Michael would not be seeing much of her during working hours. No matter, he would see her after work, either at his place or hers.

Without her distraction, albeit welcome, Michael was able to plough all his energy into his work so that time passed swiftly. As yet, he had no answers, but he was determined to find a solution.

For the next few days the laboratory became home. He developed a punishing routine that few could match. When finally he finished for the day he would shower in the changing rooms and sleep for what remained of the night on a couch in the staff lounge. His breakfast, lunch and dinner came from the canteen and he became the only staff member in the whole laboratory complex to receive from Maggie, the Coloured catering manager, an extra portion of whatever was on the menu. Not only that but she even extended credit to him—unbeknown to her employer. She had a soft spot for Michael and always enjoyed their friendly banter at the counter.

Michael reviewed the programme again and decided to tackle the problem head-on. He went in pursuit of Geoff and Chris, researching in an associated area. He found them both with heads down, peering into the twilight world of otherwise invisible invasive micro-organisms through powerful electron microscopes.

'Hi, guys! Just a quickie.' He startled them out of their concentration. 'Off the top of your heads, what presents the greatest post-operative problem with transplants?'

'Pneumonia!' Chris responded without hesitation.

'That's what I thought you'd say,' said Michael.

'Funny you should ask—it's what we're working on right now. The *Pneumocystis carinii,* or the *P.carinii* for short, it's a nasty one. Here, take a look.' Geoff vacated his chair for his colleague.

Adjusting the lens, Michael peered at the cells, magnified many thousands of times. 'Look like typical cysts in tissue section!' he exclaimed.

'Yes, they appear harmless enough, don't they! I've coated them in methenamine silver to highlight their features,' Geoff explained.

Michael could clearly make out the chromosome DNA—the building blocks of life. The chromosomes contained the genes, so minuscule that not even the microscope could magnify them enough to see. Yet each of the genes held its own unique programming information for replication and life support.

'Well, what do you think of those little buggers?' asked Chris.

'What's its classification?' For once Michael was unsure.

'Good question, that's just it—we can't classify it. No one's sure. I think it's a fungus but Geoff reckons it's a protozoan. Whatever, it can kill! Pneumonia, I suppose, is the real problem—and its associated complications. If you really want to know more about this bug, ask the Cape Doctor. I'd swear they are related the way he speaks about it! Believe me, he's a mine of information on the *P.carinii.*'

Michael declined further consultation with Tinus. 'No thanks, but I do need some of these—with antibiotic-resistance.'

'Help yourself,' offered Chris, pointing to the micro-organism repository in the far corner. 'But be sure not to take the container on your left!'

Michael keyed in the security code number, pressed the button and stood back as the airtight freezer door sprang open. Donning protective clothing he stepped inside. Misty white vapours of liquid nitrogen enveloped rows of stainless steel flasks which contained plastic vials, keeping their contents frozen and safe. Seeing an ice-cream tub wedged into the left-hand corner, he smiled to himself, making a mental note to refuse further offers of snacks from his colleagues at tea breaks. He found what he was looking for and selected a flask. The label confirmed the specimen was a multiple drug-resistant *P.carinii*.

Michael dipped a probe into the solution containing the *P.carinii* with infinite care, then scrapped the probe in a zigzag pattern across selected plates, transferred the *P.carinii* into a mix of agar, a gelatinous substance, and the antibiotic. Placing them in an incubator at a pre-set temperature and humidity, he hoped the cultures would grow. Then he double-checked all the necessary laboratory conditions in minute detail to ensure survival through incubation.

The cultures were the subject of continual monitoring for the next few days and when, at last, viable growth spread over the surface of the plates. The resistant micro-organisms were present and testing began in earnest.

'Great theory, now for the practice,' Michael muttered to himself. There was little chance of getting it right the first time round. It might be that it would never work, but it had to be tried.

The in-vitro tests proved interesting. The *P.carinii* was indeed resistant to all the drugs he tested it against. There was nothing more to do but to repeat the procedure as many times as it might take to get a positive result. He kept focused by constantly reminded himself that apart from the tissue rejection problem, it was the antibiotic-resistance factor that could kill the transplant patient. Just when he thought the repeated experiments were hopeless it produced a result.

He had plied it with a combination of two new agents. One drug, when used against a non-resistant strain, usually killed the *P.carinii* by attacking the membrane wall. The other was a new chemical compound that attacked the chromosome, breaking up the DNA chain to prevent replication of the micro-organism. It was untried in combination with the first drug and against the *P.carinii,* as far as he could ascertain. The assault with this chemical cocktail gave conclusive results. The *P.carinii* proved no match against the synergistic effect of these powerful drugs. It was eradicated.

Excited and encouraged, he pressed on further. In-vitro tests provided only a measurement of the pathogens' growth rate, based on their spread over the agar plates and their sensitivity to drugs. Whereas in-vivo tests offered a far greater opportunity to study the *P.carinii*—through white blood cell counts, blood serum levels of the drugs and lung biopsies alike— and clinical features of the disease. He introduced the *P.carinii* into several test rats. They would give him an opportunity to fight antibiotic-resistance firsthand. His experiment had reached the point of 'wait and see' when he finally went home, and to bed. He stirred briefly, wondering if he had found a new means to fight antibiotic-resistance, before succumbing finally to a deep sleep.

Michael returned early to the laboratories, eager to check the results of the animal tests.

'Morning.' Paul greeted him on his arrival, 'Shame about the rats.'

'What do you mean 'shame about the rats'?' Michael was totally unprepared for the devastating news that Paul greeted him with. Every animal he had injected was dead—had died within hours of introducing the pathogen. Paul's expression was one of sympathy.

Michael barely acknowledged Carla in the corridor as he dashed past on his way to the laboratory in a state of near panic. What could possibly have gone wrong? He arrived breathless and there, confronting him behind the glass partition were nine, very active, rats. His initial confusion turned quickly to relief and then anger at the tasteless 'joke'.

It took until lunch-time when he met Carla in the canteen before Michael's sense of humour returned to anything near normal.

'Oh come on, Michael, this is not like you,' Carla coaxed, mindful as ever. 'Paul didn't mean anything by it. It was only a bit of fun. You really have been overdoing it, haven't you?'

'Yes, I suppose you're right,' he conceded.

Paul walked past with his tray. Though he had made no further reference to the rats during the morning, he found it difficult not to smile each time their eyes met.

'Come and join us, Paul.' Michael's voice was amiable but he could see Paul was uncertain.

After a moment's hesitation, Paul said, 'Okay,' and went round the table to sit opposite Michael, facing the servery. For a while they ate in silence, Paul giving Michael nervous glances between mouthfuls, until Michael felt uncomfortable.

'Paul, don't worry. It took me a while but I do now see the funny side.'

Carla had been observing Paul's furtive glances since he sat down. 'Your jitteriness has nothing to do with that, has it, Paul?' she said, watching the servery. 'It's Nina.'

Michael swung round to follow her gaze and saw the new canteen assistant.

Paul looked startled at this revelation. 'Carla, please!' he hissed nearly choking as he turned away to look anywhere but toward the servery.

Nina was striking, with long auburn hair and pale skin, but she was Maggie's daughter, a Coloured.

If Paul had a crush on her he had every reason to be nervous.

It was dangerous for a White to admit even a mild attraction to a Non-White. The penalties for a conviction under the Immorality Act of 1950 were severe and most Whites were strongly supportive of these stringent rules of apartheid.*

Michael saw a chance to get back at Paul, but hesitated. It would not be amusing. After finally convincing him that they were not about to tip off the Bureau of State Security (BOSS), Michael and Carla left him to savour his third cup of coffee while they returned to work.

'He's really taken with her,' Carla whispered outside the canteen. 'You had better warn him to be careful if he's thinking of chatting her up.'

'Doesn't it worry you that she's Coloured?' he enquired.

'No! Should it? She's a woman the same as me.'

'I thought with your background and...'

'Michael, I am my own woman. As an Afrikaner, if that's what you mean, I feel strongly about certain things and in others I don't.' Her chin went up and she walked ahead of him seemingly offended by his insinuation.

Michael held back and smiled to himself, pleasantly surprised at her liberal attitude to the sensitive issue of inter-racial relationships.

By the middle of the second day, after the introduction of the *P.carinii*, it became apparent that all the experimental rats were infected. Antibiotics had been deliberately withheld to ensure the pathogen had taken a good hold, to simulate a worst-case scenario.

Tests confirmed that massive colonies had invaded their systems. Their condition deteriorated rapidly and on the third day and they showed every sign of distress. Michael began to administer the drugs hoping that the synergistic action would save them. Low doses of the drugs were administered which also meant he was not saddled with the problem of countering their side-effects. Slowly the rats began to recover. His strategy was working. Further encouraged he decided to take the experiment a step further. The rats immune systems were assisting in the destruction of the *P.carinii* and he wondered to what extent. Michael administered one of Tinus' experimental immunosuppressants in order to find out just how effective the drugs were by themselves.

Hours later he made an unwelcome discovery. The *P.carinii* began to display some unexpected characteristics. The new drugs he had used previously, suddenly had no effect at all. He increased the strength and plied it with numerous other drug combinations, still the *P.carinii* survived.

'Bloody hell—it's going the wrong way—the damn thing is more resistant than ever!' Michael complained to no one in particular and filed his report.

It intrigued him that the micro-organism persisted, regardless of the fungicidal and bactericidal qualities of the variety of drugs ranged against it, at ever-higher levels. Regardless, the rats began to die.

That afternoon Michael went to the stores only to find a 'Closed' sign on the door. It rankled that, not for the first time, the storeman had left his post causing inconvenience to other laboratory staff. The Cape Doctor had insisted on the storeman's authorisation for all withdrawals. Michael, however, was not deterred and cast a furtive glance in both directions.

Once inside, he closed the door quickly and felt for the light switch. He turned the light on and there before him was an obviously intimate and very embarrassed couple. Another minute and he would have caught them in an even more compromising situation.

For a moment they all froze, Michael astonished to find Paul and Nina entwined in one another's arms. They both looked worried, concerned more for the repercussions if the authorities became aware of their relationship than for being discovered.

It occurred to Michael that this might be the reason the store had been shut on previous occasions. He looked directly at Nina. 'What do you see in this reprobate?' asking in the most serious voice he could muster under the circumstances, 'Besides, he's far too ugly for you. Can't even tell a dead rat from a live one!'

Paul let out a deep sigh. Michael had let them know his position clearly.

To save further embarrassment, Michael grabbed the nearest piece of apparatus and promptly left, waving it in the air saying, 'Sign this out for me, will you?'

From that moment on, the three became firm friends but it was understood that Paul and Nina's relationship would not be an easy one. All laboratory personnel used the canteen at one time or another and most knew Nina was Maggie's daughter, though from the look of her pale skin she could pass for a White. An unguarded word in the wrong place would spell serious trouble for both of them. For his part, Paul was smitten beyond caring.

Michael arrived at work to find an urgent message waiting for him from Professor Mueller. Tinus' office door was ajar, but still Michael knocked.

'Kom binne, come in, Michael,' said Tinus congenially. 'What have you been up to my boy? I hear your last test batch produced an unwanted result.' He had read Michael's latest report, but nevertheless preferred to hear the details firsthand. 'So, you had little success. What's the problem?'

'Well, that depends on how you gauge success. I had an interesting result with one specimen. It's in my report.'

Tinus maintained a patient silence, allowing him to proceed.

'I'm sure I'm close to a breakthrough on this one. The initial results with the *P.carinii* were promising, although the test animal's survival rate did not improve. Maybe, if I had started treatment sooner it would have fought off the infection...it seemed to regain its former drug-resistance very quickly.'

Tinus grew impatient, 'What you mean is, all your test animals died? Michael, in view of the micro-organism you are dealing with, you need to exercise every precaution. I don't wont a Marburg incident occurring in these laboratories. Do you understand?'

'Marburg incident! I don't follow?'

The Professor crossed the room to withdraw a file from his cabinet.

'Let me enlighten you.' Tinus opened the file and, adjusting his half-moon glasses, checked its contents. He returned to his seat and scanned pages from the file. 'It's believed by some to be a simian virus that causes *Marburg* disease.' He paused only briefly, peering over his glasses to see if the name rang any bells. On seeing no sign of recognition, he continued. 'It is otherwise known as Green Monkey Fever.' He paused again. This time Michael's reaction was plain to see. 'Ach! I see you have heard of it.'

'Yes, we studied it briefly but I don't recall...'

Tinus did not let him finish, he leaned back in his chair, removing his glasses and continued from memory, gazing into space while he spoke. 'I was called to Germany late in '67 to the small town of Marburg, where an outbreak of a new and acute disease appeared in some laboratory workers who had been handling vervet and their close cousins, the grivet green monkey. Both had recently arrived from Central Africa.'*

Michael drew up a chair and listened intently. He had never seen the Cape Doctor so animated about anything.

Tinus continued, seemingly unaware of his audience. 'Other centres were also affected—one in Frankfurt and another in Yugoslavia. Of the twenty-nine victims I saw in Germany, seven died within seventeen days of the onset of the illness. Fortunately, the two Yugoslav cases, though serious, were not fatal.'*

Michael chanced an interruption as Tinus paused. 'How on earth did the disease manage to go undetected all the way from Africa?' There were checks on the traffic of live animals around the world and it seemed incredible that such a tragedy could have occurred.

Tinus grimaced. 'I can say with some certainty that two batches of monkeys sent from Uganda via London were implicated.* I assisted in isolating the virus and returned to South Africa with specimens for future analysis.'

Michael knew that this scenario was a biologist's worst nightmare and the potential for disaster was always present.

'Let me make this absolutely clear. It was a biological accident that should never have happened. For that reason I have stringent rules at these laboratories. You may proceed with this *P.carinii* of yours, but only under the Code 10 security procedures and a Category '4' laboratory. Is that understood? This *P.carinii* is displaying very unstable tendencies, and there can be no mistakes with this one.'

What Michael was asking for, was permission to experiment further with the micro-organism in its already altered state.

'You will be careful, ja?' Tinus considered the proposal for a moment longer. Then rose, and Michael followed, as he led him away from the main laboratories to a new wing to which the Cape Doctor alone had access. Tinus hit a switch and a pneumatically sealed door hissed and swung open to reveal a bright-red door displaying the distinctive three circles of the 'BIOHAZARD' symbol: indicating the potential danger within. Until then, Michael had not been aware of the existence of this wing.

They stepped inside and the door closed behind them. Putting on protective suits and sealed breathing apparatus, Tinus keyed a code on a pad by the door. It swung open to reveal a Category '4' high security laboratory and another door. Beyond this lay an isolation unit used for accommodating test animals.

'This is where you will work,' was all the Cape Doctor said.

Back in his office Tinus summarised the briefing. He remarked that if ever there was a time to wear a protective suit, it was now. Michael merely expressed his dislike for their restrictive movements and was taken aback when Tinus suddenly rounded on him severely.

'You will exercise every precaution, and I do mean every,' he finished.

'Don't worry, I had no intention of doing otherwise!' Michael answered.

Michael's research was quickly transferred to the Category '4' laboratory in the high security wing. He fulfilled all the stringent Code 10 security requirements for working with highly dangerous micro-organisms. Code 10 governed not only the procedures for operations within the working area but also the researcher's conduct outside. Curiosity was rife among his colleagues and ancillary staff. Part of the requirement of Code 10 was that Michael did not divulge details of his research to anyone except other classified personnel; that meant only Tinus and a handful of senior technicians. His research notes had to be secured, either within the Category '4' laboratory or in Tinus' safe.

Before Michael was allowed to proceed, Tinus himself validated all the security arrangements culminating in Michael's signed agreement.

All the cloak-and-dagger arrangements mildly amused Michael, when they weren't frustrating his efforts to get started, but it was clear he wasn't going to make any headway until he had agreed to the rigid protocols.

Time spent working in the laboratory was drastically reduced by rigorous decontamination and preparation procedures. All surfaces were scrubbed thoroughly with disinfectant.

The entire contamination area had to be slightly depressurised to ensure that, if the airtight door seals failed, any subsequent leak would be into, rather than out of, the laboratories. All the specimens used had to be carefully secured in their containers before Michael could withdraw to the decontamination chamber—the area between the doors where he had to spend many minutes having his suit scrubbed down with a powerful disinfectant. While this was in progress, the air within the laboratories and chamber was extracted then recycled through an incinerator. Entry and exit routines were never allowed to vary.

The final checks completed, Michael donned his protective suit, adjusted his respirator and stepped into the laboratory.

Having recovered the multiple drug-resistant *P.carinii* from the rats, Michael cleared the way to start anew. Carefully he repeated the experiment with a new culture. The work was intricate and time-consuming and beneath the protective clothing he perspired freely, more from nervous tension than from the heat. His expectations of a result in the early stages were not high; he knew the procedures would have to be repeated time and time again with minuscule adjustments to numerous variables.

Aware that he was dealing with a potent pathogen he chose a larger test animal. He reasoned, with complementary drug therapy, their hardier immune systems would be better equipped to fight against these invasive resistant micro-organisms. In the adjoining isolation unit, he installed five monkeys which Tinus had imported.

Michael introduced the newly altered *P.carinii* and before long the monkeys were confirmed as being infected.

Immediately, he started them on a drug regimen. Again he briefed his technicians on what to look for and how to administer the combative agents. Michael stood, staring at the test animals and reviewing the question of drug-resistance as a whole. He was aware of the dangers of using antibiotics that broke up DNA chains. Theoretically these free fragments of DNA could recombine with any other micro-organisms to create a hybrid with possibly disastrous consequences. His concern was, GPs worldwide administered low dose antibiotics similarly without any thought to the consequences of their actions. The ease of administering user-friendly capsules was the real problem. Previously, antibiotics had been administered by injection directly into the bloodstream. But now, compounded by the fact most patients never took their capsules on time, and the absorption rate of individuals could differ and varied dependant on when, and what they had eaten—caused blood levels of the drug to drop, thereby giving the pathogens a chance to 'resist'. The greatest benefit of low dose treatment was it produced minimal side-effects. Simply he saw this as a recipe for disaster, and the cause for the recent emergence of resistant strains. This time he wasn't taking chances and increased the drugs to almost toxic levels, determined to wipe out the *P.carinii.*

It seemed he had just fallen asleep, though it was over eight hours since his head had hit the pillow, when the insistent ring of the telephone woke him. It was his senior technician. For a fleeting moment, Michael thought this might be more of Paul's humour, but the hour and the anxiety in the voice quickly brought him round and convinced him otherwise. Awake now, he listened, but the technician was adhering conscientiously to the rules of Code 10—not to divulge anything that was not absolutely necessary over the telephone. Even so, the message was clear enough: something serious had occurred and needed his presence urgently.

'I monitored everything as you insisted,' he reported, 'but I've never seen anything like it.'

Michael rushed to the laboratories.

'Jesus! What the hell happened here?' Michael stood gaping through the glass partition into the laboratory. He expected the two monkeys to begin to show signs of infection. After all, his chemical cocktail probably would have had no effect against the resistant micro-organism, but their immune systems should have checked the infection for some time. But they were both dead!

Michael and the chief technician suited up and entered the 'hot zone'. The technician's description of events leading up to the deaths was graphic and terrible. The evidence was clear.

The cages were covered with copious amounts of black blood and fluid faeces, congealing with torn out hair as the monkeys had thrashed about. The mouths gaped wide with froth still present around their jaws. Even fragments of teeth were among the foul debris, cracked when the animals began convulsing violently in the confined spaces.

Death had come very quickly—about seven hours after the first signs of distress, he was told.

'My God! What's in this *P.carinii*?' Stunned, Michael was about to order the containment of the area before collecting samples for investigation, when a technician called him from the isolation unit.

'I think you should come and look at this!'

Preparing himself for the second chamber, Michael was full of anxiety. What he found stretched credibility to the limit.

'Impossible!' the word exploded from his lips. 'How could these have become infected? What in God's name have I created here?'

In the laboratory each animal had died in its cage, here the remainder of the monkeys had been kept together in a much larger enclosure. At first, Michael could not readily identify individual bodies. The same disgusting mix of blood, faeces and hair had swilled about in the bottom of the cage and seeped onto the floor. It seemed as if the animals had melded together in their death throes. Michael felt real fear. The rest of the monkeys had been separated from the experimental subjects by a connecting corridor where decontamination also took place.

'I want all the equipment rechecked for faults, and fast,' he ordered brusquely, after his second decontamination within the hour, 'and check both rooms for leaks. That bloody bug got in there some way—I want to know how!' How could this happen in a modern lab with security as tight as this? he wondered.

Michael knew they would find no fault with his equipment, so thorough had he been in the preparation, yet he had to be sure. There must be a breach between the two laboratories and it must be found.

Tinus had authorised the use of the two monkeys for the experiment while the others were earmarked to be used elsewhere. He was livid to find the entire group dead within a week of their arrival and even more so, because of a stupid error.

Ignoring Michael's feelings, he immediately stepped in to supervise a thorough biopsy on parts of the internal organs left intact from the largest monkey, liquidizing the matter and drawing off cells in a centrifuge. The electron microscope confirmed their fears—the presence of the mutant *P.carinii* in its altered state. Biopsies on the other animals confirmed they too had died of the same disease.

That afternoon they found the cause of the leak. A cable duct passing between the labs carrying the power to the electron microscope, fitted after the construction of the laboratory complex, had not been properly sealed.

Michael was relieved by the discovery. 'At least this will get the Cape Doctor off my back. It proves it wasn't my fault,' he told himself.

Despite the lifting of the blame for the recent catastrophe. Michael returned to work to find Tinus had taken him off the project and it had been halted. The results of his first attempts in the new field of genetic engineering had not exactly been the success he had hoped for. Admittedly, as far as the object of the exercise was concerned, he seemed no nearer to finding a solution. Nevertheless, through the experiment he had gained from a steep learning curve and now he was convinced, more than ever, that resolving drug-resistance had significant implications in organ transplant surgery.

Michael had been summoned to Tinus' office—and it suited him just fine. Disregarding the protestations of his secretary, he burst into his office.

'Why have you stopped the project? The contamination wasn't my fault! You might think there's little to show for all this work, but we have made advances. We need to analyse the real benefits to date,' he stated flatly, depositing the original research volume on the desk along with three more just like it.

Tinus ignored the rudeness of the interruption. He continued to speak calmly into the telephone. 'Excuse me, General, something urgent has come up. I will call you later.'

He replaced the receiver, looked up at Michael over the rims of his spectacles and, with elbows on the desk, pressed his fingertips together waiting for him to continue.

Unconcerned that he had interrupted Tinus' conversation, Michael launched into what he hoped was a convincing argument. Apart from being taken off the project, Tinus had offered him his full support, thus far, but now he needed to convince the Cape Doctor of his objectives in order to have the project reinstated.

'You just can't stop work of this importance because of a bloody building defect. We had begun to get interesting results. Consider the risk assessment. I admit this is not what we had expected but...'

'Precisely, my boy, and because of that I have put it to bed immediately. I have your rogue pathogen sealed securely and stored safely away from all the other material in the main repository. Let me remind you of the Code 10 classification. News of any of this could have serious repercussions for all of us, if it was to leak out from these laboratories. Do you understand me?'

'But what did you find in the biopsy?' Michael rushed on, trying to evoke a positive response. 'Is it possible that there was some genetic cross-species contamination from the monkeys? A simian virus or perhaps...?'

'Enough!' Tinus exploded, holding up his hand, 'It's done. There is no more to be gained by following this path. You must realise that these laboratories are like any other business. Bad public relations could cause untold damage. It is time your obvious talents were utilised in more profitable pursuits.' A momentary silence prevailed.

The dejection written in the younger man's face was obvious.

'It's not the end of the world, Michael,' he said, more softly than usual. He scanned the last few pages of the final volume of research notes. 'You have been very thorough, I can see that. If there was a way to succeed, then I'm sure you would have found it. This branch of research is too risky. I'm closing it down now before there are any more mishaps. Anyway, I have something else for you.' He offered a rare smile, trying to lessen the young man's disappointment.

'Come and see me in the morning and we'll discuss it then. I know you will find it appealing,' and with that, Michael was dismissed.

On the way out he turned, about to say something else, but he saw that Tinus was lost in thought. He closed the door softly behind him.

Michael met Carla in the outer office.

'Hi!' he said glumly.

'What's up?' She detected something was wrong.

'My project's shelved. What about you?'

'Oh, Michael, I am sorry!'

'Forget it,' he forced a smile, 'we'll talk about it later. More importantly, where have you been these past few days?'

'Don't ask. Tinus has me transferring all his confidential documents onto a new computer he's had installed in the east wing. And I can only gain access in the evenings and at weekends at the moment.'

'But why?'

'It's a government computer and we can rent time on it when they are not using it. Only the Cape Doctor and his deputy have the code.' She lowered her voice and whispered, 'And I'm that deputy.'

'Really!' he said, conspiratorially. 'So what is it?'

'I can't tell you that, silly. There will be hell to pay if I do.'

'That's why I haven't seen you lately—up to your neck in reports?'

'Afraid so, sorry.'

'Bloody computers. Haven't been around for five minutes and already we're slaves to the damn things. When am I going to see you?' he asked. He looked downcast.

'Come on, it's not that bad. It'll only be for a few more weeks, and he's also planning to have other terminals installed for the rest of the staff. Guess who has to teach them! Promise I'll phone you when it's all quiet, how's that?'

'What can I say?' Michael was resigned, only half pretending to sulk. He kissed her goodbye and idled away the rest of the day in his office, clearing the decks for whatever the Cape Doctor had cooked up for him.

On reflection, Michael thought that Tinus Mueller had been extremely fair, for it had cost him dearly. Tinus had even given Michael the rest of the day off, while personally taking care of incinerating the carcasses.

Michael left early and made his way to the car park. He sat for a while in his car pondering his situation.

Almost ten months' hard work at Mueller Laboratories had come to nothing. It crossed his mind to leave Cape Town, to see Africa in all her glory; an immense and beautiful continent and like most South Africans he had seen next to nothing of it. He could leave, but then again there were no other laboratories in South Africa with enough prestige to attract him, with the possible exception of Groote Berg Hospital. Even that was not such a good prospect because, as a government-funded Public Health Department, all the advantages rested with Afrikaners—and the pay was atrocious!

Still, he was confident his qualifications would open doors for him wherever he happened to be, if only he chose to knock on them. Perhaps he should go even farther—to America, to where his father had emigrated from his native Latvia.

But there was Carla. He had met her less than a year ago and their relationship had blossomed, slowly at first, then with ever-growing intensity as they spent more time together. He'd had fleeting relationships in the past, none of which were memorable. But Carla was different; Carla was always on his mind. She was not just a lover, but also his best friend and confidante. It was only now that he was contemplating leaving Mueller Laboratories, Cape Town and Carla, he came to realise that for the first time in his life he was desperately in love.

Carla was enough to change his mind. He wondered what she would say if he asked her to go with him, but knew she was happy working where she was. The Cape Doctor clearly had a soft spot for her, and as a result Carla had certain opportunities which she would be unlikely to realise elsewhere, at least in the short-term. It would be unfair even to ask her.

'No. I think I'll stick around a while and see what Tinus has to offer.' He started the engine and felt the sports car immediately respond to his handling. Feeling slightly less depressed, he drove away.

Neither Tinus nor Michael made any real effort to reconcile their personal differences. They maintained a professional working relationship and face-to-face contact occurred infrequently. Michael no longer attended the regular review meetings now that he was assisting another team, as only the team leaders were required to attend. He had effectively been demoted though his salary remained unchanged.

Tinus himself attended fewer of them, leaving the chair to his deputy. Activities elsewhere accounted for much of his time and, even when at the laboratories, he was frequently engaged in talks with a stream of visitors.

Michael now found that most days he had time on his hands, and he spent many idle moments in reflective mood, gazing out of his office window overlooking the car park.

Over the weeks, he noticed the same faces returning to visit Tinus. In particular one elderly man, whose posture was ramrod straight, greet Tinus with a shake of the hand and a click of the heels as he bowed stiffly. Curiosity aroused, he asked Carla if she knew who all these people were.

'He's pretty vague about his callers,' she said, resting her elbows on the canteen table. 'He doesn't discuss them at all. But the tall elderly gentleman you saw, that's Rolf. I asked Tinus because he made a pass at me. He just laughed and said he was harmless—they were in Marburg together.'

'Marburg!' Michael picked up on the name. 'So that's it. He must be one of his old colleagues from the laboratory in Germany where he went to consult on the Green Monkey Fever outbreak.'

'He didn't mention anything like that. Like I said, he keeps very quiet about his callers.'

Though most visitors seemed to be from the Cape—Michael knew because he had seen them leave in locally registered cars—others were from farther afield and he had even seen one with diplomatic plates from a neighbouring country. In a way this made Michael unexpectedly proud that these laboratories were so highly thought of in their profession—here in South Africa and beyond.

Partly because of Michael's geniality and partly perhaps as a lesson in humility, Tinus assigned him to a public relations function. It fell to Michael to conduct visitors around designated areas of the laboratories, explaining their function and a little of the work undertaken. Visitors included local dignitaries and interested scientists—a never-ending stream of them.

In this role, however, his tolerance waned. Shepherding yet another group around the laboratories, he explained once more the difference between DNA and RNA.

'DNA,' he said mechanically, heaven knows he felt like a robot, 'stands for deoxyribonucleic acid and RNA stands for ribonucleic acid and, no,' he said before someone asked the obvious question, 'I have no idea why it's DNA instead of DRNA—perhaps it's because they like TLAs.' When they looked at one another and shrugged, he explained wearily, 'Three-Letter Acronyms!' They had hardly had time to register this before Michael strode off to continue the tour, concluding in the auditorium with a short question and answer session.

Tinus pulled him aside for a quiet word. 'For God's sake, man, what's the matter with you? Try to inject some enthusiasm into your work.'

Michael agreed to try but he knew it would be difficult.

CHAPTER 2

"I want to state here unequivocally...that South Africa is a White man's country and that he must remain the master here. In the reserves we are prepared to allow the native to be the masters...."

Hendrik Verwoerd
Prime Minister of South Africa, 1958 - 66
Assassinated in 1966

Michael had accepted with trepidation Carla's invitation to stay for the weekend with her family on their estate. Carla, he knew, was an anomaly among Afrikaners, who were best at ease with their own people, preferring to remain aloof from all others. The racial division was not only between Black and White; a huge gulf divided Afrikaans- and English-speaking South Africans. Michael's standing would be further diminished in their eyes because he was a Jew, a fact which though seemingly irrelevant to Carla would not, he suspected, be entirely ignored by her parents.

For his part, Michael bore no animosity towards Afrikaners nor, for that matter, any of the homogeneous races that made up the colourful mosaic of humanity in Southern Africa. He vowed to try to make the best of this visit.

4 December 1971
It was a comfortable forty minute drive from the heart of Cape Town to the verdant valleys of the Western Cape wine estates. This was the area known as the Drakenstein, where Carla's ancestors had lived for almost three centuries. Michael drove with the top down, and Carla let her hair whip wildly behind her, finding the rush of wind exhilarating and making the heat of the day more bearable. The road was bordered with vineyards, interspersed with orchards of apple, peach and apricot trees, the ripe fruit sweetly scenting the air. She sensed the promise of an enjoyable time ahead.

They arrived at the Boshoff estate in the late afternoon. The long gravelled drive was canopied by aged oak trees, planted by Carla's ancestors when the first settlers founded the nearby town of Stellenbosch. The imposing manor that appeared at the end of the long drive was of the traditional Cape Dutch design; an ornate facade and an impressive central door flanked by tall symmetrically placed, rectangular windows. High, thick white lime-washed walls reflected the heat and promised a pleasant cool interior beneath a roof thatched with dark reeds.

Andries Boshoff greeted his daughter stiffly at the front door. He held out his arms to take her hands, leaning forward to offer his cheek for her to kiss.

There was little evidence of the affection one would normally expect a father to bestow on a daughter he hadn't seen for weeks. Carla seemed to accept this as normal.

Michael watched this rather cold reception from the driver's seat. He lifted his weekend case and approached his host with some misgivings.

'This is Michael Bernstein, I phoned you about Papa,' reminded Carla.

'Mr Bernstein,' Andries extended his hand. The handshake was brief and very firm and Michael was treated to a curt nod of the head. He half expected Andries to click his heels together like Tinus' visitor. Michael sensed the father's hostility. What had Carla said to him about their relationship? He wondered if this was the reason for the cool reception.

'How do you do, sir,' he gave a generous smile, allowing it to reach his eyes. Get the parents on your side and it's plain sailing, Michael thought, but there was no further response from the man. Michael was all but ignored as Andries Boshoff led them inside.

The tall windows made the interior light and airy; the spacious rooms had high ceilings with exposed beams. There was little in the way of furnishings. What was there were mostly solid and functional, a heavy wooden coffee table in the lounge typifying the style. It stood before a large open fireplace surrounded on the other three sides by equally solid sofas. Michael pictured cosy family get-togethers and felt a pang of envy. An assortment of well-worn animal skins adorned the polished wooden floors, likely evidence of earlier hunting safaris, judging by his host.

Carla's mother, Hettie, was a fine looking woman with green eyes and fair hair plaited and wound on top of her head. It was plain to see where Carla's good looks came from.

'So you are Michael,' she said with a faint smile when Carla introduced him. She kissed Carla lightly on the cheek, excused herself and left the room.

'Where's Louise, Papa?' Carla asked.

Her younger sister '...who was afraid of spiders', Michael remembered Carla telling him, was not there to meet them.

'How should I know? I am just her father. She went off this morning with some of those hippie friends of hers to God knows where. I told her to be back for this evening's meal.'

'Hippie', Michael suspected, meant any person under the age of thirty whose clothes were anything other than grey or beige.

Carla left the two men in the lounge and went to help her mother supervise the two Coloured cooks in the kitchen.

'Tell me, Mr Bernstein, what is it that you do?' His guttural Afrikaans accent was harsh and his manner abrupt.

Michael was surprised that he did not know. Surely Carla must have said something to her parents. 'Please, call me Michael,' he said. 'I'm a microbiologist at the Mueller Laboratories in Cape Town. I work with Carla—hasn't she mentioned me?'

'I wouldn't know, Mr Bernstein,' he replied pointedly. 'My daughter mentions many people. She's a very popular girl. Perhaps she has spoken about you—I don't remember.' And then, after a brief pause, a look of recognition crossed his eyes. 'Ah! But, of course, you are the Jew. Ja, she has mentioned you now I come to think of it. How is it you come to be a minor biologist?'

From Andries Boshoff's tone it was evident to Michael that he had known exactly who he was but he didn't allow himself to become ruffled. 'Microbiologist,' Michael corrected him before answering. 'I qualified at Wits University and came straight from there to Mueller Laboratories. I'm involved in heart transplant research.' He answered politely, wanting desperately to say, 'And what qualifications do you have to tread grapes?'

'I see.' Andries grudgingly conceded a point scored and changed the subject to one with which he was far more comfortable. 'My family has worked this estate for nearly three hundred years and today we produce more wine than any other estate in the region.'

He omitted to add, Michael thought, 'with the exception of the Stellenbosch Farmers Winery and Gilbey Distillers and Vintners,' which were far larger, though he had to admit that old Boshoff could turn out a good wine.

'You will come with me tomorrow around the vineyards and I will show you the results of honest hard work,' said Andries.

It was not so much an invitation as an order and Michael was reminded of Tinus Mueller who used the same method of communication. Whose hard work was it anyway? It was highly unlikely, Michael thought, that Andries Boshoff spent long, hard hours toiling on the land.

Michael had been keen to tour the estate—Carla had already told him a great deal about it—but he had hoped she was to be his guide. He fancied they might even get bored before it was over and find a quiet spot to relax. His intentions were evidently not to be realised.

'I look forward to it,' he lied. Carla returned to show him to his room and he was grateful for the interruption. Andries Boshoff was going to be hard work.

Dusk approached and, as lights were switched on, they heard a car pulling up outside, the music blaring. A Chevrolet convertible, with what seemed like a dozen teenagers enjoying a mobile party, slewed to a stop at the front steps of the house. Three of the youngsters leapt out noisily to let Louise Boshoff extricate herself from the back seat. The party continued as they said their goodbyes and the car disappeared down the drive. When they had gone, Louise rushed into the house, heading for her room.

Minutes later a Ford Granada, gleaming black with highly polished chrome trim, arriving sedately and almost silently pulled up alongside Michael's MGA. The driver walked to the front door and pressed the bell.

Near on six feet tall, he was a handsome young man with smooth dark hair accentuating his sparkling blue eyes. The door was opened by the servant who impassively viewed the immaculate visitor dressed in a dark lounge suit.

'Please tell Mr and Mrs Boshoff that Jan DuToit is here,' said the visitor.

'Yes, Master.' The servant inclined his head and stood aside to admit him to the foyer.

Michael and the Boshoffs, except for Louise, were in the lounge drinking apéritifs when the servant announced the arrival of their guest.

'Ah, good.' Andries Boshoff rose and, without excusing himself, went to greet Jan DuToit. He shook his hand warmly.

'Jan, good of you to come at such short notice. How are you?'

'Fine thanks, Andries. It's no trouble. When you said this morning that Carla was home, how could I refuse your invitation? You've told me so much about her, I thought it's time we met.'

'Ja, good man,' Andries glanced towards the lounge, then lowered his voice putting his arm round Jan's shoulders to speak close to his ear. 'I hear you have a promising career in the government. Remember, I am not without influence.'

'Of course, I understand.' Jan DuToit's thoughts were occupied with Carla. Mutual friends had said Carla was stunning and headstrong. He was keen to find out more about her directly.

'Good. That's settled.' Andries steered Jan towards the lounge and stopped suddenly, adding as an afterthought, 'Oh, by the way, I almost forgot. We have another guest tonight. One of Carla's colleagues from the laboratories. A Jew,' he almost spat out the word. 'Carla felt sorry for him and thought Louise might make a friend of him. Thought you should know!' he said conspiratorially. 'Now let's go and meet everyone.' He led Jan DuToit into the lounge.

Louise, having showered and changed for dinner in record time, was about to enter the hall when she heard the muted exchange between the two men. Giving in to her natural curiosity she stayed out of sight, peeping from the shadows of her bedroom doorway. It was easy to overhear her father, even when he whispered, so resonant was his voice. The two girls had joked about it when they were children, often repeating things to one another they were not supposed to know. Now, as when she was a child, Louise listened in fascination to what was clearly not meant to be heard by anyone but the guest. Jan DuToit, whom she knew from several visits to their home in recent weeks, was nodding in agreement. All she could deduce from it, however, was that Jan had come to see Carla and Carla had invited a friend. 'Pity,' Louise thought, with a pang of disappointment. 'I like tall, dark-haired men.' She waited a few moments before bouncing into the lounge to meet the two guests.

Dinner that night was a little unusual. Andries and Hettie were seated at opposite ends of the heavy oak table with Michael on Hettie's right and Jan on her left. Carla was next to Jan, much to Michael's chagrin. Ever since they were introduced, Jan had not left Carla's side. Andries now only spoke Afrikaans and was visibly put out when Michael had the good grace to converse fluently in his host's language. Louise, who was a trifle flippant for Michael's liking, added to his discomfort by sitting too close to his right arm.

When Michael had been introduced to her, Louise was pleased to find he was dark haired, and as tall as Jan DuToit though more solidly built, but wasn't half as stuffy! All Jan talked about, when he bothered to speak to her at all, was politics. Her best efforts had failed to get him off the subject for long. She no longer even bothered to try, leaving him to talk to Carla and her father. However, Michael was much easier to get on with. He had a ready wit and, even better, knew most of the Beatles and Rolling Stones albums. There was potential here for some cosy nights with the record player and a kindred spirit. Jan was into classical music and, as he was monopolising Carla anyway, she was welcome to him.

'Jan is a budding politician, Carla.' Andries' statement was designed to help the conversation along between those two to the exclusion of the others. 'We have been exchanging ideas and I see a great future ahead of him. Isn't that right, Jan?'

Jan directed his answer to Carla as if she had asked. 'Well, I don't know about the future, but right now I'm committed to what our Government wants to achieve, and it is exciting. Are you interested in politics?'

Andries Boshoff smiled behind a glass of one of his best reds when he saw that Carla was animatedly engaged in conversation with Jan DuToit. He sat smugly savouring the full bodied wine, rolling its rich smoothness around his tongue. It was a bonus to see the pained expression on the face of his other guest. Occasionally Carla caught Michael's eye, shooting him apologetic looks, but her attention was always drawn away by Jan's monopolising conversation.

Louise furthered her cause with Michael by moving closer still so that he had difficulty using his fork. She twittered on about rock music, beach parties and barbecues, giggling and becoming more flirtatious as the wine flowed.

The only respite for Michael came in the regular intervals when the servant, resplendent in his white uniform and cotton gloves, separated them to pour more wine into glasses that never seemed to become less than half full. At one point, Louise became a little too boisterous and Hettie tried to calm her but her husband frowned at his wife, shaking his head almost imperceptibly, and intervened by speaking to Louise.

'I am glad to see you are making friends, my dear,' he said, laying a fatherly hand on Louise's arm. 'But please don't burst our guest's eardrums.'

'Oh, Papa, of course not. Michael is such fun—he likes rock music too.' Louise, in her present state of inebriation, mistook Michael's affability for attentiveness. In fact he was merely being very polite out of respect for his hosts and a desire not to upset Carla, but he doubted that Louise's announcement of his liking for rock music would endear him any better to her father. A glance in that direction confirmed this. Louise returned her attention to Michael, continuing exactly as before, though slightly more quietly. Jan DuToit had managed to ignore the exchange despite Carla's attempts to draw his attention to it by looking pointedly across at the other side of the table. Andries, now delighted with the course of events, nodded at Hettie.

After dinner, they all gathered in the lounge. Michael declined port, settling just for coffee. He calculated that the best way to rejoin Carla was to be rude and butt in on their ongoing conversation. He had entertained the faint hope that Louise or her parents would have distracted Jan. It was clear that politics was the only subject which was going to interest his rival and Michael was thinking how best to phrase a probing question about Jan's stance on apartheid without offending anyone, but Andries side-tracked him.

'What do you think of my wines, young man—they are rather good don't you think?'

Andries had made no effort to be pleasant since their arrival earlier in the day but now the self-satisfaction in the older man's attitude became apparent.

'I'm no expert but I thought the white was extremely good indeed,' Michael answered evenly, and Andries puffed with pride. Innocently, he added. 'It is easily as good as the Hassenberg I usually buy.'

Hettie, wide-eyed, stared anxiously at her husband, watching his reaction to the unintended insult, while Carla choked on her coffee. Michael had never seen an expression change so suddenly and so drastically. It was nothing short of murderous.

'I am sorry if my life's-work cannot produce a wine to better the quality of the local supermarket's offering,' he said between clenched teeth.

His reaction would have been quite satisfying had it not been laced with such pure hatred that Michael immediately regretted his tactless remark.

The venomous retort was the only thing all night to have stopped Jan DuToit in his monologue. Carla looked bewildered, having been oblivious to what had been going on from the moment of their arrival. Michael thought Louise had failed to perceive the gravity of the situation. She laughed uncontrollably, rolling about on her chair and finally pummelling Michael's arm. 'Hassenberg!' was all she could say before she succumbed to another bout of laughter. Michael found it infectious and wanted to laugh with her but thought better of it, though he was unable to stop a broad smile stretching across his lips. It did nothing to change the thunderous look on Andries' face.

'Oh, Papa, your face is a picture,' Louise managed to blurt out between gasps.

When Louise finally quietened into breathless giggles, Carla intervened. 'It has been a long day,' she yawned, 'and I for one am ready for bed.' Hettie took the cue and, rising, signalled an end to the evening.

Sunday in South Africa is a day for church for most Afrikaners, but Andries and his family, although nominal members, did not often join the local congregation. Politics and vineyards were his religion and he had no regard for the church except when it suited him. This Sunday it suited him. He was adamant that today they should all attend, including Jan, who would have gone anyway, and Michael, who would not. No matter how much Michael protested that he would be happy to stay on the estate, Andries became heavily insistent that he join the family; so in the end Michael went along if only to keep the peace.

Religion had never really been broached in their relationship and now Michael sat wondering if Carla and he, had inadvertently avoided the subject, afraid of offending each other. For his part, Michael was fairly relaxed about Judaism, never observing kosher laws and ate pork, but not out of choice for he disliked the taste. As for the rest, he hated religious constraints. Each to their own, he thought, though he had to admit he had a few prejudices about Boshoff's church.

'You'll enjoy it, really you will, Michael.' Quietly, she added, 'It's quite an eye-opener. Anyway I'll sit with you.' It was as close as he'd been to her since their arrival the day before.

Michael sat uncomfortably through the service, not because of the spartan seating arrangements, but because the service itself appeared to have little to do with religion as he understood it and more to do with political indoctrination of the Afrikaner viewpoint with which he was quite at odds. The sermon was given by the imposing figure of the Dominee. It seemed to Michael as if he were the preacher's sole target. Whenever he looked up at the pulpit, the Dominee stared straight back at him, punctuating his sermon with a stabbing accusing finger. His words were delivered in a powerful voice, demanding attention. The Dominee was clearly an important figure in the community and respected by all, or more likely, Michael thought, feared.

'The Bible tells us,' the Dominee began at an almost intolerable volume, 'that God found it good to establish boundaries between people and groups of people. Therefore, because of the differences in culture, biology and political aspirations between Whites and Non-Whites, we must all stand under different laws of life.' He paused, waiting for nodding heads and murmurs of agreement to subside before continuing. 'But what about compromise?' I hear the liberal and communist elements ask. To them I say, that compromise would imply that we accept we are partly wrong. Yet, the Bible tells us we are not wrong in what we do.' Again there were murmurs and nods and Michael thought how convenient it must be for a public speaker to be preaching to the converted—nobody standing up and saying, 'I don't bloody believe you!' A sneer tugged at the corner of his mouth.

He held a strong suspicion that these 'sermons' were occasionally delivered to strengthen the resolve of any waverers who had been exposed to other doctrines. Coincidental, then, that such an address should be taking place on the very day that he was present. Perhaps that was why Andries had spent so long talking to the Dominee when they shook hands before the service.

'Liberals and communists,' the Dominee proclaimed, 'are both subversive and dangerous and their misguided calls for unity must be rejected as anti-Christian. We must endeavour to convert these opponents of our faith but we must not waste time listening to their misguided arguments. We have already stated that compromise is not acceptable—then, if that is so, discussion is pointless.'

He was in full flow now and Michael drew a mental comparison between him and Joseph Goebbels. He had seen monochrome film of the Minister of Propaganda in Hitler's Nazi party. A powerful orator, Goebbels had directed his energies into a 'final solution' aimed mainly at Jews. 'Yes,' Michael thought with cynicism, 'there are striking similarities.'

'And change?' The Dominee's voice was becoming almost maniacal now. 'We cannot accept change. How can we? To do so is to admit error and wrongdoing in the past. Yet everything that has happened— does happen—is the direct expression of the will of God.'

The sermon continued and Michael found himself shaking his head in exasperation and disbelief.

'God found it good to establish boundaries between people and groups of people....'

The whole system of apartheid was justified by the doctrine being preached, leaving no room for manoeuvre, no hope for change and every reason for Afrikaners to have a total belief in their superiority.

Michael's attention was on what the Dominee was saying, when he realised the man was staring directly at him as he spoke.

'...I quote Professor J.J. Muller of Stellenbosch Theological Seminary who said, when questioned as to whether a person embracing the Jewish faith can go to heaven like Moses and Elijah, *"For Jew and heathen the same demand is put by the Gospel. No one goes to the Father except through Jesus Christ".* '*

A murmur of agreement rustled through the congregation and Michael shifted uncomfortably in his seat. He did not care to glance around for he felt the whole congregation was watching him and he could see from the corner of his eye that Andries Boshoff was well pleased with the sermon.

Outside the church, the congregation gathered in small groups. Michael stayed close to Carla. He had managed to leave without shaking the hand of the Dominee who was accepting praise for his service from the rest of the congregation.

Michael glanced around as they stood waiting and was surprised to see Tinus Mueller, who inclined his head slightly acknowledging his presence, then turned to address the two portly men to his right. It was quite a large congregation and Michael hadn't noticed them until now, when he recognised they were cabinet ministers from their press photographs.

His eyes alighted on Andries Boshoff whom they all gathered around and whose group had now swelled to five or six, all dressed in severe black suits and, except for Andries himself, all wearing a white carnation on the lapel of their jackets.

'What's he doing here?' he asked Carla, pointing out Tinus.

Carla saw Tinus Mueller had gone over to talk to her father. Leaning closer to Michael, she said quietly, 'Oh, probably checking that his funding is secure.'

'What do you mean?'

'His funding for the laboratories. Papa invested a lot of money in the Mueller Laboratories. Didn't you know?'

'No! No, I didn't. They look pretty friendly to me—I guess it's secure!'

Carla looked back at her father and Tinus Mueller. 'It's safe enough. They go back quite a long way, Papa and Tinus. It's supposed to be a secret but it's well known they both belong to the Broederbond.' Carla nodded towards the two men Michael had recognised, and whispered conspiratorially, 'They're cabinet ministers! Most of them are members of the Broederbond as well,' referring to the secretive organisation that's sole purpose was to further the ideals and aims of Afrikanerdom.

'So what other family skeletons are you hiding from me,' he hugged her gently. 'From what I've seen and heard here today I can believe the Dutch Reform Church and the Broederbond have greater influence on our country's policies than I ever imagined,' said Michael.

'I told you it was an eye-opener, didn't I? You know, Papa is very involved in politics. He is the head of an elitist group who call themselves the ARB.'

'Who are they?' Michael enquired, full of curiosity.

'Afrikaner Regte Broederbond—they're a fairly small organisation— consisting mainly of prominent people. Papa doesn't say much about his affairs, but they're an offshoot of the Broederbond. He says they maintain a low profile so as not to worry our English-speaking friends because they further only Afrikaner aspirations in the economic sector. It seems silly but he has his own private army to protect him.'

Michael wondered just how high up Andries Boshoff was in this organisation which he had never heard of, to warrant several bodyguards?

'Look,' Michael nudged Carla, indicating the two cabinet ministers. 'They are talking to your father and Jan.' Most of the congregation began to drift away to their homes and Sunday lunch, while Andries' group swelled further.

'Oh, they often do.' Carla linked her arm with Michael's. 'Papa doesn't come to church very often but when he does they all like to get together like this. I'm sure that the real politics in our country is conducted on Sundays outside churches like this.'

'Your father certainly has done well,' he commented.

She turned to see if she could read anything into his statement but Michael's face was impassive.

'Papa studied oenology and viticulture in Germany, then France. If you must know, he has a number of degrees in science,' she gently admonished him.

'Got that wrong,' Michael thought, smiling to her. But now there was a more pressing matter which he had not got wrong. Her father had insisted he did not know Michael worked at the laboratories. As a major investor, he struck Michael as a man who would make it his business to know who worked in his organisation. Had he been trying to put him down earlier or just making small talk?

Andries Boshoff insisted that Michael accompany him on a tour of the estate immediately after lunch, using a dusty and battered 'bakkie' pick-up truck. Andries drove the bakkie slowly so as not to raise dust which might spoil the crops. The roads were rutted by the tractors and trailers laden with hand-picked grapes that would eventually become the product which provided the Boshoffs with their luxurious lifestyle.

The Coloured workers were hard at their labours, lost among the sea of vines. So vast were the fields that it seemed there was only a handful of them, but closer inspection showed dozens more were scattered throughout each of the fields. Even so, it seemed impossible that they could ever complete the task of tending the whole estate, whether planting, ploughing or picking.

'Do they always work over the weekends?' Michael asked.

'We gather the crop as quickly as we can,' Andries replied simply.

Michael wasn't so sure about the 'we'. He wondered if there was any substance to the rumours that many wine producers supplied the workforce with a measure of wine to start the day—thereby ensuring that by becoming dependent on their daily drink, they never left. He cast another glance at Andries Boshoff.

'You'd be surprised how much a single kaffir can do in a day,' Andries boasted. 'I have a handful of good supervisors—White, of course—and they don't allow any slacking. They know how to get a good day's work from a lazy kaffir.'

Michael was not surprised by the derogatory use of the word *kaffir*, only that this was usually reserved just for Blacks, and not for the descendants from the union of Blacks and European settlers who were known as Coloureds. Tactfully he let the issue go and could only guess at the sort of treatment that was meted out to the labourers in order 'to get a good day's work' out of them and imagined what it must be like to spend long hours toiling under the hot sun.

For nearly an hour they bumped and jolted their way between the fields, stopping half a dozen times for Andries to get out and talk to one of his supervisors. Michael was not invited to join them. From where he sat, with his elbow resting on the door-sill, he could not hear their discussion and so he whiled away the time observing at close range some of the activity at the edge of the field. Many of the workers wore nothing more than rags to keep the midday sun from their backs and battered cloth hats to protect their heads, yet despite it all they appeared to be happy. Those close enough to their neighbours laughed and joked as they toiled. Some were singing working songs with a rhythm to aid the pattern of their movements as they bent, deftly separating the bunches of ripe fruit from the vine and then turning to toss them into the baskets. The action was so smooth and rhythmical that Michael began to understand how such a vast area might be worked efficiently.

Andries returned just as Michael was beginning to wonder why he had been dragged on this tour of the fields. He tried to engage him in conversation but Andries remained uncommunicative. Revving the engine

Andries took off up the slope of the gently rolling hillside, now leaving the vineyards behind. They crested the brow of the hill and descended into another smaller valley, passing vacant fields on either side, the harvest already reaped.

The road was no less bumpy, yet the bakkie's speed increased down the long straight road, leaving a cloud of trailing dust. Michael had to brace himself against the roof to avoid injury. He glanced at Andries whose thin-lipped grin and jutting jaw gave him a demoniac look. 'For Christ's sake, slow down!' he yelled.

Andries gripped the steering wheel with fierce determination, and ignoring his passenger's concern, laughed aloud, and pressed the accelerator yet further towards the floor.

The bakkie went even faster, forcing Michael to push his feet hard into the foot well and to grip the door handle as tightly as he could to prevent himself from been thrown from his seat.

Bucking wildly with its engine screaming, the aged bakkie reached a sudden dip in the road causing its weight to press down on tired leaf springs. The road began to rise again revealing a large ridge jutting out from the centre of the dusty track, but Andries saw it far too late to take evasive action. They hit the bump at 95 kph. There was a terrible jolt as the sump hit the ridge, the force of the impact lifting the bakkie causing all four wheels to momentarily lose traction, then too late the springs began to uncoil. It came down heavily and the suspension did little to absorb the impact. Andries fought desperately with the steering-wheel as the front left-hand tyre caught in a furrow, taking the vehicle on a wild course of it own making. Suddenly, the tyre blew out and the front end dug into the track, gouging a furrow and sending a bow wave of thick orange dust to the sides of the vehicle. The bakkie was still sliding forward amid showers of grit when it left the road; with a sickening crunch it came to an abrupt halt in a drainage ditch, leaning over at an impossible angle.

For a moment there was no movement from within. Then Andries emerged through the cloud of choking dust. He looked round then went back, reached in and unceremoniously grabbed Michael's collar and pulled him out. Michael, badly winded, fell onto all fours and then, unsteadily, rose to his feet.

'There's no spare,' rasped Andries.

They both surveyed their transport, or lack of it, covered now in the settling dust. Badly shaken and bruised, Michael's temper exploded.

'Bloody hell! What the were you trying to do—kill us?'

'Pah! It was nothing. Just a blow-out,' the older man said dismissively. Suddenly, he turned menacingly on Michael. 'But now you listen to me and listen carefully.' Andries Boshoff's cold-eyed expression matched perfectly the threatening tone in his voice. 'All this,' he indicated the surrounding countryside with a full sweep of his arm, 'belongs to me and my family. We have owned this land for nearly three hundred years and it is more successful today than it has ever been which makes me a very powerful man. This power will pass to my son-in-laws' but it will not pass to you, Mr Bernstein. It will remain under the control of an Afrikaner. Do I make myself clear? You will stop making overtures to Carla. She is young and wilful, but she is confused. It's only a matter of time before she sees things our way—the Afrikaner way—and her future will not include you. I don't want my daughter's mind tainted with ideas and beliefs of liberals and communists—and especially not of Jews. This country has given us Afrikaners a good life and I will protect that future for us. Accidents can happen as we have seen, and today we both walk away from this,' he indicated the bakkie. 'But I will give you no assurances about tomorrow.'

Michael drew a breath, about to respond vehemently, but Andries Boshoff cut him off.

'Don't waste your breath, Bernstein. You will stop seeing Carla. If I find that you do not, I promise you'll wish you had never set eyes on her.'

There was no suitable reply.

'I take your silence as agreement, then. Now you may collect your belongings and leave—the house is that way—about three kilometres. And I warn you—do not speak to Carla of any of this.'

Michael knew that nothing he could say would make the slightest difference to the man who stood resolutely before him, so he held his peace. All he could do was show his disgust, but Andries was already striding away in the opposite direction. He watched until he had disappeared over the crest of the hill. The man was totally irrational; his behaviour nothing short of madness. Why had he sped like a maniac? Had he intended to frighten Michael, if so, he had succeeded with the accident. At that moment he could almost have believed the flat tyre was deliberate. Michael began the long walk back to the homestead. Soon he was perspiring freely, his shirt stuck to his body and his head throbbed behind his eyes; a culmination of the accident, the intended threats, and the scorching heat.

o0o

Carla was confused by Michael's sudden mood swing on their departure from the estate. He had returned dishevelled and dusty, explaining they had had a puncture and her father had gone in search of a spare tyre, heaven knows where. After the walk he simply had wanted to take a shower. Knowing her father, she wondered if Michael had told her everything.

'Are you sure everything's okay?' she shouted over the roar of engine.

'Shouldn't it be!' he responded.

Michael was intent on driving fast and it was almost impossible to hear over the noise from the exhaust and wind, so they lapsed into silence during the drive back to Cape Town. Later, he dismissed her further enquiries as being unreasonable. Yes, he had had a perfectly pleasant weekend, and yes, he liked her mother, and no, he had no fixed opinions concerning her father, or Jan for that matter. Carla smiled to herself, she thought he was just a little jealous over Jan's attentions.

In the following weeks he was not only evasive about his feelings but, she felt, was deliberately avoiding her. She couldn't help wondering if she had done something to cause this change in him but all her efforts failed to elicit a reason. Their burgeoning relationship cooled until they were barely on speaking terms and Michael became friendlier than ever with Paul. Carla tried to get Paul to find out what was going on but without success.

'As soon as I try to discuss it, he brushes it aside and changes the subject. I can't get a thing out of him.' Paul rubbed his temples. Peering through microscopes gave him a headache—so did this rift between his two friends.

'You're not just saying that? You're not hiding anything from me?'

'No, of course not, Carla. If I knew anything I'd tell you. Honestly. He just won't give. What on earth did you two get up to? Everything seemed to be going so well.'

'Yes, I thought so too. I don't know what happened. We spent a weekend at my home and he's changed after that. He came to our church and didn't like it much but he's not that sensitive. That wouldn't be it. I can't figure it out. Keep plugging away at him, Paul. I need to know.'

'I'll try,' he promised. 'But if these flu symptoms get any worse I expect I'll be taking a couple of days off,' and he massaged his aching back to emphasise his condition.

'Thanks, Paul, you're an angel. I really don't want to spend Christmas alone,' she said. 'Hope you feel better soon.'

It was a week later when Carla's telephone rang in the middle of the night. She reached for the bedside lamp and squinted at the alarm clock. Who the hell could be calling at three in the morning?

'Yes?' she said tersely. She listened for a moment and then said, 'Michael! What is it? Do you have any idea what time it is? Two weeks of nothing and now you call in the middle of the night. What the hell are you playing at?'

'I know. I'm sorry. Look, I'm at casualty...'

Her anger switched suddenly to concern. 'Are you all right? What's happened?'

'No...I mean yes. I'm fine. It's not me. It's Paul. He's in a bad way. He's contracted some sort of weird bug. Do you know if he's been working on anything hot lately—anything dangerous?'

'I haven't seen him for a week or so. He was all right then.' She thought back to her last meeting with Paul. 'But he did say he thought he was coming down with flu. Said he was going to take a couple of days off. I assumed he was angling for some time with Nina. How bad is he?'

'Very. I can't tell you over the phone. I'll stay here at the hospital tonight and call you in the morning. Sorry to have woken you but I needed to know if you'd any clue what might be wrong with him.'

'No, sorry. I'm glad you phoned anyway—really. Look, I'll come down to the hospital.'

'There's no need. We can't do anything. He's not even conscious at the moment.'

'My God! That's awful, I'm coming straight down. When he comes round some friendly faces will do him good. I won't be able to sleep now anyway.'

'There's really no need for you to come. They probably won't let us see him anyway'

'Look, Michael, I don't know what it is with you lately but it's not for you I want to come—it's for Paul, okay? I'm coming. I'll bring coffee. The stuff's lousy from the machine.'

He walked from the public phone booth annoyed. She was coming to see Paul—he hadn't assumed otherwise—he had only tried to be considerate.

A short while later Carla met Michael outside the casualty department.

'How is he, what did they say?' she asked.

'He's in a bad way. They didn't tell me much and frankly, I don't think they know what it is. They've placed him in isolation! Come on,' Michael beckoned her to follow, 'We can't see him but we can wait inside.'

They made their way to the visitor's area along cold corridors; the clinical smell of antiseptic permeated the austere surroundings. Michael told her of the events of the evening. He'd had a call from Nina.

'She's been seeing Paul and secretly staying over sometimes. Recently he'd started getting headaches and backaches. Says she gave him aspirin and hot drinks but his symptoms became worse, with vomiting and then nosebleeds. He was in severe pain and she didn't know who else to call, so she rang me.'

'Poor girl!' exclaimed Carla.

'That's what I thought. I went straight round to his place and found him coughing blood. He's lost a lot of weight and wasn't quite with it—didn't seem to know me at first, poor sod. He could just about walk so I brought him here immediately. We waited over an hour before anyone saw him,' he added acidly.

'What do you think he's picked up?'

'No idea! Maybe a form of viral pneumonia or something.'

'What about Nina?' enquired Carla.

He glanced about, and said in a quieter voice. 'She seems fine—no signs of any infection. I told Nina she'd done the right thing, and not to worry. Told her to collect her things and slip out and go home. She's a good kid.'

'Lucky for Paul she was there,' said Carla. 'What happens now?'

'We wait. They did say, they didn't think it was worth me waiting and to come back in the morning. I wanted to stay anyway.'

Uncomfortable on the armless padded chairs in the waiting area near the isolation units they dozed fitfully. There was little activity in the early hours of the morning and time passed slowly. They hardly spoke at all, just waiting for any news of their friend's condition. Carla watched Michael as he unconsciously thumbed through another magazine from the coffee table. He appeared to be uneasy about something. Yes, of course he was concerned for Paul but she was sure there was something else too. She had caught him shooting sidelong glances at her more than once. At that moment the sound of footsteps heralded the arrival of the doctor, who was struggling into a white coat as he walked towards them.

'Ah! It was you who brought the young man in,' he sought confirmation.

'Doctor! How is Paul doing?'

'Sorry, are you both together?' as if noticing Carla for the first time.

'Yes,' we're both friends of Paul. How's he doing?' Michael asked again.

'We can talk in here,' he said, indicating a small office off the waiting area. He looked at Carla 'I think you had better wait here, Miss, this won't take long.' Less than five minutes later the doctor emerged and, without a glance in her direction, disappeared along the corridor. Minutes passed before Michael appeared, visibly shaken.

'Can we see him?' she asked.

'It's too late for that...he died a half hour ago.'

Carla's stomach muscles clenched so tightly that she winced. 'What do we do Michael? Can we say goodbye?' she choked.

'No!' Michael exclaimed vehemently, then more gently. 'No. It's best you remember him as he was.' He wanted to spare Carla the full horror of seeing Paul's condition some hours earlier. He would never forget it. It was difficult to believe that a human being could have looked so dreadful and still be alive. Paul, semi-conscious at the time, had no idea what was happening to him. He had not recognised Michael and was barely able to speak. He had become nauseous and Michael had seen that his vomit was strangely black. His skin by that time had turned a ghastly blue, as if he had been beaten all over, and the whites of his eyes had turned red under drooping eyelids. Had it been only the eyes, he would have looked like a drunk who had been on a binge for a week, but his skin had become wrinkled and the flesh seemed detached from the skull. Blood had seeped from his body through every orifice, soaking his clothes. Massive haemorrhaging had taken place within that haggard frame, yet no one had been able to determine the cause.

oOo

The health authorities were baffled. They immediately placed the entire personnel of Mueller Laboratories under quarantine. Michael remembered vividly having seen such fatal results in his laboratory animals, and went to the Cape Doctor with his suspicions about the cause of Paul's death.

Tinus was extremely concerned and personally supervised the investigation, confining everyone to the laboratories in a bid to contain any possible spread of infection, insisting that Paul must have become contaminated by some pathogen or virus on the premises. Blood samples were taken to establish if the agent was contagious. No, it was not *P.carinii* and he drove them nearly insane in an attempt to isolate the security leak.

Eventually they all conceded that Paul had probably opened the wrong vial and, realising his error, simply replaced it without recording the possibility of contamination, or the breach in procedure. Tinus immediately introduced a new policy which made merely walking into the building as time-consuming as entering the hot zone itself.

oOo

Paul was cremated, while they remained restricted to the premises during the mop-up operation. There was little joviality over the festive season due to the circumstances surrounding their forced confinement, nor any New Year's celebration, but it brought Carla and Michael closer together until, in a quiet moment in the canteen, he cornered her.

'We have to talk before we get out of here tomorrow.'

'Yes,' she said. 'At last!'

Michael fidgeted a little as if seeking the right words. He sat next to her and, throwing an arm over the back of the chair, turned to face her. She mirrored his posture and waited for him to speak.

'Look, Carla, I have to explain.'

'Yes?' she said again, offering no help.

'But first I want you to tell me what your father had to say after we left that weekend.'

'Not much, though I've spoken to him several times over the phone.

He said you were quite rude when he was showing you round the farm—said you were angry when the bakkie broke down and that you took off by yourself and walked back to the house. Is that right, Michael?'

'Ha!' He snorted in disbelief. 'The sly old ba...' and then he remembered that he was talking to the sly old bastard's daughter. 'That's not quite how it happened, Carla. Your father told me to tell you nothing of this, and he actually threatened me with I don't know what, if I did. He also told me not to see you again...' recounting the details of that Sunday afternoon to her and she listened quietly until he had finished.

'I don't believe it,' she said, shaking her head. 'Papa wouldn't do that. He wouldn't say those things.' She stopped short of calling Michael a liar.

'What else can I say to convince you, Carla. What other reason could I have?'

'I don't know—but Papa...no, he wouldn't.'

'He could, Carla, and he did.' He saw that she didn't believe him. 'Okay, then what about the bakkie?' He remembered she had seen them leave together in the pick-up. 'Where was the bakkie? Did you see him come back in it? Of course you didn't, because he put it into a ditch on the far side of the estate! Why didn't he come back with me?'

She could see he desperately wanted her to believe him. She recalled that her father had not reappeared before their departure from the estate and she had not seen the bakkie since. She was trying to believe him. 'Yes, but Papa wouldn't actually do anything. He may have wanted to frighten you off but he wouldn't hurt a fly.'

'Bloody hell! It wasn't very funny. First he nearly killed me, then threatened me. I'm telling you, Carla, he wasn't messing around.' Michael looked at the ceiling for guidance. 'He's a very powerful man, you know that, so what am I expected to do? Of course he wouldn't do anything himself, but a word in the right quarter and he could make my life sheer hell if he wanted to. Do I take the chance and have him mess your life up, too?'

She loved her father dearly but she knew he could be a hard man and had probably been a little rough on Michael. While growing up she had ridden her horse around the estate and often seen him dealing sternly with his supervisory workers and more harshly with the pickers...even striking one in her presence. She had told her mother, who sympathised but forbade any mention of it again: the control of the labourers was entirely his responsibility and he would stand no criticism from wife or child.

On another occasion she had found his 'sjambok', a small rhinoceros-hide whip, in his study and had thrown it away. Later, when it was discovered to be missing, the servants were immediately blamed and to save them from physical abuse she had confessed. Her mother had reprimanded her for entering the study, while strangely enough her father had said nothing and the matter was summarily dismissed. She admitted finally to herself, 'Yes, his side of the story is believable! Why Papa? Why!'

'So why are you telling me all this now?' Carla enquired.

'It's been eating me up inside, I can't go on pretending. Dammit, I want to marry you!'

Accepting what Michael was telling her, she now realised how painful it must have been for him. 'Oh, Michael. You poor thing. Kom,' she said and opened her arms. They embraced briefly, clasping one another tightly.

'Well?'

'Well what?' She teased, gently pushing him away.

'You know what. Will you marry me?'

His recent behaviour had not led her to expect a proposal of marriage now—she had harboured the hope of that happening during their weekend at the family estate.

'You don't really expect an answer right this minute do you?' Seeing the look on his face she knew that he did. 'I need more time, Michael. What with Paul's death and now Papa's threats, I need time,' she said lamely. She had been sure of Michael before that weekend on the farm, but the change in him since then made her uncertain of her feelings and, while she thought she believed him now, she had to be sure.

'All right then,' he conceded. 'After tomorrow I'm going up to Durban to see Aaron. He wants to discuss the business with me. I should be back in a couple of weeks. How's that?'

'Two weeks will be fine,' she said, relieved that he did not try to push her for an answer. 'Thanks, Michael.'

CHAPTER 3

Apartheid, experienced first-hand: "The hardship to
which I was subjected was superficial—only
a symptom of the deep disease of colour prejudice."
Mahatma Gandhi
Natal, South Africa, 1893 - 1914
Assassinated in 1948

Within the province of Natal on South Africa's eastern shores, where
the subtropical land meets the clear blue waters of the Indian Ocean,
lies Durban. It owes its existence to the almost landlocked bay discovered
by Vasco da Gama in 1497. From small beginnings as a settlement of traders
from the Cape, it grew to be the most important cargo port in all Africa.

It was to Durban that Michael's brother Aaron Bernstein had moved
Coronet Chemicals' headquarters from Johannesburg in 1970, almost before
his father had gone cold. Samuel had bequeathed the firm in equal share to
his two sons.

Michael never had any enthusiasm for the business and Aaron assumed
complete responsibility for the company. Now he had summoned Michael
for discussions. Michael had been expecting it sooner or later. Aaron didn't
like loose ends and most probably wanted to legalise his full control over
the business. Michael knew that for this he would have had his lawyers
draw up a watertight legal document and, no doubt, needed Michael's
signature before he could relax. Of course, Aaron wouldn't come straight
out and ask—that was why he had been invited for a fortnight. Michael
reasoned it would also give Carla the breathing space she needed.

Aaron would begin by buttering him up for a few days and then, Michael
guessed, he would be wined and dined while Aaron talked about all aspects
of the business, knowing he would be boring his brother. Only after these
ploys, would Aaron come to the point and ask for Michael's signature,
agreeing to hand over his legal interest in the company. Aaron had tried
twice before but Michael was reluctant on the grounds it had been their
father's wish that the two brothers actively participate in the company.
Maybe now the timing was opportune if he and Carla were to get married.

Aaron sent one of his drivers to collect Michael from the airport.
A short drive brought him from the southern freeway into central Durban
and they skirted the natural harbour following the Victoria Embankment.
The dark Chrysler swept into an underground car park. The lift took
Michael and his luggage up to the tenth floor where he stepped out into

Aaron's new penthouse. The panoramic view was amazing—encompassing the Bay of Natal. The harbour and ships lay in the foreground below and he could see clearly across the estuary to the villages on the far side of the bay. Michael was suitably impressed. Aaron would arrive home about 5.00pm, he was told. The houseboy showed him to his room and made tea while Michael showered and changed after his flight.

With no one around except for the servant, he spent time investigating his surroundings, walking from room to room inspecting every feature. Aaron had spared nothing on the decor. Still something was missing. The apartment was large but too austere—Michael decided it needed a woman's touch. He smiled to himself—there was a good chance he would be married before his brother. He found a locked door and knew instinctively it would be Aaron's inner sanctum and that he would be invited in—in due course.

Promptly at 5.00pm Aaron arrived home and the two brothers greeted one another stiffly. It was always the same; as children, they used to squabble and fight incessantly but as men, after they had gone their separate ways, their reunions began with a certain formality, like strangers. After a couple of days of getting to know one another again, the bickering would begin again. It was never serious, just a difference of opinion on politics or any one of a thousand other topics. That's why Michael usually restricted his visits to a couple of days at most, but this time he needed a holiday and Aaron's place was convenient.

Michael had guessed right. Aaron was particularly pleasant and complimentary, all the time steering well clear of business matters. He booked a table for dinner at the exclusive Durban Country Club and, during the meal, made plans to take in a show the next evening.

Both events were enjoyable and relaxing. During the days while Aaron worked, Michael joined the thousands of holidaymakers exploring the city's many attractions.

On the beachfront Michael was stopped by one of the few remaining Zulu rickshaw drivers in the city, resplendent in his colourful beaded garb and horned headgear, who tried to coax him to ride on the two-wheeled cart. Michael was tempted but was beaten to the post by a young couple who climbed on board before he could accept. He watched enthralled by the colourful spectacle as they disappeared down the road with the Zulu driver leaping high into the air, using the long yoke of the rickshaw as a fulcrum to give him purchase.

To get out of the midday heat, Michael turned away and headed for a lounge bar in one of the many hotels that bordered the shoreline. As he sipped a brandy, he thought of Carla and wished she had said 'Yes', and was with him now.

By the fifth day, Aaron finally broached business matters. The evening meal was taken at home and he used the opportunity to raise the subject. Michael refused the proffered cigar but accepted a Cape port. Used to his brother's economical hand he checked the measure, then went to the cocktail cabinet and filled his glass.

'We've had some good news today,' Aaron began. 'I had a meeting with some government officials and they have agreed to renew our contract with the Ministry of Health and even to expand it. The deal should be worth 2.5 million.'

'That's good news,' Michael responded dutifully. 'But I didn't know it was up for renewal!'

'My dear brother, we have to tender along with all the others. The results are usually a foregone conclusion, but we have to go through the motions. A formality you understand, but it gives them the opportunity not to renew if we default.'

'Default! On what?'

'Anything. Absolutely anything, but usually it's politics. It's their way of ensuring that businesses toe the line. Put one foot wrong and they may not only decline to renew the contract but they could actively inhibit our progress. We don't want that sort of thing, Michael, or we could find ourselves out of business altogether.'

Michael became wary. He had expected to be asked to sign over his say in the company but Aaron's tone suggested something else. 'What exactly are you driving at, Aaron?'

'Look, Michael,' Aaron went on, 'I need hardly remind you about your performance while at university...your political viewpoint concerning the Non-Whites is no secret. You've made it clear to the board on many occasions. But if you were to seek a wider audience for your political views, it could reflect on the business and then where would we be?'

'A lot better off, I should say. What would you think if your fate was decided for you and you had no say in the matter, because of the colour of your skin? And what if that fate dictated that you should be treated no better than a stray dog? What if you had no access to a decent education and were forced to live hundreds of kilometres away in a place where you had no family or friends and no prospect of work? I tell you, man, this 'Homeland Citizenship Act' is an abomination. Don't you think these are views that should be aired...?'

'Michael, Michael,' Aaron interrupted, trying to placate him, 'I'm not arguing with you. Of course these things are important but I am not a politician—I cannot change them—I am a businessman and my responsibility is to the business and the shareholders. I must protect these interests. I cannot get involved—and what's more neither can you.'

'What do you mean neither can I? How dare you presume to decide what I can or cannot do.'

'This is not the first time...' Aaron stated.

'I will do what I like and if I want to, to...' Michael thought briefly, 'write another letter to the paper I'll damn well write a letter to the paper.' Until that moment, it had not crossed his mind but now it seemed the obvious thing to do. He had done so in the past, voicing his opinions on the injustices in his country. He hated the way the White minority chose to ignore the hardships suffered by the Non-Whites. Again he felt he should have the courage to stand with those who had not flinched. He blurted out, 'If enough people made their dislike of the régime known, things might change. Just maybe.'

Aaron's voice and colour rose. 'Let me spell it out for you, little brother. We are a well-known family in these parts, thanks to our father. People don't know that you have nothing to do with the company. If you start spouting all that commie crap it's likely to do a lot of damage to our standing. The government won't renew their contract and others will follow their lead. It wouldn't take long in a business like this for a healthy profit to turn into a crippling deficit. I'm telling you, you can't get involved publicly because you will involve me as well!'

'Commie crap? You bloody hypocrite!' Michael shouted. 'You can't see past the end of your nose. Anything that goes against the grain you label 'communism'. Open your eyes, Aaron. Look at what's happening to people. They won't stand for it much longer. They want change—they want to control their own destiny and they will fight to get it. Why can't you see how much better it would be if we could all work together?' Michael calculated that this tirade would form the basis of his letter to the *Cape Herald*, a leading Cape Town newspaper.

'Michael, I'm asking you not to do this. For my sake. For the sake of the business. Don't you know how much damage you could cause? You say you're concerned about the Blacks! Think about all the Indians, Coloureds and Chinese working for us. If the company fails, what will happen to them? Please reconsider.'

'Not a chance, Aaron. My mind's made up and I very much doubt that anything I have to say could harm the business. Your precious company is safe. Just don't try to dictate to me. Understand one thing,' he fumed, 'the main difference between us is that you and most Whites in this country believe you are still Europeans. Well, you're wrong: we are all Africans.'

'You're either very naive or very stupid,' Aaron shouted. 'I warn you, Michael—you'll regret this if you go ahead with it.'

'Thanks for your hospitality, Aaron,' Michael yelled back, refusing to be intimidated by his elder brother. 'I'm leaving! I've better things to do than stand here arguing with a bigot like you.' He stormed off to collect his gear. Reaching the lift door he turned to face his brother and said, 'Oh, and another thing, I'm not signing my authority in the company over to you either.' The last thing Michael saw before leaving the room was his brother's dark brooding expression.

oOo

From a beachfront hotel, Michael composed a letter of protest to the editor of the *Cape Herald*, censuring the Homeland Citizenship Act of 1971. The Act decreed that every Black must be a citizen of one of ten newly created 'Bantu homelands'. The inference was that if they belonged to these homelands then they were not citizens of South Africa. It was clear that the aim of the Act was to ensure that all remaining South Africans were White.

He pointed out that the coincidence that the homelands were of no particular value, as far as mineral wealth, farming or strategic military use were concerned, had not gone unnoticed. 'Coincidence my foot!' Michael muttered to himself.

Still, the disagreement with Aaron troubled him. It was not unusual for the brothers' meetings to degenerate into petty bickering, but there was usually nothing important at stake. This time it was different. Aaron was protecting his business interests—interests which satisfied his need for wealth and its attendant power. Michael now saw the opportunity to do something useful at last: to stand up and be counted—to make a difference.

It seemed that they had always been at loggerheads since his childhood. He thought of his father Samuel, who had sold a prosperous industrial chemical plant in America to seek a new life in South Africa with his bride. With the healthy profits from the sale he had opened a new plant in Johannesburg and immediately found a market in the mines.

After his wife's death Samuel threw himself into building Coronet Chemicals into a successful company quoted on the stock exchange, leaving Sophie, their large and kindly Black nanny, to attend to the newborn infant and his elder brother, Aaron. Sophie became their surrogate mother. She reprimanded them when necessary and gave generous praise when they reported their triumphs to her, accepting her care without question. It made no difference to them that her skin was a different colour. Michael's saddest day in all his fourteen years was when Sophie died. His father took them to the funeral where he had wept openly for her. Michael's sobbing drawing the attention of all the Black mourners who had stared at the White boy's tears for a Black woman. He had been embarrassed, not that he was crying for her but because they were staring at him.

At Jeppe High School he had excelled in the sciences and knew early that he wanted a career in the medical field. Later, at Witwatersrand University, the news came that his father had died, worn out by hard work and the grief he never overcame. Aaron, soon after, moved the company headquarters to Durban and Michael, having no interest in the firm, stayed on in Johannesburg to complete his degree.

While there, he enjoyed a peripheral involvement in left wing politics and joined a protest meeting against 'The Prohibition of Political Interference Act of 1968', which prevented different race groups from belonging to the same political party. He and some fellow students were arrested and interrogated for twenty-four hours before being released with threats of dire consequences if they were to pursue such an odious involvement with communism. He knew the government saw any criticism as a threat to their policy of apartheid; any opposition, a communist plot to overthrow them. They didn't even consider him to be a true South African for God's sake. Being a Jew, rather than of Afrikaner descent rendered him an alien in their eyes.

He finally put the pen down. His letter was hard-hitting and he suspected it would not go unanswered, but he didn't care. If there were repercussions, then Aaron would feel the brunt of the government's wrath but, in truth, he believed his brother's fear of reprisal to be grossly exaggerated. Aaron tended to over-amplify situations concerning him and, while he was thinking about it, he wondered if Aaron's resentment stemmed from a sibling rivalry—or even if in some way he blamed Michael for their mother's death. They were not close and for his part, he had given up trying. Aaron had never shown him any brotherly warmth. After the row, Michael knew it would be best to stay away for a while.

Michael strolled along Marine Parade and posted the letter to the *Cape Herald* plus a copy to his brother, before telephoning Carla on the off chance she had already made a decision.

Carla was distraught. 'Oh, Michael, where have you been? I've been trying to reach you.'

'What's wrong, Carla, what's happened?'

'It was horrible. One minute they were there and the next they were gone. It was awful, just awful,' she said hysterically.

'Calm down. You're not making any sense. Who was there? What was awful?'

'Geoff and, and Chris—on the mountain—they fell,' she stumbled over the words telling him how their two associates at the laboratories had died tragically. 'We were climbing on the mountain. It was an accident. There was nothing we could do!'

'Jesus! Are you all right?'

'No, I'm not, I need you here. Come back, Michael. Please!'

'Okay, okay. Take it easy. I'm on my way, I've finished my business here anyway.' Carla's breathless plea was a powerful incentive to be on the next plane southwards to Cape Town.

The flight passed swiftly without incident. Michael thought of the turbulent meeting with his brother which had ended with a feeling of finality. He knew it might be a while before they would reconcile their differences, but he didn't care. Now the news of the death of his friends occupied his thoughts even as the Boeing 727 touched down at Cape Town in the late afternoon.

Carla met him and they drove to her apartment in silence.

'I'm glad you're here,' Carla said when they arrived, entwining her arms tightly around him for the comfort she needed.

He was just glad to be holding her again. Finally, reluctantly, he prised her arms open and led her to the sofa. 'I love you Carla...you must feel dreadful.' He watched while she composed herself.

Hesitant, she reached for the half-filled glass which had been left standing before her departure to the airport. She drained its contents, too distraught even to think to offer him a glass.

Michael rose and helped himself to a drink. 'What happened up there?' he asked as he refilled Carla's glass. 'In your own time,' he added, gently encouraging her.

With obvious effort she began to recount the ordeal, reliving the moment the two men had become the latest victims of Table Mountain.

'Tinus had invited us to tackle a more difficult route. We all agreed. We had separated into teams. Chris and Geoff were roped together on a parallel climb to Tinus and myself, to our left. It was all going so well until Chris shouted he was in difficulty on a rocky promontory close to the summit. Tinus secured me before traversing the rock face to assist Chris.' She shivered involuntarily. 'I couldn't see them—Chris or Tinus—only Geoff alongside me. I was in a kind of hollow and could barely hear Tinus calling instructions to Chris. The wind...it had become violent, but they seemed to be doing all right. I could see Geoff looking up, waiting.'

Michael, now sitting next to her, held her trembling hands.

'Then I heard Tinus shout to Chris that he was clear now, and Chris called to Geoff to start moving again. That's when it happened! Suddenly their rope went slack and Chris yelled out. I only saw him as he hit Geoff.'

Carla was still trying to block from her mind Geoff's ghastly look of terror in the instant before Chris smashed into his face with the full force of his climbing boots. 'Then they were both falling. I heard them scream but the wind was blowing hard and all I could hear after that was the roar of it in my ears. I closed my eyes. I didn't want to see where they fell. Michael, it was dreadful,' she shuddered involuntarily.

Terrified, Carla had clung desperately to the rock-face, helpless; her mind now blanking out her wide-eyed stare riveted on the bodies of her two climbing companions cartwheeling into the abyss. Surging winds off the Atlantic, channelled through the breach at False Bay had tugged fiercely at her clothes, she recalled. With enormous force the gale had enveloped the Cape Peninsula, and a clawing, violent gust had torn them away from the mountain, snatching away their screams of terror. Then suddenly they were gone. Instantly, her rope had jerked tight...

'Next, Tinus was pulling on my rope, but there was nothing we could do.'

Michael drew her close, whispering into her hair, 'I love you.' He tightened his hold on her, gently, while she sobbed: cathartic weeping that seemed to wipe away the horror she had experienced up on that mountain. Slowly she became calmer and, sitting up, wiped her eyes.

Michael drained his glass—the tragic accident adding to his abhorrence of heights. He listened while she filled in the details.

Even before Tinus and Carla reached the safety of the station on the summit, the alarm had been raised by several people who had seen the accident from below. Tinus, as party leader, dealt with the formalities and Carla had been treated for shock before being taken back down the mountain and home by Tinus' friend.

'That's strange,' she paused, 'now I come to think of it. He asked where you were.'

'Who? Tinus?'

'No, his friend. The one who drove me home. I haven't seen him before but he seemed to know you. I didn't catch his name—tall man, fair hair, big build. Looked more like a wrestler than a biologist, but you never can tell! Do you know who I mean?'

'Can't say I do. What did he want me for, did he say?'

'No, not that I recall. I was still in shock, I think. Told him you were away in Durban and we expected you back in a few days or so and certainly for Geoff's cremation—tomorrow. Hope you don't mind.'

'Just curious, that's all,' and Michael drifted into thought for a moment, unable to place anyone fitting the description of the man who had driven Carla home.

They lay entwined in each other's arms on the sofa while Michael caressed her back, kneading the tight knots out of her muscles. Slowly, she stood up and led him to the balcony where she leaned back against him. Michael wrapped his arms around her from behind and breathed in the scent of her hair while they gazed out at the setting sun.

She caught him unawares. 'The answer is yes, my love.'

For a moment his mind was a blank, trying to understand what she was talking about, then he saw the smile as she half-turned to face him.

'Yes? You mean yes, you will marry me?' he asked.

'I mean yes, I will marry you,' she mimicked and as she swung round he gathered her in his arms even more tightly than before.

Michael knew she was emotionally overwrought with the death of their friends but he didn't care. He wanted her—forever. This time they kissed long and passionately.

That night they lay in bed making plans for the future. Where they'd buy a home, having children, even down to the family saloon. 'You can have everything, but not my car—it was my graduation present from Papa,' Carla laughed happily. They held each other long after their lovemaking until they fell asleep.

The next morning, Carla and Michael arrived early in Carla's more sedate blue BMW to join the people quietly waiting outside the crematorium. After subdued exchanges of condolences with friends and relatives, Carla noticed the man who had given her a lift home and pointed him out to Michael. He was with another man of similar dress and build, scanning the congregation. Seeing Carla, the man spoke to his associate and they approached.

'Good morning, Miss Boshoff,' he smiled politely. 'Is this your friend Michael Bernstein?'

Carla smiled automatically but her expression quickly changed to curiosity when she realised he did not know Michael.

Michael said, 'Yes, I am Michael Bernstein. What can I do for you?'

The man looked at his colleague and nodded. Stepping forward they grabbed Michael by the arms, brushing Carla brusquely aside, 'Come with us, Mr Bernstein,' they ordered.

Michael's reaction was to struggle out of their grasp, but together they were far too strong for him. 'Hey what's going on?' he yelled, attracting the attention of the other mourners, 'What do you want with me?'

Carla pounded ineffectually on the receding back of the first man, screaming at him, 'Leave him alone. You can't do this. Who the hell do you think you are?' But she was shrugged off easily and they bundled Michael quickly into a waiting car which sped away. The whole scene was over in seconds, leaving Carla trembling with confusion and fury.

Tinus Mueller had also witnessed the arrest. He voiced his anger at the plain-clothes policemen's untimely and heavy-handed tactics. He tried consoling Carla and continued to do so after they had returned to the laboratories directly from the cremation.

She twisted her handkerchief; while a tear ran down her cheek.

He put an arm around her shoulders to comfort her. 'There, there. I'm sure everything will be all right, my dear. It's all a mistake, you'll see.' He spoke calmly, soothing her with comforting words until her tears subsided. 'I know people,' he said. 'So I will see what I can do for you. How's that?'

'Could you?' Carla said hopefully. 'I would be so grateful for anything you can find out.'

'It's no trouble, though it may take some time—and I cannot promise you anything.'

'Yes, I understand. But anything—anything at all. I know I'm probably worrying needlessly but it was the way they snatched him away from the funeral,' she pleaded.

He was back within twenty minutes. 'It's all right, my girl. He was only taken in for questioning. The police say he was released an hour ago. I suppose he'll be along shortly to explain what's happened. So, why don't you take yourself off home and, if he comes in, I'll tell him where to find you.'

oOo

Michael did not return. Several days passed without a word and his disappearance remained a complete mystery, while Carla fretted.

'Where is he?' she pleaded to anyone who would listen. 'What have they done with him?'

Andries Boshoff was plainly concerned at his daughter's distress and came over day after day to her apartment, before insisting she return with him to the farm until they could establish Michael's whereabouts. Even though he stated openly that he didn't particularly like her choice of friend, he promised to place his resources behind the search for Michael.

'What's happened to him?'

Carla was tearful most of the time. No rational explanation accounted for his sudden disappearance. Michael had left his MGA outside her flat the morning of the funeral, but later it was gone. He must have returned before her from the police station and taken the car. She went over events time and again but still there was no clue to indicate any motive. Had he cold feet about marriage? Did she appear too anxious in giving her commitment and now he had turned and run? Carla was angry and hurt at the same time.

Turning on the light, he glanced at his bedside clock. 'Who the hell's ringing at this time of the night?' he wondered, picking up the receiver. 'Aaron Bernstein,' he answered sleepily.

71

'Hello, Aaron,' she paused, 'I'm sorry to disturb you, this is Carla Boshoff. It's concerning your brother.'

Immediately Aaron thought the worst, 'What! Has something happened to Michael?' he demanded.

'No, no, he's not had an accident or anything...I was hoping you could help—he's disappeared!' Quickly she apologised for the late hour, ' I did try to contact you sooner, but your office said you were away and would only be back tonight!'

'Oh! God, I'm afraid my brother is unpredictable at times. Now what's he gotten into...' Aaron could throw no light on his brother's whereabouts. No, he had definitely not returned to Durban and he didn't expect him to, not after the way Michael had behaved.

Aaron replaced the receiver. Michael's disappearance was odd to say the least. And where did this girl fit into things? Michael had never mentioned her! She had intimated that their relationship was a serious one and hence her anxiety. Boshoff! Aaron let that bounce around for a moment. Michael and an Afrikaner! Well that was one for the books. Possibly the only thing he shared with his brother was a liberal religious attitude and they had both agreed, they did not have a problem marrying out of the faith. Still, an Afrikaner! It was too much to believe. He shook his head and turned out the light but sleep evaded him. Where was his brother? She had seemed very concerned.

Almost five weeks had gone by and still there was no news of Michael. The laboratories no longer had a vibrancy about them. It was almost as though they had served a purpose and were winding down. Everyone seemed listless and some talked of leaving. The general apathy filtered from the top as even Tinus seemed preoccupied by interests outside the laboratories. He didn't bother to show up most days. But today was different.

Tinus arrived at 10.00am and almost immediately received two visitors. They had been with him, behind closed doors, for half an hour before Carla was summoned.

'I'm afraid I have some grave news, Carla. About Michael.' Tinus' expression was anything but comforting that Carla feared the worst.

'You mean he's dead?' she gasped.

'No, no. Mercifully Michael's not dead,' he said and Carla relaxed a little.

'Please sit down, Carla. These gentlemen have something to say to you.' With a wave of his hand Tinus indicated the men sitting in the guest chairs. Carla had hardly paid them any attention since she entered the office. Now she stared at them intently. They had the same appearance as those who had arrested Michael weeks earlier yet somehow they looked different.

The older one was in his mid-thirties, perhaps nearer forty. He looked as if he had recently been used as a punch bag. There was something about him that looked familiar. Both men were solidly built and wore sombre suits and matching expressions. Even before the older man spoke, she had a sudden attack of anxiety—they were plain-clothes policemen she had little doubt.

'Good morning, Miss Boshoff,' he began. 'Commandant Van Heerden of the Bureau of State Security,' he introduced himself proudly as though reverence went automatically with the title.

This view was not shared by Carla. She went on the verbal attack.

'What does BOSS want with Michael for God's sake? Where is he?'

'We are here on a very serious matter, Miss Boshoff,' Van Heerden began solemnly.

Carla was losing patience. 'Then get on with it! Tell me what's going on?'

'I will, if she shuts the fuck up,' thought Van Heerden. 'We believe Mr Bernstein stole important research papers and subsequently fled the country. We think he went to Botswana. You were known to be his girlfriend at the time. What can you tell us about it?'

Carla stood gaping as the words sank in. She did not like his use of the past tense, even less his accusation that Michael was a thief. 'Michael! No! He wouldn't—not Michael—he wouldn't do that. You must be mistaken. As for Botswana, what nonsense! These are wild accusations! Where's your proof?'

'There is no mistake Miss Boshoff. We also understand your boyfriend was known to be friendly with kaffirs.'

Her eyes flashed. 'Don't you call them that. They are human beings, do you understand?'

There was no response from Van Heerden but his contempt for her was clear. 'We want to know what your part was in all this.' Van Heerden was having difficulty being patient himself.

'My part! Are you mad? I've had nothing to do with the theft of any research papers.'

She turned suddenly to Tinus. 'What research papers?'

Tinus leaned forward, resting both elbows on the desk, removed his spectacles and rubbed his eyes. 'Sorry Carla, I should have told you before, but at the time it was only a routine matter. I have tried to tell them that Michael wouldn't do it but the research papers are missing. He knew their value. It was the project he started—you helped him with some of it, I believe. I took it a stage further because I saw some commercial value in it. Now it's gone and so has he.'

'Yes, but he was arrested. They took him,' she said glowering at the two visitors. Then it dawned on her that Tinus had initiated the enquiry and she turned her focus on him.

73

Van Heerden interjected. 'He was only brought in for questioning after Professor Mueller reported his research notes missing. He was released that afternoon and subsequently disappeared. We put two and two together...'

'And came up with five,' Carla interrupted.

'No, Carla, I don't think so,' said Tinus. 'I told them it couldn't be Michael. But they persuaded me to search his locker yesterday. It looks like he was preparing to leave us anyway. His personal effects are gone and we found these,' he held up some laboratory notes. 'They were with the missing research papers but they are of no particular value. I'm afraid I find myself agreeing with these gentlemen. Michael may have stolen the papers before he left for Durban. I took the liberty of phoning his brother, and he said you had phoned, but Michael's not there. He didn't seem surprised and said Michael is capable of doing something this reckless.'

She winced but did not let on. It was what Aaron had said to her, '...I'm afraid my brother is unpredictable at times....'

With sudden realisation Carla said, 'You searched my office too, didn't you? I thought my things had been moved. You couldn't have thought I had any part in this?'

'No, not really,' Tinus said, 'but—well, we had to be sure. You must understand. The research is very valuable. If they are right, I can see how Michael must have been tempted.' He turned to the senior BOSS agent and said, 'I'm quite happy that this young lady had nothing to do with the theft, don't you agree?'

'Ja, sir, of course,' Van Heerden answered deferentially, 'I think we can safely say the lady had nothing to do with it.' He turned to face her and said, 'But I would choose my friends more carefully in future if I were you, Miss. He was a Jew, I understand. They are always out for a fast buck. Take my advice—stick with your own kind. You know where you are with an Afrikaner,' he smiled. Carla saw a flash of stainless steel wire in the corner of his mouth. With that the two men rose and left her with Tinus in the office. A picture of abject misery Carla sat slumped in the chair, staring into a void of shattered expectations.

Tinus came from behind the desk to lay a consoling hand on her shoulder, 'I'm truly sorry. I thought very highly of that young man.'

Carla waited vainly for Michael to contact her. She forgave Tinus, but even in the face of the damning evidence she still couldn't believe that Michael had absconded with valuable research material and exiled himself. She knew him too well and loved him even more.

CHAPTER 4

Pre-Independence: "We are not concerned solely with
the rights of Africans, we are struggling for human
rights—the inalienable rights of all men."
> Kenneth Kaunda
> President of Zambia, 1964 - 91

5 January 1972

The young doctor paced the veranda of his parents' home. He was deeply
concerned about the future. Only last year the White government had
transformed the region known as the Transkei into one of many self-
governing 'homelands' in order to contain the 'Black' problem. Dismayed
and alarmed by their arrogance as they carved up the country, he knew they
were taking the wealth for themselves and leaving soil-eroded barren tribal
lands for the so-called newly 'independent' Blacks. In real terms,
as a Black he had become a disenfranchised person who could not now lay
claim to being a 'South African' citizen. He knew a further motive was to
create even larger labour reservoirs for White South Africa as in the case of
his parents, whose home was in Soweto, bordering on Johannesburg.
This Black township provided the affluent White community with cheap
labour. He had been born here and had grown up under the apartheid
system. David Nyamande had cause to feel depressed. With a sigh he
flopped down into his father's favourite chair, fingers absently stroking the
armrest. He reviewed his circumstances.

Thirty-six years earlier his father, the son of an Ndebele chief, had broken
from the old ways and joined migrant workers from across the Limpopo
River—in what the Whites called Rhodesia—taking the long road south to
here, the Transvaal gold reef, in search of employment. They were attracted
by good pay, despite the harsh working conditions on the mines.

His Xhosa mother had likewise come to Johannesburg seeking work and
his parents had fallen in love at first sight. She was from one of the largest
tribes in South Africa. Not long after they met, a tribal committee
approached his father, suggesting it was unwise to contemplate wedlock
out of his tribe. They considered the Xhosa even lower than the Amaholi
social class; tribes conquered by the Ndebele and whose members were not
fit to marry an Ndebele of his status.

David's father had stood his ground and eventually the delegation
conceded that possibly an exception could be made on this occasion.
Standing near on two metres, his powerful upper body may have had
something to do with it; and the son had inherited his fine physique.

David remembered the pride he had felt the day his father returned home proclaiming, *'I have been promoted to a 'White' position, I am now a foreman.'* Recalling the moment he smiled: the mining corporation had recognised his father's years of loyal service and his status within the community. It had been his mother who explained that his father was the first Black to hold any authority on the mine. The organisation had seen his father's potential and attempted to get him to study, but he had brushed the offer aside, saying: *'Better you teach my children,'* and had won a small grant to assist with their education. Besides this, the company had provided a modest pension on his retirement. Even at that early age, David had been aware that this was not common practice and saw his father's friends were proud of his achievements.

He realised now that it must have been a continuous struggle for his parents to support two academically inclined children through university. Nyamande senior had restated his position many times. David and his younger sister Nandi must not be deprived of an education, saying that this was the way to meet whatever the future held for them in South Africa.

David patted the armrest. Throughout his childhood he had sat for hours on the edge of this chair, enthralled as his ageing father related accounts of their tribe's past.

At David's prompting he would recall the warring ways of the Ndebele: past battles with the Zulu and rival Shona, always pleased to see his son enthused in these tribal recounts.

'Our family's past is rich. When we, the Ndebele, split from the great Nguni tribe in the early 1800s, General Mzilikazi led us away to avoid the expansion of the Zulu nation after a disagreement with their leader Chaka. Later, in 1872, Dingaan plotted the death of Chaka his half-brother, and gained control of the Zulus.'

David's realisation that it was now a hundred years since that event did not distract him for long. He drifted back, becoming again engrossed in memories of his father's words.

'Dingaan pursued Mzilikazi, who had settled in the Transvaal, not far from where we live today. If this wasn't enough, Mzilikazi and our people were being hounded by the newly arrived Dutch-Afrikaner settlers from the Cape in their push to steal our lands. It was what they called the Great Trek northwards. So we moved yet again—travelling north—conquering and absorbing smaller tribes on our way and eventually crossed the great Limpopo River to settle, after many months of hardship, in a fertile land. Here our mighty Ndebele nation was born near the Matopo Hills. *

Momentarily his father's eyes had misted over. *'David, those are the mysterious stone hills where our chiefs are buried in caves—I will show you our homeland someday.'*

At the time, David remembered having imagined correctly the vast plateau of monolithic granite mounds creating a surrealistic landscape with an all-pervading atmosphere of mystery and foreboding.

His father, seeing the excitement in his son's eyes, had continued. 'Before long the smaller tribes to the east were to feel our presence. On Mzilikazi's death in 1870, his son Lobengula became Regent, eventually giving concessions to the White settlers who followed us. They, too, wanted the land.'

David recalled his father's bemused expression when he said, *'Our king's council advised him that the White men believed they could own the earth and its riches, while they thought no man could control such things. I'm afraid, son, our leaders were naive to the ways of the White man. The settlers continued to arrive in ever increasing numbers. Even I remember them, always making new demands.'*

David thought of his grandfather, who could not have been much older than himself when facing this invading army with a spear, for the last time.

'The trouble, David, was greed. The White men saw land and wealth far beyond their wildest dreams. Our land, I believe, offered them a life Europe could not provide but, remember, their circumstances were much the same as when we, the Ndebele, arrived.' His father stopped and reflected for a moment; his expression changed.

'Soon jackals like Cecil Rhodes arrived and caused much blood to spill. His ruthless band of mercenaries changed the course of our history forever. Our new king, Lobengula, stood in their way and, disregarding his hand of friendship, they turned on him like a pack of hunting dogs. They hounded our impi warriors until, with their superior fire power, they defeated our disillusioned king and his army.'

David was reminded that his father had hesitated for a while...

'The White settlers recorded the killing as a great victory, and our kingdom was taken, as if swallowed by a crocodile, whole, into the British Empire. This, they claimed, was in part fulfilment of Rhodes' dream to control our continent from Cape Town to Cairo.'*

Falling silent, David had then tried to get him to tell of the battles of his grandfather with the settlers, but Nyamande senior had grown tired.

With a start, he had looked up at his son as though coming out of a trance. 'No! That is enough for one day. Now go and study,' and David had known better than to press his father too far.

Reflecting back he smiled with the knowledge that his parents—living in Soweto—succeeded against all odds in instilling self-esteem and a pride in both himself and his sister, Nandi, his junior by seven years. David, at the age of twenty-six, had recently qualified as a general medical practitioner.

Soweto for the most part was nothing more than a migrant town of monotonous cheap red brick and asbestos-roofed houses, replicated a hundred-thousand times. Yet, David had thrived in this environment, absorbing every facet of the town's rich tapestry from its million-plus inhabitants and the aspirations of people who wanted more from life.

Whenever the subject of apartheid had arisen, which became more frequent as he grew older, his father would say, *'Apartheid will go, but first these Whites must learn to be Africans. Be patient!'* David now wondered if his father had feared for them living under this oppressive régime?

David momentarily thought of his mother. He was saddened by the course of history on her side. The Xhosa had been crushed by the Dutch and British settlers in what the Whites had called the Kaffir Wars over two hundred and fifty years before. From the time the settlers first landed at the Cape they had slowly forced the Xhosa back from their lands into the territory across the Kei River, which became known as the Transkei.*

Even in their early teens, the two children had often sat late at night talking in the dark, with Nandi perched at the end of David's bed, discussing how, together, they would rid the entire continent of this White menace. In time, their loathing of the apartheid system intensified, seeing how it deliberately impeded intellectual growth by robbing individuals of economic independence, human rights and dignity.

That now all seemed so distant as he recalled the recent tragedy. A feeling of despair swept over him. Quite suddenly within weeks of his graduation, his father had died and utterly crushed by the loss, his mother had soon followed.

Nandi had decided to take responsibility for the family home, provided David could maintain it until she qualified, as she was away completing her medical degree in Natal. The long-standing offer of a partnership for him, with a nearby medical practice dovetailed neatly with their respective plans to stay on in Soweto, but first, he had other priorities.

David had decided long ago that on graduating he would travel abroad—extend his horizons. He knew this would not be easy. Because of his colour the Nationalist Government might take months to grant him the rare privilege of a travel document, if at all.* He was told by friends to prepare himself for the inevitable interviews he would have to go through simply to convince the authorities he was not a Communist bent on bringing down the apartheid régime—why else, after all, would a Black man want to travel?

In reality, he knew their fear stemmed from outside influences. Even television—available to the rest of the world—was withheld from the people of South Africa.* It was said '...television will turn a native's head with ideas that he is on an equal footing with us White men.'

What he needed was a respite before taking up this demanding post.

Home had become a depressing place, a constant reminder of happier days. David mourned the loss of his parents and longed for the closeness of family around him. He needed to get away for a while to adjust to the loss.

Pulling himself out of the chair he went inside to telephone Nandi.

'I have to take a break—I'm going down to see Josh.'

Nandi was not surprised. Their cousin Josh and her brother had been inseparable over the years before he went to university and she knew Josh would be good for him right now.

'Hell! Nandi, I miss our mother's homeland.' His mind filled with images of the Transkei stretching along the eastern seaboard nearly 1000 kilometres to the south. The gentle rolling hills covered by a myriad of coarse brown grasses and aloes of the veldt, crazed in places by distinctive deep eroded gorges, provided a nostalgic memory. He knew the terrain as well as he knew Soweto itself. The two boys, barefooted, had roamed valley and krantz and every nook of territory widely, while herding his uncle's cattle. It had been an indelible experience and he felt at one with the land.

'Okay! But please write or telephone at least once a week. I do miss you, big brother,' came Nandi's appeal.

oOo

David felt his spirits soar, exhilarated for the first time in months as the clusters of huts, scattered across the landscape, came in view. Such huts and thousands like them formed the rural vista of the Transkei. To the north the distant peaks of the Stormsberg Mountains sketched an inky blue graph on the skyline, reminding him of the route he had travelled.

Five kilometres out of the small township of Cofimvaba, he turned off the asphalt to follow the dirt road farther southwards. 'Hell it's hot,' he muttered to himself. Even so, he wound up the window, for the heat was preferable to the choking dust.

He raised a hand to passers-by and fellow motorists. They always returned his greetings. David viewed speculatively the occasional young girls, who in their exuberance waved back, sweeping both arms wildly in the air, their firm bare breasts inviting. He recalled that the coloured beads covering their genitalia showed them to be chaste—promiscuity remaining contrary to the orthodox practice of the amaThembu tribe. Some women carried infants strapped to their backs in blankets, while others bore heavy gourds of water or bundles of firewood on their heads with indifference, balanced impossibly on slender swaying necks, enhancing the feminine grace so often the envy of western women. He smiled at other elderly folk he passed smoking their traditional thirty-centimetre wooden pipes.

Nearing his destination it was impossible to avoid raising thick billowing clouds of choking dust. He mouthed a silent apology to the pedestrians who were left behind in the red mist that hung in the air long after his passing. The shadows of the late afternoon were creeping over the landscape when David eventually reached a dip in the plateau. He braked to negotiate the steep valley, down to the Kei River; snaking his way across the road's pitted surface in a bid to miss the deep potholes. The road petered out and he slowed, then was forced to stop. Peeling himself out of the sweat-dampened seat, the shirt-like safari suit jacket plastered to his back, he stretched, then inhaled deeply the clean invigorating country air.

David strolled over to greet the group of young men who stood watching him with keen open interest, intrigued by his 'White' appearance—white safari suit, white socks and shoes. Each carried a knobkerrie, the traditional fighting stick. He gauged their ages to be about fifteen. They were entirely naked except for the white clay painted over their bodies and faces. David did not find their appearance strange for they were the *abakwetha;* initiates into adulthood about to go through the circumcision ritual and he was well acquainted with the custom.

He asked where he could find his uncle. The boys looked blankly at one another appearing not to understand him. Immediately he broke into Xhosa, with its 'click' sounds inflected into virtually every word, learnt from his mother's family as a young boy. They pointed affably—to the nearby *kraal* consisting of four thatched circular huts, with limewashed geometric designs painted in stark relief against the red mud walls. The dwellings, surrounded by aloes with their profusion of long fleshy leaves edged with raking devil thorns, seemed impenetrable. In the past, these aloes would have deterred marauding lions or the Zulu impi.

David found the gate to this *laager* and strode up to the largest hut. He stood outside and called aloud, waiting politely for a response.

Immediately a cackling laugh erupted from inside and two young girls emerged, their smiles dazzling as they came forward to greet him. David looked over their heads to see his uncle's gummy grin appear in the doorway. His cousins were bare breasted like many of the young women he had seen on his way here. Bowing their heads out of respect, they extended their hands which he briefly touched in turn while they curtsied, only to break away giggling. Finding their mood infectious, he too smiled.

David's uncle was getting on in years. He noticed how grey he had become since his last visit, but it befitted his status as headman of the village. They clasped hands. All the while David was amused watching him gesticulate and at the toothless mouth, listening politely to the cordial greeting. It seemed to go on forever as the old man sought to mention the entire family and appraised the qualities of each member.

Seated in the largest of his uncle's huts with a crackling fire taking the chill out of the Transkei night, David consumed, not too reluctantly, liberal amounts of maize beer before learning of his cousin's whereabouts. It turned out Josh had been living for the past year in the coastal city of East London, some three hours' drive farther south. It became increasingly apparent that his uncle was displeased by his son's departure.

'You young men want it all,' he said. 'Now it's cars—tomorrow you will want to take away the Whites' houses.' He pointed a sinewy finger at his nephew. 'I'm telling you there's going to be trouble in this land.' He sat back and chuckled to himself. 'That stupid son of mine says he wants to be a politician.'

David noticed his uncle's lack of co-ordination when leaning forward.

His tone became more serious. 'David, what does he want? A house like the Transkei Prime Minister? To be a puppet of the Pretoria Government?' He stopped to collect his thoughts.

David, too, was beginning to feel the effects of the beer. A cousin filled his mug once more while the other arrived with food. Bidding the men goodnight the girls quietly retreated.

In the flicker of the paraffin lamp David watched his uncle wrap his blanket more tightly about his shoulders, then reach for the food. 'No, not my son. He thinks he is going to be in the South African Government one day.' He shook his head in disapproval.

David sympathised with the older man. He had spent a lifetime being subservient to the régime. Did he not realise that his son Josh, and David himself, had a far different view of the future than their forefathers? Almost instantly David corrected himself. Of course this notion was foolish. How could his uncle understand the desires and aspirations of another generation—it was no longer his uncle's time.

Quite late and decidedly intoxicated, he staggered out of the main hut and found his way to the empty nearby dwelling prepared for him earlier by his cousins. Moving around in the dark he collided with the central post. Cursing the absence of conveniences like electricity, he located the edge of a matted grass bed and felt the soft texture of a sheepskin blanket. Undressed, he lay down on the ground mat, pulled the cover over his head against the evening chill and, closing his eyes, was whirled into a vortex of alcohol induced sleep.

David's uncle gave him Josh's address in Duncan Village, the Black township of East London. He was preparing to leave when a commotion from the far side of the village caught his attention. Curious, he strolled over to observe. That night the *abakwetha* youths had feasted having completed the period that marked their transition from boy to manhood, learning about sex and the conduct expected of them in adult life. During the circumcision ritual they had shown neither fear nor pain— to do so would have brought shame on their families. Now washed clean of the white clay in the Kei River, where he and Josh had played as boys, they were clothed ceremoniously in new blankets. He thought they stood taller, prouder than yesterday, strutting around the hut in which they had spent their seclusion from the rest of the tribe over the past three months. David watched the dwelling being set alight. Following custom, the young men did not look back at the blaze. He knew this was symbolic. They had left their childhood behind them in the glowing embers.

David found he was unable to tear himself away from the demons that seemed to dance in the flames. Then, as if released, he turned to go, sensing that he too was about to leave his innocence behind. Quickly he strode over to his car. He climbed in and sped off down the dirt road, unaccountably pleased to be away from this place.

By midday David was in East London, crawling in third gear through the old quarter of Duncan Village looking for the address he had been given. The blue corrugated shack had one small window with a black-gloss painted front door. Only its number differentiated it from other houses in the busy street.

He was ushered into the front living-room by a young child who promptly excused herself. Left alone, his gaze centred of the photographs on the bookshelf. They gave him no clue as to the owner. About to inspect them more closely, he heard his cousin's voice.

'Dave!' The door burst open and Josh rushed in. 'Jesus! Where've you come from?' Shorter and at least fifteen kilos lighter, Josh punched his cousin's shoulder lightly. 'Last time was, what, maybe three, four years ago?' he said excitedly.

'Must be about right,' and David grinned, pleased that Josh hadn't changed. Since their childhood he had always been a buoyant extrovert getting them into trouble with every step he took.

'My God! I don't believe it, you look well. How long are you staying?'

David explained he was taking some time off before setting up practice.

'Good!' said Josh, 'You can open up a surgery in Zwelitsha township. It's only 15 kilometres away.' He saw by David's face that an explanation was required. 'They're moving us out of here. This part of the town has now been zoned for Coloureds. These streets will be the last to go and next month we have to move, but it's okay. Zwelitsha is good. It's away from the prying eyes of BOSS and the police.' Seeing David's expression change, he added, 'Don't worry, I'll explain later. Now let's hear about Nandi and the family news.'

Josh gave him all of a minute, then interrupted to say that, as it happened to be a Saturday, he hoped David liked football. Fifteen minutes later David found himself driving to the football stadium in Zwelitsha township, acting as chauffeur to Josh and four friends who had miraculously appeared at the front door at the moment of their departure.

The match was uninspiring and the achievements on the field unequal to the noise of the crowd. Then, abruptly, with twenty minutes left to play, the players stopped and seemed to mingle pointlessly in the centre of the pitch. Not making any sense of this inactivity, David turned to Josh, who was waiting for his reaction.

'Wait and see, cousin,' was all he would say.

Presently a voice came over the air speaking Xhosa. 'Good afternoon all. I am pleased to address this gathering. As you know, it is illegal to hold a political rally with more than five persons. Therefore, except for the four on my right, I must ask the rest of you sitting elsewhere in the stadium, please not to listen.'

Immediately there was a tumultuous roar from the crowd and those outside the stadium might have been excused for thinking that a goal had been scored.

The speech was well modulated and the message carried clearly to the attentive audience. David estimated their numbers to be well over three thousand. He knew instinctively that the speaker had won both the hearts and minds of the spectators. They listened intently, eager to accept his ideas and vision of a new South Africa, free from oppression and racial hatred.

'Do we want this Homeland Citizenship Act? What about our people who have been settled in one place for many generations who are now being forcibly removed to new 'homelands' sometimes hundreds of kilometres away from their homes. I say to the Government, you are turning five and half million citizens into refugees in their own country.'*

David felt anger begin to well up inside himself, being swept along with the crowd. When the speaker finished, the applause drowned out all further communication for several minutes. The realisation that the game had simply been a decoy for a political rally left him under no illusion as to the person responsible for its audaciousness—Josh of course! The security and planning process necessary for this event left David in awe. He watched Josh issuing orders to various persons who materialised from out of the crowd, receive their instructions then rejoin the mass of humanity moving towards the exit gates. David's respect for his cousin rose appreciably. He shouted into Josh's ear.

'Who was that?'

'A friend down, from Natal University. He's causing all sorts of problems up there for the Boer,' Josh smiled. 'You'll meet him later if you want to.'

Now that the noise was diminishing, David peered thoughtfully at his cousin. 'What do you mean, later?'

'We're going to Cape Town to attend a South African Student Organisation rally at the University tomorrow and we'll be picking him up later this evening. You're welcome to come along if you wish.' He saw the look on David's face. 'Yes, it's over a thousand kilometres but this Students Organisation rally is important: there's talk about a Black Consciousness movement. Anyway, we'll be back by Monday morning. So what did you think of that promising young politician?'

David shook his head. It was a devil of a long way to Cape Town and the trip, if Josh's past was any indicator of the future, would not be dull. He had an uneasy feeling that trouble lay ahead but despite that, he would go.

They returned to Duncan Village. On the way Josh filled in the details. He had joined the banned African National Congress (ANC) as an administrator, setting the political agenda and organising events in East London and the surrounding area. During the day he had a job as a messenger for the Department of Justice. Speaking Afrikaans fluently, Josh overheard much of what was said in the halls and corridors of the courts. He prided himself in being able to read a letter or brief upside down at four paces. It suited him to work in a government office, as the position offered an insight into the enemy camp and provided invaluable information for the ANC's covert network. Josh confided that, although he loathed the people in the department, it was the environment he enjoyed, hoping one day to practise law himself.

Josh reassured David they would return by 6.00am on Monday, as he needed to be back in time for work. David set aside his doubts, impelled to go along for the ride by the sheer recklessness of it all. Besides, he had never seen Cape Town.

They snatched a quick bite to eat and on David's enquiry, Josh told him that the house belonged to a relative. David was once more staying with the extended family. 'She's great, our aunt Rosie. I'll explain the family connection later. You'll meet her on Monday,' Josh assured him.

'Where's she now?' He enquired, while hurriedly unpacking to sort items needed for the trip.

'Housemaid to a White couple from Rhodesia. She pays more attention to their children than her own,' Josh laughed. 'Hurry up and don't forget your passbook. Without a bloody *dompas* the cops will have you inside before you can shout *Amandla*!' A squeal of tyres announced the arrival of his friends, and he went outside to greet them.

David ran after him with his bag under one arm. They bundled into the back of the van, joining five more travelling companions. Josh made the introductions. Some were from the ANC while others represented other Black organisations. As they pulled off, a thought struck David.

'Hey, Josh, what about my car? I can't just leave it outside in the street.' This was promptly met with laughter all round.

When they quietened down, Josh explained their amusement. 'Dave, it would take a very brave or stupid man to steal anything from the front of that house! There are eyes watching it day and night.' He sensed David's apprehension but did not bother to tell him their network covered the entire area and nothing moved or happened without his knowledge. 'Don't worry your car will be there on Monday.' He changed the subject. 'Next stop's King William's Town, to pick up young Steve and a friend.'

The journey was uneventful. Lion lagers were passed around and they sipped the lukewarm beer, indulging in idle chatter. An hour later they pulled up, the sliding door was pushed back and two men climbed in. They met with friendly ribbing—it was clear these were no strangers. David was introduced to the young politician he had heard speak at the rally earlier in the day, and a friend whom he was seated beside for the remainder of the trip.

The van climbed out of King William's Town and headed for Cape Town to the south-west. Presently, Josh cut in on the banter. Obediently they fell silent, listening intently as he spoke.

'Right! So if we're stopped, remember the routine. It's just another funeral. I know what you're all thinking, but honestly it doesn't matter what we say to the cops. I'll give them a line they always accept is a lie but which they'll be content to live with. Please, Reverend Makanda, will you fill us in on the details.'

David glanced sideways and saw the white dog-collar half hidden under a sweatshirt.

'Yes. The Archbishop of Cape Town has informed me he would be most appreciative if we could attend the funeral of Gideon Matiwane. He died last week in a police cell. They say it was suicide but in these times who knows?' He continued, 'Matiwane has no surviving relatives and will be buried tomorrow afternoon. Provided we have time after the rally we would be advised to attend this funeral, to justify our presence in Cape Town, purely as a precaution.'

This was apparently standard procedure. It began to dawn on David how wide was the reach of these banned organisations. These were all otherwise ordinary working men and the subterfuge they resorted to in the furtherance of their cause astounded him. This poor wretch's demise had been an opportunity for these brave men to defy the Government.

They settled down as the evening wore on and David, now curious, asked his companion next to him what the rally was about.

Laughter erupted again from the group, and Josh chipped in, grinning, 'You'll regret asking, Dave. Steve loves a captive audience.'

Well into the early hours, long after even the hardiest of them had fallen asleep, David listened to Steve Biko's every word.

After the last fuel stop David sat in the front passenger seat next to the driver. Now he was the only passenger awake. They were descending Sir Lowry's Pass to the Cape Flats far below as daylight broke. In the distance he could see, for the first time, the Cape Peninsula materialise out of the early morning mist as the first rays of sunlight threw a golden glow over the mountain range. Within the hour they had reached the outskirts of Cape Town. The trip had passed without incident and they were fortunate not to have met the customary police roadblock en route.

This was encouraging.

The driver evidently knew the city well and turned left into Adderley Street, which led from the seafront through the heart of the city. Being a Sunday morning, he made his way swiftly through deserted streets towards the beginning of De Waal Drive, the main commuter highway from the city centre to the southern suburbs. David craned his neck for glimpses of Table Mountain between the high-rise buildings. He was impressed.

A sleepy voice over his shoulder said, 'The bastion of White supremacy over the last four-hundred years. Pity they still hide in its shadow—time they came out into the light.' Nothing else was said, nor needed saying, as they passed the Houses of Parliament.

They skirted the mountain to the left, then took the junction sign-posted University of Cape Town. The driver crossed over the motorway and entered the university campus lying at the base of the mountain range. David looked at the clock on the dash. It was seven-thirty in the morning and yet three students were already sitting on the lawn at the entrance to the campus, waving as they passed, and at least two dozen more were on the steps of the hall to greet them. David noticed students posted at strategic points around the buildings. He realised that those he had seen sitting on the grass verge near the motorway were there with a purpose.

The group was quickly ushered inside and provided with a hearty breakfast prepared by sleepy staff in the canteen.

Josh briefed David: the meeting was scheduled for eleven so they had time to kill. They were led by members of the student committee into a common room. This had been set aside so that they could meet a few of the lecturers and other guest speakers. While everyone stood around talking quietly, David found a comfortable sofa in a corner, flopped down and, as the affable chatter receded, he fell asleep.

Josh shook him. 'Come on you lazy 'Nkonka',' using his nickname, the bushbuck—a clever and stealthy antelope—from their youth.

'Leave me alone, 'Mpunzi',' came a tired response from David.

'Ah! So you remember. The 'duiker' may be smaller but it is more cunning antelope than the 'bushbuck',' he quipped.

David climbed to his feet and stretched. He looked down at his cousin. 'You want to fool around when a man needs sleep? Anyway, that's not how I recall it. The 'bushbuck' always knocked the crap out of you.'

Josh grinned, feigning a blow to David's solar plexus. 'Come on. They're about to start. We're needed in the hall. I'll be up on stage but you've got a front row seat and, so help me, if you fall asleep during my introduction....'

The hall was packed with over three-hundred people. By word through the grapevine, White students had arrived with friends and sympathisers from other political parties, to listen to the viewpoint of these opponents of the Government. Leaks were inevitable and raids likely, so the organisers were prepared for police intervention with contingency plans to spirit away the speakers as soon as they had wind of trouble.

The rally started right on time and after the opening remarks Josh went up to the rostrum and began his address, 'I wish to outline the objectives of the ANC....' Twenty minutes later, while introducing the next guest speaker who was about to talk on the Homeland Citizenship Act, Josh was interrupted from the floor.

The otherwise attentive mood of the audience was rudely shattered by a fracas erupting somewhere in its midst. Seemingly from nowhere, a dozen or more plain-clothes police and BOSS agents, having masqueraded as students, sprang into action. They lashed out indiscriminately with short batons at anyone within reach. Instantly, pandemonium broke out. A shouted order for everyone to sit still went unheeded and, when repeated, was drowned out as the noise level rose alarmingly.

Students began to retaliate. David saw a chair fly through the air. He was unsure what to do next, and looked around for his cousin for guidance, but Josh and the other speakers had disappeared.

Half the assault force surged forward trying to take the stage by storm. Countering their advance, more White students emerged from the wings to form a human barrier kicking out at the BOSS agents, thwarting their attempts to gain access to the stage.

David swung round, startled by the static of a radio transmitter which had been secreted into the hall in a camera case. Someone was yelling into the receiver above the noise. 'Kom nou. Kom nou.' David scanned the entire assembly—there wasn't another Black face to be seen anywhere. Unexpectedly someone gripped him by the lapels and jeered, 'Got you kaffir!'

Commandant Piet Van Heerden of BOSS, the Bureau of State Security, waited attentively in the command vehicle. The radio suddenly crackled into life. 'Agh! That's it boet, let's go.'

The driver rammed the accelerator to the floor. The idling motor suddenly roared into action and the van tore off down the feeder road. The light-blue vans of the SAP, the South African Police, sped past the three lookouts who not fully comprehending what had happened until the last vehicle passed from their view, turned, and ran in the opposite direction—instead of heading back towards the campus to give warning, as planned.

The screech of brakes was audible inside the hall. Police, together with plain-clothes members of BOSS, began to pour out of the vehicles even before they had come to a stop.

Van Heerden screamed, 'I want a bloody cordon around the building now.' Watching the Alsatian dogs eagerly pulling their handlers along, he shouted, 'Get your arses moving—to the sides and back.'

Meanwhile, inside the hall, David had hit the BOSS agent, a rocketing blow to the side of the head, and his shirt ripped away from his chest as the man went down still holding the torn away cloth.

Two more agents were also about to challenge David, but stopped abruptly in their tracks. After witnessing the power of his delivery, and taking in his height and breadth, they weren't taking chances. Instead they shouted at him not to move and drew their revolvers, adopting a firing stance a mere metre away. The threesome froze, surrounded by bedlam.

Students were now diving into the fray from the stage and inside the building, the situation was getting extremely ugly for the undercover agents of BOSS.

Outside, Van Heerden barked an order, 'Arrest them! Anyone coming out of this hall.' Over the din he could still hear the plea for assistance coming from the radio. He needed a way to get through, to lend support to his men on the inside. Having lost or discarded their batons, the police now drew out sjamboks, deploying the short whips effectively, slicing open exposed flesh easily like butchering pig meat with a panga. The battle raged unabated and the tide of people attempting to leave the building found themselves being crammed in the foyer, as those in front hesitated, horrified by the gauntlet they would have to run on the outside.

Van Heerden screamed, 'Throw in the tear gas.'

Several canisters were lobbed into the crowded foyer, spewing out their disabling vapour and immediately there was a rush from the building as terrified students and friends fled in panic from the stinging gas. The dogs were set loose and went berserk in a frenzied attack. Within minutes Van Heerden knew he had achieved crowd control. More police vehicles were coming up the drive and those students still standing, together with the prostrate and injured, were being manhandled into 'protective' custody.

As the tear gas cleared, Van Heerden led the charge into the main hall with fifteen men and two dogs. A few stragglers offered token resistance. They were severely dealt with. In total defiance a last remaining student on the stage continued to hurl chairs at his pursuers. As he raised another above his head Van Heerden's bullet caught him above the left eye. He fell backwards, crashing to the ground beneath the chair. Inside the building the deafening report from the gun brought everything to a halt.

Van Heerden's crazed eyes flashed around the hall, and his disappointment was evident.

They had escaped his cordon.

His sight rested on a solitary figure near the edge of the stage being held at bay by his men. He strode over.

Standing before his captive he looked up at David. 'Ja! Kaffir, so you thought you could bloody well escape?'

David stared at the sneering face, not liking what he saw.

'No! I have no intention of escaping as you put it. I only came here to listen to the speakers.'

'So we have an 'educated' one here,' he jeered. 'Look, you Black commie bastard,' he almost spat at David, 'I'll deal with you later.' He gave a signal to the dog handlers, which David did not understand.

He knew soon enough. The handlers slipped the leashes and gave the command, 'Sic hom!' One Alsatian came in low like a jackal, burying its teeth deep in his calf muscle. As the dog bit hard, it shook its head from side to side. The other sprang high—trying to ignore the pain—he concentrated on the killer going for his throat. David caught the animal in flight by the front leg, jerking it downwards in one swift fluid movement while bringing his other free hand round in a hammer blow to the topside of its head—its neck gave. Off-balance, David fell but the dog was already dead. He reached for the other dog still savaging his leg.

The handler saw what was about to happen and started to rain kicks into David's side. With their quarry on the ground the other two BOSS agents vented their frustration at not having been able to tackle him sooner. They lashed out at him with their sjamboks, across his chest and back.

A punishing minute later David relaxed his grip on the dog and lay still, watching the handler yank his injured charge out of the fray while his colleagues continued a relentless barrage of vicious kicks to his head and upper arms. He was barely conscious and no longer felt the pain.

Van Heerden interceded. 'Nee man! Stop. I must first interrogate this kaffir. Take him to the charge office.'

Four of them lifted David carrying him outside, then threw him unceremoniously into the back of a van. He passed out.

Hours later David came round in the police cell, but the nightmare continued unabated. He lay on a cold concrete floor becoming aware of the eight knife-pleated trousered legs that surrounded him and thanked God they weren't bent on kicking him to death. He heard himself pleading thickly, 'Please! Something to drink.' The beating had been thorough and already his face was so swollen as to be unrecognisable.

'Okay, Karl, give him something.' Van Heerden chuckled menacingly.

Before David could react, one of the group urinated onto his face. There was a roar of laughter as he swung out of range, and he sat up abruptly and wished he hadn't as his body was racked by pain. Certainly they were not going to allow him to stand. He looked at the officer busy tucking himself away.

Surprised, the sergeant had not expected the eye contact and could not tear himself away from David's piercing stare. Then he let fly with his boot catching David in the stomach. They started on him again and David endured relentless beatings to his body.

The pain inflicted by Van Heerden was of a different kind, excruciating, and executed with a precision that was bringing him to the point of breaking, almost. Always the same questions, 'What's your name? 'What Black party are you from? Who, and where, are your co-conspirators?'

By the end of the interrogation he recollected that he had given them virtually nothing other than his first name. Realising his friends must have escaped, he was now thankful that he had left his passbook in the van. Clearly they had no idea as to his identity but he wondered how long he could hold out. David knew, whatever the cost, he must protect Josh and Nandi. Reprisals were certain—BOSS would stop at nothing—they would traumatise and systematically beat people into total submission. He kept reminding himself, 'That's how this system works!' It had done so efficiently and effectively over many years: domination by terror was still a powerful weapon in the hands of the Afrikaner.

He drifted in and out of consciousness. In more lucid moments he took stock of his situation as best he could. It felt as if all his ribs were broken. Going over and over in his mind a self-diagnosis, listing every injury to every muscle, every possible bruise to his internal organs, every fracture. He was certain all his fingers were either broken or dislocated. Through the excruciating pain he had heard some crack as Van Heerden personally administered the torture. Now his fingers remained useless, painful extremities to an aching and battered body. The cigarette burns had had the opposite effect. Searing deep into his flesh they dredged up an anger he had not experienced before. Even as he bellowed out in pain at their inhumanity, he vowed vengeance from a dark side of his being he had not known existed.

David awoke, face down on the cold floor where they had left him. He had no idea how long he had lain there. He was only thankful that they had stopped the assault. His nose was a bloody pulp and he could no longer smell his burnt flesh—his right nipple was no longer there. His sense of smell, or rather the lack of it, worried him least of all. He was more afraid that they might have seriously impaired his ability to father children. His testicles felt like red-hot rivets stabbing at him even when he lay still.

o0o

10 January 1972

Michael Bernstein was confused as the car cut a clear path through the traffic. The driver headed directly for the main Cape Town police station where he was dragged, protesting, through an inconspicuous doorway and along stone walled corridors to a cell. Thrown unmercifully into the corner of the tiny room without so much as a glimpse of the charge office, he lay sprawled on the concrete floor. He knew from experience in his student days that this was fairly typical treatment, though the last time he was arrested the charge officer had laid into him with a tirade of anti-communist abuse before slinging him into a similar cell 'to wise up'.

'What's the charge? What am I supposed to have done? You can't do this,' he screamed at them at the top of his voice when they locked the door.

Impassively they walked away down the corridor, ignoring his angry protest echoing round the cell block.

'Hey you! Come back here, you hairy ape, let me out,' and he instantly regretted this abuse as the tall man with fair hair turned and came back to face him menacingly through the bars of the cell.

'I have a name—Commandant Van Heerden of BOSS. I should be very careful what you say, *Mr* Bernstein. To me you are just another fucking commie like all the rest. You'd better be careful you don't leave here feet first. Ja, *Mr* Bernstein, I should be very careful if I were you.'

Michael fell silent contemplating the warning, unable to work out why he had been dragged away. 'Commie' he had said. It was the term used for any opponents of the Nationalist Party's policies, however minor, and yet he had done nothing. Nothing except write a letter to the editor of the *Cape Herald*, that is. Could that be it? Surely not. He had only posted it a few days ago and it wouldn't even be printed yet, if they were going to print it at all. But then if the editor had seen it and reported it to BOSS... but would they react so fast...could they?

Van Heerden sat tapping the desk with his pen, waiting for his telephone call to be answered.

'Hello! General Meyer here. Can I help you?'

'Ja! General, it's Piet Van Heerden here in Cape Town. We are sending the two up to you in the Transvaal. The kaffir won't talk and Bernstein is best handled by yourselves.'

There was a pause, then: 'Everybody talks when I want them to talk. Anyway, what does this Bernstein know?'

'We haven't questioned him yet, we only picked him up this morning. Your instructions were explicit!'

The General seemed satisfied. 'Okay, I want these prisoners here by tomorrow. You'd better bring them up here personally.'

Van Heerden replaced the receiver and promptly shouted orders to his junior officers to make the necessary preparations. When General Stoffel Meyer, the head of BOSS requested your presence in Pretoria, it was as if God himself had spoken.

oOo

They came for both men that morning. David was hoisted onto a stretcher, then transferred to the back of a van where he was roughly manacled to the side rail. He overheard his tormentors discuss their destination and his worst fears were realised.

Farther along the dank corridor, the door to Michael's cell opened. Two uniformed constables, their batons held loosely, motioned him to come out. At Michael's reluctance to pass between them in the doorway, one constable stepped inside. He promptly lashed out, hitting Michael's arm with a violent swing of his baton, causing him to cry out in agony.

'Come with us, kaffir-lover,' he ordered and Michael did as he was told without further resistance. This did not deter the constables from prodding and pushing him along the corridor ahead of them, inflicting painful jabs to his kidneys with their batons until they reached the rear courtyard. Outside stood a police van and, as one constable opened the rear door, the other shoved Michael from behind sending him sprawling headlong into the van. The door slammed shut and locked behind him. He was in a box-like trunk with nothing but a minute grille in the front for two-way communication, and another in the back for light and ventilation. Unaccustomed to the gloom, he was temporarily blinded. The van smelled of sweat of countless previous occupants. He lay still for a moment trying to catch his breath. Suddenly, he became aware of another presence in the darkness.

'You'd better hold tight if you don't want to break anything. It's a long way,' Van Heerden warned through the front grille.

With that Michael heard the cab door slam shut and the engine cough into life. The van began to move and Michael felt round expecting to find a side-seat. There wasn't one, just the bare floor. Reaching the street, the sounds of the city became louder and a faint breeze blew through the grille. Already the heat had begun to rise. Michael couldn't help thinking the back of the van resembled an oven as he was thrown from side to side. The vehicle rounded a sharp city street corner and he collided with the other occupant whose drawn-up knees thumped into already bruised ribs.

The unseen figure groaned softly.

'Sorry,' Michael said automatically settling into a more stable position beside his travelling companion. Some distance on, the road straightened out and he tried to make himself comfortable. He peered closely at the shadowy figure, his eyes beginning to adjust to the dim light. He could see that the man's skin was ebony and glistening with sweat. Part of his face was obscured by something. Finally, Michael could make out that it was his forearms: his hands were bound and manacled together to a side-rail above the height of his head as he sat on the floor.

Michael moved his position to get a better look at the man and, as the van changed direction, a shaft of sunlight from the small opening of the grille pierced the gloom striking the man full in the face. That instant registered as a snapshot on Michael's mind and it horrified him, that he recoiled from it. Whereas the forehead was ebony with beads of sweat, the rest of the face was swollen, a mask of bright pink cuts and a lattice-work of abrasions so that it was impossible to imagine the man's normal features. He had been subjected to the most terrible beating.

Michael felt his own bruised arms and the horror of what might have happened to him suddenly registered and he felt sick. He choked back the feeling, drawing close to the man again.

'Jesus, what have these bastards done to you? Are you all right—is there anything I can do?' Michael enquired, feeling helpless.

The man spoke in a cracked, educated voice, barely above a whisper. 'I am okay, thank you,' he said politely. 'There's nothing you can do for me. You had better look out for yourself. It is a harsh place where we are going.'

It dawned on Michael that he had no idea where they were taking him. 'You know where we are going? Where? They didn't tell me!'

'We are going, my friend, to the detention centre at Pretoria Prison.'

'Pretoria...no, that can't be right. It's nearly 1500 kilometres away,' he realised he could no longer hear the sounds of the city. He sat back uncomprehendingly. After a while he could feel the vehicle straining up a steep incline. He moved to the grille at the rear of the van and rose, steadying himself, and peered out as they climbed through the north-eastern pass leaving the Cape Flats below.

For a moment he crouched, with mounting dread, watching the Cape Peninsula fading into the distance. Most people had heard of the notorious detention centre at Pretoria with its alarming statistics of deaths. The authorities always maintained that nothing untoward went on there, but the number of suicides and of those killed while trying to escape stretched belief to breaking point. It was said that political prisoners never left there alive.

'Are you sure that's where we are going?' Michael questioned as he returned to his place beside the injured man, but he knew the answer even before he could reply.

Van Heerden bellowed through the front grille over the engine noise, 'Shut your bloody mouths or I'll shut them for you.'

They fell silent.

The kilometres fell away. Michael began to think of what might be about to happen to him. Each time he tried to comfort himself with the thought that it would all work out in the end—that they had made a mistake—he would glance at his companion and know that reason was not on the agenda of anyone who could do this to his fellow man. Tendrils of fear crept along his spine. This was a journey he did not want to complete.

After a while, Michael, sweat oozing from every pore, crawled over to the rear grille, to breathe the cooler air and immediately felt guilty that his companion could not indulge in the same luxury. He sat down again.

'I am sorry I cannot make you any more comfortable, er...'

'David. My name is David'

'David, I'm Michael,' he said, touching the man's shoulder gently, keeping his voice below the sound of the engine. 'I am sorry there is nothing I can do for you, David.'

They both peered at the front grille anticipating a barrage of verbal abuse and were relieved when there was none. They continued in hushed tones.

'It is not necessary, my friend. It is enough that you would help if you could but these are not reasonable men. I am beyond help now. Even if I was free of these,' he nodded towards his manacles, 'I could not run and if I did they would seek me out. You are right to be afraid, Michael. But draw strength from your fear and use it against them.' He lifted his head a little higher. 'They are strong in the arm but soft in the head. Intimidators, not clever men. Be afraid, Michael, and if the time comes, be free.'

Michael felt a bond develop quickly between himself and this beaten but unbroken man and he drew comfort from the thought, yet he knew that he would have to abandon him if an opportunity to escape presented itself. They fell silent again.

About 100 kilometres out of Cape Town they reached the town of Worcester, where the van stopped. The rear doors flew open. The bright sunlight was blinding after the darkness but the air was cool in comparison to the stifling conditions in the back of the van. Michael immediately recognised the front passenger as the man who had arrested him. Van Heerden ordered him out while the driver unlocked David, and they were allowed to relieve themselves.

Looking around surreptitiously, feigning difficulty with his fly, Michael checked for an escape route but it was impossible with both guards so close. They were armed with batons and each wore a holstered pistol. Even if he managed to escape the reach of the baton, he would not be able to make cover before one or the other was able to draw his gun and fire. No, there was no opportunity of escape here. Michael flexed his leg muscles to revive the feeling he had lost from sitting on the floor, then he turned to look at his companion. David was hanging onto the van door for support— he could barely stand. Michael flinched at the sight of those terrible injuries and went to assist him.

Van Heerden smirked, 'Silly bugger fell down the stairs. Bloody kaffirs are always doing that,' he pushed Michael towards the vehicle. 'You've no time to help the kaffir. Better make sure you don't fall down the stairs too.'

Ordered into the back of the van, a lock and chain were thrust into Michael's hand and he was told to manacle David to a side-rail. He did so, deliberately finding a lower position in the hope this would benefit David.

Though the doors had been open for a few minutes it had done little to cool the interior. If Michael were to escape he would need his legs to work properly so he changed position frequently to encourage circulation. He could not afford to be crippled with cramp at a vital moment.

For three more hours they were bounced and tossed around in the dark. They talked little for the heat drained them of all energy. David's reserves had been depleted by the beatings and now he was barely conscious. Several times Michael had to support his head, cradling it on his shoulder to save David from smashing into the sharp metal struts behind him. This leg of the journey became torturous, seemingly interminable as the temperature inside continued to rise until the sides of the van blistered the skin. At last the vehicle began to slow and he thought again of escape. He prepared himself knowing it would take vital moments for his body to respond to his will.

They stopped and the doors were thrown open by the uniformed driver as Van Heerden stood back to cover him. Michael saw immediately that escape would again be impossible and made the most of the fresh air, breathing gratefully while flexing all the muscles in his body. He replaced lost moisture with the lukewarm water passed to them in a canteen.

He helped David to drink. Too soon they were locked in the van again while Van Heerden and his driver strolled into the roadhouse. Michael tried the door but it held firm. The only way he was going to get out of this oven was if their guards unlocked it.

By 6.00pm they had reached the outskirts of Bloemfontein, about two-thirds of the journey, for another stopover; they had been cooped up for almost ten hours. Michael's shirt was wet through with perspiration generated by heat and fear. At each halt now he was becoming more desperate to find the chance to escape. How many more stops would they make? Already they were nearing the northern province of Transvaal, their destination. He must not allow them to get him to Pretoria.

The Transvaal, of course! The natural southern boundary of the province was the Vaal River. He knew the area well from his student days and an idea quickly formed—it was flimsy, and would have to wait, but what were the options? For now, Michael decided to try to convince his captors that he was weaker than he really was by adopting an exaggerated stagger. Every little bit would help when, or if, the time came. As Van Heerden looked away to light a cigarette, Michael straightened and moved towards him.

'Okay. Back inside, you bastards,' the driver called as he approached from the blind side of the van.

'Damn!' Michael oathed silently, resuming his hunched posture. The opportunity lost, they were yet again locked inside the metal box.

Now the evening sun was setting giving them a little respite from the unbearable heat but they were still pounded by the metal struts of the van's interior. Unexpectedly the van slowed. He felt the van swing to the right in an arc and bump off the road. It came to a halt. The driver walked off on his own and Van Heerden came round to the back. Michael hardly dared to breathe. This was it—it must be now.

The door swung open. He squinted in the bright light. Light? That couldn't be right. The luminous dial on his watch had told him it was past 8.00pm. Michael climbed down from the van and his spirits fell as his eyes adjusted, taking in the surroundings. Compared with this, every stop before had been an ideal opportunity for an escape.

They were in the floodlit courtyard surrounded by buildings linked with high walls. The van had entered the police station through a narrow arched gateway and there were policemen everywhere. The first hint of trouble would bring the entire force into the yard and he would be brought down under a hail of bullets before he covered twenty paces. For a fleeting moment he wondered if they had arrived in Johannesburg but as the single-story buildings came into focus he realised they were not in the city. Desperation almost made him chance the thirty metre bolt to the courtyard gates but in that instant a key was thrust into his hand and Van Heerden shoved him towards the van.

'Unlock the bloody kaffir. I suppose we'd better feed him too. Waste of time if you ask me. You know how many ways you can commit suicide in detention? Hundreds, kaffir boettie, hundreds. Which way do you think it'll happen to you, eh?'

The casual taunt, with its inference that he was going to die no matter what, served as a powerful incentive to flee. Michael took an unsteady step towards the open gate.

'Ja kaffir boettie. Run you bastard. Reckon I'll get you between the shoulders before you get halfway, and for good measure I'll shoot the kaffir here too.' Van Heerden laughed as he dared him to run—hoping he would—but Michael knew he could not make it.

Resigned to thinking that there would be little, if any, opportunity to escape, Michael climbed back in to free David.

They were fed meagre rations and halfway through the meal Michael found the nerve to ask, 'Where are we?' He had a desperate need to know.

'Shut your bloody mouth and eat,' was the only response he received from Van Heerden.

Twenty minutes later they resumed the journey. Michael was already reviewing his previous plan. 'It might just work...' he thought. The van jerked to a stop a hundred metres on. They heard the occupants up front get out followed by the smell of petrol fumes as they refuelled the van. Then they were on the road again. Though cooler now and much revived by the meal, Michael still felt incapacitated by fear. Every minute took them another kilometre closer to their destination, the infamous Pretoria Prison.

Michael was worried. Had he miscalculated the distance! He knew this part of the country fairly well from his student days at Witwatersrand University and he could almost picture the unseen landscape beyond the walls of his mobile cell. He moved again to the grille at the rear but saw nothing except indistinct grey shapes that could have been anything.

Suddenly the drone of the tyres on the road changed pitch and he knew exactly where he was. It was the sound he had been consciously waiting for. He and his student friends had come here for riverside barbecues. The Vaal River swirling eight metres beneath them was inhabited by nothing more ferocious than Transvaalers in speedboats. Nothing else had caused as many injuries on either side of this wide bridge—the only one for many kilometres. They were two hours from Johannesburg, which in turn was merely a short distance to Pretoria. From the rear grille he saw light faintly reflected off metal girders and hastily scrambled forward, past his companion.

Watching with fascination and understanding, David from his manacled position on the floor, saw Michael hammer frantically at the front grille.

'Stop. I can't breathe,' he yelled. In that instant Michael knew what he would do, his fear of pursuit overpowered by fear of what lay ahead.

'Be still,' came the curt reply, though Michael noted a slight check in the speed of the vehicle.

Michael hammered on the front again with renewed urgency and gasped, 'Help! I can't breathe...' and fell instantly silent, crouching beneath the grille out of sight of the peering eyes on the other side. The vehicle slowed as they reached the far bank and he heard their guards swearing at the unscheduled interruption. They, too, were tired after almost 1200 kilometres on the road. Michael was banking on it.

'Go, my brother.' David's voice was stronger now, the sudden chance of escape lifting his spirits.

Michael knew only too well that he could do nothing for this man who, even in his battered state, had helped inspire him to his present course of action. The van was almost at a stop.

Michael bent over David clasping his shoulder for a fleeting second. He could find no words suitable to comfort the man. Spurred on by a surge of adrenaline he slid to the back to await the opening of the doors.

The doors opened to a torrent of expletives. The driver had left the engine running—they didn't anticipate stopping for longer than a couple of minutes. Both men had come back to check on him. They weren't taking any chances. Michael took in the scene. He staggered out, his hands clutching his throat. He doubled up beside the van and began to retch, his body heaving convulsively. Van Heerden stood nearby, watching, while the driver turned away in disgust, fishing in his pocket for a pack of cigarettes.

With explosive speed Michael unwound from his bent position, lunging upwards. His head connected with tremendous force catching the underside of Van Heerden's chin, cracking the bone and splintering teeth.

Van Heerden's legs buckled and he dropped to his knees, then twisting sideways, fell grasping his face.

The driver saw nothing but, hearing the awful crack, ducked instinctively as Michael swung his elbow wildly towards his ear. He missed. The force of the intended blow swung Michael off-balance and he fell backwards onto the prostrate BOSS agent. The driver launched himself at Michael, whose reaction to the airborne figure was to kick out. His shoe caught the driver squarely in the groin. Instantly the man's savage glare turned to wide-eyed agonising disbelief. He collapsed momentarily on top, sandwiching Michael between him and Van Heerden.

Michael lashed out and twisted furiously to extricate himself from the heap, then sprinted in full flight towards the bridge. The winded driver managed to suppress his pain. He drew his pistol and let off a shot in the general direction of the fleeing prisoner.

Michael felt a rush of air as a bullet zipped past his ear. A second shot ricocheted off a girder with a shower of sparks and instantly he veered to the left, disappearing from view down the embankment and diving headlong into the Vaal River.

Even as he hit the water the current tugged at him. Michael surfaced unexpectedly under the bridge and with a few strokes reached a pier and found a hold. He could not tell if one, or both men, were now emptying their side arms at the point where he had been, just thankful he was temporarily hidden from their view. Above the crack of shots and the blood pounding in his ears, he heard the faint cry, 'Freedom, brother, freedom.'

Any second now they would reach the embankment and see him. The newly risen full moon illuminated everything—and not a cloud in sight. He seemed not to notice the water was ice-cold and glanced around in desperation. The far bank was just that—too far! Keeping to the same bank, he judged the distance to an overhanging willow tree beyond the bridge and letting go his grip, dived, allowing the sluggish current to carry him away. Kicking out, he resurfaced and managed to grab the trailing branch. It held and Michael hung on while frantically thinking of his next move.

Breathlessly scrambling up the muddy incline he could hear their angry shouts. Cover was sparse but as long as he made no sound or sudden movement he should be safe for the moment, but he would have to get out of there and be pretty damned quick. With one eye on the bridge he worked his way along the bank keeping out of sight, not daring to raise his head to look at the spot where he could hear voices cursing the night. To his amazement he found the swearing getting fainter. They were going across the bridge to the other side!

'They're going the wrong way!' He estimated they were now about a hundred metres from the van and making so much noise that he was able to move swiftly but carefully, that if the sound died suddenly, he too, could stop instantly.

He worked his way around through the denser undergrowth. Suddenly, he froze. With heightened awareness a familiar sound rose into his consciousness. The van's engine was still ticking over! He crawled closer, closer until he was parallel to the vehicle. In a desperate bid, he broke cover and dashed towards the cab.

Instantly Michael heard the driver's shout of alarm!

They must have heard him or turned back and seen him. He realised that if they could have fired they would, either they were reloading or they couldn't see him clearly enough to get a clean shot. He ran until he thought his lungs would burst, yet it was fleeting seconds. He could hear them now, thundering across the bridge towards him from behind the vehicle.

Reaching the van he made for the driver's door, flung it open and leapt into the seat. Stamping on the clutch he threw the gear lever into first. At full revs he let the clutch out and the vehicle strained forward desperately slowly, until his hand found the handbrake. With a squeal of rubber and clouds of blue smoke the van lurched forwards.

Firing in unison two out of four shots went through the open door. A second volley went wildly overhead but they were closing rapidly on the van. More bullets whined nearby, one shattering a side mirror. Coming within ten metres Van Heerden wanted to scream to his colleague to shoot out the tyres, but the pain in his jaw prevented any such command.

Michael heard them emptying their pistols in frustration. Into second gear, third and finally fourth, then when he was sure he was out of gunshot range he eased his foot a little off the accelerator.

Michael laughed aloud with relief, then thought of his next move.

He must leave the country. Botswana was the obvious choice—it was his only chance! The road ahead was clear. Determined now, he turned off the main road and headed towards the north-west, still laughing when he heard an echo. No, it wasn't an echo. It was a different laugh.

'David!'

In the excitement he had forgotten all about his travelling companion manacled to a strut in the back. 'My God! With the rear doors open he was exposed to that hail of bullets,' the thought belatedly struck him. It was remarkable David was still alive.

'You okay?' he shouted back.

'Yes! I think so, but I'd prefer it if you didn't drive so recklessly and shut this bloody door,' came the response from the grille. In fact the way Michael had taken off, it was only his bindings that had stopped David falling out.

Michael slowed the van and found a clear spot to pull off the road and stop, out of sight of passing traffic. He switched off and went round the back. By the moonlight he could see David's smile.

'Son of a bitch,' Michael swore, 'you lead a charmed life,' and they both laughed out loudly at their good fortune. Neither had been hit.

Michael climbed into the back to inspect David's bonds.

'When I said take your fear and use it against them, I didn't exactly mean use me in the middle. I was resigned to dying in Pretoria Prison but I wasn't ready for you to kill us on that bridge,' lamented David.

'Believe me, it was a scary moment!' Michael grinned. 'I didn't come back for you—I needed these wheels! I didn't like the idea of a three hundred kilometre walk to Botswana!'

'I don't give a damn for your reasons, but I'm very glad you did.'

'You can owe me one. Right now we need to get you out of these manacles and to a doctor.'

'Just the manacles please! I am a doctor,' said David.

The tool-box and a jack found behind the driver's seat offered the necessary hardware to work on the rivets of the manacles and though he had David free from them in under half an hour it was still too long. They knew their guards could have been picked up by a passing motorist almost immediately after their escape and certainly by now had notified the authorities. They must assume they were now being hunted.

At a glance Michael could see David was tall and powerful and somehow he had become used to the sight of the doctor's injuries. The blood had dried over open wounds and the puffiness around the cheeks was subsiding. 'We have to leave the country—agreed?'

'Agreed,' David answered.

'Sure you're okay, and up to this?' Michael's concern was for his injuries.

'I'll be all right—except for my hands.' He held them out, now bound in rags which they had found in the cab. 'Just let's get the hell out of here.'

'All right—but we can't go far in this thing.' The police van was peppered with bullet holes and one of the rear lights was smashed. It would stick out like a sore thumb. They would have to ditch it somewhere in the dark. 'We'll either have to walk or steal another vehicle. It's not exactly what I do best. How about you?' Michael asked in jest.

'No. But you're right. We must have our own vehicle. I'd be very conspicuous like this on public transport.'

Michael's mind raced. It was essential they get out of South Africa. The authorities did not take kindly to losing prisoners. They would stop at nothing to get them back, preferably dead. Botswana was the nearest suitable haven, but it was almost 500 kilometres to its capital, Gaborone, and sanctuary. There, the Government was known to be sympathetic towards South African refugees. The greater the distance they could put between themselves and their pursuers, the happier he would be, and the sooner the better. He sped into the night.

David was curious. 'Excuse me asking but what did you do?'

'You mean why was I arrested? Well, in the past I've written a few strong letters of protest to the press condemning apartheid. It appears my last letter did the trick. You might say the authorities and I differ on this issue.' Michael glanced at the man he now considered to be his accomplice. 'And yourself, David, why were you arrested? Where will you go?'

'I'm in this condition because I happened to be listening to some members of the African National Congress.' He looked at Michael to see if he understood. 'The ANC is a banned organisation...'

'That much I know!' Michael interjected.

'It was an illegal gathering and we were raided. They had no intention of arresting us peaceably. I was beaten unconscious. When I came round, I was in a police cell.' His head dropped forwards and he looked at his hands. 'Peaceful protests are not the way to change things here. I see that now. I'll head north to the land of my father, where I'm needed. What else do you want to know?'

They fell silent, temporarily lost in their own thoughts.

They headed into the Western Transvaal following signposts until they reached the outskirts of Carletonville. Slowly Michael drove through the deserted mining town. On the other side he stopped.

'Did you see that hotel we just passed?' Without waiting for an answer he said, 'I've an idea that might just work.'

They backtracked past the hotel and stopped in the shadows of some trees. Several vehicles passed and the hours seemed to drag by when a solitary figure came out of the public bar; even in the dim light they could see the man was unsteady on his feet and was having difficulty unlocking his car door. Eventually he started the car and drove slowly around, coming in their direction.

Michael followed, tailing the drunk for a while, then flashed his lights several times. 'Dammit, the idiot won't stop,' he said and hit the accelerator. The police van lurched forward to overtake the car. Michael suddenly cut back in and braked hard.

The startled driver swore, realising it was the police, applied brakes and ground to a halt.

'Out you get,' Michael jerked the car door open. 'You're under arrest for drunk driving.'

The man was not as inebriated as they had at first supposed, but nonetheless was terrified by the 'wild man' standing over him brandishing a car jack. Within minutes he was bound and became the sole occupant in the back of the police van.

Michael drove the van off the road. Getting out, he peered into the night in all directions, confident that their captive could shout himself hoarse and remain undetected from any passers-by for some time. He threw the keys into the bush and ran back to the car where David had already installed himself in the passenger seat.

Looking skywards, Michael briefly held his hands together in prayer. Without a word he turned the ignition key. The engine burst into life. Holding his breath he swung the car round and drove slowly away. A check in the rear-view mirror confirmed the road was still clear. They both heaved sighs of relief.

The Peugeot 403 was old and rusty but the engine was sound, if a little noisy. It was impossible to tell how full the tank was because the needle swung from one end of the gauge to the other with every bump in the road. Michael prayed they had enough fuel to get them to the border.

An hour out of Carletonville saw them passing through the small town of Koster where Michael reduced speed in case there was an over-zealous traffic officer lying in wait. The last thing they needed was to be pulled over for speeding. Michael would have preferred another route altogether but this stretch of road was unavoidable. The Mooi River guarded the left of the main R509 road and the railway the right. Once through the town, he accelerated again. Now the national road lay ahead of them leaving a clear run to the border.

David saw it first. A police van was parked sideways across their path. 'Dammit! A roadblock...what you gonna do?'

Michael swore too, when he saw the vehicle, and a man waving a torch at the side of the road.

'Don't know! But I'm not stopping. You'd better hang on.' Michael slowed for what he now saw was a group of men standing at the roadside. Drawing closer, the Peugeot's lights illuminated the scene. Barely visible on the opposite side of the road was a narrow space between the van and a civilian car. Instantly, Michael hit the accelerator and aimed the Peugeot for the gap. The tyres spun and the 403 lurched forwards. Both men waited for the rendering screech of torn metal. It never came. They were through with a hair's breadth on either side.

'Hell!' exclaimed David incredulously.

'Bloody fantastic!' Michael was caught up in the adrenaline-rush of the moment. Already, he was looking into his rear-view mirror watching the frantic activity behind them as he floored the accelerator.

David's wounds appeared to be worrying him but he kept a watchful eye in all directions and a kilometre farther on there was still no sign of pursuit. Suddenly he was flung forward as Michael hit the brakes hard. Picking himself up he turned to look out the front, expecting to see something.

'We just passed a dirt road.' Without further explanation or apology Michael killed the headlights and reversed. He swung off the asphalt and they crawled away from the national road in second gear. Michael was relying on the police assuming they had continued along the R509. After several hundred metres, he flicked the headlights on. From here, they kept to secondary roads and headed due west. This had the undesired effect of slowing them down, finding it difficult to see their way in the weak headlight beams of the stolen vehicle, but they stuck to the dirt roads into the early morning.

At times the dusty tracks were good for travelling at speed but errors of judgement were severely punished by rocks and gullies which threatened to smash the suspension or damage the oil sump in an unguarded moment. They felt very vulnerable because the car would then be useless.

In the east, the sky was paler, heralding the new day. Michael checked the fuel gauge. It was still swinging back and forth but now alarmingly the needle registered lower as it swung to the left. He drove on. David, unable to assist with the driving due to his injuries, remained alert, talking to Michael to keep him awake, acting as lookout despite his pain. Both men were now very tired.

They hadn't reached the desert yet but the closer to Botswana they came, the closer came the eastern edge of the mighty Kalahari. The terrain was flat and without cover. Even the vegetation was thinning out, giving way to thickets of prickly pear.

Michael supposed that it wouldn't have taken the authorities long to figure out that they had headed off the beaten track, nor much longer to realise they were using the secondary roads on a parallel course to the R27, towards the north-west.

His thoughts were interrupted by David. 'Headlights...long way back.'

Michael shot a glance in the rear-view mirror but the hint of pre-dawn obscured his vision. He adjusted the mirror.

'Can't see a thing. Are you sure?'

'It's there. I'll keep an eye open.' David watched intently for some minutes before he spoke again. 'It's still there and moving fast. I think we have company. Probably BOSS!'

'How far back?' Michael peered frequently into the mirror until he caught a momentary speck of shimmering light. 'I see them,' he said. 'About two kilometres I'd say.'

'More or less. Can you go any faster?'

'Not if you want me to stay on the road.' Ahead of them they could see only darkness and their headlights were dim and badly adjusted. Michael's head was throbbing from concentration and lack of sleep. Nevertheless, he pressed the accelerator pedal a fraction further and, old though it was, the Peugeot responded. Each bend became a battle with the steering wheel to keep the lumbering saloon on the dirt road. The dust billowed behind them like a smokescreen in the ever-lightening eastern sky.

David was right. The pursuing car was moving very fast. Suddenly a T-junction came up on them and Michael took a turning to the right onto asphalt, scattering dirt and stone scree.

David shouted as a sign flashed past. 'Zeerust up ahead, eight kilometres north. Do we want to go in this direction?'

Michael gave his answer by swinging sharply onto another dirt path to their left which led west once more. 'No. I reckon they will have radioed ahead. Zeerust is probably crawling with cops by now. Anyway, they would have caught up with us within minutes on the asphalt. We keep heading west.' As a bend came up he barely slowed to negotiate it.

In less than a minute the lights behind changed direction to follow again, confirming that they were in pursuit. It was left unsaid but they both prayed this road would carry them across the border.

That they were now speeding through the pre-dawn light at breakneck speed would tell their pursuers that they were aware of their presence. It would also be obvious that their quarry was heading for Botswana, its border a mere 50 kilometres away.

Michael knew, once across, they would be safe—the South African authorities had no jurisdiction there. A sprint to the finish then.

Michael's feel for the handling of the old Peugeot was improving with every bend and now he could anticipate the rolls and slides. More importantly this meant he could increase his speed, yet still the pursuing car drew closer. David braced himself into the back of the seat, expecting to leave the road at every turn, but somehow Michael managed to keep control of the wildly bucking saloon.

The headlights in the mirror confirmed that the gap between them had narrowed. About thirty seconds separated them now; at this pace that was approximately a kilometre. Michael held his foot to the floor, going flat out, the motor unable to deliver more. The edge of the track was ill-defined in the dim light. The back of the car slewed left as the road fell away beneath the wheels on that side, and Michael steered hard left to reduce the power on the rear wheels to correct the skid. There was a strong urge to stand on the brakes but he anticipated the consequences; that the back would continue to break away and they would spin and probably roll over. The rear of the car snapped back into line, and beyond; it now swung out to the right. Michael see-sawed at the steering wheel as they fish-tailed for the next hundred metres applying power and regaining control.

David raised his voice over the staccato sound of stones tumbling in the wheel arches. 'With these hands I cannot drive,' he said drily, 'but has anyone told you that you can't either?'

Michael shrugged. 'Must be the tyres,' he said. 'I'll check them at the next garage,' but, despite the humour, he knew that they were losing valuable seconds to their pursuers.

Having found the car's limit, he maintained steady progress; the car behind was no longer gaining so rapidly. There were times, in fact, when it lost ground, probably experiencing the same difficulties on the dirt road. A powerful car was no advantage if there was no traction. But still they were there and the light in the eastern quadrant was spreading to the north and south as dawn approached.

David caught sight of something to their left. He was not sure what it was at first but then he exclaimed excitedly, 'Border fence!'

'I see it!' Michael shouted, spotting it moments later.

The borders were patrolled regularly by both South Africa and Botswana, neither side trusting the flimsy structure to provide security against illegal immigration. The fence was hardly ever totally intact anyway. Posts, rails and wire were all stolen at regular intervals, mostly by the local villagers whose goats grazed in the region.

Michael thought that this would be useful now as they could hardly use a border checkpoint to cross. He told David to keep an eye open for a break in the fence while straining his eyes to see the terrain and calculate the distance between the fence and the track. The surface seemed not much different to what they were driving on except it was strewn haphazardly with boulders of various sizes. Striking one of these at speed would almost certainly mean the end of their bid for freedom. Slow down further and BOSS would capture them. The fuel gauge seemed not to register any change since the last check. They could not afford to squander a drop.

'Over there,' David shouted urgently, his bound arm outstretched pointing to their right, 'it's a break in the fence.'

Michael hesitated long enough to scour the terrain for the best path, then checked his speed by using the handbrake. This method of slowing did not operate the brake lights, preventing their pursuers from being alerted to his actions. When the car had slowed sufficiently he crashed into third gear for more control of his speed, then swung the wheel to the right. The car careered onto virgin ground. Immediately, more small stones were thrown up from the tyres into the wheel arches and the underbody, creating a deafening roar. The dust swirling behind them increased and the car bucked as Michael ignored the smaller boulders, weaving round those most likely to cause serious damage. A rise caused the nose to lift into the air then it dropped with a bone-jarring crunch into the dirt. A hub cap tore from its mountings and flew back past the window like a tossed silver coin. The car maintained its erratic bronco motion. Michael was concentrating so hard on the boulders and gullies that he failed to see that he was past all that remained of the border fencing.

'We're through!' David yelled, and Michael thumped the steering wheel with his clenched fist.

'Thank God!' he shouted, and slowed the car to a more manageable speed to search for a proper road on the other side.

They saw their pursuers had fared no better across the boulder-strewn wasteland. The dawn was far enough advanced so they could see intermittently through their own dust trail that they were being chased by a dark sedan. Michael and David watched the wildly bucking bonnet behind them as the driver fought to control the car. When they reached the border, they would of course stop, curse in frustration and, finally, turn for home.

106

'Oh shit!' Michael exclaimed, his eyes wide as he examined the rear-view mirror closely. 'They haven't stopped. They're still coming. The bastards can't do that. It's against the law!' But still they came.

'We'd better get going, my friend,' David spoke calmly. 'Keep close to the border and look for a friendly patrol. They won't want to risk an incident.' His unruffled manner and logical reasoning were steadying influences.

Michael hit the accelerator. The car leapt forward again, slithering until the rear wheels gripped, spraying stones in its wake. The headlights were now of no benefit as the dawn sky lightened so Michael switched them off. Without the beacons of the red tail-lights to chase, he reasoned, their pursuers would have only the dust cloud to follow and they would not be easily visible in the grey dawn light.

The ground suddenly became uneven and, before Michael could react, the nose of the Peugeot dropped into a trough. It bottomed out at about two metres, enough for the car to disappear momentarily from view, and then it rose up the far side and launched into the next trough, all four wheels leaving the ground. It landed heavily, ripping the muffler from the exhaust pipe on the down slope with Michael's foot pressing the brake pedal to the floor. The car rose to the next ridge and dropped again into yet another trough. Still too fast!

'Hold on!' Michael shouted. Crossing their path was a gully. It was about a metre deep and two metres wide but with sides so steep that only a tank could have crossed it. Fighting the wheel, the tail of the car snaking wildly, Michael spotted a low narrow concrete causeway spanning the gully almost dead ahead. It didn't look wide enough but it was all there was. He guided the bucking car towards it. Seconds before reaching the causeway, he lifted his foot from the brake and the car straightened, speeding across the concrete strip with the outer half of each tyre overhanging the edge. Michael slammed the brake pedal again as they rose to crest the next ridge.

The chasing car was within a quarter of a kilometre and closing fast. Michael made a snap decision. In the next dip he wrenched the handbrake on and swung the wheel to the right. The tail swung out to the left and the car pivoted on its front wheels until it was facing the direction they had come. He gunned the engine and returned to the causeway over the gully and stopped the car short of the approach.

'What! What the hell are you doing?' David demanded. 'They'll be onto us in seconds.'

'Trust me,' Michael stared determinedly ahead. They could not see the advancing car, only a trail of dust as it went in and out of the dips. There was no time to explain. He waited precious seconds. While revving the engine to its upper limits and engaging first gear, he kept his foot pressing the clutch pedal to the floorboards.

Michael was gambling on their reactions being the same as his. Suddenly, the black sedan reappeared on the ridge between the two dips before swinging in a downward arc towards them. Michael, his jaw set grimly, released the clutch pedal and the Peugeot moved forward painfully slowly, the unbaffled engine roaring, the wheels fighting for grip. Their pursuers could see them. Twenty metres separated them—moments from collision. David shut his eyes against the impending impact as the tyres fought to grip the concrete.

'Aaarrh!' Michael yelled defiantly, buoying up his courage; at the last moment he hit the brakes and turned his head involuntarily away from the impact, and then...!

Then nothing. At the very last instant, the black sedan veered left, raking them in a hail of stone and grit, before plunging headlong into the far side of the gully. The front section crumpled as it struck. The bonnet flew up on impact and the windscreen shattered as a body was flung through it, in a shower of blood and glass. The man bounced off the twisted bonnet to land in the dirt. The tail of the car lifted into the air and hung motionless for several moments before falling back to the ground, its weight buckling the chassis further. Lying half out of the windscreen frame, a second figure lay slumped forward impaled on the steering column in his chest.

Michael turned the car at the top of the incline, and they faced the wreckage. Steam rose from the mangled radiator but otherwise nothing moved as the dust cloud settled. He wanted to stop and search the car and its dead occupants for any clue that might explain why they were being chased so relentlessly. There would be money and firearms on board which they might need later—but others would be following not far behind. He hesitated, but let caution prevail.

'Come on, let's get going,' and he carefully drove back across the gully.

'That was close,' said David wryly.

Michael could have sworn his passenger looked pale.

THE BUSH WAR

Matopo Hills, Zimbabwe

1972

African Affairs

Apartheid had crept as a darkness across Southern Africa—a callous and iniquitous act forced on its indigenous population. A kind of madness had possessed the minds of otherwise normal men. They were White and they were being confronted with the threat of Black Nationalism for the first time. Their hatred stemmed from fear that this would destroy their lives, their faith, their spoils and gains. Christianity would be doomed, their enterprises and industries would be nationalised, absorbed by this menacing tide of humanity: they were under siege.

Colonisation of Africa by European powers had placed generations of White settlers on a foreign shore. They now believed the land to be theirs by succession of conquest.

Slowly and ominously for the Whites, the Black descendants of ancient nations, patient over centuries of abuse under harsh rule, stirred, then marched. West Africa, Central Africa, East Africa, country after country acquired its independence, then lastly the South. Here, South Africa, Rhodesia and Mozambique, and to a lesser extent Angola, stood as the final bulwark against freedom.

Blacks watched in dismay as the colonial powers pulled out of their countries with no thought to train key personnel for the take-over. Usually they left behind a decimated infrastructure. Without the rudiments for a stable economy, a vacuum formed into which poured accusations from Whites blaming incompetence on Blacks for failures in the wake of their departure. In attempting to rebuild their economies, these African countries were forced to fall back on loans from the West and the World Bank, loans they could never hope to repay.

To White South Africans and Rhodesians these were real and perceived threats, a recipe for disaster. To this was added a threat of world domination by communism. They became even more entrenched in their thinking. In South Africa the White minority consisted of fractious elements: liberals, left-and right-wingers. There was one other element which has to be taken into account: hate.

Hatred and division were inherent in a country ravaged over many generations by Whites for its land and phenomenal mineral wealth.

The Afrikaners hatred for the British stemmed from the time when they were displaced as rulers of the Cape Province, culminating in the Great Trek in the 1830s northwards where they confronted the 'kaffir'. Here their hatred was transferred to the natives, fighting bloody battles to dispossess them and occupy their lands.

Their hatred against the British revived when they fought them in the Boer War from 1899 to 1902, when they strove to annex their ill-gotten Boer territories of the Transvaal and Orange Free State.

At last, the countries were united as the Union of South Africa. But they believed in their covenant with God, that it must remain forever a White Afrikaner-dominated country. Much later, into this cauldron of evil, poured Nazi war criminals who found sanctuary with Afrikaner sympathisers. Then, under successive Afrikaner administrations, they legislated for the segregation and separate development of race groups, known as *apartheid* and opted for a republic in 1961.

The country had become an open sore—now it was festering.

The South African Government deliberately misinformed its White population, keeping them ignorant of what was happening within and across its borders unless, of course, the news was negative and could be used by their propaganda machine, which had systematically spread its tentacles around the world. At home, the structures of government and church reinforced the belief that they were right.

The White population's biggest crime was that they remained aloof, unconcerned and chose to be ignorant about all things of import to its indigenous people.

Rhodesia, too, had its problems. Occupied mainly by British settlers, they were not looked favourably upon by the Afrikaners to the south. Rhodesia still remained a British colony and Britain believed the country should revert to majority rule. The White settlers took things into their own hands.

Meanwhile, Black 'Rhodesians' had striven for eight years, through democratic channels and their main political party, to attain parity with the Whites. But their opinions were ignored and it became perfectly clear that the Whites, like their neighbours to the south, were not going to concede power-sharing or the prosperity with which the country provided them.

The Black party was banned because Black aspirations were felt to threaten the White minority. In response, the party changed its name. The White government reacted swiftly and banned the new party in December 1961. Not to be outdone, the following month the name was changed yet again, once more throwing the White Rhodesians into turmoil. Realising that another banning order was imminent—it came in September 1962—the party went into exile and moved their headquarters to Dar es Salaam in Tanzania, together with its military wing, the Zimbabwe People's Revolutionary Army (ZIPRA), far from Rhodesia's borders.

Zambia (formerly Northern Rhodesia), to the north of Rhodesia (formerly Southern Rhodesia), had not yet acquired independence from Britain. In Tanzania, at least, President Nyerere was sympathetic to Black liberation movements in Southern Africa. Besides, he advocated socialism, believing it offered hope to Black African people, whereas under capitalist rule they had gained very little from the White colonial powers.

Here, too, had come Black Mozambique refugees. That country had been held in an iron grip by the Portuguese. The Black population there were similarly fighting for freedom from White oppression and their political parties were likewise exiled in neighbouring Tanzania. A coalition among their three main political parties in 1962 formed the liberation movement, the Front for the Liberation of Mozambique (FRELIMO).

In June 1963, followed a second Black political party from Rhodesia into exile in Tanzania, with its new military wing, the Zimbabwe African National Liberation Army (ZANLA). The Whites paying little attention to this threat.

In October 1964, Zambia gained its independence from Britain and the newly elected president, Kenneth Kaunda, then extended a hand of friendship to ZIPRA, still stranded in Tanzania. President Kaunda did not allow both rebel forces to operate from Zambia, believing that two foreign armies operating on Zambian soil would be untenable.

Still, the two rebel armies were poised, if necessary, to send their freedom fighters across the Zambezi River to liberate their country from its White oppressors, ZIPRA being supported by the USSR in Zambia, and ZANLA supported by China in Tanzania.

The White Rhodesians had taken a more liberal stance than Whites in South Africa but it was not to last. They saw the threat of 'terrorists' building up strength over the border, refusing to recognise them as legitimate political parties or liberation armies. It now suited these White racist régimes to instil fear in their White electorate, propagating the belief communism and Black nationalism were synonymous.

On 11 November 1965, Rhodesia announced a Unilateral Declaration of Independence (UDI), to the chagrin of the British Government.

When Ian Smith, the Rhodesian Prime Minister, tore these people away from the bosom of the British Empire with UDI, he created a sense of unease—almost an identity crisis—because most White Rhodesians still had strong ties with their 'mother country'. And when, almost overnight they became responsible for themselves without the protection of the Crown and were punished by sanctions, they eagerly rallied round the new Rhodesian flag. The die was cast then for what was to be a long, bitter and protracted 'Bush War' of attrition. The 'armed struggle' in Zimbabwe would cost over 30,000 lives.

The South African Government, seeing their worst fears realised needed to counter this Black onslaught. They deployed their paramilitary troops on Rhodesia's borders to bolster the Rhodesian security forces and systematically set about attacking their opponents outside the country.

Meanwhile, the West wittered on about the virtues of democratic rights for world citizens but gave no tangible support to these repressed peoples. On the face of it, it seemed they had little desire to stop the exploitation so long as they had a vested interest. Rhodesia was no different: Black people lost their basic freedoms, while a world appeased its conscience by saying oil embargoes were the answer to the Smith régime, but allowing trade to continue unashamedly via the back door, at a high cost.

In Tanzania, FRELIMO was an effective force under the leadership of Samora Machel. They re-entered Mozambique in March 1968, and in 1970 captured and held the central province of Tete. The Portuguese continued their relentless attack on FRELIMO forces.

For ZIPRA things weren't going well. Their initial efforts to infiltrate into Rhodesia from Zambia and Botswana proved ineffectual. It appeared that the White Rhodesians were successfully containing the Bush War.

In April 1971, came a major split in ZIPRA with many experienced fighting men crossing to ZANLA. The rift considerably strengthened ZANLA who still operated out of Tanzania, because of Zambia's sworn support for ZIPRA alone. ZANLA soldiers had to cross Zambia in order to reach Rhodesia, mostly under the guise of FRELIMO troops, but the Zambians took a relaxed attitude towards them in transit.

FRELIMO then offered the beleaguered ZANLA forces a launch pad in Mozambique for their new offensive on Rhodesia, even before the departure of the Portuguese. This changed everything. They were partisan to Mao Tse Tung, learning the lessons of the Chinese on how to mobilise the masses. ZANLA was to have a profound effect on the Bush War.

The White governments of Southern Africa with their misguided thinking were dangerous men. They saw and felt the effects of the ZANLA offensive from 1972 onwards, and knew time was fast running out.

Rhodesia remained the last buffer state between Black Africa and the White-held south. They needed desperate measures if they were to hang on to White rule—not hesitating to use a 'quick fix' and to hell with the consequences—they would deal with worldwide condemnation afterwards.

CHAPTER 5

Announcing UDI, 11 November 1965: "We have struck
a blow for the preservation of justice, civilisation and
Christianity and in the spirit of this belief we have this
day assumed our sovereign independence. God bless
you all."

Ian Smith
Prime Minister of Rhodesia, 1964 - 79

18 February 1972

David was nursing his body back to health—he knew the pain would
subside in time but the mental scars would stay. Although it was over
a month since he had started out on that fateful journey to Cape Town with
Josh, the events nevertheless remained raw.

This quiet and desolate place suited his mood. He sat on a rocky-ledge
surveying the sacred burial ground of the Ndebele, where their chiefs,
including his grandfather, lay buried. The sombre atmosphere of the place
didn't disturb him, although it was pervasive, spiritual, commanding
a respectful silence. His father, knowing his request for his body to be
buried here would be denied by the authorities, had asked that his ashes be
scattered close by and David had come nine months earlier to this very spot
for that purpose.

Another man's remains lay close by. From his vantage point, out there on
the crest of the granite hill, David could see clearly the symmetrical burial
stone and the Black guard who stood in day-long vigil over the tomb.
Beneath lay not an Ndebele but a man whose memory defiled this hallowed
ground. The plaque read Cecil John Rhodes.* David turned away and gazed
into the distance.

His arrest by BOSS and his subsequent beating remained fresh in his
mind. Still recovering, his left hand was splinted and the right was still
painful when he clenched his fist. Through the mental turmoil and physical
abuse that he had endured, one good thing had emerged: Michael, to whom
he clearly owed his life. This man, at grave risk to himself, had got them out
of South Africa into Botswana. Despite his protestations about having
escaped only to secure his own freedom, Michael had refused to leave him
until he was sure he was in safe and capable hands. Over the next three
weeks Michael had called at his bedside, daily, attending to his needs and
bringing him the latest news concerning their flight from South Africa.
A close bond developed between them but now he almost resented the

friendship. It threw him off-balance—it would have been easier to hate Michael for being White. He recalled what Michael had said when he had asked why Michael had bothered to help him—a Black man!

'Scratch my skin, and underneath you'll find I'm as Black as you,' he had joked. Even now it brought a wry smile to David's lips and he struggled to push Michael from his mind.

Beneath an outward calm, David seethed. The torture meted out to him had acted as a catalyst engendering the hatred he now felt. Here, in Rhodesia, Ian Smith, the Prime Minister, had taken the country down the road of apartheid. Before then, on frequent visits with his father, they had shared a spontaneous and genuine camaraderie with many Whites, but since the minority White government had introduced its illegal Unilateral Declaration of Independence, severing links with Britain, that had changed.*

White extremists were now speaking openly of introducing a scorched earth policy, rather than hand the country over to the Black majority. They were threatening to destroy their farms, industries, mines, even the Kariba power station on the Zambezi River. Hydropower was essential for economic stability. Kariba provided the shared power to the hungry copper mines in Zambia and the coal collieries of Rhodesia alike—a legacy from the time when both countries had been part of a federation of states. There was loose talk of the Rhodesian Special Air Services (SAS) having mined the dam wall. The devastation, if it were blown up, would prove catastrophic, causing unbelievable loss of life in the wake of a tidal wave, sweeping villages and towns before it. Its effects would be felt as far away as Mozambique on the east coast.*

Feeling betrayed, it rankled David that few Whites had ever travelled out of South Africa or Rhodesia and yet they spoke with authority about the persecution of Whites in other Black countries, or about the so-called inherent inadequacies of Blacks in general. He asked himself, 'Yes! But then, by whose standards are we being judged? In truth, Whites in Africa want for nothing.' He knew there were not many who thought of themselves as Africans. Instead, they still called themselves Europeans.

What hurt him more was that most found it unnecessary to have any kind of social contact with people of his colour; hence, few understood Black African culture or their feelings. He was sure the blind belief in their own superiority would eventually cost them dearly.

David knew what he had to do and stood up to leave.

Michael had wanted to walk up the path to see Rhodes' burial site in the Matopo Hills, but held back patiently in the car park out of respect for David's wishes. He tried to doze but the heat was stifling, when David returned.

'Do you still want to see Rhodes' grave?' he asked laconically.

'Yes,' Michael replied. 'This is probably the one and only time I'll come this way.'

'Okay, I'll take you up.'

Michael followed in silence as David retraced his steps along a narrow path winding its way upwards through the massive wall of granite. After a short distance they arrived on a plateau seemingly stretching across the horizon. Michael gazed across what resembled a lunar landscape. Nearby lay Rhodes' graveside.

Presently he asked, 'Is this it then? Hardly seems worth the effort.' He glanced down again at the brass plague inscription mounted on the granite slab, then took in the surroundings once more. 'Come on, let's go. This place gives me the creeps.'

Michael felt enervated as they motored steadily north. It did not help that there was minimal traffic and the main road through virgin bush was cut straight. The long spells of driving and the heat had made him drowsy and to keep his mind alert, he whiled away the kilometres reflecting on their short stay in Gaborone, the capital of Botswana.

After dropping David off at the hospital, his first thoughts had been for Carla. He had tried in vain to telephone her. Later, he had managed to make contact with the ANC on David's insistence.

The following day Michael had visited the Standard Bank and requested his account be urgently transferred from South Africa. To his relief, on the third day the transaction was completed without a hitch. As he had hoped, his statement reflected the recent substantial deposit from Coronet Chemicals; his director's annual dividend on shares held in the company. This would be the last for some time. He had been fortunate to catch the South African authorities napping, knowing it would be days, if not hours, before they froze his account on discovering why he had left the country. Michael had immediately made a sizeable withdrawal which now lay tucked into his bulging wallet.

His mind turned to Carla. Eight days ago he had managed to get through to her and he wondered what she was now thinking?

oOo

The receptionist buzzed her extension. 'Carla, I have a call from a Mr Semillon. Says he's seen your advertisement and wants to buy your BMW.'

She was about to say the caller must be mistaken; she wasn't selling and

117

hadn't advertised, when a shiver ran down her spine. With a rush of recognition she realised it was him. 'Ja, ja, put him on.' There was a short pause, 'Michael!'

'Carla, my God I've missed you. I've been trying for weeks to get through.'

'Where are you? Are you all right? I've been so worried.'

'Carla, slow down, and just listen. I'm in Botswana. I was arrested, but I managed to escape.'

'I see...they said you were there.'

'What! Who said I was here?' Michael asked anxiously.

'BOSS. Something about you stealing the Cape Doctor's notes. Tell me you didn't do it for God's sake.' She began to weep audibly.

'Carla don't! They are lies. What was there to steal? Has Tinus gone mad?'

'Michael, that's unfair!' This seemed to force her to become defensive and the crying stopped, 'He's tried to defend you over these past weeks. If you didn't take the documents, then why did you leave? Why were you arrested?'

'Because I wrote a letter to the *Cape Herald* and you can guess what it was about.'

There followed a dreadful silence.

'Come off it, Michael, they don't arrest you for writing letters to the paper. What did you say that was so awful? No, Michael, if you love me, you will come back to Cape Town and tell me the truth.'

'But how can I? BOSS will flay me alive. Honestly, Carla, you don't understand, you're asking me to commit suicide...you've no idea what's happened in the past few weeks.'

'Michael, I've spoken to the police, Tinus has too and I've even had Papa use his influential friends to ask after you. They are most insistent you were only pulled in for questioning concerning these bloody missing documents, then released. What am I expected to think? I want to believe you but your staying away only seems to worsen everything.' She was getting angry now. 'Why have you waited so long to contact me?'

'Carla, believe me, I've tried almost every day. There's been no answer from your apartment; the farm telephone is out of order or at least I cannot get through to that number, the laboratories always say you are out or otherwise engaged. I'm sure it's only because I gave them a false name that I'm talking to you right now. Carla, please, about these documents...'

She had been biting her lip and now cut him off. 'Michael, if you love me you'll come back and we'll sort this mess out. I'll only wait so long.' She sobbed again and put the telephone down.

'Papa, please, I need your help. You know the editor of the *Cape Herald*. Would you find out if they received an anti-government letter from Michael any time over the last few months. It's important to me, Papa.'

'Is there no end to this young man's talents for getting into trouble!' said Boshoff senior scornfully. 'Has he also been dabbling in politics? I'm sorry—I know how much you miss him—I'll see what I can find out.'

Within days he was back to Carla with an answer. 'The editor is adamant. No, they haven't received any mail, letter or any other form of communication from Michael. He personally checked the records for me going back over the past six months.'

oOo

After getting through to Carla, the days seemed to drag by and Michael experienced a bitter-sweet hell ever since, knowing she was just across the border, yet out of reach. To go back would be folly, spelling certain death. She couldn't possibly appreciate his predicament. He had been tempted to return, to see her, to hold her, but reason dictated otherwise. He would bide his time—wait for the dust to settle. She had said she would wait!

Something up ahead darted across the road and disappeared into the dense bush. It brought him back to the present and Carla slipped temporarily from his mind.

With David now recovering from his injuries, they had decided to cross the border from Botswana into Rhodesia earlier in the day. It was agreed to detour to the Matopo Hills for David's sake, but they still had a long drive ahead of them. They wanted to put as many miles between them, and South Africa, as possible—Botswana was still dangerously close. Besides, Michael had reason for wanting to go to Zambia, and quickly.

The kilometres slowly fell away and eventually they passed through the city of Bulawayo. From here they headed north towards the Victoria Falls, many hours drive away. Michael checked the speedometer and glanced over to see if his passenger was awake.

'Don't reckon we'll reach the border post tonight. How about if we book into a hotel at the Falls?'

'Suits me, provided they'll take Black customers,' David replied without sarcasm.

'Money talks, David!' Michael felt reassuringly for his wallet in the driver's side-pocket. 'Leave the finances to me but you hold onto this,' handing the wallet over. 'Sure as hell, I'll lose it, and then we'll be up the creek. It's all we have to tide us over for a while.' He patted the dash, 'I'm afraid eight thousand on this rust heap has already made a dent.'

David thought of the salesman in Gaborone who had haggled, then argued and, finally, given up when he realised Michael had subtly beaten down the price. In so doing, he had demonstrated an in-depth knowledge of what went on under a bonnet. Then came the test drive, an experience David wished he had missed. Michael had gunned the motor—driving out into the desert where the vehicle severely overheated.

They barely made it back. He had then pointed out to the dismayed salesman that there was something very seriously wrong with the vehicle to cause the overheating but, nevertheless, agreed to take the car provided new tyres, an entirely new exhaust system and track-rod-ends were fitted—the list went on. Once out of Gaborone, Michael had stopped and opened the bonnet. With a spanner he had removed and discarded the thermostat. Grinning like a cat who got the cream, he was back behind the wheel in the space of a few minutes. Thereafter the vehicle ceased to overheat.

'How much do you think you'll get for the car in Zambia?' David asked out of curiosity.

'Don't know, maybe twelve thousand. I believe vehicles are in short supply given the current situation. War tends to create a demand.'

David fell silent for a while, then asked. 'How long do you think this Bush War will last, Mike? It's already been going for six years.'

'I've no idea, I know precious little about Rhodesia,' Michael confessed, 'or its political history. What do you know about it?'

David gazed out the window, the view unseen. 'Not much to tell really. Suppose it's much the same as South Africa, except here it has already developed into an armed struggle on a civil war footing...my father was born not far from here.'

'That makes you a Rhodesian!' Michael deduced.

'No, I am half Ndebele. My mother was Xhosa.'

'Different! Your parents certainly moved around.'

'You might say that. My father loved this country and I think, when the fighting started, it broke his heart.'

'Why did this bloody war start anyway?' Michael asked.

'Because Whites here don't want to share the country's wealth with people like me. So they introduced apartheid like yourselves in the south.'

'I'd rather you didn't include me. We're not all the same.' Michael added with a wry grin, 'That's if you'd prefer not to walk the next 100 kilometres,'

'Sorry, Mike, you're right. It's just that most Whites profess a liberal attitude but do nothing. Anyway, as I was saying, they banned the Black political parties.'*

Michael appreciated David's bluntness and, glancing fleetingly at his passenger, sensed his friend's need to talk. 'Then what happened?' He listened with genuine interest.

'They went into exile and moved their headquarters to Dar es Salaam.'*

'Why Tanzania of all places? It's a communist country,' Michael frowned.

'That's White rhetoric for you. Black Nationalism is not communism,' he grimaced, then gave a rueful smile. 'That Karl Marx was a Jew, like yourself, does that make you a communist?' he questioned.

'Not likely. David, how many Jews do you know who are willing to share their livelihoods with the masses? I can honestly say I don't know any, including myself.' Michael grinned at his companion, 'Maybe Marx left greed and incentives out of his theories?'

David thought for a moment of the wealthy, mega-wealthy, Jews of Johannesburg. 'You might be right!' And they both chuckled.

'Communism,' David continued, 'isn't the African way. The way I see it they are simply helping liberate us Blacks from White oppressive régimes. Or maybe you think the South African régime isn't oppressive?'

Michael caught his sideways glance, 'I've no argument with that statement!'

'What really pisses me off are sanctions,' David swore. 'The West says oil embargoes are the answer. That this will bring Rhodesians to their knees. But did you observe any shortages when we filled up?'*

'I see your point!' Michael conceded, finding it difficult to concentrate on the road, but fortunately the asphalt stretched in a straight line almost to the horizon. They hadn't passed another vehicle in the past hour. He was becoming more and more intrigued with the history of this neighbouring country which he, admittedly, knew little about. He was also impressed by David's knowledge, but then his friend had a stake in the country.

'Go on!' he encouraged.

'What do you want to know?' asked David.

'Well, where does that leave the 'armed struggle' as you call it?'

'If only we knew. I'm afraid that's in the lap of the gods and possibly ZANLA—that's one of the liberation armies.' Even so, David sounded optimistic.

'I see. So what do they propose to call Rhodesia, if they win the war?

'Zimbabwe!'

'Tell me one thing more, David. Why is it every time a Black nation gains independence they have to damn well change the names of everything—you know how frustrating that is?'

'Frustrating! After centuries of colonisation and forced impoverishment, it's us who are frustrated. Mike, it's simply a way of expressing our pent-up feelings. We want to be free of your imposed, no sorry not yours, but White rule. We don't want reminders of the past.'

'All right, but you'd better study the map because I don't recognise any of the names of the towns in Zambia any more.'

David smiled. 'You don't have to, just keep heading towards Lusaka. They haven't changed that name.'

Dusk crept up on them as they drove into the border village of Victoria Falls. Fifteen minutes and a greased palm later they were both installed in a local motel supposedly catering only for White patrons.

'Hungry?' asked Michael.

They could not find a take-away and within an hour they had exhausted all the restaurants in this small tourist mecca, being refused entry because of the colour of David's skin. Returning to their motel they were too late for the dining-room and had to settle for sandwiches in their room. Despondent, and knowing that the night held no attractions, they turned in.

The Victoria Falls was breathtaking and Michael wished they could have stayed on to enjoy the sights. But the border post was tantalisingly close and he had an important appointment to keep in Zambia.

At a crawl their vehicle crossed the high-level bridge. They were both full of expectations of what lay ahead on the other side of the Zambezi River. The Falls filled their view, the white waters thundered down the rock face, boiling and bucketing through a series of rocky gorges far below, from where a rainbow-filled cloud billowed up to tower majestically above them in an otherwise empty sky. Free Africa beckoned.

The eight-hour journey from the Victoria Falls to Lusaka gave the two men their first insight into, and taste of, life north of the Zambezi. Here was a pulse, a vibrancy which they had hitherto not experienced in South Africa or Rhodesia. The pace was different. Wherever they stopped, which was frequently, they found the people more relaxed and definitely friendlier. By mid-afternoon they entered the outskirts of Zambia's capital.

David folded the road map he had being studying intently. 'It's hard to believe we've travelled nearly 5000 kilometres since leaving Cape Town.'

'Seems ages ago—but at least we made it here,' Michael replied, but something was troubling him. 'Dave, are you sure that ANC fellow in Botswana was on the level?'

'How can I answer that? You will have to wait until Monday morning. Isn't your appointment at 10.30am?'

'Yeah, I suppose you're right. I just hope your pals in the ANC are right when they say they can swing it with residence permits for us both.'

'Mike, must I remind you again, I'm not an ANC member. However, they're normally sympathetic to anyone in our predicament and when I mentioned Josh things just happened.'

'Your cousin Josh seems quite a lad—let's hope he can pull a few more strings.'

As they approached the city centre, David voiced what was on both their minds. 'All we need to worry about now is where we're going to put our heads down over this weekend.'

Sunday was spent leisurely cruising around Lusaka, a pleasant city with sprawling green suburbs and wide, tree-lined avenues. The air was warm, laden with the scent from the profusion of flowering vegetation visibly in abundance. Here the tempo of life was slower than they had expected. At one point they had stopped at the intersection where the Great North Road split: north to the Copperbelt and onto Zaire; east to Malawi; or south, the way they had come. It seemed as if the city had sprung up over the years by enticing travellers like themselves who, once stopped, never moved on.

That was yesterday. Today, Michael had driven a few kilometres south to the township of Chilanga to keep an appointment. The long single-storey building was set back from the roadside. It was singularly unimpressive except for the two massive elephant tusks that towered over the entrance. The sign read 'Game & Fisheries Department'. He strode up the front steps in his khaki shorts and T-shirt, found the personnel director's office and before long was being interviewed.

Simon Kalabo had worked his way through the ranks in the national parks, from game scout during colonial rule to his present position as the personnel director. He had served under many White South Africans and had a deep respect for their commitment to their work. He reviewed Michael's credentials. The letter from the ANC offices in Botswana outlined his recent experiences and, in addition, they had supplied him with an exemplary reference and testimonial.

'I can sympathise with your predicament following your departure from your country and I see you certainly have your supporters,' Simon Kalabo cleared his throat. 'Of course, you are aware the ANC has contacted us directly concerning you?' He picked up the application form as if weighing it and placed it down again on the desk. 'Your qualifications are impressive but I'm not altogether sure they are appropriate for the post we wish to fill, Mr Bernstein. While our department is inundated with zoologists and botanists, we require the services of an entomologist to research 'sleeping sickness', more specifically trypanosomiasis—which, as you know, is transmitted by the bite of the tsetse fly. Nasty insects, believe me, Mr Bernstein. And 'sleeping sickness' is not restricted to cattle. It can be a killer in man.'

'Yes, we encountered some of the little buggers on the way up from the Vic Falls,' Michael interjected.

This seemed to amuse the personnel director. He continued.

'Wild animals in the Zambezi Valley are generally immune to this disease but it devastates domestic cattle. We are currently working closely with other departments. There is joint funding for this project in the belief that, if we can establish and then isolate the mechanism of this immunity, it may create an economic boom for Zambia. We could effectively range more cattle and sell the technology to the rest of Africa. A lot is riding on this research.' He fell silent, waiting to hear the applicant's response.

Michael hesitated momentarily, considering what he'd been told. 'Mr Kalabo, I cannot guarantee to find a solution but certainly the work falls well within my capabilities. Frankly, I would enjoy the challenge. On a personal level, I'm sure you'll appreciate that I can't return south and I should very much like to focus on something positive. You have my assurances that I will do everything I can to further the project.'

The interview dragged on with Simon Kalabo firing question after question at Michael. 'Are you prepared for the isolation this job entails? You may be out in the bush on your own for months on end.'

'I am a conservationist and I love the bush. I'm happy in my own company. No, I see no problem in staying out alone for long periods. Mr Kalabo, I really want this job and I want to know if you are going to give me a chance....'

Michael found David talking to the barman in the hotel. His expression gave nothing away.

'How did it go, Mike? Did you get the job?'

Michael's face lit up. 'Yes! And I'm really pleased. Why didn't I think of a career in this field before? It's going to be challenging—but there's still one major hurdle, a residence permit in order to work in Zambia.'

'No problem, Mike!' He called back the barman. 'Two lagers and keep them coming. We're celebrating!'

They settled into a quiet corner and David announced his good news.

'While you were out I had a visit from the Zambian ANC representative. He's promised to attend to all the formalities. Apparently Josh interceded for us and the ANC has offered to place its services at our disposal. I honestly think Josh's conscience is worrying him after what happened in Cape Town.' David chuckled to himself.

'At least that's reassuring,' Michael agreed. Then chipped in, 'You'll be pleased to know I've got quarters in Chilanga and there's room for two. It's a small township with a cement plant or something, a few houses and a pub close to the Department building that will do nicely.'

David was less confident. 'Sure your boss won't mind?'

'Simon Kalabo! No—he seems like a regular guy. They're all very relaxed in the Department and I've already got the keys to the bungalow. By the way, I explained your position and Simon said there's no problem with you staying as my guest until you sort yourself out. We can move in any time and, assuming the permit's granted, I start work next week.'

The relief showed on David's face. At last the pieces were falling into place and were going their way.

They moved into the bungalow and before long it seemed most of the residents in the village knew more about them than they knew about each other. The local pub was the social centre for the small community and they were made to feel welcome.

Still Michael was getting anxious about his work permit. He was about to bring up the subject yet again when the telephone rang. David reached it first. The message was brief.

'The ANC representative wants to see me in Lusaka—didn't say what it was about.'

'Okay, I'll drive you. Let's go and maybe you can press him to contact the Zambian immigration about our work permits.'

'After your persistent daily calls, I dare say they'll appreciate the change,' David muttered wryly. On the way into town he enquired, 'Still no news from your girl?'

'No! Nothing. Not since Botswana when she slammed the telephone down on me.' It was a statement tinged with bitter resentment. 'Now when I ring, she isn't in or else doesn't want to talk to me.'

'I'm sorry, Mike,' he said, thinking it best not to refer to the matter again.

David came out of the ANC offices waving an envelope in the air and Michael knew instantly what he was holding—he sprang from the car and hurried to meet his friend.

'Your residence permit, Mike,' David held out the papers. Michael reached out as a silver-grey car slid alongside them. The screech of brakes drew their attention. The front seat passenger was pointing a camera in their direction. He seemed to snap several shots before the car accelerated away.

'What in hell's name was that about!'

'They took our photos!' David yelled back, 'Come on, Mike...' already having started after the car.

Michael was hot on his heels. For a second they gained on the car as it slowed fleetingly, then disappeared around the far corner.

They stood on the pavement, breathless, their fear evident.

The residence permits represented the first platform of stability in their lives since escaping from South Africa and they were determined not to let this incident spoil the moment, but nagging doubts remained for days. They had been photographed, but why? Who were the occupants of that car?

o0o

In Cape Town, the final blow came for Carla when she arrived at work one morning to find Commandant Piet Van Heerden waiting for her in the foyer.

'I am afraid we have the proof you wanted, Miss Boshoff.'

'What do you want me to believe this time?' She tried to sound irritated but doubt had already crept in.

'See for yourself.' Van Heerden produced photographs.

Carla looked briefly at the set of four enlargements. They tore her apart. Taken at slightly different angles, the photographs clearly showed Michael handing an envelope over to a Black man.

'Mr Bernstein fled to Zambia—see the date in the corner. The camera cannot lie, Miss Boshoff,' and with his index finger he pointed to a clearly visible sign on a building in the background. 'That has been identified as the ANC office in Lusaka.'

The tears welled up into her eyes.

'I'm sorry, Miss Boshoff, but we have it on good authority that he has sold the research notes to an Eastern European pharmaceutical company.'

oOo

Settling into his new job was easier than Michael had expected. He was pleased to get back into a routine. Simon Kalabo insisted on accompanying him on his first field trip and they hit it off from the start. The research proved exacting. Michael adopted a two-pronged approach. He collected tsetse fly specimens in the hope of isolating the *trypanosomes*—a parasitic single-celled micro-organism found in the infected flies, which causes sleeping sickness. He used these on trials with domestic animals and became adept at darting game with a tranquillising gun to draw blood samples in the hope of isolating the immune factor in their bloodstream.

The weeks passed with Michael seeing less of David as he became more involved in his work. He realised too, that he needed to try and push Carla from his mind. Unconsciously his calls became less frequent, then suddenly aware of the time lapse, he would phone almost obsessively for days on end. Attempts to reach her always met with the same negative response— her apartment and parents were unreachable. And every time he tried to make contact at the laboratories she was somehow unavailable.

David's departure was sudden.

Determined to use his qualifications wherever they might best serve the struggle to liberate Rhodesia, David sought out the leaders of the liberation movement in Lusaka. His services as a doctor received an enthusiastic welcome from ZANLA but the Black leadership had a more demanding role for him to play, as a member of their intelligence network within Rhodesia.

Michael was camped on the Zambezi when he received the news over the radio from Simon Kalabo.

'Got a friend here who wants to see you—says he's leaving Zambia. If you want to come in to Chilanga for a few days, it's okay by me.'

Michael broke camp immediately and, following the steep and treacherous bush tracks running up the escarpment, climbed out of the sweltering Zambezi Valley. On reaching the Great North Road, he turned right onto the asphalt and headed north towards Chilanga.

'You look after yourself and don't get killed in this bloody war of yours.' David smiled. 'And you make sure you don't dart yourself in the arse or get carried away by the tsetse when you're asleep.'

'I'll miss you, you silly bugger.' Michael felt his depth of attachment for David. 'You'll stay in touch won't you?'

'You can count on it, Mike, but for now, I'm going to kick the hell out of White Rhodesians.'

'Thought you should know I'm behind you all the way,' Michael said ardently. They wrapped their arms around one another.

'It's been one hell of an experience, hasn't it, Mike? I trust you'll have a quieter life from here on.'

They held each other at arm's length.

Michael watched his friend disappear down the road, his destination Dar es Salaam initially, for military training. David was someone special in his life, more than even his brother could ever be.

Michael stayed in the bush for as long as he dared—the months slipped by. Only when rations ran out or when his cook was on the point of desertion did he return to Chilanga, and then fleetingly. At times Simon had to threaten to go down and personally drag Michael back to civilisation. On this occasion Simon took it upon himself to call.

'Michael, I'm serious. If you stay out there too long you'll go bush-crazy. I insist you come in tomorrow.'

Reluctantly, and to the relief of his cook, Michael agreed. The following morning he presented himself in Simon's office.

'Have you had a look at yourself? I bet that face hasn't seen a razor for at least two months. As of this instant you're on ten days leave, like it or not.'

Michael knew it was pointless to argue. He asked if he could use the Land Rover allocated to him while off duty, so that he could go down to the Zambezi to do a quiet bit of fishing.

'What's with you, Michael? You've just come out of the Valley and now you want to spend your leave there. No, you can't. I'm confining you to

Chilanga or you can go into Lusaka: I hear the night life there for a bachelor is good. Now get out of my office. I've got work to do.'

Dejectedly Michael turned on his heel.

'One thing more...I'll see you at the watering hole tonight,' Simon tapped his desk with his index finger as if to hammer home his point to stay in town. 'And you're buying!'

By eleven-thirty Simon was a little unsteady on his feet and Michael, slightly less under the weather, promised to drive him home to an anxious wife who had already phoned the club twice. Simon insisted he was fine and disappeared out of the club door into the night. Last drinks were called and Michael ordered another lager and carried his glass through to the adjoining lounge as the pub closed.

Someone followed him and sat at the opposite table. Michael had become aware of the man earlier and was under the impression that he had been watched for most of the evening.

'Hellish hot this evening,' said the stranger.

'Bloody hell! Man, we could do with some air-conditioning in here,' Michael replied.

'Ah! So you are a South African.' The other had not missed the inflection in his speech.

Michael tensed. 'Yes,' he asked cautiously, 'and yourself?'

'Oh, from here and there.' He dropped his voice to a whisper, 'Actually I'm a Rhodesian, but I don't broadcast that fact around.'

'Understandably,' said Michael, though not entirely sure that he did.

'Do you mind if I join you?' the man asked.

Michael gestured toward a chair. It was obvious he was intent on their sitting together anyway.

He introduced himself: 'Captain Monarch—Steve actually.'

Not being able to resist the temptation he reciprocated,

Mr Bernstein—Mike actually.'

'What are you doing in this neck of the woods, Mike?'

Stupid bugger, Michael thought, sitting there in his parks uniform. 'I'm in the Game Department!'

'But of course, the epaulettes. Reckon you get around the bush a lot!'

Another bloody silly remark, he thought. What else did the Game Department do? 'Yes! You might say that.'

Further desultory conversation followed before Captain Monarch rose to leave. Michael finished his pint with a feeling of relief. Outside the club he found Simon in his car, dead to the world. He left him to sleep it off and strolled down the road to his quarters wondering who Monarch really was.

Michael found Captain Monarch in the pub the following night. He was there again the next night—and the night after. He felt that on each occasion Monarch was waiting for him to appear, before coming over to attach himself for the entire evening. By the fifth night Michael was feeling decidedly uneasy. What was Monarch up to? He sat trying to gauge his drinking companion but without much success. He was about Michael's age, maybe a year or two older. His wispy blonde hair and cravat gave him a somewhat cavalier air. The man was starting to grate on his nerves and he was beginning to regret that this was the only pub in Chilanga. Maybe he would take Simon's advice and go into Lusaka after all. Yet he was curious to find out what Stephen Monarch wanted? Then without asking he provided the answer.

'Mike, what do you think of the war in Rhodesia?'

In was a sensitive subject and most White residents in Zambia tried to avoid the issue, especially with a comparative stranger. Michael wrestled with the question. How the devil was he to answer? He decided to remain noncommittal.

'Steve, I have no interest in wars of other countries. As a South African, I'm not really involved.'

'Ha! Dear boy, that's typical. I must admit you chaps know how to sort out your Blacks...and screw the rest hey?'

At least he had indicated what side of the fence he was on and Michael decided to play along. He dropped his voice to match Monarch's.

'We take no nonsense from the 'kaffirs'!' And for good measure he added, 'God help the bastards if they cross our border and try to give us any grief.'

'Yes, yes! I can assure you we are very grateful for your support in Rhodesia, and I have to say, I entirely agree with your sentiments,' he added enthusiastically.

Then to Michael's amazement, Stephen Monarch came right out with it.

'Actually, Mike, I'm in what you might technically call the Rhodesian military intelligence based here in Zambia. '

Michael looked furtively around the room. 'I'd keep that quiet, Steve, if I were you.'

Stephen Monarch laughed aloud. 'Have another on me, but I really must be off, old chap.'

Simon listened carefully to what was being said and, when Michael finished, he settled back into his chair.

'You mean he was in the pub the other night—the night I, erm, slept in the car park?'

Normally such a remark would have been the cue for some gentle ribbing but Michael had more serious things on his mind.

'Yes, and he's been back every night since!'

'I see! Michael, all I can suggest is you continue to string him along while I make enquiries and alert the authorities. I can assure you that if he is up to no good, he will be prosecuted. I know you are new to our country but, believe me, you have done the right thing to report this. We Zambians feel strongly that the Rhodesians should fight their battles elsewhere, not on our doorstep. President Kaunda won't stand for it.'

'I'll keep you informed,' Michael gave his assurances.

That night, however, Stephen Monarch was nowhere to be found. Michael wondered if he had seen the last of him. Looking round the lounge and bar, he became aware of faces he had not seen in the club before.

Captain Monarch was back—so, too, were the new faces.

Appearing harassed, he came straight to the point. 'Mike, we need to talk. Let's go to the lounge.'

Michael obliged and followed him through.

'What's up, Steve? You look worried.'

'I am but I'm not sure how to tell you this.' He stared at Michael as if searching for something.

'Try me.'

Monarch hesitated momentarily, then seemed to make up his mind, 'I'm expecting a few of our chaps to cross the border near Chirundu in a couple of days time...reconnaissance work, that sort of thing. It's nothing as gallant as a contact with the enemy...just an exercise and they'll return within a few hours.'

Out of the corner of his eye Michael watched the newcomers enter the lounge, chatting to one another. Seating themselves at a table nearby they seemed anything but inconspicuous. Stephen Monarch didn't seem to notice.

'So why are you telling me this, Steve?'

'Because you're in the Game Department! Something has come up and we have a hitch. Our usual contact was injured last night in a car accident. I'll be frank with you. We have another agent who works at Chirundu but we don't want to compromise his cover. Besides, he hasn't the knowledge of the bush or the river where they intend to cross.'

'I see. So you want me to stand in for your injured agent because I've told you I know the Zambezi Valley like the back of my hand, right?' Michael asked.

'Precisely.' Captain Monarch sounded hopeful.

Michael had to make a decision.

'No, I'm sorry, Steve, I can't do it. Of course, I'll keep this in confidence and I wish you luck. But, as I said the other evening, this isn't my war and

I'm not going to get involved.' Michael wondered if he could push Monarch further and stole a glance across at the other table. For all he knew his companion was a very dangerous man but, judging by the appearance of the three men at the opposite table, he'd take his chances.

'Steve, tell me one thing. If your agent has just injured himself, how come you approached me over a week ago? I'm sure you won't insult my intelligence and say it's coincidental!'

Silence followed. 'Very shrewd—but no, Mike, I won't insult you. I recruit on behalf of our secret service and I am always on the lookout for suitable candidates. Of course, as you no doubt realise, there is no border crossing. We wouldn't dream of violating Zambian sovereignty—I was simply putting you to the test. My operatives keep an eye open wherever possible and report back on Rhodesian terrorist strength and movements, which Zambia insists on harbouring. This way we keep tabs on where terrorist incursions into Rhodesia are likely to take place.'

'You really had me going there for a while,' Michael lied. 'I'm not really a fighter but I suppose, maybe, I could be of some assistance to you.' He saw the interest in Monarch's eyes. 'I'm always working somewhere on the border and I've seen a number of soldiers around lately. Heaven knows what army they're from but if you want me to keep a record I'd be more than pleased to help. But, I stress, that's as far as I'm prepared to go.'

'Excellent!' His hand shot out to grasp Michael's, 'I'm pleased to have you on board. But we need to do something to improve your knowledge of the various terrorist units based here in Zambia.'

22 October 1972

'That's about it, Simon, word for word but please tell the Zambian secret service fellows, or whoever they are, to stay away. I don't want any embarrassing moments. If I can spot them, he'll see through them in seconds. He's coming back tonight, and tomorrow he wants to come over to my quarters. You can tell your authorities he intends to brief me on how to identify the various fighting units of ZIPRA and ZANLA. And the whereabouts of their bases, so that when I'm in the area I can keep an eye out for them.'

Simon pondered this for a moment. 'This could be very useful.'

'Exactly! That's what I thought. If he's thorough, which I think he will be, he'll disclose what information they have on the Zimbabwe freedom fighters' bases in this country.'

'Yes, it would pay them to move their bases if the information is correct but, more importantly, something still worries me. Do you think his denial of a border crossing was on the level?' Simon asked.

Michael gave an honest answer. 'I don't know but my gut feeling says no, he meant it, they're going to cross.'

'I think you're right,' said Simon. 'Incidentally, as you might expect, a 'security' gentleman will be here this afternoon to interview you. It's only a formality and I'll be outside if you need me.'

Everything went as scheduled. The Zambian secret service interviewed Michael. Captain Stephen Monarch briefed him and provided a contact number. Michael rang the number—he reached an answering machine and left a message as suggested by Zambian Intelligence.

Simon agreed when Michael said that, in view of what had gone on, he needed a break from 'civilisation' and wanted to return to the bush. Things returned to normal—almost!

oOo

25 October 1972

Moses sat smoking under the large fanlight of the operations-room. He was one of two dozen Black civilian batmen who provided the spit and polish for Rhodesia's elite battalion, the Rhodesian Light Infantry (RLI), and the Rhodesian SAS unit based at Cranborne, Salisbury. He had made himself indispensable to the non-commissioned officers, honing boots to a mirror finish, cleaning their rooms and attending to the menial chores. Occasionally he was thrown a cursory glance by one of the sergeants, then dismissed as a *munt,* who obviously posed no threat. They spoke openly in front of him, seeing him as part of barracks life. He had been around too long and was too timid and slow—interested only in his simple tasks, but Moses kept his ears and eyes peeled.

The Whites had aptly named October as 'suicide month'—and today the op.'s-room window was open because of the unbearable heat. The angle of the glass deflected downwards any sound from within the room making every word clearly audible outside. In full view of the main administrative building Moses seemed outwardly relaxed as he gazed across the parade square. He did not move when the young sergeant strode by.

'Moses, you lazy *munt!* Don't let the sergeant-major catch you sitting on your arse.' The sergeant gave him a conspiratorial wink and disappeared into the orderly room.

Moses ground the stub of his cigarette into the dirt, climbed to his feet and ambled back to his station.

At 5.30pm that day he made his way to the main gate, collected his bicycle and together with his fellow workers started the long ride back to the Black townships of Highfields and Harare, on the outskirts of the 'White' city of Salisbury.

Near the township Moses deliberately slowed and hung back. Eventually he left the group. Some knew where Moses was going but said nothing—their turn could be next.

The public telephone box was empty but he waited for a full thirty minutes to ensure his call fell within the prescribed monitoring time before dialling and feeding the meter.

'Hello. Is that you, Father?'

At the other end, the voice of Gideon Chitiyo, the ZANLA representative in Zambia, confirmed it was indeed his 'father'.

Moses asked him to call back, giving him the number of the public telephone before ringing off.

Shortly the telephone rang. The instant the connection was made, the call was relayed from the central telecommunications department in Salisbury through to a new office set up by the Central Intelligence Organisation (CIO), which monitored all international calls—particularly Zambia.

Moses spoke to his 'father' fluently in one of the many dozens of regional tongues spoken in Zambia. He heard a 'click' as the listener gave up in frustration. Unless a conversation was held in a principal language 'they' were generally at a loss to understand what was being said.

'I'll be there ten days from now. Can you meet me at the Chirundu border post?'
'Of course, my 'son', but how are you going to get there?'
'My friend who lives three kilometres to the east of Highfields will be coming up by truck.'
'Okay! I will meet you. How are the children?' asked the *'grandfather'.*
'They thank you for the plastic toys. I thought the batteries were dead but it was only a break in one of the copper wires...otherwise they're fine.'
'Good!'
'The three boys send their love and will come up to see you and Mother early in the New Year.'
'We look forward to that,' said the *'grandfather'.*

Moses rang off. Traces were always possible. Their Zambian HQ had provided a sequence of twenty other call-boxes scattered around Salisbury as a countermeasure, if one or more were out of order, or worse. He pedalled faster than usual away from the telephone booth. Moses, like many others, played his part in the silent war.

Gideon Chitiyo of ZANLA, relayed the deciphered message in a coded telex to his *comrades* in Tete, Mozambique.

The message read:

> *Rhodesian SAS officer accompanied by three men to cross the Zambezi River 4 October 1972, approx. three kilometres east of Chirundu. Carrying plastic explosives. Will be met by unknown contact on the Zambian side. ETA...possibly early morning?*
> *Target: powerlines on the copperbelt.*
> *Reported by: M—Salisbury.*
> *This proposed attack confirmed last week by a National Parks official in Lusaka. What defensive action is to be taken?*

oOo

The mighty Zambezi River is the natural boundary between Zambia and Rhodesia. It begins its journey in north-west Zambia, near to the Zaire border. By the time it reaches the Victoria Falls it is already an immense river. Plummeting down the cataract into a deep chasm cut by the river, nearly two kilometres wide. The white water races eastwards towards Kariba where man has checked its flow, panning out into the vast expanse of Lake Kariba.

Checked, but not silenced, here, the river waits for the seasonal rains. Once more, reverberating with a thunderous roar beneath the dam wall, the Zambezi becomes a vibrant force, dashing between rocky crags, breaking the eerie silence of the dense bush covering its banks. Suddenly, the waters spill out into the broad crocodile infested river in the Zambezi Valley basin.

Flanked by escarpment walls, in places 80 kilometres across, which trap the sweltering, still, heat, the Valley has remained virtually unchanged through the millennia, teeming with Africa's big game. Determined, the Zambezi forges a slow, snaking-course through this hostile terrain, devoid of human habitation because of the humidity and soaring daily temperatures, and sweeps effortlessly past the Chirundu border post.

The Zambezi presses on relentlessly to Mozambique where its flow, threatened by some unseen geological fault, suddenly courses southwards in a final thrust across a vast unforgiving landscape. Travelling over 2700 kilometres from its source, the river has run its course emptying into the Indian Ocean on the Mozambique coast.

This was, for the most part, the inhospitable theatre of war where the Black freedom fighters were struggling to free their country.

3 November 1972

The operation which followed up Moses' report began near the Chirundu border post, on the Zambian side of the river, 82 kilometres south of Lusaka. Here, an asphalt road cuts its way through the dense bush to reach the bridge, to form one of the three link roads between Zambia and Rhodesia.

The soldiers had lain in ambush, a few kilometres downstream from Chirundu, for the past fifty-two hours waiting for their quarry.

Soon the sun's appearance above trees would cause shimmering heat to rise from the Valley floor and wilt the soldiers again. Their discomfort was heightened by some of the smallest creatures in the bush. Already mopane bees the size of match heads, although quite harmless, had crawled into some of the men's ears attracted by wax, at times becoming lodged and causing acute irritation as they buzz-sawed inside. Worse were the tsetse flies, which settled weightlessly on unprotected skin, driving their proboscises into the unsuspecting victim, who, forced to lie still, would smart from the resulting sudden needle-like bites. Night brought little relief. Hordes of mosquitoes took over the onslaught, intent on sucking the last vestiges of blood left from the daytime tsetse fly attack.

Their commanding officer, like all his men, had assumed a war name, the 'Major', to prevent reprisals back home. Outwardly unaffected, he lay in the undergrowth rarely taking his field-glasses off their suspect since he had first emerged from his tent. His scouts had confirmed that this was the only White man within 20 kilometres east of Chirundu.

The Major studied the map again—they had taken the only accessible track from the asphalt road near the Chirundu border post, leading through thick bush, to this point. This had to be the man the report referred to. It was just a question of time before the SAS contacted him. Then the Major would spring the trap.

His men had kept the camp under continuous surveillance. The camp's occupants had cleared the brush from the high river bank providing them with a wide view of the Zambezi and of the far shore. The layout was basic: Land Rover and bath to one side, two cottage-tents and a cooking fire on the other side.

Their target was certainly a cool customer. The contact was imminent yet he moved around like a man without a care in the world. Apart from a shotgun across the bonnet of the Land Rover there was no sign of weapons. The smell of meat and coffee on the open fire reached across the clearing to where he and his men lay hidden. It made the Major swallow hard and caused his stomach to growl with hunger. His patience was wearing thin as he watched the man go through his daily routine for a third time. He had waited long enough.

The old enamelled bath, balanced on loose bricks, was supplied by a 44 gallon drum raised on a platform above the cooking fire. A length of black PVC piping snaked past the tent and over the lip of the bath. Watching, they saw the man give instructions to the cook and then stroll beside the tent, where he threw his clothes over the tailgate of the vehicle before stepping into the bath. He seemed content to stand there buck naked, soaping up, oblivious to all except the snorting hippo in midstream.

The Major's arm came up.

Stealthily his men moved in. On the other side of the Land Rover a hand gently removed the shotgun from the bonnet, while the cook was silenced by a hand clamped over his mouth from behind. The man in the bath heard a noise and swung round. He stared at six men in camouflage uniforms forming a half-circle around his bath. With shock he saw that they were armed and that their guns were trained on him.

The Major spoke first. 'You...Mr Bernstein?'

'Yes...of course!' Michael stammered. 'Who the hell are you?' There was no time for modesty.

'Never mind. Get dressed. I want to talk to you.' Orders shouted, he and his men began a search of the camp and Michael's belongings, leaving the Teacher, his second in command, behind with his AK rifle trained on Michael.

'What the hell's going on?' Michael felt a mixture of fear and anger, 'And point your bloody gun somewhere else.' He reached for his towel, watching intently the smile, or was it a grimace, on the Teacher's face. 'You realise I'm a government official...why is the Zambian Army interested in me? Or are you always this friendly?'

Dropping the flap of the tent, the Major came back to face Michael. 'That mouth of yours will get you into trouble. Shut up, and get dressed. Then come over to the cooking-fire. I want to talk to you.'

Michael felt disinclined to argue further while the rifle remained pointed unwaveringly at him. It took him a minute to dress. He walked to where the Major stood facing the fire. The cook sat dejectedly on the ground. The Major and some of his men were already enjoying Michael's breakfast.

Suddenly the Major rounded on him. 'Where and when are they crossing? Are you here to meet them?'

Michael was confused. 'Who? What on earth are you talking about?'

'So you deny it. Very well, Mr Bernstein, we can play it your way but you will quickly learn I'm not a patient man.' He thrust a finger close to Michael's face. 'You know damned well who I mean, the Rhodesian SAS. You reported they were crossing in this vicinity.'

'I didn't say that, I simply said that I understood they might cross somewhere on the Zambezi. Honestly, I've no idea where or when. Anyway, I'm not saying another bloody thing until I know who you are,' he said flatly, trying to stare down the Major. 'And another thing, I'm hardly likely to report a crossing, if I was supposed to pick them up?'

'How do I know that? How do I know you're not a Rhodesian agent? We know with certainty that they are crossing tomorrow. You could report the matter to throw suspicion off yourself if they're caught in this area. And how do I know you are who you say you are?'

Michael's feeling of unease grew steadily stronger. He was having to explain his situation to armed men, and to a man who was not going to win any congeniality awards.

'Okay, Mr Bernstein, my men and I are freedom fighters of ZANLA. I must tell you, we know they are crossing close to this position. What I want to know from you is, where?'

'But I've said, I don't know!' He could feel the situation was getting out of hand. 'I want to radio the Game & Fisheries Department in Chilanga. They'll confirm who I am. You've got it all wrong!'

A soldier shouted from the river bank.

'Stay where you are, Mr Bernstein.' The Major stepped over to see what it was that had caught his *comrade's* attention. In seconds he was back.

'That boat! I suppose it's for fishing then?'

'Yes! It belongs to Simon Kalabo the personnel director of the Game & Fisheries Department who's due here any day now. He lent me the boat.'

'Don't lie! It's for taking the SAS over the river, isn't it?'

'No it's not. I want to radio my headquarters, now,' Michael demanded. He was angry and afraid.

The Major glared at Michael for some moments, then reached a decision. 'Okay, radio your headquarters!'

Simon was away and a colleague came over the air.

The Major and the Teacher looked on menacingly as Michael spluttered out what had happened.

'For God's sake, tell him who I am and that it's Simon's boat. He says they're from ZANLA, a bloody major or something.' Michael took his finger off the transmitter switch to address the ZANLA officer.

'Your name is Major...what?'

'Just say the 'Major'. He'll understand.'

Michael repeated the message into the mouthpiece and waited.

There was a pause.

'Did you say the 'Major'! Yes, I know who he is. For goodness sake, Michael, don't piss him off...just do as he asks.'

The Major was Shona, a proud and powerful man, revered by the cadre of ZANLA. He had joined up after Ian Smith's illegal régime tore the country apart. His training started in Russia and was completed in China. He held the rank of Major in the Soviet Army which he now used as his nom de guerre. Conventional ranks were not used in the field by the liberation armies of Zimbabwe.

Michael broke in. 'Thank you very much—thanks. The man's standing right next to me. I think you should have a word with him.' Michael understood nothing of the exchange that followed; his eyes darted anxiously back and forth from the Major to the Teacher's gun that still pointed threateningly at him.

The Major signed off and faced Michael. 'Your Department seems to think you are innocent enough. Now convince me.'

The Teacher was the first to alert the Major. They all listened to the distinctive whine of a four-wheel-drive vehicle labouring over rough terrain. In a few minutes it would arrive along the solitary track.

'See! I told you. It's Simon, my boss. When he gets here you can ask him if it's his boat.'

Simon Kalabo did not appear. Instead, it was a White immigration officer from Chirundu who insisted that he was only intent on fishing farther down the river, being his afternoon off. The Major knew it was unlikely that anyone would risk this trip alone. Anyway, what was wrong with the fishing at Chirundu? He made a quick call on Michael's radio to the border post. They confirmed the official was on three days leave—claiming he was going to Lusaka. The Major placed him under arrest. Unflinchingly he stood his ground. No amount of questioning, not even the threat of being taken to Mozambique, would get him to reveal the SAS rendezvous point.

The Major came over to Michael, who now appeared to be a little more relaxed than he had been twenty minutes earlier.

'Sorry, Mr Bernstein, it seems I got you wrong.' Without waiting for a response, he turned on his heel and strode towards the immigration official, drawing his automatic pistol out and calculatingly, he pressed the 9mm pistol to his forehead. The man's reaction was one of speechless horror but it was about to get the Major the information he sought.

Michael's reaction was instinctive.

'You can't do that. You can't shoot him in cold blood!' he shouted.

'Shut up or go!' The Major shouted back, adding, 'Stay out of this business. It doesn't concern you.'

'Well, you have involved me. So shoot him and I'll make it my business.'

Had they been on the other side of the river the Major knew he would most probably have pulled the trigger. Too many Whites in Zambia supported the Rhodesians. He wished they'd leave, if they preferred conditions across the river that much, but many earned way above average salaries in Zambia and this was inducement enough to stay.

The Major glared at Michael—this man was becoming tiresome.

Thanks to his interference nothing further would be gleaned from their prisoner who had been at the point of breaking, but now he knew he wasn't going to die, had become defiant. His prisoner's arrival had told the Major a number of things: they were at the right location and the SAS had not yet crossed. Judging by the kit he was carrying in his vehicle it was evident that he was planning to spend at least one night out here alone—but longer seemed unrealistic. Therefore, he realised, that placed the time of the crossing in the early hours of the following day. This verified the information received from their agent in Salisbury.

Ignoring Michael, he walked off a distance to study his field map in detail, carefully judging their current location against possible landing sites. There were a dozen or more places where the Rhodesian SAS might rendezvous on the Zambian bank. The Rhodesian side of the river, however, presented an altogether different picture. Given the distance from Chirundu and that at one spot the road ran parallel to the river, the co-ordinates crossed on where the track was within easy walking distance of a natural inlet. The contours shown on the map could provide the initial cover necessary for the enemy to launch a raid. Repeatedly he stabbed the map with his forefinger, with growing conviction that this must be the chosen point. Under his breath he said, 'Yes! They will cross here tomorrow.' He felt sure of it. He turned back to a dispirited Michael who now sat staring morosely into the oily dark waters of the Zambezi.

Gripping the branch of an overhanging tree Michael held the boat steady against the current, the dark languid waters belying the force of the river which threatened to drag the craft away from the Zambian shore. He was nearly five kilometres upstream from his camp. Anxiously he stared into the pre-dawn gloom, barely making out the far bank. He ran through the events of the previous evening.

Listening to the Major outline his plan, Michael had felt a surge of excitement. 'It's sheer madness, I shouldn't be getting involved, it isn't my war,' he had thought. But something, something deep inside, had compelled him to side with this man's cause, immediately knowing he was going to regret it. He didn't care much for the Major, but he kept thinking of David. Like the Major, his friend too had become a freedom fighter and Michael firmly believed they had every justification to join ZANLA. There had been something else nagging at the back of his mind, recalling David's biting condemnation on their journey to Zambia, '...most Whites profess a liberal attitude but do nothing....' Michael's mind made up, he had said, 'Okay, Major, but we do it my way.'

The Major wanted to take the boat across and leave it there, returning later. Michael had refused because if anything went wrong, Simon's boat would be stranded in Rhodesia. He would ferry them across instead, provided it was dark. The Major had wanted him to stay and wait, but Michael declined, insisting it would be too dangerous.

'You know what they'll do to you if you're caught. Can you imagine what they'll do to me, a White guy helping 'terrorists'?'

Michael had proffered an amicable solution. 'If it's over in seconds, as you suggest, then, from the time the gunfire stops, I'll give you ten minutes to reach the drop-off point. If it's still dark, signal me with a flash light and I'll collect you immediately. If you are later than that, be prepared to swim, crocs or no crocs, or else make for this point,' he indicated a position on the map, 'and I'll pick you up the following night at 23h00.'

Now he waited for a sign from the far bank.

Before sunrise, two Land Rovers left the main road at Chirundu on the Rhodesian side of the river, turned right onto the dirt road and travelled east parallel to the river towards the old sugar estates and Mana Pools. The drivers stayed in second gear with their speed below 20 kph, keeping the noise of the engines to a minimum. Without headlights, the lead driver strained to see the track ahead; the trees cast ghostly silhouettes across their path and seemed to leap out at them from the roadside. Presently the lead driver checked the distance they had travelled. Once confirmed, he cut the engine and rolled to a stop.

With military efficiency and in total silence the men unloaded the canoes, then carefully pulled out their lethal cargo. Thirty-six kilograms of plastic explosive and primers were carefully stacked into the craft. The SAS sergeant-major signalled silently to his men to apply camouflage paint. Within seconds their White faces and hands merged with the grey-mottled shadows of pre-dawn light. He signalled again and they hoisted the laden canoes onto their shoulders and moved out in single file through the bush towards the river.

While they walked the sergeant-major went over the plan once more in his mind. His brief was to meet their contact on the Zambian side, then travel north of Lusaka, 24 kilometres past the town of Kabwe. Here they would locate the power lines, lay their explosives and blow the pylons which led towards the rich copper mines of northern Zambia. The sabotage plan would cause a total power cut to the towns of the Copper Belt near the Zaire border and bring the entire copper production of Zambia to a standstill severing its economic lifeline.

At the base camp briefing, the sergeant-major had been told that, in time, the lines would be repaired by the power corporation in Rhodesia, while the Zambian Government would pay the bill, but not before causing untold disruption to the Zambian economy. This strategy was intended to discourage the practice of harbouring terrorists—by making President Kaunda realise Zambia's vulnerability.

'Moses' had heard all this during his vigil beneath the open window.

The sergeant-major was still dwelling on these instructions when the firefight broke out. His lead man never heard the shots, dying instantly, as bullets tore through his chest and head. The sergeant-major and his men hit the dirt, frantically scanning the bush to find where the firing was coming from. Their weapons were still in the canoes. He heard the other sergeant gasp in pain as he was hit in the hip.

Cursing, he saw that the *terrs* had picked their ambush well, above them on the crest of the ridge. He rolled over, then leopard-crawled alongside the canoe and lifted the canvas edge. The craft hid his movements but offered no protection against the searching bullets. Several shots sliced through the flimsy craft ripping away flesh and leaving a numbing pain in his side.

Again he cursed. The guns had shifted forward into the prow of the canoe and were wedged tightly against the frame. Frantically probing, his hand closed over familiar objects. The sergeant-major drew out the bag of plastic explosive, pulled back the wrapping and feverishly inserted a timing detonator. In the half-light he set the fuse for a five-second delay. There was a fleeting lull in the firing—the only sound that disturbed the break came from his wounded sergeant. He seized the opportunity, knowing he alone held the weapon that might still save the last two men and himself. He crouched ready to lob the improvised grenade over the ridge—then sprang upright and leant back, his body flexed to give maximum thrust to the swing.

The Major saw what was happening—he emptied his weapon into the exposed target. The bag fell from deadened nerves; for a moment the SAS sergeant-major still stood. The Major screamed at his men to get down.

The firing had hardly died away when all hell erupted. Thirty-six kilograms of plastic explosive blew up in sympathetic detonation, instantly disintegrating everything around; the SAS men simply ceased to exist in any recognisable shape or form. The violent explosion scoured the ravine floor sending a maelstrom of small rock shards over the ridge. The shock wave immediate, hurling the prone ZANLA soldiers from the ground while a barrage of rocks, branches and burning debris rained down on them. Already all vegetation had been pulverised, uprooted, or shredded for several hundred metres—the flash visible for 80 kilometres—followed by a stunned silence.

The sudden burst of gunfire from across the river cut through the still air alerting Michael. The flattened shatter of gun shots seemed far away, as he reached quickly for the starter on the outboard motor.

Apocalyptically, the opposite bank lit up in a blinding flash—immediately followed by a massive crack, as the detonation boomed its way across the valley. The flash shrank back. A billowing fireball welled up into the sky. He witnessed the burning debris cascade back to earth. The blast buffeted the boat, causing Michael to lose his grip on the overhanging branch. 'What in hell's name happened—a land-mine? Impossible!' he thought, the explosion had been too huge. A cloud of nesting egrets, weavers and other birds rose into the early morning sky. Frightened flocks screeched overhead, circled and then scattered. A startled heron broke cover a few metres from the boat almost causing him to capsize. Then he became acutely aware that an eerie stillness had descended over the Zambezi.

He cursed aloud, 'The whole bloody Rhodesian army must have heard that!' Could any of them still be alive? Surely nothing could have withstood that blast. Michael waited anxiously glancing at his watch and lifted his binoculars to scan the opposite bank. Nothing. It was already six minutes past the allotted time. They were not coming. He better get as far away from here as possible, he thought. He struggled with the outboard. The motor caught and he headed out into the main stream but then throttled back. He knew he should have gone, but found himself checking his watch yet again. A further ten minutes—still nothing! He let the boat drift with the current, the motor idling.

Now seventeen minutes past the deadline and almost out of sight of the point where he had dropped the Major's men, when he saw movement. It was a man. But who? Against his better judgement he pushed the throttle forward, picked up speed and swung the boat around, slowly retracing his route. Narrowing the gap with one hand on the tiller, he refocused the field-glasses. He now saw several men waving frantically while a couple appeared too weak to walk, were being assisted by *comrades*.

He pushed the throttle forwards.

oOo

The events of 4 November, proved a devastating blow to the morale of many White Rhodesians. Their arrogance was shaken with the loss of their fighting men, for this came with the realisation that they were just as vulnerable as the enemy.

Days later Simon said, 'Someone to see you in my office.'

Michael was surprised to find the Major waiting for him.

'I wanted to thank you for coming back for us,' he said.

oOo

In Cape Town, Professor Tinus Mueller closed down the laboratories and retired, having arranged for what little work was left outstanding to be undertaken by a new research wing at Groote Berg Hospital under Carla's direction.

Carla's disillusionment with Michael was Jan DuToit's gain. She gave up her apartment and returned to live with her family on the slopes of the Drakenstein where the young politician became a frequent visitor, much to her father's delight. Andries Boshoff and Jan DuToit would argue good naturedly for hours, each trying to convert the other to his own style of Nationalism—Andries to the far right and Jan to his more liberal stance. But it was not these political discussions which drew Jan DuToit to the Boshoff estate.

At the end of the year he and Carla were married in the local church. The only shadow on her special day was in her heart. Before setting out to the church, her mother remarked that she hadn't thought that Carla was one to cry at the prospect of marriage. Only her sister, Louise, knew the real reason why.

Michael had tried to call Carla numerous times, but had spoken to her just the once while in Botswana. After many frustrating attempts trying the estate, he got through. Her father had answered and passed on the news that Carla was engaged to be married and told him in no uncertain terms that his call was not welcome.

Out of the blue he had received a copy of a South African newspaper through the post. He read of 'the society wedding of Carla Boshoff, elder daughter of the prominent owner of the Boshoff Wine Estates, Andries Boshoff, to a rising Nationalist Party politician Jan DuToit.' Besides the postmark, there was no indication who had sent it or where it had come from.

CHAPTER 6

"Let us deepen our sense of belonging...and engender
a common interest that knows no race, colour or creed.
Let us become Zimbabweans with a single loyalty.
Long live freedom."

Robert Mugabe,
Prime Minister, 1980
President of Zimbabwe, 1987

Eugene Vermaak was a hardened Afrikaner who had immigrated to Rhodesia ten years before and still shared the narrow view held by so many of his fellow countrymen. With stubbornness and ruthless determination he had forged virgin bush into a productive farm, showing no clemency towards the original occupants on *his* grounds, who were uprooted from their homes and moved off the property. Recently he had acquired an adjoining tract of land, as a concession for farming during the war, to add to his thousand acres. For a second time he planned to have the 'squatters' removed.

5 December 1972

Seeking justice and attempting to avert trouble, the headman, on the villagers' behalf, approached the Chief Inspector at his home. Revenge for what this man had done to his wife must wait; for now his hate would lay buried.

Resplendent in his starched uniform and regulatory knee-length shorts, Chief Inspector Victor Hammond strolled onto the veranda to meet the solitary figure. He stared down with obvious disdain, oblivious to the respect he was being shown by the headman who hastily knelt before him in the dust. He considered all natives to be subservient and would always remain so.

His elderly houseboy cautioned, 'My baas, the headman, he says there will be much trouble if they have to go.'

Hammond flapped his hand with irritation at a persistent fly, eager to return to his gin 'n tonic and air-conditioning behind fly-screen doors. Did these people really think that he had nothing better to do with his time than attend to such trivia?

'For God's sake man, don't be crass.' He wore his arrogance like his badge of office. 'Tell the cheeky bastard if he wants trouble, then the Rhodesian Government will be pleased to accommodate him. And he must report the matter to the police station. Not worry me at home.'

'Eh?' came the response, serving to irritate Hammond further when he realised the message was lost on his houseboy. Fluent in Shona he refused to speak the language, and deplored his servant's lingual limitations.

'Oh! Very well, tell him he has two weeks, then I want the whole bloody lot of them cleared off the land. Mr Vermaak now holds the title deeds. Understand? They must go! Is that clear enough?' Without waiting for an answer he turned on his heel and strode inside. The screen door banged shut behind him.

He did not see the houseboy shake his head as the headman wearily stood up, nor would he have understood the brief exchange between the two elderly men, before the headman returned with the distressing news to anxious families. The houseboy returned to the shade of a nearby mango tree, resigned to waiting for further orders from his master.

Hammond was immensely pleased with his demonstration of authority and reached for the telephone.

'Vermaak, Vic Hammond here. Consider the job done, old chap. You'll be glad to know your property will be free of these fellows within two weeks. Pleased to have been of assistance.'

Without waiting for any acknowledgement, he replaced the receiver with a satisfied flourish.

At the other end of the party line Vermaak scowled at the dead receiver and swore, 'You pompous arse-hole!' but inwardly felt pleased that the matter was finally settled.

Hammond was an expatriate who had served time with the Kenyan police and left under a cloud after the Mau Mau rebellion had been put down. Some of his superiors had not agreed with his robust methods. Since then, he had been in Rhodesia and he contrived that under his current contract two-thirds of his wages would land up in the UK through the backdoor.

His wife had become bored with him and his drinking. She understood only too well that his failings and the continuous harking back to 'the good old days' were inextricably linked to the lifestyle of the expatriate community. Quietly and without warning she had walked out, never to return.

Her desertion had humiliated, and angered him. Other expats commiserated, pouring out sympathy and gin in equal measure, though any regrets he may have felt did not last long. He satisfied his needs with a succession of nubile young Black girls whom he managed to coax or coerce into submission. This helped make his stay in Africa tolerable. Admittedly, he had thought of returning to the UK, still hankering after the quiet of the English countryside but the lifestyle and conducive weather weighed heavily in favour of a delayed departure.

Content with his handling of the Vermaak affair, Hammond reached for the gin bottle and reflected on current events. He had recently achieved his ambition of joining the Central Intelligence Organisation, with a little help from General Rocco Bastion-Smythe, Supreme Commander of the Rhodesian Armed Forces, possibly the second most powerful man in Rhodesia after Ian Smith. They had met while the General was completing one of his many field trips around the country. There had been an instant rapport between them, largely helped by recognition of their English public school upbringing. The General had departed with the promise of getting together when Vic was next in town.

With his new CIO position went the responsibility of overseeing anti-terrorist activities in the field. No more tedious reports or the submission of copious recommendations on the native situation to gather dust in Salisbury, and lately, the terrorist situation had kept him fully occupied. The Major had been active in his area again. Even a bounty, which was one way of dealing with the *'terr'* problem, had not produced a result.* Now he would have the authority to implement a few of his ideas on how to capture or kill terrorists; in particular the Major who had eluded him over many years.

Hammond's position and rank enabled him to socialise with the upper echelons of the farming community and hence to a seat of power in the government—Ian Smith himself, was a farmer. Here, Hammond believed, he would gain support for his new speculative venture into weapons-brokering for the security forces. Procurement officers were always needed. Few had the guile or tenacity or indeed the right connections.

What made this new opportunity attractive was it would not interfere with his current career. Further, Rocco had promised him an entrée into South Africa's defence circles both at home and abroad. Had he not said at their last meeting: 'Vic, it's a closed shop. Though it's widely claimed that the West isn't breaking the arms embargo, discreet dealings are always possible. I'll put the word round with a number of old chums in Pretoria on your behalf...come to think of it, there may be something in the offing in Cape Town.'

o0o

10 December 1972

Zimbabwe as a free and independent state seemed an elusive goal. The two liberation armies had fought relentlessly over the past six years, gaining little ground against the strongly entrenched White Rhodesian settlers. It was time for reappraisal and new strategies. ZANLA took the initiative.

The Major was being briefed by Gideon Chitiyo, the ZANLA representative in Zambia. They had gone into exile together, and there remained mutual respect even after joining different forces. Earlier in the year, at the request of Chitiyo, the Major had left ZIPRA and joined ZANLA which was now proving to be the more effective army of the two, against the Rhodesian security forces.

The Major listened closely to Chitiyo outlining the objectives for his intended raid. The order had come directly from the Chimurenga High Command. 'It is vital to the war effort that your mission be accomplished successfully. We are poised to attack from Mozambique if it fails.'

'Read this.' Chitiyo handed a file to the Major and rose to stand by the window from where, across the street, he could see the State House, residence of the Zambian President. Momentarily he reflected on Kenneth Kaunda who, at great personal and political risk, had made their war effort possible. He had taken Zambia along the road from colonial rule to independence. Now Kaunda was proving to be an invaluable ally in Zimbabwe's struggle against White oppression. He had stood firm even in the face of illegal attacks by both the South African and Rhodesian security forces who crossed the Zambian border time and again, to kill the opponents of apartheid by any means possible.

Gideon watched the Major replace the file on the desk.

'Of course you realise this office represents the political wing of our party. Officially you and your men don't exist here in Zambia.' He laughed without humour, becoming serious.

'Clearly I cannot stress strongly enough the importance of this mission,' for a moment he rested a hand on the Major's shoulder, 'but I know, with you in charge, it will be efficiently executed.'

17 December 1972

In the early hours of the evening, two assault teams swiftly negotiated the Zambezi River, crossing silently and simultaneously at different locations. With a brief farewell to the fighting men, Michael returned with an empty boat to the Zambian shore. At that precise moment, his colleague Simon Kalabo, completed a similar task 64 kilometres downstream—their present employment providing perfect cover for such covert activities.

Across the river, the teams set out on foot in combat formation. They were the elite, carefully chosen by the Chimurenga High Command of ZANLA. To a man they had received intensive training abroad in guerrilla warfare under Russian, Chinese or Cuban instructors. The Major led the main assault force; their strategy was straightforward. Both teams were to proceed with haste up separate tributaries of the Zambezi into the heartland of Rhodesia to a common destination.

Their objective was to unsettle the White community who, a decade earlier, had listened to Ian Smith's speech on no Black rule in Rhodesia during his lifetime,* and who might now conceive the 'terrorist' problem was contained and presented no real threat to the country—or rather, to its 600,000 White minority. The Major was determined to prove Smith wrong, as in time were six million other Blacks.

He had crossed so many times on sorties of this kind that this seemed a fairly routine matter, except for one thing. This mission was going to prove most unusual in that the Chimurenga High Command wanted this attack to have a very different outcome.

The Major set a fast pace for his five companions, but he never allowed his concentration to flag. They still had several hours' march to reach the Rhodesian border because of the strange way the colonial powers had carved up the territories, they were currently in Mozambique. He had taken the Hunyani River, the more dangerous of the two routes. They would follow well-worn game trails near the river through the valley and move up and over the escarpment. Aware that the Rhodesians knew this to be one of the main trails taken by 'terrorists' he was wary of ambushes and had sent the other four freedom fighters up the Musengezi River to the east to maximise their chances of success. The terrain was hard-going and even at night, the Zambezi Valley remained warm and humid.

During the next two days they rested and travelled only after sunset.

On the third night, they climbed to the top of the escarpment. Reaching the high plateau, they were grateful that the temperature dropped perceptibly. Before them lay the farmlands of Rhodesia.

Following instructions they reached a given co-ordinate, and turned away from the tributaries aiming to converge at a location called Mulingura Hill. It was a massive, domed granite outcrop formed when the earth's crust was cooling. Super-heated gases had thrust upwards from the earth's core, causing a huge bulge to form inside the molten rock creating a vast cave. When it blew out at the weakest point, bursting through the cooling rock, which had then splintered, it formed a horizontal cleft less than a metre high between the dome and newly created floor. The resultant thirty-foot cleft concealed the blow-hole, the entrance to the cave, undetectable to the casual passer by.

In silence and allowing only brief rest periods, they accomplished the manoeuvre in the still dark hours of the fourth night. With Mulingura Hill dimly in sight, the Major called a halt and, accompanied by the Teacher, went ahead to scout for the other team. This was a dangerous phase of the mission. If the teams did not arrive at precisely the right location and within the prescribed time, it would have to be assumed that any presence here was an enemy patrol—with possibly devastating consequences. They sat crouched, waiting; their over-heated bodies quickly drying of perspiration in the cool air as their ears strained for the faintest sound.

Suddenly, the shrill cry of a nightjar broke the silence. The Teacher answered the call. Almost immediately the throaty click of an impala buck cut through the night and then the bird call was repeated—a flash of white teeth revealing their relief at finding their *comrades*.

The Major broke cover first, to be met by a member of the other team. Within the hour the reunited unit reached the base of Mulingura Hill. The huge dome of rock loomed silent and seemingly undisturbed, like a giant hippo's back in a sea of grass. Their approach was hidden by thick vegetation, providing cover right up to the base of the rock formation. Cautiously they began to negotiate the steep granite slope.

Taking off their backpacks, the men crawled into the horizontal cleft. In the pitch darkness they dragged their packs in behind them, testing the ceiling while edging forward until they could stand upright. Bracing hands and feet against the smooth rock, they lifted themselves upwards and rolled over the lip of the cave floor which extended back into the centre of the hill. It was as though they had passed through the rock face itself.

Four months earlier, local villagers had seen the Rhodesian security forces use the hill as their base camp while sweeping the area for terrorists. After their departure, inspection showed the ZANLA arms cache had lain undetected—literally beneath the feet of the security forces. Discovery would have brought down 300 tons of collapsing granite on the luckless soldier who might accidentally have stumbled on its existence, as the hill was heavily mined. The cave still remained the main hiding place for ZANLA operatives and arms since first used by the Major five years previously. After the last man had come over the lip, they relaxed—resting in the cave until near dawn.

The Major woke two of his men. He gave orders for them to meet an agent in a small village about two kilometres to the east. Beyond lay Centenary, a farming centre for Rhodesian tobacco growers. It was typical of small farming towns with scattered houses, police station, army garrison and a sports club.

They slipped out of the cave and cautiously made their way to the surrounding cover. Pausing briefly, they looked back as the dawn washed a cloudless sky with soft rose and saffron light, tinting the grey granite of Mulingura Hill. Satisfied that they not been seen, or followed, they moved swiftly through the bush to reach the village.

Although the sun had already dispelled the chill of the night, long shadows still lay across the village clearing as a solitary woman knelt to stir the embers of a cooking fire. She became aware of their presence.

She had heard nothing. Through a drifting veil of smoke which stung her eyes she stared at the two armed strangers who stood a few metres from where she knelt. Her initial alarm subsided when one of them called softly, *'Chimurenga'*.

'Aawhe!' she cried. *'Vakomana'.'* Running from hut to hut she repeated the cry, 'The 'boys' are here.'

Startled from sleep, the villagers spilled from doorways, blinking in the bright morning light, some still pulling on hastily gathered clothing or wrapping blankets around themselves. They remained cautiously silent, watching the 'boys' until someone ventured to speak.

'Where's the Major?'

The freedom fighters made no reply. The same villager, a *mujiba,* spoke again. 'I know him. We were told last week by one of your *vakomana* that *the chimurenga watches our village at night.'*

The *mujiba* was their agent. This was the prearranged signal they had been waiting for, indicating that no one had informed the security forces of their impending visit. The freedom fighters visibly relaxed and one went back with the news that all was well. Three hours later the Major walked into the village alone, dressed much the same as the villagers themselves. The *mujiba* recognised him immediately and told the headman that this was indeed the redoubtable Major.

His reputation, already legendary, contributed to the fear and hatred felt toward him by the security forces. The Rhodesian Government had raised the reward on his head to $40,000. They wanted the Major—preferably dead.

Excitement quickly filtered through the growing crowd. Cries of *'Pasi ne vadzvanyiriri'* [Down with the oppressors], and *'Pambereri ne chimurenga'* [Forward with the revolutionary war], rang out with other shouted greetings. The Major took the headman aside. They needed to talk.

The village elder gave vent to his frustrations, pointing an accusing finger at every farmer in the vicinity. Such accusations were often well-founded. The Major knew that a few White farmers were honest men, genuinely liked by their employees, but most were despised for their greed and mistreatment of their staff.

'They make us work in their tobacco fields or as servants in their homes,' said the headman, 'and we are forced to listen to these White dogs while they insult us, without thought for our feelings. I've heard them say they have earned the privileges they enjoy because they brought civilisation to our land. But what about our ways, Major? Haven't we closer family unity than these Whites? They talk nonsense. They've a lot to learn.' The headman shook his head in disgust, before continuing.

'It's always abuse, saying we are ungrateful after what the White man has done for us. They curse us and say, if we want more—we should earn it! But with the Government laws this is impossible...'

The Major was acutely aware that the Whites deliberately maintained a wide gulf between themselves and the Black population, who owned no land and were unable to live much above the subsistence level.

The Major stopped him. 'Hold it! What I want to know is which White farmers are well known and respected by the others in this area?' These would be the targets of choice.

The headman glared at the him, shaking his head from side to side. 'No! Not them. You and the 'boys' must go to Baas Hammond, the policeman, and kill him—today!' he spat out with real hatred.

The Major was surprised by the other's vitriolic attack 'Why?' he asked.

'He raped my wife,' came the reply. The old man's head fell forward in shame, his dignity shattered.

Slowly the Major coaxed the facts out of him. The headman had three wives, according to custom. Because of his advanced age the marriage to the youngest had never been consummated. Paying a handsome dowry to her father in a neighbouring village, he had parted with this willingly and loved the girl dearly, like the daughter he never had. Besides, there was the benefit of uniting the villages. The girl was in her teens and had worked for the Hammonds as a servant.

One afternoon, while Hammond's wife was away doing their weekly shopping in Salisbury, he had coaxed her into their bedroom and forced himself on her. Afterwards he had watched with cruel pale blue eyes as she attempted to tie her torn dress.

'My dear, I've been observing you for weeks. I know you wanted it—just keep your mouth shut. I don't want to have to make things difficult for you or your family,' Then, bestowing an unctuous smile on her, 'Next time I'm in Salisbury, I'll bring you back a present. A dress perhaps! Would you like that?' He licked the spot of blood from his sun-cracked lips where he had bitten himself in his lust.

The terrified girl nodded, agreeable to anything—just to escape quickly as possible.

Hammond tried to fondle her breasts again, laughing when she recoiled from his groping hand. 'Okay then, off with you. Be a good girl. We'll do it again some time.' He had watched as she fled through the front door, down the path, and then he had headed for the shower.

Sobbing hysterically, she had gone straight to her husband. He felt powerless. There was no one he could turn to. The local district commissioner would only refer the matter to the police. There were no other channels open to him by which he could seek justice, so he had delivered an anonymous letter to Hammond's wife. Soon after she had left.

The Major found himself consoling the headman. He held his hand, 'One day I will come back and deal with this Chief Inspector of police. He will be punished, this I promise.' He waited allowing the headman time to compose himself and take in what he had said before continuing.

'Right now I need your help concerning the other matter. The ZANLA High Command want us to attack a farmer in this area, and I need a name, but the location must be remote...' He went on to explain why.

21 December 1972

The following evening the unit closed in stealthily on the targeted farmhouse. First, the telephone wire was cut then the approach road mined. The perimeter fence posed little problem and the Major quickly silenced the dogs. Finally, he checked that his men were in position. When ready, he fired off a burst from his AK assault rifle taking out the strategically placed searchlights.

The Vermaak family had been settling down for the night when the Major opened fire. The short burst stopped abruptly—so did the screams coming from inside the house. The sudden silence that followed the shock attack was broken by the Major's shouted warning to the farmer.

'Mr Vermaak, I'm the Major. I come from ZANLA's Chimurenga High Command. We have a message for you.'

There followed a deathly quiet.

The Major and his men had received explicit instructions as to the outcome of this attack. This was to be a stark message directed at Rhodesia's White farming community and the country at large, marking an escalation in violence, which would now become a way of life until they accepted change. No longer would Whites enjoy peace or inalienable rights. It would be their fault if they did not listen to ZANLA's final warning.

The events which led to this confrontation were beyond Vermaak's comprehension. Everything he had striven for was being threatened. His wife listened to him unconsciously mouthing his thoughts as she frantically tried the dead phone.

'Why in God's name did we leave South Africa! Why did I bring my family to this forsaken place...' In his confusion Vermaak turned to her, rubbing a clammy hand on his pyjamas. 'Why us? What have we done to these people?'

The farmer was half tempted to go out and face his attackers...maybe they would spare his wife and children. Vermaak's wife pleaded for him not to leave the house. She feared the worst.

152

The Major waited no longer and gave the order to open fire. Eight semi-automatic weapons discharged simultaneously. The roof of the house came alive—tiles danced, shattering under a hail of bullets, while a grenade exploded against the base of the concrete plinth of the house shaking the foundation. Emptying their weapons into the sturdy brick walls, the murderous racket was replaced by an ominous silence.

Reloading the curved magazines of their AK-47s in seconds, his men waited for the command to fire again.

The stillness of the night was shattered by a second raking burst of fire ripping into the homestead—ricochets found their way through the windows. Just as sudden as the attack, the Major and his men disappeared into the night.*

oOo

Eugene Vermaak was overwhelmed with relief, but just as bewildered—to find his family were still alive. Besides superficial injuries to one of the children and himself, they were otherwise unhurt. He was confused because he had offered no resistance—there had been no time—and he knew that had their attackers pressed home the assault, they could easily have killed the whole family. Clearly that had not been their intention.*

The dead telephone forced him to cross the three kilometres of open country to a neighbour to raise the alarm.* In flight, he did not see the ten men crouched in the dark not five metres from him as he hurried past.

It was daylight before the security forces reached the farm, following security procedures they had found and defused a land-mine en route. Chief Inspector Victor Hammond headed the investigation. The Special Branch team arrived shortly afterwards.

Before they began their search, Hammond walked round the outside of the house to inspect the damage. He pulled the khaki cloth hat further down onto the bridge of his nose to protect his sensitive skin from the sun. He had become used to not wearing sunglasses in the operational area; it was highly dangerous because the slightest reflection from them could draw a bead from an enemy rifle. His white-lashed lids, reduced to slits to filter the harsh light, opened wide as his pale watery eyes caught sight of a freshly cut wooden stake driven into the middle of an otherwise unblemished lawn.

Held fast in a groove was an envelope. Hammond's young colleague caught sight of the note as well.

Together, they read the message left by the Major:

Communiqué from: The Zimbabwe African National Liberation Army.

Operation Hurricane - demonstrates our commitment and capacity to strike where and when we please. This attack serves to notify the Rhodesian security forces, under the control of the Smith régime, that ZANLA is entering into a new phase of the war to liberate our country. The Rhodesian Government is urged to negotiate a peaceful settlement immediately or place its entire White community at grave risk. While we have no desire to wage war on the civilian population and have executed this attack with that principle in mind, we shall wreak havoc on this land should you care to ignore this warning. We are ready to negotiate a cease-fire through diplomatic channels.

The message was signed by two high ranking executives of the ZANLA High Command and countersigned by the Major.

Hammond's colleague was the first to speak. 'Jesus, Vic! It's the bloody Major again. They're threatening to hot things up.' It was a clear ultimatum to White Rhodesians.

Hammond rounded on him, 'Bollocks! We've been winning the Bush War from the start, what in hell's name does the Major think they can do now?'

His colleague seemed less certain. The fight had dragged on year after year. It wasn't a conventional war in the sense the enemy could be crushed. A contact in the bush meant the terrorists could be put to rout, but they always reappeared causing mayhem somewhere else. It seemed improbable that they would ever be utterly defeated. He watched Hammond stuff the note into his jacket pocket. 'You are going to report this to HQ, aren't you?'

'Not bloody likely!' Hammond said with finality. 'That's exactly what this bloody *terr* wants us to do. Create fear among our White farming community and next we'll be at each other's throats and handing this country over to the fucking *munts* on a platter. Anyway, you know as well as I do, this is unverifiable and not worth a damn.' He glared at his subordinate, 'You never saw this! Got that?'

'Look, honestly! You've nothing to worry about. If he said he was the Major I have no doubt he was. The cowardly bastard and his mob are probably across the border by now, but our forensic boys will need time to carry out a thorough inspection. A few days at most, if that's all right with you?' Hammond felt he had the situation under control and wrapped up.

Eugene Vermaak was not entirely convinced but, resigned to the inevitable, he would have to go along with the Chief Inspector.

'By the way you were wise not to drive last night. We found a land-mine and there may be others, even in your fields. We need to make the area safe.

Have you anywhere to stay while we attend to this matter?'

'Arthur Douglas our neighbour has offered to put us up,' he sounded relieved.

'What's the name of his farm if I need to contact you?' Hammond asked unnecessarily. It was a small community and they all knew one another by name at least. Still, he felt it necessary to adopt the official approach.

'Whistlestop Farm.'

'Good, then I'll leave you and your wife to make the necessary preparations to move out,' adding, 'please...soon as you can.' Hammond was anxious to be outside to search for further evidence. He knew now for certain that this had been the work of the Major. To have been so close, and yet again this terrorist leader had eluded him. For years, he had pursued the Major, making it a personal challenge to hunt, capture and kill him.

oOo

The young ZANLA *mujiba* came to the cave after dark and confirmed that no one had been killed in the attack and that the terrified family had gone to stay with a neighbour. A smile appeared at the corner of the Major's mouth.

All day long they heard helicopters overhead, the search patterns criss-crossing their hiding place. At one point two Canberra bombers flew low over Mulingura Hill and the sound reverberated through the cave. They held their breaths until they had passed, knowing that the Rhodesians sometimes resorted to bombs in order to ferret them out. Pretty soon the area was crawling with RLI and Rhodesian SAS patrols, and the nearby village had been singled out and visited four times during the day. Every male was interrogated. The Major and his men laughed when told what the old headman had said to the Chief Inspector.

'The Major is like the leopard: he kills at night and is gone by day. My baas, if we catch this 'mbada', we will put him in a cage and keep him there until you come.' The troops had finally left to search elsewhere.

They had provisions for a month. And the Major was content to sit it out, however long the security forces took to search the area but, first, they had one further mission to complete.

23 December 1972

Eugene Vermaak and Arthur Douglas talked late into the night. Arthur listened with morbid fascination as Eugene recounted the horrors of the attack. They checked their weapons before retiring. Next time they would be ready but, for now, they were not too concerned. The intermittent audible evidence of air and land patrols was comforting.

And had Victor Hammond not reassured them, that the Major and his men would still be running for the border!

Arthur spoke for them both, 'Thank your lucky stars they're ill-trained and can't shoot straight.'

They laughed uneasily and bid one another good night.

For a moment Eugene Vermaak thought that he was reliving the nightmare of two nights ago. But it was no dream. All hell had broken out in the early hours of the morning. Plaster was ripped from the walls and ceiling as windows smashed, while a dozen jack-hammers bore away at the galvanised roof. Bullets, sound and slivers of glass seemed to fly in every direction. Neither man had time to reach his weapon.

The family came under an unyielding attack for a second time. There seemed no end to the onslaught—followed by an abrupt shocking silence.*

Surprisingly enough, again nobody had been injured but the house was virtually destroyed, raked by gunfire, the garden beds littered with spent cartridges.*

The Vermaaks gathered in the living-room. Eugene almost apologetically told his terrified family, 'I think there's a message here somewhere. It's time we moved on!' He remembered what Victor Hammond had said and was on the steps to meet him on his arrival at daybreak.

'So you think they crossed the pissing border, do you?'

The security forces, as it happened, ran out of luck in their haste to secure the area. A Land Rover detonated a land-mine. The driver was killed instantly.*

oOo

The Major awoke to a deafening shot even as it echoed around the cave. Before he or his men could react, troopers from the Rhodesian Light Infantry poured over the lip of the entrance.

'Move!' he bellowed.

They all reacted instinctively. The Teacher grabbed his rifle and returned fire in one swift action. He saw two infantrymen crumple to the floor before diving for a safer position. Stalagmites offered cover but little protection in what was threatening to become a slaughterhouse. Bullets ricocheted off walls and the ceiling splintering rock, trebling the danger of each shot.

In that instant the Major saw his men flee as one, down the main passage. 'Why aren't they returning fire?' he screamed at the Teacher. Then he remembered—before his nap, to kill the boredom, he had ordered them to strip down their weapons and clean them.

He and the Teacher darted after them. Diving into a side passage, he yelled to the Teacher above the chatter of sub-machine-gun fire, 'Hold them! I'll fix it.'

The Major found what he was looking for and quickly set the timer. Rushing back to the Teacher he shouted, 'Run brother!'

Together they ran deeper into the cave, the Major swinging his AK over his shoulder to give a short burst as he ran.

They both knew what would happen next. Bullets zipped past them as they rounded a corner. A muffled thud followed, accompanied by a deafening roar. The ground shook once—then again—the blast hurled them forward three metres, slamming them hard against the far wall. Deadly stalactites from the fractured ceiling rained down around them.

Battling to breathe through the choking dust—dazed, the Major lifted himself from the floor and peered into the pitch dark. Momentarily disorientated, having lost his hearing and all sense of direction. After countless minutes the ringing in his ears eased and he heard a cry. It was the Teacher!

One of his men stumbled into the dust cloud brandishing a lighted piece of cloth torn from his clothing. Slowly others appeared. The Major knelt down, his immediate concern was for his brother. The Teacher sat looking disbelieving at his leg—hit in the thigh, while running, the bullet had gone straight through. Quickly the bleeding was stemmed. The Major's headcount confirmed six survivors including himself. He had seen the fallen sentry in the entrance—it was academic, but had he been asleep at his post before the attack? He looked back. Not four metres away in the direction from which they had come, their path was now blocked. Behind this impenetrable wall of stone some of his men lay entombed.

'There's no time to attend to his wounds now, carry him. Quickly!' Their plight was precarious. 'We must get out of here before we lose the light.' They lifted their injured comrade and followed the Major, who was desperately searching for a left fork in the seemingly endless underground network of passages. He vividly recalled being told that this passage linked up with the Sinoia Caves, over a hundred kilometres away. If they became lost now it could be their death warrant, taking literally a lifetime to try and find a way out. They veered left into a tight passage which rapidly narrowed further until it eventually forced them to crawl. Twice they stopped to light new torches.

The Major urged them on, 'This way! Keep going.'

Their wounded comrade moaned aloud.

'There's a small chamber up ahead. We'll halt there,' said the Major.

Arriving they found there was room to stand and the medic immediately attended to the injured man.

'How is he?' the Major enquired.

The medic shook his head pessimistically. The Major knelt at his side and saw his brother's breathing was shallow—symptom of shock! In a few hours the Teacher's leg would stiffen and it was obvious that he would be incapacitated for many days. A quick search round produced a dozen sulpha tablets but no pain killers. The medic made the teacher swallow four and said he would administer more, every six hours. Ripping off his shirt sleeve he fashioned a further pressure bandage, and gave instructions to the men. They held the Teacher down while the medic deftly removed the already blood soaked dressing and introduced a sulpha tablet into both the entrance and exit wounds.

The Teacher winced, gripping the Major's arm. 'Mbada! What will happen to me?'

'What's this—Mbada!' re-uttering the Shona word for leopard. He looked down at his *comrade* with concern—this man was really his younger brother. Since the armed struggle began he had been called the Teacher, as that was his profession, and his head had always been buried in some book or other, since childhood.

'You'll be all right. I'll work something out.'

He realised his brother had been fortunate. The bullet could have fractured his femur or worse, hit an artery. He left the medic to apply the improvised dressings to the wounds—at least that would stem the flow of blood from the punctured flesh that had saturated the Teacher's trousers. Relieved, the Major stood up and walked with determination to the far wall of the chamber.

Kneeling, he dug away loose soil from the chamber floor with his hands, revealing several metal boxes. Pulling them out he rummaged through their contents. Thousands of rounds of ammunition and precious little else! Then he found a torch and it worked. He grabbed several belts of ammo and reburied the containers. Straightening again, he looked over to where the men were still fussing over his brother. Momentarily, he became distracted as the dim beam from the torch picked up Bushmen paintings surrounding them. The chamber walls were alive with stylised warriors, some poised to throw assegai in their direction, while others rained arrows which appeared to cascade down even from the roof.

His attention focused again, taking stock of their situation. They had no supplies bar what his men were carrying, and only two weapons between them. He needed to come up with a plan—and quickly.

It was time to press on.

Again they were reduced to crawling until eventually the Major called a halt. They had reached the root system of a large mukwa tree. He worked his way upwards, clawing away at the loose debris to expose a side of the main tap root. As earth and small rocks fell away he glimpsed the paler light of the star-studded sky. Fifteen minutes later they emerged from the ground into the fresh, sweet night air.

In the distance the activity was plain to see. A dozen torches flashed to and fro as the security forces moved over the granite koppie like ants. Overhead a helicopter flew in a tight search pattern, its bright beam piercing the surrounding bush. The Major took in the scene and issued orders.

Within minutes two sturdy saplings had been cut to form carrying poles. Knowing that in the bush chopped, sawn or cut branches were as noticeable as traffic lights on city streets, they took care to slice through beneath the ground cover and smooth over all traces of disturbance. The poles were inserted through the sleeves of two shirts and lashed together with the string-like strips of bark peeled from the saplings, to form a litter.

His men were to head 170 kilometres west, in the opposite direction to which they had come along the Zambezi escarpment from their Mozambique base on the Ruenya River. Already that way home would be ambushed and crawling with patrols. For the same reason, the Hunyani River to the north was definitely a place to be avoided for the next month or so. Instead, they were to travel with all haste along an escape route which he had used occasionally from the beginning of the war, taking his injured brother to a location well known to his men—an abandoned mine. He would head south to the small town of Sinoia, to seek medical assistance for his brother.

'Give me five days and I will meet you at the *chindunduma*.'

Confident that everything would go according to plan, he parted from the group. To catch up to them, he would have to maintain a fast pace over the rugged terrain and calculated that he would arrive at the abandoned mine, north-west of Sinoia, about the same time as his men. From there, they had originally planned to head north to rendezvous with the other members of his unit, and cross Lake Kariba into Zambia and safety, but now he realised they would not make the deadline.

oOo

Unaware that he had been followed from the village for the past two nights to Mulingura Hill, the young *mujiba* had led the security forces to the guerrillas. Now he lay dead in the police station as a result of an interrogation by Hammond. He had said nothing. But Hammond claimed it didn't take a brilliant mind to piece the *terrs* movements together. Some of his colleagues agreed—he was right on both counts.

Victor Hammond sat alone on the granite koppie scratching his cancerous sunspots, while desperately trying to figure out what had happened. He looked down at the scaly scabs on his freckled arm then, frustrated by his own distraction, he forced his hands into his pockets.

The RLI lieutenant had led his men in and Hammond had heard distinct shots. Ahead of him, his young police colleague became temporarily wedged under the overhang because of the radio-pack strapped to his back. Hammond, in his eagerness to join the firefight, had started to pull the luckless lad out by his boots—when suddenly the ground shook. The shock wave had thrown him backwards and rolled down the granite slope to the soft earth five metres below. Hammond had jumped up. Slowly it penetrated what he was holding. He dropped the severed legs in disgust.

'What in hell's name am I going to report?' He had ordered the army in and now there were eight men missing in this 'contact', trapped somewhere inside this granite tomb. Were they still alive? Of his colleague, he knew his fate. Blood still oozed out of the collapsed overhang, now a centimetre gap—at least his secret was safe! He would not be telling anyone about the note they had found from ZANLA. Were the Major and his band of terrorists inside too? Had they died?

oOo

As he ran, his mind raced: he was well known to the Rhodesians as the Major and was aware that they had placed a bounty on his head. However, he smiled thinking of what his brother had said; perhaps the time had come for him to change his nom de guerre to Mbada—the Leopard.

Fifty kilometres of uneven terrain lay between the abandoned mine and the rendezvous point in the Umniati Gorge at the southern end of Lake Kariba, a wild and desolate place frequented by elephant and crocodile.

He had instructed two other members of his unit to dress as fishermen and make the twenty-five kilometre lake crossing from Zambia, in canoes, to a point where the upper branches of drowned trees rose starkly above the shimmering surface. Patrol boats avoided this forest's watery grave for fear of fouling their propellers. It was an eerie place at the best of times, but one where his men could rest undisturbed. A few kilometres farther would take them into the mouth of the gorge, where the Umniati River spills into the lake. The landmark chosen for the rendezvous was three kilometres upstream—a rocky outcrop crowned by two giant boabab trees. Their enormous girth and short but massive branches gave the impression of upended trees. The occurrence of two such giants growing together was rare and scarcely possible to miss.

He speculated on his brother's prospects: if nothing was done for him quickly, he could die when infection and inflammation set in. It was clear that his brother would not be able to make it to the rendezvous on time. Due to their hasty departure they were running a day ahead of schedule. Alone, he could easily make it, but now it would take an extra three days at least to assist the Teacher to the gorge. The 'fishermen' were under instruction not to wait later than sunset of the following day, then return.

On the other hand, if he went on ahead to the rendezvous and stalled their departure until the rest of the team caught up, it would still be too many days before crossing the lake. Time was of the essence if his brother's life was to be saved and that meant, at best, it would be nine days before he could receive adequate medical treatment in Zambia. Just before dark he arrived at the Hunyani River and turned south towards Sinoia—two days away.

On the following day, his men, in their haste to stay on schedule, were scurrying across the main road that leads from Salisbury north to the Chirundu border post in broad daylight, when a car suddenly came into view. They dived into nearby bushes.

A few hours later the farmer was reporting the incident to police headquarters in Salisbury. 'I'm not sure, but I think I may have seen some *terrs* crossing the road north of Sinoia. It was too far away for a positive ID. Thought it best to inform you, anyway.'

By late afternoon they had reached the point where the farmlands descend from the high plateau. Picking up a dry river bed they followed its course downstream throughout the night, to where it joined the Biriwiri River. The following morning they reached the confluence with the Umniati River, dry except for a *dambo* that would not flow until the next annual rains. Heading north, with the Umniati to their left, they forged a parallel course keeping a distance of a few hundred metres from the river bed. Experience had taught them that, for easier walking, the Rhodesian army patrols tended to favour the sandy river courses. His men were worried, sure they had been seen and the security forces could not be far behind or, for that matter, might even be ahead. Nearing midday, not far from their destination they slackened their pace, ever watchful for enemy patrols and ambushes.

'*Chindunduma!*' said one of the men. The area was littered with old mine diggings, reminders of earlier White prospectors searching for gold and, later, copper—the perfect cover for their purpose. Their solitary gun covered the surrounding bush as they stealthily backed into the mouth of a disused horizontal mine shaft, careful to dust away any signs of their approach with mopane branches.

The Teacher felt light-headed and drowsed at intervals. Suddenly he was jerked out of sleep. Something was coming into the shaft. His awareness of the intruders was heightened by their pungent sickly-sweet smell. Fear gripped his throat. Damp palms tightened around his weapon. There was no doubt in his mind what they were or what they sought. Hyenas had smelt blood, his blood.

One crunching bite from their jaws would shatter the thigh bone of an elephant. Not one, but several animals crammed the entrance three metres away. He could hear them breathing and knew with terrifying certainty that within minutes the pack would rush him—rip him apart—then swallow his flesh even before he had a chance to die.

Without warning the comrade next to him squeezed the trigger of the AK assault rifle and held it down. The magazine discharging its thirty rounds.

By first light the Rhodesian Light Infantry was at the site of the assumed terrorist crossing. Two Allouette helicopters had each flown a *stick* of five men straight from their barracks at Cranborne into the contact zone.

Before long they were joined by Chief Inspector Hammond and a police patrol. They began to scour the surrounding countryside searching for anyone even remotely connected to the attacks. Hammond took charge and by midday local tribesmen were being subjected to harsh, sometimes brutal, interrogations by Black members of his police force in an effort to get them to talk.

This proved futile. It served to heighten the already strong resentment felt towards the Rhodesian security forces by the local populace. No one had heard or seen anything—it was as if the terrorists had evaporated into thin air.

The sun was coming up and Mbada no longer took bearings on the stars. Having stopped fleetingly that night, he now began to run to make up for lost time. Later, he reached and crossed the main road leading to the Zambian border. Judging by the sun's current position he realised, it was around 9.00am. and, approximately 60 kilometres to the north his men would be negotiating the same road. Staying out of sight, he turned south, heading in the direction of Sinoia. Nothing on the map he carried indicated the position he was searching for in case it fell into enemy hands. Mbada, like all the cadre, had committed to memory the location of this and other observation points, just as he had memorised dozens of arms caches across the country. Soon, his goal came into sight.

Climbing the hill he reached the crest and coming around the ridge caught sight of a young *mujiba* lying on the ground, using binoculars to watch the road below.

The lad was visibly shaken as Mbada's shadow fell across him. He swung round wide-eyed to see a looming figure soaked with sweat and holding a gun. Recognising the uniform, the boy quickly recovered with a show of teeth, causing Mbada to grin. Seeing he was near to collapse, the boy offered a gourd of warm milk and several loose cigarettes.

Mbada held his head back and emptied the container, then ignoring the offered cigarettes said, 'Go and fetch water and bring the doctor, now.'

The youngster shook his head. 'I am under strict instructions not to go near the mission hospital.' Clearly he was nervous.

'Look at me—would you rather face the bull or the calf?'

The *mujiba* didn't need further encouragement and leapt to his feet, took off down the path ready to bring the doctor back even if he had to tie, gag and drag him up the hill.

Some while later, Mbada saw two figures approaching. Using the *mujiba's* binoculars he saw that the boy carried two water bottles; he continued to scan the surrounding bush to ensure that they were not being followed.

Dr David Nyamande climbed the steep slope and at the crest caught his first glimpse of Mbada sitting on the ground. Mbada made no effort to rise as he approached. He simply reached up to grasp the doctor's palm, wrist and palm again.

'Doc, I have a job for you!'

oOo

After several months at Mgagao training camp in Tanzania, David had quietly slipped across the border into Rhodesia. It did not take long to find a suitable post with a mission hospital near Sinoia, a small farming town on the main road, 130 kilometres north of Salisbury. He was pleased with the salary and working hours which gave him the flexibility he sought.

David began by familiarising himself with the activity of military vehicles up and down the road from Salisbury to the north. From a granite outcrop that flanked the main road he set up an observation post. It was manned round-the-clock by either a young *chimbwido* or *mujiba* using a pair of 'day & night' field glasses, purchased on one of his frequent trips to Salisbury. The lookouts provided accurate reports for ZANLA's intelligence department on the numbers of men and vehicles which passed, together with their registration numbers. It would have caused considerable consternation to the Rhodesian security forces, had they known that their movements in the operational zone were being monitored around the clock with alarming accuracy. Provided his unit exercised caution, there was every reason to believe that this surveillance would continue until the war ended.

The only threat to his operation had arrived one morning in a police Land Rover. He and several other staff members had watched with disdain a rather unpleasant character shout at his driver to park in the shade to keep the vehicle cool.

The man, with white, wispy hair, had then disappeared inside the administrative offices. Minutes later a messenger arrived to say David's presence was required immediately—by Chief Inspector Hammond.

The interview had been brief. The mission fell under Hammond's jurisdiction in that part of the country and David's appointment had aroused his curiosity. He believed any Black in a position of authority was potentially dangerous, because they held sway over others; he decided to make it his business to find out who they were and what they did.

Hammond was naturally rude but had also been exceedingly insulting, showering him with derogatory remarks, but David, refusing to be intimidated, had kept his dignity. This had infuriated Hammond even more.

'You'd better watch out, *munt*,' he had spat out in undisguised hostility. 'Make a wrong move and, so help me, you'll know about it,'

'I see!' said David drily. He stared directly into Hammond's contorted face, 'If that's all you wanted, Inspector, I'll be on my way.'

'Chief Inspector to you, you Black...'

'Doctor!' David cut in.

'I...I'll be watching you, whatever you call yourself...'

'Doctor Nyamande. Now if you'll excuse me!' David had turned on his heel and walked out. He in turn had seethed with anger—that was a face he would never forget!

On two other occasions freedom fighters had sought his services in cases of emergency. Shortly after his arrival he had been contacted through the usual channels and led into the bush to where the rebels had carried an injured soldier for over 70 kilometres. Raked across the chest with semi-automatic fire during a sortie, their trek had been in vain—the man died while David tended to his wounds. His *comrades* had buried him right there. Smoothing over the disturbed earth to hide the last traces of the shallow grave, they had slipped from sight with whispered words of thanks. David had stared after them as they melted into the bush and simply disappeared. Not a footprint remained to mark their passing nor the place of death.

The other incident had been less serious. A freedom fighter had tripped in an anteater burrow at night and, in an attempt to break his fall with arms outstretched, had sustained a painful fracture. David had set the arm and sent him on his way.

oOo

'My *comrade* was shot. He is badly injured and lying up twenty-four hours' march from here....' Mbada stopped mid-sentence, sizing up the doctor. 'For you it's thirty hours' march. You must come with me and attend his wounds and bring antibiotics.'

David stared hard at the grim face, hesitating before replying.

'You understand my purpose for being here. I can't leave and jeopardise all this!' He turned to indicate their vantage point above the road and the binoculars; becoming aware of the blunt manner of this soldier, and perceived that this was not a man to toy with.

'I know, but if you don't attend our *comrade* will die. Leave this to the children...' he glanced at the *mujiba*, 'I realise your work here is important, but Doctor, you have more to offer our cause than just the gathering of information.'

'But I was given this assignment in Dar es Salaam,' David protested.

'Who's your field commander?' Mbada asked, irritated by what he saw as David's prevarication.

'Justin Chauke, of...' Mbada raised a hand, cutting him short.

'I know him. You may know me as the Major and I outrank him. Therefore take it as an order...you're coming with me.'

So this was the revered Major he had heard so much about. David was not sure who outranked whom and he was used to issuing orders not taking them. He looked questioningly at the man facing him—he had the build of a heavyweight boxer but lacked David's height. There was something else here that David had never sensed before, an aura of barely controlled power. The Major's presence was decidedly unsettling.

'Okay! You say thirty hours. Where do I go to from there?' Patiently he waited as Mbada half-drained the second bottle of water.

'Zambia!' came his stern reply. 'What's more, please don't call me the Major. You may address me as Mbada. I'll explain later.'

David thought better than to question him on the matter. 'First, I have things to do.' He expected Mbada to protest but he didn't. 'I must arrange with this young *mujiba's* father to take over my post. You realise that when I leave here my absence will not go unnoticed by the authorities. They will suspect something and investigate—they always do—I will not be able to return.'

Mbada agreed abruptly. 'Now let's hurry.' He knew, it went without saying, that when Blacks disappeared it was accepted they had gone over to join the freedom fighters.

On the way back to the mission, Mbada explained the nature of the Teacher's injuries and indicated what might be needed. Three hundred metres short of the perimeter fence he stopped and crouched out of sight in the long grass. He told David he would wait for him there.

It was Sunday and the compound was quiet as David made his way to the hospital. Working quickly he stripped the covers from two pillows, thrusting one inside the other, then headed for the dispensary. Here he gathered the necessary supplies: disposable syringes, anti-tetanus and antibiotic vials, a wad of field dressings and a roll of plaster. Glancing around, he grabbed a small bottle of acriflavine liquid to apply as an antiseptic to open wounds, adding other useful items to his growing bundle. Opening the scheduled drugs cabinet, he selected a bottle of powerful analgesics and several ampoules of morphine. He peered into the pillowcase and, pleased with his haul, ran to his quarters.

Changing his duty uniform, he dressed quickly into a green safari suit with shorts. Mbada had been insistent that he wear suitable shoes and David dug out a well-worn pair of veldskoens—bush shoes much favoured for comfort. Opening his bedside drawer he reached for his passport and wallet, together with other small personal effects and a saving book. He remembered: it was one week to pay-day! He paused to look around the room with a moment of regret—he would not be coming back. Two new suits hung in the open cupboard. He had purchased them the week before, and his hi-fi system, worth over three months' wages, sat in the corner. He made for the door, then came back for the white coat. Mbada had said 'Act naturally and no one will question you on leaving.' On the way through the complex he saw his old and trusty car which he would miss most of all. He passed several members of staff who, on seeing the doctor, thought he was on duty—no one went around the bush in a white coat. He tried not to hurry to the point where he had left Mbada.

He strolled out of the front gate, past the whitewashed stones that lined the road. Nonchalantly he looked back to see if he was being observed. Secure in the knowledge that he wasn't, he made a dive for the bush and discarded the coat.

Mbada was where he had left him.

Taking the white pillowcase from David, he emptied its contents onto the ground.

'No rope?'

'Um! Sorry, I couldn't find one.' David mumbled an apology. It had slipped his mind entirely.

'Not to worry. Hold this.' He passed his rifle over.

Mbada poured the remaining water from the cola bottle over the pillowcases, dropped them onto the bare earth and ground the damp cloth into the red soil with his boot. When he was finished they were camouflaged. He spread them flat then thrust his bayonet through the centre of each one and ran the cut upwards to the open ends leaving the lower third intact. The contents were quickly thrown into one and a knot tied to secure them. Then the cut ends were again knotted to form a loop, acting as a sling. Mbada handed it back to David.

'Now you can carry it over your shoulder and run when you have to. That's if you don't want a 762 shell up your arse.'

'I see your point.' David was learning fast.

'Okay. Let's get to a shop. We want as much food as you can carry in the other pillowcase.' He judged David's expression correctly. 'I won't carry anything. First, because we only have one gun and, second, I'm the one who knows how to use it.'

David did not disagree.

'Then I want to see the boy's father to arrange for him to take over your duties here. Let's get going...' then, as if an afterthought, 'and fill these with water,' giving him the two empty plastic bottles he had been carrying.

David attended to the buying while Mbada waited a safe distance away. On his return, Mbada filled the second pillowcase with the purchases and slung it over David's other shoulder. Surprisingly, they were not uncomfortable. They slipped their belts through the handles of the plastic bottles and hung them from their waists.

David half expected his new-found companion to take control of the situation when they met the *mujiba's* father. But he didn't. Instead, Mbada left the negotiations to David.

The arrangements made, Mbada finally told the worried parent that he would be remembered in his report to the Chimurenga High Command. This seemed to go some way toward mollifying the father.

A kilometre out of town, Mbada stopped abruptly and went down on one knee. David followed suit and Mbada glanced back, pleased with the response, realising that the doctor could use his head.

He took a compass bearing in silence before speaking.

'I have one chance to tell you this so listen carefully: our lives may depend on it.'

'Okay. I'm all ears,' David replied facetiously.

Mbada looked him over before making up his mind.

'Sorry, Doc, but I must be firm with you. By now the RLI and SAS will be combing this area and, if we meet them, I'll take off at a run and I'm not going to stop to help you whatever happens. Thought I'd tell you now so there are no surprises later.' He let that sink in. 'You either keep up or I leave you behind, is that clear?'

David simply nodded.

'Good, now observe closely: if I kneel you kneel, if I run you run. Just mimic my actions. If I hold my arm up, it means stop; a clenched fist means danger ahead; fingers up means soldiers; a circling finger means a flanking move, followed by pointing to the right, you head in that direction at a run, but if my hand is clenched, then use stealth, and the same applies to the left. Now repeat what I've said.'

David did so to the letter.

'Very good, now we will not speak again until I feel it is safe to do so. Any questions?'

'What if I want to attract your attention?'

'Give a dove call.'

'How?' David asked.

'It sounds like 'twooh, hooo'. Make the first syllable explosive.' Mbada gave him a perfect imitation of a Namaqua dove calling its mate.

'I'm not sure I can do that!'

Mbada accepted his forthrightness. He didn't want someone attempting a call like a deranged parrot in the vicinity of the enemy. He gathered up some small pebbles and handed them to the doctor.

'Here, take these, throw one lightly at my back.'

The pace was fast and the midday heat sapped David's strength, leaving him to wonder how the man in front was still on his feet after the gruelling hours of intermittent trotting and brisk walking. Time crept by and soon the long shadows of the late afternoon were upon them. They picked up the course of the Biriwiri River. The terrain had changed from grassland to forested areas of thorny acacia and the ground sloped noticeably away to the west. Mbada tried to stay in the shadows to provide cover but this was not always possible, so when they encountered open ground he would cross in advance, then beckon David over. Whenever these moments occurred David felt extremely vulnerable but resolved not to show fear in front of his companion, and pressed on. He was starting to experience a new-found pride by doing something tangible in the fight for his adopted country. He also had a growing respect for the man in front.

Two hours later that enthusiasm waned somewhat because Mbada had definitely increased the pace, leaving David exhausted and beginning to falter. Cans of tinned meat dug into his sides and no amount of shifting alleviated the discomfort.

Mbada sank to his knee and David just managed to prevent himself from tripping over him. It all happened so unexpectedly. David glanced around intently but he saw nothing to alarm him in the fading light.

'It's okay, Doc,' Mbada whispered. 'I stopped to tell you I am slowing down because it's nightfall. I don't want either of us falling down an anteater hole and breaking a leg or something.'

David's mind flashed back to the previous occasion when he had treated a ZANLA soldier who had broken an arm in just this way.

'Let's go,' and with that he set off again. David was unconvinced the pace slowed at all until much later into the evening.

The stars were bright as jewels in an indigo sky. The Southern Cross rose to hold centre stage until other constellations contested its place in the southern hemisphere. The combined light of the stars and a waxing moon made the landscape visible for quite some distance. The air was warm and David felt strangely invigorated.

By 2.00am it had become decidedly cooler when Mbada stopped for a second time. David heard it as well—a helicopter. For a moment it came nearer, then the distinctive whup-whup of its rotor blades receded into the distance until they could hear only the familiar nocturnal sounds of the bush once again.

David felt every aching muscle as they moved on.

Mbada realised how exhausted his companion was and called a halt.

'No, don't drink now. You will need it tomorrow. We will sleep for four hours.'

The ground was hard and unforgiving; nevertheless, David, fatigued, was dead to the world in a few minutes.

Mbada was relieved that they had made it this far. He did not want to travel during the daytime but there was no alternative. They must get back to his brother. He shook David. 'Up you get. We've overslept by half an hour.'

He couldn't believe it. David could have sworn he had just shut his eyes; overtaxed muscles had stiffened and his body ached fiercely. They set off once more. Surprisingly, after an hour of moving at a steady pace, he began to feel better.

Slowly the night yielded to a greyness and the quiet stirrings of dawn. All too soon a golden rim of light flared above the distant hills and the bush again gave way to the incessant sounds of day. David brushed ineffectually at the persistently biting tsetse flies. Soon the sun beat down relentlessly from a clear sky, which the sand and rocks beneath their feet reflected back in their faces until even the tsetse flies retreated into the shade.

David was thankful that Mbada had insisted they conserve their water. Without it he could not have gone on. They stopped at midday but Mbada, ever vigilant, would not allow them to rest long. With eyes nearly closed against the heat and the glare, David plodded mechanically close on his heels. The day passed slowly until, finally, darkness again shrouded the bush. The intense heat still radiated from the ground, David walked guided by the soft sound of Mbada's footfalls on the dry grass and his dimly seen form in front of him. He cursed silently whenever he stumbled in the dark over some unseen object.

Suddenly Mbada grabbed his shirt and shook him. He had missed the hand signal indicating danger ahead. David crouched and froze, eyes intent on Mbada's every movement, for now the silence was pierced by frightful screams, and the sounds were not far away. David's skin crawled. Haunting myths about she-devils preying on unwary travellers in the night flashed fleetingly through his mind. Mbada indicated to go left, to avoid crossing the path of a pack of scavenging hyenas; the beasts' yelps sounding like gruesome laughter.

Mbada went into a crouch again. At first David did not identify the sound that his companion made. Mbada pursed his lips a second time and repeated the shrill cry into the dark and this time he recognised the nightjar's call. There was no answer.

'Stay here,' Mbada sounded worried and, before David could remonstrate, he found himself alone. He could still hear the blood-curdling screams, though now some way behind them.

The minutes dragged by, when suddenly Mbada appeared from out of the gloom.

'Come on, Doc, we're here.' Seeing David look back in the direction of the sounds, Mbada added, 'Hyenas! They've smelt blood. Strange, they don't normally hunt in packs—must be hungry I suppose!'

David followed him into the mine entrance; the atmosphere was damp, cold and smelt of decay. Inside he was aware of shapes shuffling around on the floor. 'I can't see a thing!' As he spoke, Mbada struck a match. The light was almost blinding.

The Teacher smiled back at them with undisguised relief as did the other men. Mbada posted a sentry to cover the entrance, while he lit a fire in a shallow hole to hide the light, so David could see to the wounded man.

Despite the welcome he had managed, the Teacher was obviously in considerable pain and slightly delirious. David quickly administered a morphine injection and the effect was dramatic as his patient became extremely vocal.

'He killed the devil with his bare hands and I had to fight off a pack of them.' Confused, he grabbed David's hand. 'Be careful, Doctor, they are still in here somewhere....'

David attributed the symptoms to shock, unaware of their encounter with the hyenas. Had he known, the eroded wall of the mine shaft would have told the story—a spray of bullet holes was clearly visible across the soft surface. The Teacher had been fortunate. The hyenas, thoroughly discouraged by the AK's retort, had gone in search of easier prey. Mbada's men had found one dead, and removed the body, leaving it in thick bush away from the mine-shaft. In time the pack would have returned....

Meanwhile, Mbada called his men together in the entrance. He issued the command to move out, but first they would eat. He dug into David's horde and dished out tins of meat and fruit. Normally they would have dispersed in pairs, travelling no more than eight kilometres, then burying their firearms and uniforms to be retrieved at some later date. This way the small cache of weapons would be retrievable even if one of them was killed or captured. But circumstances had changed. Days of forced march without provisions had exhausted them. They had little gear and two of the men had sacrificed their shirts for the litter, but there was no time for sentiment, if they were to survive.

Sticking to his original plan, he sent two men south-east towards Mt. Darwin to recruit in the tribal trust lands; the others south, to the small town of Bindura with the same objective in mind. He, the Teacher, and the doctor, would return to his unit in Mozambique.

David found the *comrade's* wounds swollen and inflamed.

He removed the dressing and sniffed for the tell-tale smell of gangrene. Thankfully there was none—he didn't fancy having to perform an amputation in these primitive conditions. He cleaned away the necrotic tissue as best he could with gauze and a liberal dousing of acriflavine, then squirted a full tube of ointment directly into the suppurating wounds, left them unsutured so as not to harbour infection. He applied fresh dressings, then administered an anti-tetanus shot into the Teacher's buttock, together with 2cc of penicillin.

Fleetingly the Teacher tried to sit up and, seeming quite lucid, said, 'You remember me, Doctor? You buried my comrade in the bush...' He fell back and shut his eyes.

David remembered the incident but not this man. When sure that the morphine was having the desired effect, he picked up the empty water bottles at his side and went to join Mbada outside the mine.

He found Mbada crouched not far from the entrance and was surprised to find the rest of the men had already departed.

'He's asleep—I'm afraid he won't be able to walk for the next couple of days. He'll feel stiff and bloody sore when he moves. Otherwise he'll be all right.' In the dark David could sense Mbada's relief.

David handed him the empty water bottles.

Mbada turned and said, 'I'll fill these at first light. You go and sleep while I stand guard. We must rest up during the daylight hours—but not here— the hyenas will attract too much attention.'

'Hell!' David thought, 'With men like this how can we lose the war?'

'Sorry, Doc, could you go in and put out the fire? The glow can be seen from a distance.'

It seemed that for the first time Mbada was making a request and not issuing an order. David did as he was asked, but after what this ZANLA soldier had been through over the past few days, he felt compelled to stick it out with him. Even though he craved sleep more than anything else, he rejoined Mbada in silent vigil outside the mine entrance until morning.

Daylight crept up on them and by 5.00am it was light enough to see the hills in the distance. The night creatures had fed and were by now settling in their lairs to sleep out the heat of the day.

Mbada stretched and beckoned David to follow. At the river they filled the bottles, then warily returned to the mine.

He moved over to the still sleeping figure of the Teacher and nudged him with his boot. A second gentle kick and his brother was wide awake.

'Okay, on the stretcher,' he said, helping him onto the frame. In minutes, their kit assembled, they lifted their patient carefully to test the litter and, with Mbada leading, moved cautiously out into the early morning mist that still hugged the ground.

The sun had already crested the horizon and they knew that within a few hours the heat would again be unbearable. Turning north they moved along a parallel course to the river. They hadn't gone a hundred metres when Mbada halted.

'Stay here. I won't be long.' He returned to the mine and combed the mine shaft floor, picking up everything from dressing wrappers to excrement and burying the dead embers of the fire. In ever-widening circles he swept the entire clearing eradicating all traces of their stay.

They passed the Chiwi Rapids without incident and had settled into a comfortable pace when suddenly Mbada stopped and slowly lowered the litter. Again the subdued command to halt, accompanied by a warning to keep very still. Cautiously, Mbada walked back past them, towards the thicket on their left. David noticed that he had his gun at the ready. Reaching for a stone he lobbed it into the undergrowth. Nothing happened.

He repeated the manoeuvre, only now throwing a large rotting branch into the centre of the thicket. David began to think his actions were pointless when deep throaty growls came from the dense undergrowth. Mbada threw another stone. Suddenly the bush shook and to David's horror a large male lion erupted from the thicket, stopping abruptly, its muscles taut. Magnificent in its prime, it stood defiant, angrily protesting; an arrogant flat nose held high and massive head raised in menace, framed by a mantle of black mane which flowed down its chest and extended back between the shoulders.

Mbada watched intently—the rich dark ochre hair on the dorsal ridge bristled as it seemed to make up its mind—the tail twitched. He watched the muscles flex and bunch but was thankful the ears remained cocked. Another accurately placed stone caught the lion above the right eye, cutting deeply. Instinctively the head went down and in a flash the lion disappeared into the thick vegetation along the riverbank.

David stood open-mouthed.

The Teacher, propping himself up on one elbow, laughed aloud.

Mbada turned to them. 'Okay, now in you get. We'll hole up here for the rest of the day.'

David, hardly recovered from his astonishment at what he had witnessed, was astounded when Mbada ordered him to crawl into the thicket.

Dragging the Teacher in behind him, with Mbada bringing up the rear covering their tracks, he edged his way in.

The pungent feline odour permeated the thicket and smelled dreadful. Otherwise they were comfortable and had a commanding view through the foliage of the terrain outside. David thought of the lion which had vacated this vantage minutes before!

'Tell me, what would you have done if there had been another lion in here?' he enquired cynically.

Mbada laughed. He knew it had been solitary—he had seen the spoor outside the lair. 'Why do you think I sent you in first? Here, have a marula,' he offered David some of the overripe fruit he had picked up off the ground. The laden marula tree formed a canopy over the thicket which normally would have been stripped bare this late in the season. The thorny bush alone, in which they hid, would not deter baboons or vervet monkeys from this feast, but the fruit tree had remained inaccessible because of its previous occupant.

They settled down and Mbada patted David on the shoulder, 'Get some rest. You'll need it later—we're heading for the border.'

Within minutes both men were asleep. The Teacher lay on his stomach, fortified by mild analgesics and a further jab of penicillin, drowsy but awake, his gun pointed outwards.

Ever watchful, Mbada's men crossed the lake from the Zambian side in two stages. Gliding through the low choppy waves in dugout canoes, cut from the forest along the northern shore, they made steady progress against a strong head wind. Dressed as fishermen they carried their weapons openly. If challenged on the lake they would drop their guns overboard and claim to be poachers or else, if the odds seemed right, fight it out. They paddled rhythmically over the vast expanse of water to reach the upper branches of long submerged trees, ending the first leg of their journey.

Here the waters were still: only the lapping of their paddles, or a tiger fish leaping and the occasional thrashing tail of a crocodile as it submerged suddenly in pursuit of prey, disturbed the mirror-like surface. They rested for a few hours in their canoes, unconcerned by the reptiles that swam by. In the early morning they stirred to the repetitive cry of a fish eagle and pressed on, entering the gorge at daybreak. They did not expect to see anyone on this stretch of the Umniati River. Fleetingly, a helicopter had flown over but it had just as quickly disappeared. They were unperturbed. It was an inhospitable and extremely remote part of Rhodesia, and the authorities knew that the Tonga tribesmen occasionally fished the area; after having been displaced when the Kariba Dam was built and the waters rose, flooding their lands.*

The pilot in the lead helicopter sighted in the distance the canoes cutting bow waves through the oily languid waters of Kariba, heading towards the Umniati Gorge. Banking away sharply, the pilot radioed his base.

Later that morning, Vic Hammond accompanied by a patrol of two *sticks* from the Rhodesian Light Infantry, surrounded the area. Leading, he spotted the fishermen busy on the river bank below. Watching them cast a fishing net he approached cautiously, then fired a warning shot.

Dust kicked up at the feet of the ZANLA freedom fighters as the crack from his 9mm pistol echoed along the canyon. They froze while armed men worked their way down the high banks on either side.

An hour later, Hammond was still trying to force a confession out of them and any clue to the Major's whereabouts, as a kill at Mulingura Hill remained unconfirmed. They stuck to their plea of poaching on the Rhodesian border, because food was scarce in their village in Zambia—when a shout from a zealous RLI trooper stopped them.

'Hey sir, here! It's the terrs' *gats.*' He had found hidden, inside the cavernous folds of the boabab tree, two loaded AK assault rifles.

Victor Hammond had had enough. He spoke to the army lieutenant who in turn called his soldiers to one side, out of view of the interrogation. Levelling his pistol to the back of the head of the nearest kneeling terrorist, he fired at point-blank range. Glancing with stirring excitement at the shattered skull of the man that lay in the dirt, he turned to the dead man's companion.

'Now, you fucking terrorist, I want to know where this Major is, or so help me I'll waste you next,' he threatened, raising the pistol.

The ZANLA soldier looked up. 'I'll show you, but it's a long way.'

Vic Hammond did not mind the distance. He had come a long way from Centenary. Now he was determined to score another kill. Two *floppies* in a day would give him something to talk about in the office but if he was able to bag the Major....

Within minutes the *sticks* were reassembled, the doorless choppers recalled, and they climbed aboard.

The prisoner was made to sit on the outer edge of the rear seat with Hammond's 9mm pistol pressed into his side. Three RLI troopers sat on the other side of the Chief Inspector. The lieutenant, together with the other *stick,* followed behind in the second helicopter.

At first they followed a westerly direction, then backtracked. The area they were flying over was sparse of vegetation and undulating. They could clearly see the game trails criss-crossing the dry ground below and occasionally they overflew small herds of elephant which panicked, in fright turning this way, then that, unsure of where the threatening noise was coming from. The wiser bulls stood their ground, raising dust clouds while they milled anxiously about, trying with their poor eyesight to see the passing threat, with ears flared and trunks high, testing the air.

After a half-hour of flying, following Hammond's directions in what seemed to be an aimless search pattern, the pilot shouted back over the noise of the rotors, 'What the hell's going on? I can't keep this chopper up here all day!' He throttled back and commenced a wide circling path to await further instructions.

It occurred to Hammond that he had been taken, literally, for a ride—the area that the terrorist was continually pointing to was much too far to the west. He was thinking about his next course of action when suddenly their captive launched himself at the Chief Inspector knocking him aside.

The freedom fighter leapt forward and grabbed the pilot's arm, trying to pull him from the controls. The helicopter reacted violently. The nose tilted down hard causing the occupants to stare directly ahead at the ground, leaving everyone frantically reaching out for something to hang onto. A nervous finger tightened involuntarily on a trigger. The shot was deafening in the confined space. The bullet seared the pilot's shoulder and punched out through the transparent canopy. The helicopter veered round, climbing almost vertically and near to stalling point as the pilot fought desperately with the controls.

Hammond glanced at his smoking firearm, stupefied, and in panic dropped it—then he reacted. Hanging onto the framework of the craft he braced himself against the trooper next to him and kicked out viciously at their captive.

The blow caught the ZANLA soldier off-balance, and at the same time the helicopter lurched to the right, sending the man sprawling backwards out of the helicopter. In a desperate bid to save himself he reached out for a hold and caught the lower edge of the door frame, to find himself hanging ninety metres above the ground and flying through the air at over 80 knots.

Victor Hammond waited until the pilot had regained control and virtually brought the craft to a hover, then he moved over. Holding on tightly, he raised his heavy boot and brought it crashing down on the fingers of the man as he flailed through the air. He saw the face contort as an agonised scream left his lips, lost on the wind. Again Hammond brought his boot down. Still the man hung on. This time he raised his foot and delivered a paralysing kick to the head. The ZANLA soldier's grip slipped and instantly his body was whisked away, cartwheeling towards the ground.

Hammond leant out of the helicopter to watch its descent.

Their captive smashed into the hard sun baked ground, his spine and pelvis shattering even as his abdomen and skull spilt, splattering their contents onto the ground. The pulverised body bounced once, then settled in a cloud of dust, the limbs distorted grotesquely in death.

Hammond smirked, satisfied by the full graphic impact of the man's death; and content he pulled himself back into the helicopter and instructed the pilot to return to the Umniati Gorge.

The Teacher, drowsy in the midday heat, heard a sound jolting him wide awake. Seven paces away was an army patrol. Slowly he counted ten soldiers as they passed, and a civilian who wore no uniform to speak of, bringing up the rear. He reached out and gently shook Mbada who in turn placed a hand over David's mouth to stop any sound as he woke. David peered through the undergrowth and immediately recognised the civilian—Chief Inspector Hammond. He wished he had a gun.

Remaining motionless and scarcely breathing, they watched intently as the patrol halted not more than thirty metres farther on. The commanding officer ordered his men to fan out. After making certain the area was safe, he called them back in. To their dismay he posted a sentry a few metres from where they lay.

Suddenly a soldier came running from the direction of the mine diggings. He was waving something. Hammond and the officer promptly went off to investigate. Mbada knew that they had found something. But what? He was sure he had been very thorough in sweeping the area.

At the same time he became aware of the attention the sentry was paying to their position. The trooper appeared to be peering into the bush where they were hiding. Suddenly it struck Mbada that it was the tree against which he was resting that was the object of the sentry's focus.

The sentry, determined to get some of the ripe fruit hanging from the lower branches, was unaware that less than three metres away an AK rifle was aimed directly at his sternum. At that moment Hammond and two soldiers reappeared from the direction of the mine to rejoin the group.

Observing their gestures, it was obvious that a heated debate had ensued with Hammond pointing in the direction of the river and Sinoia. The presumed officer, for he wore no insignia that they could readily identify, seemed to be trying to persuade him to take a different route. Finally, Hammond appeared to win the argument and the officer called his men back into formation.

By then the sentry had worked his way into the thicket staring up at the tantalising fruit just out of reach, brushing up against David's knee, Mbada's AK now mere centimetres from his genitals. They heard him swear under his breath, withdrawing empty-handed to rejoin the group. The patrol moved off warily in the direction of the river and Sinoia.

Sleep was impossible after that and they lay waiting for the sun to go down. Earlier than David had expected, Mbada made a decision to move on.

'We could wait until dusk but there's a chance the lion will return. By then, I want to be well away from here.'

David's relief at leaving their hiding place soon disappeared as their patient seemed to get heavier by the kilometre and he found the going difficult. His arms felt as though they were slowly being wrenched from their sockets. Every few metres the terrain would interrupt their rhythm and even Mbada seemed to feel the pressure, stopping frequently for them to rest. They were aware of their vulnerability in the open and welcomed nightfall. The compass bearing they now followed pointed north-east and as they moved through the bush their senses became highly tuned to every sound and movement, ever watchful for another army patrol.

Though it was past eight it was still quite warm and they perspired freely. Again the moonlit sky illuminated everything, bestowing ethereal properties onto moving objects.

Mbada halted suddenly causing David to stumble. They lowered the litter and David, who had become used to the long periods of silence, instinctively watched for Mbada's hand signals, first a clenched fist, then fingers pointing to the right.

The entire horizon to that side seemed to be in fluid motion and, looming larger by the second, was accompanied by a rumbling sound which grew louder. But David could not make out the cause of the movement. Mbada gave another hand signal which he didn't recognise. The Teacher read the sign and clutching David by the shirt pulled him down.

'Elephants. Back up!' he whispered.

They retraced their steps until David felt Mbada tug at the litter, bringing him to a halt. A large herd passed some seventy metres away. The old bull stopped and turned to face them. He raised his trunk to test the air and held his ground until the females and their young had passed, then cautiously he swung round to join the trek down to the lake shore 40 kilometres farther on.

No sooner had they passed, than Mbada lifted the litter, pressing David to move on. The bush thinned out, but the terrain became hilly and they negotiated even steeper ravines. Twice in the night Mbada slipped and on both occasions managed to hang on without throwing his injured brother from the litter.

Descending a particularly steep slope David spotted the antelope first. On the far ridge a massive kudu, with horns nearly two metres on the curve and almost as high at the shoulder, stood imposing, silhouetted against the full moon. Mbada saw the animal and momentarily checked their advance. At the same moment the kudu's nose came up, its horns lying against its back, and in a flash it disappeared. They pressed on, yet somehow the kudu had lifted their spirits and they toiled until, without warning, the clawing vegetation gave way to open ground. They lowered the litter. Mbada came back to speak with David, keeping his voice down.

'Pylons from Kariba power station. I reckon it's probably sixty kilometres plus from here.' Mbada was silent for a moment, then added, 'We'll go that way,' he said, pointing in the direction of Kariba. 'I'll explain later.'

They knew that the security forces were paranoid about sabotage to the power lines from Kariba, which supplied electricity throughout Rhodesia. The pylons were fenced off and protected by land-mines for hundreds of kilometres, the only casualties being inquisitive baboons that occasionally strayed over the barbed wire. A three-hundred-metre firebreak cut through virgin bush, following the pylons from Kariba Gorge on the Zambezi to the main cities in the heartland of the country. The freedom fighters, however, had no intention of destroying the lines. To do so would have disrupted the Zambian supply as well. Furthermore, it would provide the Rhodesians with the excuse to cut the supply in retaliation.*

Besides, Mbada had often used the firebreak as a pathway to the interior of Rhodesia on his many incursions. ZANLA was deeply grateful to the Rhodesian Government which conscientiously maintained and cleared the route year after year.

A hundred metres farther on they picked up the service road. After the terrain they had endured, slipping and slithering with the litter in the dark, the dirt road brought immediate relief. The imminent danger of injury to one of them in a fall, should they continue to stay on rough terrain, outweighed the threat of an enemy ambush. With another man down their fate would be sealed. Mbada decided the risk was acceptable—they kept to the dense bush by day and ventured back onto the service road at night.

Lights from Kariba Heights township finally came into view, appearing to hang in the northern sky. Sprawled over the mountain, the small settlement housed the many employees who worked in the power station below. Firmly entrenched on the crest of the mountain was a permanent garrison of the security forces.

Pressing on, the next sign of civilisation they encountered was the airstrip with its solitary control tower, still some kilometres from the township. Two helicopters stood to one side in isolation, silhouettes against the night sky. Mbada, aware that a detachment of soldiers would be in the immediate vicinity to guard the machines, gave the area a wide berth. They veered east.

Soon they arrived at the main asphalt road which led from Kariba to Makuti, a name on the map that laid claim to a hotel, petrol station and little else. It was the T-junction from where the main road led southwards, past Sinoia where David had worked and on towards Salisbury. Northwards, it led to the Zambezi and Chirundu, the border post with Zambia.

Mbada called a halt.

They found a comfortable patch in which to settle their injured comrade. David waited with him while Mbada reconnoitred the area. In under twenty minutes he was back, crouched down next to David and his brother, outlining his plan.

'The way I see it, we need to cross the Zambezi and soon. If we head towards Makuti—east of Chirundu, we can signal our contact in Zambia between eight and nine at night—it's an emergency arrangement—and he will cross to pick us up. All we need do is flash a light continuously until we see two return flashes. It won't be dangerous because the only person to see our signal will be on the far bank and a friend.'

David pointed out that they didn't possess a flashlight.

Mbada smiled. 'I'll sort that out later. Right now we need to move on up the road a few kilometres towards Kariba to where there is a tsetse fly barrier. I'm afraid we'll have to take a parallel path through the bush—it will take longer but it'll be safer.' He knew that the security forces favoured ambushes on main and secondary roads. The fact that freedom fighters had no vehicles made these ambushes seem futile, though he had to admit that on previous raids a few of his *comrades* had been spotted crossing, as had happened earlier to the Teacher and his men. He never ceased to be amazed by their failure to grasp that freedom fighters would never dream of using the roads to move around the country. 'We'll stop there for the night. Tomorrow, Doc, you can show us what you're made of...'

David interjected as they lifted the litter, 'But aren't we going the wrong way. I thought you said we needed to get to Chirundu?'

Mbada lowered his end. 'All right, let me explain....'

Freewheeling his bicycle down the steep road from the township high above, the elderly Black guard from the Tsetse Fly Control Department slowed as he came to the road that skirted the lake shore. He took the left fork towards Makuti.

On reaching his post, the guard dismounted, carefully placing his bicycle against the side of the shelter, which would later, provide the only shade from the harsh sun. He attended to his first duty of the day—lowering the six-metre-long barrier—effectively closing the road to all daytime traffic from entering Kariba township or the holiday resorts that lined the lake shore, and beyond to the dam wall itself. As the sun rose, the tsetse flies would become active and it was his function to stop and spray all vehicles, which might accidentally have trapped or were harbouring these insects.

The guard checked his uniform over. His khaki shorts and jacket being immaculate, he straightened the askari hat, then went back to the shelter to retrieve his hand spray. While shaking the cylinder to check that it was still full, he found himself staring down the barrels of two guns.

Mbada barked an order, 'Over here—fast.'

The guard, disinclined to argue, was led at the point of an AK into the thick bush, while David reopened the barrier and ran to catch up.

Some way on Mbada stopped. 'Now get undressed!'

'Excuse me?' The guard was unsure that he had heard correctly.

Mbada repeated the order, prodding the man with his gun, and watched as he hastily stripped off.

David, too, stripped down to his underwear.

'No. Keep your underclothes on. We won't harm you provided you do as we say.' The guard didn't take much comfort from this reassurance.

'Give me your clothes,' said David.

Elasticated plaster from David's medical kit, together with remnants of his torn safari suit, enabled Mbada to tie and gag the guard.

Though they were of similar height the guard was painfully thin. Fortunately the jacket was standard government issue, and far too big. Donning the hat, he dusted down his new outfit while walking back to close the barrier again.

They hadn't long to wait before a vehicle approached. A Mini drew up to the barrier and the woman driver stuck out her head.

'Morning. You're new aren't you? Where's Tobias?' she asked.

'Morning, madam, he's off sick...' David returned her greeting, 'I'll spray the car for you.' Having had his car sprayed once before, he attended to the wheel arches, then thrust the nozzle through the back window, all the time watching Mbada, hidden, out of the corner of his eye. The plunger jammed at that moment, so he pushed down harder. Something gave and he nearly emptied the entire cylinder's contents into the back of the vehicle.

The woman coughed and, catching her breath, spluttered, 'Good God! Are you trying to kill me or something?'

'Sorry, madam, they pay me to be thorough.' He smiled.

'Oh! To hell with it. Just don't do that again. You Blacks are all the same!' Totally unaware of any immediate danger, she started her car. David lifted the boom and, crashing the gears, she sped off in the hope of ventilating the vehicle to rid it of the noxious pesticide fumes.

Mbada was chuckling as he stepped out from behind the shelter.

'It was too small for the stretcher. Leave it to me to decide on a suitable vehicle—and take it easy Doc, with that spray.' He laughed again.

'You're bloody dangerous with that thing.'

David shrugged, then sauntered back to the barrier. He was beginning to enjoy the role of tsetse fly eradicator. Less than an hour later they heard the approach of another vehicle and David tensed. It was an army Land Rover but the two uniformed occupants had no visible rank. He went through his routine and was in the process of asking the driver to open the door, in order for him to spray the interior, when Mbada appeared at the passenger side and thrust his gun in the soldier's face.

'Out, gentlemen!' he rasped. With his free hand he opened the door.

The driver turned off the engine resigned to the inevitable.

Mbada held both men at gunpoint while he instructed David to turn the vehicle round. This done, he led their captives behind the hut into the long grass to join the guard. The Teacher, from his prone position, covered the two men while Mbada tied them up to the repeated pleas from the passenger not to be shot.

'Don't be bloody stupid,' said Mbada gagging the man. 'You think I'm mad, with your soldiers up there?' He glanced up indicating the army garrison. But for the foliage that grew on the mountain side they would have been visible from above. He checked their bonds before returning to David at the barrier.

'Come on, Doc, help me with our patient.'

They carried the Teacher out to the Land Rover, opened the tailgate, slid him into the back and secured the litter. David was making for the driver's door when Mbada shouted at him to stop. They both listened.

There was the distinctive drone of heavy vehicles approaching. A large military truck came into view, followed by another, and yet another...there seemed no end to the convoy.

'Quick—the barrier and act normal. Christ! Where's your spray?'

David grabbed the pump. 'What now?' he demanded.

'Spray the bloody lot,' Mbada hissed, ducking into the Land Rover.

There were now nineteen vehicles in sight and every indication that more were following. The leading vehicle in the convoy was slowing for the barrier. It was just their luck to intercept the Rhodesian Light Infantry's, 1 Commando, en route from Salisbury to Kariba to relieve 3 Commando, guarding a power station that no one had any intention of attacking.

Mbada stepped out of the Land Rover, leaving his gun behind, and brazenly walked to the front and placed his foot on the bumper. His ZANLA uniform was clear to see.

The lead driver came to an abrupt halt not ten paces from the ZANLA major. The young sub-lieutenant next to him could hardly believe his eyes. Jumping out, he ran back down the convoy to speak to the occupants of the command vehicle, at the same time pointing at Mbada.

A group of men moved menacingly towards Mbada led by a high-ranking officer. Mbada's eyes narrowed as he took in the man in the lead.

'What's the meaning of this?' snapped the dapper little man.

Mbada was relieved that no guns were pointing in his direction and his hastily devised plan seemed to be working—so far. His deception now depended on how he handled the inevitable questions he would be asked.

Mbada jumped to attention. 'Sorry, sar, I didn't recognise you. Corporal Vambe, Selous Scouts, sar.'

'Yes, yes! The Scouts, I see!' The little man glanced back with a withering look at the young sub-lieutenant, turning again he carefully studied the Black soldier who stood rigidly to attention before him.

He smiled. 'One of Tom's lads,' he said. 'What are you doing here...corporal?'

Mbada was ready with a reply, 'Waiting for Sgt Van der Merwe, sar.'

'Oh! Where is he then?' asked General Rocco Bastion-Smythe, Supreme Commander of the Rhodesian Armed Forces.

'Can't say...classified, sar,' was all Mbada offered.

Bastion-Smythe broke into laughter, for he had brought about the Selous Scouts formation earlier in the year, to undertake covert operations behind enemy lines. He had also sanctioned the use of enemy uniforms.

The General was impressed. He appeared to fit the part of a terrorist perfectly. He would mention him to Tom Bailey, the Selous Scouts legendary leader, who had come up through the non-commissioned ranks and risen to colonel in command of the most feared fighting force in the country.

'Keep up the good work.' Glancing back, he said, 'I think it's time we were on our way and let this man get on with his duties.'

He looked past Mbada and barked at David, 'Open the bloody gate and let's not fool around with this nonsense.'

Mbada saluted.

Word passed on down the convoy that the Selous Scouts were up ahead and that there was probably a dead terrorist in the back of the Land Rover. In passing, the men in the rear of the trucks craned their necks to look at Mbada. He acknowledged their interest with a wave and, as the General passed, he snapped to attention. The vehicles rolled by and, as the last of them rounded the bend, David began to laugh, experiencing a mixture of almost hysterical relief, amusement and admiration.

'I'm pleased you liked the performance but I'd hate to be around when they discover who we really are.' Mbada started for the passenger door. 'Leave the barrier open. Come on, let's get the hell out of here.'

David checked the fuel gauge. It was half-full, more than enough to get them to the border via Makuti junction which lay 30 kilometres ahead. It was also the Selous Scouts main base camp.

Several kilometres from Makuti, rounding a bend, they nearly ran into a military vehicle. A large RL truck blocked the road.

David shouted, 'Ambush!'

Immediately Mbada countered, 'Puncture!' He had seen two soldiers removing the rear wheel. 'It's okay, they're stragglers from the convoy,' he explained, reaching for his weapon.

They slowed for the trooper who flagged them down, and drew to a halt. Reluctantly Mbada slid his rifle from view.

David spoke first. 'Selous Scouts...your convoy passed us farther back with the General.'

The soldier looked relieved.

'Can we help?' enquired David.

'We've had a blow out. Could you give me a lift back to Makuti with the wheel?'

David shot a glance at Mbada who was studying the dozen or so other occupants of the truck and simply inclined his head giving his consent.

'Sure. Hop on but we're in a hurry.'

The trooper shouted to his mates, 'Get the fucking thing onto the back.' He spoke warmly to David, 'Thanks, *china.*'

David restarted the engine and moved off slowly round the truck, now carrying an additional passenger and a large wheel.

The RLI trooper stared at the Teacher. The Teacher gazed back at his new travelling companion with as much interest.

'What happened?' the trooper asked.

'The Teacher hesitated, 'We had contact with *terrs* up at Kariba,' and he half-turned to show the field dressings.

'Jesus man, did you *slot* the bastards?'

David and Mbada listened to the shouted conversation through the open window at the rear of the Land Rover's cab. Mbada swung round to watch them both, his AK resting gently on his lap.

'Kill them! No, man. We tortured the bastards, then threw them alive into the Zambezi—for the crocs. Look, I've got one of their AKs as a souvenir.'

'Shit!' The soldier had heard talk about the Selous Scouts barbaric practices. 'How did you get injured, my *china*? Were you ambushed?'

'Nae! I'd just managed to kill the Major—you know—The Major!' He emphasised the deed by thrusting an imaginary bayonet down for the killing blow.

'The Major!!! Jesus....'

'Some of our blokes mistook me for one of the *terrs*,' he shouted to be heard. 'Took a burst from an SMG in both legs. Really I'm as White as you. It's the camouflage paint we use in the Scouts.'

'You're bullshitting me.' Smiling back, he looked harder at the Teacher but he felt unsure. Previously imagined glory of joining this elite fighting unit hastily dismissed from his mind—they were too mercenary for his liking.

The Teacher grinned wickedly at him knowing he had killed further conversation.

Mbada, embarrassed by his brother's fertile imagination, shot a glance at David and jabbed him in the ribs in time to prevent an outburst of laughter. They rounded a sweeping left bend and Makuti came into view. David drew to a halt at the T-junction and Mbada climbed out, still smiling.

'Sorry we can't take you into camp but we're in a hurry.'

The trooper unloaded the wheel and thanked them for their assistance. He was pleased he had met the Selous Scouts and equally pleased to be out of their company. He shouted to Mbada as the Land Rover moved off, '*Slot* the next *terr* for me.'

Mbada waved two fingers and the soldier grinned back.

David turned left, heading north towards the escarpment that runs the entire breadth of the Zambezi Valley on the Rhodesian side. They remained silent for a few minutes, then as they entered the steep pass that cuts its way down the plateau wall to the valley floor below, all three burst into uncontrolled laughter.

The small settlement that supported the personnel at the border post lay ahead. Before reaching the Chirundu bridge, they turned right, off the main road, and followed the bush track on a parallel course downstream in the general direction of Mozambique.

Mbada told David to slow-down and glanced again at the map. 'Yes!' he said, 'This is near to the spot where we ambushed the SAS last month.' He saw David's questioning glance. 'It's a long story. I'll tell you about it sometime...drive on for five kilometres, then we head towards the river.'

Further on, David pulled the vehicle over and, engaging four-wheel drive, turned north, cautiously negotiating the short distance of virgin bush towards the green fringe of vegetation lining the bank of the Zambezi.

It did not take long for Mbada to find the clearing he sought, and he indicated that David should stop. Together they climbed out and walked to the river-bank. Across the wide expanse of water they could see what appeared to be a camp on the opposite bank. The swirling, dark, Zambezi water lay between them and safety.

'We'll talk round any stray patrol in this part of the valley,' said Mbada as if answering David's unspoken question. 'If they need confirmation of who we are, they simply have to contact General Bastion-Smythe at Kariba. No doubt he'll vouch for our bona fides.'

They hid the vehicle in the undergrowth at the river's edge, while Mbada disconnected one of the headlights. They settled down to await nightfall.

Promptly at 8.00pm Mbada began to flick the headlight switch on and off repeatedly. Almost immediately came an answering flash from across the river and Mbada sent a coded reply. All they had to do was sit out the remaining hours before their rescuer arrived. The seasonal rains had come early and Kariba Lake had swollen alarmingly. The flood gates on the dam wall had been opened to lower the water level and as a result the Zambezi was swirling faster on its way to the sea. David wondered who in his right mind would attempt such a crossing at night.

oOo

10 February 1973
Simon stood in the doorway to the bedroom in the single quarters which Michael used whenever he came in from the field. 'Are you coming into Lusaka with us, or are you aiming to get mindless again at the club tonight?' he enquired.

Michael did not answer but glared up at Simon from the bed where he lay. Since his return from the bush he seemed more distant than before, content to survive purely on a liquid diet, to the concern of his boss and fellow workers.

'What's eating you, Michael?' Simon persisted, coming into the room and leaning against the dresser.

'I don't know. Suppose it's our involvement with ZANLA that's getting to me. What do you think?'

Simon took a good hard look at Michael. 'What? About you, or ZANLA?' but he knew what Michael had meant. 'I know, I've been thinking the same thing. Tell me, Michael, what do you make of the Major?'

'To be honest, he scares the hell out of me. God help the poor sods who meet up with him on the other side—but I respect him for his commitment.'

Simon searched the unshaven gaunt face. There was something there, puzzling him. 'Why are you helping ZANLA, Michael? I mean, I was born here so I've a vested interest, but you, you are a White South African. This isn't your war!'

Michael felt his chest tighten as he inhaled and sighed audibly before answering. 'You've answered that. 'Cause I'm White I share the blame—I've had plenty of time to think—us liberals, we've done nothing to stop this.' His penetrating stare held Simon's attention. 'Call it a guilt trip, appeasing my conscience if you like, but I'm ashamed. Without South Africa's interference this would never have happened.' He hesitated, adding sullenly, 'Then there's Carla! It helps to get her out of my mind.'

Simon wondered if the mention of Carla was merely a ruse to play down his emotional outburst. He felt uneasy, he had not intending to dig too deeply into Michael's motives for having become involved in ferrying ZANLA soldiers, preferring to steer the conversation away from personal matters. 'Do you think ZANLA stands a chance of winning this war?'

'Well, somebody's certainly stirred up a hornet's nest,' said Michael drily. 'I hear Smith's closed the Rhodesian border with Zambia, claiming it's in retaliation for us supporting 'terrorist' bases here in Zambia,' a smile curled his lip, 'while ZANLA's openly claiming to operate out of Mozambique.'*

'Never seen a ZANLA soldier in Zambia. We can vouch for that, can't we?' Simon said with a grin.

'You know the ridiculous part of all this: Smith hasn't given any consideration to the fact that Rhodesian exports to Zambia amount to a few million dollars every year, while South African exports to us are about three hundred million.' His voice conveyed his scorn, 'Can you believe it, the silly bugger neglected to advise the South African Government of his intentions. It'll certainly cost him. Already the PM—Vorster, has made it clear he doesn't support the boycott and I see the Afrikaans press is attacking the Rhodesian Government.'*

'I heard. According to the media, Smith's realised he's committed a diplomatic blunder which threatens the very alliance he needs for survival.' Simon shook his head, mystified, 'The arrogance of the man! Now he's saying he intends to reopen the border because a special Zambian envoy visited Rhodesia...and agreed to his terms.'*

Michael saw the funny side. 'You heard President Kaunda's response?' By Simon's expression he hadn't. 'Well, the wily old fox is keeping the border closed and has severed all direct links with Rhodesia. He's challenging the Rhodesian Premier to produce this fictitious 'dishonest broker', and still denies the existence of guerrilla bases.'*

'I bet Kaunda's having a quiet chuckle to himself,' said Simon. It's a brave move, what with us being landlocked and totally dependent on rail exports.' He realised he was becoming as solemn as Michael. 'Hey! Enough of this. Politics depresses me. I came in here to invite you to a party in Lusaka. Coming?'

The party offered more than he had expected. Whereas Carla was beautiful, Trish was attractive with a wide, generous mouth that usually wore an engaging smile. She began to remind him of Carla more and more as the evening wore on. Her golden blonde hair seemed to bounce in the same way each time she turned her head. His interest was reciprocated, confirmed later when Simon and his wife sidled up to him. 'She wants to know if you're married. You lucky devil, go for it, Michael.'

Their courtship was brief. Trish had come over from the United States and, having served three years with a UN aid organisation, was due to return shortly. She was vivacious and outgoing, whereas Carla had been quiet and reserved.

By May 1973 they were married and, to the amusement of his colleagues, he whisked her away to honeymoon alone at his camp on the Zambezi. Michael had installed all the available mod cons to accommodate his new bride. The rudiments were all there, though admittedly crude. Trish thought the idea romantic and she was determined to overlook this to please him.

Trish was good for him and he was content and happy, but within months he found unnervingly that, whenever he was away from her, within a day or two, haunting memories of Carla would materialise to play havoc on his mind. Carla somehow never seemed far from his thoughts. He was sure, given time, these would disperse and she would be remembered only as his first true-love. Their relationship endured despite his nagging doubts.

Then came the news, Trish was pregnant.

oOo

Victor Hammond sat sipping a gin 'n tonic on the terrace of the George Hotel in Salisbury, a guest of General Rocco Bastion-Smythe, listening to him lament over the current state of affairs.

'At least my tours boost the morale of our troops, especially with the Bush War having changed to one of military significance,' declared the General. He felt it was a deplorable situation that ZANLA's cross-border raids were slowly gaining them the upper hand. All the more remarkable since the ZANLA leaders were languishing in a Rhodesian prison.* 'It seems our Government is in a cleft stick, similar to what's happening in South Africa,' he added.

'What do you mean?' Hammond looked puzzled.

'Like Mandela and other prominent ANC figures, there's no way Mugabe or Sithole can be eliminated. Let's face it, both governments fear mass violence that terminating them would inevitably bring.'

'If I had my way...' Hammond left the sentence unfinished.

'On the contrary, my dear chap, imprisonment is the only solution— a small price to pay to keep them out of circulation,' the General was being more circumspect, 'but I'm concerned how these men, locked behind bars, still hold total control over their external forces.'

Hammond looked at him blankly. He was as much in the dark as the rest of the White Rhodesian authorities, who were dumbfounded how these incarcerated leaders communicated with the outside world. It mattered not that they were held on frivolous and fallacious charges. Besides, he had no real interest in the intricacies of the politics of this war—only of his mastery in inflicting his perverted authority and power over others.

'What's happening on the war front, Rocco?' he asked innocently.

'There's been a dramatic escalation of attacks, Vic. The tide has turned and some of our strategists seem to think the raid by ZANLA on that Centenary farmstead the December before last, was probably the start of a new offensive. I do not understand why this should have happened. My security forces have dominated this Bush War from the start of UDI, but the truth is, we are now unable to hold back these terrorists.'*

The follow-up counter operation to the Centenary attack, code-named Operation Hurricane,* led by one of their most senior men, namely Victor Hammond, had yielded nothing. To make matters worse, the Major was reported to be alive and active in Hammond's area.

Hammond swilled his drink round, then burying his nose in the glass, downed his gin and looked aimlessly at reflections in the thick-bottomed tumbler. He sucked on the ice cubes—his face flushed, remembering the note that he had deliberately withheld from his superiors.

'Since that attack, there has been an increase of trained insurgents infiltrating across the border. Attacks are becoming more frequent,' continued the General, oblivious to Hammond's discomfort. 'It seems that every day, Black children leave home or our mission stations, and cross into Mozambique to take up arms against us. Frankly, I'm at a loss to find a way to contain this offensive, but we do need to regain control, at any price.'*

oOo

29 March 1974

Jan DuToit had heard the same words from the pulpit ever since his childhood: 'God gave us this country. He delivered us from the Zulu at the battle of Blood River, commemorated by our *volk* each year on the Day of the Vow.' These words were a powerful symbol of Afrikaner unity and their ability to survive. In his youth he had not questioned the policies of the National Party nor the South African Prime Minister, Hendrik Verwoerd— the father of apartheid, who had been assassinated eight years earlier in the parliament building, Cape Town.*

Jan now served in the cabinet of Verwoerd's successor and friend, John Vorster, who continued to implement the policies of his predecessor with enthusiasm. Jan, as a junior minister, found himself more and more a confidant of a senior member of the cabinet. The elder statesman appreciated Jan's refreshingly honest approach and his ability to bring forward new ideas while still remaining dedicated to the cause.

'The message from the 'North' is clear. If we continue to support the Rhodesian Government, especially with our paramilitary police in that country and the supply of arms, we will fail to resolve the conflict there. And there are veiled threats that the war may be on our borders soon. Let's face it, ZANLA is gaining ground in Rhodesia and simply is not going to go away. What makes matters worse, our sources indicate a coup in Portugal is imminent, and if so, the Portuguese will pull out of Mozambique, leaving FRELIMO with a free run of that country,' said Jan.

The elder statesman understood the gravity of the situation and he had listened intently. These were separate issues and each front-line State posed its own unique problem.

'Jan, let's tackle one difficulty at a time. What's your assessment of Mozambique?'

'South Africa needs the Mozambique port of Lourenco Marques to relieve our own over-worked harbours. Hydro-electric power is about to flow from the new Caborra Bassa Dam on the Zambezi in northern Mozambique. It rivals Kariba and will provide a valuable supply of power to our industrial base. Above all, migrant workers from Mozambique still represent twenty per cent of the labour force in our mines,'* said Jan.

For a moment he thought about what his protégé had said. 'Let me make it abundantly clear, Jan, while FRELIMO will not engage in open dialogue with us, we need to set the stage for winning them over. FRELIMO's leader, Samora Machel, poses a greater threat to South Africa than any other Black leader. Once FRELIMO comes to power, it will offer the ANC a safe haven under the protection of their forces. We need to negotiate with FRELIMO, but, I stress, we will continue secretly to support RENAMO with arms and training.'*

As far back as 1972, fearing reprisals from FRELIMO, forty Resistencia Nacional Mocambicana (RENAMO) soldiers had secretly crossed into Rhodesia to become known as the 'fifth column' in support of the Rhodesian security forces. Ever since, RENAMO had continued to recruit and build up arms within Mozambique against FRELIMO.

'Is that wise? RENAMO is seen abroad as a terrorist movement formed largely by dissident Black soldiers from the Portuguese Army in Mozambique.'

'Ja, it is necessary. We will continue to provide aid to RENAMO. This is the most effective way we can counter the communists on our eastern border. Even so, Rhodesia is our more immediate problem!'

Jan had always held the elder statesman in high esteem and agreed with most of his sentiments, but now for the first time he began to question this radical foreign policy. 'I see no change and agree, we need to continue supporting the Rhodesian security forces with arms for as long as we can.

While they are engaged with ZANLA, it keeps insurgents away from our northern border. And it is only a question of time before the Rhodesians lose the war.' There was something else nagging at Jan's mind, 'Surely Zambia remains the primary issue? We need to regain our export market. What we need to consider very carefully is, that this border closure and Smith's support for RENAMO, has not been received well by Kaunda in Zambia nor Machel in Mozambique.'*

'You are absolutely right, Jan. Zambia holds the key. All the Black front-line States will listen to Kaunda, including Machel. If we can get them to believe we are sincere about changes to our apartheid policies, then maybe this will allow us to open up the export market again and create an opportunity for dialogue with FRELIMO. Call a meeting with the Zambians and tell them we are sending our emissary to Lusaka to negotiate a deal with Black Africa. The message must be clear—let them think the prize is Rhodesia.'*

'Who will you send?' Expecting to be delegated the unenviable task.

'General Meyer. I will inform the Prime Minister of this and you can break the news to the cabinet.'

'I don't wish to question your judgement, but is Meyer the best choice? After all, they know he is the head of BOSS.'

The elder statesman gazed at him for a while before replying. 'Precisely! You know, power can be a convincing tool in itself. Even Prime Ministers can sometimes believe they have total control Jan, trust me on this—but maybe you're right, he should be accompanied by a neutral representative.'

Jan worked diligently on the terms of the proposal and in time the South African emissaries delivered their message.

'Have the subversive forces withdraw and Smith promises to discuss a cease-fire and peace negotiations in Rhodesia. Of course for their compliance...a show of good faith...certain guarantees concerning Zambian copper exports would be forthcoming.'

Landlocked, Zambia desperately needed a seaport. Hence, South Africa had made sure that all rail links out of Zambia were threatened, except the one leading south. It was economic blackmail and the leaders of both countries knew it.*

The delivery of Jan's speech was not going down well with the cabinet. Furthermore, it was causing the Prime Minister some disquiet. Apart from the PM, the elder statesman and Jan himself, none of the other members of the cabinet had been aware of the dialogue with Black Africa—and it showed.

'...so gentlemen, with the initial steps taken, we are now engaged in dialogue with the Zambians. I might add, this has not come a moment too soon. I'm afraid time is running out fast for Smith. The good news is the Rhodesian episode is still a useful diversionary tactic.' There were murmurs, but Jan proceeded, 'They continue to serve their purpose as an expendable buffer, allowing us to implement, uninterrupted, the policy of apartheid by introducing independent Homelands for Blacks.'

A minister asked, 'Concerning these Homelands—would this legislation not seem to confer on ourselves a spurious legality through the ballot box, as then, legally, all Blacks will be classed as citizens of these new satellite states and not citizens of South Africa?'* The minister turned to face his colleagues. 'What we are really talking about here is making our White minority appear to be a majority?'

Jan denied this, but the charge worried him. He knew the plan would have worked in time, except for one thing—they had underestimated the worldwide hostility towards apartheid. More importantly, he realised that from the floor had come support for his own unvoiced yet nagging doubts.

The United Nations had never accepted the concept of separate development and the Foreign Ambassador was hastily recalled from the UN to explain this failure to the régime.*

Jan heard the distinctive sound as her car pulled up in the driveway. He looked up as Carla entered, radiant and beautiful. She gave him a loving smile and placed her shopping parcels on a chair.

'What did you buy?' he asked.

'I'm not telling. You'll have to wait and see at the function tonight.' Adding coyly, 'And I bought something for afterwards!'

His eyes lit up in anticipation, and he looked approvingly at his wife's perfect figure, imagining her scantily clad in silk. Lingerie was Carla's one weakness and, he had to admit, on her it was his as well.

'Maybe we should skip the do,' he said. 'There'll be the same old boring ministers and their wives.'

'What! And spoil my fun.' Carla gave him a disapproving frown and changed the subject. 'Anyway, why are you in the lounge? You've got a perfectly good study which you never use.'

'Because I like to be with you and there's more room in here.' He started to retrieve piles of notes he had stacked on chairs and the floor while working at the large low coffee table. Clearing a space for her on one of the chairs and returned to the sofa they sat down.

'Phew! Cape Town was hectic.' She let her arms fall freely over the sides of the armrests and, discarding her shoes, stretched her legs out straight. 'What are you up to, Jan?'

'I'm worried, Carla...'

Before he could say another word she was on her feet. She knew what was coming. It had happened so many times before—starting like this, using her as a sounding board, then unburdening himself. Carla was always attentive. 'Coffee?'

Their lives had been full up to this moment and, as a minister's wife, life was never dull. She herself hosted several social parties a month. Then there were the customary duties of a minister's wife and events to attend, besides the more solemn side of her husband's career which meant he was often away from home. Jan always asked her to accompany him; sometimes she declined, but it was a good feeling knowing he cared. Minutes later she returned from the kitchen with two steaming mugs.

'All right, let's hear it,' and she cocked her head to one side.

'What concerns me is we have invested millions to secure the support of influential politicians in many countries abroad. I know you don't approve, but we have effectively lured those prepared to sell out for krugerrands. In this way, if I say so myself, we have spread our influence into media companies and businesses throughout the Western world .'*

'So write it off to expenses!' Carla quipped.

'That's not the point! The point is, our plans are not working!'

He had carefully avoided mentioning an incident when at one stage a leak had been imminent, and a prominent White professor of economics had threatened the régime with exposure. He and his wife were ruthlessly gunned down by agents of BOSS, not in some foreign capital but right in the heartland of South Africa.*

Jan spoke quietly. 'I'm becoming disillusioned with our party, Carla,' he said with some trepidation.

'No! Don't say that Jan,' she countered, concerned for his political career. It was his life!

'If anything, our plans have been ill-conceived from the start, and there are others in the cabinet who think like me.' Lately, he had begun to examine his politics more closely. 'I'm afraid apartheid has been a gross misjudgement in timing, what with the communist bogey being discredited. Now the tactics of BOSS are likened to that of the KGB.'*

'But communism is a threat to us, is it not?' She seemed unsure.

'Ja, of course, but in reality there is little chance of Blacks marching down Adderley Street brandishing communist slogans. They are not embracing communism in the way we first feared. What makes things worse for us is that Vorster still remains defiant in the face of worldwide condemnation. If everyone is against us, then surely something must be wrong! Are our policies too oppressive?' he asked.

'You know my opinion. We're not going down that road again are we?'

'No, darling, but I am also concerned with our involvement in the supply of arms to Rhodesia. Vorster always meets these accusations with categorical denials. If he can lie to the world about that, what *other* lies are *we* being fed?' Jan knew South African arms were being unloaded at railway sidings in Salisbury at that very moment.*

'Tomorrow the cabinet will consider our support and continued presence in Rhodesia...I will vote with my conscience.'

Jan returned home late the following evening, the burden of defeat weighing heavily on his shoulders as he walked into the room. He collapsed onto the sofa.

'What is wrong, Jan?'

'We lost by a wide margin,' he stated without emotion.

She had never seen him this depressed. Disregarding changing attitudes, the Cabinet had stood firm on its policy of support for the war against 'communist insurgents' in Rhodesia. It was felt this would take the focus off South Africa and delay the inevitable civil war within its own borders.

'Our Government's military strategists have devised a master plan to destabilise the whole of Southern Africa through violence, and the majority support this view. They reason, with cause, that the front-line States will be in so much turmoil as to forget us. I admit it's clever, because even if the White electorate find out, they will continue to convince themselves that this is essential to preserve our civilisation—while outwardly our propaganda machine will be busy calling for racial equality.'*

'My God!' Carla exclaimed, 'have they all gone mad?'

'The Prime Minister has asked me to set up another meeting with the Zambians. They are the only receptive channel open to us at the moment. And guess what! I might have to go along—this time to Paris—offering détente to the Black states. The question is, will they accept?' With lowered head he groaned 'Oh, Carla, what a mess!'*

30 July 1974

Dialogue with the Zambians almost collapsed at the outset. General Meyer of BOSS rudely thrust the Peace Manifesto back at the Zambians, saying that it would be South Africa who dictated the terms. *

Wiser counsels prevailed, however, through the mediation of Jan whom the South African Premier had, at the last moment, added to the team. He saw that the manifesto clearly contained concessions agreeable to South Africa which the General had seemed to overlook. News of the agreement was carried back to a jubilant John Vorster in Pretoria.*

CHAPTER 7

Addressing the 11th summit of the OAU, prior to
independence: "One does not ask a slave if he wants
to be free, especially after he has rebelled, and still less
if one is a slave owner."

> *Samora Machel*
> *President of Mozambique, 1975 - 86*
> *Killed in plane crash, South Africa, 1986*

The Overall Co-ordinating Committee (OCC) was inaugurated with the
express purpose of overseeing the defence of White Rhodesian
sovereignty. Its members consisted of top military personnel from the
Special Operations Committee; the Director of the Central Intelligence
Organisation; the Ministry of Foreign Affairs and Special Branch. Together
they formulated strategies to combat all internal and external threats.
The Committee met at Milton House in Salisbury every Wednesday.*

25 October 1974
The duty sergeant eyed the General's secretary, then glanced back at the
boardroom door.

'What's going on? They've been in there for ages.'

The secretary shrugged, pointedly emptying the ashtray again,
and continued to pound the keys of her typewriter.

She was curious herself. It was Friday, and usually she would be asked in
to take the minutes.

On this occasion General Bastion-Smythe was addressing the OCC on
a matter so secret that, for once, she was excluded. She felt it was a slight
on her trustworthiness.

Vic Hammond was a regular visitor to the General and he had turned up
a week ago for scheduled meetings held behind closed doors.

For the past hour the General had faced the members of the Committee,
who now listened to other senior members of the security forces give their
detailed appraisal of the current state of military play in the war zone.

Bastion-Smythe took the floor again and summarised the situation.
'Our forces are having great difficulty in containing the terrorist situation,
particularly with ZANLA escalating the war on our eastern border.
Unfortunately, they have made advances into the tribal trust lands.
Another potential threat is posed on our western flank by ZIPRA, entering
from Botswana and Zambia. If the terrorists continue to recruit at their

present rate it may be impossible to contain this onslaught, even if we maintain our kill rate. Gentlemen, we need is a new strategy.' He reached for a glass of water.

'What I propose is a revision of our Terrorist Release Programme of the sixties, except this time deployed in conjunction with a new 'agent'.'

This was met with silence.

The General continued undeterred. 'I know what you are all thinking but it was effective in Zambia and, if used in the manner described, it may yet prove to be the solution to our problem in Mozambique. With your indulgence, I have asked Chief Inspector Hammond to fill in the details. Before he begins, let me say that I cannot stress strongly enough the importance of this action, if we are to preserve civilisation in this part of the world, and ensure our hold on this country.'

Three hours later Hammond wrapped up his address with important bullet points highlighting the benefits to be derived from the new 'agent'. They desperately needed a solution. Time was given to debate while they appraised his proposal. Others were asked to provide opinions in support of the General's programme.

The vote was unanimous.

The chairman summed up the meeting, 'That's it then, gentlemen, we shall employ a two-pronged attack. In the first instance, we make conciliatory gestures to the enemy, in the hope that they scale down their operations, if only temporarily. This should give Vic's strategy enough time to take hold and allow us to regain control in the eastern sector. Should this fail—then God help us!'

The secretary outside suddenly stopped typing.

As if by some instinct, she pushed back her chair and approached the heavy wooden double doors to the main conference hall. Cocking her head almost imperceptibly, for a moment, she listened, then opened both doors. The Committee had concluded its business for the day and she stood aside to let the members pass.

The General and the Chief Inspector emerged together. Hammond was looking particularly pleased with himself, she thought.

'Thanks for your support, Rocco. I assure you, you won't regret it.'

'I sincerely hope not, dear boy. What is your next move, then?'

'Now we have the green light, I'd better get down to Cape Town and renew my acquaintance with our old friends.'

'I hope you know what you're doing.'

oOo

To the South, in Cape Town, at that very moment, Jan DuToit and the rest of the senate hung on every word of the Prime Minister.

Vorster was revealing his détente mission with Black Africa; coincidentally, it was ten years to the day since Zambia had gained its independence. His speech received mixed reactions from ministers who were only too aware of the recent 'swearing in' of the transitional Mozambique Government, which effectively placed that country in the hands of a Black majority. Appeasement and Black independence were not considerations any of them wanted to contemplate.*

oOo

To the North, in Zambia, the reaction was one of mixed blessings.

Gideon Chitiyo, the ZANLA representative in Zambia, was worried. He had been summoned to this meeting at the insistence of these four heads of front line-States, who had convened in the Zambian capital to resolve the 'Rhodesian' affair, but he was privy also to other matters. At that very moment there was a power struggle going on within his party. Besides, there was something of even greater concern and he voiced his anxiety:

'Gentlemen, if we can trust what the South Africans say we can expect a speedy end to this war. However, I have my doubts, I need hardly remind you that they have blown up the rail link to Dar es Salaam, besides supplying Rhodesia with arms and military personnel.' He turned to Kenneth Kaunda, 'And what is the cost to Zambian copper exports since the border closure with Rhodesia?'

He addressed President Machel, 'In Mozambique you are fighting a bitter war and your FRELIMO forces are hounded day and night by RENAMO bandits from Rhodesia, and within your borders. We know they are aided and abetted by the South Africans.' He stopped and glanced around the room. Assured of their undivided attention, he continued, 'Likewise, we hear from government in Luanda that the South Africans have committed full-scale attacks across the border into Angola in open support of Savimbi's rebel forces. It would seem to me that South Africa is intent on destabilising our countries! Is this not a policy of divide and rule?'

He spoke directly to Sir Seretse Khama, 'How many times have they crossed the border into Botswana, killing your people in pursuit of the ANC? They have an economic noose around the necks of Lesotho and Swaziland as well as the rest of us. And now they are advocating peace talks of behalf of the White Rhodesians. Gentlemen, I doubt if there is a shred of truth in their claim to this new-found generosity. Even so, I think we should give support to their proposal in the hope I am wrong. But I must warn you, it will not succeed unless the Zimbabwe liberation armies are unified, for it cannot be in the interests of White colonialists to deal with factious elements. May I suggest we err on the side of caution and be vigilant. If you wish, I will inform both Zimbabwe liberation armies of my suspicions. We know the South Africans have orchestrated this kind of subterfuge before, over many years. Why should they change now?'

Chitiyo glanced around the table.

'Vorster has said that if the ZANLA freedom fighters stop the war in the north-east of Zimbabwe, the Smith régime will be ready to talk to us about majority rule. If this is so, gentlemen, then ask the Rhodesians to release our leader from prison and let him come to Lusaka so that the South African proposal to end this war can be put to him.'

President Kenneth Kaunda of Zambia gave his consent, as did President Nyerere of Tanzania and Sir Seretse Khama of Botswana. They waited for the last man to deliver his verdict: eventually President Samora Machel of Mozambique agreed through his interpreter.*

16 November 1974

Lusaka still buzzed with excitement. The week before, Chitiyo's worst fears had been realised when, instead of the Reverend Sithole—Robert Mugabe, temporarily released from prison, arrived to see the four presidents. They had not accepted him as the new leader of the Zimbabwe African National Union (ZANU), the political wing of ZANLA, despite his election in prison by their Executive. Suspecting foul play, they sent him back to Rhodesia and insisted on the former leader, the Rev Sithole's presence instead.

Sithole had duly arrived in Zambia two days ago, accompanied by another member of the Executive, Maurice Nyagumbo. Maurice had reluctantly agreed that Sithole could represent ZANU/ZANLA interests and they went on to Dar es Salaam to meet Presidents Nyerere and Machel who had left Zambia shortly after Mugabe's visit. The following day saw Sithole's and Nyagumbo's voluntary return to prison in Rhodesia.*

Gideon Chitiyo pushed these bigger issues aside and concentrated on matters of immediate concern. He reviewed the report on his old friend the Major, now better known to his men as Mbada, 'The Leopard'. It indicated that his last sortie was his forty-eighth into Zimbabwe. It was an achievement made all the more remarkable because he had survived despite the bounty placed on his head by the Rhodesian Government. He was now a living legend among the freedom fighters. Chitiyo smile evaporated as he read the last page of the report, paying particular attention to the comments

Mbada had made about the conditions in his base camp in Mozambique. Something was wrong. A number of Mbada's men had fallen ill and there had been several fatalities. Disease was rife in his camp and Mbada was expressing concern for his cadre and requesting urgent replacements to keep his complement of men up to strength.

This kind of report was all too common. Something had to be done and he needed someone qualified to handle the situation immediately. He made his recommendation to the Chimurenga High Command.

David had been surprised to receive an urgent communication from Gideon Chitiyo requesting his presence in Zambia. Over the past two years, since his harrowing escape with Mbada from Rhodesia, he had been stationed at Mgagao training camp in Tanzania as the resident MO. The few times he had returned to the Zambian capital, he made a point of looking up Michael and on each occasion had found Mbada at the camp on the Zambezi.

He leaned closer to Chitiyo and listened.

'Dr Nyamande, you have no idea how hectic the last few weeks have been. I've had consultations with President Kaunda and many others...' as if this explained why David was there at such short notice. 'Thank you for coming down. Now, to the point: let me outline our position.'

David decided that the face opposite him was giving nothing away. Chitiyo, with his quick barrister's mind, was largely responsible for heading up ZANLA in Zambia, and there was talk that he would one day hold the highest office in a new Zimbabwe. The Rhodesians quite rightly, feared him.

'Both liberation movements have had their differences in the past and now our own party's suffering from a leadership crisis, though in the broader context of the war, this is of little consequence.' Chitiyo leaned back in his chair watching David's reaction. 'You will be aware that since 1973 we have tended to lean more towards Mugabe's leadership. Since then we have acquired new bases in Mozambique. These are for our continued offensive into the Eastern Highlands of Zimbabwe.'

This much David knew.

'It's no secret that our Executive has suspended Sithole, and that Robert Mugabe is now our leader. You can imagine what confusion it's creating within the Rhodesian Government. David, I am curious to find out where your allegiances lie.'

David was quick to respond, 'I am told they are calling Sithole a *Zvimbgawasungata,* a hunting dog or an Uncle Tom, for selling out to the settler régime. Apparently he is saying we must agree to a cease-fire. Of course, I want this war to end as much as anyone but Sithole is wrong to believe the settlers are sincere. Frankly, I care little for politicians but if Robert Mugabe has the foresight and sense to say we fight on, then...'

David thought possibly he had said too much, but threw caution to the wind. 'I'm right behind him and for continuing this war.'

Chitiyo smiled. 'We all want Robert out of prison, then watch out Rhodesia!'

David noted the reference and could not resist the question, 'It is odd that you call it 'Rhodesia', when we are told to call the country 'Zimbabwe' and the Whites...'settlers'.'

Chitiyo leaned forward. 'You are a South African although your father was Ndebele. Why didn't you join the ANC in South Africa instead of ZANLA?'

David cleared his throat. 'My father was a Zimbabwean. Anyway, I was on the brink of joining the ANC, when BOSS intervened. When this war is over, I'm returning to South Africa to fight on until the racist Boers are driven out.'

Chitiyo considered this. 'That's what I thought,' he said. 'Thanks for being so candid. Now let me answer your question. While the White settlers go on calling themselves 'Rhodesians' they distinguish themselves from us. We are really all Zimbabweans and when the régime falls Rhodesia will disappear. In the meantime I can focus on Rhodesians as the enemy.'

He paused, then continued. 'Your work in Rhodesia, or should I say Zimbabwe, and in Tanzania, has been invaluable to our war effort. But now we need a man of your calibre for a specific assignment in Mozambique. We have a nasty problem on our hands and urgently require a field MO to undertake an investigation of our front line camps as well as active medical duties. You come highly recommended.'

David could not think of what could be so important as to warrant investigation, so he asked.

'Can't be sure except...' Chitiyo handed over a thick dossier, 'we are extremely concerned that our cadre are dying, not in the fight to free our country, but from disease. The Chimurenga High Command says these figures are too high. I'm no doctor but looking at them I have to agree. To lose your life in the liberation struggle is one thing but to throw it away because,' he hesitated for a moment, 'it has been suggested that the lack of hygiene is the cause—is something else! Of course, if you accept the post you can expect to be in the combat zone for some time. I'm sure the transfer details can be sorted quickly at your end?' He did not wait for an answer but continued, 'You will operate from bases near to the Rhodesian border. We have fought alongside FRELIMO in Mozambique for most of this war. Now, as you probably know, the coup in Portugal last April means that FRELIMO will wrest power from the Portuguese in Mozambique next year. After their withdrawal, Machel has promised free elections and has assured ZANLA of continued support for our fight. We will be allowed to move our headquarters to Maputo, which means your transfer is simply premature. In the meantime, you are to make recommendations on hygiene, so we can issue new guidelines to the camps and their medical units.'

There was no reason for David to hesitate. He would go wherever he was needed. 'I will first have to clarify the position with my senior officer before I can give you a firm commitment.'

Gideon Chitiyo held up a hand as if to restrain him. 'Your commanding officer has already been briefed. All I need is for you to accept the post now. The alternative would be for you to be posted here, in Zambia, or you could return to Dar es Salaam.'

'In that case, I accept.'

Chitiyo leant forward and signed a document on his desk. 'Good! I expected as much.'

David watched him knowing this was the end of the interview, yet there was still unanswered questions. 'Can I have a straight answer. Why was I picked for this task?'

With that Chitiyo sat back and smiled. 'I suppose you have every reason to be curious Doctor. I see no harm in you knowing that you have your good friend Mbada to thank. It is on his recommendation that you are here and I suppose you will want his address in Mozambique. David, I'll be straight with you, my colleagues and I have been watching you for some time. There is a great future for you in our country. Let me say, most of what you hear about our current situation is just 'talk'. If you know anything about the origins of our party, you will remember that we had to change our name several times, each time the government banned us. That worked then. Now much the same can be said of our current tactics. I think we have confused the enemy in that they are not altogether sure of where the real threat lies. I will bet a million to one they try, at some stage, to create an alliance with either ZANLA or ZIPRA, so they can play one off against the other.' He hesitated, 'That's their way; you, as a South African, should know that's what the Nationalist government has managed to do for many years.' He leaned forward. 'We are playing them at their own game. If necessary we will continue to splinter our political parties and military alliances until the enemy is never entirely sure who they are attacking or negotiating with from one minute to the next.'

He rose and extended his hand. 'By the way, you might like to know that your appointment to Provincial Field Medical Officer was approved last week in Tete Province, with the blessings of our Executive in prison. As the representative in Zambia, let me welcome you to ZANLA!'

oOo

David read the dossier given to him by Chitiyo. There were medical reports of sporadic outbreaks of disease here and there covering a wide range of illnesses. He noted that someone had already sifted out deaths arising from trauma and war injuries, or attacks by wild animals, as well as snake bites and drownings. He was mildly surprised to see they included documentation from both liberation armies spanning the last seven years.

Picking up another sheet he read on:

ZIPRA Medical Secretariat, Zambia, July 1967
Report by Dr Able Padwera
Lusaka—Zambia

During the course of my duties I visit the various satellite posts on a rota system. Since my arrival I have become increasingly alarmed by the number of deaths that have occurred within my area. Recently, I have become aware of outbreaks of a number of different diseases in ZIPRA camps in Zambia. Within the limitations of this field unit, I have been able to evaluate slides and establish the causative micro-organisms that have simply not responded to a broad range of antibiotics. The high incidence of pneumonia infections is alarming. On several occasions I sent lung-biopsy specimens for analysis to the Zambian Centre for Tropical Diseases. The results came back always showing Pneumocystis carinii infections. This suggests that many of our soldiers are not battle-fit, for this micro-organism is usually associated with some kind of lung impairment. I can only conclude that the standard of hygiene and sanitation is a main contributory factor and therefore will introduce corrective measures.

Subsequent files presented similar patterns of illness to the previous report, highlighting only too clearly that a very real threat existed behind the front line. The fatalities seemed higher than normal, considering the causative micro-organisms responsible for the outbreaks. The next report read:

ZIPRA Medical Secretariat, Zambia, Sept. 1969
Report by Nurse Winnie Tangweno
Mkushi Camp—Zambia

Last month the Rhodesian SAS attacked our base on the Copperbelt, where I am stationed. On my return from an excursion into town, my Land Rover was ambushed and the

201

driver killed. I only just managed to escape. Making my way back to the camp through thick bush, I narrowly missed running into the Rhodesian SAS, who were escorting three captive ZIPRA soldiers from our base.

Hiding in thick undergrowth I observed their departure in four helicopters. On arrival at the camp I found most of our men dead or wounded. I was surprised to find that all the prisoners I had seen were patients from my sickbay. They all had influenza. They couldn't have put up any resistance to this attack....

This account was odd to say the least and he wondered why it was included.

He compiled a breakdown of all the reported cases, listing the prime causes of death: pneumonia, tuberculosis, cholera, enteric fever, malaria, amoebic dysentery, tetanus, sleeping sickness and, finally, causes unknown. Next he counted the number of fatalities against these headings and noted whether the causative micro-organisms had been isolated and their origins ascertained. The figure for pneumonia seemed excessive.

He calculated the death rate of soldiers and found it far higher than the normal index, well beyond acceptable levels. He wondered how many unreported cases there had been from these outbreaks, and without records, whether they had cleared up once proper medication had been administered. Then there was the civilian population to consider which was not included in these figures.

The final entry was from the medical directorate of ZANLA which wanted to establish the sources of these increased incidences of disease. The directorate wanted him to evaluate the data and make firm recommendations before the situation got completely out of control. Of one thing David was sure already: there was an acute shortage of medically trained field personnel to deal with the problem. Especially given the increase in numbers of young recruits from the eastern provinces of Rhodesia, arriving on a daily basis at these remote bases in Mozambique. He established that over a seven-year period there had been nearly fifty deaths a month. The figure was far too high. He had to act—and act quickly.

He set about planning the arrival of personnel and vehicles from Tanzania for his new field unit—he would meet the convoy near the Mozambique border the following week—then began the logistic nightmare of listing and ordering the required equipment and supplies.

David used the little free time he had to visit Michael and found the new home his friend and wife had moved into. Trish answered the door.

'Can I help you?'

'Morning. I'm David Nyamande. Is Mike around?'

Her surprise was followed by a heart-warming smile. 'Come on in, come in, David. I have heard so much about you.' She ushered him into the lounge. 'Can I get you a coffee or something to eat?'

'Coffee's fine.'

'I am so pleased to meet you at last. You know, Michael never stops talking about you—he will be so sorry to have missed you.'

'Sorry, but my last stay in Lusaka was such a rushed affair, much like this trip, I didn't have time to come round. Where is he then?' David asked.

'Working, where else!' she said irritably.

'What! On a Sunday?'

She realised what he had meant. 'No, no, not in Chilanga. He is out in the bush. You know Michael, he's married to the bloody Zambezi. A field trip he calls it—for the past six weeks!'

'Any idea where he is?' enquired David.

'At his Chirundu camp, but it is difficult to find if you are thinking of going down there. Four hours' drive at least.'

'I see...' he was mildly surprised. He had expected to find Michael with his wife and child in Chilanga. He caught her puzzled expression. 'Sorry, I was thinking—last time I came down to Zambia, Michael was in the Valley then. I take it, he's at the same camp where he rescued Mbada, his brother and myself from Rhodesia?'

'Yes, he seldom moves from there. He told me about your escape. Typical of Michael!' She smiled and did not seem in the least bit surprised in the knowledge that her husband was ferrying soldiers across the river.

David tossed the decision around. 'I think I'll go down and see him.'

'Let me get that cup of coffee.'

He heard the kettle boiling as she returned with an infant in her arms.

'Meet Bernstein junior.'

David rose and peered into a cherubic, if unimpressed face.

'Ah! So this is the young man, Michael wrote about—looks a lot like his dad. How old is he?'

'John's just on eight months,' and, gazing adoringly at her son she said, 'I'd better put him down.'

An hour later David was trying to get away.

'And you won't forget to give him the message?'

David promised and, with deliberation, engaged first gear.

'You have a nice day,' she said, waving him goodbye.

He drove south towards the Zambezi, reminiscing about the night of their crossing. Mbada had expected to see Michael, but for Michael and David the surprise had been total. Because of the treacherous road and late hour, they had decided to stay overnight. The Teacher was made comfortable and the three men had stayed up until dawn, draining Michael's bar and catching up on each other's news. At dawn they had loaded the Teacher into the back of Michael's vehicle and he had been driven to a Lusaka hospital. A memorable week had been spent by the three trying to drink the city dry before David was transferred to Tanzania...he almost missed the dirt track and turned off into the dense bush.

Michael speculated on who was coming down the track. Simon was currently touring the wildlife sanctuary on Lake Tanganyika in the northern province, so it was would not be him. He half hoped it might be Trish, who came down now and then, if simply to plead with him to return to Chilanga and his son.

His surprise was complete when he saw David and they wrapped their arms around one another.

'What do you mean for the night? You must stay longer...'

Michael was persistent and eventually David gave way.

'You win, Mike, but I must be back in Lusaka by midweek. I leave for Mozambique on Friday.'

Now he had time to inspect the camp, David marvelled at his friend's improvisations. Michael had built a lean-to which acted as an open-air laboratory. It was kitted out with microscope, test tubes and innumerable bottles containing an assortment of liquids, all meticulously labelled.

Time flew. Michael dragged David off every morning in search of tsetse fly or to capture game. He was trying to dart a 'nyala' which he maintained was a fairly rare antelope with a long, striped shaggy brown coat and a white chevron between its eyes, thought to be immune to 'sleeping sickness'—he wanted a blood sample. After several gruelling days of walking through the maze of dense undergrowth, along the river bank and ploughing their way through razor grass, that left paper fine cuts on their exposed limbs, they negotiated yet another thorn bush. David was convinced that there were no nyala within 100 kilometres of the Zambezi Valley. The only redeeming aspect of the trek was that they had talked and laughed virtually non-stop, which he thought, on reflection, probably accounted for the absence of game. He looked forward to the end of each day when, on returning to the camp, they were greeted by the smell of meat cooking over the open fire. The brandy would come out and he made a discovery: the paraffin refrigerator in the laboratory contained little else but ice. Bathed and fed, they would sit by the fire on the river bank and drowsily while away the evenings to the sonorous calls of hippos.

David's last day seemed to come suddenly. Sensing that their parting might be permanent, Michael took a break from his work and they made an early start and short work of a new bottle of brandy, his refrigerator producing the ice and the Zambezi River the mix.

Michael pressed David, not for the first time, to recount his and Mbada's escape from Rhodesia. He roared with laughter, picturing their encounter with the security forces at the tsetse fly barrier at Kariba.

'I'll get you a job in our Department, if you like!' He doubled up.

'You can laugh. Your face was a picture when you realised it was me you were collecting with Mbada,' said David.

'Collecting?' said Michael incredulously. 'More like rescuing! Admittedly you're the last person I expected to see crossing the Zambezi.'

'Enough about the war, Mike. What about you and Trish? She looked as miserable as sin when I left Chilanga.' David hid his true concern. Over the past few days he had received the impression that Michael was withdrawing not only from civilisation but from family and friends as well.

'Oh! It's nothing. Just domestic blues.'

'Come off it, Mike. We've been through a lot together. You know there's more to it than that.'

'Yeah! Yeah! I suppose you're right. It's just that she's always socialising in Lusaka when I'm at HQ, and expects me to go along. Why can't she reciprocate and spend time with me in the bush?'

'Because, dammit, she's got an eight-month-old infant. As a doctor I can assure you, no mother would be prepared to take the risk of bringing a child out here.'

'I suppose you're right,' Michael agreed. 'Maybe I should wait a while.' He grinned without any sincerity, 'She'll come round!'

'You're incorrigible,' David laughed. 'Here, it's empty,' he said, passing his glass for a refill.

By late noon and more than a little hung-over, David was ready to go. He engaged the four-wheel-drive and turned to say farewell. Michael, he thought, already seemed distant—almost vulnerable out here alone.

'You look after yourself, Mike, and thanks for everything.' He felt depressed, not knowing if they would meet again and searched for something to say. 'Oh! Grief, I almost forgot. Trish said to remind you, Paddy's arriving this coming weekend, and she's expecting you to meet him at the airport.'

'Bloody college friend of hers from the States,' he grumbled.

'I know...Trish said,' David replied. Waving goodbye, the last words he heard his friend mutter were, 'Bet he's a teetotaller!'

oOo

Mozambique was different to Zambia and Rhodesia. In the distant past, the Zambezi had created vast flood plains on its relentless thrust towards the Indian Ocean. The region was now flattened and sparsely populated except for small herds of game that roamed the horizon-stretched sea of flowing tawny grass. Dotted here and there were clusters of tall palms etched against the molten colours of the setting sun. The palms, reminders of Arab traders who had come this way in the distant past.

Seemingly out of place in this vast landscape, David's small convoy, consisting of two Fiat ambulances and three diesel trucks, cut a dust trail crawling south-west towards the eastern border of Rhodesia. He and his accompanying staff, comprising two female nurses and four male orderlies had made painfully slow progress all day. With the approach of evening he decided to stop and make camp near a small settlement.

Early the following morning they arrived on the banks of the Zambezi River at one of its widest points near the town of Tete in central Mozambique—the far side barely visible. The convoy negotiated the swift current by pontoon and landed downstream from Tete.

The sun climbed to its zenith while they traversed the road south, climbing the hilly terrain that forms the western border of the country, until they crossed the Ruenya River. Studying the map intently, David realised Mbada's outpost was no more than 30 kilometres east of their present position according to Chitiyo's directions. He decided he could afford the time to make a personal detour without delaying the convoy's progress. Besides, he had calculated that even if the road restricted his speed, he would catch up to them by morning.

Three hours later, approaching Mbada's camp, David braked suddenly. In front of him were the remains of several huts. He hesitated a few minutes scanning the terrain, then quickly climbed out of the vehicle and cautiously made his way down the road towards the camp. He was sure he was in the right place and it was deserted. Not only that, but every hut had been burnt to the ground, and some of the remnants still smouldered. There were several fresh graves to one side and little else to suggest the camp had been recently occupied. He searched the ground for tell-tale signs of a fire-fight and was relieved to find no spent cartridges. Still, he felt uneasy. There was nothing here to explain the absence of all life from this camp. He looked back towards the freshly turned mounds. The graves were unmarked. He did not want to speculate, but with dread he found himself wondering if Mbada's remains lay under one of these mounds. Hurriedly, he made his way back to the vehicle and just after nightfall he had caught up with his convoy.

Having travelled south all day on a parallel course to Rhodesia's eastern border, David's field unit arrived at its destination. Their base was

Nyadzonya camp, situated near the Rhodesian border to the left of the main road, alongside the Nyadzonya River—close to its confluence with the Pungwe. This small refugee centre for victims of the Bush War served as a staging post for those joining up to fight for ZANLA. It was within easy reach of two other military camps—Tatandica and Chimoio—where FRELIMO troops were garrisoned.

David climbed stiffly from his vehicle, when an orderly ran up to him.

'The Commander wants to see you in your office, Sir.'

David had hoped that these formalities could wait until the morning. He was tired and depressed still thinking of the deserted camp, but followed the orderly inside.

He found Mbada installed behind a desk. With open arms Mbada gestured as if in answer to his question, 'Beat you to it! Arrived a few days ago. Asked for a transfer and here I am. Meet your new Provincial Field Operations Commander for Manica Province.' A grin softened his leathery face. 'I believe that makes me your boss.'

David was elated and relieved. 'What happened to you base camp—I've just come from there?'

'Bad news I'm afraid.' We had an epidemic of some sort; lost many good men but the rest of us seem to be okay,' he hesitated as if remembering something. 'I would rather forget what happened, anyway I'm pleased you are here, you can check us over tomorrow. Come on let's get you fixed up.' In under fifteen minutes of David's arrival he had ousted an irate Sectional Logistics Officer to have his friend billeted in the closest accommodation next to the building allocated as the hospital.

David was satisfied with his quarters but shook his head in disbelief. 'You're not serious, there's hardly enough room for a sickbay.'

Mbada laughed, 'Come on, we can sort that out tomorrow. Best have your staff unload your equipment now—you are going to be busy first thing in the morning, what with the illnesses around! Then let's get over to the canteen so you can tell me your plans.'

Over a drink and in answer to Mbada's probing questions and genuine interest, David outlined his new ZANLA role in the war zone. Their bond of friendship was stronger than ever. Mbada put the empty glass down.

'It's too hot in here, let's grab a few beers and go down to the river.'

'Suits me, better than brandy, any day!' said David. Mbada looked on questioningly, so he told of his last visit to Michael.

'...I take it young Bernstein is still at his camp on the Zambezi?'

'Yes. He sends his regards,' David passed on the greeting as promised, if somewhat overdue.

'Strange one, that Michael! Can't say I know what makes him tick!'

David smiled. He was aware they had had their differences but still, Mbada and Michael shared a marked respect for each other.

They stood up to leave. 'If you insist on celebrating I brought a crate of beer with me—you can help me carry it down to the river,' suggested David.

The late afternoon was spent in idle chatter on the river bank. This was one of those rare interludes in the armed struggle when the two friends found time simply to relax.

'...indeed 'he' was a blow to justice, civilisation and Christianity.'

David coughed and spluttered at the end of Mbada's rendition of Ian Smith's infamous independence speech. He wiped the mirth from his eyes. 'A nice play on words, you missed your vocation. You should consider TV.'

'I don't suppose you know this, Doc, but I trained to be a radio announcer for the Rhodesian Broadcasting Corporation before the war. After this is over though, I don't think I want to continue with it.' He turned to face David. 'I've been considering a bit of a career change. Possibly wildlife conservation, or maybe write—someone has to tell the story of our struggle.' Mbada raised the beer to his lips, glancing again at David, trying to judge his reaction.

'Get on with the story then.' Smiling, David stretched out, finding a more comfortable position on the river bank.

'Maybe I'll describe some of my experiences when I trained in China.' Unexpectedly he added, 'Hell, I hated their food! It's all fish and soup, you'd starve Doc. Give me *sudza* and meat any day.' Lost in thought he lobbed the empty bottle into the river and contemplatively watched it bob downstream.

David interjected, 'Haven't you lost the thread of your story a bit?'

Mbada eyed him disapprovingly. 'All right, but first give me another beer.' David dutifully removed the bottle tops and passed one over. 'You'll like this...I'll tell how ZANLA and ZIPRA gave the White settlers a bloody hard time,' really warming to the part and punctuating his words with his fist. 'Ah! But it was ZANLA that caused the problems for the Whites, and annoyed the heads of the front-line States, who had stupidly supported the Ndebele dogs...'

David glanced up. 'I think my friend is forgetting what tribe I come from! Besides, our forces are not divided on tribal grounds.'

Mbada grinned. 'No *mukoma,* it's just the beer talking, but honestly, I get angry when I think how short-sighted ZIPRA is. You are right, it is not the Ndebele.' He slapped his chest. 'In here we are all Zimbabweans.'

The baking sun and brew had its effect. They lay back on the river bank, silent, watching the silhouettes of two young boys fishing for bream oblivious to the blood-red orb that formed a backdrop to the trees behind them. The boys' energetic antics, trying to avoid their catch's poison-spiked dorsal fin as it flapped on the mud bank, brought back childhood memories. An egret started the cry, and a riot of sound erupted as others joined the evening chorus. Both men grew melancholy—the perfect day was ending and tomorrow would bring back the realities of war. They stayed a while, until the sultry day had all but vanished and the first mosquitoes began to appear, driving them indoors.

Mbada was as good as his word. The whole camp seemed be lined up for sick parade in the morning. By lunch-time David was exhausted and went to lie-down. An hour later he strolled back into the hospital and found Mbada sitting there.

'What's up?' he enquired.

'Nothing Doc, other than the fact you've been holding out on me.' Seeing David's perplexed smile, his head fell back in laughter. 'I'm referring to your nurse, Jessica, who is at this moment making me tea. Now that's a beautiful woman.'

As if on cue Jessica entered—tall and slim, the khaki uniform accentuating her curves. They were not altogether sure if she had overheard their conversation, but her smile suggested she was aware of being the centre of their attention.

Within days David had the hospital organised and running. He realised that Gideon Chitiyo had grossly underestimated the situation. Existing facilities were meagre and disease rife. Immediately, he introduced strict hygiene measures to reduce infection. The daily treatment of illnesses and minor ailments soon became routine and he set himself a tough regimen of biweekly inspections of all ZANLA camps up and down the border.

David saw little of Mbada over the next few weeks despite living next door and, not surprisingly, as little of nurse Jessica. Eventually he had to hunt Mbada down and confront him. 'Either marry the bloody girl or give her back. I am short-staffed enough as it is.'

oOo

2 February 1975

Near an isolated tourist resort in the Rhodesian Eastern Highlands, two Australian hitchhikers zipped up their anoraks against the bitter cold. Leaving their overnight stop in the hope of catching a lift with early morning traffic, they rounded a bend in the pine forest to find a camouflaged figure lying sprawled by the roadside. They approached cautiously, fearing the worst, for frost still lay on the ground.

Having established that he was still alive, if barely, the young man sent his female companion running back to the mountain inn they had just left—a kilometre down the road—while he waited. Holding the man close, he tried to provide warmth from his own body. There was no telling how long he had lain there—with freezing temperatures in the Highlands it was a miracle he was not already dead.

The figure stirred, then spluttered, 'ZANLA...freedom fight...' and lapsed into semi-consciousness.

The young man heard a car coming towards them. Suddenly, without warning, the freedom fighter had a seizure. The spasm ceased abruptly and he went limp—he appeared to have stopped breathing, the young man fought desperately to revive him with mouth-to-mouth resuscitation. The car jerked to a stop and the girl jumped out, followed by the hotel manager.

'Strewth, he almost died on me. We must get him to a mission hospital.'

oOo

20 March 1975

The Nyadzonya camp was bustling. Mbada had chosen the former option, making David his best man at the open-air wedding—a short and unpretentious ceremony held on the parade square which sometimes doubled as a football pitch. The *camarada* rallied, making up for absent families and friends. The day's celebrations had offered brief respite from the anxieties of war.

Later, David lay under the mosquito net, listening to the sounds of the ebbing marriage party. The laughter of the last of the revellers still mingling with the sound of drumbeats, as the dancing carried on. He envied Mbada and Michael: right then he too wanted a woman he could love. He wondered what Michael would be doing at that precise moment...probably still sitting on the banks of the Zambezi! He was saddened that their friend could not be here on this day, but Zambia was too far and anyway here, he would be in danger as the war zone was a no-go area for White civilians.

With his arms behind his head, staring at the ceiling he thought again about the communication which he fortunately intercepted that morning. It would have marred the day, and he had deliberately withheld it from Mbada—Gideon Chitiyo had been assassinated by a car bomb in Zambia two days before. There seemed little doubt as to who was responsible. The Rhodesians had placed a significant bounty on his head.*

oOo

In time the Rhodesian CIO, the Central Intelligence Organisation, in Salisbury, where Vic Hammond had recently been transferred, received news through *skuz'apo* infiltrators of Mbada's presence at Nyadzonya and of his recruitment drives in Rhodesia. He now considered the information with fervid interest. Suddenly it struck him what lay behind the report.

'Bloody hell!' His associates glanced up from behind their desks. 'The bloody cunning bastard. Do any of you realise who we have here? I can't believe it! For the past year we have been looking for the Major, who seems to have evaporated into thin air. The bugger was here all the time. Gentlemen, I hate to inform you but the Major and Mbada are one and the same person.'

Hammond knew that Mbada's elimination was now paramount. If anyone else in the Department got to him first, and alive, Mbada could cause his dismissal by mere mention of the missing communiqué left at the farm.

While cross-border raids were routine from either side, it irked him that the CIO had previously ruled out large-scale attacks on prominent bases such as Nyadzonya. It was deemed that to target those bases would be folly in view of current world opinion.

Vic Hammond came up with an idea on how to get Mbada.

oOo

1 June 1975

David saw something was troubling Mbada as he strolled into the hospital, his head down and bunched hands shoved into his trouser pockets.

'It's Jessica. She received a letter this morning from our Sectional Operations Commander in the Nehanda operational area. Her mother is dying and obviously the poor girl wants to go home. Doc, what do I do?' This was the first time he had asked David for advice.

'I wont let her go alone and I can't leave my duties here!'

The question caught David by surprise. 'I never thought I'd hear you ask for help...!' The look that passed across his friend's face left the reply incomplete. Instead he said, 'I'm sorry. I was thinking—you don't have a problem. If I understand correctly from our Political Commissar, you had a recruitment drive over there last month, didn't you?'

'Yes!' Mbada said, 'So what?'

'Simple—follow it up with a personal appearance—that's bound to boost recruitment figures.' The inference was plain.

The transformation was remarkable as a smile spread across his face.

oOo

17 June 1975

Victor Hammond paced the operations room floor. He had received confirmation that Mbada had been co-ordinating large-scale recruitment drives for young Blacks in Rhodesia. They would then be sent for clandestine training in Mozambique, later to return and join military cells in specific sectors of Rhodesia. He knew, too, there had been was a sizeable gathering of *terrs* in the area over the past few days.

His informants, who had infiltrated Nyadzonya camp, now assured him the recruitment drive was scheduled for tonight. News that Jessica was in the village had been received less than an hour ago. Her mother was ill, of that he had made certain. Dysentery was not difficult to pass on to an unsuspecting person with the help of the *skuz'apo*. He had baited the trap: now it was a question of whether Mbada would fall into it.

The cordon was roughly six kilometres square. The Air Force's combined strength of sixteen helicopters, three Provosts, four Dakotas and seven Trojan aircraft had carried a dozen companies of troops, supported by an engineer squadron and a mortar platoon. That night the cordon closed in and, by first light, reports came in confirming small groups of terrorists moving in the general direction of Mauswa Village.*

Hammond punched his fist into his palm. 'I've got that son-of-a-bitch. All I need do now is close the door,' he said exultantly.

By nightfall the brigade major reported six kills and one terrorist captured. The radio crackled into life again. 'Two large parties, moving east—we're in hot pursuit.' The radio went dead. Moments later the voice was back, 'We have them pinned down—at least eight *terrs*!' Amongst the background static Hammond could hear gunfire. The military commander gave specific orders as Hammond listened anxiously then the radio went quiet. He could only imagine the battle raging out there in the night. Suddenly the voice on the radio snapped, 'They're gone! One minute they were here...but they've just disappeared! We're searching for their tracks...'

As the night drew to a close, his hopes diminished he mouthed quietly to himself, 'Please don't let him slip through the net.' By morning twenty-six freedom fighters, including Mbada, had managed to do just that.

Within the hour a Land Rover pulled up inside Mauswa Village.

Jessica was brutally arrested and taken to the operations HQ. Realising the girl was not going to co-operate, Hammond vented his rage on her. The interrogation was violent and obscene. Having beaten her almost senseless he proceeded to rape her in front of his men. Then he shot her. Later her limp, lifeless body was thrown out of a moving vehicle in front of her mother's hut. She would serve as a grim reminder to others in the Kandeya Tribal Trust Land, the consequences of harbouring terrorists.

oOo

Everything at Nyadzonya camp changed. David tried to console Mbada but he refused to discuss what had happened. Not even the news of the new FRELIMO Government, celebrating its independence and granting ZANLA the right to operate legally from within Mozambique, drew any response.

'Come on, Mbada, let's go down to Chimoio. I understand Robert Mugabe and Tekere are there, setting up the new headquarters—our government in exile.' Their leaders had been set free by the Rhodesians in the hope that this would stop the attacks.* David's attempts to distract Mbada from his grief were ignored and he decided to leave him alone, watching him go about his duties as if he were an automaton. Besides, David was saddled with a growing problem of his own.

A number of their rank and file, who had been captured during engagements with the Rhodesians, suddenly reappeared in the camp. They claimed they had been released in the hope that, on their return, they would convince their *comrades* that the Rhodesians were sincere in wanting to end the war. Why else let them go? What concerned David was that most of them were seriously ill. The fatality rate was rising alarmingly. He had nagging doubts. These were opportunistic infections, too frequent, yet in not one case did their immune systems appear to be suppressed. Then there were unsubstantiated reports of men simply dropping and dying in the bush but nobody would show David where they were—too afraid of whatever had caused their deaths. Superstition became rife and he noticed attendance at the sickbay dropping daily, despite an increase in illnesses.

Later that morning he received a radio call from Chimoio camp, 65 kilometres to the south, where FRELIMO currently shared the old Portuguese garrison town with the newly installed headquarters of ZANLA. Their doctor had been out into the field to investigate an outbreak of disease in a remote village. On his return he stated he had found everyone dead. Now he, too, was ill. Could David come and assist? Glad to be able to help, he picked up his medical bag and shouted for a driver.

What he found shocked him. The doctor lay unconscious, and examination showed he was haemorrhaging from the eyes, mouth and nose. The running discharge from his bowel was mostly bloody, as was his urine, evident from the fouled sheets. There had been massive blood loss present in the now congealed vomit that threatened to overspill from the stainless steel kidney dish at the bedside. His entire body was covered by scaly skin, fluffing off leaving behind exposed bleeding and suppurating tissue.

'It's haemorrhagic fever!' David exclaimed. 'I've never seen anything like this but I would bet on this being a classic case.'

Quickly he took stock of the situation.

'Who else has come into contact with this man in the past seventy-two hours?' he demanded.

Several of those present raised their hands.

'I want all contacts isolated immediately. As of now, nobody enters or leaves this hospital. Is that clear?' David turned to the senior nurse. 'You were right to call me. Frankly, I do not know what we are dealing with here. It may be airborne so we are going to take every precaution. First, are the telephones working? Then, we need blood samples.'

Issuing urgent instructions to the nursing staff to gown-up immediately and to wear disposable gloves and masks at all times, he then ordered all surface areas in the entire medical block to be liberally doused with phenol, followed by formaldehyde.

By late afternoon the sound he had anxiously awaited could be heard approaching. A light aircraft buzzed the building, then landed in a nearby field. The pilot reluctantly took the boxed vials left conspicuously on a table alongside the improvised airstrip. Five minutes later he was taxiing down the runway, ready to fly north. David's patient had died three hours ago. Over the next few days there were no further outbreaks.

David waited anxiously for the inevitable call.

'Hello, Dr Nyamande?' The voice sounded hollow and distant and he was forced to shout over the static. 'This is the Director of the Tropical Diseases Centre in Zambia. I can confirm that in the blood sample we received is *Marburg*—a virus sometimes called Green Monkey Fever. Your patient was probably bitten by a vervet monkey which I understand is a possible host.'

David cut in, 'Not likely. By all accounts he caught it from some villagers. They're all dead.'

'How is your patient?' the Director asked.

'Also dead!' David replied bluntly.

'Not surprising,' the Director stated matter-of-factly. 'Frankly, not many people walk away from this one. Strange though, yours is the second most southern case yet recorded. Two Australian hitchhikers in Johannesburg went down with *Marburg* disease in February. One confirmed fatality. There is speculation about them being in the Eastern Highlands of Rhodesia earlier this year.* Not far...' Static broke up the radio call.

'Sorry, I missed that!'

'I said, not far from you. I wonder if there is a connection between the cases? Well, let me know how you are getting along and if I can be of any further assistance....'

David thanked him, then referred him to the Chimurenga High Command for payment. David replaced the telephone and sat perplexed, '*Marburg*! What in hell's name will come along next?' Ten days later he lifted the quarantine and drove back to Nyadzonya camp.

5 July 1975

'David, I have come to say goodbye.' Mbada was having difficulty in getting it out. 'I've given up this post and talked HQ into giving me active duties again. I can't stand being around here any longer.'

David tried to say something but Mbada cut him short.

'This place reminds me too much of her—I'm leaving tomorrow. Apparently they want someone to scare the hell out of travellers on the Beit Bridge road. At least it's better than this!'

He looked up at the ceiling. 'David, I think I'm actually cracking up. These bastards have finally got to me. You know I went back and found her body—just dumped in the dirt. These men are mad.' He corrected himself. 'No, they're not men, not even dogs. On the way back here I passed through a small village. The Rhodesians had been there first.' He paused, and then with a tremor in his voice continued: 'David, a child, a small child not more than two, had been picked up by its feet, and...and impaled on a stake in front of its mother. I'm not ashamed to admit that I didn't cry for Jessica, but I cried then. Where's their humanity gone? Are they all mad? I heard yesterday that the Selous Scouts raided a defenceless mission station, killed the priests, then burnt it down. Of course they are blaming us but my men were not in that sector at the time. Why, in God's name, did they do such a thing?'*

oOo

The damn pub was out of tonic water, so Vic Hammond sat at the far end of the bar on his sixth double 'gin and it' made with a liberal shot of vermouth. He had driven south that morning because it was a harrowing journey from Salisbury down to Fort Victoria at night. Holed up in this one-horse town en route to South Africa, he was waiting for a friend from the local police station to join him. In the morning he would join the civilian convoy and receive a military escort to the border—to minimise the risk of a terrorist attack.

The pub was filling up and two more farmers joined the regulars in a night of social swagger. They propped their FN rifles in the gun rack, never far from reach. The farmers were angry because *terrs* had raided their respective farms the night before. Drinks flowed and Hammond listened as one gave a detailed description of the damage to his burnt-out barn and tractors, while the other complained bitterly—he had lost fifteen heifers, hamstrung by the *terrs*.

As he started drinking his seventh gin of the night someone said, 'Sterilise the *munts*, put something in their mealie meal.' There was laughter

215

followed by a consensus of approval from most of those at the bar.

Hammond caught the mood. 'Why bother when you can shoot the bastards. More fun that way,' he insisted. His comments drew a few laughs and he enjoyed the attention. 'That's why I am going south. I have a deal with the South African Defence Force. Just watch for the new shipment of arms come up by train, the moment I get back.'

Someone commented, 'A bullet's too good for a *munt.*'

Downing his drink, Hammond stood up, unsteady on his feet. 'I have one better than that...' and promptly received what felt like a mule kick to his right side which did not help his cirrhosis.

'Sorry, my friend seems to have overdone it a bit.' A uniformed officer steered him in the direction of the door. Outside Hammond spewed up gin and kudu *biltong* leaving the bitter taste of juniper in his mouth.

Sobering up enough to glare at his assailant, he croaked, 'Christ's sake, what did you do that for?' It was the first time he had managed to speak since leaving the bar.

'Vic, you know loose talk in a public place can be dangerous, particularly when it concerns the matter in hand,' his companion warned.

Hammond pulled his car over and joined the queue. It was nearing sunrise and the civilian convoy already consisted of three vehicles waiting to travel south. He knew from previous trips to South Africa that they would incur a delay before being escorted to the border. There was always the underlying fear of attack from terrorists. Recently some sales representatives from Johannesburg had tried to run the gauntlet through the Lowveld. They had driven straight into an ambush. His friend from the night before had said they had died before their vehicle had even left the road.

Hammond saw a soldier approaching in his rear-view mirror. Winding down the window he waited until the soldier was within earshot. 'Is there going to be the usual bloody wait?'

The young trooper was clearly used to irate motorists and, barely checking his stride, cocked his head. 'Noth'n stopping you driving on right now without the escort....' Leaving the rest unsaid he strode out of earshot.

'The sassy little twit, I'll...' Hammond muttered under his breath. The effrontery of the lad needled him and he was tempted to find his superior officer, obviously in the lead Land Rover. His side still ached from the kidney punch he had received the night before and he dismissed the idea, deciding it was too bloody early in the day to vent one's spleen—especially after a particularly heavy night.

Instead, he reached for an antacid tablet and a copy of a confidential report lying on the passenger seat.

Hammond laughed, then doubled up in pain. Wheezing, he said to himself, 'Nice touch, Vic me old son. Spare them indeed!' He had witnessed the post-mortems at the new laboratories in Salisbury. Nine small children, four women and seven men had been slaughtered. Their execution had been necessary. The aluminium box at his side contained tissue samples, all that was left of their earthly remains apart from their ashes. Besides, he could not understand all the fuss—after all, they were only *munts!*

He faced a tight schedule but he was looking forward to the trip, assured as ever of being well dined by the Defence Force in Pretoria. Even so, Cape Town remained at the top of his agenda. His contact had promised to come up with an even more potent weapon than before. He had to have this weapon at any cost...the war in Rhodesia was in the balance, and if current field tests were any indication, this kind of weapon would tip the outcome in their favour...he was even prepared to steal it, if that was necessary.

Hammond read his report again and smiled. He had deliberately fudged the account and hoped this would get what he saw as wet liberals, in the newspaper and the other concerned government departments, off his back.

oOo

Mbada had chosen the spot well: a small game ranch tucked between the Nuanetsi and Liebigs Ranches. Their names simply did not do justice to these vast stretches of territory. Both were greater in size than some counties in the UK, and reputed to be among the largest ranches in the world. A narrow strip of land not more than a kilometre wide divided them. The terrain was flat and densely covered by mopane trees. The region had seen drought conditions for years and now ground cover was sparse. Yet the bushveld teamed with impala, zebra, giraffe and buffalo, sustained by the head-high leafy branches of the mopane. A short distance into this maze, visibility fell to a few metres. It was said that many an unwary hunter had succumbed to Lowveld mopane fever—the trees high enough to prevent a man from getting his bearings and too low to offer shade. Blinded by the sun and parched by the severe heat, a wrong turn and hundreds of kilometres of horizonless wilderness would lie ahead—sending its victim bush-mad—slowly dying, provided lion or leopard did not scent him first.

It was through this wasteland that Mbada had brought his men from the Mozambique border, confident they would not be tracked or followed. Now they lay by the side of the main road in the deep depression, which had been excavated by the rancher to create a waterhole, in his bid to attract game from neighbouring ranches. Game ranching and cattle were the only viable resource this region could sustain.

The day before, they had observed passing convoys to assess their strength. Mbada drew the Teacher's attention to detail.

'See the long-wheel-base Land Rover in front, the machine-gun mounted on its roof.' Several vehicles passed. 'Right, here they come again. Look at the rear—a vehicle carrying four soldiers, and another. Always the same formation!'

His brother nodded in silent acknowledgement.

The convoy disappeared and Mbada sat up. 'The civilian vehicles are always placed in the centre. So tell me, little brother, how do we tackle this situation in the morning?'

oOo

Through a mist of fitful sleep, Hammond heard the driver of the lead Land Rover sound his horn. He saw the soldier running back towards him. 'About bloody time!' he muttered to himself.

Coming alongside, the young trooper shot a glance at Hammond, '*Terr* Alley up ahead—next stop Beit Bridge.'

'Cheerful sod,' Hammond murmured.

The convoy snaked out of the town and Hammond counted nine civilian cars along with the three security forces vehicles. They passed the signpost pointing to the Zimbabwe Ruins which lay off the main road, to their left. Hammond involuntarily tightened his grip on the steering wheel—this was the last outpost of civilisation before the border 280 kilometres to the south.

Presently the drivers in the convoy were pacing one another at 90 kph along the narrow asphalt road. The occasional oncoming vehicles would force them onto the dry sandy verge with two tyres gripping the road surface while the others spun on loose dirt, throwing up blinding clouds of dust and stones—a serious hazard to the cars behind. Hammond concluded that this precarious method of passing at speed was not for the faint-hearted.

In sections the road widened and they relaxed as they sped on through the sweeping bends past massive granite koppies, then on to the flat terrain of the Lowveld again. The sign up ahead read Nuanetsi and they drove on without incident.

Suddenly, tail-lights flaring bright-red caught him unawares.

Hammond hit the brakes hard. 'Shit!' he exclaimed—then audible above the squeal of hot rubber on molten asphalt, he heard the riveting chatter of automatic gunfire. 'Shit!!' Everything happened so quickly that there was no time to be afraid. Instinct took over—he pulled the wheel to the left to avoid colliding with the VW Kombi in front.

'Bloody hell! The bastards are on this side,' he shouted to no one but himself, looking directly into the white flashes coming from the ditch. He yanked the steering wheel to the right and the car slewed across the road as the attack was pressed home.

In blind panic, the driver behind attempted to overtake; instead he landed up ramming his vehicle into the side of Hammond's Renault. The momentum carried them both off the road into the depression on their right and to an abrupt stop. Hammond was stunned, trying desperately to comprehend what was happening. Horrified, he saw the lead Land Rover, or rather what was left of the smouldering chassis, roll down the road—the cab and its occupants were missing. A rocket had hit dead centre.

'Oh! Christ!' he moaned, still gripping the steering wheel. A bright flash and flying debris caught his eye and he sat riveted in the seat, watching the drama unfold in his rear-view mirror as a second army vehicle disintegrated.

Now under heavy fire, the last remaining vehicle was putting up token resistance. The MAG fell silent—the trooper slumped lifeless over the weapon, raked for a second time by the deadly AKs fired from concealed positions around the waterhole.

'I'm going to die,' Hammond thought as his vehicle was hit. Above the gunfire he heard the right front tyre explode and his car slumped down on one side, then he felt, rather than heard, the two rear tyres deflate as further bullets tore rubber from the rims. He was vaguely aware of the firefight that now seemed be developing somewhere to the rear of the convoy. He fumbled in the glove compartment for his police issue 9mm pistol.

The attack was over in less than three minutes: now the silence was unnerving. Mbada viewed the prostrate body of the dead RLI soldier, not more than twenty paces from where he crouched. The trooper had shown great courage in the face of overwhelming odds. He had charged their position with his Sten gun blazing. He must have known that he was unlikely to hit anyone. When he was twenty-five paces away, Mbada shifted from the prone position to the half-kneel and pumped the trigger. Five rounds found their mark ending further resistance from the security forces.

His men waited until he raised his hand, then as arranged, all but two climbed to their feet and ran in the direction from which the convoy had come. A kilometre down the road they set up another ambush in case there was a rearguard.

Covered by his two *comrades*, Mbada checked the vehicles to make certain the soldiers were dead, and rounded up the civilians.

'Get out,' he bellowed at the white-haired man in the Renault—he poked him in the chest and raised his gun menacingly.

'Okay. Okay. Don't shoot,' Hammond pleaded as he joined the small group by the roadside. Mbada and his men pushed their terrified captives towards the waterhole. Fifteen minutes later the Teacher and his patrol returned, confident that there were no vehicles following.

Hammond feigned ignorance of the language as he listened to Mbada giving orders in his native Shona.

'Taking out their radio means contact was broken with their HQ. By now they will have realised something is wrong.' He looked at his watch. 'They should be with us within the hour.' He hesitated. 'I'm not sure if they'll come from the north or south, or by helicopter.'

The Teacher cut in, 'Maybe all three?' Mbada shot a glance in his direction.

'You could be right, so get busy and be quick. I want everything of use to us taken out of those vehicles.'

While the search was in progress, Mbada turned his attention to his captives. He had no way of knowing that the white-haired man was the same person he had vowed to kill and avenge, for what he had done to the headman's young wife the year before, let alone the score to settle for Jessica. For Hammond that was not the case: he recognised Mbada instantly as the Major from the hundreds of photofits and posters he had personally organised over the years. This was the terrorist he had pursued for so long.

Hammond was incensed as he looked at the faces of the survivors. The women were crying while young children clung to their skirts, the men, petrified with fear—they would all die. His hatred was all-consuming and threatened reason.

'Search them,' Mbada barked the order. A cry from the Renault drew his attention for a fleeting second. 'Mbada, come and look here—in this briefcase.'

Momentarily distracted, Mbada glanced over to where the Teacher was waving something. A movement caught his eye and he turned back to the body search, to find himself staring down the barrel of a gun which had materialised in the white-haired man's hand in the middle of the group. His men, unaware of this new development, went about their search.

Mbada dived for the pistol, grabbing Hammond's wrist even as he fired. A hammer-like blow hit Mbada high up in the chest, ricocheting off his left clavicle and, burying itself under the scapula. The impact of the 9mm bullet threw him backwards. Surprisingly there was no pain—just a numbness.

In shock, his reflexes seized but his mind raced. As if in slow motion he saw the children duck, their mothers scream open-mouthed, while the men flung themselves to the ground, as if to dissociate themselves from the attack. Staggering under the blow, he saw the white-haired man step out of the crowd and advance towards him, the weapon now centimetres from his temple. In that instant, the nearest of Mbada's men brought his weapon to bear in a scything arc cutting ruthlessly through the crowd to take out the assailant. The AK's 7.62mm rounds found their mark, tearing into Hammond's body. The pistol fell from his hand and he crashed to the ground, together with two other fatally wounded travellers.

Galvanised into action, the Teacher was at Mbada's side even before he had sunk to his knees. Mbada glanced up at the Teacher standing over him. Unlike Mbada, he was of slight build. They had fought many battles together and always he had addressed him as Teacher in an attempt to hide his affection for his younger brother...Mbada fell silent. He thought, 'Why does he have to see me die? No! I cannot let it happen, not like this.' He pushed all notion of death from his mind.

Through a haze Mbada sensed what would happen next.

'No! Teacher, leave these people,' he moaned. 'It was this white-haired

221

devil and he is dead.' Hammond lay face down where he had fallen and Mbada managed to glance up at the pitiful group of travellers. 'Go now, before I change my mind.'

Transfixed, they stared, not daring to move.

The wound was beginning to make itself felt and he looked down to see blood spreading over his tunic. 'Teacher, get them out of here, now—send them off down the road. Then get the medical bag and be quick!' he ordered urgently. A wave of excruciating pain hit, sending him onto his back and blinding him temporarily.

After fifteen minutes, the powerful analgesics had dulled the searing sensation sufficiently for him to sit up. Enduring the discomfort, with a field dressing stanching most of the bleeding, he whispered to the Teacher who had taken on the role of medic, 'It's agony! Every time I move this arm, the pain shoots across my chest. Can't you put it into a sling?'

Mbada was worried. Thirty-five minutes had elapsed while his men attended to him. And his injury made it impossible for him to tackle the arduous escape route back to Mozambique.

He stood up gingerly. When he was sure he was not going to keel over, he pulled the Teacher aside. 'If you all go now, not even the Selous Scouts will track you. You'll only be slowed down...!'

'Forget it, Mbada,' he snapped, but concern was written all over his youthful face, '—and don't argue. I have already spoken to them and it is agreed, we're staying with you.'

Mbada gave an uncharacteristically quiet order to his men. 'Okay! Get one of those civilian vehicles back on the road and change tyres around if you have to. I want it running in ten minutes. We'll head for the mission station near Fort Victoria. I can get help there and there'll be less chance of them finding us among friends.' A shallow cough sent stabbing pains through his chest and shoulder and he fought to stay upright. He checked his spittle for blood, then looked up. 'Come on. Don't just stand around. Get moving,' attempting to stifle another involuntary cough.

Relieved to hear him bark the command, if weakly, his men had the VW Kombi back on the road in under five minutes. They were climbing on board, when one of his men emerged rapidly from the bush.

'Where's he come from?' asked Mbada quietly.

'I sent him into the mopane with the settlers...' the Teacher tried to explain.

'Did I not say, to take them down the road?' snapped Mbada.

'I know! But when the security forces arrive, they'll tell them exactly which way we went. Now they'll waste hours rounding them up, before they start looking for us.' Mbada managed a smile but was dubious about the delay. This road led straight to the enemy. Either way they would meet soon enough.

The engine burst into life. The vehicle suited their purposes admirably and there were two spare wheels, unwittingly provided by a young family who were leaving the country for good, to seek fortune and security elsewhere. The vehicle climbed back onto the asphalt. Mbada lay on the camper bed, and the Teacher sat next to his elder brother holding his hand. Aware that Mbada was trying to hide his distress only served to increase the Teacher's anxiety. They headed north and he found a suitable distraction.

'I think you should look at this,' said the Teacher. He gave Mbada a file from the briefcase which he had managed to hold onto in the confusion.

Its contents concentrated his attention despite the pain. Scanning the pages quickly he became increasingly agitated, not because of the wound, but in appraising the gravity of the information his brother had found.

'We have to get this back to the High Command!'

His voice was back and he was seething with anger. 'The bloody murdering bastards!' Propped up on an elbow he flipped another page. 'This is utter madness!'

He reached for the briefcase and rummaged through its remaining contents with one hand, finding medical slides and other less important documents. Handing the file back to his brother he said, 'Hold onto these whatever happens.'

He lay back, desperately trying to formulate a plan. All he knew was that he had to find a way back to Mozambique with these documents. They held information so important that the outcome of the war possibly hinged on their notifying the Chimurenga High Command of their findings.

Suddenly the vehicle slewed left; the swaying jarred his elbow into the side panel causing a searing of pain to grip his shoulder and chest. The Kombi straightened and shot round a bend.

The Teacher answered his unspoken question. 'We just passed an army vehicle going in the opposite direction—doing at least 120 kph.'

The helicopter landed at the ambush site and the RLI troopers fanned out. A soldier knelt down. 'Hold on *china*,' then he shouted, 'Live one here— at the water-hole.'

Hammond lay where he had collapsed. He held on to consciousness by a tenuous thread knowing he had to act, while he still could. He made one final choking effort. 'The *terrs*—Fort Vic—in a Kombi!' Then overcome with loss of blood and shock, his body slumped and he passed out.

'Fox-trot Tango to Fox-trot Bravo. *Terrs* coming your way in a VW Kombi, over.'

'VW? Watch out!!! Eh! Fox-trot Tango, bloody hell, we just passed them. Okay, we're turning round. Fox-trot Bravo, over and out.'

Mbada said what they were all thinking, 'It won't take them long to figure out what's happened, then they'll be onto us like a pack of dogs.' Sure enough, fifteen minutes later they saw a vehicle fleetingly in the distance. All too soon they could identify it as a Land Rover and slowly it closed the ground between them.

He was more worried because the Rhodesians could deploy helicopter gunships and, if so, it would not be long before they arrived. He glanced back. The gap had narrowed even farther.

'What weapons were on that vehicle?' he asked urgently.

The front passenger had had a clear view when they passed. 'Machine-gun on the roof and at least half-a-dozen men in the back.'

Mbada scanned the passing landscape. 'Dammit!' he swore. The terrain had changed to savannah grasslands. There was no ground cover. He voiced his doubts. 'We can't stop and fight and it won't be long before they bring in more men and block the road. Our one hope is to press on and try and lose them.'

The aged vehicle was running at maximum speed. Mbada shouted as he looked around the cab. 'Quick, kick out the windows.'

Within the confined space of the Kombi there was a hive of activity as first windows were kicked out, then every removable object was flung into the path of the approaching vehicle. The windscreen blew out beneath a well-placed boot and the rush of air was exhilarating after the stifling heat of the interior; but now increased wind resistance slowed their speed perceptibly—the vehicle behind was making alarming headway.

The driver momentarily lost concentration while shielding his eyes from the wind and cut onto the verge. Through the dense dust cloud thrown up by the Kombi's wheels, he caused the driver behind to lose valuable seconds as he swerved to avoid the hurtled scattering debris before him.

Suddenly there was a burst of gunfire, kicking up the ground to their left. Mbada realised their pursuers were, as yet, still too engrossed in the obstacle course to be able to take an accurate bead on them. Thankfully a bend came up and they were concealed briefly behind a clump of trees.

Their vehicle now bristled with guns, two at the front and the rest aimed in the direction of the pursuing army vehicle.

The Land Rover rounded the corner after them but the occupants had not opened fire. Mbada was momentarily puzzled noticing further, it had slowed.

'Roadblock!' shouted the driver above the rush of the wind.

'So that's it!' Mbada thought and swung round abruptly. A thousand metres ahead were two Land Rovers blocking their path.'

'Keep going—all guns to the front!' Mbada yelled.

The gap closed rapidly and at five hundred metres the RLI opened up. Mbada's driver did his best to weave from side to side, aiming at a small opening to the right of the roadblock. Inevitably bullets found their mark. The RLI soldiers, though revealed by their gun flashes, were impossible targets for the men in the lurching Kombi. Mbada staggered forward to lean over the driver's shoulder. At three hundred metres he screamed into the driver's ear, 'Go left, go left.' The vehicle shot off the road. At the last moment he shouted, 'Fire!'

Half-a-dozen soldiers sprang from cover, running for their lives. The Kombi bore down on them. It struck a knee-high anthill a glancing blow and veered to the right, striking one man as he tried to evade its path. The vehicle bucked over the fallen trooper, flinging two of Mbada's men out through the open sliding door. One managed to grip onto the side, his legs dragging over the rough ground, while the other catapulted directly into the path of the fleeing soldiers.

The driver fought desperately to regain control. The sound of rending metal from beneath the Kombi drowned out all other noise. He pressed the pedal to the floor and gunned the motor to its limit, fighting the jostling vehicle back onto the asphalt. A fresh hail of bullets hit them from behind.

Mbada screamed, 'Off the road! Get on the verge!' The driver hesitated, knowing this would slow them down.

'Now! Do it now,' Mbada bellowed, his injury forgotten.

Immediately those behind were enveloped in billowing clouds of choking dust. Unable to see them, the soldiers hit the vehicle intermittently. Rapidly the gunfire receded and within moments had ceased. They were alone.

'Okay! Back onto the road and go like hell.'

First satisfying himself that his brother was uninjured, Mbada's eyes darted from man to man. The attack had taken its toll. The guerrilla who had dragged himself back into the cab was little the worse off for his experience. Four were dead. Another had minor injuries, leaving the Teacher and three others unharmed. Then there was the driver.

Blood was oozing over his lap; he had been hit, at least once in the stomach, but gripped the steering wheel with a fierce determination, refusing to look down.

A signpost loomed up. It read 'Zimbabwe Ruins' with an arrow pointing to the right. 'Take it!' Mbada ordered and the driver nodded grimly. The road seemed to go on forever and, in what may have seemed to be a callous move, Mbada had them jettison their dead *comrades*. He reasoned their departure might make the groaning Kombi go a little faster, with every second making the difference between their living or dying.

The Teacher yelled a warning, 'Helicopter! Coming up fast to our left.' Flying at ground level to intercept their path, above the trees, the Allouette was visible, yet still distant, then briefly it disappeared behind the bush before reappearing.

Zimbabwe Ruins—the ancient stone fortress came into view.

Mbada ignored the fast-approaching aircraft as he assessed the terrain. Stone workings ranged over much of Rhodesia but nothing matched the scale and magnitude of these structures. He took in the remains of the high outer-walls on the plain—it was too exposed.

He tapped the driver on the shoulder. 'Straight ahead...to that hill.' It was a natural fortification, away from the main ruin.

Cutting over the empty public car park, the driver reached the base of the granite outcrop. The neat signboard, to one side, read 'The Acropolis'.

The driver killed the engine.

'Out everyone! Out—follow me.' Making his way painfully uphill, Mbada stumbled and turned to look back. He saw his men assisting their injured *comrades* and beyond them, on the open plain, he could see a number of White archaeologists who, having deserted their dig, were now scurrying for cover together with several Black security guards.

The climb grew more difficult and Mbada was eventually forced to rest. In the distant past, defenders of this unknown civilisation had the foresight to fortify this hill with closely packed stone walls. He glanced up, half expecting to see a gunship bearing down on them, but silence still reigned—a solitary vulture circled overhead in an otherwise empty sky. Mbada reached a parapet wall and ducked down waiting for his *comrades* to catch up. By the lack of activity it was obvious that the helicopter had landed and, glancing over the rampart, he saw enemy soldiers cautiously moving in to surround their stronghold. Slowly the cordon was being pulled tighter and reinforcements would arrive soon. He looked at his watch. There were four hours to nightfall. Could they survive that long?

'You men spread yourselves along this wall and cover the approach.' He looked around, 'They must come up the same way we did.' Satisfied, he gave fresh orders, 'Teacher, come with me.'

The gradient became steeper and the pain in his chest intensified but he pressed on until they reached the crescent-shaped summit. The view was not a pleasant one. From this vantage point they could see the concentric ruins on the plain below, already swarming with troops.

Military vehicles continued to arrive in the public parking area and men disembarked, all intent on the same objective. A second helicopter landed but the pilot did not switch off the engine. Vic Hammond lay on a stretcher in the back with a medic fussing over him regulating a drip. These *terrs* had tried to kill him—now he wanted revenge, wishing he could lead the assault.

Hammond demanded the presence of the commanding officer to whom he explained his predicament. He pointed out that it was imperative that they recover the briefcase and its contents, and the possible consequences should anyone escape. He carried the appropriate authority and, confident that the situation was understood and that his orders would be adhered to, he allowed himself to be evacuated out of the battle zone. Lifting off, they circled the Acropolis fleetingly and he caught sight of movement near the crest—then they were gone from his view.

High on the hilltop, the two brothers stared at one another. Mbada put down his weapon and reached out with his good arm, draping it round his younger brother's shoulders. Mbada spoke gently to him.

'I will not be leaving this place, but you must. It is vital you get back to Mozambique. I want you to find the Doc at Nyadzonya and give him the file. He will know what to do with it.' Mbada had an anxious moment, 'You still have it, don't you?'

His younger brother smiled and tapped his chest. 'I'm going to keep it with me at all times.' He looked at Mbada. 'They've been killing us off all along and we didn't even know it.'

Mbada studied the sensitive face. 'That's right—that's why you must get back. This information might stop this war.'

'But I cannot leave without you,' the young man pleaded.

Mbada was beginning to feel distressed and held his young brother at arm's length. 'That's a direct order. This information is more important than either of us. You will leave later—when it's dark.' He softened his tone. 'Look, I'm almost finished. I couldn't walk a kilometre in this state,' and he spat into his palm. The crimson-tinged spittle betrayed signs of internal haemorrhage. 'Not as lucky as I thought! Promise me one thing, you'll go home when you have the chance and tell our family that I love them dearly.' Mbada had to steel himself. 'Now go and bring the rest of the men up here—then we'll talk later.'

The sun was setting and his men sat grim-faced watching the enemy move from cover to cover, until finally they secured the base of the fortified hill. Mbada studied their movements, thankful that whatever their reasons they had decided to spare them until the dawn. Of one thing he was sure, there was no risk of being bombed by a Canberra. This site was a national monument which precluded the usual kind of assault. Floodlights were now being set up below, bathing the hill in stark relief.

The driver died during the night, leaving the others to wait for the dawn. They had no illusions as to their fate. At times they fell silent or spoke openly to one another about their lives and of loved ones. At 11.30pm Mbada called the group together.

'Thank you for your loyalty over the years. I could not have expected more...I am honoured to have served with you.'

There was a quiet chorus of, 'And with you Mbada.'

After a moment of silence he continued, 'Tomorrow is our last battle. It is fitting we fight from a place of our ancestors. These settlers wage war and, by God, tomorrow they will know what it is to fight Zimbabweans.'

Just before 3.00am Mbada nudged his brother. 'Come, it is time for you to leave. I think I've found a passage that will take you down to the plain—and it's in the moon's shadow, but you will have to cross open ground.' Mbada crawled along an overhang that seemed to protrude into space. Towards the edge, he ran his hand over the hard granite until he found the root system he was searching for. 'Earlier, I crawled down some way, but with this arm.... There seems to be about a three-metre drop to a ledge. From there on, maybe another thirty metre climb to the base. Seems fairly easy, but you must be careful!'

They fell silent.

Mbada embraced his brother. 'When this war is over and the killing stops, come back here one day...now go, please.'

Turning his back, he heard the Teacher's boots scrape the granite walls as he descended. He prayed it would lead him to safety. He sat waiting for the dreaded sound of gunfire which would indicate that his brother had been seen—possibly killed. It still had not come as the sun rose and he felt the crushing weight lift from his heart.

oOo

25 August 1975

Victoria Falls saw the meeting of Kenneth Kaunda, John Vorster and Ian Smith; together with Bishop Abel Muzorewa and overshadowed by the presence of General Meyer of BOSS. Normal trade relations would resume. In a seemingly conciliatory gesture, the South Africans agreed to withdraw their military personnel from Rhodesia.

Jan DuToit was troubled at the conclusion of the talks. What had not been said, however, was that they were leaving behind fifteen officers attached to Rhodesian Combined Operations Headquarters and fifty helicopters, together with pilots and technicians seconded to the Rhodesian Air Force, for another year—in a secret assistance programme code-named Operation Polo.*

CHAPTER 8

"The Blacks cannot gain political rights through
violence. Constructive change can come only by
acquiescence of the Whites."

Henry Kissinger
US Secretary of State, 1973 - 77

February explained the inclement London weather. Inside the cavernous
halls and corridors of Whitehall, however, huge ornate Victorian radiators
suffused the air, countering the cold.

2 February 1976
Settling behind their desks, staff from the Foreign Office prepared to begin
their daily task of sifting through dispatches from around the world.

Suddenly the silence was broken. 'Good Lord! This will cause a stir.'

The supervisor was not given to a sense of the dramatic and he did not
expect it from his subordinates. There must be something quite out of the
ordinary in the communiqué. This happened from time to time. He took the
telex from his hapless clerk 'Interesting!' was all he said as he handed back
the report. 'Have your summaries on my desk by noon, please.' He quietly
left the room and made his way to the Department Head's office.

'I think you had better take a look at this, Godfrey.'

It was from the British-based International Defence and Aid Agency
in Mozambique. Godfrey Macmillan read the short message.

> *TOP PRIORITY STATUS*
> *Alleged use of chemical or bacteriological agents by the*
> *Rhodesian security forces against ZANLA, FRELIMO and*
> *Mozambique civilians. Report from ZANLA medical officer*
> *confirms outbreaks of unexplained illnesses....*

The scrambler sprang to life as a green light flashed above Godfrey's head.
There was absolute silence, the acoustic insulation dampening out the
background noise of the transmitter.

The supervisor spoke over the intercom, 'Your satellite connection—
you are through to Tete, Mozambique—Sally's on the line.'

Immediately, the intercom went dead and he waited for the security beep.
The booth was equipped for normal two-way transmission without the use
of a handset. His senior operative came on the air.

'Morning, Godfrey.' She never broke the Department's cardinal rule by calling him 'sir'.

'Hello, Sally. What's this I hear about chemical warfare? A bit over the top isn't it?'

Sally hesitated. She knew her boss had at some stage in his career been stationed in Southern Rhodesia before UDI and often referred to it as 'God's own country'. In the end she decided there was no sensitive way to say this.

He waited impatiently for her reply.

'With respect, I questioned Dr Nyamande myself. His credentials are beyond reproach.'

He cut in curtly. 'All I'm asking is why would they want to do it?'

There was no hesitation in her response. 'Because they are losing this war both militarily and ideologically.'

'Steady on, old girl. I see your point but do you really think they would go *that far?*' He knew these people. 'My God,' he thought, 'they're nearly all British!'

'It might explain why the Rhodesians are stepping up their border raids...'

Godfrey interrupted her. 'Hold it right there. It is all circumstantial. Give me facts, girl—facts. This, and your previous concerns about atrocities does not in any way prove that the Rhodesians are using these weapons, as you imply. They simply suggest that the situation has deteriorated further.'

'I hardly need reminding. We have a wealth of reports on the atrocities committed by both sides in this affair.' She waited for his response. When there was none she continued, 'The Rhodesian security forces are annihilating civilians—entire villages of men, women and children. There definitely appears to be an emerging pattern to these events. What's really worrying is not the frequency and the totality but also the timing of these attacks. We need to know what has triggered the use of these appalling methods?'

'What do you mean?' he asked.

'Remember when, back in August 1971, Rhodesian troops shot an 'alleged' terrorist...after cutting off his hands and feet, and then began reprisal raids in the Mukumbura area in Mozambique, even after admitting they had made a mistake?'*

'Yes, yes! I do read your reports. Please get to the point.'

'And you recall the Singa massacre where they shot the chief, his pregnant daughter, villagers and even babies? Everyone, except for two children who were, thankfully, overlooked. Well! I now suspect the reason behind those attacks has to do with what we are now confronting.'*

He frowned. He did not allow for sentimentality.

Sally paused, then continued more quietly. 'Countless others have died in similar incidents. Since then the Rhodesians have been systematically wiping out entire villages. We also understand they have taken prisoners back to Rhodesia for interrogation who have subsequently disappeared.' She added quickly, 'You don't go around annihilating all the inhabitants without a strong motive. If you take Dr Nyamande at his word and put these raids together they form a definable blueprint for eradication...'

'But you still haven't explained the relationship between these attacks and chemical warfare,' he said irritably.

'I believe there is something very sinister behind these killings. Most of these people were civilians.' At times like this her boss aroused an intense animosity in her. 'What concerns us here are as yet unconfirmed reports of illnesses resulting in too many unexplained deaths. Our operatives are currently engaged in field investigations collecting data from mission hospitals with the help of Father de Costa.'

Godfrey looked down at his nails. Here was the beginning of something. He knew the gut feeling well. There would almost certainly be substance to her allegations.

'What is your summary of the situation then?' he asked.

'It certainly seems as if the Rhodesians are trying to cover-up this flagrant misuse of power, by eradicating all evidence of some prior covert experiment, with either a chemical or biological agent. What we don't know is how long they've been using these agents or, for that matter, what they have deployed. It may have been going on for several years. What we can be sure of is that this supposition seems to fit the facts on the ground.'

'It's all so hard to believe. Where on earth would the Rhodesians get this kind of weapon? They do not have the expertise or capability!'

She came back on cue. 'I know, that's just the point. But the South Africans do, and South Africa has a military presence in Rhodesia.'

He was starting to feel decidedly uncomfortable. He was privy to certain classified information which had not been passed to the Prime Minister. Suddenly, for the first time, past events and Sally's allegations seemed to fit in the most frightening way. 'My God, Sally! If you're right on this, it would be too horrible to contemplate. Please correlate the evidence you have. Come to think of it, map out a timetable of events relating to the situation. Let's see...' he thought fleetingly, 'I want you here, in my office, by Friday.'

6 February 1976

Godfrey was appalled. The debriefing, concerning Rhodesian security activities in Mozambique had taken several hours. He did not like the sound of it at all. After the door had closed behind Sally, he sat and read the dossier from cover to cover. Putting it aside he was forced to conclude that the Rhodesians had indeed deployed some kind of chemical or biological agent in the war zone; of that there seemed little doubt. What sickened him was that he, personally, had made certain recommendations to the Prime Minister, who—on the basis of what he had been told—had tried to reason with the Rhodesians in the decade since UDI.

Now Godfrey was being forced to see the consequences of not having faced up to the Rhodesians' treachery from the outset. To have done so might have meant that none of this would have happened. Military intervention, proposed by some quarters, might have diverted this tragedy.

The repercussions to a senior civil servant were obvious—heads would roll and from the top. But even if he was to be one of the sacrificial lambs, his resignation would be handled with absolute discretion. These facts could not be divulged; if this leaked to the media, it would certainly topple the government—except this went much further!

Godfrey pressed the intercom. 'Margaret, come in here for a moment.'

His secretary entered. She had never seen him so upset before.

'Will you get the PM on the phone...no, on second thoughts I'll contact him in the morning.' He looked at his watch. 'Contact the CIA. I need to speak to the Director.' Godfrey was becoming very agitated. 'And when I am done, put me through to MI6.'

'Are you sure you're all right, Godfrey?' she asked.

His response was curt. 'Yes! Now please do as I ask, the Director of the CIA—immediately.'

oOo

18 March 1976
The recently appointed Director of the Central Intelligence Agency, George Bush (DCI), was now settled behind his desk. His sudden introduction was unique in that he was the first 'politician' to take up the post of director with the agency. His appointment followed the dismissal of his predecessor by President Ford. There were extremely sensitive issues that had to be dealt with urgently. Bush, had the backing of the President, and immediately replaced fourteen Agency department heads with carefully chosen successors. He in turn wanted 'his' men in the right places.*

Ellis, as a department head in the CIA, was immediately asked to lead an investigative team and submit recommendations concerning certain allegations in Southern Africa. The headlines in the newspaper in front of him screamed 'Harold Wilson resigns. PM gives no reasons.'*

He listened intently to a senior officer on his team who concluded with, '...there have been other resignations—God dammit! It'll be our turn next.'

232

'Okay, let's get a grip on ourselves. The British Prime Minister's resignation is probably unrelated to this matter,' said Ellis, but inwardly he did not believe that—it was too convenient. Turning to his team, he continued, 'All right, now let's look at the salient facts. The British say the Rhodesians have used some kind of chemical or biological agent in their Bush War against communist terrorists.' He let that sink in before continuing.

'What do we know about the situation?' He proceeded to hand out copies of the National Security Study Memorandum prepared for President Nixon.

'Here's Kissinger's report on Southern Africa. I'm afraid NSSM39 doesn't give adequate coverage to this matter. If anything, it holds next to nothing to enlighten us what actually is happening out there.'*

The senior officer came to the defence of the US Secretary of State. 'Sure, Ellis, but remember it was written in '69. At the time we were preparing for a communist onslaught on Africa.'

'I was not aware things had changed!' he said acidly. 'All it says is that we should leave it in the hands of White extremists in that part of the world. And this is Kissinger's assessment!!' He looked around questioningly, then turned his attention to the officer who had spoken, 'Do you believe he had the answer?' He did not expect a response and none was forthcoming so he continued, 'As you are aware, we are currently re-evaluating the situation in Angola and I want to get a feel for what's going on in Rhodesia. There is a distinct possibility we may need Kissinger's services in that part of the world—very soon.'

Ellis turned to the CIA's military advisor. 'General, by now you and the Pentagon will no doubt have deduced that our intelligence services in Southern Africa is abysmal, with our agents having provided scant information. But the assertion that the Rhodesians have deployed chemical or possibly biological weapons in their civil war is of grave concern. What is more, this matter does not seem to be localised; it seems that they may have deployed these weapons in neighbouring countries. We need to investigate immediately and this is where you can assist.'

'If what they say is correct,' the General considered, 'then I agree, this poses the worst threat to the Western world since Cuba and the Bay of Pigs debacle. Am I correct in my thinking?'

'Affirmative,' Ellis knew he had grasped the size of this potential disaster.

'Then why doesn't the British Government use force to get rid of the Smith régime?' the General asked. To him this seemed a perfectly logical solution to an otherwise insoluble problem.

'I'm afraid if what we have discussed here today holds water then they can't—well, not openly. You might even say it's political blackmail.

Forced removal of the Rhodesian Government by the UK or the West will result in exposing what they have been up to for the last decade. And, of course, the rest of the world will blame us for not interceding sooner.' Ellis addressed the team, 'I hardly need remind you, the USSR currently has operatives all over the subcontinent. Our agents report that the Russian Ambassador to Zambia, Salodnikov, is a general in the KGB.* If he gets onto this we can kiss our arses goodbye.' He drove the point home, 'Gentlemen, both Russia and China would exploit this development to the full at the UN. It could give them a 'legitimate' excuse to invade Rhodesia and, God forbid, South Africa.' He turned to the General, 'If they get wind of this you can be sure, we'll be up to our necks in another war.'

The General held Ellis' gaze and, leaning back, ran his fingers roughly through his close-cropped hair. 'Yeah! I see what you mean. Can you expand a little on the political implications?'

'Well, yes,' Ellis continued, 'given any excuse the Russians will jump at the opportunity to take over Southern Africa. I'm sure you'll agree, these two White régimes wouldn't survive a month if we didn't intervene. The prize is the mineral wealth of South Africa, and control of the sea route to the east. Strategically this would tip the balance of power clearly in their favour. In my opinion, we would need to stop them at all costs, even if it meant engagement in another Vietnam-type operation.'

The General considered this. 'Congress wouldn't stand for another war. Darn it, they ain't fully aware of our involvement with the South Africans in Angola.' He paused for a moment, then asked, 'Are you saying that at this moment we don't know precisely what the Rhodesians are up to? If so, how the hell do we know how to avert this crisis?'

'No, we don't have answers yet and yes, I agree this needs to be addressed urgently. The UK is providing every assistance, but is forced to stay out of this. We must not give the Rhodesians a lever to use against the British.'

He looked slowly around the table from his aides to the General. 'You gotta believe it, this is the worst crisis we've every had to face. Use everything at your disposal and give me progress reports daily. Is that understood?' He looked around again and felt the need to emphasise the point. 'Do you know what this means if it leaks out?'

They knew.

'It rests in our hands entirely and, I want to keep the lid shut tight. From now on this matter is classified, absolutely no releases. I alone will notify the DCI directly.'

Ellis then put his proposal to the General.

Fourteen hours later a plan had been devised. Removing his glasses, Ellis rubbed his eyes, 'General, I believe these are the very men we need.'

oOo

3 May 1976

North Vietnamese forces launched their final offensive in 1975 and the South Vietnamese capital Saigon fell in April. By May, the new communist régime was in complete control of South Vietnam. US troops, after fighting a hopeless and bitter war, had all supposedly withdrawn the previous year. However, a few units remained in a covert capacity supporting anti-communist elements which operated on the Laos and Thailand borders.*

The *USS Odyssey* cruised through the South China Sea off Cambodia's coast. She was to pick up one of the last remaining contingents of the 25th Infantry. They were a phantom unit, continuously active behind enemy lines over the past three years, almost on the doorstep of Hanoi.

The men of the 25th expected to sail straight home after completing their extended tour of duty in Vietnam, and regarded the prospect with mixed feelings. Many found the thought of withdrawal from active service a depressing one. The threads of their lives 'back home' had been completely unravelled by time and ravages of war. Few felt they could readjust to the tameness of barrack life in the US. Rumour started to circulate around the ship: they were not heading for the Pacific after all.

At first light a siren wailed. Already routine, on their sixth day at sea, the listless GIs made their way to the briefing room.

Their commanding officer raised his hand and the murmuring ceased. 'I know some of you have been wondering where we are off to next.'

Colonel Porter studied the front row of faces. 'Thought you were going straight home—yeah? Well, you got it wrong!'

They remained silent.

'Some of you may be thinking about the Middle East? Wrong again!' There was a sound of shuffling from his men. The colonel went on, 'For the past three hours the Big 'O' has been heading due west through the Indian Ocean.' He picked up a pointer and pulled down the chart showing the continent of Africa. He tapped the map. 'From this point she travels south, down towards the Cape of Good Hope, here,' he pointed to the southern tip of Africa, 'into the Atlantic, and then home,' pausing to let that sink in. His men would be wondering why they were taking the long route back to the US. 'But first we have a little diversion. As I always say, no pain, no gain!'

There was further shuffling from the men.

'You twenty guys have been selected for a special assignment. We're travelling halfway around the globe, with a specific goal in mind—to drop you into Mozambique for tactical reconnaissance at this point here.' He prodded the chart. 'This mission is classified and comes straight from the top.'*

His men looked at one another, then back to their commanding officer. He had their attention.

'You are going in with one primary objective: to contact and engage communist-backed guerrilla forces in Rhodesia and Mozambique—we need to assess their firepower. Our generals think we may have to launch the next major offensive against the commies, here,' tapping the map again, 'in Southern Africa. If this is going to be another 'Nam', the US needs to evaluate the enemy's capabilities.'*

They drummed with enthusiasm on their armrests, pleased at the prospect of further action.

'Okay, guys, settle down. This ain't going to be no picnic. You'll not wear any insignia. The intention is for the commies to think you're a White Rhodesian task force and you're not to inform them otherwise.'

There was not a murmur.

'Because of the nature of this mission you will be accompanied by two medical officers and, yes, myself. But I stress: if you get zapped you're not coming home. Do I make myself clear? Besides present personnel, there ain't more than five other persons out of this room that know where you are heading. I'll say this only once: the US has not and will not deploy our military in Rhodesia. Do we understand each other?' He waited for their assent, then pointed to the map. 'Good! We will be dropped at this location at 04h00 on day one. Then here, here and here, we will engage the enemy.' The pointer moved next to Mozambique's coast. 'Our reconnoitre of the area is estimated to be a five-day march to this location, giving us ten hours' leeway. The Big 'O' will be off the coast and, at precisely 15h00 on the 20th, four whirlybirds will be sent in to collect us.'

To break the tension he added, 'We need to meet that deadline, because the next cruise ship doesn't pass this way for some time. Any questions?' The next hour was spent confirming operational details.

15 May 1976

Here and there white caps broke an otherwise gentle sea and purple streaks were beginning to vein their way across the eastern horizon. It was three-thirty in the morning, yet the activity on the flight deck was frenetic. Packs, weapons and ammunition were loaded aboard the helicopters as the men of B Company made last minute preparations for departure. At last, the tower gave clearance for take-off. Simultaneously the four craft lifted off the flight deck, tipped their noses and hung motionless while the carrier cruised on. The lead helicopter manoeuvred to the left, tilted slightly, then, turning sideways, raced for the coast. The other three followed in close formation.

At first they followed a north-westerly bearing to avoid the more densely populated coastline. Twenty minutes later the gunships were over land.

After forty-five minutes they swung south-west. The sky in the east was getting pale and, two hundred metres below, the ground was now clearly visible. The navigator spoke into his headset; the pilot glanced to his right and nodded. The Pungwe River lay beneath them. He throttled back and lost altitude. The other pilots did likewise, assuming the hover position—while searching for a suitable landing site.

Within minutes they were down.

Colonel Porter took control. He shouted above the whine of the motors, 'Get going. Secure the area!' The platoon fanned out to take up defensive positions, while the flight crews unloaded jerry cans and carried out rapid refuelling. This completed, they boarded, the pilots hit the throttles, fanned the rotors, lifted off, skimming the treetops disappeared in seconds. The whole procedure had been completed in under ten minutes.

The Colonel gave command to the platoon lieutenants and they moved out in classic battle formation: one squad two hundred metres ahead of the other, ready to outflank any contact by moving the rear squad to the right or left, as the situation demanded.

Nine kilometres farther on they found their first objective. Porter leopard-crawled the last few metres to where Lieutenant Miller lay.

'There, Colonel.' He passed the field glasses. 'Over to your left—gun emplacements. I count at least four 23mm ack-ack guns. Now take a look to your right. See the tanks, next to the hospital.'

Colonel Porter grimaced. 'Affirmative, they're Soviet T54s. There's the HQ and water tower. This is it, Miller.' Porter picked out the landmarks while noting the four men in camouflage uniform milling around the T54s. 'Yup, it's the ZANLA camp all right. Okay, assume attack formation and have Brown take the left flank.' Seizing his lieutenant's arm he added, 'Get back and have those two doctors stay well out of our way.'

Miller nodded—his sentiments entirely! He resented having passengers thrust upon them, more so because they were not from their unit. A veteran of many campaigns, he knew the chances were they would have to pull them out if things became too hot.

'Okay, Doc, you and your partner, back to the rear with me.' The medical officers dutifully followed Miller, who went back to instruct Brown on the attack formation.

Satisfied his snipers had secured a commanding field of fire over the entire area, Porter issued the order to move in. They approached stealthily forming a semicircle around the perimeter of the camp. On his command, they charged into the clearing. The element of surprise was complete. Two rockets were launched simultaneously at the HQ building with devastating effect—part of the galvanised roof lifted into the air as doors and windows blew out in the fire-flash. As they ran, the advancing GIs opened fire from the waist with their sub-machine-guns. The ZANLA soldiers stood no chance and many dropped in the first hail of bullets. A lone soldier managed to find temporary cover behind an ambulance. Panicking, he bolted for the bush fifteen metres away across open ground. He had not covered more than half the distance before one of the snipers brought him down.

At the far edge of this isolated camp lay the sickbay where David was starting his monthly round. Startled, he ripped the stethoscope from his ears.

'Gunfire!'

He bolted past a bewildered orderly heading for a window. He saw White soldiers moving in fast, zig-zagging across the open ground, coming in their direction. Out of nowhere the roof of the HQ crashed down onto the parade square, as the sentry on the water tower opened up with a 12.7mm heavy machine-gun in the first token of resistance so far. David turned abruptly, to find three of the patients in pyjama pants at his side. Behind them stood the male orderly and two terrified female nurses. He glanced at the other five patients, too badly injured or too sick to get to their feet. Their pleading looks heightened his own desperation as he ran past them.

'This way!' he yelled. And led the terrified group back down the ward and out of the rear door. Their flight was obscured by the hospital wing, as they ran headlong for the trees edging the camp perimeter. Ten minutes later, exhausted, he called them to a halt, far into the bush. In the distance they heard sporadic gun shots which were soon replaced by a strained silence.

Between bouts of coughing one of David's patients managed to gasp, 'Doctor, please...I think we should...' he battled to regain his breath, 'get under cover. They may have seen us leave, and come after us.'

David required no further prompting and he started to search for a suitable hiding place.

Colonel Porter was confident that all resistance had been subdued. He radioed for the medical officers to come in. Within minutes they had attended the two marines who had sustained relatively minor injuries, one with a bullet through the wrist. The other had been hit by flying debris. 'I'm all right, Doc. Better attend to the others.'

The doctor looked him over. 'You ain't going nowhere until I've arrested this bleeding,' and he tightened the field dressing to halt the flow of blood from the GI's thigh.

Another casualty lay dead, hit by small arms fire, while a fourth had received a burst from the machine-gun all but severing his right arm.

He lay in shock, repeating over and over that there wasn't anything wrong with him. The medical officer kneeling at his side spoke soothingly to him, while administering an intravenous toxic shot of morphine ten times above the prescribed dose. Withdrawing the needle he pulled the plunger back on the syringe and reinserted it into the vein and, depressing the plunger, expelled air directly into the man's bloodstream. He felt for a pulse and shortly, lifted the GI's eyelid, then moved on to the next victim.

Seconded for the mission from the US Army Medical Research Institute of Infectious Diseases (USAMRIID), the MOs set about examining the wounded ZANLA soldiers. They made no attempt to treat their wounds. They simply filled syringe after syringe, drawing blood from each of them.

Lieutenant Miller stood next to one of the doctors, watching, unsure what to make of this highly irregular procedure. 'What gives, Doc?' he asked.

The MO glanced up. 'What the hell does it look like?' All but ignoring the lieutenant and going on about his business. In the sickbay the terrified patients were very much alive. Powerless to resist, they made no protest as the doctor extracted blood samples. Eventually, he went to find Porter. 'Okay, Colonel, I'm through here.' Porter immediately had his men regroup.

Eight hours later there were still no signs of pursuit.

David called the orderly over. 'You and I are going back.' It was already late afternoon and long shadows were falling.

The patient, who had suggested that they hide, spoke. 'I'd better come along as well, Doctor. At least I know how to use a gun, if we find one.'

David glanced at his skeletal frame. The man's flesh had wasted away leaving him debilitated and of indeterminable age. Initially his persistent cough had concerned David in case it revealed their location to the enemy. David was full of admiration: how this man had run so far was beyond him and now he was volunteering to return to an uncertain reception.

The camp was deserted, except for the victims of the attack who lay where they had fallen. David and his companions split up, running from building to building, to be met by the same sickly smell of death. The dead lay in thick waxy pools of their own blood, the grotesque bodies already attracting hordes of flies.

The orderly called, 'Quick, Doctor, over here!'

They gathered round a solitary figure. David approached, half expecting to find a survivor. Instead he gazed down into the unseeing eyes of a White soldier.

His skeletal patient knelt down and rifled through the dead man's pockets. 'Nothing! Not even a pack of cigarettes,' he slowly peeled away the clothing while feeling beneath the prone figure. His hand touched a round metal object.

'*Skuz'apo!* Selous Scouts,' he exclaimed in alarm. 'Get down.' They dived for the ground. Carefully, the patient extracted the hand grenade taking care to make sure to hold down the handle firmly. A glance confirmed that the pin was missing.

'Doctor, have you any syringe needles I can use?'

David ran to the hospital, with the patient and the orderly close on his heels. The sight was gruesome.

He walked from bed to bed: every patient had been shot. David felt tears misting his eyes, almost forgetting the grenade.

With trembling fingers he peeled back the yellow wrapping from a disposable needle and gave it to the skeletal patient who pushed it through the aperture to replace the missing safety clip. A second needle was introduced for good measure.

They began to check the bodies and David felt his anger build-up. He had spent his career endeavouring to save lives and in a few seconds these butchers had come and slain his patients.

Pulling up the last blood-soaked bedspread to cover the body beneath, he saw something flutter to the floor and instinctively picked it up. About to discard it, he realised it was a wrapping from a disposable needle.

He studied it carefully.

The wrapping was of blue transparent polythene. Turning it over, the silver paper backing revealed the US proprietary trade name. He retrieved the wrappers he had discarded in making the grenade safe.

They were definitely yellow!

David went to the cabinet, opening all the drawers, but could not find a single needle with blue packing. He showed the other two the blue wrapper. 'See if you can find any more of these!'

Soon they found one, near to the front door, and then another in the bedclothes of a second victim. He was stunned. It did not make sense. He sat on an empty bed and moments later leapt purposefully to his feet.

'Help me with these bodies. See if you can find where these men were injected. You check that one—look at the arms, the upper iliac crests, on their buttocks—anywhere!'

Almost immediately the orderly shouted, 'Here, come and look!'

David dropped the arm of the corpse he was examining and joined the skeletal patient who was peering over the orderly's shoulder at the extended limb of the second victim.

'See! If I press with my thumbs on the elbow joint, the blood serum still oozes out of the puncture.'

They looked at the clear bead of fluid.

David gripped the orderly reassuringly by the shoulder. 'Well done.' He proceeded to examine the rest of the bodies. Sure enough, the results were the same. Outside, they found further wrappers near to corpses scattered around the camp.

The orderly turned to David, 'What did they inject them with, Doctor?'

'Nothing!' came the reply.

David covered another body. 'It's just dawned on me—you don't administer an injection, then proceed to shoot your patient. No! You withdraw blood.'

'But why?' asked the orderly.

o0o

By the beginning of July things began to happen. The CIA's senior departmental head, Ellis, was working late when his telephone rang.

A laconic voice said, 'It's the CDC here.'

Ellis had asked the Centres for Disease Control (CDC) in Atlanta—the public health body responsible for investigating epidemics—for assistance, because orders had come down: this was not to be treated as a military operation. He pushed aside the documents on his desk.

'Excuse the late hour but I thought you should know immediately.'

'That's okay. What have you got?' enquired Ellis.

'Our guys made a major breakthrough several weeks ago. We have been waiting to confirm the findings. But I am afraid it's the worst scenario imaginable,' he paused not wanting to be the purveyor of bad news. 'The Rhodesians definitely used biological agents. You can rule out chemicals entirely, if...'

'How come?' Ellis interrupted impatiently.

'I was about to tell you. The specimens taken in Mozambique have revealed some rather unusual pathogens. The British Ministry of Defence at Porton Down has grown cultures taken from patients in mission hospitals in central Mozambique, which they say corroborate our findings. A full report is on its way.'

Ellis sounded troubled. 'I see. It's not what I wanted to hear but thanks for your assistance anyway.' He put down the telephone. Placing both elbows on the desk, he leaned forward, shutting his eyes and cradling his forehead in his hands. 'Biological warfare! What'll happen if the Russians find out what's going on?' he wondered.

He rubbed his eyes with his palms, then stood up. On his way out he gave instructions to his secretary, 'Tell the team I want them here by 10.00am tomorrow and arrange an appointment for me to see Kissinger,' adding sarcastically, 'at a time convenient to him.'

It was 4 July, Independence Day. While most American families were celebrating the holiday, however, the senior staff of the CIA were not at home. They had dropped their engagements to attend what Ellis called a 'crisis meeting'. The team was now gathered in the main auditorium at Langley. There was no hint of an agenda nor what would be under discussion.

Ellis began by distributing the CDC folders to the officers. The reports contained therein had been sent to him, overnight express, by government messenger. He opened the meeting, skipping unnecessary formalities and came straight to the point. 'We have confirmed reports that the Rhodesians are engaged in biological warfare. Please read your notes.'

CDC - Atlanta

Specimens taken from the blood samples received from Mozambique have been isolated and cultures grown. Our research confirms a number of micro-organisms present, mainly the Pneumocystis carinii and the filovirus, Marburg. The latter was found to be morphologically identical to that isolated in Germany in 1967, although the current specimens are antigenically distinct. The Pneumocystis carinii has also been altered in some way and genetic manipulation is suspected in both cases....

A full technical report followed.

Porton Down - UK

A number of other pathogens have been isolated: in particular, the Pneumocystis carinii, from specimens taken at mission hospitals near to the border. Concerning the Pneumocystis carinii, the taxonomic position remains unclear. Certain authorities regard it as protozoan, while others consider it to be a fungus. The micro-organism has a strong predilection for the lungs and is transmitted aerobically and acquired through inhalation. This micro-organism is especially common in rats. The human strain appears to display differing characteristics. It first emerged after World War II in Europe among undernourished infants. Rarely seen in healthy adults, it is usually associated in humans with lung impairment and is most often found among patients undergoing organ transplants and who have had their systems immunosuppressed, resulting in Pneumocystis carinii pneumonia (PCP).*

There have been several other reported outbreaks in Southern Africa of what doctors have described as a 'new' disease. Lacking the necessary equipment to isolate the causative micro-organisms, they have assumed that it is a highly contagious disease of unknown epidemiology, possibly a viral haemorrhagic infection but one with a high mortality rate. Several accounts point to symptoms associated with Marburg disease. There seem to have been spasmodic outbreaks along the eastern border of Mozambique with Rhodesia, all the way up to the Zambian border. The spread of the disease seems to have been contained. Since there are no survivors in this remote area it has not been possible to procure viable specimens....

The report went on at length.

What had interested the British scientists was that the physiology of the *Pneumocystis carinii* had somehow changed. Of major concern was that the pathogen did not usually invade organs other than the lung, but the specimens from the Mozambique mission hospitals had been found in the thymus, salivary gland, liver, spleen and even the skin. They were remarkably prolific and displayed marked resistance to standard chemotherapy. Co-trimoxazole was the most effective agent found to date. This drug was not readily available in the devastated regions of Mozambique.

A further report hinted that a ZANLA doctor had confirmed hundreds of cases of pneumonia in the war zone. It suggested, in the absence of adequate test facilities, that the *Pneumocystis carinii* might be the micro-organism responsible.

Colonel Porter's mission had also found the *Pneumocystis carinii*. The US scientists stated that, in their estimation, the genetic structure had been tampered with. The altered DNA, giving rise to the apparent new characteristics, was not likely to be a natural mutation. They gave their reasons why.

'Anyone want to dispute what they have to say?' asked Ellis.

They remained silent.

'Good!' Ellis leaned forward placing his hands on the table, 'Then can someone tell me why this report has taken so long?'

'From what I can gather, it falls under the new field of genetics and they need time to carry out extensive trials and evaluations,' an advisor commented.

This agreed with what the CDC had said, so Ellis pressed on. 'It is of paramount importance to keep a lid on this or else the Russians will be hightailing it down to Cape Town. In the circumstances who could blame them! Gentlemen, I have been in consultation with the White House. There is consensus regarding this grave matter: the US cannot condone the use of, or allow the proliferation of, these weapons. They're too god-damn dangerous. Therefore we cannot afford to let the Rhodesians get away with this—we need to stop them and I mean stop them now. The way I see it, we have a number of options,' and he annoyingly kept them waiting while he reached for the water tumbler.

'Make this public, and it will clearly provide sufficient provocation for the Soviets to invade Southern Africa—give them access to gold, platinum and diamonds, not forgetting plutonium. And this, without so much as reproach from the free world and, you better believe it, possibly even with the backing of the UN. This is not a situation the US wishes to contemplate.'

He paused again. 'On the other hand we could go in and, if necessary, crush the Rhodesians. I am not ruling this out, but I fear South Africa may be mixed up in this affair somehow! Or, we can confront them with the facts and force them to capitulate. This means handing the country over to Black majority rule immediately.'

He turned to his attentive audience. 'Your comments please!'

A studious young man wearing glasses, seemingly not as discreet as his elder colleagues, responded immediately. 'I don't believe the Black nationalists can possibly make a success of ruling the country. I'd advise against the latter course of action. If they take over immediately, there would be a mass exodus of Whites, resulting in economic collapse and possible chaos overnight. Besides, we would be placing the country in the hands of ZIPRA or ZANLA, and we all know they have an empathy with the communists. I suggest we present the Rhodesians, and South Africans too if necessary, with the facts—give them an ultimatum couched in the strongest possible terms and leave them to disengage from the war. A transitional government could ensure a lengthy hand-over to the Blacks. This would cause the minimum amount of disruption to the Rhodesian economy, and possibly Smith would see this as a way of saving face for the White minority. At the same time, we'd insist that they take steps to eradicate all traces of their recent activities and, hence, prevent this from leaking out.'

Questions flew round the table. 'What if Smith defends himself and quotes our deployment of Agent Orange in Vietnam?'

'A defoliating agent to cut down the forests harbouring the Viet Cong is not the same thing as targeting humans. We weren't to know of its long-term side-effects.'

'What if the Rhodesians simply refuse to co-operate?'

'Then we take them to the cleaners. Threaten everyone with war crime trials, Nuremberg style, if they do not comply.'

Ellis asked, 'What stance do you think the South Africans will adopt on this issue?'

The studious young officer cleared his throat. 'Kissinger's last trip in April confirmed what our agents have been telling us. The South Africans have supplied the Rhodesians with arms and a token force of paramilitary personnel on the Zambian border for the past decade. Now they have withdrawn because Rhodesia has decided to close its border with Zambia. Rhodesia may be prepared to lose its R7,500,000 annual turnover in trade with Zambia, but the South Africans stand to lose R300,000,000 as a result of the closure.* I'm sure Vorster doesn't think the sun shines out of Smith's...'

Ellis cut in with a smile. 'We all see your point, but please continue.'

'Well, it's fairly clear they have fallen out over Smith's political gaffe— it was a punitive move closing the border in the hope that Zambia would stop harbouring terrorist bases. Especially after ten years of warring! It's worth noting that up to now South African has used Rhodesia for their own ends, and I'm sure Vorster, their Prime Minister, will be amenable to any recommendations we make in this arena.'

He paused but Ellis waved him on.

'I've been wondering how the Rhodesians might have acquired this *carinii* thing! They don't have the capabilities to produce it and, I'm told even our scientists, who are daily breaking new ground in genetics, cannot lay claim to this one. On the other hand South Africa is highly advanced in this field, what with their pioneering research into heart transplant surgery.'

'If so, they are, excuse the pun, playing it very close to the chest,' Ellis cautioned, the smile on his lips never reaching his eyes.

'Of course! Vorster has already denied all knowledge of germ warfare weapons. He is even on record as saying they'd have more chance of developing a nuclear warhead, which is also probably close to the truth.'

Ellis had heard enough.

That afternoon he briefed the Director of Central Intelligence and gave firm recommendations.

o0o

Victor Hammond was beside himself with fury. Besides, he hated having to ask General Bastion-Smythe for help, particularly when it smacked of incompetence on his part.

'Rocco, we have a real problem on our hands and it's not something I can resolve on my own.' Cleverly he had twisted it around to become their mutual problem rather than his alone and was relying heavily on the General's vanity for support.

'You know that terrorist we captured at the Zimbabwe Ruins? Well, for bloody months I've been giving him the full treatment, trying to extract information out of him, but the stupid *munt* stuck it out right until we released him. Now he's given us the slip, dammit!'

General Bastion-Smythe did not need a detailed account of what that treatment might have been. He knew only too well how Hammond operated. He himself had sanctioned field trials on captured terrorists back in 1967, when they were infected with relatively minor diseases, then released under the guise of conciliation, in an attempt to spread infection within terrorist camps in Zambia.

The theory was that a weakened and debilitated army would soon lose the zest for war. Now the newly inaugurated Germ Warfare Unit attached to the security forces* was deploying new biological weapons in Mozambique to achieve the same, perhaps more permanent, end.

After months of applying intensive physiological conditioning techniques and brutality in even measure, Hammond would change tactics and approach his captives by using a new ploy, subtly devoid of menace. The Teacher had been no exception.

In a friendly manner Hammond had told him he could return to Mozambique provided he told his *comrades* to lay down their arms. In return, the Rhodesians would extend a hand of peace.

Before his release the Teacher had received what seemed to be a thorough medical. Told that he had a mild bronchial infection, a 'remedy' was administered by intramuscular injection.

'As I expected the bastard went back to the Ruins,' said Hammond scornfully. 'This must have been to retrieve the documents he had hidden, and then he hightailed it to Mozambique. I knew I was right all along because we only found the specimens and my briefcase in their vehicle at the time.'

The General frowned. 'So why didn't you pick him up there and then?'

A worried Hammond revealed his frustration. 'Damn it all, Rocco, I issued the order but he took three days to reach the site and our tail claims the suspect gave them the slip. Frankly, I think the short incubation period scared the hell out of our Black agents and they let him go.'

The General knew how they felt—this weapon terrified him too. 'So your informants' say he is heading for Mozambique?'

'No! I have confirmed reports from the Selous Scouts that he is already there, at Nyadzonya camp. If this information falls into the wrong hands...'

'From what you've told me, dear boy, it already has.' He drummed the table with his fingers. 'I really see no choice! We must to go in and retrieve this information as a matter of urgency.'

oOo

16 July 1976

From dense forest the vegetation changed to grasslands as David approached the coastal belt. He drove through vast sugar estates stretching as far as the eye could see, now derelict, deserted by the Portuguese in their haste to leave the land when FRELIMO came to power. For these self-deluded settlers, in June 1975 the sun had set on a rushed exodus...their dreams shattered. Many crossed over into South Africa, while others sought refuge in Rhodesia or returned to Europe. The colonialists gave little thought to the chaos they left behind; they simply condemned the FRELIMO Government for taking back what was rightfully the indigenous people's in the first place. Making no effort to reconcile past differences with the new régime, they left, full of acrimony and resentment, to be met by sympathetic White brethren across the border.

David now sped south, along the road by which they had departed, on his way to Maputo, the Mozambique capital, occasionally passing small rural settlements alongside the highway. After the horror of the past days he pressed on, reluctant to stop; hardly aware of the scenery as it changed from lush forest to palm, then abruptly to plantations of tall glistening emerald green cashew nut trees.

On arrival he headed for the Polano Hotel.

The following day David set out to find the new ZANLA HQ in Maputo. The debriefing was to the point and he felt nauseated recounting the events of the past week, describing what had happened during, what he was convinced of, was a Rhodesian attack. He outlined his fears that they might have deployed some type of biological agent; this explanation would account for the strange syringe wrappers, if they had taken blood samples.

Admittedly the evidence was flimsy and their scepticism showed. 'Battle fatigue...take a rest,' was all they had said.

Maybe they were right! He needed a break from the front line. He collected his mail—two letters. Recognising the Zambian postmark on one and seeing his sister's handwriting on the other, he pocketed them to read later. On the way out of the HQ he picked up several old newspapers in the foyer, the first he had seen for months. Admittedly the news was dated but the headlines caught his attention as he went out into bright sunshine.

A few minutes' walk through the city centre brought him to the foreshore, he strolled along the busy esplanade and sat down under the shade of a tall palm—one of many that graced the shoreline. The war seemed remote as, lazily, he watched the ships anchored offshore, then turned to the news-papers.

April 1976
Britain
James Callaghan elected leader of the Labour Party. *

He wondered why Wilson had suddenly resigned and if this change in leadership would in any way affect the Bush War, then decided it would not. A second lead story promised to be more interesting.

Kissinger's whistle-stop tour of Southern Africa. *

David smiled. Like most Africans he questioned whose side the Americans would be on. Until now they had shown little interest, although CIA agents were scattered around Southern Africa. Everyone deliberately avoided them, or else fed them misinformation. It was known locally that these agents could not work out how the population knew they were CIA, apparently not realising that there were few Whites in Africa with American accents! Still, he hoped their new peace initiative would work.

British agents were harder to identify, and the smile remained on his lips as he thought of Sally Thomas. During one of his many trips to collect medical supplies from Tete, they had 'bumped' into each other and struck up a casual friendship. Not long afterwards he had experienced doubts concerning her role with the International Defence and Aid Agency in Mozambique, and wondered if their meeting had been that accidental after all. David openly expressed his concern, to which Sally had replied, 'Whatever you might think, David, I promise you, I am on your side!'

The memory of their first meeting remained fresh in his mind. His encounter with Trish and others had been fleeting, which left Sally as the only White woman he could count as a friend and he had found it strangely pleasing.

On his last trip he had told her of his suspicions about the opportunistic diseases he was confronted with in the field—he was currently treating drug-resistant diseases he would not normally have expected to find in physically fit combatants.

He remembered the letters. Pulling them out of his back pocket, savouring the moment while he smoothed out the envelopes, he tore open the one dated 2.6.76 with the Zambian postmark.

It was from Michael! A sad chronicle of two people who, after their marriage, had discovered how little they had in common. Michael wrote about his son John, now two years old, and how Trish had finally agreed to accompany him on a field trip to the Zambezi. John had been quite seriously injured when their vehicle had overturned in the bush. Trish, worried by her son's condition, had flown back to the States with him and blamed Michael for what had happened. Michael sounded depressed as he explained that Trish had decided not to come back.

He rambled on, depressing David further about having to try for John's sake, admitting fault and how he hadn't worked at their relationship; that possibly Simon was right—that he should leave the bush. He had added a few lines saying he was unsure whether he was still running away from his past.

The only light note in the letter was a reference to Paddy. If David remembered, Paddy was the friend of Trish who had come out to visit them from the States. He said:

> *...thankfully the 'mad Irishman' isn't a teetotaller and has promised me temporary employment in his clinical laboratory in Houston, so I can secure my green card. Paddy feels sure that all I need, as a microbiologist, is to sit the local Texas Examination or its equivalent and, after the required internship, I can practise in the States. He is finding out and will let me know. I am seriously considering the offer and will drop you a line when I'm settled...*

At the end of his letter Michael wrote that he was going over to the US to see if he could patch up his marriage.

David put the letter down feeling thoroughly downhearted. Judging by recent events, it was unlikely that any more post would reach him for some time. The war was escalating daily and he could be transferred anywhere at a moment's notice. He did not expect to hear from Michael again.

He ripped open the second letter. Nandi, as always, would cheer him up.

> *10.5.76*
> *...over the past six months 600 pupils have died...*
> *...they have taken to the streets in protest against the inferior education they are receiving. My God! Once again, our children have come under fire. Hundreds are dead, or simply missing. The violence is getting worse every day and more of our men are leaving to join the party in exile.**
> *I have been told this letter will reach you by the usual means.*

Please join us. I know how strong your loyalty is to our father,
but Zimbabwe's problems are rooted right here in South Africa.
'Umkhonto we Sizwe' needs men like you...now!
Always thinking of you.
Love Nandi

'No, not now Nandi!' he whispered.

David slipped the letters back in his pocket and gazed at the ocean. His thoughts returned to the events of the past week.

With their transport and radio destroyed, he and the small group of survivors had been stranded at the 'death' camp. Two days after the attack, a FRELIMO patrol had arrived on a routine tour of the camps, to foster good relations with ZANLA, on the express orders of President Machel.

He had felt relief flood over him the moment he recognised the emblem on the side of the first truck. He learnt that they were not the only casualties that week. A FRELIMO outpost had been attacked in much the same manner, as had two villages farther towards the coast. Then the attackers had simply vanished. It was rumoured that nearby villagers had heard helicopters in the night and he surmised that it was the Rhodesians on one of their many raids. With their work done they had left, leaving chaos and mayhem in their wake. What was worrying was that they had never penetrated this close to the coast before and he felt sure that denials would be forthcoming and accepted, as usual, by the international community. The world's attitude towards Mozambique was that its fate was of no consequence—there were no exploitable resources!

The FRELIMO truck had dropped him at Chimoio, a substantial garrison town, swelled by two thousand refugees and ZANLA soldiers. From there he had made his way back to his unit at Nyadzonya, contacted his commander in Maputo, and had come down here for the debriefing.

David remained uneasy. He had provided a detailed account and yet felt he had missed something. Was it the mystery still surrounding the syringe wrappers? No, that was just part of it! What troubled him more was that there were too many unanswered questions concerning his work. He would go back to Nyadzonya for the answers....

Frustrated, he read Nandi's letter again, knowing the future was uncertain until the battle for Zimbabwe was over.

Right now he had a few weeks' leave ahead. He thought of Mbada, who might walk into Nyadzonya camp at any time and, if so, wondered what it would take to get him to come down and join him in Maputo.

The unexpected happened, cutting David's leave short by a week. Returning from the beach one afternoon, he found a driver waiting for him in the hotel foyer.

'Doctor, you're wanted at HQ. It seems you need to contact Nyadzonya urgently.' More than that he did not know.

Thirty minutes later David was on the scrambler to the camp commander.

'David, it is a matter of urgency otherwise I would not have disturbed you. The Teacher has arrived. Apparently he was captured over the border but managed to...'

There was a terrible noise, then a break in transmission. David stood listening, hearing nothing except static. Seconds later the camp commander came back on the air.

'Sorry about that,' he laughed nervously, 'we had a Canberra bomber overfly the camp. They were low—you should see the panic outside— we *were* playing soccer against FRELIMO,' followed by another nervous laugh.

David visualised the scene, then picked up the thread of conversation again. 'You were saying something about the Teacher?'

The radio clicked. 'Yes! He's standing next to me. Walked into camp last night after escaping from the Rhodesians.'

David cut in, 'Where's Mbada?' He received no reply.

Instead the Teacher's voice came over the air.

'Hello, Doctor, Mbada's brother here.'

David realised he did not even know the Teacher's real name.

'Doctor, I need to see you urgently. Mbada said I must contact you— I'm afraid he is dead.'

David felt his throat constrict, unable to say anything for a few moments.

'We were caught in a fight at the Zimbabwe Ruins. They all died... I managed to escape but was caught by the CIO. Their Chief Inspector Hammond released me ten days ago.'

David had met Hammond once at the mission where he had worked, then seen him again while on the run with Mbada. On several occasions he had treated injuries which this man had inflicted on freedom fighters. ZANLA wanted him more than anyone else for these heinous crimes.

'They questioned me but I didn't tell them where I'd hidden the papers.'

David caught his breath and interrupted, 'What papers?'

'Sorry, Doctor. We found documents which I hid, and I went back for them...they prove the Rhodesians are using germ warfare against us. I have them with me now.'

David could not believe what he was hearing. His skin crawled. This was the missing piece of the puzzle. The supporting evidence!

A bout of coughing filled the air. Presently the camp commander came back on the line.

'Our young Teacher isn't complaining but I am afraid he's in bad shape. It seems the trip back has left him weakened.'

David was concerned but he wanted the evidence. 'Can you send him and the documents down here? I really need to see the information he holds.'

'David, you're not listening. This man is desperately ill. Our orderly says he's bleeding internally; blood in his stools and urine. He's in no position to travel. It's only at his insistence, and because of what Mbada said, that I allowed him out of bed to speak to you.'

'Okay. I'll make arrangements to return immediately.'

Try as he might David could not stop thinking about Mbada...he would do what he could for his brother. He knew his dead friend would approve of what he was about to do. If these documents contained information that could be substantiated, they could destroy the perpetrators of this weapon as easily as the germ itself.

His first move was to phone Sally Thomas at Tete.

'You'll never guess what's come up. We have the bastards.'

She could hear that he was excited. 'David! Slow down, tell me what's happened?'

'I thought you'd want to know there is concrete evidence of the Rhodesians having used germ warfare against us...' he went on hurriedly, explaining the circumstances.

The Teacher was probably dying. The evidence was there and he wanted to drop everything and return as quickly as he could, but there were necessary medical supplies he had requisitioned which stalled his departure by a day. Irritated by the delay and with a feeling of growing urgency, he arrived late at Chimoio on the evening of 8 August. Tomorrow he would complete the trip to Nyadzonya camp and, all being well, see the Teacher by midday.

oOo

Colonel Tom Bailey, Commanding Officer of the Selous Scouts, came out of the final briefing with the General. Cross-border raids in hunt-and-destroy missions on small villages were one thing, but to attack an entire camp was an altogether different matter. There was reported to be up to five thousand trained terrorists at Nyadzonya, poised to attack Rhodesia.*

According to the General, the CIO's view was that they had to be stopped. Aerial photographs, supplied by the newly appointed head, Victor Hammond, indicated near on a thousand men surrounding the parade square, with what looked remarkably like a football match in progress. He was concerned that the CIO had never adequately explained why the Air

Force had not been called in. Dropping fragmentation bombs into a camp that size would have eliminated the threat in one fell swoop and the matter would have been dead and buried, in every sense. Instead, Bastion-Smythe had said that the CIO had asked him to come up with a plan. In response he had suggested that the Selous Scouts go in and reconnoitre the area, then attack to assess enemy strength and capabilities. The CIO had intimated that dependent on the outcome of this mission, it might pave the way for future cross-border raids on other camps.

Bailey welcomed the challenge but, with the CIO pressuring him to take prisoners for interrogation, especially from hospital beds in the camp, he hesitated, having reservations. However, one look in the General's direction and he reluctantly agreed.

He passed the order down to his men. If they were to go in search of ill and dying terrorists in the heat of battle, so be it; but under no circumstances were they to compromise the mission, not even for the CIO.*

His Scouts questioned what was wrong with taking healthy soldiers? Were there not purportedly five thousand in the camp from whom they could choose at random? Besides, in hospital pyjamas, how the hell were they going to differentiate between soldiers and civilians? It didn't make sense, and to a man, they could see that the mission was fraught with potential disaster.

As the day drew nearer it became increasingly clear how hazardous this action would be. The dangers of transporting sick or dying terrorists, in their vehicles on the return trip, was something Bailey found unacceptable. He would handle the protests from the CIO and his superiors later.

9 August 1976

Operation Eland* swung into gear. The heavily disguised convoy of Selous Scouts crossed the border just after midnight. A foot patrol sent ahead to cut the telephone line were picked up several kilometres before Chimoio and the convoy turned left, taking the main road to the north.

By early morning they reached Nyadzonya as the camp was beginning to stir, in expectation of a public holiday's festivities. The Selous Scouts vehicles parading as FRELIMO troops advanced to the gate in a convincing display. The men were dressed in the full battle fatigues of FRELIMO, using balaclavas to conceal their faces and camouflage paint to cover white skin. In the lead vehicle, which had previously been captured, stood what appeared to be a FRELIMO soldier.*

He shouted to the sentry, 'FRELIMO has arrived to join in the celebrations.' The barrier lifted and the sentry stood to attention as they went through, passing the billets of a detachment of fifty FRELIMO resident guards.

Early morning muster had drawn most of the young men and boys onto the parade ground and they turned collectively to watch the column arrive at the far edge of the square. The line of heavily armed vehicles drew up to face the crowd. The plan was to have the crowd gather in orderly fashion. The Selous Scouts were then to ask for Mbada's brother on the pretext that FRELIMO needed information which he held. Once they had retrieved the sensitive documents, they would attack.*

A Scout lifted his loud hailer. 'FRELIMO expresses its solidarity with your struggle. We have come to celebrate....'

The crowd surged forward.*

But there was nothing orderly about the sea of faces in front of them. Boys not older than nine or ten ran ahead, shouting 'Viva FRELIMO'. The cry was taken up by others across the square and yet more people swarmed out of their shelters—women, children and their grandparents joined in the prospect of an early start to the festivities.

The Selous Scouts opened up with two Hispano cannons, taken from a scraped Vampire jet fighter, MAG's, fifty calibre Brownings and a Russian 12.7 millimetre heavy machine-gun, firing at close range with deadly effect into the crowd. Scores fell in the first burst, the bullets ripping through several bodies at a time. People collapsed in wave after wave. For a moment the crowd still pressed forward, unable to comprehend the slaughter scything its way towards them.*

Realising at last what was happening, the camp guards began to return fire as the Selous Scouts mortars came into play. Ferret cars, with thirty calibre Brownings flanking the crowd, swept the area with a hail of shells cutting off any escape. Buildings caught fire. Men, women and children fell, or rushed panic-stricken in every direction. Pressed towards the Nyadzonya River, hundreds ran terrified into the dark water, trampling one another in their efforts to escape. Many drowned. Still the firing frenzy continued. In under three minutes it was over. It took a further fifteen minutes to kill those injured or too infirm to escape the cordon.*

The Selous Scouts were never given the opportunity to ask for the Teacher but their informants' had said he was in the hospital. They watched with resignation as the building blazed fiercely, destroying all within.

With FRELIMO in hot pursuit, the Selous Scouts withdrawal from the operation zone was not without hazard; but by 13h45 the following day they re-crossed the border safely into Rhodesia.*

For a second time the Canberra bomber flew over the camp. But this time the reconnaissance pictures told a different story. Bodies lay three-deep on the parade ground and hundreds more were scattered around the camp.*

Later that evening the CIO reviewed the results of the raid with the help of Bastion-Smythe's commentary and a slide projector which graphically illustrated the impact of the attack.

'Conservative estimates are 675 dead. Some thirty FRELIMO soldiers were also killed. The total figure is probably closer to a thousand. The wounded are estimated at around three hundred. We had no casualties and I understand the Selous Scouts weren't able to bring back any captives, or the documents. Unfortunately the Teacher died in the attack and apparently the missing papers were destroyed in a fire.* But still, in all, a truly satisfactory result.' The General cleared his throat. 'Now we are facing ridiculous charges of genocide from the UN. How else do they think we can defend our country and our families against communism and armed terrorists?'

David drove into the killing ground with the main task force from Chimoio base. They had come to salvage what they could from Nyadzonya.

He was repulsed by what they found. The previous attack on the ZANLA camp and hospital had been horrific. Here, the carnage was on such a scale that it staggered the imagination.

A bulldozer was immediately set to cutting a wide trench, while a second, moved slowly along gathering up the dead. The stench indescribable! After several hours in the sun, the victims' bodies were already bloated and decomposing—their smell clung to the living, forcing them to cover their faces. The bodies in grotesque attitudes of death, were toppled into mass graves. Search parties brought in more dead from the surrounding bush and dragged the river for further victims.

David stumbled into the remains of the hospital. The wooden poles which had supported the walls were burnt down to stumps. The row of twisted metal bed frames, with remains of human skeletons fused to the springs, stood stark in hideously regular formation. All were covered in ash. Nothing else remained. He searched among the few survivors coming in from the surrounding bush. There was no sign of Mbada's brother, nor of the documents of which he had spoken.

o0o

18 September 1976
In the week running up to this day, Ian Smith was still telling the world at large that White Rhodesians would never capitulate. His military advisors had assured him that they were now on top of the situation and still boasted about the success of the Nyadzonya raid; within months terrorist activities would be reduced to an all-time low.*

Henry Kissinger's second visit to South Africa came as a surprise. He first met the South African Premier and then requested the presence of the Rhodesian Prime Minister.

Before Ian Smith left Salisbury to fly to South Africa he was brimming with confidence, certain that US support would be forthcoming. The Americans would back his stance against the communist onslaught, of that he was sure. Besides, the Secretary of State's wife was accompanying her husband on his visit. She was an avid fan of his. Surely this was a good omen!*

He joined Henry Kissinger and John Vorster in a succession of private meetings lasting several hours. At times, Jan DuToit and other aides were present, but they were not privy to what was said between Kissinger and Smith behind closed doors. When Smith emerged from the talks he appeared ashen. The Rhodesian delegation flew home the same day. It appeared that Kissinger had issued an ultimatum, leaving little room for manoeuvre or barely time for Smith to present the facts to his cabinet. Within the week Ian Smith flew back to South Africa, where Kissinger waited patiently to accept Rhodesia's capitulation.*

The country's leading newspaper carried the full text of Prime Minister Smith's statement:

25 September 1976

As you are all aware, I have recently had a series of meetings in Pretoria, firstly with the South African Prime Minister, then with Dr Kissinger and finally with Dr Kissinger and Mr Vorster together.
At these meetings the position of Rhodesia in relation to the rest of Southern Africa, and indeed to the Western nations, was discussed in great detail. It was made abundantly clear to me, and to my colleagues who accompanied me, that as long as the present circumstances in Rhodesia prevailed, we could expect no help or support of any kind from the free world....
The alternative to acceptance of the proposals was explained to us in the clearest terms, which left no room for misunderstanding.... *

After a decade of announcements of no surrender and despite the promise made by Ian Smith of no Black rule in his lifetime, there remained only one thing to do—hand over power to the people of Zimbabwe. This turnabout was so sudden that it caught the Black leaders unprepared.

The Rhodesian Herald announced:

MAJORITY RULE IN TWO YEARS

Interim government to be established

THE GOVERNMENT HAS ACCEPTED *the proposals put forward by the US Secretary of State, Dr Kissinger for majority rule in Rhodesia....**

oOo

10 February 1977

On this day, Cape Town's parliament building saw the last meeting of the two White racist régimes in Southern Africa. The Rhodesian cabinet sat on one side facing the South Africans on the other. Time was fast running out for both countries. The fact that the policy of apartheid was beginning to unravel was slowly being recognised and both sides needed someone to blame for their own failures.*

Jan DuToit, who had served as a minister in the South African cabinet for the past three years, now turned to the Rhodesian delegation and opened the meeting by questioning Rhodesia's attitude to his country's export market with Zambia.

A member of the Rhodesian delegation rose to reply. 'Gentlemen, we understand your concerns about the border closure and your trading position with that country. We regret the incident and do not wish to repeat that affair any more than you do.'

'Your forced capitulation may very well rectify the situation anyway,' said Jan. 'But nevertheless,' he went on, 'of even greater importance are the accusations levelled against you, that you have indulged in germ warfare. If we are to avert a crisis we must know exactly what weapons you have deployed in the Bush War.'

The Rhodesian minister was clearly annoyed. 'We have heard the rumours and as a cabinet we are innocent of any atrocity. There has not been, nor will there ever be, any government approval for such drastic measures.'

His response brought derisive snorts from the South Africans. Long-standing resentments still simmered among Afrikaners. They still recalled the ill-fated Jameson Raid when Cecil Rhodes' soldiers from Rhodesia had attempted to capture their heroic leader, Paul Kruger. And the treatment meted out to their women—prisoners in British concentration camps during the Boer War—rankled even more deeply. Such old wounds still festered over half a century later.

Jan could not contain himself any longer. 'Haven't you forgotten that our Defence Force has fought alongside and in support of yours on the Zambezi?' He looked around at his colleagues and caught the Prime Minister's eye. 'I take it from your comment that there are certain measures that you would take, then please tell us, what measures would you use?'

'I resent that remark.' The Rhodesian was acid, ignoring the question. 'Yours was a token force, more of a hindrance than any help to us. What did they do apart from languishing behind barricades the whole bloody time, while we were fighting an honourable war and...'

'Enough!' A senior minister's voice boomed across the room. Both speakers sat down. 'I've heard enough of this. This meeting must not turn into a slanging match. We are here to resolve a problem that concerns us all.' He moved across the chamber before speaking again. 'This is the place where my dear friend Hendrik Verwoerd was assassinated. His dream of apartheid has assured us all of a Christian and civilised way of life in Africa. We will not throw it away. Your sacrifice is necessary and we share your loss in handing Rhodesia over to the Blacks, but there was nothing we could have done, it was out of our hands as you well know. It is now vital that we discuss a strategy that leaves us in a position of strength when this transition comes. I understand you are talking to your native chiefs. I always advocated a policy of dialogue with Black leaders who want separate development for their own peoples.' He paused. 'But, if there is to be any hope for the Whites, we must crush the communists before you hand over.' He glanced at the cabinet, 'We shall not tell you how to orchestrate your affairs,' then smiled at the Rhodesians, 'but you would be wise to take a leaf out of our book—we have been very successful in Mozambique and Angola.' His point made, he caught Jan's eye, who waiting for the barely perceptible nod, rose to take the floor.

'As to the matter in hand, I understand that this disease, or whatever it is, has been contained.' Jan squared up and stared directly at his counterpart, 'Whatever its origins. If that's right, well and good; but our leading authority on this subject who has been studying its effects in the field doesn't share your optimism, that is, unless you have been more successful in your efforts to eradicate it than I understand to be the case. He will explain to us what the potential threat really is and what further measures you may need to take in order to prevent it from becoming endemic.'

He signed to one of his aides and Professor Tinus Mueller was ushered into the chambers.

o0o

Vic Hammond was delighted. His promotion had given him awesome powers. The Rhodesian Government had sanctioned the CIO's revised policy, secretly planning to implement Hammond's strategy of escalating the war in the months ahead.

Meanwhile, through May 1977, they talked peace and continued to negotiate with the Black nationalist leaders within the country, who in turn faced ridicule for their naivety from Robert Mugabe, the newly emerged political spokesman for ZANU and its ZANLA guerrilla forces. He justifiably viewed this new-found benevolence with suspicion. While some bravely grasped the opportunity at whatever the cost, on any terms, to wrestle power from the White settlers, a few negotiated for their own more devious ends.*

Then, without warning, the security forces intensified and pressed home their offensive and seizing Mapai, their first major town in Mozambique.*

Unbeknown to the Rhodesian Government their deceit pleased Hammond further, for it also suited the objectives of his other benefactor.

oOo

The war was escalating and, as time passed, David became more and more concerned. It was now late September and the base hospital at Chimoio had already been extended into two further barrack rooms threatening to take over an entire section of the camp. Beds for those with minor ailments had already been moved outside under a lean-to. Every day the injured arrived after skirmishes with the Rhodesian security forces. Two other camps had been attacked and overrun and now those survivors were also trickling in, some having walked for days to reach Chimoio.

The situation threatened to deteriorate and he was having great difficulty in isolating patients with opportunist infections from those who were injured. Even the news that Robert Mugabe had been elected President of ZANU at a congress in Maputo did nothing to alleviate his anxiety.

oOo

Attacks by the South African-backed RENAMO forces continued to pose a constant threat to FRELIMO. In effect, South Africa was slowly bleeding Mozambique to death by fomenting civil war.*

In South Africa itself, BOSS pursued its enemies with renewed vigour, striking out violently at those who were seeking no more than basic freedom and rights for all citizens.

259

That evening in the canteen David learnt of Steve Biko's death in detention, having been tortured in a South African prison at the hands of BOSS.* When asked, the South African Minister of Justice, Jimmy Kruger, had replied, 'Biko's death leaves me cold.'*

David sat quietly in a corner remembering how this had all started at a certain political rally in Cape Town where he had waited in anticipation for Biko to speak. Recollections of his own mistreatment fanned his smouldering anger. He glanced down at his hands. Though they had healed the mental scars would always remain.

oOo

28 October 1977

In Pretoria General Stoffel Meyer, head of BOSS, was adamant. 'Van Heerden, I want you on tonight's flight to Rhodesia.' Wishing to terminate the conversation he said, 'Ask my secretary for your ticket on the way out.' He was at a loss to understand how Van Heerden had managed to work his way up to the position of commandant. 'Contact our agent and ensure everything runs according to plan, then...'

Van Heerden enthused, 'Ja, General. I understand your orders.'

It annoyed the General the way Van Heerden always tried to pre-empt his statements. 'You'd better, and you can tell him from me, we don't pay good krugerrands for nothing, and Mapai achieved nothing. Attacking that town has not resolved the problem. Do you hear me? This time we bloody well insist that the Rhodesian security forces eradicate this disease. I have reports here that confirm it has now spread to RENAMO.'

Van Heerden was not sure why the General was getting so worked up. 'But they're kaffirs!' he said.

'Who?' the General demanded.

'The RENAMO—kaffirs!'

Meyer's exasperation boiled over. 'My God, man! Don't you realise these Blacks are working for us? We finance, train and arm them to fight in Mozambique against FRELIMO.'

'Ja, General,' Van Heerden was perplexed, 'I realise that, but if they die as well, then you'll have got rid of two problems.'

Meyer became angry. 'Don't you realise, not before...' He stopped himself. 'Forget it. Tell this Rhodesian fellow from me that I demand they take prompt action and stop this disease spreading into RENAMO camps. This thing of theirs is out of control. Only last week we had to eliminate an entire RENAMO-held village. Reports indicate that the ZANLA bases at Chimoio and Tembue are centres for this disease. I want them hit, and hit hard. And you can tell our agent that I hold him and his men personally responsible for doing so. Is that clear?'

Van Heerden's clandestine meeting with their Rhodesian agent went according to plan. The BOSS commandant related what General Meyer had said, leaving their agent under no illusions.

'The bloody bastard means it. Fuck up this time and he'll roast your balls, boet.'

The agent's pallor seemed waxen and he sweated a lot. 'Okay, okay, I get the drift. Do you have the goods?'

Van Heerden handed over an ostrich-skin briefcase; when opened it revealed a small fortune in newly minted krugerrands.

An hour later the message was relayed to General Rocco Bastion-Smythe.

'He says the South Africans will not make a direct approach. Firstly, they don't want to be implicated and secondly, they feel our government might not comply with their request,' said Hammond.

General Bastion-Smythe snorted. 'Doesn't sound much like a request to me. Did he give you a deadline for us to act?'

Hammond shook his head. 'No, Rocco, but Van Heerden gave me the distinct impression it should be sooner rather than later.'

He was still holding onto the ostrich-skin briefcase.

Van Heerden's diplomatic visit to Rhodesia had been brief and executed without a hitch. With the confirmation he required tucked firmly into a file in his briefcase, he strode out onto the Air Force base tarmac at New Sarum, towards the waiting aircraft for the return trip to South Africa.

He would be able to report to his superiors in Pretoria that, in compliance with the South African directive, Rhodesian security forces were about to launch hot pursuit forays. These included land and air strikes on the two main ZANLA camps in Mozambique—with the objective of annihilating the occupants.

This would ensure that the disease was effectively eradicated.

oOo

Almost a month to the day since his return, Van Heerden received a copy of a Rhodesian newspaper forwarded with the compliments of Vic Hammond. Attached was a note: 'Thought you would want to read the headlines concerning Chimoio and Tembue.'*

261

The Rhodesia Herald
29 November 1977

1200 TERRORISTS KILLED

Forces smash two camps

Security forces have killed more than 1200 terrorists in what are acknowledged as their biggest and most successful raids to date against terrorist bases inside Mozambique.... Rhodesians greeted the news of the successful operations with delight. A group of Mozambican journalists who went to the area on Saturday with Mozambique's Vice-Minister of Defence Mr Armando Gubueza reported that the base was a "horrifying sight with pieces of bodies scattered everywhere"...that about 700 wounded had reached the hospital.... One of the worst-hit spots, according to the Guardian News Service, was a school where the bodies of more than 100 children were counted....*

Another article on the same page read:

Welcome in S.A. for peace bid

Johannesburg: The Minister of Foreign Affairs, Mr Pik Botha had welcomed the move by the Rhodesian Prime Minister, Mr Ian Smith, to achieve a domestic settlement in Rhodesia. SABC-TV reported last night....*

oOo

When the attack on Chimoio took place on 23 November 1977, David counted his blessings that he had been transferred to Moputu a month before. The Rhodesians might have expected such attacks to have shaken their enemy's confidence but, on the contrary, ZANLA was more determined than ever to strike back. David had revisited Chimoio shortly after the attack together with representatives of the UN. The scale of the massacre was massive. Again bodies were bulldozed, then cremated, before being covered over in more than a dozen mass graves.*

The Rhodesian Government faced international criticism, which came from many sources and not only from countries that might have been expected to condemn them. Quietly a number of cabinet ministers planned to resign and secrete their money abroad. In certain circles it was suggested that further negotiations with the Blacks at this point might divert attention from these atrocities and, more importantly, might hide the true purpose behind the barbarous attacks.

oOo

21 March 1978
The Chimoio 'incident' had shaken Jan DuToit and a number of the younger cabinet ministers, forcing the government to call an emergency session to discuss South Africa's involvement in Rhodesia's affairs.

'Gentlemen,' said the elder statesman, 'I can report that in Rhodesia a transitional government of Whites and Blacks was sworn in today, in a bid to stop the war. This, of course, ends White rule in that country. The Black militant African nationalists were invited to join the new government but I understand that these moves were rejected outright. The Rhodesian affair is now out of our hands.'*

Jan and his colleagues had been appalled when they learnt of South Africa's indirect involvement in the Rhodesian offensive. Carla's husband felt compelled to speak out.

'I'm sorry, but I cannot sit back and remain silent and I'm not alone. Some of us no longer trust senior ministers who have taken things into their own hands.' He stared defiantly at the Prime Minister. 'We will not stand by and see our country destroyed by a few egotistical and arrogant men with misguided beliefs.'

There were murmurs of approval from both sides of the House. A few senior politicians, for a moment, thought Jan was referring to their leniency in handing Rhodesia over to Black rule. They quickly realised their mistake.

'I promise you we will force radical change if we have to,' he shouted. 'We demand a revision of our security organisations' which, it seems, almost runs this House.' He waited for his words to sink in. The effect was electric! This was the first direct challenge issued to the old order. A split was imminent!

The elder statesman accepted the challenge. 'I hear what has been said here today. Let me make it abundantly clear. I did what I thought was right for our *volk* and this country...' but his words were ignored. Before he sat down he knew he had lost.

Later, when the House had emptied, he alone remained in his seat.

The tide had turned and he knew the cause—if it hadn't been for this confounded germ warfare! He looked at the spot where Verwoerd had been killed, and shuddered.

Vorster resigned as premier, and shortly afterwards his presidentship, before retiring altogether from politics.*

oOo

Hammond was furious, the transitional government of the settlers' choosing was doomed to failure. His plans had not worked and he had not foreseen the events that unfolded. The two major political parties in exile, the Zimbabwe African National Union (ZANU), and the Zimbabwe African People's Union (ZAPU), had formed an alliance early in October 1976.*

Now they presented a united front and he knew this put paid to all his future plans. For him, and many Whites, the end was in sight.

By March 1978 hundreds of freedom fighters had crossed the border from Mozambique and Zambia into Rhodesia to consolidate and defend newly gained territory. By mid-year there were over thirteen thousand ZANLA guerrillas in the country, besides those trained locally.*

The *Chimurenga* had defeated the enemy of the people, leaving the Rhodesians with no option but to negotiate with this new movement, called the Patriotic Front. A cease-fire was agreed by all parties and a settlement ultimately negotiated.*

Hammond knew the game was up. Soon, as had happened in Kenya, he would have to move on. When the time came he would know what to do; already there was an offer of an interesting position with an associate in Cape Town.

8 January 1980
Before new elections took place the Rhodesian ministries and security forces, in a bid to conceal their nefarious activities over the past decade, burnt their records. A pall of smoke hung over Salisbury for days.*

Vic Hammond called on General Bastion-Smythe and advised him clearly to destroy everything.

'We don't want files turning up or faces coming back to haunt us in the future. Rocco, make sure that all signs of the Germ Warfare Unit are eradicated.'

This immediately led to protests from Bastion-Smythe, 'It will take weeks—months—to eliminate the evidence!' he exclaimed.

Hammond provided the solution.

'After the elections you will have to answer to Mugabe about what went on here! Burn the lot now! We destroyed our department's entire interrogation records and archives yesterday. Took the bloody lot down to the city crematorium.'

The General promised to do the same for the Germ Warfare Unit's records.

oOo

David went in search of his superior officer. Within a week the necessary documentation had been completed and his bags packed. For him the war was over.

He contacted the African National Congress in Mozambique and they offered to put him in touch with John Gama, a long-standing supporter of the ANC. With the assistance of Gama's network he could slip quietly over the border into South Africa.

The ZANLA Chimurenga High Command had also suggested that he might think of returning to Zimbabwe. Men of his calibre were going to be needed in the new government.

David was undecided as what to do.

African Affairs

Rhodesia - renamed Zimbabwe

In February free elections led to a sweeping victory for the Patriotic Front, and on 18 April 1980 Robert Mugabe was elected the first president of a free and independent Zimbabwe. Another chapter in Africa's colonial history was over.

South Africa

After Vorster's resignation the new South African President, P.W. Botha, was slow in bringing about reform. Trade unions were eventually legalised and in some areas exclusive job reservation for Whites was relaxed. The government, for the first time, began to question details of its 'petty' apartheid laws; but segregation of the races remained firmly intact.

Over the next five years, the South Africa Defence Force tried desperately to destabilise the Black front-line States. Cross-border raids became routine.

Playing for time, South Africa signed the Komati Accord with Mozambique in 1984. If Mozambique stopped harbouring ANC terrorists, South Africa would in turn stop assisting RENAMO forces in northern Mozambique, who were threatening to overthrow the FRELIMO Government. Within months it became clear that South Africa had never intended to honour the agreement.

Internally South Africa had become unmanageable. Black workers staged a series of national strikes and, if their voice was not clearly heard, their action was certainly felt. The mood of the populace had changed irrevocably. The yoke of apartheid was being cast aside by people who would wait no longer for their freedom.

EXPOSURE

Houston, Texas

1985

CHAPTER 9

"In the end, the essential triumph has been that of the people of Zimbabwe themselves. Transmuting their suffering, their faith in the processes of peace has exceeded their courage in war."

Commonwealth Nations Report, 1980
on the free elections in Zimbabwe

2 March 1985

There was no respite—no hope. The attack, ferocious. A relentless onslaught against its victim, overwhelming the defences with lethal effect and closing down the system now awash in a sea of chemicals, plasma and a writhing mass of replicating and dying life forms. The electronic monitoring equipment, recording vital signs, sounded a warning. Alarmed, the nurse returned to check her patient.

The still figure lay sweating freely, his temperature 105°F. An oxygen mask covered his nose and mouth while a saline solution fed into his arm. The drip rate had already been increased to the maximum over two hours ago, to combat fluid loss. Each time the nurse came near, he wanted desperately to talk to her, to hear her say everything was going to be all right but the mask prevented this and it was too great an effort to lift an arm. After a minute and a sympathetic smile, the nurse resumed her other duties. Even though he could see her in his blurred peripheral vision he felt alone and afraid; he sensed that something very serious was happening. His head pounding—craving sleep, he closed his eyes.

Michael Bernstein's bedside telephone jarred him awake. Answering automatically, he glanced at the clock—2.00am. He listened to the caller. He sprang bolt upright, his face draining of colour. 'Oh, dear God. No!'

'Mr Bernstein? Are you still there, Mr Bernstein?' the voice enquired. A physical pain as from a blow, struck him in the stomach with unbelievable force. He worked his jaw, trying to answer but there was no sound.

'Hello! Mr Bernstein? Are you all right?'

His voice returned slowly and he spoke despite the knot of anguish in his stomach. 'Yes...I'm still here. When? How...how can it be? For God's sake, what the hell have you done? He was fine when I left him this evening. He was getting better.'

'Is there anyone with you, Mr Bernstein? A family member or a friend? I think it would be better if someone brought you to the hospital.'

'What? No, I'm alo—er, yes! Yes, I have a friend nearby. Paddy can drive me. I...I'll be there in twenty minutes.' The telephone went dead. He sat numbly holding the receiver in his lap, the full meaning of the news sinking in. It was no more than—he looked at his wristwatch—five hours. Five hours ago his son had been alive. Certainly he was unwell but his condition had seemed stable. It was only some kind of bug he'd picked up. How could this have happened?

The dial tone in his lap changed and Michael looked at the telephone quizzically, as if seeing it for the first time. After a moment's consideration he replaced the receiver in its cradle with a leaden movement, then immediately picked it up again and pressed one of the memory buttons. He raised the instrument to his ear like an automaton.

Sitting on the edge of the bed, he saw through unblinking eyes a cloudy vision of his son who had managed a faint smile when he had last seen him in his hospital bed a few hours ago.

'See ya tomorra, Dad.' John had whispered as Michael was reluctantly about to leave the hospital ward.

In under two weeks, John Bernstein would have been eleven years old.

'Yeah. Who is it? This had better be important.'

The gruff American-Irish voice brought Michael back to the present and he blinked away the vision. A tear escaped from his left eye; as it ran down his cheek, he rubbed it away with his hand.

'Paddy...' he croaked. He felt his voice about to break and gathered himself. 'Paddy, it's me, Mike—John just died. I have to get to the hospital. Can you come now? I'm at home and I could do with the company.'

'Christ!' Paddy swore. 'Wait right there, Mick—I'll be five minutes.' Padraig Duffy, co-partner of the clinical laboratory in Houston, Texas, where they worked together, was the only person ever to call him Mick. This had been Michael's first job in the US and somehow he had never moved on. Paddy had offered him a share in the laboratory and he had accepted. Michael knew he could rely on him for anything, despite Paddy's close friendship with Trish from college days.

Dr Winslow was kind and sympathetic. His years as a paediatrician had trained him to be so, but he had never become used to the task of reporting a child's death to bereaved parents. He dreaded it. He could not develop the technique, as some of his colleagues had, of hiding his own intense distress at relaying such news.

Michael guessed the doctor's difficulty but this was not the time where he could consider anyone else's feelings except his own. He pushed for an explanation.

'There have been at least a dozen other children in recent weeks,' the doctor explained uncomfortably, 'and a handful of adults too, who've been admitted with similar symptoms—high temperature, lethargy, nausea. There's a virulent bug going round the city and most hospitals have dealt with a large number of patients. I have to say, all ours have so far responded well to treatment. All except John, that is.' He found himself voicing perfunctory statements to a grieving parent. 'At the moment it is too early to tell exactly why it developed into such a virulent form of pneumonia. Tests will be done, of course, but it'll be a couple of days before the results are known.' Michael felt the doctor had effectively told him nothing—there was nothing as yet to tell.

'I want to see John now,' he interrupted.

The doctor considered this for a moment, nodded and picked up the telephone to make arrangements for Michael to see his son one last time.

After the ordeal, Paddy drove to his own home in River Oaks, with Michael in a state of semi-shock.

'You want me to call Trish?' Paddy passed him a glass containing a large shot of whiskey and poured one for himself. It was a rhetorical question.

'Eh? Oh! No...you're right. I'd better tell her.' Michael knew Paddy was not really offering to perform the task of telling his ex-wife the tragic news. He was suggesting that it ought to be done right away. Michael had phoned earlier to give her an update but Paddy was right of course. Although Trish had left him almost five years ago there was no enmity between them. If Trish and he hadn't separated when they did, Michael reflected, they could quite easily have become embittered. Neither had another partner until after the divorce. No, that wasn't it, Michael reminded himself. He had sometimes thought that if he could have taken a greater interest in her life, or she in his, then...but those considerations were well in the past. He was pleased that Trish had remarried two years ago and was happy. He took a large swig and dialled.

Trish was disbelieving at first—unable to accept what Michael was saying—but then it sank in. She cried out, an anguished wail that climbed dangerously near to hysteria.

Michael waited silently for her to compose herself. 'He didn't suffer,' he lied, trying to console her. He knew John had been in a lot of pain and hardly able to breathe but she didn't need to know that now. He hated lying but there was no point telling the truth.

Michael let her go in silent tears and promised Anthony, her husband, who took over the telephone, that he would inform them of the test results. 'Look after her, Anthony,' he said, hanging up without delay to let him go and comfort Trish.

Paddy returned from scrabbling around in the medicine cabinet and handed Michael some tablets while pouring another liberal portion of Irish

whiskey into Michael's glass. 'Take these, Mick. They'll help you relax.'
'Into blissful oblivion', thought Paddy, 'Thirty milligrams of Diazepam will
knock him out.'

Michael took the tablets as ordered and gulped them down.

For nearly thirty minutes Paddy listened dutifully to his friend's
outpourings—about the unfairness of life and death—before Michael
yielded to the heavy dose of sedative and spirit. Paddy raised Michael's
head and made him comfortable on the settee, removing his shoes and
covering him with a bedspread. 'Sleep well, my friend!' He closed the door
and went through to his bedroom to finish off the bottle of whiskey.

Michael's thoughts drifted back to John's early childhood. Like all children,
he had suffered cuts and bruises, measles and chickenpox; but he had
recovered faster than average. Hardy, and ignoring minor illnesses,
he had simply got on with the fun and excitement of being a boy. Colds and
influenza had been very rare.

There had been the accident of course, when John was a baby. Michael
had talked Trish, against her better judgement, into accompanying him on
a tour of the Zambezi Valley in Zambia. John had been two at the time and
they had set off in the early morning with him squealing in delight. Working
his way down a treacherous dirt road on the Zambezi escarpment, Michael
had slowed down to negotiate a deep erosion donga cut into the road.
He had been unprepared for the charging rhinoceros that seemingly came
from nowhere. Although he was an experienced driver he had lost control.
They had crashed heavily, after the one-ton beast had hooked its horn
under the chassis from behind and heaved them over the steep embankment,
sending the vehicle somersaulting down the slope. The rhino, apparently
content with its performance, had trotted away with not a care in the world.

John had been concussed and sustained internal bruising which required
emergency treatment. With intensive care he had recovered quickly and
Trish had gathered up her son and flown him back to the US after his
recovery. She had never forgiven Michael for that near tragedy, even
though he had left Zambia and had come over to the US in an attempt to
reconcile their differences. In time they simply drifted apart and, not wishing
to hurt Michael further, she had left but consented to her son's wishes to let
him stay with his father.

On one other occasion John had received a nasty laceration to his leg
while out playing on his bicycle that had required a blood transfusion.
He had proudly displayed the scar to his father like a battle wound. Lately
though, now that he thought about it, John had been getting more than his
fair share of colds and taking longer to get over them. He had seemed a little
lethargic too, which was unlike him. Michael had assumed it was because
he missed his mother and would have liked to have seen her more often.

After her remarriage, visits had become less and less frequent.

Suddenly he was horrified by a further thought. Being a microbiologist he had administered erythromycin to try to combat the symptoms of John's most recent attack leading up to his fatal illness. After two days his son had shown no improvement—in fact he had deteriorated. His action had been highly irregular. What if the drug had aggravated John's condition? What if he had taken his son into hospital those two days earlier? Might that have been soon enough to have saved his life?

Michael called at the hospital determined to see the doctor. What had killed his son? He wanted answers. The nurse ushered him through.

'The Doctor will see you now.'

'Please take a seat, Mr Bernstein,' said Dr Winslow softly.

'I know it's only Monday but do you have any more information? Why did John die?' Michael enquired tensely as the doctor flipped through the folder in front of him. He knew that the paediatrician had done everything in his power to save John. His eyes started to mist over again.

Dr Winslow, knowing Michael's profession, looked up. Making his mind up, he came straight to the point with no preamble or condolences. 'You must realise we haven't had time over the weekend to evaluate the tests. But I can tell you, Mr Bernstein, that your son died of pneumonia, sparked off by this confounded virus that's doing the rounds.' The doctor's frustration over what seemed to be a relatively minor, but nevertheless unsolvable, problem was evident. Dr Winslow recalled, however, that the common cold still baffled the world's best medical minds.

Michael appreciated Dr Winslow's professional candour. He knew of this virus, of course. The laboratory had been inundated with specimens by local doctors who had prescribed a variety of drugs to cure the problem but none cleared it. They only alleviated the symptoms. A few days' rest were usually enough and the body eventually took care of itself. It was the type of indiscriminate bug which caused headaches, tiredness and lethargy, that people sometimes used as an excuse for an extra day off work.

'Your son was clearly suffering from this virus and I am afraid things were complicated by the presence of another micro-organism...he simply failed to recover. The drugs did not seem to make him feel any more comfortable. Quite frankly, we are at a loss to explain why this should be.' He picked up a report and studied it thoroughly.

'Initial tests showed John's white blood cell count was very low and there was little we could do to fend off the infection. I have ordered further tests and will keep you informed. Please be assured, we tried everything possible. He did not respond to the Co-trimoxazole and, after its failure, there was a rapid deterioration in his condition. We even administered Pentamidine, but that made no impression!'

In the days that followed, he was full of self-reproach, while a dark, heavy suffocating cloud hung above him as he cleared John's room and organised arrangements for the funeral.

Michael cast his mind back. After leaving Zambia he had arrived in the US to start a new life in a new country. He now regretted the lack of direct contact with his brother, Aaron, since leaving South Africa for Zambia thirteen years before. They had managed to exchange letters on occasion through Poste Restante addresses around the world. In this way he had learned of Aaron's marriage to Ruth and the arrival of their twins—a boy and a girl—and had passed on news of his own son. By then, John was almost three years old.

Now it was time, he thought, to re-establish contact with his brother. Aaron had moved but he soon traced his telephone number through international directory enquiries.

Ruth answered and he introduced himself before she handed the telephone to his brother. Aaron sounded pleased to hear from him but Michael cut him short and came straight to the point.

'Aaron...John died a few days ago. It was a stupid bloody virus. He contracted pneumonia and whatever they did they couldn't stop it.'

'Oh dear God! I am sorry, Michael. Are you okay? Is there anything we can do?' It was the type of question everyone asks at such a time and, despite the fact they were talking from different continents, it did not seem ridiculous. Michael's answer was just as standard.

'Thanks, Aaron, but I'm okay. I've a damn good friend here, Paddy— I mentioned him in my last letter. He's being very supportive.'

'All right, but if you need anything...'

'Well, I was half hoping to visit you and your family sometime soon.' Michael desperately wished he were there now.

Aaron hesitated momentarily. 'Of course, we'd love to have you. Just name the day.'

After the funeral Michael remained apathetic. Paddy tried to convince him that he was needed at the laboratory. Michael resisted but, nevertheless, allowed himself to be persuaded.

Paddy was right—after four days of hell, he returned to the lab—the daily routine helped distract him from the pain and life went on. Attempting to push John to the back of his mind, he busied himself with the preparation of slides taken from the latest batch of specimens.

Michael hadn't been back seventy-two hours, when, before their lunch break, a courier entered carrying a package. Paddy had gone round to the other side of the partition, which served as a reception area, in answer to the bell. A sample pack of heaven-knows-what this time, thought Paddy.

These were usually accompanied by a pushy representative but occasionally deliveries of trial offers were sent by courier. No doubt the rep would be around soon enough to press for an order.

'Delivery—Michael Bernstein,' said the courier after pressing the bell.

He nodded and, with an engaging smile, held out his hand for the package.

'You Michael Bernstein?' the courier queried, holding the package close to his chest. 'This is addressed to Michael Bernstein personally—you're sure you are Mr Bernstein?' he repeated.

Michael heard the exchange and noted the delivery man's clipped foreign accent with a faint smile, as he finished his work for the morning. It reminded him of his homeland. About to declare himself, he held back as he heard Paddy's reply.

'I'm pretty sure. I was Michael Bernstein yester...' Paddy's flippant answer was cut short.

'Sign here,' said the courier.

Paddy shrugged and signed Michael's name on the delivery note as he had done so often. The courier barely glanced at it before striding out, leaving the parcel on the counter. Michael finished tidying up his worktop with an exasperated shake of the head, but he was grinning as he came around to the reception area.

'One of these days, Paddy, you're going to be caught out impersonating me,' Michael warned his friend.

Paddy grinned back at him. 'Bloody Germans—no sense of humour!'

'Not German,' contended Michael. 'South African. I should know, I grew up there. I couldn't mistake that accent.' Hanging up his white coat, he collected his jacket from the coat-hook behind the door and said, 'You open the parcel. I'm going down to see Frankie. Won't be long.'

Frankie owned the diner downstairs. He was terminally ill—dying of AIDS and on maintenance therapy. To make things worse he had a pathological fear of hospitals and all things medical. Susceptible to disease, he lived in mortal fear his customers might find out. He maintained that the consequences would be disastrous as the small business was his only livelihood. Michael was happy to take on the responsibility of administering the medication himself. It took only a few minutes.

'Take your time, Mick. It's quiet today. I'm fine here by myself for a while—see you down there for a bite, later.' Paddy knew Michael and Frankie would probably have a cup of coffee or two, and talk about betting on the horses and better times...he had called on Frankie himself in the past. He picked up the parcel and carried it through to the laboratory. He was in the habit of opening all the post anyway.

Michael went through the same performance every time. Coaxing his reluctant and talkative friend through the kitchen into the rear apartment. Then on seeing the syringe, within seconds Frankie was reduced to a quivering wreck and he spent several minutes calming him down. Michael never accepted payment for the medical attention; besides, the diner wasn't doing that well and Paddy and he enjoyed the free coffee and bagels which Frankie sent upstairs in an endless supply.

Paddy was annoyed at first by this generosity with their profits. They had even argued about it in the early days, but now he budgeted for Michael's benevolent disposition.

Frankie was refilling Michael's coffee cup when the apartment windows rattled violently, followed instantly by a deep rumble, like a roll of thunder overhead. It was punctuated by the clatter of pans and smashing cups and plates, and plaster dust showered down from the ceiling, followed by silence that was almost immediately broken by frantic screams and shouting as horrified customers stumbled from the diner.

Michael joined the rush for the exit. On reaching the sidewalk where a number of people stood in shock, unaware of their injuries inflicted by flying debris and glass, he followed their fixed stares. Looking up he froze in disbelief. A cloud of dust and smoke billowed from the laboratory.

'Paddy!' Michael raced up the stairs.

It took a few seconds to reach the landing. Inside the shell Michael found himself surrounded by flames that licked the ceiling; the air was thick with smoke mingled with masonry dust. Glass crunched underfoot as, with handkerchief held to his face, he stumbled through the remains of the lab. It was difficult enough to see at all but then a gust of wind wafted a pall of acrid black smoke into his eyes, blinding him completely.

'Down! I must get down!' Falling to his hands and knees he gashed his palms on the shattered remains of hundreds of bottles, slides and test tubes, yet he felt no pain.

'Paddy!' he yelled, coughing spasmodically, then croaked, 'Can you hear me?' Tears brought on by the stinging atmosphere cleared enough of the dust from his eyes for him to make out a fire extinguisher and he grabbed it. He felt for the mechanism. Blinking rapidly, he aimed the flexible hose at the shattered wooden partitions and shelving which had caught alight.

'Paddy!' He screamed again as he stood up. 'For Christ's sake, where are you?' He stumbled about in the semi-darkness, searching desperately as he went, dousing small pockets of fire.

The smoke and dust were beginning to settle. He could see a lot better but there was still no sign of his partner. The extinguisher spluttered, spent, and he threw it down among the rubble.

Where would he have been? Michael crashed against the sagging counter which he used to steady himself. Of course! He raised himself up to look over the counter and was totally unprepared for what he saw. A flash-burned torso, mutilated beyond recognition by the direct force of the explosion, lay on the floor. There were no hands on the charred arms and the head was missing. He stared for a moment in disbelief, then vomited.

Paramedics had the unenviable task of removing the body—considering the force of the explosion it was a miracle there was only one casualty. While the fire department made the building secure, the police detectives made enquiries of Michael and neighbouring establishments. Michael drank coffee, strong and black, courtesy of Frankie's Diner—thankfully pretty much untouched, if you discounted the broken crockery.

'What was it—the gas boiler?' Michael asked the lieutenant.

'The gas!' The streetwise police officer checked himself. 'You're havin' me on, right?'

'What do you mean?' Michael gave him a quizzical look. Before the police officer could answer, they were interrupted by the fire chief emerging from the building.

'Yup. I was right. This confirms it.' Hooked on the end of his pen, he held out what looked like a charred piece of twisted metal about the size of a small coin attached to a thin strand of wire.

The police lieutenant eyed the object briefly and simply said, 'Detonator?'

'Sure looks like it,' the fire chief confirmed.

The policeman took the object, carefully dropping it into a plastic bag, and turned to Michael.

'Your friend was Irish, right? IRA connections?' It seemed more of a statement than a question.

He stared with stunned disbelief at the realisation of what he had heard. It was ridiculous. Why should the laboratory be bombed? Paddy had no enemies. In fact he enjoyed a very good relationship with all the neighbouring businesses and they were both well liked by their clientele. He could not recall anyone ever having been upset or angry. Yet he knew there was no mistake. This was no gas explosion. There was the acrid taste and smell of the dust which had made no impression at the time, other than to choke him. Now it was obvious. And Paddy. My God, Paddy. A picture of his headless body flooded his mind, he felt cold and proceeded to shake uncontrollably. He was dirty and his hands and knees, lacerated from crawling in the debris, began to hurt. The policeman gave him a sideways glance and called over to one of the medics.

He woke from a sedated sleep in the late afternoon—they wanted to keep him in overnight, despite his protests. Whatever it was that they had smeared on his hands and knees, it stung like hell. They hurt more now than before the treatment and were swathed in bandages.

His first thoughts were of John, then immediately returned to the day's events that had put him here. The massive blast in a confined space had clearly been meant to destroy the laboratory. Where had the bomb come from? His thoughts were interrupted by a visitor.

Lieutenant 'I've heard it all before' Pinkerton backed into Michael's room, berated by an unseen nurse with Michael's welfare at heart. 'Just five minutes, I promise,' he told her. And closed the door in her face.

'How ya doin?' he greeted. Pulling the bedside chair closer.

'I've known better days,' Michael replied.

Pinkerton eyed the dressed hands and forehead.

'You'll live!' he said drily.

'Have you come to fill me in or interrogate me?' Michael expected that, in view of the circumstances, he might well be a suspect himself. After all, he was conveniently out of the way at the time of the blast.

'Both!' he said. 'First, you can start by telling me if you or your partner had any enemies. Anyone who held a grudge, that sort of thing. Yeah, I know it's a cliché but I've gotta ask.'

Michael assured him that Paddy had no enemies nor knew of anyone who held a grudge. No, he did not think Paddy had any IRA connections, and no, there was no animosity between him and his ex-wife. Yes, they did get on with all their neighbours. No, Paddy was not refusing to pay protection money—they had never been asked for any as far as he knew.

'What's the connection with South Africa?'

The question came like a bombshell. That one question switched the focus of the attack from Paddy to himself.

He had left all things African behind when he set up a new life here in America. To all intents and purposes he was American. Even his accent was so modified as to be indiscernible, except to an acute ear which might pick up the odd inflection here and there.

'What makes you ask that?' Michael tried to keep his answer casual but his reaction did not go unnoticed by Pinkerton.

'Okay, what gives?' he asked again. 'What had Mr Duffy to do with South Africa?'

'Not Paddy. Me!' he said. 'It's no secret. I was born there. I left in 1972 because my political leanings didn't exactly endear me to the state, and I went to live in Zambia, that's a country to the north of South Africa.'

'Yeah! I reckon I know where it is,' said Pinkerton. 'Are you saying you were forced to leave, a refugee?'

'There was—er—shall we say a minor 'disagreement' between us as to which policies I should support. It's not like here, you know.'

'I've heard,' Pinkerton replied without humour. 'How minor is minor?'

'Minor. I mean at the time it seemed serious, but I still can't understand why they overreacted. I merely attended a couple of political meetings on campus when I was a student and later, after I qualified, I wrote to the media condemning apartheid. But in South Africa when BOSS—that's their Bureau of State Security—is interested in detaining you for questioning, you're not interested in being detained by them. Do you get my drift?' Pinkerton knew what he meant.

'So why are you asking about South Africa?' Michael enquired anxiously.

'Oh, it may be nothing. The bomb guys picked out a few fragments from the rubble and they say that some of the identifiable parts are possibly of South African origin. Darned how they know, but they're usually right. Thought you would want to know that the FBI will want to speak to you, and about your buddy.'

Pinkerton watched intently as Michael's eyes opened wide.

'My God! I'm being slow,' he said angrily. 'It was intended for me. Don't you see, it was meant to kill me.' He felt cold fear begin to well up inside. 'I can tell you that a parcel was delivered today for me. I didn't touch it. Paddy...' he swallowed hard as he remembered the last time he saw his friend in the rubble of the laboratory. 'Paddy must have opened it.' Remembering the man delivering a package—he had thought from one of the pharmaceutical companies—obviously he wasn't. Neither, he supposed was the package all that it had appeared to be. What was it he had said? 'This is addressed to Michael Bernstein personally.' The courier had a South African accent.

'It must have been in that package! He didn't stand a chance. The bastards didn't give him a chance. It should have been me. Oh Christ, Paddy.'

The cumulative effect of recent shocks—the loss of his son whose birthday would have been the following day, Paddy's death, and now fear for his own life—overwhelmed him. He broke down and wept unashamedly.

The detective knew that further questioning would be futile and touched Michael's arm sympathetically, rising from his chair to leave just as a nurse arrived to tell him in no uncertain terms that his time was up. He held up his hands in resignation. 'Okay, lady. I'm outta here,' he said in his soft, southern drawl.

o0o

At first, after fleeing from South Africa, Michael had looked over his shoulder for the unexpected, though he did not know exactly what he was looking for. That was the peculiar thing about his self-imposed exile—he was never quite sure why he had to flee! Certainly he had rubbed the South African authorities up the wrong way and, while no accusations were actually levelled, his escape had been a matter of life or death.

Admittedly, in Zambia he had felt edgy with every wrong number received on the telephone, or the squeal of tyres from a nearby car. Gradually, as time went by and each event was rationalised, his paranoia had evaporated. Here in the US he had not felt at all threatened and resumed a normal lifestyle.

'But now! I was the target. Me! Paddy is dead because of me.' Michael's anguish was deep. His heart ached knowing that he was responsible for his friend's violent death.

Retreating from the painful present, he cast his mind back. He had defied them once; then, despite their heavy-handed threats, again, when arrested for a second time after submitting a letter to a newspaper. This had ultimately led to his sudden departure from his homeland. Why would they still be interested in him? Not even the South African Government could be that insane, or could they? What about the accusations Carla had once levelled at him about some stolen research papers belonging to the Cape Doctor? Had they found the perpetrator? He could think of no other reasons—after all this time it didn't make sense.

'So what now?' he thought. 'Should I go to the authorities here in America? The South African Embassy?' Neither course of action inspired confidence. What could the Americans do even with the strong evidence of bomb fragments? Possibly give him a new identity! But if, as he believed, BOSS was behind the attack—how long would it take them to find him once more? It would clearly be folly to go to the South African Embassy.

He considered his situation. All that he had held dear was destroyed: his son, his friend, his livelihood—all gone. There was nothing for him here any more. Michael brooded on his contact with his brother and he could almost see and smell the country of his birth as he replayed their conversation in his mind. He needed answers and they were not to be found in Houston. He had known it all along—he simply needed to convince himself that the course of action he was planning was the right one.

The retrieved wall safe was still intact although scorched on the outer surface from the laboratory fire. He withdrew its undamaged contents.

'Paddy, my friend,' he mumbled to himself. 'I need your passport.'

Michael knew he must return to Cape Town where the nightmare began.

CHAPTER 10

"There are as many Communists in this [Black] freedom movement as there are Eskimos in Florida."

The Rev Dr Martin Luther King Jr
Negro integration leader, 1964
Assassinated in 1968

18 March 1985

It was a strange feeling, returning to one's homeland after such a long absence. Disembarking from the jumbo jet at Cape Town, Michael felt a familiar vibrancy that he had not experienced since he was forced to flee years ago. More than that though, he felt strongly that this was where he belonged and all the years away had been a temporary absence. This was home.

He joined the queue at passport control with apprehension. It was a scheduled flight and the officials were being thorough.

This was a mistake, he thought; he should have booked onto a charter flight with a holiday company. They would not be so thorough then. Michael had every reason to worry—he was travelling on a false document.

'Good afternoon, Mr Duffy.' The immigration officer spoke in the heavily accented English of the Afrikaner as he opened the passport. Michael nodded matter-of-factly, trying to convey an impression of boredom he did not feel. The passport was real enough but it wasn't his. The photograph bore some resemblance to himself and it should pass a cursory inspection—he was counting on it.

'American?' the immigration officer asked.

'Yeah, that's right,' Michael emphasised his acquired American accent.

'The reason for your visit?' The official pressed the keys of a computer, scanning the resulting data on a small screen.

'Vacation.' Michael was uneasy.

The official looked up sharply. 'Where are you planning to travel to?' The challenge was explicit.

'Oh! I'm told the Cape Peninsula and the Garden Route are worth seeing,' Michael answered smoothly, his story well rehearsed in advance. 'It's something I've always wanted to do and everyone who's been to Africa keeps telling me how beautiful it is, so I thought I'd start here.'

The official looked carefully from Michael to the passport, then back to the screen, for what seemed like an eternity.

Michael managed a weary smile. His heart was beating so strongly that he was sure it could be heard in the baggage hall. He realised he had made a dreadful mistake. This was anything but a cursory glance. The likeness between Paddy and himself ended at being approximately the same height, brown eyes and hair. Paddy's photograph was old but Michael knew it would not pass this close a scrutiny.

The official snapped the passport shut and handed it back. 'Welcome to South Africa, Mr Duffy. It is a beautiful country. Hope you enjoy your stay.'

'I'm sure I will. Have a nice day,' Michael answered, pocketing the passport with a deep but silent sigh of relief.

With little luggage and nothing to declare, he quickly found his way outside and hailed a cab. He asked to be driven to a central hotel. On registering, the receptionist relieved him of his passport as required of foreign visitors the world over. Michael asked about a hire car and was told the clerk who dealt with rentals had gone off duty. He would have to wait until the morning.

Because of the time difference it was later than he had realised. Room service brought an evening meal on a tray, after which Michael settled on the bed to relax and think. Throughout the long flight he had tried to work out a plan of action but there had been too many distractions: the constant interruptions for meals, the film, the passenger on the inside seat with a weak bladder. Even when there was a quiet spell, he had found himself watching the legs of the hostesses who brushed past his shoulder on their way up and down the narrow aisles. One in particular had reminded him of Carla as she had looked years ago with her hair tied up. He had summoned her on the pretext of wanting to watch the in-flight film. Treated to a professional smile, she had brought him a set of headphones, then she was gone again—and so was the similarity. But he couldn't stop thinking about Carla.

Even now he still had no idea what he was going to do, or how he was going to go about it. 'What are my objectives?' he asked himself aloud. 'Why am I here? I'm here because...because I shouldn't be. I should be dead. Only I'm not dead. Paddy is.' Unbidden pictures of the carnage at the laboratory filled his mind. He dismissed the images angrily. 'Think objectively, damn it,' he reprimanded himself and rose from the bed to pace about the room with his hands thrust deep into his pockets. 'Question: Why should anyone want me dead? Answer: I don't know! So find out. How do I find out? Find whoever it was that wanted me dead and ask them. Is that such a good idea? I don't know! Why am I here?' He paced the room silently for a while as he pondered the questions. 'The American police said there was a South African connection.

That's why I am here. So who in South Africa wants me dead? And why?' Michael returned to the bed to lie with his hands clasped behind his head, staring blankly at the ceiling.

He drifted back to 1972 when he had fled, along with David Nyamande to Botswana, with BOSS in hot pursuit. 'The Doc. I wonder what became of him?' he pondered. 'Somebody wanted me dead then, too. They said as much! They would've made it look like another suicide at Pretoria Prison; after beating the crap out of me, as they did to David. But why? It couldn't have been over that letter to the newspaper about the Homeland Citizenship Act, surely? Many letters as strong as mine were published. Well, almost as strong. And what about the missing research papers Carla mentioned? Dammit! I should have done something about all this long ago, then I wouldn't be in this mess.'

Carla invaded his thoughts again. He wanted to clear up the controversy surrounding these stolen research notes and, he needed to enlist her help. 'She'll be different now. I wonder what she's like? Perhaps she's where I should start.' He remembered the hurt and frustration it caused when reading the newspaper announcement of Carla and Jan's wedding; and screwing it up and flinging it across the room, because until then, he had harboured the faint hope that he would somehow straighten things out with her. Aaron had since told him they were still together.

'Perhaps now I can explain what happened?' he thought, trying to console himself that time is a great healer and, possibly, after all these years she would listen and understand, even if she did not forgive him.

'That's it! In the morning, I'll start with you, Carla.' Satisfied that at least he had a starting point, Michael showered and went to sleep.

Over breakfast in the hotel dining room Michael planned his next move. Appealing for Carla's help was one thing but first he had to find her. What then? Would she refuse to see him? Meeting her unannounced, by surprise even, would she turn him away? If he could get to see her, he was sure he could make her listen to his story. What on earth did she think he had done anyway?

'Mr Duffy?' A page enquired as Michael thoughtfully sipped his coffee. Michael looked up to see who was being addressed. 'Mr Duffy?' The page repeated uncertainly, looking directly at Michael.

'Oh...er, yes. Yes, I'm Mr Duffy,' Michael said hastily, suddenly remembering who he was supposed to be. 'Sorry, I was miles away. What is it?'

The page seemed relieved. 'Reception asked me to tell you the hire company will require a current international driver's licence.' He handed Michael an assortment of pamphlets. 'For the car, sir,' he explained. 'You did ask about a hire car at reception, didn't you, sir?'

His hesitancy returned. 'Oh...yes...yes I did, thank you. Incidentally, will they deliver to the door?'

'Yes, sir, most companies do. We can arrange delivery within the hour.'

Michael watched the page depart and cursed silently. It was an oversight. He hadn't thought to bring Paddy's driver's licence with him. Michael had a licence in his name but now, booked in as Padraig Duffy he could hardly use it and, besides, it would be foolhardy while in South Africa—computer checks were not far from his mind. No, he would have to take cabs everywhere.

Michael went to the public telephones in the foyer where he thumbed through the directory for DuToit. There were many, a few with addresses in the wealthier suburbs of the city. He dialled the numbers one after another. Twenty minutes later he had exhausted every J. DuToit in the book. It was likely that a public figure like Jan DuToit would be ex-directory anyway. So much for plan A., move on to plan B.

Adderley Street led him to the Houses of Parliament buildings. For security reasons, no one would give him the address or private telephone number of a member. Instead he was directed to the Nationalist Party headquarters, a few blocks away, where he was told he might be able to speak with the administrator or leave a message with the secretariat.

The building was a five minute walk away. 'Hi, Paddy Duffy, freelance journalist,' Michael said brashly, by way of introducing himself to the receptionist. He flashed his US driving licence swiftly in front of her eyes before returning it deftly to an inside pocket. 'I've flown in from the US to do a piece on one of your up-and-coming 'progressives' for *Time* magazine. Henry Kissinger's press office said I could do worse than try...' pausing to check a blank piece of paper, 'Jan DuToit. Can I speak to Jan DuToit, Miss?'

'Henry Kissinger? The Henry Kissinger from America?' the girl asked, impressed.

'Sure, the Henry Kissinger from America,' he mimicked with a smile. 'Is there another? I've done a piece on him. Nice guy. Said he was looking closely at South African affairs and had spotted some political talent over here on his last visit. He mentioned this...' checking the piece of paper again, 'Jan DuToit. Is he here now? Can I speak to him?'

The girl chuckled with amusement at his French pronunciation of the Afrikaans name and at his naive expectations. 'I am sorry, Mr Duffy,' she said, maintaining her smile. 'Our ministers are very busy people. You will need to make an appointment if you want to interview him and you will have to speak to one of his secretaries for that.' She stifled a laugh with a small cough, consulting the list in front of her. 'I'm not sure I've heard the 'Nats', being called 'progressive' before.' With a conspiratorial whisper she informed him, 'The Progressive Party are our major opposition, here in South Africa.'

'What's he like, then, this DuToit? Fat and bald I shouldn't wonder.' The girl smiled again as he deliberately mispronounced the name. He remembered Jan DuToit from his weekend at the Boshoff estate. Jan had commandeered Carla's attention practically the whole evening. He was good-looking then but perhaps he had not weathered the intervening years so well. Anything detrimental would be encouraging but the girl said, 'Oh, no. Not our Jan,' with genuine affection. 'He is really quite handsome and very nice with it,' keeping her secret desires and ambition well hidden.

She returned to consult her list. 'Here we are.' She dialled an internal number. 'Marie, hi, it's Stella. I have a gentleman here in reception who wishes to make an appointment with Jan. Is Hettie there? Oh, I see. Okay then. Thanks anyway.' She hung up. 'Mr DuToit's secretary is not in today. Could you possibly call back tomorrow?' she asked.

'I'm afraid not,' Michael lied. 'I have rather a busy schedule. Never mind, Henry gave me another name—someone in your opposition party—I could do him. Tide and *Time* wait for no man, you know,' he joked. 'Pity, though. I particularly wanted to do the 'Nats'. They have by far the most attractive receptionists.' He gave her a practised look of sincere regret. 'I thought we might have been able to squeeze your photo in with a shot of the reception area. Thanks anyway.' He turned to go.

'No, wait,' she said glancing around the otherwise deserted reception area. She unlocked a desk drawer and extracted a book. 'I shouldn't do this but if you really think it will help him...well, I'm sure it will be all right just this once. But you mustn't tell anyone how you came by it. Promise?'

'Promise,' flashing his engaging, and genuinely grateful, smile.

She flipped through the pages of the book and copied the home number of Jan DuToit onto a notepad. She tore the page out and folded it neatly before slipping it secretively into his hand.

Michael found a public telephone and dialled the number. The houseboy answered. Michael forced his South African accent. 'Let me speak to Mrs DuToit, please.'

'Yes, baas. Whom shall I say is calling?' the houseboy asked in a cultivated telephone manner.

'Please tell Mrs DuToit it's an old friend,' Michael thought that a little mystery would be irresistible.

'My madam has instructed me to ask the caller for a name, baas,' he said functionally.

It was clear that Michael was not going to get past this fellow without giving a name. His mind raced for something alluring but he could not think of anything clever to say.

'Tell Mrs DuToit that Mr Michael is calling.'

'And what may I say it is in connection with?' came the response.

'It's about...er...the laboratories. Tell her Mr Michael is calling about the Mueller Laboratories.'

'Yes, baas. Mr Michael about the Mueller Laboratories. But my madam is not at home. She and the master are away and will be back by tomorrow lunch-time.'

'Well, why didn't you.... Oh! Never mind, I'll call back.' Michael's teeth were clenched in exasperation; his frustration due to this unexpected circumstance. He had hoped to speak to Carla and now there was a delay. He replaced the receiver with exaggerated care. He checked his watch— there remained the rest of the afternoon to kill. He walked around the city centre, familiarising himself with old haunts.

Michael rose early and, without any real purpose, caught a taxi to the foot of Table Mountain, near the cable-car station, and had the driver agree to return after two hours.

He strolled on the familiar slopes where he had first made friends with Carla. Now, as then, tourists disembarked after their twelve-minute descent from the top of the mountain. In all his years in Cape Town he had never once ventured to the top. The thought of being suspended from a cable high above the ground lacked appeal. He could imagine how splendid the views must be—everyone said they were magnificent. He wandered further up into the foothills, as he had with Carla, until they became too steep for comfort and then he settled on a boulder and gazed once again across the cityscape to Table Bay and beyond to Robben Island where, Nelson Mandela still languished as a prisoner of the Government. Thoughts of the youthful Carla filled his mind. He could see in his mind the image of her stepping between the boulders strewn about the hillside below; his heart filled with sadness. If only...

He was surprised to find the stipulated time had passed while he was daydreaming of what might have been. It was time to return to the city and try to make contact with his first real love.

Michael hoped Carla would be there and had not gone straight out again after her return. On the third ring his call was answered.

'Hello, it's me again. Is Mrs DuToit back yet?'

'Sorry sir, but whom shall I say is calling?'

'Now please don't start all that again,' Michael pleaded. 'If Mrs DuToit is home, please tell her that Mr Michael is calling about the laboratories.'

'Yes baas, I will call my madam immediately.'

Michael heard him retreat rapidly across a tiled floor.

Now other footsteps approached the telephone—the measured clip of high-heels—and his heart began to pound with nervous excitement. He tried to imagine how she might look now. Had she gained weight? But imagined she had not. Was she going grey? He saw fair hair with perhaps a streak or two, swept up and tied elegantly. Possibly wrinkles at the corners of her eyes, evidence of the smiles and laughter of a happy life. How would she sound? Probably as sweet as he remembered....

'Hello, Mr McGill? How can I help you?'

Michael was momentarily lost for words.

'Hello, is anyone there?'

'Oh, er, hello. Carla?' he croaked.

'This is Mrs DuToit,' she said, 'and you are...Mr McGill?' she raised her voice at the end of the sentence, making it a question, unable to place him.

'No, Carla, not McGill.' He paused briefly, listening for her reaction to the sound of his voice, but there was none that he could discern. It had been so long and he had acquired an American accent. It was clear that she did not recognise his voice.

'Who is this?' her annoyance was evident.

'I'm sorry. I didn't mean to alarm you, it's...' hesitating, wondering what he should say next, knowing that this line would not be secure.

'I beg your pardon! Who are you? Do I know you?'

Michael thought he detected a hint of doubtful recognition in her voice. He concentrated on his South African accent. 'Please don't say anything, Carla. I did not say McGill, I said—Michael.' He heard her catch her breath and knew that she recognised him now. 'I can explain...'

'You!' she exclaimed in disbelief. 'How...why...what do you want? You left...'

'Stop, Carla,' his voice urgent, cutting her off. 'Please don't say any more—just listen to me—you must! I need your help in a delicate matter and I need to keep a low profile for the moment. We can't talk on the phone. Please, will you meet me somewhere?'

There was a long silence as Carla gathered her thoughts. The nerve of the man—after all these years. He had absconded like a thief in the night with valuable documents—after she had decided to marry him!

Michael could imagine what was going through her mind. She was trying to make sense of his call. He wasn't sure what she knew of his sudden departure but, from the abortive attempts he had made to reach her, he guessed she felt betrayed. 'Please, Carla,' he encouraged her, 'I need to explain the truth to you. You don't understand, do you? Don't you want to know what really happened?'

Carla thought she knew the facts. She had accepted the story Tinus Mueller had given her. The evidence supplied by the Bureau of State Security was overwhelming but, she admitted to herself, that was only one side of the story. Still he had destroyed their love....

'No, Michael, I don't think so. You have absolutely no idea how much you hurt me, have you?'

'Carla, I'm not asking you to forgive me. I understand how you must feel,' he heard his voice break. 'It's made my life a living hell as well. I know we cannot go back...this is not about us. What I have to say is extremely important. Carla, someone is trying to kill me!'

It took her by surprise, but he had said it in earnest and she could tell he believed it.

He waited for her response but her silence was enough.

'I have never been more serious, Carla. An attempt was made on my life, very recently—my friend was killed! I'm sorry, I have probably said too much already, but I need to talk to you.'

There followed another long silence.

'Very well then,' she agreed reluctantly, her voice unsteady. 'I will meet you. Where and when?'

'Thank God!' he said with relief. Without her, his tentative plan to find out why someone wanted him dead could not get off the ground. 'It must be soon—but we need to be careful. Do you remember a certain beach where we used to walk? It was our favourite. There was a hotel there, remember. We had been walking on the beach late one evening and then we...'

'Yes, yes,' she said hurriedly, 'I know where you mean. When?'

It disappointed him that she was embarrassed to remember the time when they had made love urgently in a quiet spot on the Muizenberg beach in the twilight, excited all the more by the possibility of discovery.

'Today, this evening,' he said, trying to control his excitement lest she misinterpret his eagerness. On balance, he thought, it would not be a misinterpretation.

Carla thought for a moment. Jan had a political meeting at home with some of his colleagues. Such meetings were inclined to drag on for hours and it was not unusual for her to visit a friend on such occasions.

'All right, this evening. I will be outside...the hotel at...at eight o'clock. I warn you, this had better be good.'

'You'd better believe it, Carla, it will be.' And he knew that for him, at least, just being near her again would be good.

Michael took the late commuter train southwards to Muizenberg. He watched the city workers disembark at the outlying suburbs, and was surprised to see most of the surrounding countryside had been absorbed into the greater metropolis of Cape Town. His stop came up and he joined the rush for the exit and was taken aback by the changes to the village since his departure.

Muizenberg was now strewn with modern developments, high-rise buildings and billboards depicting sprawling new residential areas. A quick walk from the station and he was on familiar ground. Even so, what had once been a small, picturesque village had expanded almost out of all recognition. Saddened, he strolled past the spot near the hotel where Carla and he had shared intimate moments.

He had allowed ample time before their rendezvous in order to find a place from where he could see clearly in either direction, to ensure that she was not followed. Such paranoia might not be necessary but, with recent events still frighteningly fresh in his mind, it was expedient not to take chances.

With time to spare, he walked along Baden Powell Drive towards Sunrise Beach, as he and Carla had done so many times. He looked at his watch and turned back towards Muizenberg, his thoughts of happier times fading. He stopped at a spot almost a hundred metres from the hotel. From this vantage point he could watch her approach. He still had half an hour to kill.

He found a bus shelter and sat down to wait, watching the regular flow of traffic with fascination. At this time of night it was a mix of late office workers returning home to their families and evening revellers on their way to the hotel bars, clubs and shows to join friends and colleagues; or maybe to make an illicit rendezvous with other men's wives...?

Watching the cars, he realised that he did not know what Carla would be driving. Her blue BMW must have been traded-in long ago and anyway, he surmised, it was not suitable for a prominent minister's wife. He scanned the traffic carefully. Which one would it be? He watched each car that drew up at the hotel but the occupants either disappeared inside or went onto the beach for an evening stroll, some hand in hand and in love.

By 8.15pm it looked as though Carla was having second thoughts about their meeting. Michael stood up and had begun to walk back towards the hotel when a sleek, black Porsche approached at speed and slowed smoothly to a measured halt immediately in front of the main entrance. A lady in her mid-thirties stepped out with practised ease from the low sports seat despite the tightness of her short skirt. She ignored the stares of passers-by and stood elegantly on the pavement, looking first in one direction and then in the other. Twenty paces away Michael came to a standstill with a sharp intake of breath. Carla was much as he had pictured her, yet even more beautiful. The smoothly tailored skirt and jacket accentuated her figure, while her blonde hair was swept loosely back and held by a clasp.

Her eyes stopped searching abruptly, as she caught sight of him for the first time in years. For a moment they stood, transfixed, staring at one another. Michael could feel the blood coursing through his veins and his skin tingled. She smiled fleetingly before her eyes narrowed and her expression hardened. Her look broke the spell and he moved towards her.

'Carla,' he said, fearing to trust his voice.

'Michael Bernstein,' she nodded slowly as she looked him up and down as though evaluating a racehorse. In a matter-of-fact voice she said, 'You haven't changed much. The years have been kind to you.'

It certainly didn't feel like it, after his son's death, Paddy's murder, he felt more than a little haggard—but she was beautiful, he thought!

'And to you.'

Carla inclined her head in acceptance of his understated compliment.

It was difficult to know what to say next. After an uncomfortable silence Michael nodded at the Porsche and said, 'Nice car.'

Carla sighed heavily with impatience. 'For God's sake, Michael, we are not here to talk about my car. You have a lot of explaining to do. Hadn't you better get on with it?'

'Yes, of course, but not here. Can we go somewhere quiet?'

Carla hesitated for a moment and then said brusquely, 'All right, get in.' She drove off swiftly in total control, confidently easing the powerful car smoothly into a gap in the traffic. Towards the edge of town, as the traffic thinned, she hit the accelerator and sped past Sunrise Beach. They did not speak during the seven-kilometre drive along the False Bay coastal road until Carla slowed, then pulled off before Strandfontein and turned onto a secluded dirt track. Michael had not even been aware that the turning was there. Carla stopped the car on the rise overlooking the beach. They were surrounded on three sides by grassy dunes, out of sight from the main road only a few metres away. It was evident that Carla had been here before and Michael guessed why.

'Jan and I used to come here sometimes,' Carla said in reply to his sidelong glance and the unspoken question. 'Years ago when we first started going together. We never even went down to the beach. I couldn't even tell you if it's a Black beach or a White one.'

Michael felt unreasonably resentful of the intimacy she and Jan would have shared in this tranquil place above the breakers.

'What did you think? That I was going to wait all this time in case you came back?' she said.

'I didn't say a word,' he replied.

'You didn't have to. It's written all over your face.'

'You wouldn't take my calls. I tried so many times,' he countered. 'Why wouldn't you talk to me?'

'What was there to say? You stole those research papers and left me after I had agreed to marry you. Was money so important to you? You knew I didn't care about that. What made you think I would marry a thief? And anyway you only called twice after I had spoken to you.'

'That's why I want to get to the bottom of, but first, how can you say I phoned only twice! I called dozens of times. Your damned father told me you would not talk to me. He told me you were marrying that politician. Directory enquiries said you had moved and I even tried phoning the Laboratories again under another assumed name. Every time I was told to hold and then the line went dead. I tried repeatedly, until I realised it was pointless. Can't you see, someone deliberately prevented me from speaking to you. Anyway, why didn't you bother to reply to my letters. Dammit, Carla, you didn't wait a moment before marrying...'

'Kindly leave Jan out of this...but what are you saying? It was almost a year after you left before our wedding was announced. I never received any more calls or any letters! And I don't hear you denying that you stole the research papers you sold in Zambia. How much did you get for them? I hope it was all worth it.'

'I have no idea what the hell you're on about. Look! I did not come all this way, after all this time, to pick a fight with you, Carla. By my life, I'm no thief—and if you'll let me explain—I don't know anything about stolen research papers and I certainly haven't sold any. I came here to tell you what happened back then, because I believe it has something to do with recent events...and to ask for your help. Don't you want to hear my side of the story?'

'I've already heard what happened. Tinus told me and it was confirmed by those BOSS apes.'

'BOSS! So I was right.'

'Michael, perhaps you would like to explain what this had to do with State Security? What was in those missing documents? Carla frowned. 'I think you owe me an explanation now.'

'I will,' Michael sighed, 'if you'll give me half a chance.'

Carla listened in silence to the tale of his escape before reaching the infamous detention centre in Pretoria. He told her of his flight into exile in Zambia, his career switch, then across the world to America and of his ill-fated marriage. She stifled a gasp at the tragic loss of his beloved son, and was shocked as news of the sudden violent death of his business partner, Paddy and evidence of South African involvement, unfolded.

'That is why I have come back now. It all started after I wrote that letter to the newspaper....' He stopped to take a deep breath, 'There is nothing left for me in America and I need to find out what's going on. Whatever else you may have heard, whatever you have been told, this is the truth, Carla,

I swear it. I have no reason to lie to you. But I need your help now if I am to get anywhere at all. Will you help me, Carla?'

'Michael, it all seems a bit far-fetched. Why have you left it until now to do anything about it? Didn't you want to know why you were chased halfway round the world? I'm bloody sure I would have wanted to know.'

'Of course I want to know. But don't you see? I couldn't do anything because, if I had, I would have given my position away and these guys play for keeps. I've kept my head down, dropped out of circulation in Zambia, and after I settled in the US it didn't seem to matter anymore. With John dying I thought of coming back and called Aaron—he's the only family I have. Then they blew up the laboratory. Now I have to find out what's going on. God knows how they found me there.'

'Phone tap,' said Carla matter-of-factly. 'It's quite common, I understand.' The casualness of her statement alarmed him and she explained. 'Jan often has colleagues round for meetings. I hear things.'

'That's probably how they pinpointed my location. My God, we even exchanged addresses!'

'One more thing. After you disappeared BOSS showed me photographs and claimed you were in Lusaka. You were with a known criminal— a 'broker' they called him; the sort who acts as a go-between in illicit deals. You were handing him something. How do you explain that?'

Michael's brow furrowed as he tried to recall events, which had occurred so many years ago, in Zambia. At that moment it came to him. 'This guy wouldn't have been over six feet tall and Black, would he? Wearing a brown leather bomber jacket and blue jeans?'

'Yes...I suppose so,' she said hesitantly. 'I only saw it briefly...'

'Ha!' Michael scoffed explosively, 'The bastards. David Nyamande, he is the doctor I was telling you about. We escaped across the border into Botswana. From there we went to Zambia together. He came from Soweto. He's the one who arranged for me to get a residence permit and that's when those shots were taken. We didn't see the car at first. David was handing over my residence permit when suddenly it did a U-turn and some bastard in the passenger seat stuck a bloody camera with a long lens out the window, then they sped off...it had us wondering at the time. We thought it was the Rhodesians or BOSS. I can tell you, I was bloody worried at the time. I didn't want to be around if they identified me. That must have been what you saw in the photograph, Carla.' He let her analyse his explanation for a while and then said, 'So what's it to be, Carla ? Will you help me?'

'Another thing. Why didn't you use your MG to escape ?'

'For God's sake! Because I was thousands of kilometres away. I have just explained! The car is probably still outside your flat where I left it,' he pleaded.

Carla considered it all, watching him intently, silently, trying to penetrate his mind for signs that his story was in any way fabricated. It had been a leading question to trap him if he was lying. If he had not been arrested, as he claimed, why would he not collect his beloved MG? She remembered the car not being there on her return from the funeral and she had assumed he had taken it to escape in. Somebody had removed it! Why would he deliberately lie about this, knowing he would be caught out. He believed the car was still 'there'...he would, only if he was telling the truth!

At last she said, 'I suppose I have to believe you. Nobody could make that up...it's all too incredible!' She noticed for the first time how strained he had been because, as she spoke, his anxiety seemed to ebb away. 'But how are you going to clear yourself?' she asked, 'And what exactly do you want me to do?'

'You don't know how relieved I am to hear you say that,' he said and leaned across to kiss her cheek. Carla was unresponsive but, Michael was happy to note, she did not object either.

She was bewildered, unsure of her emotions.

Michael continued quickly. 'I am not sure exactly what to do next. I thought perhaps a word with the 'Cape Doctor' if he is still around might help. It seems more than a coincidence that his research notes went missing around the time of my departure...I wonder what was in them? He had connections in high places. Do you know if he's still around? If he's still alive even?'

Carla put aside her conflicting emotions. 'I don't know. I haven't had anything to do with him for years. I hardly saw him at all after he closed down the labs and transferred the work to Groote Berg Hospital. I wound up his work there and he left before I took on responsibilities of my own. He really stuck up for you, you know, when those BOSS agents accused you of selling the research papers. Do you really think he could help now?'

'There's no harm in trying. I haven't anything else up my sleeve at the moment. He could be a good ally. Would your father know where he is? They were pretty close at one time, weren't they?'

'Yes, they were, but Papa lives in the UK now. Well, for six months of the year anyway. He has business interests over there. I could ask Jan, I suppose.'

'Would you? But er...'

'But what?' Carla saw his anxiety return.

'I would rather no one else knew I was here.' Michael was gambling but he had to trust her. 'The truth is I am travelling on Paddy's passport. Could you be discreet? At least until I know what is behind all this.'

'I see. Yes, I'll be careful, you needn't worry. I think your presence is best kept secret.'

They fell silent for a while, watching the brightening stars in the southern sky cast a shimmering light over the calm waters of the bay.

Michael tried to steer the conversation towards more mundane matters. For so long he had wanted to speak to her about normal things, to recapture their past, without this threat hanging over him. 'How's your family?'

'Oh, fine. Mama is the same as ever and my sister Louise lives in Paris... close to Papa. That's about it.' She did not elaborate.

Whatever Carla was thinking Michael could not tell, but his own thoughts turned to analyse his situation now that he had at least one ally. Carla's father was a friend of Tinus Mueller, another possible ally who, in turn, had powerful connections. She was also the wife of a prominent politician with connections, presumably, to the top. A powerful assembly indeed, yet at this moment Michael could trust none of them. Access to the corridors of power was useless until he could tell friend from foe. He must have more information. But where to find it?

He broke the awkward silence, 'When did the labs close?'

'Not long after...after you left. Tinus had other interests and the various projects gradually wound down. Tinus transferred what remained to Groote Berg and put me in charge of it. I still work there on occasions, mostly on a consultancy basis. Jan understands that I need to have a life of my own but obviously my main responsibility is to him. At his level there are times when we must function as a team, so part-time consultancy suits us both. Why do you ask?'

'What happened to all the records—the work we were doing? It wasn't all for nothing was it?'

'Oh no, far from it. You remember...? All the research was copied onto the computer and transferred to Groote Berg Hospital.'

'Bloody computers,' Michael said, 'but we can't do without them. I seem to recall you taking to them like a duck to water. Do you still use one at Groote Berg?'

'Yes, but mostly I copy my files onto a disk and take them home to work on my PC there.'

Michael lost in thought, turned away to gaze at the sheen on the breakers lapping the shore.

Carla let out a small cry of alarm. 'Look at the time, for God's sake. How did it all go so fast? Come, I must get back.'

She turned the key in the ignition and Michael struggled to find something important to say, reluctant for the evening to end, but there was nothing more. He knew he must let her go and he consoled himself with the fact that he would see her soon, hopefully with the information he needed.

Carla asked where he was staying.

'I had better take you back to your hotel.'

She dropped him at the car park. With regret Michael watched the Porsche pull out onto the feeder road and disappear, leaving him with a lonely, empty feeling. He glanced over at the hotel and sighed resignedly.

Carla left a message at reception for him to call her before lunch. Reading the note it seemed that she might have news. To be safe, he rang from a public booth in Adderley Street.

'Tinus is still here in the Cape,' Carla informed him. 'He has a place over at Hout Bay. I told Jan I needed to talk to him about my work, so he found the number for me.' Her excitement transmitted itself down the line. 'I called Tinus earlier and he will see me this afternoon—as yet he doesn't know you're coming along. Mind you, he was reluctant to see me at first, but changed his mind when I said it concerned your work.'

'Great! But I didn't mean you to get this involved. I'm *persona non grata* around here you know. What if things don't go according to plan?'

'What else could I do? I could hardly tell him I was sending you round instead, could I?'

'No, I suppose not. Thanks, Carla. When do we see him?'

'I will pick you up at your hotel in an hour.'

Taking the scenic route to Professor Mueller's home, they hugged the steep slopes above the many coves and bays that lay beneath the watchful gaze of the Twelve Apostles—the so named craggy mountainous peaks of the Cape Peninsula. It was a relatively slow drive because of the many twists and turns as the road followed the rugged coastline.

'What has the Cape Doctor been up to since he closed the labs?' Michael still harboured a tremendous amount of respect for the Professor abilities, curious to know how his old employer had been keeping busy.

'I don't know exactly. As I said, I didn't have much to do with him after we moved our research to the hospital. I think he was doing some work for a government agency though.'

'Yeah? What makes you say that?'

'In the last days he had a lot of visitors. Some of them were definitely military because I heard him use their rank. At least one of them was a colonel or a captain or something—I forget now—but I remember thinking 'military' at the time. Can't think what he was up to. He kept it all very quiet at the time.'

'Yes, now you mention it, I remember that. Others were diplomats, or at least they drove cars with diplomatic plates. They had started to come even before I left.' For reasons unknown to himself, Michael felt that this information was significant in some way and spent the journey trying to reason why.

Mueller's luxurious house nestled into the rock face overlooking the picturesque harbour, where fishing boats bobbed gently at their moorings. Tinus opened the door himself and greeted Carla with genuine pleasure. He stooped a little more than Michael remembered and had aged noticeably. His eyesight was failing and he was plainly unaware of Michael's presence until Carla stepped into the house.

'Wha...who is this? A friend of yours?' he said, squinting over Carla's shoulder.

'Professor, it's Michael, Michael Bernstein.'

Tinus Mueller was numb with surprise. 'Bernstein? But you're...you're...'

'Hello, Professor,' Michael offered his hand, unsure what to expect. Tinus was clearly stunned by his presence and scrabbled for the half-moon glasses balanced on top of his head. He had been so certain Michael Bernstein would never show up in South Africa again.

'You said it was about Michael Bernstein,' he accused Carla. 'You did not say he was here.' He peered at Michael through his glasses and saw the proffered hand for the first time. He hesitated and then, to Michael's relief, he took the outstretched hand and shook it briefly. The thin smile returned. 'You had better come in, both of you.'

They were ushered into a cavernous split-level lounge with a magnificent panoramic view, of the whole bay. The floor was tiled, scattered with rugs and animal skins. Plain white walls set off enormous modern paintings in bold colours. A sunken fireplace was the focal point of the room with seats arranged around it. Outside the wide windows was a large patio with wicker furniture, colourful cushions and potted geraniums. Beyond that, there was a sheer drop to the rocks below, then a gentler slope that tumbled down to the shoreline. Michael stayed well away from the patio.

A Coloured servant entered from the far end of the lounge carrying a silver salver with a Meissen ware coffee service which she placed on the glass-topped coffee table between the two settees. Tinus ordered her to bring an extra cup after which he dismissed her. He poured the coffee himself with a slightly trembling hand.

The social graces having been observed, Tinus abruptly became very businesslike. 'So, do I have to guess what this visit is all about? I take it you have some explanation for your behaviour, young man? Do the authorities know you are here?'

Michael shifted uncomfortably at the thought. 'No, sir, they do not and for the time being I would like to keep it that way if you don't mind. Please, if you would hear me out, that's all I ask for the moment.' He waited expectantly as Professor Mueller regarded him coldly.

'You have my undivided attention.' Tinus reclined comfortably, crossing his legs, and sipped from the delicate china cup.

Michael looked nervously at Carla who nodded her encouragement. He took a deep breath and recounted the same story he had told Carla the day before.

Throughout Tinus watched Michael impassively. His mask-like face gave no hint of his reaction to what he was hearing. When Michael had finished, Tinus sat motionless and silent for several moments.

'Very interesting,' he said at last. 'You expect me to believe this tale of yours?'

'I do, sir, because it is the truth,' Michael replied firmly. 'Would I dare to come here if it were not?'

'Then how do you explain the missing research papers? And why would BOSS fabricate a pack of lies?'

'Before I have a stab at that, would you answer me one thing, Professor?'

'And what is your question?'

'In the last few weeks before I was arrested, you had a number of visitors, some who arrived in government cars. Were you working on a project with other government departments then, Professor?'

Professor Tinus Mueller hesitated momentarily but recovered swiftly. 'I had a number of visitors, certainly. Our work was not confined to heart transplants alone.'

'Might I ask the identity of these visitors, Professor?'

'It is not something I would have broadcast but neither was it a secret. I was consulted by the South African Defence Force on a number of matters and from time to time by foreign governments. Surely you are not suggesting that they were responsible for the theft? That is preposterous.'

'Is it?' Michael asked. 'Let's face it. Military men the world over have often proved to be incompetent and irresponsible when it comes to chemical and biological warfare. They see the potential for a weapon and they want it regardless of the longer term consequences. Did you give them everything they wanted, Professor, or did you hold anything back?'

Tinus rubbed his chin, deep in thought. 'Well, ja, there was something,' Tinus admitted. 'I advised against a number of their requests on the grounds that they were too dangerous.'

'Yes,' Michael thumped his fist into the palm of his hand. 'I knew it. Don't you see, if what you held back was as sensitive as you say, I believe there is a good chance the military stole the documents and BOSS put two and two together and came up with five. They didn't have all the facts.' He looked excitedly from Tinus to Carla, seeking their agreement. Carla smiled uncertainly.

'All right, young man,' Tinus agreed reluctantly. 'What you are suggesting is possible. But is it likely?'

'Under the circumstances, frankly yes,' Michael spoke with feeling.

'If you assume what I say is true, and it is, what other explanation is there?'

'I confess I can see no other explanation,' said the older man.

Michael waited for Tinus' judgement.

'All right, if one accepts you are speaking the truth it should not be too difficult to prove if the Defence Force have my research, which I very much doubt. With my contacts it would have been known to me anyway.'

Michael felt his hopes being dashed in those few short seconds.

'So who else had access to your notes?' asked Carla.

Tinus appeared deep in thought, suddenly his face lit up.

'My God! The Rhodesians. Back in those days they were always onto me to supply them with the technology we were developing for the South African Defence Force, but of course I refused. It was in those stolen notes.' Professor Mueller looked truly shaken. 'I didn't like the Rhodesians much but surely...!'

Both Carla and Michael held their breath.

'In the light of what you have told me, I find that I am forced to reconsider your position, Mr Bernstein. This is not a line of investigation that has been considered—until now.'

Michael made no effort to conceal his relief. It had occurred to him that he would be in an extremely awkward position if Tinus had not accepted it.

'But why have you come here? I assume there is something else you want from me? Ah! I think I see. You want me to use my influence to reopen your case—put in a good word for you, is that it?

'That's it precisely,' Michael agreed. 'Can you do that for me, Professor Mueller? Will you do that for me?'

'Of course, you have my assurances. Clearly this matter needs to be looked into. As Carla will tell you, I didn't really believe you were responsible in the first place, but the evidence was overwhelming and I had no choice.' He hesitated momentarily, then showed Michael one of his rare smiles. 'Do not worry, I will say a word in the right ears. Hopefully that should do the trick. Let me know where you are staying and I will be in touch when I have some news.'

Michael was elated. Tinus' friends were powerful people and they would undoubtedly have connections. He had thought it would be more difficult to convince the Cape Doctor. Yet, after all this time in exile, after all the heartbreak, the problem was almost solved. Still, his elation was tinged with some reservation—how long would it take to resolve this matter? He told Tinus where he was staying. Thanked him profusely for his time and the proffered help, before parting with a warm handshake, to await his call.

Starting up the car in Tinus' driveway, Michael and Carla stared at one another. Michael could not hold himself back, leaned closer and kissed her. Tinus' friendly demeanour remained unchanged as he waved them goodbye, his small figure receding as they drove away.

Excitement is a poor sleeping partner but Michael had no complaints. Carla had agreed without undue persuasion to spend the next day with him. 'Be ready by nine,' she had said, but he had no intention of oversleeping. After a cool shower and a closer shave than usual, he made his way downstairs for breakfast with a lightheartedness he had not felt in weeks.

He crossed the marble foyer towards the reception desk, eager to allay his dread that Carla might have left a message postponing their meeting. His attention was drawn to a heated exchange between the pretty receptionist and a man who obviously believed that the louder he shouted, the more likely he was to get what he wanted. He was about Michael's height, powerfully built, and he exuded menace. Michael waited his turn.

Michael understood something of what was being said, even though his Afrikaans was rusty. At the same time he noticed another burly character, a carbon copy of the first, propped nonchalantly against the counter nearby, waiting patiently for his argumentative friend.

'Here, give me that,' the man said, snatching the register from the receptionist's grasp. 'He must be booked in here. What are you trying to hide, eh?'

The receptionist's voice rose. 'I have told you, sir, there is no Michael Bernstein registered at this hotel.'

Michael froze.

'Damn you, move!' Michael said to himself. He saw a sign and turned towards the public toilets. He was sure that everyone around him must have sensed his fear but miraculously no one seemed to notice. He made it to the door unhindered. His mind raced as he splashed water onto his face and dried off with a paper towel. Mopping perspiration from his neck, he looked at himself in the mirror. 'Who are they? Intelligence Service? They must be BOSS. They're all the same—bullying and bloody surly!' He cursed himself for not having spotted them straight away.

How had they found him? The Cape Doctor! Was it possible? 'It must have been Tinus.' He had gone to Tinus for help and Tinus had shopped him! 'He didn't believe me? No one else knows I'm here!'

It struck him like a hammer blow.

'Carla! Carla betrayed me? No, not Carla—she's not capable of that.' His mind was in turmoil; it had happened so suddenly. But the facts were damning. How naive he had been. Carla's husband was a cabinet minister. Distraught, he told himself, 'She told Jan to protect him from possible scandal. There is no other explanation—if I discount the Cape Doctor!'

There were no other exits from the toilets. Michael checked his wristwatch. Five to nine. Carla, if she was coming, was due any minute. The only way out was across the foyer. He was beginning to panic. If she had reported his presence she would not be keeping the appointment. There was one way to find out.

He took a deep breath and strode as calmly as he dared across the foyer to the main doors, hoping the men did not have a photograph of him. Even if they had, it would be out of date.

Both BOSS agents had become engrossed in a heated argument with the receptionist, now aided by a concerned manager, as to the whereabouts of the elusive Mr Bernstein.

Outside on the marble steps, Michael squinted against the morning sun. He noticed two more plain-clothes BOSS clones dressed in three-piece charcoal suits who gave him a casual glance. Each had the regulation cigarette clamped in his lips as they lounged against a white sedan drawn up beside an empty dark blue one. Both vehicles carried six foot antennae, the unmistakable sign of an 'unmarked' police car. Michael gave them a wide berth and started walking in the direction from which Carla would be approaching. He scanned the heavy traffic for her car and checked the time again. Seven minutes past nine. She was not coming—sadly he had been right. He noticed the two BOSS agents looking at him with renewed interest. What now?

At that moment he saw her car weaving between lanes. His mind raced. 'My God! Of course, I'm registered as Paddy. The bastards are looking for a Bernstein. Carla would have told them to ask for Mr Duffy.' Michael gave silent thanks to Carla and his late partner for the use of his name.

Carla reached the slip-road towards the hotel as Michael rushed forward. She must not reach the hotel. Asking for him within earshot of those thugs would have catastrophic results—both for him and for her. With no time to think of his actions, he leapt in front of her car and with nowhere to turn she slammed on the brakes squealing to a halt centimetres from impact. He flung the passenger door open and scrambled into the bucket seat.

'Drive on! Get out of here, now!' he ordered. Carla reacted with cool presence of mind and flipped the powerful Porsche through its gears. The car shot into the heavy traffic. Michael twisted in his seat to look over his shoulder and saw that their actions had not gone unnoticed by the men outside the hotel.

Half-finished cigarettes were hastily flicked aside as they leapt into the white car. Having parked too close to their colleagues, they lost seconds as they first scraped the side of the blue car, then reversed into a taxi that had drawn up. The car sped forward along the hotel slip-road in hot pursuit; losing further seconds they forced their way into the mainstream traffic.

Michael smiled grimly, the colour draining from his face. He had spotted another antenna some cars back. Suddenly a dark sedan cut out fast, moving up on them—so there had been a tail on Carla all along.

'There's another police car right behind us, lose them,' he urged.

He discovered a new dimension to Carla as she raced through the city.

She drove like a professional racing driver, weaving this way and that through busy streets, forcing gaps where none had existed. The speedometer read anything up to 140 kph. Michael checked behind again; there was no sign of their pursuers. Carla darted down a side road into a multi-storey car park. She pulled up in the lower ground-level near to the exit ramp, ready for a quick getaway.

'Well, that was fun,' her voice was heavy with sarcasm. 'What the hell's going on?'

'They're onto me, Carla.'

'Who?'

'BOSS, who else?' They were at the hotel looking for Michael Bernstein.' He forced himself to take a deep breath. 'It wasn't a social call. They meant business all right.'

'How did you get past them?' Carla reached over to hold his hand. 'And how on earth did they find you?'

'Only two people know I'm here, so it's not exactly difficult to figure it out...'

'Tinus!' she exclaimed. 'No, he couldn't—he wouldn't. He was going to help you clear yourself. Why would he do it?'

'I would like to know the answer to that myself. It must have been him. There's no one else! I'm registered here as Mr Duffy. That's the name I've used all along, only Tinus knows me as Michael. It has to be him. I managed to get out because, in the excitement yesterday, I forgot to tell Tinus my assumed name.'

'Where does that leave us now?' Carla included herself in Michael's predicament. Under other circumstances he might have taken more notice of that. He might have deduced that she wanted, even if unconsciously, to be linked with him because of the chemistry that still existed between them. But this was not the time and place to ponder on this. At the very least Michael felt that his liberty was in jeopardy; at worst, his life.

'I'm not sure. I don't have a step-by-step plan on how to keep Michael Bernstein alive. Tinus was my first port of call after you. I guess I was placing too much faith in him and his contacts. If it failed...well, I haven't thought beyond that.'

'Something's been worrying me,' said Carla. 'Forgive me for saying this. But if what you told me is true and you didn't steal the research papers and sell them, why did BOSS try to convince Tinus and me that you did? If they thought you had stolen the papers they would simply have arrested you.'

'They did, and I escaped, remember? They came to the labs to see if I had tried to get in touch with you.'

'Yes, but they didn't question you about missing documents, did they?'

'No, but maybe they had that in mind for later.'

'You are missing the point, Michael. Initially they told me you had been brought in only for questioning...why didn't they tell me you were arrested? And, another thing, why try to convince Tinus? If the papers were missing, Tinus would have been the one to report the loss. Therefore he would have approached them knowing it was you. In fact he said he had found evidence in your locker. If the truth is that you did not steal the papers, it seems he is framing you, either for someone else's crime or for no crime at all—don't you see?'

'Not if it was someone else's crime, I don't. Let's say the military stole the papers or one of Tinus' other visitors. It would be understandable if he suspected me, because I didn't return.'

'Okay. But why didn't you return? Because you were arrested, supposedly for something that was not discovered until after you escaped. Something is definitely very fishy about this whole thing. The pieces just don't fit.'

Michael considered Carla's logic. No matter which way he looked at it, he had to agree with her. It didn't add up. 'So what's Tinus up to? What's he hiding?' The question was rhetorical. He wrestled with the problem a little longer, going back to the days before his arrest. Suddenly a thought struck him. 'Oh my God,' he said.

'What is it?' Carla's brow furrowed at the gloom in his voice.

'Do you realise that we are the only two left out of Tinus' original team? All the others are dead. The mountain, the virus—Jesus, what's going on here? I'm beginning to think Geoff, Chris and, God forbid, Paul's death, were no accidents! And then there's the attempt on me.'

Taking in this revelation, Carla shuddered. 'Coincidence, bad luck, that's all,' she said, trying to convince herself it was so but it was obvious she did not believe her own whispered words.

'Until today I would have agreed with you. But now! There's something going on here that we are missing. If they had taken me to Pretoria Prison or if I had been in the laboratory when the bomb went off, I would be dead too. That would leave only you and Tinus. It keeps coming back to Tinus. Why the interest in me? What did we all know, that we had to be eliminated?'

'It doesn't make sense!' said Carla. 'When you think about it, I knew more than anyone else. So why wasn't I eliminated? I've been here all this time.'

'I agree, it doesn't make sense. What precisely was he working on back then? You never did tell me,' Michael asked.

'It's difficult to be specific. All I was doing was creating a filing system for his work on the computer. I was mostly concerned with sorting directories and organising his files and even then it was disjointed. I've no idea what was in the files he had already entered but I did add some data, a bit here and there, into new files. I had the impression he was working on genetic transference.'

Genetic transference was not too far removed from the work Michael himself had been doing. He recalled that their aim had been to convince recipient tissue that donor material was friend rather than foe, in the hope of preventing the natural rejection mechanism, while he had tackled antibiotic-resistance. This was highly relevant at the time because the field of human heart transplants had been in its infancy. Michael had been excited to be engaged in this brand new science.

'Interesting,' he said. 'As I recall, I had some success in that area but not enough to be of any use. The process was too slow and it produced a very dangerous strain. Did Tinus play around with that, I wonder?'

'I can't say, though if he did, it may be in his notes.'

'It seems to me that we need to take a look at those notes. Where are they now?'

'I don't think they exist on paper any more, or if they do, I don't know where they are. As far as I'm aware, Tinus never published anything connected with his work around that time, or I'm sure I would have known about it. If the notes are anywhere they will be on the computer.'

'But where, Carla? Would they still be at Groote Berg? If we are to make any headway we really need to see them.' Michael's acceptance of Carla as his partner in this affair was as automatic as Carla's co-operation. If the notes were on a computer he would need someone who was familiar with the system to be able to extract them and Carla was the obvious candidate. She had processed some of the original material.

Carla thought for a moment. 'If they are still in the hospital's database I might be able to find them. But they will be protected by a password. If he changed it we'll have little chance of getting at the files.'

'So how do we find out?'

'We could access the information on the main computer through any of the remote terminals or workstations in the hospital. As a consultant I come and go more or less as I please and I have exclusive use of an office with a link to the mainframe with my access code.'

'When can we go and have a look?'

'Right now. The way things are going I don't think we'll have another chance, but it would be less conspicuous if we used my office.'

'Well, if you say so but only if you're sure.' Michael turned to face her with genuine concern. 'You realise they know you are with me. Tinus would have told them—that's why you were tailed.'

'Yes, Michael. And now Jan will know too—I will have to deal with that later. Come on, let's go.'

Carla parked the Porsche in its reserved space outside Groote Berg's administrative block. There were no formalities on entering the building and Carla led him straight to her office, nodding greetings to acquaintances they passed in the corridors. The office furniture was of a standard modular design, purpose-built in light oak veneer with a desk and a side-table. A three-drawer pedestal unit for office stationery and hanging files fitted neatly under the desk. A remarkable lack of paperwork or reference material was testimony to the confidence placed in modern technology, represented by the desktop computer and attached printer. The pictures on the wall were of similar style to the framed prints that adorned the walls in the corridors of each floor. All that distinguished Carla's office from any other in the corridor was a personal photograph beside the telephone, which Michael recognised as Jan DuToit. The face staring out was still youthful but his thick black hair was now slightly tinged with grey at the temples. The office chair behind the desk was high-backed and contoured, with armrests—as if to confirm the seniority of the occupant.

Carla settled into it now and swivelled to face the blank computer screen as Michael looked on. She switched on and the cooling fans whirred as a series of rapidly changing images flashed on and off too fast to read, until 'Enter User name' appeared in the centre of the screen. Carla tapped the keyboard. 'Enter Password' flashed up. Again she used the keyboard and the screen went blank for several seconds before a message said 'Welcome, Carla DuToit, your access request is accepted—press ENTER to continue or ESC to quit.' She pressed ENTER and a numbered list of options replaced the message.

'You had better pull up a chair,' Carla advised. 'This might take a while,' and she began selecting options from the menus that presented themselves.

Time dragged for Michael and he muttered, 'Can't this thing go any faster?'

Carla cursed occasionally at her inability to access certain menu selections. 'You are not authorised for this option' or 'Access failure' flashed across the screen causing her intense frustration as she probed the databases. Michael moved to the window to scan the car park for vehicles with unusually long radio antennae. It was almost an hour since she began searching—he was beginning to think it was a waste of time when Carla herself confirmed it.

'Nothing,' she muttered. 'Not a damn thing that I can get at. I can see a list of all the other users but I can't get at their areas. I've tried everything I can think of. I'm out of ideas! Unless you can think of something, we may as well call it a day. We're not going to get anything more from this heap of junk,' she said spitefully, banging the keyboard.

'Changed your tune a bit, haven't you?' said Michael. 'I've always said the damn things are a waste of space...I usually forget the backups and lose everything.'

'That's it!' Carla exclaimed with delight. 'How stupid of me,' and she returned to the keyboard and attacked the keys.

'What is? What have you found?' Michael leaned forward.

'You may not know it but I think you have given me the answer. Backups! Look here,' she said, making selections from various menus, then tapping away at the keys. 'I backed up my work and his files from time to time.'

Michael peered over her shoulder with renewed interest.

'Now where are you, you little beauty?' she murmured. 'Aha! There you are—look, Michael.'

Michael stared obediently at the monitor as she selected 'ARCHIVES' from a menu of administrative functions. The selection came up with a list of dates and Carla made mental calculations before choosing the option RESTORE. After a few moments the screen displayed 'FILES ARE BEING RESTORED—PLEASE WAIT'. They had been anxiously watching an unchanged screen for the past minute when the telephone rang, startling them both.

Carla answered. After a brief exchange, Carla said. 'No, no mistake. I know the files are old but I really do need them. Can you do them now? Thank you.'

'What was that all about?' Michael asked.

'The operator was checking because restores are done on our mainframe computer downstairs. When I selected it, it showed up as a request on his console. The operator has to get the tape from the archive library and load it to a mainframe disk. When it's done, I can access the files.'

'And what do we do if we find anything interesting?'

'I'll copy the file to disk,' she said, producing a floppy disk from a box in her desk drawer, 'and then we can take off.'

Fifteen minutes passed. Michael started to agitate before the screen confirmed 'RESTORE COMPLETE'.

'Look here...' she selected 'MUELLER_T' from a list of user names and pressed Enter which prompted 'ENTER PASSWORD'. 'I hope this is still it,' and she keyed in 'MARBURG'. She looked up to see his astonished grin and anticipated his question, 'Well! I was his deputy.'

Carla scanned through the old files.

'Here we go, some of these look familiar.' She settled down to read the original version on screen. She scanned a few pages, making noises of recognition. 'Aha, I remember this,' and Michael came to look over her shoulder again at the research notes.

His name appeared several times in the notes against research he had almost forgotten. The notes refreshed his memory and he was transported back to the Mueller Laboratories in the '70s.

'Grief! What's this?'

Carla interrupted Michael's reminiscences, drawing his eyes back to the screen. 'What is it?'

'Look at this,' Carla pointed to some notes halfway down the screen. There in front of them were details of Tinus Mueller's further research after Michael's departure.

'What's he been playing at? Look here—that is what I was working on,' he continued to read in disbelief as Carla scrolled through the file.

Carla read parts aloud, intermittently, as Michael followed. 'Look what the Cape Doctor says here...*P.carinii* has been developed into a powerful weapon...administered intravenously...could be widely distributed via military...of pandemic proportions—bloody hell, Michael, this is serious stuff. Do you see what this could mean?'

'Yes! The man's insane. He cannot do that. Why, it would...'

'What do you mean he can't do it!' she interrupted. 'Look at the dates. If he was going to, he's already done it. My God, that could explain...'

The shrill ring of the telephone interrupted her again. 'Carla DuToit,' she answered automatically. There was a pause as she listened.

Michael could not make out what was being said and watched as she inserted the floppy disk into the computer as she spoke.

'What do you mean I shouldn't have access?' The telephone clamped to her ear by her shoulder, she tapped frantically at the keyboard and pressed the key to copy files to the floppy disc. 'I do have access. These are my files—well, strictly speaking they are Professor Mueller's files but I was working for him at the time and most of the work on them is mine,' she lied.

'No, I'm afraid I cannot come downstairs. I'm rather busy at the moment. I'll come later, goodbye.' Carla hung up quickly and spoke to Michael over her shoulder as the screen informed her that the copies were completed. Her hands flew across the keyboard a second time. 'We seem to have rattled somebody's cage. We'll have to go in a sec.'

'What's up? Who was that?'

'Computer admin.' She made her final selection. 'They say I don't have authorisation to restore these files...want me to go down to explain myself and insist I delete the copied files. They'll be up here soon.' The computer transferred further files as she spoke. Safely copied, she ejected the disk and switched off. 'We had better get out of here and take this with us— we need to take a closer look—I'm afraid we only had time for this one. Here, you had better hang onto it,' and she handed over the floppy disk which he slipped into his trouser pocket.

'All right, let's go.' Michael opened the door and checked the corridor before leading the way to the lifts. One was arriving at their floor as they reached it but instinctively Michael grabbed Carla's arm and tugged her through the fire exit doors. Peering through a gap in the door he watched as a small man in a grey suit hurried along the corridor towards Carla's office followed by two uniformed security men. 'They didn't waste any time, did they?' he whispered. 'Come'n, let's go.' Gripping Carla's arm, he led the way rapidly down the fire escape with Carla doing her best not to trip in her high heels.

They heard shouted words from above, exaggerated by the echoing in the enclosed stairwell. 'She's gone down there. You—follow her. You—come down with me in the lift. Don't let her leave the grounds.' The little man snapped instructions to the guards and heavy hob-nailed boots clattered on concrete steps.

At the bottom, the fire door opened at the side of the building onto a paved footpath leading to the car park. The car was a short sprint round the corner. They paused momentarily.

'Here, quick. Give me the keys,' Michael demanded and Carla handed them over dutifully. 'Right, let's go.'

They reached the car as the guard in the stairwell emerged from the fire escape. Simultaneously the small man and the other guard burst through the swing doors at the front of the building. Michael and Carla were in full view, scrabbling with the door handles.

'Stay where you are. You cannot leave here,' the small man ran towards them shouting.

Michael ignored him while fumbling with the key. Hurriedly he climbed in, reached over and opened the passenger door. Carla leapt in as he turned the ignition switch. The engine caught with a roar as the guards converged on them. Throwing the gear level into reverse, he backed out with smoking tyres. Then into first gear as the nearest guard lunged at the passenger door handle but Carla managed to snap the lock shut.

Rubber shrieked as Michael pulled away. The guard screamed an oath and shook his fist before tucking it into his armpit, nursing bruised and bleeding fingertips. The other guard hesitated a split second as the Porsche bore down on him—it was evident its occupants were determined to escape—he flung himself from its path, narrowly missed by the tyres which kicked up a spray of fine grit, stinging his eyes. The small man screamed his wrath at the guards watching the Porsche speed out of the grounds.

'Bloody hell! They don't want us to have this information, do they?' said Michael, glancing in the rear-view mirror. The guards were running for one of the security vans.

'Are you surprised?' Carla answered. 'But we'll have to load these on another computer before we can read them through properly. Where the hell are we going?'

'I haven't a clue but we're not alone,' he nodded into the mirror and Carla turned to see the security van weaving through the traffic in pursuit. 'It won't take them long to phone the police and report the theft. It's a government establishment after all. Just keep your eyes peeled for six foot aerials!'

oOo

The BOSS Commandant picked up the telephone. 'Van Heerden.' He had been as mad as a snake ever since leaving the hotel reception area. He almost had Bernstein within his grasp but his men had lost the cunning Jew once again. He listened intently to the security man at Groote Berg Hospital.

Dropping the telephone, he shot out of his chair. 'Quick! Get the helicopter pilot—we've got the bastard this time.' Two of his subordinates ran after him.

oOo

Carla watched the surrounding traffic, searching for the tell-tale signs of short-wave radios while Michael concentrated on staying ahead of the security van. It was not difficult; the van was a utility vehicle and no match for the sleek sports car. It soon fell behind. Nevertheless, it would not be difficult to become caught up in traffic; so he headed away from town along Rhodes Drive and the Simon van der Stel freeway towards Muizenberg, half expecting roadblocks.

They drove for minutes, weaving through the free-flowing traffic. Suddenly Michael became aware of lights flashing in his side-view mirror.

'We have company,'

'Where? I haven't seen anything,' she said.

'In the opposite carriageway.' At the same time he saw another patrol car coming up from behind. He stamped the accelerator to the floor and the Porsche sped towards the rear of a station wagon in front. Michael tugged the steering wheel and the car swung into the next lane.

Their speed increased whenever a gap appeared in the traffic; the Porsche, responsive to his commands, swerved from lane to lane. If there was no gap, Michael forced one by leaning on the horn and flashing the headlights as he approached at high speed. Every move he made was shadowed by the patrol car from behind.

On the opposite carriageway, the patrol car gained then steadily overtook them, siren screaming and lights flashing, but was unable to cross the central reservation for another half kilometre. Suddenly there was a shriek of brakes, blue smoke streaming from rear tyres as oncoming traffic slowed the patrol car, and it fell far behind. Michael went faster still—every second putting greater distance between them.

'What can I do?' Carla pleaded. Until now it had been exciting, but now that capture seemed inevitable, real fear crept into her voice.

'I don't know—I've only done this once before. We do not want to get trapped in town. We had better head for the country.'

After ten kilometres the freeway ended abruptly at an intersection. The car ahead was making slow work of turning left, so Michael burst across the road turning right, leaving havoc in their wake, and headed for the Cape Peninsula—an isolated mountain range that jutted out to sea. It was virtually uninhabited—a vast conservation area. He did not have many options but the openness, away from the city, seemed the most likely route to escape. There would be places to hide in the forests or mountains. There was no sign yet of the pursuing cars but they could not be far away.

The M64 became hilly and twisting. Skirting the Silvermine Nature Reserve, conditions over the tortuous road were ideal for the Porsche but not for patrol cars. Cutting their way deftly through the rugged terrain, Michael increased his speed, knowing he could also outdistance most other vehicles on these stretches. The countryside flashed by in a blur. False Bay came back into view intermittently; the liquor-free coastal resort of Fish Hoek on their left passed unseen; the parched, boulder-strewn slopes dotted with thorny brush and wild flowers passed without a glance.

For a moment the tension began to ease.

Carla spotted it first. It was a helicopter coming up fast from the city in their direction.

'I think we have a tail,' she pointed it out to Michael. 'A helicopter— up there, behind us, slightly to our right. I don't think he has seen us yet.'

He glanced back fleetingly. What had been a speck in the sky was quickly becoming larger by the second.

'Let's find out shall we?' He stamped on the accelerator and the car sped on. 'It won't be easy to shake off a helicopter. He just has to sit there above us with a bird's eye view and radio everything we do to the patrol cars.'

Still the helicopter trailed behind like a kite on a string but moving up fast. Something drastic would have to be done to avoid capture. Michael knew they were becoming boxed in on the Peninsula, with False Bay on one side and the Atlantic on the other. To make matters worse the land mass was rapidly narrowing to a point and they were on a scenic drive which ultimately led back to the city; in a sense they were trapped. The aerial surveillance would undoubtedly culminate in a roadblock ahead.

An idea suddenly formed in his mind. It was crazy but it could work. It would have to work. There were no other options. They must not be caught. If they were, there would be but one terrifying foreseeable conclusion. The decision made, he raced on.

Negotiating some sharp bends, a straight came up. 'I have a plan but hang on for the turning up ahead.' For a few minutes they were out of sight and arrived at a T-junction. Michael took the direction he believed would cause the pilot the most consternation as he agonised over which way they might have gone. He sped on towards the west coast of the Cape Peninsula and pressed the accelerator down even further.

The helicopter was close now and Michael was sure they must have been seen. He raised his voice to make himself heard over the engine. 'I know this road. Up ahead there's a hairpin bend and, if that helicopter is consistent, we should be unsighted for a few seconds as we round it. I'll slow right down so we can jump from the car and let it go over the cliff. If we do it right they'll think we have had it and will give up the chase. What do you think? Can you do it, Carla?'

Carla's expression was one of disbelief. But she knew that Michael's life would be forfeit if he was caught. His plan was a dangerous one, which at the very least would wreck her car. At worst...she preferred not to think about that. She considered the importance of the information they had. It had to be made public.

'Dammit, Carla, can you do it?' The point of decision was imminent.

'Yes...yes, I can do it,' she responded.

'Good girl,' he reached over and squeezed her arm, smiling encouragement. It was a shame about her beautiful car.

'Michael, I'm scared! What will we do after we jump?'

'There are gaps in the cliff face to the right. Run for those and then keep your head down, okay?' he encouraged her. 'We'll only have a few seconds to get there but they won't see us if we keep still.'

She nodded. 'Okay, I can manage that.' She braced herself, 'Ready when you are,' she said.

They passed through woodlands which hid them momentarily from above. The hills to their right steepened with the road dropping towards the coast. They crested a slight rise and the Atlantic Ocean came into view, shimmering with silver streaks where the sunlight reflected from the waves. On a Sunday this road would be busy with sightseers vying for the best views high above the ocean. Thankfully, today it was deserted.

The road seemed to end abruptly as it disappeared round a sharp right-hand bend.

'Hold tight, here we go—you'd better unfasten your seat belt.'

Carla unbuckled the belt and pushed it out of the way. Michael reduced his speed imperceptibly, then changed down a gear, and pressed the accelerator pedal hard to the floor. The car responded, catapulting away towards the cliff face with a blast of white exhaust smoke. The helicopter fell behind for a moment and disappeared giving them vital extra seconds. Was it enough? Michael took the bend at breakneck speed hugging the cliff edge. Then several more bends.

The hairpin approached with alarming speed, so fast that Carla thought he wasn't going to make it but, at the last possible moment, Michael pressed the brake pedal hard and coaxed the car round the bend. The helicopter had not reappeared.

Now in neutral he kept his foot on the brake until the speed dropped near to walking pace. 'Ready?'

'Ready,' she confirmed.

At the last minute he warned, 'Be careful—the barrier!'

He steered towards the edge where the safety barrier ended, and thrust the car into gear, reached down and pulled the protective floor mat onto the accelerator pedal. He turned towards Carla. 'Now!' he yelled. 'Go, go, go!' He saw Carla pull on her door handle as he flung his door open and tumbled out, releasing the clutch pedal as he went. The car leapt away from him and he rolled once before scrabbling to his feet. Hearing the helicopter nearing the corner, he raced across the road towards the cliff face to hide in one of the many fissures. Running, he heard the car hit the end of the crash barrier, and then the sound of the engine revving hard as the wheels lost contact with the road. He dived for cover.

The helicopter came up quickly and rounded the bend, its rotors beating the air, drowning out all other sound, as the car plummeted from view.

Nose-diving into the rocks below, the Porsche crumpled to a third of its original length; windows and debris exploded outwards, as the engine compressed and obliterated the passenger cabin. It balanced for a moment, as though it had always been there, and then, in the blink of an eye, a wave crashed over the rock face and sucked the wreckage out into deeper water.

The helicopter manoeuvred into position on a level with the road, thirty metres out to sea.

Michael wedged himself deeper into a crevice and froze. From the shadow of his hiding place he saw the helicopter flutter above the cliff like a giant insect as an updraught caught the blades. Slowly it disappeared from view as it descended.

The occupants of the helicopter watched the wreck impassively. The pilot, his eyes hidden by aviator sunglasses, mouth obscured by a microphone, handled the machine skilfully in the treacherous conditions at the cliff face. His two passengers scanned the surrounding area for movement but there was none.

Michael remained motionless. The helicopter hovered over the wreck of the car for what seemed like an age, then the giant insect rose and came into view again. The gusting wind caught the aircraft and tossed it menacingly close to the cliff face so Michael thought it was coming straight at him. He froze.

The pilot wrestled with the controls manoeuvring the craft safely away. It was another five minutes before they seemed certain that there could be no survivors from the crash, then the helicopter wheeled away, heading back towards the city.

Michael let out a sigh and his tension ebbed. They must still be careful as the cars in radio contact with the helicopter would soon arrive at the crash scene to see for themselves and make absolutely sure there were no survivors.

'Carla,' he yelled. 'Carla. Where are you? Quick, they've gone.' He looked left and right calling to her but she did not answer. With mounting panic, he ran from one hiding place to another calling her until he realised he was checking the same places twice.

Inside the car, Carla had grabbed the door handle. She pushed at it, leaning against the door to open it as Michael disappeared through his. It did not move. She had pounded it frantically with her shoulder but still it would not budge. Through the windscreen all she could see was the ocean beyond the bonnet. For a moment the car banged into the metal safety barrier and scraped along it. She began to scramble over the centre console, making for the other door, but the bucket seats and the mounted gear level slowed her down. Then, sickeningly, the barrier ended and the car veered onto the stony verge gathering speed—suddenly the ground disappeared. Falling into space, she remembered locking her door in the hospital car park.

The full horror of what had happened dawned slowly but he refused to believe it. It must not be true. He ran to the point where the car had gone over the edge, his eyes on the spot where it had struck the rocks below, and he knew Carla was dead.

The rocks were gouged and scratched and littered with scraps of metal. A wheel and part of an axle were trapped between two rocks and waved to and fro with each rush of the ocean.

She could not have survived. Michael sank to his knees, perilously close to the edge, but he was unaware, or uncaring, of the danger and he screamed her name into the wind.

There was nothing left—no one. He fished in his trouser pocket and found the wafer-thin square of flexible plastic. Miraculously it had survived undamaged. He scrutinised the floppy disc casing in detail for the first time.

It was strangely plain. There were no labels, just a discreet trademark on the protective cover. Nothing to indicate the importance of the data on the disk inside.

'And for this Carla is dead,' he screamed his rage aloud and drew back his arm ready to throw the floppy disk in despair into the sea far below. He hesitated, the sound of an engine catching his attention. It grew louder and he leapt for cover behind the crash barrier, stuffing the disk back in his pocket. It was not the police and the car passed, but it was enough to clear his mind. BOSS could not be far behind. The helicopter would have reported the crash site and they would soon be here. There was a long way ahead and the road would be crawling with police any minute.

Michael climbed above the road onto the steep mountainside. He began to pick a way, then ran across the rocky ground—the floppy disk forgotten.

Farther along the road, where the mountain gave way to gentler slopes, the unmistakable smell of meat cooking over charcoal wafted from a picnic area protected by trees from the offshore wind. Michael crept down towards the tell-tale signs of smoke, to where a Ford Cortina was parked in the shade. Deeper in the glade, though he could not see them, he could hear voices. The car was on an incline that led to the road and it was unlocked. Better still, the keys were in the ignition. He opened the door quietly, let the handbrake off and rocked the car until it began to roll gently down the track. Once on the road, he turned the ignition key.

'Sorry about this but my need is greater than yours,' Michael silently apologised to the owner, making his way into Cape Town.

After watching the hotel for fifteen minutes until he was sure that there were no police around, he walked brazenly into the foyer. He asked for his key at reception. The receptionist was still at her post. Michael casually mentioned the fracas in the morning.

'Oh, you mean those awful policemen? They're so rude, aren't they? I told them, 'There's no Mr Bernstein staying here' but they wouldn't listen. Said they'd been told by a reliable source that he was booked in. Well, I ask you! I should know shouldn't I?' She looked at Michael more carefully.

'You look a little unwell, Mr Duffy. Can I get you anything?'

'Thank you, no,' he said, then changed his mind. 'Yes, yes—you can send a bottle of Cape brandy up to my room. Thanks.'

Two measures of brandy and a hot shower did little to lessen the wretchedness he felt. He stood with the needle points of hot water stinging his face and chest, overwhelmed by feelings of guilt. 'If only I hadn't contacted you, Carla....' Clinging to the rail he hung his head and wept aloud, his tears washed away but not his despair.

Half an hour later he settled the bill and left the hotel in the stolen car. There was one thing on his mind—kill the Cape Doctor. He left the city centre and took the road towards Hout Bay. Would the police still be looking for a certain Mr Bernstein, alias Duffy, or did they believe him to be dead at last—killed with Carla?

'Who the hell cares?' he said aloud.

CHAPTER 11

Government White Paper 1976: "...recommendations that would amount to the recognition...of the identity of the various [established] population groups...being broken down are not conducive to the orderly and evolutionary advancement of the [those] population groups...the government...is not prepared to change its standpoint [to be retained]...in regard to the Immorality Act and Prohibition of Mixed Marriages Act."

John Vorster
President of South Africa, 1966 - 79

Tinus Mueller should have been pleased. Less than four hours had passed since receiving the report of Michael Bernstein's death on the Cape Peninsula earlier in the day. For years the man had eluded all efforts to eliminate him but now, even in death, Michael remained a thorn in his side. He had not died alone but had taken the daughter of his good friend with him. Tinus realised he must face Andries Boshoff and confess to his part in Carla's death.

He stood gazing at the scene from the patio. Under other circumstances he might have enjoyed the view—the sun glinting on the Atlantic Ocean and the fishing boats lying at rest in the harbour below but he was oblivious to the calling of the gulls as they wheeled overhead. Instead he contemplated the events that had brought him to this current predicament. He had been a young man in a laboratory surrounded by wooden, single-storey buildings, all alike except for the concrete structure with a tall chimney at the far end of the compound. His memories came flooding back, taking him to a different land and a different time.

He wore the white coat of a medical intern, his grey uniform jacket and shiny peaked cap which marked him as a junior military officer hanging on a hook on the back of the door. He did not care much for the uniform: he wore it only for parades or other official functions. It rendered him indistinguishable from all the other young officers and it was this that he did not like. It was different in the laboratory. Here he was God—his work revolving around his microscope and test tubes and experiments with sterilisation. Full of enthusiasm for a certain project, the concentration camp provided all the necessary raw material he needed, alive or dead, and he made rapid progress, then it was curtailed abruptly. Things were not going well: news that the Allies were rapidly advancing was alarming. Some of the most respected senior officers were fleeing the fatherland for South America or Africa and it was time for Tinus to leave as well.

They would never have understood that the work he was doing would, in time, have been of significant scientific benefit, not just to Germany but to all mankind. Less than three months before the Allies arrived at the death camp he was spirited away by sympathisers to South Africa, where he was given a new identity and full citizenship.

He set up a simple laboratory and continued his work, almost uninterrupted, with funds willingly donated by new friends. It did not take him long to appreciate that, in this country, wealth brought immeasurable power—even more power than could be realised by the brute force he understood so well. Even so, power was controlled by politics.

At the outset Tinus, from a discreet distance, studied many of the political organisations. He began, as they developed, to concentrate on those with a strong right-wing element until, at last, he was accepted into the most powerful of them all—the Broederbond or Brotherhood. Senior members of the organisation were also senior members of the government and the Dutch Reformed Church, a powerful influence on the Afrikaners' way of thinking. Between them, the Brotherhood and the church controlled the daily lives of most of the White population—and of course, the Black population too. Tinus' strong anti-Semitic views sat well with the Afrikaner, who thought himself superior to both Jews and the indigenous Black African peoples. The difference was that the Afrikaners wanted to control and use the Blacks for their own purposes, rather than exterminate them. The mines had to be worked—they were hard and dangerous places at the best of times; and the farms needed an endless supply of workers to labour in the scorching heat. Wherever unskilled labour was required under arduous conditions, the Blacks and Coloureds were employed on minimal wages.

Tinus' life revolved around politics and his work. He flourished as South Africa became a major player in the field of microbiology and medicine, thanks in no small part to his own contributions.

In time, however, even the tough policies of the Broederbond became too liberal for Tinus and a few like-minded hard-liners. The plight of the Black populace was raised on the world stage to the detriment of White South Africa, and apartheid began to be diluted. Thus it was, when Andries Boshoff proposed a breakaway organisation, Tinus became one of the founder members and the ARB—Afrikaner Regte Broederbond, was born. The ARB was dedicated to the maintenance and improvement of the quality of life for Afrikaners; even the English-speaking Whites were viewed in much the same light as the Blacks and Coloureds.

Many years later, in 1973, one of John Vorster's ex-bodyguards, Eugene Terre Blanche, formed a similar right-wing organisation. Terre Blanche's plans to contaminate the luxurious hotel complex of Sun City with syphilis appealed immensely to Tinus as a way of preventing Whites and Blacks from cohabiting.*

Tinus stiffened, sensing a presence behind him—it might have been a hint of a sound. Startled, he swung round and knew the form at the periphery of his failing vision to be a man. He could not see him clearly because he had been gazing unblinking out to sea—the interior of the house was dark by comparison.

'Who is that?' he demanded. 'What do you want?'

'I want you, Professor. But first I want some answers,' he said icily, stepping out from the dimness of the lounge onto the patio.

'You!' Tinus recognised the voice immediately. 'But you are...'

'I'm what, Professor, dead?'

'Dead! Why...why would you say that?' Tinus recovered quickly from his initial shock. 'I was going to say you are in Cape Town. What are you doing here? How the hell did you get in?'

'You should lock the servants' door.' Michael advanced slowly on the Cape Doctor. 'Forget it, Mueller. You can't fool me any more. I know it was you who set BOSS onto us.'

'BOSS? I don't know what you are talking about, man.' He was at a disadvantage—he had left his glasses inside. He wanted Michael to move closer where he could see him better. He tried to edge away from the patio railing indicating a seat nearer the window. 'Over there, we can sit down and...'

'Stand still and be quiet,'

Tinus froze, midway between the railing and the patio door.

Michael spoke more softly now, 'It won't take much for me to kill you Professor,' even though he had changed his mind about killing Mueller—he had other plans—and grabbed Tinus by the shirt at arm's length.

Despite his impaired vision, Tinus saw Michael's menacing expression. To shout was pointless—the house was isolated and the servants were off duty. This was a different person before him from the man who had recently sought his help. Now he appeared cold and focused. A man who had become dangerous and formidable. Tinus was wary—he held his tongue.

'You put them onto me,' Michael continued. 'You had no intention of helping at all. I told you where I was staying and you sent them to pick me up. Carla was there too and instead of killing me they killed her.'

Tinus winced and Michael saw it. 'You hadn't planned on that, had you? But you wanted me dead. Why?' Michael shook the motionless man slowly. 'And Chris and Geoff—you killed them too, on the mountain, didn't you? And Paul! What did you do to him? I saw him die. It wasn't very pleasant.' He stopped, and jerked Tinus nearer. 'Tell me, what did you do to Paul?'

Tinus' fear increased. If he was to defend himself, he needed to distract his attacker. There was no further point in bluffing. 'I thought you had all the answers, Jew, so you tell me.'

Michael suddenly pushed Tinus backwards. 'You exposed him to something, didn't you? You took my culture and engineered a new strain and you administered it to Paul somehow. What was it? What did you do?'

'You are fishing, Bernstein—you know nothing. You do not have a shred of evidence to support such accusations.'

'Oh but I do, Professor Mueller, I have lots of evidence. What did you do with your work after I left?' He did not pause for an answer. 'I'll tell you what you did with it. You had it stored on a computer. Computer files can be accessed, read and copied. I have copies of those files.'

'Impossible. They told me you hadn't got anything. You could not have accessed my files; they are protected by passwords.'

'Ah, they told you. So you are working with BOSS! Well, they were right. We could not access your files, but who administered your bloody files? Carla did and she routinely made her backups which were also archived. They make interesting reading.'

'You stupid fucking Jew,' Tinus hissed. Now he seemed to care little for the threats. 'You've no idea what you're dealing with. Leave it alone, you'll ruin everything. Bloody Jews, we should have finished the job we started.' Tinus caught Michael off guard. He grabbed Michael's arm and twisted viciously wrenching himself free from his grasp.

Michael's reaction was swift. He lunged with both hands and caught Tinus by the throat.

Tinus felt Michael's breath in his face as he was held and shaken violently.

'What did you create, Mueller?' he shouted. 'What did you do with it?'

Tinus saw his face clearly now, the eyes crazed and dangerous. Clutching at Michael's wrists to relieve the pressure on his throat so he could speak, he answered defiantly, 'Fool! I created nothing—I did not need to. The work was already done for me. By you, you imbecile. All those hours working on the *P.carinii* so there would be no antibiotic-resistance, so the prima donnas could have the glory of transplanting human hearts. You did it—all that hard work. You created a deadly strain; I had to do nothing!'

Michael took a step backwards, transferring the pressure from Tinus' throat to grip his lapels. 'You're lying.'

Encouraged by this reaction, Tinus pressed on. 'Lying, you say? I don't think so. You say you have the files. Read them for yourself. You will find that your creation was deployed as a biological weapon against communist terrorists.'

'No, it can't be. It's not true.'

Tinus pressed home his advantage. 'But it is true. You were responsible for this terrible virus and its mutations, for which I thank you. It was one of my more profitable transactions. The Rhodesians confirmed excellent results in their field trials.'

Michael's horror was plain. 'My God, they didn't! It could have been disastrous.' He shook Tinus viciously. 'Tell me they didn't use it.'

Despite his dangerous predicament Tinus smiled cynically and said nothing.

'For God's sake, you were the man at the top. Why didn't you stop them? Something like this could have wiped out half the world's population if it went pandemic. Didn't you see that?'

The more apparent Michael's horror became, the greater Tinus' gratification. He realised, too, that Michael Bernstein still had not grasped the full implications of events in the distant Rhodesian Bush War. The dumb Jew still believed they were discussing the mutant *P.carinii* that had been under trial in that small sphere of operation.

'Ha! That's what you think, is it? Let me tell you something, domkopf! It was not my idea, though it was so brilliant in its simplicity that I wish it had been. That little ploy was the brainchild of your precious girlfriend's father. It is Andries Boshoff you should be talking to, not me.'

'Boshoff! What has he to do with all of this? What was your relationship with that bastard? I want answers from you, you bigoted little kraut. Exactly where, and when, was this pathogen deployed? How widely was it used? Tell me, or so help me, I'll kill you.'

Tinus, with deceptive strength writhed in the younger man's grasp—in defiance of nemesis—fingers clawing and kicking out, his frenzied struggle surprising his opponent. He spat through clenched teeth, 'Go to hell! You will never know what was done. You will get nothing more from me, verdampt Jew!'

They wrestled, crashing into the railing and scattering potted geraniums from the parapet. Tinus managed briefly to force Michael towards the edge but he was too frail. A fist struck Tinus behind the ear losing him the advantage and Michael turned him back with ease, pinning him against the railing, his fear of heights forgotten. Off-balance, Tinus reached blindly for something to cling to; his hands clutched uselessly at the air as he pivoted on the railing.

'This is for Carla—this is how she died.' The words were as a scream, 'You like cliffs, you bastard?' Tinus teetered, staring wide-eyed for a second into Michael's eyes centimetres away; then twisting his head sideways, looking at the rocks far below. Michael planted a fist into his solar plexus. Tinus went limp, his eyes still registering terror. Michael held him there for a few more seconds, then pulled him back from the railing. 'That would be too good for you—you're coming with me.' He set off resolutely, dragging Tinus like a weighted sack through the house and outside to the secluded driveway. Tinus was still struggling to regain his breath as Michael tumbled him into the boot of the Cortina and slammed the lid down.'

He tested the lock, then tapped the boot. 'You'll stay in there until you give me a written confession.'

Michael drove mechanically. His mind filled with thoughts of Carla. All the things he should have said to her or have done in the past. All the time wasted! How he cursed their forced separation. What a fool he had been to allow himself to be a victim of his own grief and stubbornness.

At length he pushed them aside and concentrated on the Cape Doctor in the boot. He would force him to make a public confession. That way he would compel his pursuers to back off.

With no one else to turn to, Michael was constrained to fall back on family ties. He should have called Aaron first but, fearing a negative response and a phone tap, decided not to. He had filled the Cortina with petrol before calling on Tinus and now struck out on the main coastal highway. It seemed more prudent to call on his brother unannounced when he reached Durban.

The family saloon had seen better days with over a hundred thousand on the clock. It was noisy but hardly likely to attract undue attention, and he consoled himself with the thought that less than four hours had passed since he had acquired the vehicle. Still, he wanted more distance between himself and his pursuers and possible roadblocks.

By the time Cape Town receded into the distance it was dark. The drone of the tyres on the road and the pressure of the day's events had their effect as he drove through the coastal forests along the Garden Route. Fatigue forced him to stop. Michael pulled into a lay-by and climbed out. He felt unsteady on his feet. His head ached. He went back to let Tinus out and, knowing the Cape Doctor was not as fragile as he appeared, opened the boot cautiously. Noxious fumes made him cough and, as he let the lid go, it sprang up.

'Carbon monoxide!' He swore.

The Cape Doctor lay there in peaceful repose and quite still. He bent down in the dim boot light to take a closer look and shook Tinus.

He was dead.

Michael straightened up and, for a moment, stood transfixed gazing at the body. Tearing himself away he restarted the car and knelt down to listen. He hadn't noticed it before but now he could clearly hear the blown exhaust.

The Cape Doctor had succumbed to the poisonous fumes that had been sucked into the boot. Gassed! With frightening clarity Michael realised he had inadvertently killed Tinus Mueller. He felt no remorse. Looking at Tinus again he thought fleetingly that it was probably a fitting end. What had this man done to others in his dubious past? He had probably got away lightly.

'Oh! Bloody hell,' Michael moaned. 'I needed you, you miserable bastard.' He looked around and was met by the quiet of the woods. Slamming the boot down he climbed into the car and drove off slowly. Within a short distance the headlights showed a track leading into the forest. He reversed, then stopped, leaving the engine running with the headlights on. Pulling Tinus out, he dragged him away down the track, then off deeper into the undergrowth. Michael knew there was a remote chance that a forester would find the body. More likely a jackal or wild cat, or possibly something larger—would get him first. He glanced around wondering in there were any leopards left in the Cape Province.

Hurriedly he retraced his steps to the car using the sound of the engine as a beacon.

Michael drove until he felt, rather than saw, the car drift onto the gravel verge. Exhausted, he pulled up at the first lay-by, climbed onto the back seat and almost immediately fell into a fitful sleep.

He woke a little later feeling wretched with Carla's face haunting him and he tried desperately to push her from his mind. He began to think again of his circumstances.

Undoubtedly the search for Michael Bernstein would continue and he was thankful to his late friend and partner for the use of his passport. So far no one had matched their identities but, when it became apparent that there was no record of Michael Bernstein entering the country, BOSS would try to tie up his description with recent arrivals of single American males.

Another thought struck him. Whoever planted the bomb in the Houston laboratory would almost certainly have turned up Padraig Duffy's name. The local papers had carried the story over several days. They would recheck the hotel in Cape Town as a matter of procedure. It would be a matter of hours before they connected him to Paddy. His optimism faded—he had to assume his cover was blown. Where did that leave him? His only hope was that they now presumed him to be dead along with Carla—until only one body turned up! Would they eventually trace the stolen Cortina to him? He had taken it not far from the accident site. At least they had no way of knowing where he was heading. Roadblocks would be set up for certain! He would get rid of the car in Durban, even though they had his finger prints on file.

Tinus' disappearance would not go unnoticed. At best he hoped to be out of the country in a couple of days and, with Aaron's help, make it to the nearest bordering country, Lesotho, and freedom.

The information held on the innocent-looking computer disk in the pocket of his jacket was, both medically and politically, a time bomb. There was no telling what other dark secrets it might reveal but the little they had seen pointed in that direction. Tinus himself had confirmed the use of biological agents produced at the Mueller Laboratories against human beings. The thought disgusted Michael and he found it hard to believe it was not fantasy. Would the files verify the Cape Doctor's confession? Tinus had clearly stated that, despite Michael's efforts to produce a means of controlling rejection in organ transplant patients, he had created by chance something lethal. He must find out what that 'something' was.

He woke early and pushed on, with windows open as a precaution against exhaust fumes, crossing the Great Kei River, through the Transkei towards Durban. The journey was one of contrasts and tiring. Errant domestic animals had him wide-awake again. After his second close encounter with stray sheep, he lowered his speed. Still, he felt safer in these natural surroundings than in the concrete environment he had left behind, or that which lay ahead.

Late in the day he arrived in Durban and joined the early evening traffic. He was mentally and physically exhausted by strain and heat. The light was fading fast so he stopped at the first hotel on the edge of town, knowing he desperately needed a shower and sleep. After a simple meal Michael drove the Cortina for several blocks, then parked in a quiet lane. At the last moment he scribbled a note, 'Stolen. Please return to the rightful owner.' He slipped it under the dash, together with the keys, and locked the doors. Checking the vehicle for the last time, he decided it was unlikely to be discovered for weeks, perhaps months, then retired to the hotel.

Michael wondered how he should approach Aaron. The brothers had not seen one another since Michael had stormed out after their last argument, so long ago. That angry parting now lay in the past. Admittedly there had been a few calls over the years, and recent contact after John's death left him feeling things were all right, but with Aaron it was difficult to tell. Michael respected his brother as a hard-nosed businessman heading a multi-million rand consortium of companies. But, he had built this from the proceeds of Coronet Chemicals, in which he now appeared to have lost all interest. He knew Aaron had fought hard to get his foot in the door to the lucrative government-controlled markets, especially in the mining industry.

Aaron had made it clear at the time that he was not prepared to compromise his position at a delicate stage of negotiations by involving himself with his younger brother's anti-government stance. He had won the contracts he wanted. From then on he had gone from strength to strength, diversifying into pharmaceuticals. From the latest reports in the business and financial press, it seemed that he was now trying to make a large acquisition in the petro-chemical industry and, if past performance was anything to go by, he would succeed. Aaron was a master of the hostile take-over. He was also totally ruthless when it came to shedding excess manpower from the companies he had absorbed. Once acquired, the failing businesses would receive injections of capital from the parent company. When they were able to stand on their own, he would cut them loose to operate on their own. Depending on the long-term prospects of the company, he might retain a major share-holding or sell outright. More than once he had built a company into a market leader and then sold it at top price. A man in Aaron's position had powerful friends—and powerful enemies.

Before he slept, Michael convinced himself that it was Aaron's powerful friends in government who might help him right now. It would be best to turn up unannounced. He would promise his brother no anti-government activities and be willing to sell his interest in the business to him—that should please him. All he needed was a place to lie low—to rest and hide. Before he could sleep he concentrated on planning for tomorrow, in this way, trying to mask his heartache. It did not always work. Sometimes he would be transported back to happier days when he had played with John and the pain would return. God, he ached for his son, his friend Paddy, and over the tragic loss of Carla.

Aaron had moved house since their last confrontation but it was not difficult to find his new address. His homestead nestled in the lea of the North Ridge near the Royal Durban Golf Course and the taxi dropped him outside. The building was more than a home. It was a reminder of former colonial rule and at first glance Michael estimated it to have at least a dozen bedrooms.

Pausing at the double gates, Michael glanced at the 'discreet' brass plaque, 'Aarondale', and grimaced at the visible ostentation. Aaron's visions were always on a grand scale, which his house reflected perfectly. It was of palatial proportions set in an immaculately tended garden. Although it was early and a Sunday, the gardeners were already at work with rake and hosepipe. Michael walked past elegant white pillars flanking the gates, up the jacaranda-lined paved driveway. From here he could see the tennis courts and, behind that, a diving board. He wondered if the swimming pool would be as grandiose as all the other features he had seen. He arrived at the front entrance under an imposing portico. Aaron would never wittingly permit his wealth and status to be understated.

It was Ruth who came to greet him. The houseboy had taken him to the drawing room while he went to announce Michael to his mistress.

From the nervousness she exhibited when she entered, Michael could guess that all she knew of him was based on Aaron's description. He saw her appraise him, looking him up and down before smiling brightly with what Michael thought was relief. He had expected this and hoped to make a good impression. Until now she probably thought he was a drug-taking, left-wing drop-out, but he was cleanly shaved, neatly groomed and clad in a smart sports jacket, dark trousers, with a clean shirt and tie. He returned her smile and shook hands politely.

'Michael, I am so sorry for you. How does one cope with such a loss!'

'Thanks Ruth, with great difficulty I'm afraid.' He knew what she had meant, and it was kind of her to think of John. She was a slim, handsome woman in her mid-thirties with keen, intelligent violet eyes and dark hair.

She instructed the houseboy to call Aaron from his study.

Aaron appeared a moment or two later. Too many corporate lunches and far too little exercise had contributed to his overweight condition. He did not seem particularly surprised to see his brother. Michael let it pass.

'What can I say...my condolences Michael. It must be a terrible blow.' Aaron greeted him solemnly, working Michael's arm slowly and mechanically. 'You could at least have let me know you were coming.'

'Aaron, I think we need to sort out Michael first; he needs somewhere to stay.' She said eyeing his bag.

'I had hoped to use the company penthouse in town, if it's free? I need to recharge my batteries that's all, a week at most.'

'The apartment! No...the company, er...disposed of that years ago, but...' Aaron began.

'Nonsense,' Ruth interjected taking charge, 'I won't hear of it. You'll stay here as our guest for as long as you need. There's plenty of room.'

'If you're sure it's no trouble...' Michael looked for Aaron's reaction to this sudden offer and, to his relief saw his brother had no objections.

She summons the houseboy and had him take Michael's bag upstairs and prepare the room. It was not a request—she struck Michael as a woman accustomed to command.

'What brings you to Durban?' Aaron asked. 'But come, let's go and sit somewhere more comfortable.'

'You know why I'm here...' Michael began, now seated in one of the informal lounges.

Aaron seemed not to understand.

'John,' he answered.

'Yes, yes, of course. Sorry, I wasn't thinking. If you need to talk I'm always here for you, you know that. If I can be of any assistance in any way, please don't hesitate. Dad would have wanted me to do that.'

'No, not really. It won't help now; thanks all the same.'

Michael had never known Aaron to be so expansive to anyone before, and especially not to him, but he supposed time changes things. It might even have been an attempt to cover embarrassment at an unfamiliar rush of brotherly affection.

'But I appreciate the offer of a bed, if you are sure it's no trouble...'

'Don't be silly,' Ruth cut in, 'of course you can stay. To tell the truth I will be glad of the company. Aaron won't say but he is in the middle of a huge take-over bid for some petro-chemical company or other...' she said conspiratorially. 'He is so busy these days I hardly see him at all and the twins are away at boarding school. Come on, I'll show you to your room.'

Aaron smiled, 'You two go on. I'll catch up in a short while.'

Michael followed her into the octagonal hallway with its fluted pillars and intricate parquet floor. From here he could see the two lounges, drawing room and dining area. Clearly it was a magnificent piece of architecture but the furnishings and style were not to his taste. They turned to climb the wide staircase and Michael felt compelled to say something. 'You have a truly beautiful home.'

'Oh! I suppose so. You know Aaron, he always insists on putting everything into the house. At times I feel it's more like a museum.' She looked at him, her violet eyes lined with resignation as she showed him into the main guest room, before excusing herself with the promise of lunch in an hour's time.

Michael found his bag next to the bed and made himself comfortable in the guest room which contained all the trappings of a five star hotel: en-suite bathroom, balcony, air-conditioner, telephone; it even had a radio and television. Yet despite all the luxury around him, he had an uncomfortable feeling he could not account for. He was fidgety and played with all the gadgets. He flicked through all the TV channels and found only one; there was nothing there to interest him. He toyed with the air-conditioning controls until he had forgotten the original setting. He tested the water pressure in the shower and checked the softness of the towels, then looked in all the cupboards and drawers—they were empty. Finally, he tried the door to the balcony but found it locked, he went back and flopped down on the bed—sinking into its welcoming embrace. This was luxury and he stretched to the bedside cabinet and picked up the telephone. He did not want to call anyone but it was the only device he hadn't yet examined; so he listened to the tone. As he did, an extension elsewhere in the house was lifted from its cradle, immediately followed by the tones of numbers being dialled. He should have hung up but he didn't. Michael felt embarrassed listening in, but to hang up now would alert the caller that someone else was on the line.

The ring was answered quickly and brusquely, 'Van Heerden.'

The voice and the name both sounded immediately familiar but Michael couldn't place them. Then he heard his brother whispering and his heart missed a beat.

'You were right, Van Heerden,' his brother's voice said in hushed tones, 'He came! How did you know?'

'He can't be—are you sure?'

'Of course I'm sure. I can recognise my own brother,' Aaron sounded indignant.

'Sorry, it's just that—well, we thought he was in Cape Town. Does he suspect anything?'

That name—Van Heerden! It came flooding back to him in a rush. He was the BOSS officer who, years ago, had taken him and the doctor on a journey of terror from which they had barely managed to escape with their lives.

'No, not a thing. Why should he? He's staying here for a while, so you can pick him up any time you like. When will you be here?'

'Early tomorrow afternoon. I don't want the local police bungling this one, so I will supervise the arrest myself. I will be on the first flight out of Cape Town in the morning and then I will have to pick up a local team. I trust you can keep him there that long?'

'Yes, of course I can, just make sure you keep your end of the bargain. There must not be any publicity, understand?'

'Don't worry, Mr Bernstein, I shall be the epitome of discretion. Your company's reputation can remain unblemished, if you know what I mean— make sure your brother stays where he is. He is a very elusive man but this time I shall have him.'

Aaron knew what he meant: a backhander would keep his empire untarnished. Right now he could not afford to have a loose cannon around with sensitive negotiations currently in progress. Whatever Michael had done was of his own doing and he would have to answer to the State.

The line went dead and Michael found he was sweating despite the air-conditioning. The bastard! His own brother—how could he? Did he know what would happen? Did he even care? Michael waited for the click of the receiver before hanging up his phone. On his arrival in Durban he had begun to relax—just a little—now in a matter of moments the situation had changed and he was in real danger.

He checked the time. Twenty-four hours left in which to escape from this luxury prison and go—but where? Lesotho lay a few hundred kilometres to the north. He would make for the capital Maseru. From there he could fly abroad. There was no one else to turn to and certainly no friends. How he needed a friend!

His breathing steadied and he began to think more clearly. 'Yes, behave normally for the moment. Unpack and go downstairs and join your brother and his wife. Calm down and don't let on you know. Keep them off guard and look for a chance to get away without attracting attention.' He made his way to the lounge.

For the past hour Ruth had been cheerfully trying to engage Michael in conversation but he seemed distant, his answers monosyllabic.

'We thought we would dine out tonight if that would suit you. There's a new place in town we haven't tried yet. What do you think?'

'Er...yes. Sure...fine...whatever.'

'Are you all right, man?' His manner had not gone unnoticed by Aaron. 'You seem preoccupied. Is everything okay?'

'Oh, yes, everything is fine; I'm a bit tired, that's all. If it's all the same to you, I'd like to go to my room and lie down for a bit. I'll be much better after a couple of hours' rest.' It was no use trying to think of an escape plan with people talking to you all the while.

Time dragged by and yet there seemed precious little of it. He tried the balcony door again but it remained locked. Taking the risk of being seen he climbed out of a side-window onto the balcony and keeping well back from the edge, surveyed the garden for possible exits. There was no way to leave in daylight without being seen by the gardeners or, by anyone looking out from the large bay windows below. Aaron's study and drawing room overlooked the drive on one side of the house and the lounges had a view of the other side. He gauged it was at least sixty metres to the wrought iron gates and there was nothing to hide him from view. The branches of the jacaranda trees lining the drive were too high and only a couple of ornamental shrubs broke the expanse of manicured lawn. Forcing himself to the edge he saw, thankfully, that there was a sturdy trellis-work he could climb down.

Michael paced the room, racking his brains for a solution. Perhaps he should come right out and explain the situation. Maybe if Aaron knew that he was in mortal danger he would think differently about turning him over to BOSS. But, if Aaron knew already and was still prepared to turn him in, whatever small advantage he had would be lost. Maybe if he feigned illness and then slipped away after they had left for the restaurant. Chances were they'd cancel. Perhaps later, under cover of darkness, he could slip away from the house and have at least a few hours' head start before it was found he was missing. No! Michael wanted to put as much distance between himself and Van Heerden as possible. The restaurant then? On the pretext of going to the toilet, he would slip out and make his escape. Yes, it would have to be that. He would have to make it to the Lesotho border on his own. First, he would attempt to retrieve the stolen Cortina he had left downtown; it would only be a matter of forcing a window.

Michael ceased his pacing and lay down on the bed, his hands behind his head, staring at the ceiling. With BOSS on his tail it didn't matter where he went, so long as he managed to get away—but escape wouldn't improve his situation. They would eventually find him and he would be on the run again. They had managed to find him after all this time, had they not? There had to be a final solution. Something that would get them off his back completely. But what?

'The files! Where the hell is that disk?' He scrabbled in his overnight case and found it in the side-pocket. 'So much trouble for such a small thing.' He flopped onto the bed.

If he was to have his wits about him tonight, he would need to be wide-awake when the time came so, although he did not much feel like it, he tried to force all thoughts from his mind and dozed fitfully.

He awoke with a start and found that he had slept for nearly five hours. The afternoon was well advanced, the shadows lengthening before a falling sun in the western sky. The noise of gravel crunching beneath the rolling wheels of a car drifted in through the balcony window. No, not one car—two. They came to a halt near the front door and Michael rose from the bed and moved to the window, rubbing the sleep from his eyes as he went. The cars were hidden from his vision, but through the static there was no mistaking the sounds that came from the short wave radio. Police!

Instinctively, Michael stepped backwards into the room and glanced around frantically for a way to escape. He grabbed his wallet, passport and the floppy disk off the dresser and, stuffing them into his trouser pocket, ran back to the window. He was too late. Suddenly the bedroom door burst open and two armed policemen rushed in. Their handguns were drawn and they were aimed at him. Behind them, Aaron stood in the hallway half smiling.

'Bly still! Keep still,' ordered the first uniformed policeman. Michael obeyed. 'Now, raise your hands behind your head and step away from the window.' Again Michael complied and said nothing, his gaze resting on his brother. His arms were forced down behind his back and he felt pain as the handcuffs pinched his wrists. Aaron's self-satisfied look withered beneath his stony glare. A policeman nudged Michael out of the room with the point of his revolver.

Aaron stood aside to let them pass and Michael spoke through gritted teeth. 'Have you any idea what you have done? You have signed my death warrant.'

'What's going on? What are you doing with him?' Ruth demanded of the policemen as she hurried from the staircase towards them. Another plain-clothes policeman in the corridor held her aside as Michael was forced along.

'Your husband,' Michael said curtly, 'has turned me over to BOSS. By this time next week I will probably be dead.'

'Aaron?' Ruth gasped.

'Don't worry, darling,' Aaron said shuffling his feet, 'he is being melodramatic; it's a trivial matter. He'll be out and about in a few days, you'll see.'

'Betray your own brother? Dad would have been proud of you!' Michael shouted back.

'Stop them, they cannot do this, this is our house,' Ruth screamed. A policeman said simply, 'Sorry, madam, but it is our duty.' Michael was whisked down the stairs and into one of the waiting cars. They left the grounds, the wheels spraying gravel.

Michael was crushed: it was the end of the trail. The plans to have him arrested tomorrow had been changed and he had been caught napping— literally. A deep sense of foreboding overwhelmed him. He had done nothing wrong, yet he had been hounded for most of his adult life by the threat, and now the reality of capture and—who knows what! Each of his colleagues in turn had been killed. Was it his turn now?

'Why am I being arrested?' he asked indignantly. 'What have I done?'

'Shut your bloody mouth,' came the retort, accompanied by a sharp elbow in the ribs from one of the escorts next to him on the back seat. They drove to the airport where he was handcuffed to the plain-clothes police officer, making escape impossible. The man looked somehow familiar but a mere glance at the other officers was enough to confirm that they all looked alike. 'They are all cast from the same arrogant mould,' he thought.

'Where's Van Heerden?' Michael demanded but the plain-clothes officer ignored him, tugging him across the tarmac to a waiting aircraft. They were shown to the first class compartment. Michael and his silent escort were the only occupants. The pilot's announcement confirmed what Michael already guessed: they were bound for Johannesburg.

On arrival at Jan Smuts Airport, Michael was rushed through to a waiting unmarked police car. The driver hit the freeway at high speed, weaving past slower traffic on either side. He slowed only a little on entering central Johannesburg, making his way down Commissioner Street to the police station. John Vorster Square loomed over them, a dark and sinister building. The driver turned into the security car park. It seemed to Michael as though the vehicle was entombed in the walls of this notorious building, where many political detainees went in but fewer came out, unless it was from one of the upper storey windows! They made their way inside.

There were several doors leading off the corridor, each labelled according to its use or the occupant. At the far end, Michael could make out the front desk where law-abiding citizens, though rare, handed in wallets they found in the street, or were brought in and booked before being escorted to a temporary holding cell for minor misdemeanours. They passed the cells, an administration office and a small staff room where a constable was making coffee for the desk officers.

Interview room one, with its heavy door and small barred opening was bare, but for two plain wooden chairs and a rough wooden table. For an hour—maybe longer—he sat alone where they had left him, listening to the sounds of heavy boots on stone floors and the banter between police officers going about their business. Thankfully they had removed the handcuffs. A greater feeling of desolation descended on him. Not knowing what was to happen, he stared at the bare surroundings. Who was there left he could turn to for help after he had been betrayed by his own brother?

A scream came from somewhere in the building, reminding him of the catalogue of 'suicides' that frequently occurred with political prisoners. Though now on the inside, it was difficult, if impossible, to see how anyone could 'fall' accidentally from a top storey window that was protected by solid steel bars and wire mesh.* Michael was under no illusion about the length of his stay. It was going to be very brief. He reminded himself that these were the same people who had betrayed their fellow countrymen during World War II. Both Verwoerd and Vorster had been responsible for sending information to the German High Command on South African 8th Army troopship movements. They in turn had relayed the messages to the U-boats lying in wait off the East African coast, where many men had lost their lives in shark-infested seas.* His fate now rested in the hands of people who had received this legacy of corruption.

The door opened and the plain-clothes officer entered. Michael stared at him; it was his escort of the late afternoon flight. The officer said nothing but slowly removed the jacket of his dark suit and carefully hung it over the back of the chair opposite him. Still standing, he reached into the pocket and took out Michael's wallet, the floppy disk and his passport, and placed them on the table. Pressing his knuckles in the centre of the table he leaned towards Michael until his face was centimetres away and, for the first time, Michael heard him speak. 'I have a score to settle with you, Mr Bernstein,' he said with unveiled loathing.

Michael's eyes widened in surprise at the sound of the voice he had heard so recently on the telephone. 'You! You're Van Heerden.' Michael's mind flashed back to the nightmare journey from Cape Town to Johannesburg in the back of a police van which he had shared with David. At the time they were accompanied by two officers and, yes, this one could have been one of them. If so, the years had not been kind to him. He had spread around the midriff; the face was pitted and craggy, weathered by the

330

African sun and too much alcohol; his thinning hair barely covered his scalp. His nose had changed shape irreparably and his breath stank.

'Ja, I am Van Heerden. You caused me a lot of pain breaking my jaw and for that I am going to make you pay.'

Until now he had no idea that he had broken the man's jaw, and evidently his nose, but the thought of it cheered him enough to raise a faint smile.

'So you think it is funny, eh?' A baton appeared in his hand so swiftly that Michael never saw it coming before it crashed across his temple, sending him sprawling from the chair onto the cold cement floor. He sat dazed as the pain flooded through his head.

'Ja! You're a lucky bastard, Bernstein. You escaped my bomb in Houston and then you walked away from that crash—pity about the minister's wife, but messing about with you she deserved to die.'

Van Heerden lit a cigarette while he waited for Michael to regain his seat. He came closer to his prisoner and, stooping, exhaled in Michael's face. 'Ja! I am going to enjoy this.' He placed the baton under Michael's chin, forcing his head back so that his jaw ached with an excruciating pain.

'Tell me, where is Professor Mueller? His maid reported him missing yesterday morning,' he prodded Michael viciously.

'I don't know. I was in Durban. Remember?'

'Agh! Don't get bloody funny with me, mister. You're in enough shit as it is.' He picked up the disk and waved it under Michael's nose. 'Tonight you will remain here, then tomorrow I'm taking you to Pretoria Prison and this time we will get there. For now, you are going to tell me what happened to that ANC kaffir that was with you in the van. And I want to know what's on this computer disk we found in your pocket, and what else you know. You stole this information from Groote Berg Hospital didn't you?' He grinned. 'Ja! It's all right, Bernstein, we have the rest of the night ahead of us. I'm really looking forward...'

A sudden commotion in the corridor outside cut across his words. The door burst open. Two constables were trying to restrain a very large and very inebriated Afrikaner farmer.

'Give us a hand here, man,' shouted one of the constables. His right eye was already beginning to close. The big farmer bellowed and hit the constable again. They stumbled and fell into the narrow interview room. Van Heerden drew calmly on his cigarette then stamped it out on the floor.

'For God's sake, man,' he said wearily, 'can't you sort out a bloody drunk between you?' He started towards the door. The drunk and the other constable tumbled together on the interview room floor. With a surprisingly deft movement the big man regained his feet and, straightening up, drew up his trouser leg and unsheathed a knife strapped above his ankle.

'Look out, man, he has a knife.' Van Heerden reacted swiftly, unflapping the holster of his sidearm but the man was too close for him to draw the weapon. He took a step backwards, and then another, until he was able to get the gun clear of the holster. The drunk stumbled forward, waving the knife wildly in front of him. One more step back and Van Heerden would be able to level the weapon and fire.

'Van Heerden,' Michael yelled from behind and threw himself at his interrogator. The impact pushed Van Heerden forward and the thrusting blade penetrated cleanly between the ribs deep into his chest cavity. Van Heerden's eyes shot open in utter astonishment and the gun clattered to the floor. He stood frozen for a second. His knees buckled and he slumped to the ground. The drunkard seemed to sober instantly. The hilt of the knife protruded through Van Heerden's fingers as he clutched at the pain in his chest. He was barely conscious and he gasped for breath as blood began to trickle through the rent in his shirt.

'Get that drunk out of here,' Michael seized the moment, 'and get some help. Quick, man! I'll tend to him.' To his relief the constables man-handled their now docile prisoner out of the room and along the corridor towards another cell. The whole episode had taken only a few seconds.

Renewed shouting in the corridor brought the duty desk sergeant rushing over to assist. He appeared in the doorway and found Michael trying to stanch the flow of blood with Van Heerden's shirt.

Michael looked up. 'It's all right, I am trained for this sort of thing,' he said with all the authority he could summon. 'This man has a punctured lung. He must get to hospital. Call an ambulance.'

The sergeant hesitated a moment and, as he framed a question, Michael pressed heavily on Van Heerden's chest causing him to moan and gurgle on the blood rising in his throat.

'Hurry, man,' Michael snapped, 'or he'll die.' The sergeant turned and ran down the corridor to his office.

Michael bent over Van Heerden while he rapidly sized up the situation. A few metres of unsecured corridor now separated him from the outside world and the gun lay inches away. The man who so wanted him dead was lying mortally wounded before him. So far, no one appeared to recognise him as a serious threat—chances were that they had no idea what BOSS wanted with him.

'Don't die on me yet, you bastard. I need you alive just a little longer,' he whispered to the limp figure. Van Heerden stirred and raised an arm, trying to speak. Suddenly he convulsed. His eyes opened wide, fixed on Michael, then his arms went limp. Michael felt for a pulse. He found none, and closed the staring eyes. He looked around for the floppy disk. Yes! It was still there on the desk. He pocketed it and his other belongings as the sergeant rushed in carrying a First Aid box.

'How bad is he?' he asked, handing over the box. 'Shouldn't we move him to somewhere more comfortable?'

'Thanks,' said Michael, opening the lid. 'We daren't move him. There's not much damage at the moment but it's best he stays still. He'll be okay but I need to get him to a hospital quickly. Thank God he's passed out. I think there's internal bleeding—hopefully not too serious,' Michael lied as he fished for a clean dressing. 'I have to keep pressure on his chest here,' indicating a spot near the wound. He pressed it firmly to demonstrate the point.

Van Heerden appeared to groan as trapped air escaped from his lungs. Michael released the pressure quickly.

'The ambulance is on its way.' The sergeant stepped closer and frowned, 'Sure he's okay? Seems bad!'

'I'm afraid my commandant has lost consciousness.' Michael looked suitably pained, 'Who was that fellow?' he asked.

'Transvaal rugby supporter.... Couldn't happen to a nicer bloke,' the sergeant said—his voice thick with sarcasm—gazing down at Van Heerden. 'Bastard comes here throwing his weight around, telling us we don't know our jobs. At least I've never been stabbed by a bloody drunk in my years of service...' he paused. 'What's that, you said: he's your commandant?'

Michael's mind raced. He had to say something. Anything! 'Look, I'm undercover. Can I trust you to be discreet, sergeant?'

The sergeant moved closer and nodded uncertainly.

Michael remembered the gun and purposely picked it up. 'Here, you had better look after this until he asks for it back.'

'Okay, I'll lock it in the safe.' The sergeant seemed less apprehensive.

'Ja, he can be a right bastard at times. Mostly he's okay, but he has a lot on his plate just now, that's all,' Michael whispered. 'Did you know that Van Heerden,' he indicated the still figure, 'suspects subversive elements right here, in John Vorster Square?'

'No, I didn't. They phoned yesterday morning and said he was coming in from Durban with a prisoner and that we were to assist him in any way he wanted.' He seemed puzzled. 'What are you doing here?'

Michael stood up.

'We are under pressure to get results. We've been after this leak for months but the suspect is always one step ahead. We think he, or possibly they, are being tipped off by someone higher-up. So I have been working as his informant to try and to get closer to them, hoping they will break their cover while I'm kept here. Did you know we caught an SAP sergeant in Durban last month. He thought I was an American. That's the way it works.'

Michael knelt down to check Van Heerden again and, satisfied, patted him on the shoulder. 'He keeps me in overnight and I pass on the information in the interview room—this way it seems as if he is giving me a rough time for a day or two and then I'm released. It has to look real, you see.'

Michael mopped Van Heerden's forehead, then adjusted the folded jacket under his head. 'Wait 'til he gets his hands on that bloody drunk!'

'I don't blame him,' the sergeant confided.

'Where is that damned ambulance?' The concern in Michael's voice was sincere. If he played his cards right this might be his passage out. If Van Heerden was pronounced dead here, there would be no great hurry to remove the body, or himself. He had to keep him 'alive' and he had to get out of this place quickly.

'Don't worry man, it'll be here soon. He'll be okay.' The sergeant seemed to notice Michael's swollen face for the first time. 'What happened to you?' he asked.

Michael forced a smile. 'The bloody drunk hit me first.'

The sergeant nodded, then added, 'Better have that seen to.'

'Bloody hell!' Michael thought, 'He swallowed it.'

'Look, we cannot wait any longer.' Michael pulled back Van Heerden's eyelids in turn and they both peered into the dead eyes. He felt for a pulse. 'This man's condition is worsening.' Michael sounded genuinely desperate. 'Get one of our vans and some help, fast—we'll take him to hospital.'

'Leave it to me.' And the sergeant was gone.

Commandant Van Heerden's breathing was very weak according to Michael. They carried him carefully to the van and loaded him on board under the supervision of the sergeant.

'The station commander is on his way in. It's okay, I'll explain. You had better go with him. Have your face treated at the same time.' Suddenly he seemed a little unsure. He indicated one of the constables. 'Albert must go with you too, you understand, until we can clear this matter up.'

Michael forced another smile even though the side of his face ached. 'Of course, sergeant! You can be sure, when my commandant hears how you assisted, he will want to thank you personally.'

The sergeant smiled. 'I expect he'll want to kick the crap out of you for not being in front of him at the time.'

'Ha!' Michael laughed at the sergeant's humour. 'You could be dead right.' A young policeman climbed in next to Michael.

The sergeant, closing the door to the van, leaned close to Michael and said quietly, 'Don't worry, man, your cover is safe with me.'

'Thanks, sergeant.' Michael watched the figure recede as the police van made its way at speed from John Vorster Square. There was still the guard to contend with.

Michael leaned over Van Heerden's mouth as the trolley was wheeled into the casualty department.

'What's that? You want a bedpan? Okay, let me see if I can find one.' He looked apologetically at the escort. 'Do you want to get one, or shall I?'

The young constable nodded, 'You get it.'

Michael disappeared down the corridor.

Minutes later the casualty team were rushing Van Heerden into theatre. The duty medical officer, stopped the trolley, straightened and stared at the young constable in disbelief. 'What do you mean your colleague has gone for a bedpan? This man has been dead for the best part of an hour.'

Michael reached the hospital foyer with comparative ease and tried to find a way out without success. He slowed his brisk pace in an attempt to walk casually. A mere ninety minutes had elapsed since Van Heerden had struck him.

He looked around frantically for another exit—time was running out! A boisterous group of rugby supporters were milling around two young nurses who were applying antiseptic and bandages to their superficial wounds. He suddenly had an idea and joined the queue—his own dishevelled clothing, together with visible abrasions and bruises, drew comment.

'You got a good one there!' said one.

Within minutes they were all stained with acriflavine and bandaged up. Michael had difficulty seeing though the dressing swathed around his head.

The erstwhile combatants, arms draped about one another's shoulders, bore Michael through the main doors on a cloud of beery breath and antiseptic!

Out of the corner of his eye he saw the young constable, now with revolver in hand, frantically searching the casualty wards for the bogus BOSS agent. The constable barely gave them a glimpse as he ran past.

CHAPTER 12

With reference to handing over to Black rule:
"[I] was not prepared to lead White South
Africans...on a road to abdication and suicide."

P W Botha
President of South Africa, 1979 - 89

24 March 1985

Michael discarded his bandages outside the hospital, before purposefully making his way along the busy streets of Hillbrow—one of the most densely populated suburbs in the world. The night air was redolent with petroleum fumes and the smell of charcoal grills from many steak-houses. The spotlighted sidewalks and the glare of neon seemed to expose the stark reality of his situation. He felt a mixture of excitement and fear, accentuated by the roar of the early evening traffic, the blare reverberating between the high-rise buildings. Hurriedly he passed a White taxi rank, then turned to walk briskly downhill towards the quieter city centre.

For a moment Michael felt the pavement shake beneath his feet, a normal occurrence in Johannesburg. He was reminded of the terrible risks to which the miners, most of them Black, were exposed night and day. Even as he passed, they toiled three hundred metres or more underground, chasing the mother lode—gold! Suddenly the earth shuddered again as the aftershock passed. Michael pressed on.

Taking a short cut through Joubert Park, he came to the exit and a standstill. Catching his breath, he instinctively looked over his shoulder. Satisfied that he had not been followed, his attention was drawn to the line of stationary vehicles in the foreground. Watching the activity in front of the taxi rank, he could see several drivers haggling with a group of Black men and women, when a van pulled up opposite him and the passengers alighted.

Michael steeled himself. He emerged cautiously from the protective shadows of the park and crossed the last twenty paces to the back of the rank and approached the now empty van.

The Black taxi driver was apprehensive.

'Did my baas say he wants to go to Soweto township at night?' He shook his head. 'Try those drivers,' directing him to the vehicles up ahead.

There, Michael received the same response; this time the driver pointed nearer to the front of the rank.

'Try the red Datsun van.'

He felt very conspicuous, feeling sure heads had turned to watch him, the only White man in sight and attempting to use a taxi forbidden to people of his colour.

The driver listened, convinced that Michael had to be a madman or was looking for a Black girl. His regular White clientele usually telephoned and he brought the girls into town; never the other way round.

'Yeah!' Michael accentuated his American accent. 'I'm from the States...'

'No kidding,' said the driver. 'I'd never have guessed.'

Michael changed tactics. 'Okay, I'm a reporter...looking for a colleague I knew some time back. Lives in Soweto.'

The driver frowned. So this man was not after girls. Pity, he would have to make up the commission later. 'Who's this friend you're looking for?'

Michael hoped his pronunciation was correct. It would have to be if he was to have any chance of finding David or his family. 'David Nyamande—Doctor Nyamande,' he repeated, ensuring that the driver understood.

'Never heard of him. What part of Soweto is he from?'

'I have an address,' Michael lied. 'Can we go, now?' he pleaded.

Just then three large middle-aged women broke away from the over-packed vehicle in front, and headed towards them. In their rush they jostled past Michael and clambered into the back of the van.

'All right, you'd better get in quickly, my baas, but it will cost you twenty rand—one way.'

Michael did not hesitate, he climbed in with the amply endowed matrons.

He was met by a chorus of protest, then frosty silence from the other passengers. Engaged as domestic servants, for these women the day had begun at 4.00am with the trip into the White suburbs of Johannesburg. Wearily travelling home at 9.00pm it was not unusual then to cook for their large families. What was unusual for them was to be accompanied to Soweto by a White man!

The van rattled while music blasted from the radio. The driver cut deftly through the city centre. Hemming them in, Michael looked up at the glass wall of skyscrapers. Shop windows flashed by. Gazing out he thought the city was comparable with New York or London, by day or night. The passengers rocked to and fro as the van made its way through traffic lights, accompanied by the sounds of squealing brakes and blaring horns. Michael was thankful when they reached the arterial freeway which led away from the city centre's bright lights.

Heading south towards Soweto, they passed abandoned mine dumps with rusted riggings, silhouetted against an indigo sky. Far to the east, forked lightning seared the night. Michael remembered the many times as a small boy, he had watched storms crashing overhead. Once, the lightning had been so close he had heard the static crackle through the air and he had run to the protective arms of his nanny. He peered around—his surrogate mother, Sophie, could have been any one of these women. His thoughts returned to his current predicament. Without family or friends he had thought of David; it was imperative that he find him, but at best he knew the chances were slim. He had no one else to turn to.

The driver was shouting. Michael forced his attention to take in his immediate surroundings. He stared along the headlight beam. What he saw made his heart skip a beat—*Hippo* riot trucks partially blocked the road up ahead. All vehicles were being stopped and searched.

There wasn't time to evade the roadblock. 'Oh Christ!' he said aloud.

The driver slowed to a crawl and glanced back. 'My baas is in trouble?'

Michael caught his gaze. 'Yeah! Deep shit.'

The driver spoke sharply to the women—Michael did not understand. Nothing happened! The driver spoke again, then he said to Michael, 'Get down quickly. Lie flat, my baas, flat.'

Michael dived for the floor. Immediately he was buried under flowing garments as bodies landed on top of him. The women began to weave about and sing like drunks. He gasped for air, pinned beneath a swell of generous thighs and buttocks.

The sliding door was pulled back and a beam of light flashed around the inside of the cab.

There was a moment's hesitation, then a voice said, 'Bloody drinking again. Jesus, you people never stop!' The voice sounded thoroughly disgruntled. The soldier's duty as a national serviceman in the townships had become routine and it irked him to give up the comfort of wife and home in the White suburbs to spend nights checking on Blacks. He focused, with horror, on one of the women who was beckoning him seductively, and turned on the driver.

'Piss off and take these Black whores with you.' Disgusted, he waved them through the cordon.

Two kilometres on, the driver pulled over and let the women out. Michael, having regained his breath, murmured his thanks and they waved him goodbye. The taxi pulled away with a spray of gravel.

Michael studied the monotonous rows of regimented houses under the high stadium lights that substituted for street lighting, creating a surreal and alien landscape. He felt a wave of depression—it was so bleak.

'What's the address?' asked the driver.

'I don't have one,' confessed his passenger. 'All I remember is he had a sister—also a doctor, or something. I met him in Zambia...a few years back.' Michael was only too aware that the vehicle had slowed.

The driver was staring at him in his rear-view mirror. 'My baas, that doesn't help either of us. There are a million people living here.'

Passing through the half-deserted streets Michael said, 'But there must be someone who has heard of him. It's urgent. I have to speak to him.'

The taxi driver caught the worried note in Michael's voice. 'Baas, I don't want trouble.'

Michael was desperate; the hour was late and being White, he was possibly in a hostile environment. He had no alternative but to place his life in this stranger's hands.

'Look, I'm writing an article on the ANC for *Time* magazine. I must find this doctor—it's important! If not, can you please take me to the ANC, or at least to one of its members?' Michael did not know what else to say. 'I'll pay you a hundred dollars—sorry rands.'

Carefully the taxi driver looked in the side mirror. He was afraid, half expecting to see a riot van following. The road was deserted. 'What you do is dangerous—if the police catch you....' He left Michael to figure that out. 'My baas, take some good advice. Let's go back to Johannesburg—now!' He knew that if his passenger was a security man, neither of them would stand a chance with the *comrades,* the rank and file of the ANC.

Michael offered him payment which the driver reached back and took, inspecting the two fifty-rand notes as he drove.

'I'm not kidding. Take me to the ANC, or drop me nearby to where they are if you want, then you can leave me.'

The man glanced up at the mirror and their eyes met.

'Please, I must get away from the authorities. I'm in a lot of trouble.'

'Apartheid, or some other kind of trouble?' the driver asked.

'No! Just apartheid trouble. If they catch me again I think I'll be, shall we say, dead—in fact very dead.' This statement seemed to make up the taxi driver's mind.

'That's not good for your health,' the driver responded and they both laughed nervously. He glanced at the money, hesitated, then returned one of the notes. 'Fifty is enough. I will take you to an address but I do not know if they can help you. It's a place where the ANC *comrades* hang out.'

A short drive later Michael was deposited at the kerbside. There were no street or house lights—there appeared to be no signs of life at all.

'Go and knock on that door,' the taxi driver pointed across the road to a bungalow, the outline of a roof faintly visible, 'and good luck.'

Michael felt some trepidation at being in the middle of Soweto, unfamiliar surroundings where Whites were forbidden to enter. He took a few tentative steps, then thought it wise to have the taxi wait for him as a precaution. He was too late.

Crashing his gears, the driver without so much as a backward glance sped off down the road, and was soon swallowed up by the night. Michael was alone, frighteningly alone. Somewhere a dog barked. Seemingly out of nowhere two ghost-like figures appeared simply to vanish again in the opposite direction. He stood stock-still, all his senses alert. He could smell wood-smoke mingled with paraffin fumes. Slowly his eyes became accustomed to the night. He saw a flicker of light in the direction to which the taxi driver had pointed. It was now or never.

The first knock brought no response; neither did the second. After what he considered to be a respectable delay, Michael banged on the door again. Suddenly a shadowy figure loomed out of the darkness from around the side of the house. Michael stepped back in alarm.

'What do you want?' the man asked abruptly.

'I'm looking for Dr David Nyamande. I am an old friend and need to speak to him.'

Realising that Michael was White, the man immediately became defensive. 'Who is this Doctor? Anyway, what do you want with him?'

As he came nearer, Michael judged the man's height to be well over six feet and he immediately tensed in the presence of this gigantic figure. 'Please, it's most urgent that I see him, or even a member of the ANC, tonight.'

The man seemed singularly unimpressed. 'Are you alone?' He half-turned to stare back into the dark.

'Yes, I am and I'm in a helluva lot of trouble.'

Unexpectedly he gripped Michael by the jacket and swung him round with ease so that he faced the front door.

'Spread your legs, mister, while I check you out.' Skilfully he frisked Michael, removing his wallet, passport and disc.

Michael felt certain this was a practised routine!

'There are no ANC people around here. Your story'd better be good or I'll turn you over to the police.' He reached past Michael and rapped on the door, which promptly opened, and pushed him inside. The man followed.

The pungent odour of candle wax and paraffin permeated the air. There were two other men in the small room. In the flickering light Michael realised he had been right—the man from outside was a giant: tall and broad-chested, he towered over Michael.

'Sit there.' He pointed to a chair in the far corner. The room was sparsely furnished with a Formica dinette table and two chairs. Michael complied and sat staring at the three occupants. They spoke a language he did not understand. The younger of the three men opened Michael's wallet and deftly went through his possessions, then handed them back to the giant together with his passport.

Gazing around the room Michael became aware of other eyes watching him. In the dim light of the paraffin lamp, he saw two children standing in the doorway of the next room. Beneath them, a wizened face with opaque eyes also peered up at him. He realised that the old woman lying on a mattress near the doorway was blind. She was holding back the curtain so that the children could see the strange spectacle of a White man in their midst.

'My friend here says you are from the Security, that you are out to trap the ANC,' said the giant. The man lifted a chair and swung it like a toy through the air, positioning it in front of Michael. Straddling the seat, he rested both arms on the backrest.

'No, Mr Duffy, you don't have to worry. I am an ex-policeman and I can vouch you are definitely not one of them.' He raised a hand and pointed a finger the size of a banana at Michael.

'So you tell us who you are and what you want with Nyamande.'

Michael was not sure if he was relieved or not. It was a promising sign that this man had acknowledged David's name and had not denied his existence. What should he say next? He knew his career as a roving *Time* reporter was over—that would make no impression on this man. Michael decided to stick as near to the truth as he dared.

'Okay. I am being chased by the authorities because of the bloody apartheid laws in this country. I got away but if they catch me now, they will kill me.' He stopped to see what affect this would have on his interrogator.

'So they will kill you! What have you done to piss off the SAP? Got a Black girlfriend?' The two men flanking him laughed.

'No, no! Nothing like that,' Michael protested. 'You don't understand. It's not the SAP—it's BOSS!'

They stared at him, the disbelief plain in their eyes.

'I know it sounds incredible but it's true. They had me down at John Vorster Square this afternoon and one of their BOSS agents was killed. I escaped.'

An arm shot out and, before Michael could react, a huge hand held him firmly by the lapels.

'Stop fucking us about, man. Nobody walks out of the Square. What the hell's your game? I want to know—now. What are you supposed to have done and how did you get these injuries to your face?'

Michael gasped for air. 'If you let go, I'll tell you.'

The hand was reluctantly withdrawn.

'I'm a kind of doctor.' He fought to find a way to explain his predicament and how it had been brought about. 'I used to work for a medical laboratory in Cape Town.' He thought for a moment. 'I was taken...' he stopped again. No, they weren't going to believe he had escaped from BOSS a second time. 'I was employed to do some research on germs.'

His interrogator interrupted. 'When was this?'

'In 1971,' Michael replied. 'Shortly after that, I went to live in the US.

I returned ten days ago—take a look in my passport.' Michael searched the impassive face.

'Go on,' the man prompted.

'I came back to Cape Town. And found out that the work we were doing in 1971 was the development of germ warfare, here, in South Africa. BOSS found out I knew. They killed my girlfriend and this morning I was arrested.'

The man cut in again. 'This was in Cape Town?'

Michael felt exasperated. 'No! It was in Durban. I managed to get out of Cape Town. They caught me in Durban, then they flew me to Johannesburg earlier today. Christ! If you don't believe me, I was in John Vorster Square and was beaten up. Can't you see?' Hoping the swollen side to his face was self-evident. 'A man was killed in the cells and I managed to escape.'

The story was confusing to say the least, but why had this White man come to Soweto alone? His interrogator needed to find out.

'Okay! Let's say I believe you. You can't stay here—it's too risky.' He omitted to say that having Michael there made the situation far more dangerous for them than for him. 'I will be your guide and take you to another safe house.' With that, he pocketed the passport and gave orders to one of the men who slipped out the front entrance. He gave Michael back his wallet and the disk.

'We'll walk. It's a few kilometres from here. Put this on and pull it down over your face. I don't want people seeing me with a White in Soweto. They'll think I keep the wrong company.'

Michael took the balaclava, unsure if it was a bizarre attempt at humour.

They left by the back door. The guide walked lightly for his size and at a leisurely pace, insisting that Michael stay close and to his right. Michael found he could see a lot better now than when he had first arrived in the street, his eyes having adjusted to the shadows. They went in the direction from which the taxi had come. Some way on, they turned down a side road. Occasionally people emerged out of the dark only to disappear again like wraiths. Most of the way they walked in the middle of the road and eventually the uniformity of prefabricated housing gave way to uneven lines of shanty dwellings. Michael had seen photos of them but had never been so close to this kind of poverty.

Here the low-roofed sprawling mass of tumbledown structures were crowded together, some with scarcely sufficient space between them to allow for a narrow footpath. Constructed from a miscellaneous assortment of scrap building materials, wood and even sacking, they typified the millions of dwellings which Black South Africans had to live in all over the country. Though the light was dim, Michael could see that they were not much better than crudely built chicken coops, covered with sheets of rusting corrugated iron or offcuts of asbestos sheeting.

They passed close to a group of men, wrapped in blankets, huddled around the last heat of a dying fire. His guide returned their greeting as they passed and Michael found himself repeating the salutation. Shortly afterwards, Michael broke the silence.

'How much farther?'

The man stopped. 'Maybe a half-kilometre but first we wait here for my friend.' Michael watched as his companion gazed cautiously in all directions. Soon, a silhouette approached from the route by which they had come.

Michael recognised him immediately: he was the third man they had left behind at the house.

His guide spoke tersely, 'It's good for you that we were not followed. Come on.'

Michael felt enormous relief.

Borne on the still, night air he could hear a noise, growing louder. They seemed to be heading towards it. Within minutes they had arrived.

Standing in the shadows was the man who had left by the front entrance. They certainly weren't taking chances, Michael thought. The rambling shack had no visible signs of activity that he could see, but clearly, from the babble of sounds coming from within, it was occupied.

'Wait here with my friends. I need to speak to the owner.' With that, the giant ducked through the front door. Michael removed the balaclava. It had become uncomfortable and there was nobody around except his guards. Minutes later the giant re-emerged. 'Put that back on.' He eyed Michael, 'No, forget it. Just follow me!'

Michael glanced around the *shebeen*—he had never been inside one before. Men chattered affably and laughed freely. There were few women. The raw smell of perspiration, mingled with the sweet-sour aroma of the maize beer, caught in his nostrils. Working their way through the crowd, he noticed the more elite clientele sat to one side while a rowdy group was gathered around the bar. 'Miners!' Michael thought. The dusky room was broad and long. The walls were constructed of wooden pallets filled with mud and limewashed. Paraffin lamps hung from the ceiling while the central posts supported the lattice-work of the flat roof, blackened by soot over many years. Stale tobacco smoke hung in the air.

Their arrival caused a sudden silence to descend. Only the tinny sound of a soulful saxophone playing Soweto jazz throbbed from a corner near the bar. The patrons stared at Michael as he passed with his escort. His guide disappeared into the dwelling attached to the shebeen—Michael followed close on his heels, pleased to be out of sight of so many hostile eyes. Immediately after they left the room, the chatter started up again but now more subdued.

'Patricia, this is Mr Duffy. He will stay with you while I try and find a *comrade* to take care of him.'

Michael looked at the short, rotund figure who stepped forward to greet him.

'Good evening, Mr Duffy. Welcome to my establishment.'

Michael felt her warmth and was completely taken by her cherubic smile.

'Evening, Patricia.' He thrust out his hand.

'Can I get you something to drink or perhaps eat?' She smiled up at him, grasping his hand briefly in both of hers.

The guide turned to Michael.

'You will stay here until I return. Patricia will give you a bed or anything else you want.' He came close, causing Michael to look up. 'Mr Duffy, please to do not leave this room of your own accord, that's if you value your life. Those men out there will leave you alone while you are in here. Okay?'

The message was clear.

'Okay! But if you know Dr Nyamande, please contact him—he will know me by my real name—Michael Bernstein.'

The man appeared dubious, 'Bernstein! I see. I'll make sure I remember that,' then left.

Ravenous! Michael's hunger was reinforced by the smell of meat cooking on an open fire and he waited in eager anticipation, while inspecting his surroundings. The room was obviously an office and to the side of a desk and filing cabinet was a bed. A door left ajar in the far corner revealed a toilet.

Patricia brought him a plate of braaied boerewors and mealies with a bottle of chilled wine. 'Would you prefer something else to drink?' she asked.

Michael recognised the name immediately. Boshoff Estates! He saw the irony. 'No, no, I'm more than pleased,' adding, almost too embarrassed to ask, 'Patricia, do you sell many wines as good as this?' He dutifully inspected the label.

She knew what he had meant and smiled. 'Mr Duffy, some of my customers are very discerning. They want quality and I pride myself on having the best wine cellar in Soweto.' She was glad to see Michael attack the food and drink with such relish.

The bed proved uncomfortable. Twice in the night he rose and pummelled the lumpy coir mattress but to no avail. His mind was full of images of Carla; and he was worrying about whether he would ever find David. The last he knew of his whereabouts was in Mozambique. Had he survived the war and, if so, had he returned to South Africa or Zimbabwe? Was he here in Soweto? Eventually he fell into a fitful sleep.

By the time he woke, the sun was beating down on him through the curtainless window. He was sweating and felt stiff and sore in every joint and muscle. He became aware of others moving around outside in the hall. It was already 8.00am.

An hour later Patricia stuck her head around the door. 'Morning, Mr Duffy. Would you like some coffee?'

The day dragged on and by midday Michael was becoming concerned that his presence here was being ignored. He glanced out of the window thoughtfully but decided to obey the warning he had been given.

Suddenly the door flew open and four men barged in. They all seemed to speak at the same time and Michael did not understand a word of what was being said. Not knowing what to expect, he was puzzled when, after peering at him for several more seconds, they left as abruptly as they had arrived.

An hour passed and two more men entered. One asked him in Afrikaans to confirm the details on Paddy's passport. Again they left.

Soon, his guide of the night before returned and, with a menacing stare, thrust a leading newspaper into his hand. 'Look!' He gave Michael a copy. The story read:

> Last night Major Piet Van Heerden of the Bureau of State Security was ruthlessly gunned down while attending to a routine matter. A Black man and an accomplice are being sought by police....

Michael was dumbfounded. 'But I can explain!' Still gazing blankly at the newspaper, not entirely sure how he was going to reconcile the account he had told them last night with this press propaganda. He looked up but, to his relief, the face above him had broken into an expansive grin.

'It's all right, we know you're not a spy. We have our informants even at the Square,' he said and a chuckle erupted from deep in the man's barrel chest. The guide smiled at him.

Without warning, Michael found his hand being crushed in an oversized paw, while the giant exuberantly clapped him on the back, almost rattling his teeth. 'What the hell's going on?' Michael demanded.

'Hell, man! I didn't believe your story yesterday. But the newspapers are full of it.'

'Except they've distorted the facts.'

'Black!' His guide laughed, 'Last night I could have sworn you were White, or did BOSS turn you white with fright?'

Michael felt a wave of relief sweep over him.

The guide shook his head in disbelief. 'I notice they make no reference to

John Vorster Square...reckon they don't want to admit their vulnerability. How the hell did you manage it? Van Heerden, of all people!'

Michael looked embarrassed, 'There wasn't any gun and it's not an experience I'd care to repeat.'

'Well, Mr Duffy, or whatever your name is, there are many men out there today who wish they had been in your shoes yesterday, including myself.'

He looked Michael squarely in the face.

'Thank you. Now I think it's time we sorted out your problem. You are going to be transferred to another safe house until we can contact this Dr Nyamande.'

'Is he here in Soweto?' Michael needed to know.

'Sorry, I can't answer that...I don't know. I must go, but I'll be back tonight. It's too dangerous for you to move around in daylight.' He pointed to the back of his hand. 'Your skin's the problem. By the way, I hear the police are doing a house-to-house search combing the suburb Houghton. Any reason you know of?'

Michael was at a loss to know why. 'No, except that we used to live there when I was a child.'

His guide thought for a while. 'Never mind, I'll see you at about eight tonight.'

No sooner had he left when Patricia came in. 'Mr Duffy, I have prepared lunch. Are you hungry?'

The portions were overgenerous and she watched contentedly while he ate. Michael complimented her on her cooking and she was obviously enjoying the appreciation.

'You know, Mr Duffy, I heard what you have done. The whole of Soweto is talking.'

She sniffed and Michael suddenly realised that she was near to crying. Her emotion was obvious—he pushed the tray aside and put his arm around her shoulder. This brought on an uncontrollable flood of tears.

'They killed both my children, Mr Duffy. My daughter was gunned down outside her school, then they took my young son Patrick to the Square. We never saw him again. A friend of his said he saw Van Heerden interrogating Patrick. Both my children are dead.'

They held onto one another. Michael's vision blurred in sympathy.

'Mr Duffy, what you did yesterday was a good thing. Thank you.' With that Patricia pulled away and hurried from the room.

Promptly at 8.00pm Michael's guide reappeared.

'Come, we must go now.' They made their way past the throng that ringed the bar. Their reaction was completely different from that of the previous evening. Michael was convinced that everyone was smiling—then a hand shot out and on impulse he shook it—then another and another. A number of men slapped him on the back. The extraordinary thing was that nobody said anything until they arrived at the exit.

The guide glanced around outside, then beckoned Michael to follow.

Someone at the bar shouted, 'Go safely, Mr Duffy,' and, by the sound that followed them into the darkness, everybody agreed with the sentiment.

The walk was uneventful but seemed endless. The guide offered to slow down but Michael reluctantly refused. A sudden thought struck him. 'Passport?' He tapped his trouser pocket. The floppy disk was still there.

'You still have my passport?'

The guide glanced at him. 'You'll get it back later but I wouldn't use it again in a hurry. Mr Duffy is probably the most sought-after man in Africa right now.'

Michael was pleased that the guide had not seen his reaction to those words. He barely managed, 'I suppose you're right,' and lapsed into silence, welcoming the dark—it hid his fear.

They left the shanty town and continued to walk for what seemed ages until they reached an established residential suburb; then quite abruptly the guide turned into a driveway. The bungalow was set back ten metres from the road, hemmed in by a neat prefabricated garden wall. In front of the garage stood a Toyota Corolla. The guide knocked on the door. Presently it was opened by a woman.

The guide's massive frame blocked his view and Michael could not see her properly until they were both inside.

She came forward to greet him and her handshake was firm. 'Good evening, Mr Bernstein, I'm Nandi. Let me take your jacket.'

Michael handed it to her, mumbling a reply. Her voice was pleasing—distracted, he had not caught her name.

She turned from Michael and conferred with his guide. Michael watched, more than fascinated.

He sought to define her attraction. Exquisite? Yes! That was it. He watched her closely as she spoke. She was tall and slender. Her strong, yet finely drawn face with an aquiline nose delicately flared, gave her a look of slight arrogance. The effect was softened by the curve of her mouth. Her dark, lustrous eyes kept him spellbound. Michael stood still, waiting for her to look in his direction again.

When she did, she turned fully to face him, self-controlled, calm and tranquil, trying to read his expression.

The woman disturbed him, making him feel a little awkward in her presence. What was her name?

The guide interrupted his thoughts. 'You will stay here, Mr Bernstein.'

'Fine by me!' Michael found the suggestion not displeasing.

'Tomorrow we'll figure out what to do next.' The guide came forward, enveloping and pumping Michael's hand, only releasing it after what felt like eternity. Michael forced a smile and waved farewell with his other hand as the guide disappeared into the night.

Michael turned to face the woman, aware he was under intense scrutiny.

'I will show you your room.' She smiled, 'I'm sure you'll want a bath.'

After the past forty-eight hours he knew it had become a matter of some urgency. He followed, mesmerised by the way she seemed to glide effortlessly along the passage.

The room was neatly furnished and contained a single bed. Gently, she brushed past him as she walked out. He caught a delicate pleasing fragrance.

'You'll want to know where everything is.'

Michael trailed behind her into the bathroom.

'Be careful with the hot tap; it tends to scald if you're not careful.'

Michael wanted to stand where he was and have her brush past him again in the confined space. Instead he backed into the passage.

Staring directly into his eyes, she sidled past.

He had the uncomfortable feeling that she was reading his mind. It was unnerving.

'I'm making supper, so I'll let you get on with your bath.' Half way down the corridor she turned again, adding with a smile, 'I hope you like omelettes?'

'Yes, I've no hang-ups with food...eat just about anything.' It was not what he had wanted to say.

'Good, be ready in half an hour.' She disappeared around the corner, then called back. 'Do you want something to change into after your bath?'

Michael glanced at his shirt—filthy! And his trousers were ruined. 'If it's at all possible, that would be great.'

'I will leave some clothes on your bed—use what you need.'

The hot water was bliss; he lay sniffing the soap before using it. When he had finished, he stood up. Where was the towel? Looking around, he opened cupboards and drawers but found nothing. He was forced to stick his head out and yell his plight down the passage.

'Sorry, I'll get one for you,' came the response.

He was standing looking into the mirror and rubbing two days of stubble and inspecting his bruised face, when she walked in unexpectedly.

'It was on the stool next to your bed,' she admonished.

Michael was stunned. She placed the towel firmly in his hand; together with a disposable razor, and smiled demurely on the way out.

When he had dressed, Michael went through to the kitchen. The table was laid for two, with a beer opened and poured into a glass to one side.

She swung round from the stove and saw Michael standing uncertainly in the doorway. In borrowed clothes, even if a bit on the large side, cleanly shaven and with hair combed, he looked quite handsome, she thought. Raising her eyelids slowly she said. 'If I embarrassed you, I apologise, but I work in a hospital and, frankly, I never stop to think about naked bodies. It's a daily occurrence.'

'Of course,' Michael said, 'I understand!'

Again she smiled, as a flush suffused his face.

'It's ready. Let's eat. The beer's yours. I don't touch the stuff.' As if to prove the point, she carried a glass of fresh orange juice to the table.

'Sorry, I didn't get your name earlier.'

'Nandi.' She smiled.

It didn't mean anything to him, but he couldn't help noticing the whiteness of her teeth.

'The clothes are fine. A bit to big though, but thanks. 'Your husband's?' Michael enquired.

'No, I'm not married,' and she laughed, 'they were my father's.'

The meal was modest and filling. Michael found her a convivial and easy companion to talk to and he was grateful that she had not quizzed him about his encounter at the police station. He had tried to find out more about David but all she would say was that it could wait until the morning. Presently she stacked the dishes in the sink and came back.

'I hope you'll be comfortable for the night, Mr Bernstein.'

He stopped her, 'Please, call me Michael.'

Laughing softly she said, 'It suits you. All right, Michael. I have to be at work—Baragwanath Hospital—at eight tomorrow morning but you are free to get up when you like. Use what you want in the kitchen and there's a TV in my bedroom if you become bored.'

Passing him on the way out, she glanced down, her sober expression accentuating the message, 'I'm sure you don't need reminding that it's unsafe to leave this house. Better, don't open the door to anyone.' She leant over and gave him a peck on the cheek. 'You do realise you are quite a celebrity around these parts right now?' She glided off down the passage. Over her shoulder she added, 'Please turn the lights out when you are finished.'

He was alone; only her lingering perfume remained. There were questions he had wanted to ask her. He desperately needed answers concerning David's whereabouts. His mind raced, dredging up ghosts: John, Paddy, Paul and the lads from the Laboratories, and of course, Carla. Whenever he found happiness, it was destroyed. He felt the tension build up inside. How much more of this could he endure without cracking up? Distressed, he felt physically sick, barely making it to the bathroom. Michael lay awake many hours worrying about his immediate situation—his brother's betrayal preying heavily on his mind. Brooding would not resolve anything and he decided it was something he would have to deal with later.

Michael woke in unfamiliar surroundings. The sun filtered through the curtains. Slowly he remembered where he was and, because of the way he felt about Carla, he was surprised to find his hostess uppermost in his thoughts. Had she been as beautiful as he had first thought? Probably not. Possibly his senses had been heightened by the nerve-racking events that had culminated in his arrival at this house.

He realised that here, for the first time in many days, he felt safe. Still, he needed to find David or the ANC, if he was ever to get out of the country. The idea of repeating his last journey to Botswana was not an option he even wanted to consider.

He opened the curtain cautiously and peered out into an enclosed yard. 'When did she have time to do that?' he said in amazement. All his clothes were on the washing line. Looking around the room he saw to his surprise that the borrowed trousers and shirt were now neatly folded, hanging over a chair. Even if a bit on the large size, they fitted and that was all that mattered. Dressed, Michael looked at his watch—11.15am. Making his way to the kitchen, he found that she had laid out all he needed. Minutes later, he was sipping black, sweetened coffee and munching toast.

What was his next move?

A vision of Van Heerden flashed through his mind and he shuddered involuntarily.

He had to get the computer disk to someone who would appreciate its significance. He felt he owed this to Carla as well. 'Maybe through this girl! What does she do at the hospital?' he wondered. 'She might know someone who can help.'

Michael found her bedroom and entered tentatively. The TV stood on a pine table in the corner of the room. Her perfume was stronger in here.

The room revealed little. Two enlarged, framed portraits sat on the dresser. The man was strikingly handsome even in his mature years, while the woman in the photograph showed from whom the girl's good looks came from. 'Maybe she has inherited her father's personality? A man's got to contribute something!' he thought. Michael shut the door quietly and went back to the kitchen.

Minutes later, he was back in her room sitting on the bed orientating himself with the TV. Out of frustration he flicked the remote control but found only one English channel. After what seemed like endless minutes, he became bored by instructions on how to plant and nurture a Red Hot Poker and a tiresome botanical description on the parts of the flower. Apparently they were frost-resistant. 'So bloody what,' he muttered, glowering at the screen. He then learnt how to cultivate Strelitzias— thankfully, the programme ended.

The lunch-time news came on. Michael sat up—he had not long to wait.

The announcer looked suitably pained.

'The police are following up a number of leads after the murder of a senior police officer—killed while making an arrest. A Black man is still being sought. He and an American, travelling under the name of Michael Bernstein, or alias Paddy or Padraig Duffy, are believed to be responsible for the armed robbery in Market Street two days ago...'

'Christ! It's still headline news,' Michael exclaimed aloud. He sat transfixed at the photograph of himself that stared back. It pictured him when much younger and he realised with shock that they must have obtained the snapshot from Aaron.

'...members of the public are warned to contact the police and not approach this man as he is extremely dangerous.'

The announcer appeared concerned and then, on a more cheerful note, read out that twenty protesters had been shot dead in Langa township, near Port Elizabeth. He reminded the viewers it was the 25th anniversary of the Sharpville massacre. What was not said was, as on that other day, most of the victims were shot in the back.*

It was the opening statement that had fired Michael's anger. Clearly the authorities had no intention of revealing the facts about the incident. The truth was that a pathological killer had received his deserts while the public were being left ignorant, as always, of the realities of apartheid. And, of those that did know, many remained quiet and complaisant.

He had watched the South African scenario play itself out over the years, with the advocators of apartheid—well versed in deceiving the White electorate—holding centre stage. The current report was typical. He hated what they were doing—leaving people blinded. In his frustration he cursed aloud.

'Bloody lies! Can't they tell the truth?'

'No, I suppose they can't,' came the reply to his rhetorical question.

Michael's heart missed a beat. In the doorway stood a tall, imposing man staring down at him. He jumped up—'David!'

David smiled. 'Nice to see you again, Mike.'

'My God, am I pleased to see you.'

Their handshake was warm and both men were reluctant to let go as they studied one another—the years fell away.

'You haven't changed much,' said David.

Michael took a deep breath. 'Maybe not but you just aged me ten years.'

David's mouth creased. 'Sorry, but I do have a key. I see you have already taken over my bed and, by the looks of things, Nandi's too?'

'What! Nandi—the girl. I don't understand?'

'She's my sister, Mike.'

'Ah!...of course.' He glanced back at the disturbed quilt where he had lain a moment before. 'Your sister said I could watch the TV!'

'No sense of humour,' David grinned at his obvious embarrassment. 'Well, what's so important that you've come back here as someone else, killed one of our heads of the Bureau of State Security, and walked calmly into Soweto demanding a chat with an old friend—me to be precise? Frankly, I can't imagine anyone wanting to be your friend right now.'

His expression changed and it told Michael all he wanted to know. Here was a man who knew how desperate he felt and knew how to do something about it. 'I know this sounds bizarre but it's not exactly correct to say I killed him. Let's say I did my level best not to save him. Anyway, it's the first time I've been able to talk my way out of a police station.'

David looked at him quizzically. 'I'll get the kettle on and you can fill in the details. You can update me on what you've been doing since we parted in Zambia.'

They hadn't been seated more than a few minutes when they heard a car pull into the driveway. David was at the window in a flash—Michael observed his agility.

'Don't panic,' David blurted out. 'It's Nandi. That's odd! She's back early—usually comes home around six-thirty.'

With that, the door burst open and Nandi entered, wearing her regulatory white coat over her dress and carrying several parcels.

Michael immediately moved to take some of them from her and was greeted by a welcoming kiss on the cheek.

Seeing David she said, 'Oh! It's you. Hello, big brother, it didn't take you long to get here.'

David eyed Michael. 'I'm pleased to see you two are getting on so well.' He smiled. 'What my sister means is, I live in Katlehong Township, on the East Rand, where I have a practice—came the minute I heard you were here.' He winked, 'Can't live with her. Too damned fastidious for my liking.'

Nandi rose to the bait. 'Too bloody untidy is more to the point. It's about time you married, David, then I wouldn't have to worry so much about you. Look at him, he never eats.'

Michael glanced at David. He was not convinced.

'Why are you home this early?' her brother enquired.

She looked from one to the other. 'Because I took the rest of the day off. I wouldn't miss out on this for the world.'

Michael filled them in on events from the time he left Zambia, expanding on his experiences in the US and about his divorce. He described in detail John's death, attempting to simplify the language for Nandi.

'It's all right, Michael, I can follow you—I am a doctor after all!'

For a moment he lost the thread of his account...

David gently coaxed him back to where he had left off.

'I went back to work with Paddy after John's funeral. Three days later a bomb was delivered to our laboratory. It killed Paddy but I was told it was meant for me. I used his passport to come over here. You know what's ironic? Initially I thought the bomb was intended for him. Paddy being Irish—and the IRA. I subsequently found out from Van Heerden that he had delivered it himself, which was verified by Tinus Mueller, but I will get to that later. Really, I should start at the beginning.'

David agreed. 'That might help—just a little.'

Michael glanced at them both, realising that they must be struggling to follow the sequence of events.

'Remember in Botswana I told you BOSS was after me because of a letter I had written to a newspaper? Well, I was wrong!' Michael spent the next hour explaining, in as much detail as he could recall, about Mueller Laboratories and the circumstances that led up to his arrival in Soweto. He did not reveal his true feelings towards Carla, and explained their relationship as a close friendship, holding the memory of her to himself. Michael felt in his pocket. 'This is what cost Carla her life,' he pulled out the floppy disk.

They both stared at the insignificant looking piece of flimsy plastic.

'I've no idea of the full extent of what's on here, other than it contains notes of my experiments in Cape Town on a pathogen, *Pneumocystis carinii*. There's also information on field trials, dates and names, and its subsequent deployment in Rhodesia. Carla and I saw this much before our abrupt departure from Groote Berg Hospital in Cape Town.'

'You mean Zimbabwe,' David corrected him.

'Yes, Zimbabwe; and the good Cape Doctor confirmed this before he died,' Michael added.

'Whew!' exclaimed Nandi. 'If Groote Berg knew what was on their computer they'd go berserk. I want to see these notes.'

David reached over and took the floppy disk from Michael.

'I'll take this and print it out, so we can all read the files. In the meantime, I'll keep the disk in a safe place.' David's mind flashed back to a time in Mozambique. Maybe this would go some way towards confirming the cause of the opportunistic illnesses and deaths he had witnessed.

At Michael's insistence, he related his experiences in the *chimurenga* war while based in Mozambique. Keeping it brief, he mentioned Mbada and his brother, the Teacher, and the supportive evidence which was never found after the attack on Nyadzonya camp. 'This might even explain what the Teacher meant on the telephone before he was killed,' he thought. The Bush War was not something he wished to dwell on at any length. '...then I was discharged and, a few days later, I surprised Nandi.'

'Yes,' she said, 'I arrived home from work and found him sitting on the doorstep. You should have seen the state he was in.'

By the wry grin on his friend's face, Michael could imagine the attention that had been lavished on him by his sister.

David looked at his watch. 'Grief, I have to go. Late surgery I'm afraid. Unfortunately I'll be out of town for a few days. Just some prior arrangement. While I'm away, I'll have printouts made and drop them off on Sunday morning. Then we can have a good look at them together.' He stood up to leave. At the door he paused, then came back.

'I never really thanked you, Mike, for what you did for me in Botswana. Now maybe this is how I can repay you.'

Michael felt awkward and stared at him. 'I don't want to endanger you or your sister in any way.'

Stepping up to the table, David raised an open hand centimetres from Michael's face, forcing him to look.

'I appreciate that, but see these fingers. Remember? I have not forgotten.' Nothing else was said. In that instant the two men knew they shared a common purpose.

Michael felt he was going out of his mind over the next four days. Nandi would depart early, leaving him with nothing but his thoughts for company—a living hell throughout the lonely hours, waiting with growing anxiety for her return each day—she, arriving late and exhausted from work every evening. This was her weekend off.

'Patricia said you liked this wine!' She looked up, while unpacking the parcels from her weekly shopping excursion.

Michael was touched. Here, in these terrible conditions, people still cared for one another. He put his hand on Nandi's arm in a moment of overwhelming gratitude.

'Thank you for thinking of me.'

That night over supper Nandi caught him off guard.

'Tell me about Carla. You loved her very much, I can see.'

'Yes!' He hesitated, 'I think she still loved me. They set out to destroy our love from the beginning.' Michael felt his face burn with anger. 'Her life for what? A lousy computer disk?' His eyes misted over. 'I want nothing more in this life than to meet up with that evil bastard again, just once.'

'Who, Michael?' Nandi's concern showed.

'Her father, Andries Boshoff!' he almost spat it out. Michael's clenched fists were pressed hard against the table top and his knuckles were white. 'In these past months I seem to have known only death.' His head drooped and he stared unseeing at the empty dinner plate. 'I'm not afraid of dying— it's living that's the problem—I can't stand the pain.'

Nandi felt his anguish, almost tangible, drawing her nearer. She reached across the table and gently enfolded his clasped hands within the warmth of her own for a moment. Several minutes they sat in silence, gazing intensely at one another. He became aware of the deep understanding and sympathy in Nandi's dark eyes and slowly the bitterness eased.

Michael held Nandi's hands—a silent expression of thanks.

'Come on,' she whispered.

Nandi drew him to his feet. He had neither the wish nor the desire to resist. She led him into her room.

'Wake up, please Michael. David will be here any minute now.' Nandi shook him again.

He opened sleepy eyes and drew a deep breath. The taste of her was still on his lips and her scent aroused him. His arm reached out.

'No, not now. Please, Michael, you must get out of bed.' She leaned forward and gave him a peck on the forehead. 'Get a move on. I've cooked breakfast.'

David arrived with two sets of printed copy, full of apologies for not having found the opportunity to run it off sooner. The floppy disk had been left elsewhere for safe keeping. Nandi gave her brother a warm, welcoming embrace. Before David realised what was happening, she had relieved him of the top copy and beat a hasty retreat to her bedroom.

'Hey! That wasn't for you,' he protested.

'Don't worry,' Michael said. 'You read this one and I'll share her copy. Feigning resignation, he followed her through to the bedroom. The deception almost succeeded.

David sat in the lounge poring over the files. Moments later he was at the doorway, silently watching them. Lying on the bed they had their heads together, deeply engrossed in the files. Shrugging his shoulders and saying nothing, he returned to the lounge.

There it was!

Right back in 1967, the Rhodesians had completed field trials on a pathogen Professor Mueller had been working on. The research was evidently discarded but no reasons were given. To Michael's astonishment he found all his notes from 1972, on the mutated *P.carinii* were transcribed as if the experiment had been intentional and the result anticipated, clearly undertaken by Professor Mueller himself.

This was followed by a report from the South African Defence Force which, after evaluating a new biological agent, turned down the Cape Doctor's proposal, deeming it to be too unstable. A footnote, added by Mueller, stated that the agent *P.carinii* had been code-named PF657.

355

It was all there. In 1974, through Andries Boshoff's organisation the ARB, the Rhodesian Biological Warfare Unit had secretly obtained PF657, besides other biological agents from Mueller. They were administered to captured terrorist fighters from ZANLA bases in Mozambique. Subsequently the captured men had been released under the guise of reconciliation, in the expectation that they would spread infection among their *comrades* at their base camps.

The report mentioned the freedom fighters' suspicions concerning the Rhodesian security forces motives. With meticulous detail Mueller had recorded the terrorists' erroneous conclusions; believing that the return of their men was a political ploy by the White government, intended to undermine their resolve to continue the war.

The files indicated that, in 1975, Mueller had analysed samples reputedly taken from subjects at a camp in Mozambique; after testing, the findings had confirmed the presence of PF657.

Slowly they sifted through the information, uncovering every sordid detail. One name stood out: Victor Hammond from Rhodesia. It appeared that he had negotiated the purchase of PF657 from Mueller Laboratories. It jolted David's memory. Hammond! The image of the white-haired man with white eyelashes and watery pale blue eyes came vividly back to him. He recalled that Hammond had also interrogated Mbada's brother.

Mueller referred to a blanket security measure imposed over the entire project. This was said to have been demanded by the ARB, which, according to the files, had evidently insisted on the eradication of all traces of the research. Michael could see that Mueller had been careful, but there were veiled references to the 'removal' of all personnel connected with the project. It became apparent that the orders had come directly from Andries Boshoff, which accounted for Carla's survival while others were liquidated.

No mention was made of the climbing accident nor of Michael's departure, but Mueller had provided a lengthy report on the specialists who had treated Paul. The cause of death was said to have been *Marburg*.

Michael scowled at the page and left Nandi's side. He felt a desperate urge to breathe fresh air and began to pace the room like a caged animal.

She looked up at him questioningly.

'Jesus, Nandi. This is horrific!' Michael grimaced, 'Tinus never told us...yet he knew all along. He was responsible for infecting Paul with *Marburg*!' His face seemed drained of all colour, with a lost, haunted look in his eyes, 'He could have infected the lot of us. Oh! God, how can I be so stupid...that's why we were kept in quarantine,' he swung round to see David standing in the doorway.'

'I think you had better fill us in on all the facts Mike. If I'm correct these files have even wider implications.'

Michael told them what Tinus had said: he had brought back viable samples from Germany, taken from the victims of the outbreak in Marburg.

'Coffee!' Nandi climbed off the bed, leading the way to the kitchen and put the kettle on. 'Won't be a tic,' leaving David to prepare the cups, and she was back in under a minute.

'Here, listen to this,' in her hand was one of her medical books.

'The Marburg virus is inevitably fatal in monkeys and caused haemorrhagic fevers in humans. Clinical features are: high temperature, slow heart rate, headache, inflammation of the eyes, abdominal pain, vomiting, acute back pain, diarrhoea and, finally, in a large percentage of cases, death.'

Michael had a vivid recollection of what he had witnessed with Paul and his laboratory animals. Had they too, died of *Marburg* at the hands of Mueller?

'There's more. It seems, like all viruses, this one has a propensity to cross into other cells with comparative ease and with devastating results.'

She turned the page and read.

'Marburg disease is a severe haemorrhagic disease characterised by severe bleeding between days five to seven. The lungs and gastro-intestinal tract are most frequently involved with haematemesis, melaena; blood present in the faeces. Bleeding frequently occurs from the rectum, bladder and vagina, with distinctive haemorrhaging from the eyes, nose and gums. Death generally occurs from shock due to blood loss seven to fifteen days after onset. First described in 1967, when in Germany thirty-one cases were reported resulting in seven deaths with a 29% fatality rate in the primary cases. Believed to have been introduced by monkeys from Uganda. The first case reported in Africa was two Australian hitchhikers on the Rhodesian border with Mozambique. No host for this disease has been found and monkeys remain as susceptible as man himself.'*

Waiting patiently for Nandi to finish the excerpt David said seriously, 'Your book is inaccurate, in view of what Mueller says about *Marburg*. Besides, there being no mention of it on the disc, I think it's safe to assume they deployed *Marburg* as well. It would account for what I saw in the Bush War.' In graphic detail he described the condition of some of the victims he had seen in the bush, vomiting black blood, their skin falling from them like melting waxworks, bleeding from every orifice—even their eyes.

'I can't believe it,' said Michael. 'Tinus clearly states that the Rhodesian security forces literally took patients back to Rhodesia. To interrogate the sick or dying seems too barbaric to be true.'*

'It was real enough. I was there,' David said grimly.

They downed their coffee hastily and returned to read the files.

There was a detailed report concerning emergent new illnesses. From what Mueller had entered, it was clear that the situation was fast getting out of control. His notes mirrored his anxiety. It became evident that he had apparently been worried, and then later, extremely concerned by what he saw happening as these biological agents ran riot.

David heard their voices raised in excited discussion. 'What are you two up to?' he shouted. The noise level dropped appreciably, so he went back to his notes, rereading sections to verify the implications.

A new file revealed how Mueller had discovered a genetically mutated virus. The commentary was brief and indicated it was annexed to other files. Michael grabbed at pages he had already read in the hope that he'd accidentally missed some. There were no others—they had come to the end, having already read the entire print-out from the floppy disc.

'What in hell's name was on the computer that Carla and I did not copy?' He glowered at the notes.

Nandi picked up the pages and waved them around in frustration. 'Is this it? Where's the rest?'

'We only had time for these files!'

David looked up as they entered the lounge. He understood their chagrin but assured them that what they now held was, nevertheless, damning enough to bring down the whole corrupt government and the apartheid system. 'Do you see what this means? The nearest parallel I can think of is Nazi Germany—it's genocide,' he said. 'What we have here, is their political downfall. They cannot survive this!'

The two sat, scowling, taking in everything he was saying.

David was convinced it went further. 'There must be Government complicity, somewhere here. The ARB—what do you know about this organisation, Mike?'

'Not much more than it says in these files. I know Carla's father heads the ARB and it's supposed to further Afrikanerdom. But I never realised it was a covert force that would sanction this kind of atrocity.'

'This is dynamite—we must be very careful. I want to get rid of these files right now.' David took their copy and gathered up his notes. Quietly they followed him into the kitchen. They watched him set them alight, catching the edges of the paper, waiting until the flames took hold.

He explained, 'You can't be too careful. This hard copy is as good as a death warrant signed by the Minister of Justice himself.' He dropped the burning pages into the sink and when they were burnt through he ran the tap flushing away the ashes. David made up his mind—the floppy disk which he had left at his surgery, had to be made safe and spirited abroad.

'You realise that without this information it will be virtually impossible to prove,' said Michael. 'Their plan was diabolical, perfect in its execution—we are unlikely to find survivors who could testify to being injected.'

'What happens now?' Nandi frowned.

David stared long and hard at his friend. 'This proves the bastards used biological weapons on us in Mozambique. My God! This animal has actually typed a report on the very men I saw die.'

'Yes! And some of his notes cover the period of my research in Cape Town. It's my work that's caused this.' Michael sounded ill.

'No, I don't see how you are to blame,' Nandi tried to comfort him. 'You were engaged on a project to benefit mankind. They're the ones that misused and let it loose—committed murder!'

'But they didn't create this mutant strain—I did!'

'Don't be so harsh on yourself, Michael.' Nandi's rebuttal was spontaneous. 'You know that's being emotional and unscientific. If medical science let loose with what we experiment with daily, this planet would be in a hell of a mess. They must have realised that cross-species transmission was a potential danger; that it could possibly become endemic.'

This didn't lessen the guilt that Michael now felt.

Something was troubling Nandi and she turned to her brother.

'David, what are the clinical signs and symptoms of *Pneumocystis carinii* pneumonia again?' she asked.

His reply confirmed her fears. She looked at Michael. He looked dreadful.

'Michael, what I'm about to say isn't going to be pleasant but still, I feel it must be said.'

Momentarily he searched her expression, then, resigned, he nodded.

'Your son John, what exactly did he die from?'

Michael felt a growing unease creep over him. 'Pneumonia—but surely you're not suggesting...'

Her jaw was set, the expression grim. 'Do you know what the causative micro-organism was?' She watched his face—clearly he didn't.

'I was too distressed at the time. I suppose I should have checked but with Paddy and everything...'

'Sorry, Michael, but do you recognise any of the symptoms David has just described?' She felt awful.

'Yes...' he paused, burying his head in his hands.

'For God's sake!' David snapped at his sister.

She looked pleadingly at her brother. 'But we have to know. Look at the facts we have read. They used this pathogen to kill off your friends in Zimbabwe. By all accounts they used some other ungodly virus on his friend in Cape Town. Why not use it to eradicate Michael?' It was more statement than question. She continued undeterred, 'Sitting on this information, it's not surprising that he was a target and obviously he's been a thorn in their side for some time. Maybe, inadvertently John was the victim and failing to kill Michael with the *P.carinii*, they resorted to a bomb; or, maybe, they were attempting to use him to carry the infection to you,' addressing Michael. 'Is that so implausible?' There was a pregnant pause.

Michael sat up. 'I need to know if this pathogen was responsible. Can I use your telephone?'

Michael called directory enquiries and, on obtaining the number, dialled; he waited several seconds before he heard the telephonist pick up the telephone.

'Give me Dr Winslow plea...'

Though Michael saw him coming, he had no time to react. David brought his hand down on the telephone so hard it cracked the casing. He had never seen David like this before and stared down at the damage.

'I think I've lost my connection.' He looked blankly at Nandi who held her hand to her mouth.

David spoke, his voice sharp. 'Sorry, Mike. Damn it to hell! I was so wound up in this report, I didn't realise what you were saying or doing. Did you get through?'

Michael, aware that somehow things had gone desperately wrong, did not immediately appreciate the cause. 'I spoke to reception, if that's what you mean.'

David hit his temple with the flat of his palm. 'What an idiot I've been. I preach to our *comrades* about breaches in security and now I overlook something as fundamental as a telephone call.'

'What do you mean?' Michael felt he had missed the point.

'They tap our telephones, Michael. Especially international calls. Lucky you said nothing, so there's a chance they may not bother with a trace.' He did not wish to contemplate the outcome if he was wrong.

Nandi said it for him, 'If they do, it will be several days before we can expect a response.'

Michael felt culpable. 'You're kidding?'

'No, Mike, I wish I was, but this is the price we pay for living in this police state. No freedom of press or speech.' David glanced at the broken telephone, then apologetically at Michael. 'I'm afraid we will have to call from a safe phone; that's if you don't mind lying on the back seat of my car for a while, until we're out of Soweto.'

Within the hour, Michael was re-dialling the Houston number, this time from a call-box.

'Dr Winslow, it's Michael Bernstein here. Sorry I haven't been able to get in touch with you sooner, but have you the results of John's tests?'

The doctor had long been expecting the bereaved father's call and had wondered why it had taken him so long. 'I see. So when can you come down to see me? I would like to discuss our findings with you.'

'Sorry, Doc, but right now I'm in Africa on business.' As an afterthought he added, 'Unfortunately I won't be back for several months.'

Dr Winslow said nothing, thinking of a way to break the news—at least it explained his absence.

'Well?' Michael insisted, 'What were the results?'

'Really, Mr Bernstein, this isn't something I want to discuss over a telephone. I'll send you the report and then possibly we can speak again.' It was clear to Michael that the man was hedging. He knew the answer before he asked.

'Dr Winslow, you know that I am a microbiologist by profession. Therefore I'm not exactly unfamiliar with disease. Nothing can bring John back and I'm learning to live with that. When we last spoke, you said he had a viral pneumonia complicated by another pathogen. All I'm asking is for you to tell me, was it *Pneumocystis carinii*, or not?'

'You've spoken to your ex-wife then!' stated Dr Winslow.

'No. As I said, I'm here, in South Africa. Please...was it the *P.carinii*?'

'Yes! But how did you know?' Dr Winslow sounded somewhat mystified.

Michael's mind was in utter turmoil. The doctor was saying something. 'Excuse me, please could you repeat that?'

'I said, John—your son...tested *HIV* positive.'

'The *Human Immunodeficiency Virus*—AIDS? No! But that's not possible!' Michael was disbelieving of what he had heard.

'I'm afraid there's no mistake, Mr Bernstein. I double-checked the records myself. I'm sorry to break the news like this; but, well, you insisted. Would you like me to send on the reports?'

Michael could barely concentrate. 'What?—No, no don't worry. I'll get them when I get back.' His attention was drawn to the urgency in the doctor's voice.

'I know how you must feel but I must urge you to get a check-up. Incidentally, we have contacted John's mother and she tested negative. Until now we haven't known where to find you. Please feel free to call me if you need any advice.' He gave Michael a direct number and rang off.

Michael stood, gazing unseeing at the receiver in his hand. Gently, Nandi relieved him of the telephone and replaced it in its cradle.

He struggled for words. 'They say John had AIDS, but it's not possible.'

Nothing was said on the drive back.

Once home, Michael excused himself and immediately Nandi tackled her brother.

'*Pneumocystis carinii* pneumonia—an opportunistic infection, right?'

361

'Yes, and often associated with the Acquired Immune Deficiency Syndrome—AIDS,' said David.

'Precisely,' Nandi stressed, 'that's the point I want to make. Don't you see, John being *HIV* positive, it would have depressed his immune system. That in itself might have led to this infection. Nothing to do with BOSS or this mutant strain.'

'Then it's one hell of a coincidence!' David stated bluntly.

'Maybe, but you can't rule it out,' Nandi countered. 'What interests me is how did the kid get the virus in the first place?'

'I've been trying to figure that out myself. It is possible the parents passed on the infection.' David did not see the fear in his sister's eyes.

Neither of them heard Michael return. 'You're right! I need a check-up.'

'Sorry Mike, it's just that we are concerned for you,' David explained.

Michael glanced at Nandi as he sat down, inwardly praying that he had not passed on this dreaded virus to her. 'They say Trish, my ex-wife, is clear, so I will need to be tested.' He was getting over the initial shock and his mind was beginning to respond. 'The sooner it is completed the better. Does Baragwanath Hospital have any facilities?'

Nandi reached out and took his hands. 'Of course we do. But if you had asked me that last month I would have said, no. The manufacturer only delivered the first batch last week. It's called ELISA, the first blood test of its kind for infection with *HIV*. I suppose we could take a blood sample now?' She glanced at David, 'I can take it over to the lab and have it analysed right away.'

'All right, I'll get my bag.' David heaved himself out of his chair and headed for the car.

Nandi was on her way to hospital with the specimen within thirty minutes; but not before she had received strict instructions from her brother to pick up something stronger than beer on her way back.

Michael felt as if the vitality had been punched out of him. 'You hear about AIDS, but you never believe it will affect you, or your family; then suddenly it explodes in your face. It's hard to grasp that this could be my death warrant as well. The only consolation is that I will know in advance, not like poor John.'

David tried to console him. 'Let's not jump to conclusions, Mike. At least wait for the test results. We'll take it from there.'

Unable to do anything until Nandi returned, Michael fretted. 'I can't believe I have this virus. Between you and me, I've had two partners since my divorce and both of them I saw infrequently. There's nothing between us now. Neither of them is ill. If anything, they are disgustingly healthy.'

'Mike, as you know, *HIV* doesn't lead to full-blown AIDS, sometimes not for years. In other cases it may be quick. It's simply that opportunistic infections kill, because the *Human Immunodeficiency Virus* suppresses the body's ability to fight back.'

'Nicely put,' said Michael with mild sarcasm. 'First described in 1979 and brought to the attention of the medical community in 1981 by the Centres for Disease Control in Atlanta, Georgia, the US public health body responsible for investigating epidemics. It appeared as from nowhere in the spring of 1981.... I think maybe Dr Nyamande is forgetting that I'm a qualified microbiologist!'

'Touché,' David was somewhat taken aback.

Michael saw the confused expression on his friend's face.

'Sorry. That was uncalled-for. It's just that I'm so keyed up!'

David looked at him speculatively. 'Forget it. I reckon you have reason to be testy.' He maintained his vigil at the window. 'Where's that sister of mine?' By 7.30pm he was wearing the carpet thin in the living-room.

'Where the hell is she? I hope she hasn't had an accident,' he did not dare to consider other possibilities. 'Why didn't she say she was going to be late?' David's anxiety was contagious.

Michael became agitated. 'Do you think we should go and look for her?'

David checked the time, yet again. 'We'll give her another fifteen minutes, then I'll go to the hospital. You wait here, in case she calls.'

At that moment Nandi's red Toyota flew into the driveway and screeched to a stop. An automatic pistol appeared in David's hand as if from nowhere. Flattening himself against the wall, he peered out from behind the curtain.

'Get down, Mike, something's wrong!' Michael dived for cover while David watched his sister frantically leap from the car and dash towards the safety of the house.

'Where the hell are they?' He cursed, unable to see Nandi's pursuers.

The door opened and Nandi entered. She froze, wide-eyed with fear. David was flattened against the wall, gun in hand, still peering outside. Michael was almost out of sight, behind the couch.

'What's wrong?' she whispered.

Nandi still ached. 'You two should have seen yourselves.' She gasped, drying her eyes.

'Okay, Nandi, you've had your fun but we were worried stiff.'

Michael was equally upset. 'Where've you been?'

'At the hospital, where else?' She glared at David, 'And I stopped at Patricia's, as ordered, to pick this up!' Nandi placed a bottle of Cape brandy on the table with obvious disdain.

She took Michael's hand in hers. 'Michael, your tests were negative. You're completely clear,' she smiled. 'Of course the test is not for AIDS, it's for antibodies to *HIV*. I had the procedure repeated several times, all with the same result.' As if reading his mind, she added, 'No, Michael, it wasn't you; you were definitely not responsible for John's illness.'

Michael squeezed her hand—their eyes said everything.

David unknowingly broke the spell. 'Mike, this means we're back to square one as to how your son contracted AIDS...'

Michael stopped him. 'Not exactly. I've been going over and over events in my mind. It's something you mentioned earlier. Remember, I wrote to you in Mozambique after the rhino incident when John was hurt. It was serious and he required several transfusions at the time, but as I recall he was on a saline drip—the accident was one of the reasons why Trish returned to the US.' He hesitated, 'But some years later, he had a severe injury while out on his bike—I know he received blood! It was about then that the press were shouting about 'innocent victims' and haemophiliacs having contracted AIDS from blood transfusions.'

They fell silent for a while, and David was the first to speak.

'This seems consistent with the facts. It seems your son was a victim of circumstance.' He glanced at Nandi, 'I think we can rule out any involvement by BOSS.'

'Yes, but it's ironic that routine testing of white blood cells for *HIV* in blood transfusions began only this year,' she said. Then, smiling sympathetically, 'At least we know your research at Mueller Laboratories had nothing to do with AIDS.'

'Agreed!' exclaimed Michael, dismissing the fact. 'But it does not change anything. It still leaves a question mark over how John contracted the *P.carinii*. Was it an opportunistic infection or, as you said earlier, in an attempt to get at me, did they intentionally or unintentionally infect my son?'

'I'm afraid we may never know the answer to that,' said Nandi.

Michael shot a glance at her. 'Possibly. But there is one man who might know and, by God, he's going to tell me one way or the other.'

'Boshoff!' David exclaimed without any doubt in his mind.

'Precisely. Carla told me he's in the UK, just before she...' Michael fought to hold a grip on himself. 'I need to get over there somehow.'

David saw the time. 'Okay, you two, I have to be going. Incidentally Mike, I've burnt your passport or, should I say, your friend's passport. Of course you wouldn't have been able to use it—far too dangerous, but I'm making arrangements for you to get another one. I think the sooner you leave South Africa, the better.' He was pleased to see the semblance of a smile cross Michael's face. 'I think you have caused the authorities more trouble in the last two weeks than they've had in the past two years...on second thoughts, maybe you should stay and see what else you can do!'

27 April 1985

Arrangements were made to spirit Michael out of the country. Every day he looked forward to Nandi's return from work. He had been totally reliant on her while in hiding. Over the past weeks he had not dared to venture out of the house and now he felt trapped, viewing all passers-by as a potential threat. Twice in the past few days, around midday, a stranger had knocked persistently at the front door. After what seemed like ages the Black man had given up, on each occasion leaving Michael extremely edgy as he watched him walk away.

That night David visited for the first time in a week. 'You leave tomorrow. All arrangements have been made. Now here's the plan.'

An hour later David left and Nandi came through to Michael's room. 'I've told David that I'm taking tomorrow off so I can be with you.'

Checking her watch, Nandi urged her brother, 'Come on, we've been waiting for ages.' It was 5.50pm.

'Sorry, but I had to sort out my locum.' They watched as David stood in the doorway, waving goodbye to the young doctor who backed out of the drive in David's car. 'Good man and a fine doctor. He's from the Transkei.' David smiled to himself watching both their reactions. 'You should meet him, Nandi,' he said meaningfully.

Nandi turned on her heel and stalked off, to collect the meal she had prepared for the trip from the kitchen.

Michael noticed the suitcase he carried in. 'What's that for?'

David flashed a grin at him. 'Thought you could do with some male company after putting up with my sister all this time. Anyway, I've been promising myself another visit abroad. Seems like a perfect opportunity.'

Nandi came through to the living-room. She had overheard what had been said and clearly expressed her displeasure. She had become resigned to Michael's going but David's leaving was unexpected. She knew that he had deliberately kept his intended departure from her. Her brother would do something like that, knowing she would worry.

David, touched by his sister's concern, steered the conversation back to their immediate plan. 'Let's hit the road, but first we'll drop this disk off with someone in Houghton.'

'Who?' Michael asked full of curiosity.

He anticipated Michael's question. David explained that the elderly gentleman they were about to meet was a solicitor, who acted in the ANC's interests and that was all he needed to know, and he should not ask more.

They both gaped at him in surprise.

'I'm not taking chances. If we are stopped I don't want any of us to be within a hundred kilometres of this evidence,' he tapped his jacket pocket.

Leaving Soweto, Nandi drove while David sat in the front giving her directions. Michael lay flat on the back seat, out of view.

David leaned over to talk to him. 'I've left a message with our contact; he's expecting us. He will take care of the disk...'

The sudden rumble of heavy vehicles passing in the opposite direction drowned out further conversation. When the noise had receded, Michael raised himself to peer cautiously out of the rear window. A convoy of armoured trucks had swept past them, accompanied by four police riot vans. Recognising them he ducked unnecessarily.

He spoke for them all. 'Pity the poor sods on the receiving end of that.' Adding, 'Why didn't someone tell me they were coming?'

'What? The convoy? Sorry Mike we're used to it; we see patrols like that every day,' David explained.

They drove on, skirting the dried yellow mountainous dumps of sludge from the gold mines, south of Johannesburg. Bypassing the city centre, they worked their way towards the northern suburbs. Finding the quiet street in Houghton was easy, but they had difficulty in locating the house.

Nandi pulled in to the kerb. In desperation David turned round. 'Mike, you had better go and ask directions. No White is going to give me the time of day...or night, for that matter.'

Michael wasn't sure if his reception would be any better. Nevertheless, he climbed from the back seat of the Toyota and strolled over to where he could see two men in a car, parked up ahead.

He tapped on the front passenger window. The man shrank back, startled by Michael's sudden appearance. Evidently he had not seen him approach. He wound down the window slowly and the streetlight shone directly onto his face as he peered up at Michael. His scalp was severely sunburnt and the skin from his nose had peeled, exposing raw, weeping flesh. Michael noticed the eyes—pale blue, bloodshot and watery, offset by blanched eyelashes and brows. Wispy strands of white hair lay across his blistered scalp. Michael guessed he was unsuited to the harsh African sun. He could not see the other occupant who was in shadow. He asked for directions but the man was unhelpful and rude. Winding up the window, the man hurriedly gave instructions to the driver who promptly drove off. 'Bloody typical!' Michael thought, not overly surprised by the abruptness, but his accent struck a chord. 'Of course, a Zimbabwean,' he muttered to himself. He watched the disappearing tail-lights and shrugged; then he indicated to David his intentions. He walked up the driveway of the nearest house and the servant, who answered the door, gave him the information he wanted. The house they sought was virtually opposite to where they were parked.

An elderly gentleman, greying slightly at the temples and very stooped, came to the door. He had long since retired from law and now acted undercover for the ANC abroad. Michael looked past him at the interior furnishings. Here was a man of considerable wealth and impeccable taste. The owner recognised David immediately and came forward to receive him warmly, as he did to both Nandi and Michael in turn. Nandi was introduced and he replied that they should call him Ben. Michael shook his hand and looked into lively, brown eyes that seemed not to have aged.

'Come in. Come in.' Sorry, David, I've only just received your message. I arrived back from Europe yesterday. In fact you are fortunate to get me at all. Tomorrow, I leave for New York for three weeks. Now, what's this I hear about a magnetic disk?'

They were ushered into his study. David apologised for the rushed visit explaining their urgency; and in detail what they had gleaned from the floppy disk which served to confirm his own experience in Mozambique. He mentioned briefly Michael's part in the development of the deadly pathogen and the demise of Van Heerden.

Their host listened in earnest as the minutes flew by, and then, David summarised the situation concisely. 'What if the government uses this biological agent against us in the ANC, or even the Pan African Congress? We both have external militant forces operating against them. My God! It would be catastrophic.'

There followed a tense silence.

David had made his point. The elderly solicitor was convinced, and with a solemn promise to secrete the floppy disk over to the appropriate people in Washington, the matter was resolved. Afterwards, he and David went into his study to discuss several other unrelated matters concerning the ANC, leaving Nandi and Michael to wait patiently in the lounge.

David, watching the time, declined an offer of a meal, and Ben walked them to their car and bade farewell.

Ben closed the door and looked down. He appreciated the enormity of the information he now held in the palm of his hand.

oOo

They had waited until Sunday evening, knowing it was likely that the occupants would be at home. Over the past three hours the cordon had been pulled tighter around the house. By 8.00pm the Defence Force, accompanied by BOSS agents, were in position—ready to strike.

The execution was clinical and brutal—the attack designed to take out their targets swiftly and efficiently. Incendiary bombs smashed through the windows engulfing the house in seconds, while raked by automatic gunfire. A lobbed grenade landed in the living room and exploded. The devastation was complete. No one could have survived the attack.

o0o

Resigning himself to the fact that he wasn't going to get any further information out of David concerning the man they had just met, he sat back staring at the passing scene. Of one thing he was certain, Ben was Jewish, because of the mezuzah above the doorway to the house. He wondered what part David played in the ANC. Michael had tried to get his friend to open up but always David gave a stock answer, 'Believe me, the less you know the less dangerous it is for all concerned.'

Nandi found her way through the city onto the R22 motorway and headed towards the eastern border of South Africa.

It was getting late—the dashboard clock read 8.05pm.

They travelled by the shortest route towards Swaziland, the small country which lay cradled between South Africa and Mozambique.

A few kilometres before the border post, David directed Nandi south, off the asphalt and onto a dirt road. Some distance on he had her stop.

'All right, back up and take that road,' he ordered.

Nandi peered into the dark, gaping at what she saw; she frowned, glaring at her brother, 'That's no road, it's a bush track. It'll wreak my car!'

Michael glanced over their shoulders into the waist-high grass and was inclined to agree with her. All he could see in the beam of the headlights was a footpath receding into a dense thicket.

'Leave your parking lights on and I'll guide you from the front.' David went forward and sat on the bonnet, as she edged her way onto the track. This worked well for some distance and, as her confidence grew, she increased her speed until something scraped alarmingly along the bottom of her car. Nandi hit the brakes hard, launching David from the bonnet to land in an undignified heap on the track.

He stormed back to the car dusting himself off. 'Move over.'

She giggled and climbed, without protest, over the well onto the passenger side.

'I'll drive,' said Michael hurriedly. 'You carry on and show me the way.' Seeing David's unexpected departure from the front of the vehicle, he had no desire to take his place. A sideways glance at Nandi had them both trying hard to suppress their laughter as David resumed his position on the bonnet.

They made slow progress through the veldt.

Suddenly they were caught in a powerful beam of light from ahead. Michael killed the engine and drifted to a halt. David slid cautiously off the vehicle and stood next to the driver's door.

'It may be the police. Leave me to do the talking.' He walked towards the light. Drawing nearer he saw it was a spotlight mounted on a Land Rover.

A man called from the protection of its shadow. 'Stop. I have a gun. Who are you?'

David shouted his name, already recognising the familiar voice. He confidently approached the shadowy figure. He was a stocky, powerful man in his sixties. David saw that the shotgun was pointing at the ground.

'You want to die, young man! Why didn't you tell me you were coming? I could hear your car from kilometres away.'

David grinned at John Gama. 'With your eyesight, you'd never hit anything with that gun!'

Gama pointed the shotgun past David. 'That's the least of your worries. They mined the road last month. Twice now we've heard land-mines explode. After the first went off we found a dead baboon, but I've no idea why the second mine went off.'

David's blood ran cold. 'Where do you think they mined it up to?

'Right where you're standing,' he pointed to his feet. 'Here. This is where my farm ends—right on the border.'

'Okay, John, wait for us. I'm going to warn the others.' David walked back towards the car, this time leaving a good few metres between himself and the track. Nearing the driver's door he was not surprised to find Gama right behind him.

'You didn't have to.' It was really an expression of thanks.

'Forget it, you'll need the help,' Gama muttered.

'Mike, meet my friend, John Gama.' A large, callused hand was thrust through the open window. 'John owns the farm up ahead. Swaziland is less than fifty metres away.'

Michael sensed instinctively that something was wrong.

'Guess what? This bloody road is mined. We can count ourselves lucky still to be alive.'

Nandi's nails dug into Michael's thigh.

'John and I will direct you. Just follow.'

David led Michael off the road onto open grasslands. The two men walked ahead slowly, testing the ground with their feet, steering him in one direction then the other, around anteater burrows, tree stumps and furrows in the ground. It seemed ages before they drove back onto the track on the Swazi side of the border. The spotlight on the Land Rover now behind them.

'I cannot thank you enough.'

'Nonsense, David, I'm only pleased you came to no harm. You carry on while I get the Land Rover, then see you back at the house.'

David began to protest about being pressed for time but Gama would hear none of it.

Seated in the kitchen, he plied them with sweet, hot black coffee laced with cane spirit. They listened while Gama assured David that he would drive his cattle down the track, to detonate the mines. David smiled as he thought about what would happen if one of John Gama's prized cattle was killed. The South Africans knew this shrewd Swazi from past encounters. They had tried on several occasions to impound his herd when the cows had strayed across the border. John Gama had maintained that the onus rested on the South Africans to fence their territory adequately. In the South African authorities' eyes, crossing the border to kill their enemies was entirely justifiable; but it was equally important to be seen to be considerate and avert border disputes. They grasped the opportunity and, acceding to his demand, fenced off his property for 25 kilometres on either side of his farm. At least, this would finally put a stop to their long-standing quarrels with John Gama.

A month later, word was out. He had realised a tidy sum on the transaction when a trader from neighbouring Mozambique came to collect the fencing; leaving Gama's cattle to range freely once more.

It caused the South Africans extreme embarrassment. Initially flummoxed, yet not wanting to turn a blind eye to his activities, they had set about mining the road. It was simply another problem for the wily farmer to resolve in his own time.

Gama's visitors bade him farewell and pushed on towards the main asphalt road that bisected the small country. Passing through the capital, Mbabane, Nandi headed south, down the steep pass to the floor of the Ezulweni Valley. They made good time. Michael glanced at the signs by the roadside: Cuddle Puddle, hot springs; Mlilwane Wildlife Sanctuary. This was the well-known holiday mecca he had heard so much about, with its casinos and golf clubs. It was fast falling behind them by the time dawn broke.

Arriving at Matsapha Airport near Manzeni, they were met inside the newly constructed terminal by a member of the ANC. He gave them their new travel documents. There was time to kill before the national airways flight to Tanzania was due for take-off; Michael took Nandi to one side. He glanced back to see David talking to the ANC official and led her to the other end of the uncompleted building.

'Nandi, this last month has been hell and I am sorry that you've become involved.'

She looked up at him. 'Are you, Michael?'

He realised that she had misunderstood. 'No, Nandi, that's not what I meant. I mean, what we have is so special...I can't bear the thought of you getting hurt because I got you caught up in all this.'

She scrutinised him steadily, seeing if she could read the truth in his eyes.

'I want you to come with us. This place is too dangerous for a woman on her own. I don't know where I'm going next but I want you to come with me. Maybe...'

She raised a finger to his lips. 'No, don't say it, Michael. I won't leave. This is my country and I love it. Why must I be chased away from my country by some ignorant Boers? Besides my work at the hospital is important to me...'

He had no answer except, 'Because I think I'm falling in love with you.'

Nandi shook her head. 'Michael, what we had was beautiful and I will always cherish that but I can't go and you mustn't stay. If things are meant to be different—they will be.'

He pulled her close and they clung to one another for a moment.

David watched over the rim of his coffee cup. He turned the other way, not wanting them to know that he had seen their intimate embrace.

Nandi knew that to wait until they had boarded the plane would be foolhardy. Time was against her. She had to depart, and depart now, to reach home in time to be able to go to work as normal. She said goodbye inside the terminal building, refusing their offer to see her to the car. She lingered for a moment outside, holding onto the wire mesh surrounding the airstrip perimeter, watching the plane parked at the end of the apron.

Mechanics were milling around the twin jet-engined Fokker Fellowship, preparing it for the morning flight. In the pre-dawn it looked luminous; the light reflected off its white underbelly and distinctive Royal Swazi insignia. 'Please take them safely,' she begged. Soon the plane would lumber down the runway away from her and turn towards the east. The two men would be over Mozambique in minutes, then winging their way northwards towards Dar es Salaam. She felt terribly alone.

Nandi glanced at the clock on the dash. She had the timing about right. Enough for a bath, a bite to eat and to get to Baragwanath Hospital by lunch-time for the late shift. She was exhausted—the trip to Swaziland had taken over nine hours. On the homeward run, the main road shaved hours off the journey. The ANC official, a printer by trade, had provided her with the necessary exit and entrance stamps to her passport. She reached the Ngwenya border post by 6.30am. A nerve-racking half an hour later the border post opened. Nandi was first through and nobody gave her a second glance as she re-entered South Africa.

371

Nearing her journey's end, with fatigue slowing her reactions, she wondered, dully, what the commotion ahead was about. An armed *hippo* troop carrier half-blocked the road and soldiers were milling around. They waved her on. A rush of adrenaline banished the last vestige of tiredness. What confronted her was the ruin that had once been her home.

Momentarily she slowed, glimpsing the plain-clothes policemen combing through the rubble. Nandi's face contorted. She forced herself to focus on the road and crashed the gear lever into second. No one paid any heed as she drove past.

o0o

At the same time, across town, the distinguished solicitor kissed his sleeping wife goodbye. This trip would take him away for several weeks. Long ago she had resigned herself to his commitment to help in the struggle to liberate his country, preferring this to idle retirement.

Checking the contents of his briefcase, which were destined by the ANC for disclosure at the UN, he left quietly, closing the front door...and died instantly. The briefcase had changed hands before his lifeless body struck the ground.

Ben had been a known courier for the ANC who enjoyed a formidable reputation abroad. He represented a threat to the régime and he had to be eliminated.

The assassin viewed the prone figure through watery eyes, then rifled the dead man's pockets as a precaution. His task completed, he inspected the contents of the briefcase. Several documents caught his interest. He slid a floppy disk out of an elasticated grip and paused in momentary indecision. He made up his mind and tucked the disk into his pocket together with the documents. His employer could draw his own conclusions as to their worth.

He barely acknowledged his ARB companion who dropped him off at the international terminal at Jan Smuts Airport. He produced his ticket and his luggage was checked in.

The ground hostess smiled generously. 'That way to the departure lounge, Mr Hammond. Your British Airways flight to London should be boarding shortly.'

CHAPTER 13

"I have cherished the ideal of a democratic and free society in which all persons live together in harmony and with equal opportunities. It is an ideal which I hope to live for and achieve. But if needs be, it is an ideal for which I am prepared to die."

Nelson Mandela
President of South Africa, 1994 onwards
Political prisoner 1964 - 90

31 May 1985

Breaking from a holding pattern the Boeing 707 began its downward spiral. The captain announced that they were about to land, then banked—giving them a clear view of the Thames snaking its way across London. Michael leaned over David's shoulder to watch the picturesque landscape which faded into a hazy horizon, bathed unexpectedly in brilliant sunshine. As the plane straightened for its final approach, a metallic jarring came from somewhere within the fuselage—the air brakes reducing speed as they lost altitude. The aircraft touched down effortlessly on the runway to the reverse thrust of turbines vibrating through the passenger cabin.

David and Michael exchanged glances. Up to this point their lives had been fraught with danger; but at least Tanzania, where they had laid low, had been a safe haven. Now, no matter what lay ahead, they were eager to turn their weeks of preparation into action. They would become the hunters rather than the hunted.

Heathrow was the first test for Michael's new identity. He patted his passport for reassurance. Apart from his nationality, his particulars were otherwise correct. The immigration officer was polite, and efficient. Inwardly, Michael sighed with relief as their documents were returned. This was the second time he had used a false passport in as many months. The official's attention was already focused on the next passenger, repeating the standard instructions for new arrivals. The terminal seemed purely functional with nothing to indicate they had arrived at one of the world's leading capitals. They joined the throng of travellers heading towards the exits—the city centre still lay an hour away to the east.

The Underground train whisked them through suburbia, then tunnelled under the city to King's Cross. Riding the escalator to street level, Michael stood with luggage in hand, completely blocking the way for other busy commuters.

373

'I think the general idea is to keep to the right!' David reminded him.

'Damn, I'm sorry.' Michael apologised, tucking in his suitcase to allow the impatient but polite queue to pass.

David then discovered the loss of his ticket. The Indian ticket collector took one look at the pair and decided he would reserve his comments for lesser men. He waved them through!

David rang the bell at 28 Penton Street. A woman's voice sounded over the external intercom.

'Good morning—can I help you?'

They identified themselves and heard the security bolt snap back.

The voice said, 'Come in.'

Inside, ceiling-high stacks of leaflets, extolling the virtues of the ANC and denouncing the South African Government, filled much of the small foyer. A male voice shouted down the stairwell.

'David, come on up.'

Michael followed him up the stairs, two at a time, into a small office where a man greeted David with undisguised affection. Michael realised that his companion was well acquainted with the building and its occupants. The room, like the foyer, was small and cramped. Desk, cabinets and chairs furnished what had once been a bedroom of a Victorian terraced house, long since converted into business premises which now served as offices for the Chief Representative of the ANC to the UK.

Initial greetings over, the room's occupant turned to Michael, hand extended in welcome.

'You must be Michael. David has told me much about you, besides what we have learnt from the media.'

David completed the formalities. 'Remember, my cousin Josh? He secured the work permits for us in Zambia.'

Michael shook Josh's hand warmly. 'It seems, then, that we both know something of each other...I've only heard good.'

Josh chuckled, 'Don't you believe it. Dave obviously hasn't told you what we got up to in our youth!'

Several faces had appeared in the doorway, keen to meet the man who had caused such a furore back in South Africa. Introductions were made with other staff. The African National Congress was still a banned political party and many were in exile from their native land; they had fled to stay alive and to fight back.* Michael noticed a small placard on the wall: 'An Exiled Government in Waiting'. He wondered if their objective would ever be achieved.

He watched Josh and David as they spoke animatedly, reverting to Xhosa, their mother tongue. Michael, though not understanding a word, sat envying the friendship between the cousins. Few brothers could have been closer and he thought wistfully of himself and Aaron. Michael was pleased when David interrupted his thoughts.

'Sorry if we appear rude, Mike, but we were just catching up on family matters.'

'Not entirely true,' interrupted Josh, 'Dave has also been telling me why you have come to the UK. If the ANC can be of any assistance in finding Boshoff, we would be glad to help. Any idea what he is doing over here?'

'I think he could be importing wines.' It was a long shot and Michael inwardly cursed himself for not asking Carla at the time but he couldn't have known...

Josh glanced over his spectacles. 'Wine you say. All right, we'll put the word out.'

'Thanks. We both have a score to settle with Boshoff. He was responsible for the deaths of some of our friends in Zimbabwe,' said David solemnly.

'And the death of my son, Carla, Paddy and others,' Michael added bitterly.

'You can be sure if he's here, then in time we'll find him.' Josh noticed the mixture of grief and anger that crossed Michael's face. 'Let's hope it's soon.'

'He's here all right,' Michael was adamant, 'and when I meet up with him, the bastard gets what he deserves.'

'What about Van Heerden?' Josh's expression remained thoughtful. 'Can't say I'm not curious to hear the full story but that can wait. Right now,' his tone of voice changed, the creases around his eyes and mouth smoothed out, 'I have something important to tell you.'

'Nandi?' said Michael. Immediately he and David tensed.

Quickly, he set their minds at ease. 'Nandi's okay. Since you left there has been some trouble, mind you.' He looked directly at David, 'I'm afraid the house is gone, burnt to the ground by BOSS.' He raised his hand as if to stop them. 'She's fine, unhurt, being taken care of by the *comrades*.' He filled them in on the details of the attack. Josh agreed to convey a message back to her from both of them. To write or telephone could spell further disaster for Nandi.

Josh took a deep breath. 'I'm afraid I have further bad news. Since your forced stay in Dar es Salaam, a number of things have happened.' He looked down at his desk. 'I regret having to tell you, but Ben was killed; we have reason to believe it was a BOSS assassination.'

David let out a groan, and confirmed what Michael already knew. 'Ben was the solicitor we met in Johannesburg.'

'I gathered as much, but what about the floppy disk?' Michael's voice was full of anxiety.

'Disappeared, I'm afraid!' said Josh. 'There's no trace of the disk or of the other documents he was carrying.'

'What?' he expelled loudly. It was a devastating blow. Michael was overcome by a wave of depression.

'Apparently it happened as he was leaving for the airport,' Josh continued. 'We understand from his wife that he definitely had the disk on him, so we can assume they found it.' He addressed Michael. 'You do have another copy?'

'No! I never had an opportunity. That was the only...'

'Dammit!' David cut him short, 'I printed it out but I never made any back-ups. I was afraid that one of us would be caught with the damn thing.'

'Well, there is nothing we can do about that now,' said Josh. 'No recriminations—please! The fact that they killed Ben points to some sort of cover-up. At the very least, they are going to have a devil of a time explaining his death.' He glanced at his cousin, then at Michael. 'I don't want to hear what you two are proposing, but please keep me informed if further evidence comes your way. I know certain parties who would dearly love to be in on any disclosure at the UN concerning this matter.'

Both men agreed.

'What do you intend to do about accommodation?' Josh asked. 'Beds are no problem. A number of our staff have already offered to put you up. I would, but it's a bedsitter and my fiancée might find it a bit awkward,' he added with a smile.

Michael needed to be a free agent, to come and go when he pleased. He felt being tied to the ANC might compromise them, besides restrict his movements. He was ready with an answer, 'Don't worry, we have discussed this at length. I'll arrange accommodation for David and myself.' Michael glanced at his travelling companion, 'Are you sure you still want to stick with me?'

'Provided you're paying!' David replied, 'Seriously, I want Boshoff for my own reasons. We're in this together.' He turned to Josh. 'We will appreciate anything you can do for us, Josh. For the time being I'd better work from outside the party; the less involved you are, the better all round.'

Michael asked to use the telephone and made a hotel booking.

Josh seemed content to leave things at that. They arranged to meet for dinner the following evening, when Josh could introduce his fiancée to David. In parting Josh said, 'If the ANC can help in any other way, it will be our pleasure.'

It was clear that Josh had other matters to attend to and they stood up to leave. Walking them to the front door Josh stopped. 'Won't be a moment,' he said and disappeared up the stairs again. He returned almost at once holding an umbrella.

'You're kidding, Josh?' David was puzzled. 'It's hotter than the Transkei out there!'

Josh nodded, 'I know—just a precaution. When you get to the roundabout don't be surprised if the driver of a white Ford Sierra stops and asks you for directions, but keep your faces hidden.'

Their concern showed.

'They're up to their old tricks again—photographing everyone who comes out of here, have been for days,' he said matter-of-factly.

Josh's warning proved correct.

Reaching the busy intersection, a car cut dangerously across traffic and pulled up beside them. The passenger drew their attention. 'Excuse me. Would you be so kind as to tell...'

Michael jammed the umbrella just as the driver raised his camera. David moved deftly to the right, blocking the camera's aim while at the same time opening the rear door.

'Taxi, take me to Tower of London.' He threw his case onto the back seat and climbed in after it.

The camera miraculously slid from view between the seats. The two men in the front sat speechless.

'You take me to Tower of London.' David prodded the driver's arm.

The driver stared at his unwanted passenger over his shoulder, then gawked at his colleague.

'Don't ask me!' the other said shrugging his shoulders.

David beckoned to Michael and in an instant there were two passengers on the back seat. 'You drive now please. We are in hurry—straight to Tower of London.'

The driver thought of arguing as he stared again into the rear-view mirror. 'Oh! What the hell.' He engaged first gear and rejoined the traffic, working his way slowly down Farringdon Road towards the Thames. 'The Tower it is then!' He looked dispassionately at his colleague who was trying to suppress his mirth at the situation foisted upon them. Attempting to salvage the day he glanced back at Michael. 'Where are you lads from?'

Michael got as far as 'Um!...' When David cut in.

'Him no talk. Lose tongue, cut out by witch doctor.'

The two men in the front stared back over their shoulders. Michael was indeed speechless.

'Him missionary, not too clever,' said David. 'Tribesmen beat him on head too often,' aware he was getting the queerest look from Michael.

The driver made remarkably good time through the morning traffic, eventually stopping at the busy intersection on the approach to Tower Bridge. 'Where to now?' he asked.

Michael nudged David, an almost imperceptible movement conveying the need for action. They glanced at one another. Five cars ahead the traffic lights had changed to green. Simultaneously the rear doors opened and they bundled out with suitcases in hand.

'This will do nicely,' David said in an affected British accent.

'Awfully kind of you, old boy,' said Michael, as the traffic began to roll forward forcing the car to move on towards Tower Bridge.

Michael saw the subway entrance. 'Come'n, let's get the hell out of here before they can stop.' They crossed under the road and took the path that skirted the Tower away from the road. The hotel lay ahead.

'Wonder what they'll write in their report for the day?' said David as they made their way to the hotel entrance.

They were shown into a double suite overlooking the Thames. After they had unpacked Michael left David staring out over the river while he attended to a pressing matter. He telephoned his bank in Houston and asked for an immediate and substantial transfer of money to be sent to the UK, to tide them over for the weeks ahead.

In the morning Michael ordered breakfast. When room service arrived with their trays, David signed the chit.

'Bloody hell, Mike. This is going to cost a fortune. We could move to cheaper digs in Knightsbridge, or even Earl's Court, if you wish?'

Michael came away from the window. Across the road lay the Tower of London and the famous Crown Jewels.

'Thanks for the concern but what am I going to do with my money? I might as well piss it up against the wall and enjoy it while I...no, while we can. You'd better believe it. Boshoff isn't going to be a pushover.' He thought back to something Carla had once said about her father, 'He has his own private army to protect him...'

His jaw set. 'Anyway, this was supposed to have been for John's education. It seems fitting that I blow the lot on getting his murderer—kind of levels the score a bit.'

'You're convinced that John was somehow deliberately infected with the P.carinii, aren't you?'

'Yeah! You don't seriously expect me to believe otherwise? Besides, the second bullet he gets is for Carla.'

That night they met Josh and his fiancée.

Gathered around the restaurant table, ignoring the menus, the three leaned forward engrossed in Michael's account.

'As for Aaron...I have a score to settle with my brother too.'

David was watching him closely—Michael was too calm, appearing almost aloof about what had happened. It worried him. He was sure there was an undercurrent of emotions which, when it erupted, would not stop until it had run its course. He didn't want to be in Aaron's shoes when that happened.

Josh sensed something as well, and was almost loath to ask him what stance the authorities had adopted towards his business interests when he first fled South Africa, having a good idea of the answer in advance.

'They froze my assets. It was only after arduous and protracted negotiations that Aaron agreed, for a price, to bribe one of his many friends in government to override the decision. Much later, my assets were unofficially reinstated and, from then on, handled surreptitiously by our family solicitors.'

They could see he was angry.

'Initially I was really screwed—admittedly Aaron talked the Reserve Bank round but it cost plenty. So much for my inheritance, but at least now I derive a small income from the business. Enough of that. Come on, what are we all eating?'

Michael's idea that Boshoff might be marketing his wines in the UK led nowhere. Several weeks dragged by as they exhausted every possible lead to his whereabouts. The South African wine importers they tracked down appeared bona fide and, if any of them knew of his presence, nobody was talking. Michael had become despondent with Boshoff eluding all their efforts to track him down.

The telephone rang. Michael answered.

'David, it's Josh for you,' he shouted in the direction of the bathroom.

David came through, dripping, leaving wet footprints on the thick pile, a towel round his waist.

'Thanks, Josh, you interrupted my shower.' Something Josh said made him repeat 'I see—I see!' There was a long pause, then 'I'll tell Mike. See you later.'

David replaced the receiver slowly.

'Are you ready for this?'

Michael nodded.

'BOSS have crossed the border into Botswana to hit the ANC bases there.* Josh says four men were killed, probably in an attempt to find us. They must believe we left the same way as before and still think we are in Southern Africa. Apparently the Botswana Government is breathing fire down every diplomatic channel but is powerless to do anything.'

Michael sat down.

'Jesus! It doesn't look as if they're going to leave us alone.' He glanced at David still standing next to the telephone, the carpet damp beneath his feet. 'Seriously, David, you are better off out of here. Boshoff is my problem. You are of more use to the ANC. You don't want to be involved in my problems, especially not now.'

'For Christ's sake, I am already involved,' David scowled. 'Do I have to repeat myself. I want Boshoff as much as you—for different reasons. He was responsible for giving the Rhodesians that weapon and I saw the suffering. Too many friends and good men died because of him. I hear what you are saying but, trust me, I am as committed to finding him as you are.'

Michael had not missed David's expression as he referred to Mbada, his brother and the many others he had met during the Bush War.

David turned and went quickly into his room.

Of the Teacher's fate he was certain, but he wondered what had they done to him before he was released. He had been desperately ill when he had last spoken to him on the telephone. The camp commander had said there was evidence of internal haemorrhage. Had he, too, been infected? David was now convinced that the raid by the Selous Scouts, which he had so narrowly missed, had been set up to recover the evidence that the Teacher was carrying. After all these years it seemed as if time had stood still. He missed his old *comrades.*

Michael heard David hit the partition with his clenched fist and half expected the picture on the wall to settle at a new angle. He gave him a few minutes, then went through.

'I've an idea. It's a hunch mind you. I've been so focused on Boshoff's wines that I completely forgot the estate produces other crops besides grapes. Carla once invited me out there...'

'What—wheat, maize, what kind of crops, Mike?'

'Hell, I don't remember, only that there was fruit. Definitely fruit.'

'So now you want us to go looking for fruit merchants. Do you know how many there must be in the UK?'

Michael let David's abruptness wash right over him. 'It was just an idea.'

Nevertheless, the next day they began to search for wholesalers who might be handling Boshoff's produce. They continued day after day for a further week. The telephone bill soared while they exhausted every avenue. It seemed, as far as they were concerned, as if Boshoff had never existed.

One morning Josh came round to the hotel and tried to inject some enthusiasm into their search. 'Listen you two, there are virtually a thousand ways he could be connected to the fruit industry—importer, distributor, retail merchant. He may even be exporting to Europe. If so, it will simply take longer but don't worry, it's only a question of time.'

'I sure as hell wish we had something more definite to go on,' said Michael. 'This sitting around is getting us both down.'

'Incidentally, why is Boshoff in England?' asked Josh. It had been worrying him for days. 'Surely all his interests—politics, wine, family and home—are in South Africa? He doesn't have to live in England to sell fruit or wines. While I think about it, why hasn't the South African Embassy been able to give us a lead on him?'

Michael attempted to address these questions. Carla had told him her father was in the UK and Louise lived in Paris. Of the mother, he had no idea as to her whereabouts and in the end decided he had no real answers.

Josh promised to meet them later in the hope of cheering them up. Their lack of success in tracing Andries Boshoff was beginning to take its toll. They became morose and lay about listlessly whiling away the rest of the day in front of the television.

David absent-mindedly leafed through the Yellow Pages.

Michael sat up abruptly. 'What if he's using an assumed name?'

David glowered in his direction and tossed the book across the room. 'That's good! So start from 'A' and work your way through to 'Z'.'

Michael went over to the window. Twenty minutes later, he was still looking down on Tower Bridge—their position offering a spectacular view of the whole structure—when he stated bluntly, 'I think I have a sure way to flush out Boshoff.'

David caught the certainty in Michael's voice, 'Oh yeah. How?'

'There's one last card we can play but it could be dangerous. We might bring the entire South African Defence Force down on our heads. I won't risk it unless you agree.' Over the next hour Michael outlined his proposal. David listened. In the end he said, 'It might work but let's sleep on it.' He glanced at his watch. 'Look at the time. We'd better hurry if we're to meet Josh.'

Josh was waiting patiently at the King's Peg, the pub which had introduced them to the drink of the same name: champagne and brandy mixed. Once settled at the bar Josh brought them up to date with the latest news from South Africa.

'Can you believe it! President Botha has agreed to release Mandela—if he renounces violence. You know what Nelson said to our people when he rejected the Boer's offer? 'I cherish my own freedom dearly, but I care even more for your freedom...'.'*

David thumped the bar counter. 'Good! One day, you will see, he'll be our president.' With a grin he quipped, 'Have you heard the latest? After Desmond Tutu received the Nobel peace prize for his non-violent struggle against apartheid, President Botha was told Tutu had committed suicide. Botha answered, 'Oh! I didn't know he had been arrested?'.'

His comment brought disapproving looks from others in the bar, even though their laughter was tempered by the irony that underlined the humour.

Josh became serious. 'You should know too, that they're still looking for a certain Mr Bernstein and a Dr Nyamande—wanted for violent crimes in South Africa. And they say the ANC bears full responsibility for the present violence back home.'

'Violence! It's them that should renounce violence, not us,' demanded Michael.

None of them paid any attention to the group of young men with short, cropped hair sitting at a table near the bar, their conversation reduced to whispers, who left minutes before the bartender called time.

They downed their drinks. And, as on many other occasions, they were the last patrons to leave the pub. The street was quiet and Josh stepped of the kerb to hail a taxi. From behind them, someone shouted.

'Hey, Bernstein, you nigger-loving yank, why don't you piss off back to the States?'

Five men—the ones who had been in the pub—moved out of the shadows to confront them.

'Yeah! You wogs should fuck off to wherever you's come from.' The group fanned out encircling them.

Michael felt himself sobering up fast. Anger, such as he had seldom experienced before, welled up inside him but for the moment he kept his temper. 'Look, we ain't looking for trouble; we're tourists.'

David appeared as if he had drunk nothing all evening. His body tensed, anticipating the inevitable attack. 'Save your breath, Mike. These shit-heads are probably from the National Front.'

The youths were beginning to realise that they were not confronting three pushovers. Ranged against them were men quite ready to hold their own. In what seemed an attempt to save face, one of the youths stepped forward in a display of bravado, relying heavily on the knife he weaved in the air in front of him and the confidence that comes from outnumbering the opposition. He spat at David.

David, generally amenable by nature, was now fired by anger and alcohol—it made a volatile cocktail. He moved towards the youth. Expecting a punch, the youth feinted to the right. No punch came. Instead David's hand shot out and clamped itself around his throat, holding him in a vice-like grip. Slowly David squeezed, his muscles contracting and his face contorting with the effort.

The knife clattered to the ground, its owner desperately clawing to be free of the deadly hold. He heard, then felt, his oesophagus collapse under the pressure as sinews and cartilage were crushed in his throat.

At the same time David locked the man by the groin with his left hand and with ease lifted his assailant off the ground, and swung him high in an arc. For a moment he was held above David's head. He threw the semi-conscious youth at the gang. Two of them collapsed beneath the weight of the human projectile and fell to the ground. Terrified, the others ran off. Clambering upright their fallen companions hastily joined them, leaving their injured accomplice to his fate.

Michael and Josh stood stock-still trying to take it all in. The prone figure lay at their feet trying desperately to breathe through a crushed windpipe.

A young couple, who had stopped metres away, witnessed these extraordinary events. Hesitantly, the young lad came forward; his girlfriend hung back.

'Can I help? I am a nurse...from Guy's. I saw what happened.' He knelt down and examined David's attacker. 'He cannot breathe...he is choking.'

Even in the light of the street lamp David could see that the man's lips were quite blue. Asphyxiation meant he would die if nothing was done. 'I am a doctor. Quick, where's that knife?'

Michael picked up the weapon and passed it over. David tilted the man's head back while his fingers probed feverishly at the base of the throat. Carefully he introduced the tip of the knife between the rings of undamaged cartilage and, forcing the blade down, punctured the windpipe. Opening the incision caused the man's chest to expand instantly, drawing in life-giving oxygen.

The young lad and David exchanged glances.

'I think you should go now,' he said to David. 'I can keep him alive until the ambulance arrives.'

Josh shouted to the girlfriend to fetch help while David checked his victim again. 'Watch me!' he said, kneeling by his side. 'Keep the airway clear like this,' showing him the procedure.

The lad did as he was told. It was his first tracheotomy, and one he was not likely to forget. Sticking the tip of the knife into the man's windpipe he kept the incision open. He could feel the rasping breath rush over his hand. The minutes seemed to drag by. A crowd was quickly gathering. In the distance they could hear a siren coming closer.

'We had better go now, sure you'll be all right?'

'I'm fine, and so is he. Just get going,' said the lad.

David, Josh and Michael walked away without looking back and made their way to the hotel.

'That bastard got what he deserved!' Michael expressed with feeling, when they reached the calm of their hotel room. All three were stone-cold sober, a situation he planned to rectify immediately.

'No! I was wrong,' David replied. 'Thank God I didn't kill him.'

'What! And have a knife stuck in you by some Nazi punk who has nothing better to do than beat up innocent...'

'I think you both missed the point.' Josh cut him off. 'I am sure he called you were a Yank, Michael.'

'So what,' David was sceptical, 'they probably heard Mike's accent at the bar.' That seemed to provide the most plausible explanation.

'You probably imagined it,' Michael added dismissively.

'No, I don't think so,' asserted Josh, 'I distinctly heard one of them say Bernstein. That's why I turned to see who it was.'

They both stared at him.

At 6.00am the telephone rang. It was their routine wake-up call. Michael did not exactly spring out of bed but for the first time he had to go through and wake his companion.

'Tell me it never happened,' David moaned. 'On second thoughts I'd rather we didn't discuss last night,' he muttered, struggling to pull on his track suit.

Twenty minutes later they had jogged their daily four-kilometre route along the pavement to Cleopatra's Needle on the Embankment.

Leaning against the parapet to regain his breath, Michael felt the rivulets of perspiration running down his face. He turned to David, 'You look like shit this morning.'

David laboured, taking in more air, 'Have you seen yourself? I should have pronounced you dead days ago.'

They laughed, still struggling to catch their breath.

'Have you thought—about what we discussed yesterday?' Michael gasped.

David, turning from the Thames, shot a glance at his friend. 'Let's do it.' Without further word they began retracing their steps.

Michael was ready this time for the houseboy; instead Jan DuToit picked up the telephone.

'Jan, this is Michael Bernstein!'

Michael heard the intake of breath. Before DuToit could respond, Michael spoke again, his words tumbling down the line. He had to make this man believe what he was saying and quickly. 'Don't say or do anything, just listen to what I have to tell you.' He paused.

Jan DuToit said nothing. Thankful, Michael pressed on.

'Carla knew something, something important, important enough that she died because of it. I don't know what lies you've been told but, believe me, she loved you, and I am doing this for her—she said you were an honourable man.' Michael stopped. He could hear Jan's breathing.

Across the room David mouthed silent encouragement.

'They killed her, Jan. You're not a stupid man—you know I loved her too.

I couldn't possibly have harmed her,' he paused momentarily. 'If you want to know what your wife knew and if you want her killers, then come over to London. I am here now but only for the next two weeks. After that you will not hear from me again. What's it to be, Jan? Do you want to know the truth, however much it hurts? Or will you go on believing all these bloody lies you Afrikaners dish out, even to yourselves? Jan, do you want some straight answers?'

David wanted to shout 'back off' for he felt Michael had gone too far.

Michael saw him urgently shaking his head. He ignored his friend and spoke into the receiver. 'I'll call back in precisely one hour, then you decide if you want to know why they killed her, or what it was she found out. If you don't...!' Michael replaced the receiver. He checked his watch.

David exploded. 'Christ Almighty! What got into you, Mike? He's probably on the phone to BOSS by now. You blew it! I don't believe you could be so bloody stupid. Believe me, you've really pissed him off. No self-respecting Boer is going to stand for that kind of talk.' David threw his hands up in the air as he shouted, 'Why did you do it?' He disappeared into his room, slamming the door behind him.

Michael wasn't too sure if he had done the right thing. He tried to convince himself that he had needed to shock Jan into a decision. It was quite possible that Jan would overreact and prove David right. The next sixty minutes were perhaps the longest in Michael's life. He glanced at his watch over and again until finally the hands crawled round to register that the time was up. Michael dialled.

Almost instantly the telephone was answered. Before Michael could say a word, an angry voice said, 'Is that you Bernstein?'

'Yes!' he replied.

'Now you shut up, and listen.'

Ten minutes later Michael put the telephone down. He looked up to see David standing in the doorway.

'He's coming, David. A lot of threats but he's coming.'

'The Home Office are sniffing around. They say they have unconfirmed reports that a certain Michael Bernstein entered the United Kingdom illegally and do we know of his whereabouts?'

Sitting in his cramped office, David and Michael listened to Josh with a feeling of foreboding. The imminent threat of arrest and likelihood of deportation certainly would not help their search for Boshoff.

'This is a delicate situation. We need to find out how this leak occurred,' insisted Josh.

'The bank or maybe my credit card,' Michael ventured. 'I transferred my account from Houston to here a few days ago.'

'I see,' Josh mulled this over. 'I strongly recommend you draw out your savings. If you like I can hold the money for you—or you should try another bank, but traces are always possible. Incidentally, when did you last use your credit card?' he asked.

'When we booked into the hotel...for a credit check.'

'Good! So provided you don't buy anything or settle your hotel account with your card, I wouldn't be unduly worried. It's unlikely that anyone will check back on a credit clearance for an address, whereas a purchase transaction is an entirely different matter.' Josh was evidently pleased.

'That's a relief!' said Michael.

'I'm not sure I understand?' David sounded bewildered.

'Well, if you buy something, say from Harrods, on a credit card you're hardly likely to be sitting in Tanzania.' Josh then swivelled round to face Michael.

'We've already interceded on your behalf by contacting the US Embassy. We explained the circumstances of your departure but the South African police are still insisting you are dangerous—wanted on a murder charge. I suggest you stick with your new travel documents for the moment.'

Michael had an inspiration. 'What if the US Embassy contacted Detective Pinkerton of the Houston Police Department? He investigated the bombing at the laboratory. He was sure the detonator was of South African origin—they must be made to realise the significance of that!'

Josh assessed this new information. 'Leave it with me. I will see what I can do. For now, stay out of trouble and I'll see you both later.'

After they had left the ANC office Michael asked, 'Don't you think we should have told him that Jan's coming?'

'What will that achieve, Mike? No, I don't think we should involve the ANC more than is necessary. Let's face it, we've got ourselves into this; why should they carry the responsibility for what we do?'

'I suppose you're right.' Michael glanced at David. 'Hope you're not thinking what I am...was it Jan who informed on us?'

oOo

The South African Embassy in Trafalgar Square received a call from Cape Town. The instructions were taken down in detail and passed immediately to the Embassy's security chief, who doubled as the senior BOSS agent in charge of European operations. He read the message with keen interest, then reached for one of three telephones.

Above his allegiance to his country, loyalty to his political party was paramount in his mind. Now he spoke to his leader with reverence.

'Sorry to disturb you, Meneer Boshoff,' he sounded suitably subservient, 'but you did want to know if your son-in-law ever came to England. We received a message to say he's arriving the day after tomorrow. Staying as a guest of the Ambassador for two nights and he will be accompanied by a bodyguard.'

He listened intently to Boshoff's questioning.

'...No, Meneer Boshoff, his bodyguard isn't one of us. I know the fellow personally: he once played for the Springboks. We didn't recruit him for BOSS, too bloody *verligte* for our liking.'

'I trust you know why DuToit's coming over?'

There ensued a silence neither man could afford.

'I'm sorry, Meneer Boshoff, but I've had no time to check.'

'Bloody hell, man, what's wrong with you?' The silence was back. 'Well! Get on with it then, and let me know the outcome immediately.' The telephone went dead.

In under ten minutes the BOSS agent was back on the line.

'Meneer Boshoff, it's possible his trip is for personal reasons. I can confirm it hasn't anything to do with the embassy—I checked.'

'Can't we get a tap on his telephone in Cape Town?' Andries enquired.

'That's impossible Meneer Boshoff, you know what happened last time, when the Prime Minister found out.'

'Ja, ja, the man's a fool.' Andries was clearly irritated. 'Anyway, Van Heerden is bloody lucky he's not around to answer for that.'

'Minister DuToit has requisitioned an embassy vehicle during his stay and says he doesn't require a chauffeur. Do want us to tail him?'

Boshoff hesitated for a moment. He had always kept the entire cabinet under surveillance round the clock. Any indiscretions were duly noted and there were few secrets that he did not share and keep filed away. 'No! I'll take care of it myself,' he said.

'Very well, I will keep you informed of further developments, Meneer Boshoff,' and he passed on Jan's ETA and flight number. 'And another thing I thought you should know. The ANC are still sniffing around trying to find your address through the embassy.'

'Thanks. Just keep them guessing.'

Andries replaced the receiver gently into its cradle. 'Two days!' he said to himself. 'What in hell's name is Jan up to?' Over the years he had become somewhat disillusioned with his young protégé. Jan was far too liberal— a great disappointment to his father-in-law. Andries had a gut feeling that something was up and knew that his hunches were usually right. He picked up the telephone again.

'Victor, it's Andries. I think I might have another job for you.'

It had been several months since Boshoff had seen Jan, at Carla's funeral. Now his driver waited for his son-in-law outside the VIP lounge. He had not been there long before Jan DuToit emerged. Jan's bodyguard glanced left, then right, before falling into step behind his employer. The driver followed at a discreet distance. Satisfied that they were heading for the car park, he went quickly to the front of the airport terminal. Andries' was sitting in the passenger seat of the black saloon, the engine quietly ticking over.

They tailed Jan from the airport, to the embassy at Trafalgar Square. Caught at the lights, the courtesy driver climbed out and they watched Jan slide over to take the wheel. Andries frowned: what was his son-in-law playing at? They almost lost their man in the traffic as he accelerated away from the lights, around the corner, and disappeared down Northumberland Avenue. Within seconds Andries' driver had him back within sight.

o0o

A trip to a London store had procured a pair of binoculars which Michael now used from their bedroom window to scan the elegant expanse of stone and iron that was Tower Bridge. The bascule filled the lenses with its twin towers. A fine rain drizzled down reducing visibility as rivulets ran down the window-pane.

David paced the room. 'Are you sure you said 10.00am?'

'For crying out loud and for the last time—yes!' Michael responded irritably. 'And stop walking up and down. It's playing on my nerves.'

'Sorry, Mike.' David joined him at the window. He was trying to cover every possible contingency before they met Jan—and unconsciously resumed his pacing of the room.

Suddenly Michael saw Jan. 'Here he is!' He handed the glasses to David who was back at his side. 'See the guy next to the pillar. That's Jan. He hasn't changed that much. I'd recognise him anywhere—and to his left—I reckon that's his bodyguard.'

David studied the two figures, then slowly scanned the bridge and beyond. Jan and his bodyguard were the only stationary pedestrians on this damp and grey morning.

'Come on, it looks safe enough and it's right on ten. I don't want him leaving because we're late.'

They willed the lift to move faster. The doors opened. They rushed through the foyer, then round the building towards St Katharines Way; a short flight of steps brought them onto Tower Bridge.

They were still there.

Michael walked cautiously on while David slowed, stopping short and mirroring the bodyguard's stance on the other side of the cabinet minister.

Michael glanced back briefly as he approached Jan, then over Jan's shoulder at his bodyguard who was leaning nonchalantly against the bridge's railing not more than seven metres away. He appeared to be gazing out at the river but gave furtive glances to the left and right every few seconds.

Jan DuToit was in no mood to be trifled with. He curtly acknowledged Michael's presence.

'Jan, this is a trade-off...I'll explain my reasons in a moment. Namely, I want to know where your father-in-law is—in exchange, you get to know who killed Carla. Agreed?'

'I agree but it had better be good, Bernstein!' The implied threat could not have been plainer.

Michael told Jan, as briefly as he could, about the discovery which Carla and he had made. That he was responsible for the development of PF657, the mutant *P.carinii* pathogen created more than a decade ago; how this micro-organism had been used in the Rhodesian War. The facts surrounding the deaths of other members of the research team who had died at the hands of the Cape Doctor. And, finally, he recounted what Tinus had said in his last moments about Boshoff's involvement.

It was obvious that Jan was deeply shocked by these disclosures. Michael was thankful that he appeared to believe him. To his surprise, Jan said he was aware that the Rhodesians had used some type of secret weapon and recalled initiating a government enquiry into the matter at the time, but the evidence was not conclusive. Considering these revelations, he now felt that perhaps the Prime Minister himself might have been involved.

Michael rounded off with a detailed account of the circumstances leading up to Carla's death that fateful day on the Cape Peninsula. He finished and waited for Jan to speak.

'What you say could answer many questions. I never understood why the Rhodesians capitulated so suddenly after the Kissinger talks with their Prime Minister. I was there! They just handed over to Black rule for no apparent reason. I was going to say like lambs...but that would be inappropriate, because after Kissinger's visit they went into Mozambique and massacred thousands!'

'But didn't you hear what Smith and Kissinger discussed at the time?' Michael asked incredulously.

'No. That was not possible—I was only an aide. We were not privy to what was said privately between the two men.'

Jan made no mention of Carla or what had happened to her. It was as if he had wiped her from his mind. He went on to outline the current government investigation into allegations against the ARB as a third force and its role in destabilising Southern Africa. All he knew for certain was that Boshoff headed this little known organisation and that certain cabinet ministers were involved. He asked whether Michael knew that a State of Emergency had been declared? He feared the country was in virtual chaos. Suddenly he asked, 'What happened to Commandant Van Heerden?'

The two men talked openly and intensely as David watched the approach of a black executive saloon with foreign number-plates, glimpsing his reflection in the tinted windows as it passed at the regulatory 20 mph.

Andries took in the scene at a glance. He swore softly when he saw Michael. Once over the bridge, he told his driver to turn up a side road. Andries read a sign, 'Antiques since 1872'. The quiet street did not look as if it had seen much activity since then.

'Okay Victor, stop. This will do nicely.' Andries picked a spot where there were no shops and, more importantly, no shoppers or staff who might recall their presence.

His mind raced. He had not foreseen this eventuality and it worried him. Jan, in his own right, was now a powerful political figure, largely due to Andries himself. But what was Michael telling him? Suddenly he saw a way out. A hideous smile crept across his face.

His instructions were explicit. 'Kill them all.' He hesitated. 'No, leave Bernstein, I want to deal with him later. Just finish DuToit, and make sure to waste the bloody kaffir.'

The driver was concerned about the bodyguard and asked what he must do and if Michael presented a problem.

'Take them out!' said Andries. They weren't central to his immediate plan.

The car door closed and Andries settled himself and opened out his newspaper. If his plan worked he could visualise the headlines to come: *'Cabinet Minister slain by ANC.'* If Michael survived the attack he would be assumed to be an accomplice. In the country illegally; wanted in South Africa for murder; besides being a member of a terrorist organisation, the British police would make short work of the Jew, and he laughed.

Andries' driver came round the corner and headed back towards Tower Bridge. He pulled the collar of his raincoat up against the incessant drizzle. Increasing his pace, he kept to the right side of the bridge's southern approach, at the same time sliding his right hand into the inside custom-made pocket of his jacket. He slipped off the safety catch.

On the bridge he passed a group of French students, then as he came abreast of Jan's bodyguard, he checked the gun again for clearance. He could see Jan and Michael clearly a few metres ahead.

Michael peered over Jan's shoulder. 'Sorry, what was that?' His attention was drawn to a man walking briskly towards them—he was moving at a slightly faster pace, more purposefully, than the other pedestrians. Michael lost the thread of what Jan was saying.

Watery, pale blue eyes, and white, wispy hair clinging to a wet, balding scalp; the sight jarred something in Michael's memory—this was the same man he had seen sitting in the car outside the solicitor's house in Johannesburg. Why hadn't the bodyguard noticed him? Why hadn't David picked him out? Everything about the man was threatening, signalling danger!

Jan, aware he had lost Michael's attention, half-turned to follow his gaze.

'Duck!' Michael shouted. The gun came up towards Jan's back. Instinctively he shoved Jan aside and brushed the gleam of blue metal away with his other arm. There was a tiny cough from the weapon and Michael glimpsed a neat hole appear in his duffel coat, then felt the stinging pain where the bullet had seared his arm. He staggered sideways into Jan and they fell together onto the pavement. The gunman, however, managed to keep his footing. Michael lay immobilised, watching in stunned disbelief as the weapon swung around again towards Jan.

The gunman knew he would have made the hit had Michael not intervened at that crucial moment. Now in these vital seconds, Michael still obscured his target. Jan's bodyguard—coming in at a rush—was the more immediate threat. He hesitated for a split second—he would have to take out the bodyguard and kaffir first!

Intent on a kill, he was totally unprepared for the reaction from the group of students behind him. The moment the attack began, one of the students—a well-grown boy—launched himself at the assassin's back in the belief that he was witnessing a mugging.

'Au voleur! Au voleur! Arrêtez-le!' he shouted. Grabbing the gunman by the coat, he swung him around. Almost at once he saw the gun. Realising that this was no ordinary mugger, he instinctively dropped to the ground followed by the rest of the group. It was enough to throw the gunman momentarily off-balance.

David had recognised the man moments before Michael. Time seemed to stand still as images from the past flashed by: a vision of a man ZANLA had sought to capture during, then after, the Bush War—Hammond, Victor Hammond! David had met him briefly at the mission, and seen him again, while he hid with Mbada and the Teacher. Though he had changed over the years, his dominant features remained the same. Hammond still looked like a white rat. Fleetingly, Mbada, the Teacher and Jessica came back—as he snapped into action.

Hammond saw him coming.

Jan's bodyguard cursed as he ran, drawing his gun, caught completely by surprise. He darted in towards Jan—a frantic bid to protect his charge. He couldn't see exactly what was happening—Hammond had his back to him, partially obscuring his view. The bodyguard fired and the bullet buried itself deep in Hammond's thigh.

He screamed with pain, then swinging round, emptied the semi-automatic of its remaining seven rounds at the weaving target before dropping the empty gun. Miraculously the shots went wide, most thudding into the rear of a No 78 bus. A tyre blew and the vehicle slewed across the road, perilously close to the edge, before coming to a halt.

Skirting Hammond, who was clasping his thigh, Jan's bodyguard straddled the minister. Gripping his gun with both hands he swung it towards Michael, then at David. David skidded to a halt. The finger tightened on the trigger.

Jan shouted a command, '*Moenie skiet nie*, don't shoot, Piet!'

David's eyes were riveted to the barrel, centimetres from his forehead. From the corner of his eye he could see Hammond limping away. Disregarding the threatening gun, he swore, 'That bastard's mine!' And gave chase.

Unable to run, Hammond glanced back, panic-stricken, to see David gaining on him rapidly. Desperately, he lunged for the side of the bridge and swung his body over the railing in a frantic bid to escape in the fast-running tidal waters ten metres below.

David leapt forward to pull him back, caught hold of Hammond's injured leg and hung on. Hammond cried out in agony. Realising that he could not shake David off, he twisted round and, gripping David by the shoulders, threw his own full body weight backwards.

The varnished, wooden rail was wet and slippery. David stared down into the turbulent water and frantically clawed for something to hold onto—there was nothing. He was pulled over the edge; the two men plunged towards the river below, their screams lost in the rush of wind as a pleasure cruiser emerged from under the bridge.

Terrified tourists stood transfixed watching as the men hurtled down on them. A body crashed through the canvas awning before coming to an abrupt stop against the oak deck; the other shot past, and disappeared into the Thames.

Jan handled the sensitive situation, stretching his diplomatic immunity to the limit. Outraged by the attack and by what he had learnt from Michael, he was now determined to return home to enlist support from his colleagues in the cabinet. He would demand radical changes in the government of South Africa.

Before he left, he went to visit the patient in hospital.

Michael was sitting upright in bed while a nurse changed the dressing.

'You realise it was you that bastard was after!' said Michael.

'Ja! I believe he was.'

He could not resist asking Jan, 'Out of academic interest, what's it like to have a Black ANC member save your life?'

Jan smiled. 'That was a brave thing for him to have done. I'm sorry I didn't have an opportunity to thank him.' He paused. 'I thought you ought to know I'm leaving for Cape Town tomorrow.' He seemed a little embarrassed. 'Michael, thank you for what you said about Carla. I realise now we both loved her very much.' He hesitated, groping for words, 'Even though I hate to admit it, I think I know you were her first real love. I will always envy you for that.'

Michael studied Jan intently. He sensed that here was a sensitive and intelligent man. The years of resentment fell away and he found himself saying, 'I'm sorry you're going so soon...' getting no further.

The door burst open and David strode in carrying wilted roses snatched from a trolley down the corridor. His grin appeared as wide as the bridge he had fallen over. He acknowledged Jan with a curt nod and turned back to Michael. 'The doctor's come for his patient. You're out of here, man. I'm discharging you and the pubs are waiting.' He was euphoric, in contrast to the day before, when he had had the wind knocked out of him from the impact of hitting the water. He had been helpless, finding himself being sucked steadily towards the launch's twin propellers without the strength to resist the deadly, churning blades. As if in answer to a prayer, the skipper in the last seconds, had cut the engines.

David vaguely remembered being fished from the river and the wail of an ambulance carrying him to hospital. They were both admitted to private wards and kept under observation for twenty-four hours. Examination showed him to be mildly concussed. Discharging himself earlier that morning, David had returned to the hotel to collect a change of clothes for Michael and himself.

He threw the flowers and fresh clothes onto the bed. 'Hurry up, Mike. Get dressed. I'm in a mood to celebrate.' He was thankful still to be alive.

'David, I'd like you to meet Jan, er, officially,' said Michael.

Still grinning, David greeted him.

Jan took the offered hand. 'So it looks like I get to thank you after all,' then smiled. 'If you two are thinking of celebrating, I think I should postpone my departure for a while—a small party perhaps?'

Jan was attentive to their needs. Over the next few days he insisted that his bodyguard chauffeur them to and from the hotel, and to hospital for their check-ups. David joked unmercifully about having a White chauffeur—the bodyguard turned out to be congenial and took the friendly ribbing good-naturedly.

One evening David said to Michael, 'You go ahead with Jan; I will catch up with you.' An hour later he arrived with Josh. Michael watched intently as Jan and Josh initially sized one another up. But slowly a mutual understanding grew between them, and they began to feel at ease in each other's company. They found much to discuss about their beloved country; talking on, both men realised they shared a common vision for the future.

Two nights before Jan's departure, Josh broke the news. 'It seems you were right, David: the police have confirmed his identity. It was definitely Victor Hammond.'

David exchanged glances with Michael. 'See. I told you it was him. Remember what we read off that floppy disc. That bastard was the one who purchased it from Mueller Laboratories and probably was responsible for introducing the *P.carinii* into the Bush War,' he said dryly. 'He's obviously in this with Boshoff.'

'Was!' Josh corrected him. 'Now here's the interesting part,' he continued. 'The police say he was living in Southampton. If what you both say proves to be correct, and Hammond is in some way linked to Boshoff, then it's possible that you can narrow down your search to that area.'

'All right,' Jan interceded, 'I hear what you are saying. I know it sounds odd, but I don't know where my father-in-law is staying. I've never needed to know, other than the fact he is here in the UK. I've tried Carla's mom but she's staying with Louise and they are both away on holiday somewhere. Leave it with me, it shouldn't be difficult to track him down.'

Jan said his goodbyes at Heathrow's VIP departure lounge. He shook David's hand. 'What can I say? You saved my life and now, thanks to you, I'll probably die of cirrhosis. It's been great. Thank you, David,' and they found themselves grinning at one another.

He turned next to Josh. 'This trip has been far too short, but I feel we are destined to meet again—in fact you can count on it.'

Michael was surprised, watching him draw out an envelope from his breast pocket. 'I've been making enquiries and I'm keeping to my side of the bargain. Thanks, Michael. You have no idea how pleased I am that I came over. Believe me, it was touch-and-go for a while.'

Michael caught David's knowing glance.

'Now I feel I can get on with my life.' Jan clasped Michael's hand. 'We will both miss her. Goodbye, Michael.'

'Yes, we will.' At that moment he did not want Jan to leave.

He left them with parting words. 'Gentlemen, when I get back I promise things will change.'

The minute Jan had disappeared through the gate, Michael tore open the envelope. It contained the current address of Andries Boshoff.

The next day David disappeared for the morning. He returned to the hotel carrying a small parcel.

Michael stared as his friend opened the package. The contents were wrapped in greased paper.

'This is a Walther PPK Automatic Pistol.'

Michael knew from past experience in Soweto that David was familiar with handling weapons and watched as he slipped the magazine clip out of the hand-grip and checked the breach.

'Takes seven rounds.' He handed it, grip first, to Michael before picking up the other pistol. 'This one is Czech, and takes eight rounds. I don't know what it's called.' He had never been able to get his tongue around 'Brohmische Waffenfabrick'. 'The beauty of these two is that they're the same calibre, so we only need one size of ammunition.' As if to prove the point, he removed a smaller box from the parcel to reveal the bright lustre of nickel-coated shells; he tipped them onto the bed and began to load both magazine clips.

Michael watched with a mixture of fascination and unease. 'I've never had to fire one of these.'

David demonstrated how to handle both weapons. Together they worked on the load and unload drill until Michael was reasonably proficient at handling the guns.

'Good!' David encouraged him. 'There's one thing more...we must be prepared to use them.'

oOo

Packed and ready, David waited for the hire car to arrive, while Michael settled their hotel account. By midday they were out of London and headed towards Southampton.

The motorway brought them to the outskirts of the city and within the hour they had found Boshoff's home. It was set in woodlands away from the city centre and appeared even larger than the other substantial properties in the area. It was impossible to tell exactly how big the house was because it was virtually inaccessible.

A high wall, supporting a security fence on top, surrounded the extensive grounds. Cameras were mounted at strategic points and beyond the large, ornate, wrought iron gates they could see men patrolling the grounds with dogs. The driveway curved to the right and visible above the trees were several spiralling chimneys that protruded like twisted candy bars. Otherwise the house remained hidden—the place was a veritable citadel.

Walking gingerly around the property the previous day, they had kept an eye open for the security cameras. In a more secluded area, away from the road, they had found what they were looking for. A wide branch of a yew tree extended from the grounds over the wall by several metres.

Keeping the entrance under surveillance all morning, they now returned in the late afternoon to the same spot with a rope and ladder.

Resting the ladder against the wall, Michael climbed to the last rung and found it relatively easy to throw a knotted rope over the limb. Climbing onto the branch, he secured the rope. David followed, then pulled the rope up to clear the security wire that ran along the top of the wall and let it fall inside the property. Lowering themselves to the ground was a simple matter of slithering down the rope. Michael went first and crouched behind some large bushes. David followed.

'Watch it! That's my hand you're standing on,' Michael hissed.

'Sorry. Now what?' David peered around cautiously. Their entry seemed to have gone unnoticed—up to now it had been easy. From their cover in the thick foliage that lined the estate wall they could see, through the leaves, a large a manor house which stood amidst well-tended lawns. A dog barked but it was distant.

'Let's get a closer look at the house,' whispered Michael.

A large number of cars were parked on the gravel driveway in front of the house, and new arrivals entering the grounds threatened to spill over onto the lawn at the side of the building. They had watched them arrive earlier, which probably accounted for the absence of visible patrols. To one side stood a catering company van. Clearly some kind of celebration was in progress. They had gambled that with people coming and going as they had observed, that hopefully the presence of two further, uninvited guests would go unnoticed.

They saw a group of young men climb out from two cars. The carefree crowd strolled towards the house laughing and talking among themselves. The two intruders noticed that some guests were carrying overnight cases.

'Come on, I was right. He's throwing some kind of function. Maybe this fortress isn't so invincible after all! Let's go.'

Michael half stood, to venture out and join the party-goers.

'Hold it, Mike,' David held onto his belt, stalling his departure. 'Where do you think you're going?'

'I've come this far...I have to know if Boshoff is here. With all this activity going on there couldn't be a safer opportunity.' He found himself whispering, 'If they nab us what's he going to do? He's hardly likely to shoot us in front of his guests. No, he'll simply throw us out for gate-crashing his party.'

'For you maybe,' David was unconvinced, 'but he's not going to let me get away so lightly. How many black guests have you seen?' He was intent on watching another group arrive. Something was definitely wrong here.

'Fair enough. Maybe it's a good idea for you to stay—in case something happens to me—and another thing, if he's aware we're around, so what, at least we'll have a better idea on how we can get to him again.' He peered through the undergrowth and added, 'Have you noticed, all his guests are casually dressed. I shouldn't have a problem blending in.'

The latest arrivals had disappeared around the front of the building.

'All right but just take it easy.' He placed a restraining hand on Michael's shoulder. 'At least wait for the next car to arrive.'

Within minutes a Volvo estate pulled up displaying foreign number plates. David noticed that the occupants, all men, didn't appear to be relaxed, not enough to be going to a party, as they walked purposefully across the gravel; but it was Michael's decision.

'Okay! Go for it,' he said.

Michael stood up and strolled across the lawn. It did not take him long to catch up with the group and they had to move aside to allow other cars, which continued to arrive, to pass along the driveway. A guard and his dog stood at the top of the steps near the entrance. Michael's heart thumped wildly in his chest. He tried to act casually. Was the guard looking rather too intently at him? The man made no effort to stop him entering the house.

The hallway was packed with people. The guests stood around in small groups; their talk seemed strangely loud. He accepted a glass of champagne from the waiter who was attending to the new arrivals.

Michael glanced round. The hallway was huge and tastefully decorated. To one side a wide staircase curved gracefully to an upper floor. A skilful hand had blended the sixteenth century with more modern elements. Here and there he recognised the South African influence: several Gabriel de Jongh originals hung in an alcove to one side. At the end of the hall, a large, ornate window opened onto terraced lawns at the rear of the building. Michael saw guests congregated around a buffet, spread on trestle tables. He took one last look around. Andries Boshoff was nowhere to be seen, so Michael strolled onto the terrace and joined the other guests.

He found an empty table and sat down. It was a beautiful day: warm, with the fragrance of roses drifting gently on the still air. He could hear the sound of a quartet playing somewhere. The setting was delightful—he could almost relax and enjoy the afternoon. Boshoff's guests seemed fairly average, not the stuffy crowd he had imagined Andries might have invited. He wondered what the occasion was. He reached over to the side of the table and drew the bottle from the silver ice bucket and glanced at the label.

'Well, well! The Boshoff Estate, Stellenbosch. I admit the *verkramp* bastard produces a good wine.' He filled a glass.

Michael speculated on how Boshoff would react if his presence was detected. He resisted the temptation to refill his glass. Suddenly it dawned on him that he was the only person sitting alone and, given the circumstances, he began to feel very conspicuous. He glanced nervously around. 'I'm being paranoid. There's near on a hundred people here—they're not going to notice one more,' he said to himself. No one stared at him with more than the casual curiosity which decorum allowed. A smiling young waitress offered him a plate of canapés, and he dismissed his concern as unfounded.

Nothing else could be achieved out here. He looked around again and everything appeared to be perfectly normal. Boshoff had to be somewhere else in the house and he was determined to take a closer look at the layout of the interior before leaving. Michael strolled nonchalantly through the high, arched doorway. Everything looked very civilised. While he had been sitting outside, it seemed that a good many of the guests had changed from the casual clothes they had arrived in, into dinner suits. He noticed that the double doors to his left were now open, revealing a large banqueting hall with rows of carefully laid tables. It was relatively empty except for waiters milling around evidently making last minute preparations. He stepped inside to be out of the busy hall and looked around.

'Shit!' he exclaimed under his breath. Michael's eyes darted everywhere. The walls were decked with banners: Swastikas and other emblems of the Third Reich were festooned amongst the distinctive, inverted-swastika mark of the ARB, the Klan, the badge of the National Front and many other flags he could not readily identify.

He turned to leave, but two tough-looking young men were striding purposefully towards him. As if that was not enough, they were dressed in Nazi uniforms. 'Where the hell did they come from?' he thought, too stupefied to register fear.

'Excuse me, sir, but what cell are you from?'

Michael, realising with a jolt that he was being addressed, uttered the only thing that seemed remotely plausible. 'South Africa!'

'Oh! I see. You are with the party that arrived this morning, then. Do you mind if we check you against the guest list?' There was an edge to the man's voice.

There was nothing for Michael to do but to resort to bluff.

'Van Heerden!'

The men looked blankly at one another.

He had to say something, anything, to distract them before they checked their guest list.

He kept his voice down, 'I'm delivering a speech on apartheid at the dinner tonight...and where's our host? I have been here all afternoon and he

has not once put in an appearance! If you would like to call him I will wait.'
He tried to appear suitably put out, hoping like hell that Boshoff would not
suddenly materialise out of the crowd—and that the two would leave,
giving him the chance to escape via the terrace.

'Sorry, but didn't you know, Mr Boshoff flew to Frankfurt earlier today.
Strange...he didn't mention a second speaker!' Michael's interrogator
sounded confused.

'But I was told Andries would be here tonight,' Michael persisted.
Over the shoulder of the young man he noticed guests climbing the stairs in
their casual attire carrying their overnight bags, while others were coming
down in dinner jackets, wearing ribbons on their left chests that denoted
allegiance to one obscene right-wing organisation or another. Suddenly it
struck him, apart from the waitresses, the entire crowd was male.

'Yes, he will be. He has gone to fetch our other guest speaker. The jet
should have touched down at Eastleigh,' the man glanced at his watch,
'...at least half an hour ago. He should be here any minute.'

'Excellent! Now, my good man, if you'll excuse me, I'll go and change.'
With that, Michael turned on his heel and walked towards the staircase.

Keenly aware that he was being closely scrutinised from below, Michael
climbed the stairs, every step an effort. After what seemed an eternity,
he ducked down a passage taking him out of sight of watchful eyes.

The first door he tried was locked. He peered around the second, into
a bedroom—empty. Michael went in and shut the door. He gave himself
a moment to catch his breath. Cautiously he stepped out of the French
window onto the high balcony; his loathing of heights surpassed only by
the sheer terror he had experienced inside the building. Suppressing his
fear, he felt his way along the parapet wall. With a trembling hand he
reached out and located a drainpipe fixed to the main building. Gripping the
pipe firmly, he swung himself over the edge, and hoped it was secure—
thinking nervously to himself, 'Nice party, but I really must go.'

He slithered down, oblivious to the protruding bolts that tore at his
clothes and flesh and jumped the remaining two metres, just pleased to be
down on terra firma.

He waited, until sure the coast was clear, then sprinted across the lawn
and had just regained the shelter of the bush, where David waited
anxiously, when a black saloon swept up the drive. It drew to a halt and
Boshoff stepped out. Boshoff was bound to be told about his bogus guest.
Michael estimated it would be no more than five minutes before the
grounds were swarming with men and dogs. He whispered in David's ear,
'I don't know about you, but this nice Jewish boy is convinced it's bad for
his health to stick around. I suggest you view it the same way, if you want
to keep your arse in one piece. Come on, let's get out of here.'

The next day they positioned themselves close to Boshoff's mansion and, from a safe distance, took it in turns to watch the gates. The only activity of note, was the black saloon left in the morning and returned in the evening. Frustrated by the lack of any activity, they eventually left for their B&B.

David was now sure it was the same vehicle he had seen on Tower Bridge. 'We should tell someone what's going on in there,' he insisted for the umpteenth time after hearing Michael's detailed account.

'What do we tell the authorities? Sorry we broke in on a private party and guess what, some of the guests were in fancy dress—every ultra-right wing radical movement you can imagine. No, I don't think so. I don't think they're going to pay us too much attention. Dave, I think we first get Boshoff, because even if the authorities step in, it will have put paid to our objective by placing him beyond our reach.'

'But these fascists should be questioned, at least as to what they were doing here.'

'Most of his guests were foreigners anyway. They'll be long gone, so what will they find? Besides, it was you who said we shouldn't involve the ANC and, remember, I am an illegal immigrant. One thing's for sure, I'm not going back in. He'll be waiting for us. No, we wait, bide our time and find out where he goes every day—then we act.'

They made their move on the third day. Promptly at 7.30am the impressive wrought iron gates swung open as they had for the past two days. The saloon emerged, the tinted windows hiding its occupants as the car turned right into the lane and headed towards the city centre. Following, they shadowed the car in front, keeping well back.

Nearing the centre of Southampton, the saloon suddenly swung on to a feeder road and headed towards the dock area. Minutes later it slowed, then pulled off and disappeared into a warehouse the size of a small aircraft hangar. Motorised roller-doors closed behind the vehicle. Driving past, Michael saw a large sign painted on the corrugated front: 'Southern Fruits plc—Importers and Suppliers'.

They halted a hundred metres away, blending inconspicuously among the other cars parked on the light industrial estate.

Throughout the day they observed the movements of fruit merchants stopping to purchase produce.

The vans would drive up to the roller-doors and within seconds a man would appear from a small opening in the corner of the shutter. After checking the driver's credentials he would disappear back inside and the roller-door would lift allowing the vehicle to enter.

A quick glance at a telephone directory elicited the number of Southern Fruits.

17 July 1985

David came up with a plan.

At worst, they would be caught, tried and convicted, then sentenced to imprisonment—perhaps for life. Michael confessed that he found the risk acceptable—at best, he would deal with Boshoff.

The hire car was exchanged for a van which David parked nearer to the warehouse. He waited while Michael dialled from a nearby call-box.

A gruff voice answered, 'Southern Fruits.'

'What's your price on grapes, plums and oranges?' Michael asked.

'No plums mate, we only got everything else.'

'Right!' he said. 'We're on our way.'

'Better make it snappy, they're going fast—what's your trader's number?'

'Don't have one. Why! Do we need one? We're paying cash—opened our stall at the market last week,' Michael lied.

There was a moment's hesitation at the other end. 'All right, but report to the foreman and register when you get here.' The telephone went dead.

Adrenaline had Michael running back to David. 'Get going, I think we just got lucky.'

Already there were half a dozen traders with assorted vehicles in the queue. Drawing into the line they observed an old van come out of the warehouse. Fully laden it moved off down the road, rolling as a boat caught in a rough sea. Its place was quickly taken by the next vehicle.

They joined the traders who had left their vehicles to stand around chatting in the entrance. Inside, the staff were rushed off their feet, frantically toiling to move the fruit off the floor before the end of the day's trading and make room for the next shipment of apples due in the following morning. Michael nudged David, his eyes indicating the arrowed sign overhead which read: 'Gents'.

Nonchalantly, they sauntered past the loading bays and slipped through the door, out of sight of the men loading cases of fruit into the waiting vehicles. They were in a short corridor adjoining a long passage that ran the entire length of the building. It became clear that the greater part of the warehouse was partitioned off from the work area at street level. Ignoring the 'Gents' door to his left, Michael entered the long passage. Glancing sideways he saw at least a dozen other doors, and walked up to the one directly in front. He stepped inside. Two men, busy at their desks, looked up.

'Sorry, I'm after the 'Gents'.' Backing out, the men returned to their tasks. He made his way back to the toilet.

Once inside the small cubicle they fell to whispering. 'Where do we go from here?' Michael asked while washing his hands.

'Back to the van,' David sounded worried, 'before we cause a traffic jam out there and have someone come in here to look for us.'

Up front the vehicles moved forward and David edged their van along. They sat thinking what to do next. Michael felt sure this operation was a front for something else and, Boshoff was somewhere inside, even though they could not say with any certainty if he had been in the black saloon earlier in the day. So far, they had succeeded in entering the premises and, apart from having found the passage, had achieved very little else.

Pulling into a loading bay Michael said, 'Okay, this is it. You buy grapes or whatever and I'll go and take another look.' He handed David his wallet. Swinging his feet to the ground he added, 'I'll be back in ten minutes.'

Michael passed through the door they had entered earlier, into the short corridor. He peered around the corner. The long, brightly lit passage stretched away before him. He knew instinctively that Andries Boshoff's office would be at the far end. He went forward slowly.

Suddenly, a woman stepped out of an office farther down the passage and came towards him. Michael hesitated: another narrow passage opened to his right. At the end, there was a flight of metal stairs. Putting his head down he turned and took the stairs two at a time.

Reaching the landing he saw there were four glass-partitioned cubicles on the floor above. Inside the first compartment was a white-coated technician who wore rubber gloves, his head bent over what appeared to be a small operating table. He was deftly wielding some kind of thin instrument. It all appeared very clinical. Unaware that he was being observed the man went about his work. On closer inspection he seemed to be dissecting something. As Michael edged nearer, he saw to his astonishment that the technician was slicing apples. The man in the next cubicle was doing exactly the same thing. He walked on. The third compartment was unoccupied. He tried the door. It was unlocked and he slipped inside, thankful the lights were off. If anyone chanced to walk by, the relative darkness of the room offered some protection against discovery.

Michael moved towards the glass-panelled partition wall. He watched the technician take an apple from a fruit box and hold it to the bright light on his table, turning it around slowly. He examined it carefully, then threw it into another box. He repeated this procedure several times. Suddenly it dawned on Michael that he wasn't inspecting the apple at all: he was looking at the small, oval stickers stuck to the fruit.

The man, as if to confirm this, found what he was searching for and gently peeled away the 'Cape' export sticker and, placing the apple on the table, carefully sliced it in half. Using tweezers, he dextrously removed a small object from the core of the fruit before discarding the halves into a waste bin. He rinsed the object of interest in a tumbler of clear liquid, then held it up to the lamp.

One could not mistake the iridescent glitter of fiery colour and light which flashed about the cubicle from the stone, before it was placed in a small metal box. Michael saw that the box contained a number of similar objects. The technician's hand reached for another apple.

'Diamonds!' Michael exclaimed softly.

Suddenly the overhead fluorescent light flashed on.

'Ja, Mr Bernstein, you are quite right. They are cut diamonds, from our glorious Skeleton Coast.' A young man stood in the doorway, his hand still on the light switch. The plastic stock of a Heckler & Koch was firmly clamped under his other arm and held in a determined grip. His hand moved from the switch and he patted the gun affectionately. 'Don't do anything foolish,' he whispered hoarsely.

Michael recognised him instantly. The sound was different now. He was the youth David had almost killed outside the King's Peg. His neck was in a brace—and his voice strained. He appeared too calm and too confident for Michael to try anything. He had not heard him enter and there was nothing he could do, except stare in utter surprise. The young man was older than he had first supposed and Michael became aware that the technicians had stopped what they were doing to watch what was happening.

'Meneer Boshoff has been expecting you. How very clever of you to find us, when we gave you the address.' The words were laced with sarcasm. 'Unfortunately not clever enough! You missed the security camera in the passage.' He shook his head at such stupidity.

Michael was stunned, 'Jan!'

Jan had betrayed him. Of course, Carla! What had he expected from Boshoff's son-in-law? His act had been so damn convincing right up to his departure at the airport, Michael thought.

The young man moved away from the door; the gun trained steadily at Michael's chest. He moved over to the glass panel where Michael stood. Elation at his success of having captured Michael put the young man into an expansive mood. 'No heroics' please—you'd be dead before you could even touch me.' He smiled. 'This gun is capable of firing off three rounds almost instantly.'

Michael stood still. He said nothing.

'You see, our technicians are sorting apples from Mr Boshoff's estate. They are imported weekly from the Cape and require careful inspection. Do you not agree?' He gestured towards the technicians who immediately dropped their heads and turned back to their work. 'We place a small export sticker on each one. Some of those stickers are a little different from the others.' He seemed pleased with himself.

'But why smuggle diamonds? Boshoff is a wealthy man.'

'Move!' the young man snapped, pointing towards the door with a flick of the gun. He realised he might already have said to much. 'That way,' he ordered. Menacingly he prodded him in the ribs with the gun. 'Do as I say or, so help me, I'll finish you now with the greatest of pleasure.'

Michael saw his finger tighten on the trigger. He did what he was told, retracing his steps past the partitions and down the stairs. Reaching the long passage, following the young man's orders, Michael turned right and walked to the office at the far end, cursing Jan and himself under his breath.

'In here.'

The muzzle of the gun jabbed painfully against his spine.

Andries Boshoff didn't bother to rise from behind his desk, and his smile did not portray any friendliness that Michael could detect.

'I see you have met Gert for a second time. Search him,' Andries barked. 'Then tie the bastard up.'

Michael was bound to a chair. Johan frisked him and removed his weapon, then gave the nylon ropes an extra yank for good measure.

'Thank you, Gert. I trust you have made Mr Bernstein comfortable. Now you may leave us.'

Michael was once more alone with Andries Boshoff.

The thin cord bit cruelly into his wrists and ankles. He tested the knots. Already his hands were becoming numb but he continued to move them in an effort to loosen his bonds, aware that Boshoff was watching him intently.

'Why has it taken you so long to get here? I trust that it was you at the house the other evening?' Andries sniped.

'Your fucking son-in-law set me up.'

'Now, now, Bernstein, I detect a note of bitterness. I had rather hoped you'd get here sooner, but still you've saved me the trouble of calling on you.' He sneered, 'It seems you are more stupid than DuToit. He simply passed on the address to you from my people at the embassy.

'Your people?' Michael was astonished.

'Ja! My employees. You see, I have a vast organisation...' he stopped himself. 'What were you doing upstairs?'

'Looking for you,' Michael realised he was better off stating the facts. 'Your henchman showed me your little diamond scam. I don't understand, Boshoff. You hardly need the money!' Despite his revulsion for the man and all he stood for, Michael found himself being forced to admire the sheer simplicity of Boshoff's imaginative plan.

'Because, my dear fellow, people like you have messed up our country. The day is not far away when we will be forced to leave our African homeland, for good—it is inevitable. Even the young Afrikaner does not have the resolve we once had to uphold our God-given right to protect our heritage and *volk*.'

Boshoff might have had Jan DuToit in mind, Michael thought.

'You of all people, Bernstein, should know that I always plan ahead.'

Andries' laugh sounded more like a hoarse bark than an expression of amusement. 'My plans are, of course, only of academic interest to you now but it would give me great pleasure to tell you how futile your efforts have been. It'll be the last thing you will hear, I can assure you.'

He produced a small handgun from the top drawer and placed it in easy reach on the desk.

'They are extracting the diamonds which fund our new organisation— AXIS. I alone have made possible this vision—AXIS—my lifelong dream.' On average we process a thousand carats of the purest grade every week. De Beers would be proud of our efforts. Believe it or not, I have a stockpile on these premises that could keep most African countries running for the next decade.' He said with fervour, 'Haven't you noticed that people are becoming more right-wing in Europe? Well, we are the ultra-right. I have created something which many believed to be impossible—an alliance of all right-wing political parties throughout the western world. The day is not far off when we shall take over...' he hesitated. 'Anyway, Bernstein, that's something you will not have to concern yourself about.'

'And you're going to head this organisation of yours?' Somehow Michael's sarcasm fell short of its mark.

'I have taken it as far as I can, but age is against me. At least I'll have the satisfaction of knowing that I orchestrated a glorious future; and AXIS would not have come into existence without me.'

Michael played for time. 'I thought you were involved with a right-wing party in South Africa?'

'The ARB was the model for our global movement...a man must fulfil his destiny....' Momentarily Boshoff's concentration seemed to slip, but his hand reached out to touch the gun.

Was he dreaming of wielding power in a new fatherland? Michael wondered.

Boshoff chuckled coldly. 'It's only a question of time before we rid this continent of the likes of you and your Black friends once and for all.' His voice rose higher and he almost spat it out. 'Let the kaffirs have their heathen land and revert to being ignorant savages. Make no mistake! Europe will be for the White race only.'

Michael knew what '...the likes of you' would mean for people like him and fellow Jews.

'You couldn't make it work in South Africa, so what makes you think you'll succeed in Europe...this time round?'

'Very amusing, Bernstein. Suppose I told you that BOSS reports directly to me and then to the Minister of Justice, what would you say?'

Michael said nothing. He waited for Boshoff to continue.

'So you see, I already have an effective global network. Why, we have stockpiles of arms stashed worldwide to start a revolution if necessary, but why bother when you can control governments?'

What he had said was chilling enough, but his next statement Michael found even more alarming.

'I admit we got one thing wrong...the communists were never a threat. In fact our organisation's success is now assured by their support stretching across Europe and the eastern bloc straight to Moscow. We are everywhere. As you must realise, your meeting with Gert and a couple of our men at the pub the other evening was no coincidence.' He smiled, 'We even know the date you and that kaffir arrived in the UK.' He saw the astonishment register on Michael's face.

'You're lying, Boshoff,' though Michael knew he wasn't.

'By now you have probably figured Hammond worked for me, but he was no loss. There are a dozen more like him whom I can turn loose on my enemies as I wish.'

'What are you going to do with me?' Michael asked.

Andries gazed at the ceiling, then folded his arms with a sigh of satisfaction. The gun lay between them on the desktop within easy reach of his hand. 'What indeed...? I am not ready to kill you yet, if that's what you want to know.'

Michael glanced round. The office was furnished lavishly. What was there to stop Boshoff from killing him now? Could it be consideration for these surroundings, or that the noise from the gun on the desk would attract unwanted attention?

'Where is that kaffir friend of yours?' Before Michael could reply, Andries' hand moved to the console. Michael became aware of the security monitor in the corner as it flickered—the view of the security cameras kept changing. There was no sign of the van or, for that matter, David.

'You claim to have been tailing me ever since I got here—you should know.' There was a long silence. 'London, he's attending his cousin's wedding.' But where the hell had David disappeared to, Michael wondered.

Boshoff seemed satisfied with the explanation. He reached for the telephone and dialled. 'Have the boat ready at the jetty for eight o'clock tonight—ja, we have company...' he gave detailed instructions to the person at the other end. And before replacing the receiver he added, '...we will be going out into deep, very deep water.'

Boshoff's smile told Michael that he was the 'company' and was not expected to make the round trip.

In the corner a red light flashed above the security monitor and instantly Michael saw that the alarm had been triggered by the woman he had seen earlier. He watched her walk down the passage and disappear into another office leaving the view empty. Immediately a green light glowed over the monitor. Michael thought what a fool he had been to expect to find Andries Boshoff unprotected and at his mercy. He had naively entered the passage without so much as checking for surveillance equipment.

Anger at himself outweighed his fear. Now John's death would remain unavenged while his own life would be added to the other deaths that lay at Boshoff's door. How many more would die before this madman could be stopped? Besides, there were things he had to know before his life was forfeit.

The one weapon he had left, Michael told himself, was psychology—if he could unhinge Boshoff he might gain an advantage, however slight. He was playing for higher stakes. He had nothing to lose. It was his only chance. At worst, he would go to his death knowing he had caused Boshoff a degree of mental anguish he would never forget.

'Boshoff, what kind of father were you to Carla? You realise it was your selfish ambition that killed her!' He saw instantly he had hit on a raw nerve. He pressed on. 'You should never have ordered your henchmen to attack us. Carla would be alive but for your interference. You should know I heard her screaming when she went over the cliff.' Michael almost choked on the words as he imagined her terror in those final seconds. He wanted her father to feel the full horror of her death.

Andries' face paled with rage leaving livid blotches on his cheeks. He jerked forward in his chair, hands grasping the gun.

For a moment Michael thought he would use it. But almost at once Boshoff relaxed his hold.

He had realised Michael was trying to throw him off-balance. Andries smiled at his victim—two could play at this game—and there were certain things he still wanted to say to Michael before he carried out his execution.

'Let's get one thing straight. It was you who drove the car when Carla was killed!' Michael might have expected that but not what followed.

'Did you know she was nearly four months pregnant, Bernstein?' Andries hissed the words, 'Her first child...my grandchild!'

Michael felt sick—he had no idea—why hadn't she said? He had never seen such naked hatred, made all the more intense because it was directed exclusively at one man—him. He shivered involuntarily.

It made him think of his own son's death.

'Go on, admit it, Boshoff, you murdered my son, John. It was you who issued the order for the *P.carinii* to be used against me. How was it that John was infected instead of me?'

For a moment Andries Boshoff sat there watching Michael speculatively through half-closed eyes. He shifted in his seat and, placing his right elbow on the desk, aimed the gun at Michael's forehead.

'Use the *Pneumocystis carinii* pneumonia, on you? What a charming idea.' He laughed quietly.

Michael's skin crawled. The man was undoubtedly mad.

'On your son? No! Don't be so bloody stupid. We had no further interest in you once you left South Africa. We knew where you were. In fact we had to stop Van Heerden from going after you. He did not take kindly to you rearranging his face when you escaped. Your return presented a threat and you left us no option but to let Van Heerden loose.'

Reaching into the drawer of his desk he pulled out a thick dossier. He flipped through the pages until he found what he was looking for. 'Here is a transcript of your call to your brother made on 27 February, this year. You said and I quote '...hoping to visit you and your family soon.'.' He shut the folder and looked up at Michael. 'You should not have meddled in our affairs, Bernstein. If you had stayed away, your Irish friend would still be alive. I understand Van Heerden did a good job on the laboratory.'

Michael found it difficult to respond. Boshoff was right. He had been responsible for Paddy's death, even if indirectly.

Desperately he fought for some way to turn the tables on Boshoff.

'You can't get away with this, Boshoff. I know you sold the *P.carinii* and the *Marburg* virus to the Rhodesians. We have proof.'

For a fleeting moment Michael thought he might have succeeded in putting Andries on the defensive.

'Ja! We sold your mutated pathogen to the Rhodesians and ja, it was mildly effective in the field; but as for proof, I think it is safe to say that having lost your computer disk—which incidentally is now in my possession—you haven't much to go on! Or else why wait this long to threaten me?' Andries had not finished.

'Another thing, Tinus was a brilliant scientist. You think you changed the *P.carinii*, as you call it? Well, let me tell you a few truths. Tinus engineered the *P.carinii* long before you and these so-called 'geneticists' came along, unfortunately too late for the Fuhrer. It was designed to have been a cost-effective way of eradicating you Jews.'

'You're bluffing, Boshoff. I don't believe you.' Michael could think of nothing else to say.

'Is that what you think? Tell me then, where was the human form of this pathogen before the war? You see, I am right. There was only the rodent form and it was that which Tinus changed.'

'So what, this fact doesn't excuse you for using the *P.carinii* as a biological weapon. People talk, you won't be able to hide this...'

'My dear fellow we already have. I understood from Tinus that the first human trial on your young colleague at the Laboratories was largely a success, though no doubt you will disagree.' He sneered, 'And your friends on the mountain...a well placed boot in one of their faces put paid to them. I suppose it is regrettable that we had to waste so much talent.'

They had killed Paul and the others. Michael fought not to accept what he was hearing—he tugged at the thin cords binding his hands to the chair, oblivious to the pain as the unyielding nylon cut deeper into his wrists.

Boshoff's eyes never left him for a second.

'You really don't know, do you?' Andries was still sneering. 'You! You screwed it up. At the time no one knew that your *P.carinii* would make the *Marburg* virus so unstable.'

'*Marburg* unstable! What do you mean?' Michael had not idea what Boshoff was driving at, though he was sure it would be extremely unpleasant. He was equally certain that nothing was going to stop Andries from deriving the greatest pleasure from telling him exactly what it was.

The longer he spoke the more animated Andries became.

'*Marburg*! Again, it was Tinus who created this virus. He brilliantly conceived *Marburg* as a means of eradicating the Blacks from our land. He showed it to his friends in the new Germany but they seemed not to understand what he had achieved.' He watched closely Michael's pained expression.

'You know the weird thing, Tinus did all the work and they named it after his home town in the fatherland. But it was you, a Jew, who caused the *Marburg* virus to change.' He sat back in his chair and laughed at what he saw as the irony of the situation.

'No, you still don't get it, do you! You were too concerned with your project and the monkeys to find out what you had done to the *P.carinii*. Afterwards, Tinus went back to the laboratory and retrieved the material you had created. He had taken the *P.carinii* as far as he could, but you manufactured the vehicle we needed to carry the *Marburg* virus to our enemies.

He could see the lack of comprehension in Michael's eyes.

'As you know, a virus is a parasite and needs a host. You created just that. How? We may never know but your *P.carinii* mutated in that 'chemical cocktail' of yours and played host to the *Marburg* virus, which normally would never have happened, except—your *P.carinii* survived.'

Michael's face mirrored the horror he felt, beginning to appreciate the part he personally had played. It has been a biological accident and he bore the responsibility. Under certain conditions the *P.carinii* had mutated. In a thousand years he might never be able to repeat that experiment.

'But not even Tinus realised what would happen next. Ja! Your tampering turned *Marburg* into a terrifying mutant virus, antigenically distinct, otherwise virtually indistinguishable, from his original *Marburg.*'

He smiled as Michael pulled back—shocked.

'It was spawned in your *P.carinii* and is one of the deadliest known to man. Ja! The variant you are indirectly responsible for creating is, *Ebola*, now feared more than any other by the world's foremost microbiologists.' He shook his head. 'And you managed to create this thing by accident!!'

He saw a glazed look in Michael's eyes, and yelled triumphantly, 'You fool, Bernstein, it was not only the development of the *P.carinii* but also this unintentional benefit derived from your research—the *Ebola* parasite inside the *P.carinii,* code-named PF657—that we subsequently sold to the Rhodesians. There was no other way in which we could deploy this virus selectively as a weapon. Then that virus changed everything.'

'But I thought PF657 was the *P.carinii!*' Michael said more to himself; he desperately wanted to find out what Boshoff's devious mind was now referring to—something he had said. 'What do you mean, 'that changed everything'?' He had started to sweat.

'But of course you don't understand you ignorant Jew!' Andries uttered in a snarling tone. 'Let me enlighten you. Your *P.carinii* host and its *Ebola* parasite were administered to ZIPRA and ZANLA soldiers captured in Rhodesia. They were then released; a conciliatory gesture on the part of the Rhodesian Government I think they called it.'

Michael watched Andries' expression of deranged pleasure, and his eyes narrow as he continued: 'It was calculated that when they returned to their bases in Zambia and Mozambique the diseases would spread rapidly and rid Rhodesia of the terrorist threat, while at the same time reduce its growing Black population. Don't you see? Apartheid and racial segregation was there to protect us. Unfortunately we did not find out until too late that the prostitutes servicing the ZIPRA camps also worked in the brothels in the Copper-belt towns near the Zaire border.'

Michael failed to see the significance of point he was making, when Andries brought the relevance of his last statement horribly home.

'The *Ebola* virus, caused by your tampering, was responsible for the AIDS mutation.'

Michael mouthed awkwardly, 'No! No. It's not possible.' Suddenly it jarred his memory. Something that the Cape Doctor had said before he died had puzzled him at the time. He assumed Tinus had made a mistake when saying: '...you are responsible for this terrible 'virus'...and its 'mutations'.' The *P.carinii* was a fungus, not a virus. Of course! Had Tinus been referring to *Ebola* and *HIV*?

Michael knew he had lost the battle with Boshoff—he was also losing a grip on reality. He desperately wanted to believe Boshoff was lying.

He felt dizzy and struggled to hold the nausea back. He strained again at his bonds and felt them give slightly.

Andries, savouring every moment of Michael's mental demise, reveling in the thought that he had achieved his aim. Watching Michael now, agonising over this form of torture, gave him an almost physical pleasure. He glanced at the monitor—it was clear. He licked his lips and continued.

'Let me explain it to you this way. Your *Ebola* was even more lethal that *Marburg*. Then, something unexpected happened. Tinus believed *HIV's* precursor had been around for some while—until then it had been relatively stable. But by chance it came into contact with the altered morphology of your *Ebola*—causing it to change...ja, into something far more sinister.' Andries' glower was intensely hostile as he watched the anguish almost etched on Michael's face.

'How could that have happened!' Michael pleaded.

Andries' pleasure was verging on the ecstatic as he explained. 'I was told that your *Ebola* altered the genetic material in the AIDS virus,' and went on. 'I remember Tinus calling *HIV* by some other name, saying it was a harmless simian virus before it was affected by your mutant *Ebola*. Tinus said the altered genetic material in *HIV* had left it unpredictable and unstable, causing it to become lethal and ever-changing.' He watched intently as Michael tried to come to terms with his revelations.

'Tinus told me he was convinced that at this point AIDS was born...largely thanks to you.'

Michael's voice faltered. 'But how could it have spread?'

'Truckers. Those using the highway between Zaire and Zambia frequented the same brothels of the Copper-belt mining towns as the terrorists.* Possibly they still do. Anyway from there it was carried north. It was only a question of time before a trucker, infected with the harmless type of virus which Tinus mentioned, encountered your *Ebola*. Tinus estimated that within hours it would have mutated into *HIV*. From that moment on *HIV* was onto the Kinshasa Highway and moving right across Central Africa.'

It was frighteningly plausible. What had he done? Was he responsible for unleashing a deadly plague on an unsuspecting world? Bewildered, Michael tried desperately to find some other reason for the spread of AIDS, something that absolved him of such unbearable responsibility. He blurted out, 'But they say *HIV* was probably transmitted initially through contact with monkeys?'

Andries shook his head. 'No, you're reaching Bernstein. Not according to the Cape Doctor.' He wasn't going to stop now. 'That amused Tinus. He still has all you scientists around the world trying to find the hosts for *HIV* and *Ebola,* but without success, I'm afraid. We know, that man was the

411

primary contact for *Ebola* and that the vervet monkey was as much a victim as man himself, in fact even more so. Tinus always maintained it spread to the primates through contact with the Black drivers who often buy them from children at the roadside, either as pets or for resale to animal shippers in Zaire. He believed it quite probable that one of these animals bit its *Ebola*-infected owner. The virus kills monkeys as efficiently as it kills men.'

Michael was stunned. With a single bite that primate had unleashed untold horrors on humanity—the *Ebola* virus had jumped from man to primate—and the simian virus had jumped from primate to man, then, in contact with the *Ebola virus*, it had mutated into *HIV*. All he wanted was that Boshoff's voice would stop tormenting him. But Andries hadn't finished yet.

'Then, as you know, AIDS was carried from Africa to the US, we believe through the gay community. Finally—inevitably I suppose—it had to pass on to heterosexuals.'*

Michael felt as if someone had his head and shoulders in a vice and was applying pressure slowly. His breathing became more erratic and he could taste salt as beads of perspiration ran down his face. 'You're insane Boshoff. It can't be true.' His speech was slurred and his mouth dry.

'Please yourself. Tinus convinced me.' Boshoff's voice sounded even more mocking than before.

'At the time, in Kinshasa there were cases of weight loss, swollen lymph glands and aggressive Kaposi's sarcoma and in some cases the fungal infection, cryptococcosis. I understand these are symptoms often associated with AIDS. Yes or no?'*

He came round the desk and stopped to see if Michael was still capable of understanding what he was saying.

'Now, Bernstein, we have a disease that has reached pandemic proportions and is a global disaster—thanks to you. Proud of that?'

He shook Michael's shoulders as if to ram home his point. His efforts were needless. Michael reeled back, convinced that he was guilty of all the accusations levelled at him by his persecutor.

He was responsible for AIDS.

Michael felt reality slipping away. His skin was cold and clammy.

Andries had achieved the psychological destruction of the man he hated. There was no need to say more but he could not resist the temptation to twist the knife one more time. He wiped away the spittle which had formed at the corner of his mouth in the excitement of taunting his enemy and at the thought of what he was about to say.

'Do you realise,' he was shouting now, 'that Tinus was well on the way to reprogramming the *HIV* virus and finding a cure for AIDS? Now, thanks to you, the only hope of developing it is gone!'

Andries Boshoff could contain himself no longer. He positively gloated as he spoke.

'You must by now realise that you in fact caused your own son's death?'

The full impact of Boshoff's words hit Michael like a physical force. His face contorted, 'No, you're wrong, you're wrong...' Something snapped in his head. His mind reeled and sought the only possible refuge from the horror he felt. Michael's head dropped forward onto his chest and his shoulders sagged. He lapsed into unconsciousness—only his bonds stopping him from slumping to the floor.

Boshoff grabbed Michael by the hair, pulling his head upright. 'Come back, you bastard, I haven't finished with you,' he screamed with rage but the glazed eyes and lolling head told him Michael was beyond his reach.

There seemed no point in delaying the inevitable. He would enjoy the final pleasure of killing Michael. He raised his gun.

A single shot rang out.

The bullet hit Andries at the base of the skull, the force spinning him round, wide-eyed to face David before crashing to the floor.

David stood in the doorway with his gun trained on the prone body.

Andries did not move.

David had been outside the door long enough to overhear the end of the conversation. He quickly checked Boshoff for a pulse before pocketing his gun—there was none!

He now turned his attention to his friend and winced at the sight of the bloody marks gouged out of Michael's wrists, as his penknife hacked through the cords which held the limp figure.

'Come on, let's get you out of here.' He heaved Michael over his shoulder. The weight made him stagger slightly. He peered round the door. There was as yet no one in the passage but as he started down towards the corridor—his load seeming to become heavier with each pace—doors opened and heads began to appear.

Gert stepped out into the passage drawing his gun. Recognition dawned, as he realised that in front of him was the attacker from outside the pub, and he hesitated for a fatal second. Two rounds from David's Walther tore into his chest. The force of the impact threw him backwards into his office as his finger tightened on the trigger. A stream of bullets buried themselves harmlessly in the ceiling. Doors slammed shut.

Heads turned as David burst into the main warehouse. No one moved. No one was going to tackle a large man carrying an unconscious figure and waving an obviously loaded gun.

David fired three shots through the metal roof. The noise was ear-splitting. Pandemonium broke out as traders and workmen threw aside boxes of fruit. Apples rolled everywhere underfoot. Men slipped and fell; others fought to reach the cover of crates and vans. The driver of the forklift leapt from his machine. Out of control, it careered into the side of a waiting truck.

The confusion enabled David to reach the parked van. He threw Michael into the back, face down onto the open crates of fruit, slammed the rear doors and rushed to the front. The engine fired at the first turn of the key and he gunned the motor. With gathering speed he headed round the corner and away from the warehouse.

Five miles out of Southampton David pulled into a lay-by. Seconds later he climbed into the back and propped Michael up against the side of the van. He checked his pulse; it was rapid and weak. His patient's breathing was shallow. But it was the dilated pupils and the lack of reflex responses which caused him the most concern. Michael's limbs were now unusually rigid. He made no sign of recognition. After several minutes David straightened up, his examination complete. He shook his head. Michael was showing all the clinical signs of cataplectic shock.

David returned to the cab and drove on, leaving Southampton behind. He could not yet be certain that Boshoff's men were not following. He knew only that he had to keep under control the panic he was feeling.

When a motorway service sign came up, he took the slip road and swung off and headed for the parking area. Leaving the van parked well away from other vehicles, he dashed inside to find a telephone.

He punched the number and waited impatiently. The receiver was picked up on the fourth ring.

'Josh, it's me David. Look, we're in deep trouble,' the desperation was in his voice. 'Boshoff's dead and Mike's in a bad way. We were involved...'

'Slow down, Dave. Okay, what's wrong with Michael?' Josh asked.

'There's no injuries but he is comatose. I saw cases like this in the war—traumatised, he's in severe shock. We're at a motorway service area a few miles outside London. I need help. What should I do?'

'Fine, keep calm and leave it to me. Bring him here. No, on second thoughts, take him to my apartment in Knightsbridge. We'll deal with this from there.'

'Josh, it's very serious. He may even have suffered a stroke brought on by shock. He needs treatment. God only knows what Boshoff did to him. It'll take time to bring him round. Maybe we should try to contact his friends in the US—see if they can help to have him admitted to a clinic over there.'

'I will do what I can but let's take it one step at a time. For now, get going. See you in an hour's time.'

414

David dropped the telephone and ran back to the van. He pulled the rear doors open—nothing inside had changed. Michael's vacant eyes still stared unseeing at the roof. Suddenly David realised it could take months if not years for him to recover and even then there would be no guarantees that any such recovery would bring his friend back to complete normality.

Michael uttered a throaty, guttural sound. David stared, half expecting him to say something, but there was no further response. As yet, there was no telling what might have happened to his mind.

oOo

'Morning Dr Nyamande, if you will follow me.' David walked next to the nurse, listening. 'He's been very comfortable here and his condition has stabilised. The specialists are pleased with his progress'

They reached the end of the corridor and she pointed to a figure who sat with his back to them, across the lawn down by the pond.

He reached the bench, pausing, he put his hand on the other's shoulder. 'Hello Mike, it's been a long time.' He walked round to face his friend. There was no sign of recognition. Nothing at all!

David sat for a long while next to Michael with a heavy heart, telling him about Josh, Nandi and about remarkable new political developments in South Africa.

It was time to leave and he reached out and held Michael's hand. He told him he would be back again next year to see him and how much he missed him. Suddenly he felt his hand being squeezed. He studied the eyes but they remained dull and almost lifeless. He held the now limp hand a moment longer.

'I know you are out of reach, Mike, but whatever it is he said about AIDS, you're not to blame. Apartheid's responsible for this—it's damned us all.'

Jan DuToit kept his promise.

*On 11 September 1985, the South African Government agreed to restore citizenship to 15 million Blacks living in the 'homelands'.**

*In January 1989, F W de Klerk was elected as the leader of the Nationalist Party and sworn in as State President. Few then realised that the country was on the long road back to sanity.**

*On 11 February 1990, Nelson Mandela was freed and in the same month the ban on the ANC was lifted.**

*So, finally, after an epic struggle, on 27 April 1994, elections in South Africa led to majority rule and an end to apartheid as an official instrument of government policy and the last White racist régime in Africa.**

EPILOGUE

Of course the idea that AIDS was the result of an engineered biological weapon is pure conjecture. However, this novel has attempted to address these questions:

> *Did White extremists in Southern Africa have the resources and expertise to engineer a biological weapon?*

> *If they possessed such a weapon, were the proponents of apartheid capable of using it?*

> *Where could they have 'safely' deployed such a weapon? And, against whom would they have used it?*

Then there are the incidents surrounding this period which deserve closer scrutiny and other questions which remain unanswered.

Late in December 1979, in the US, a chance remark to the author from an ex-serviceman prompted the writing of this novel. The soldier stated that he had been one of a contingent of US troops, en route from Vietnam, who had been actively deployed in the Rhodesian Bush War. They were given no reasons for being in Africa. Engaging the local militia and having killed a number of persons on their march over several days to the coast, they were picked up by the US navy and shipped home. The soldier was not aware of any further involvement in Rhodesia by the US.

> *What were they doing there?*

When considering the vastly superior military strength, wealth and resources of Rhodesia and South Africa, there appears to have been no valid reason for them having relinquished power to their 'Black' enemies.

> *Why did both White governments capitulate?*

Harold Wilson suddenly resigned in 1976.

> *What was the reason behind his resignation?*

President Vorster resigned in 1978.

> *What was behind his resignation?*

When William Colby, then DCI of the CIA, exposed its activities and assassinations to a Congressional hearing, as a result of the Watergate scandal which had uncovered covert operations by US intelligence, the CIA was publicly claimed to be an agency '...out of control'. Colby was dismissed by President Ford; and George Bush, the first politician appointee, was installed in January 1976. Bush was given the express task of 'keeping a lid on' the CIA's affairs—these were not for the public domain. The following year the Republicans lost the election and the new President, Jimmy Carter, immediately removed George Bush from office after only fifty weeks and four days in the job.

> *What lay behind Bush's appointment that was so important that it had to be covered up in 1976?*

Undisclosed talks between Henry Kissinger and Ian Smith took place in South Africa on 18 September 1976.

> *What transpired so that, in a space of hours, the Rhodesian Prime Minister did a complete volte-face on his stance against Black majority rule?*

Kissinger made one serious gaffe during negotiations with Smith: he kept on making references to 'our own intelligence' services in Rhodesia. Officially all ties with the US had ceased in 1969. By the continual mention of their presence, he embarrassed the CIA who had told the President and State Department that they had been withdrawn.

> *What were the CIA doing there? What was behind William Colby's resignation and his involvement with the CIO?*

The Russian Ambassador to Zambia, Salodnikov, was a general in the KGB.

> *What was so important in that part of the world to warrant the personal attention of one of the heads from the KGB?*

The Rhodesian Bush War lasted thirteen years and claimed 30,000 lives (no account is made here of the combined loss of life as a result of all the White racist régimes in Southern Africa).

> *Why the change in heart on their racist policies? A cover-up or something more sinister?*

418

The continued annihilation of villages and refugee centres in Mozambique by the Rhodesian security forces—with no consideration given to innocent civilians, the elderly, women and children—seems incongruous with their Christian ideals.

Why was the war protracted and these atrocities committed after agreement had been reached on Kissinger's proposals?

The Rhodesian security forces operated a Biological Warfare Unit during the Bush War.

Why?

Numerous true incidents have been incorporated into this novel, such as the account of Operation Eland when, in August 1976, the Selous Scouts attacked the ZANLA base at Nyadzonya, Mozambique, and reported killing 340 'terrorists' and 30 FRELIMO soldiers. The UN later claimed the dead to be nearer a thousand. If this figure is correct it would have meant the total annihilation of all the occupants of the camp. ZANLA claimed the majority of the victims were refugees and not soldiers.

The offensive military operations undertaken by the Selous Scouts were accompanied by specific orders to take captive and bring back hospitalised patients from 'terrorist' bases in Mozambique during the raids—for interrogation! This seems strange in the extreme, whereas there were over a thousand healthy persons at Nyadzonya camp at the time of this attack, who could have been taken for interrogation.

Why were the Selous Scouts instructed to take captive diseased or injured persons from the hospital, where it would clearly be impossible to identify their military rank or, indeed, ascertain whether they were civilians rather than soldiers?

The Selous Scouts did not comply with this directive. It was said a chance tracer ignited the grass roof and all the patients were burnt to death.

Were they aware of the risks of infection from any captives or did they simply ignore the order that jeopardised the safety of the mission as this suggests?

Another equally strange event was the Karima Village massacre in Rhodesia, near the border, which was described by the media as a 'mysterious incident'. On the evening of 12 June 1975, the Rhodesian security forces opened fire on a gathering of men, women, and children. A Rhodesian Government communiqué denied their involvement and said that only twenty had been killed—by Black terrorists! The Rhodesian security forces removed all the bodies and told bereaved relatives that the corpses had been burned on a hill a few kilometres away. Later, the security forces returned and insisted on supervising the burial of the 'blood-soaked clothing' that remained behind.

What lay behind this callous and unexplained incident?

The Rhodesian security forces had a policy shortly after UDI, whereby they released certain captive terrorists, who were returned across the border into neighbouring countries to their *comrades*, purportedly to try to persuade them to lay down their arms.

Is this a plausible explanation?

Here are some documented facts and incidents in the public record.

South African, White, right-wing extremist, Eugene Terre Blanche, discussed plans to spread syphilis, caused by the protozoa *Treponema pallidum*, at the Sun City holiday resort in the Bophuthatswana Black homeland. He wanted to infect anyone crossing the 'colour bar'.

The South African (Nationalist) Government remained fanatical throughout the fifties well into the eighties, condoning the brutality of BOSS. Their agency went to extraordinary lengths, internally and externally, to murder opponents of the apartheid system.

After the second world war, many Nazi war criminals found refuge in South Africa.

The South African (Nationalist) Government supplied arms and assistance to: the RENAMO forces in Mozambique; the Rhodesian Government; and UNITA in Angola—thus bearing responsibility for the destabilisation of Southern Africa. The South African Defence Force made frequent incursions into neighbouring states to kill or capture members of the ANC.

South African medical research into the immune system was extremely advanced as a result of the work of the pioneering heart transplant unit at Groote Schuur Hospital in Cape Town.

Transferable antibiotic-resistance can occur when genetic material (plasmids) drifts from one micro-organism into another, thereby conferring on that pathogen the resistance message. The transfer is not confined to one species and cross-species transmission can occur which may even result in a multiple drug-resistance profile (to many antibiotics).

It is entirely possible that, either by accident or design, *HIV* could have been changed irrevocably by the transference of genetic material from another species.

There is strong support from leading academics in the field of genetics for the theory that a simian virus might be associated with *HIV* through cross-species transmission.

The *Marburg* and *Ebola* viruses are virtually indistinguishable: the only differences are antigenic. There have been sporadic outbreaks around the world. First isolated in Germany in 1967.

The *Marburg, Ebola, HIV* viruses and AIDS are said to have their origins in Central Africa.

A sudden outbreak of *Ebola* in Zaire 1976, had an international team of investigators holding its breath. At the epicentre of the epidemic, 13 out of 17 doctors and nurses at the hospital, lay dead. It was asked: had the Andromeda strain arrived? Again, in 1995 the disease raged. In Kikwit, Zaire, out of 315 people contracting the disease, 244 died. It has been stated: the mortality rate can range to nearly 90% in those infected.

The first outbreaks of *Pneumocystis carinii* pneumonia (PCP) occurred after the second world war, affecting holocaust victims and undernourished children throughout Europe. A rodent form had been isolated previously but was never found in humans.

Ian Smith, the former Prime Minister of Rhodesia, is quoted as saying that there would never be Black rule in Rhodesia in his lifetime.

Dates of Interest

1971

3 September—A comprehensive report by the British-based International Defence & Aid Fund, entitled Terror at Tete (Mozambique), describes how Rhodesian soldiers arrive at Singa Village, in the Mukumbura district, and shoot the villagers—men, women, and children.

A report by Portuguese army officers, published in April 1974, confirms Rhodesian activity 100 kilometres inside Mozambique. '...Operations consist of speedy paratroop actions in specified areas and the liquidation of any human lives (there being no military or civilian prisoners) and a return to their bases in Rhodesia.'

1972

21 December—ZANLA attacks Centenary [area] farmstead of Marc de Borchgrave at night. No one is hurt on *Altena* farm. The family moves in with neighbour Archie Dalgleish of *Whistlefield* farm. Remarkably, when Whistlefield is attacked—on 23 December—once more, nobody is hurt. Land-mines set on the approach road kill a soldier and injure others. A new ZANLA offensive begins with the attack on *Altena* farm; it becomes known as Operation Hurricane, marking an escalation in the war.
The same day Ian Smith addresses a Rotary Club meeting where he says that he knows what is best for Rhodesia because he knows 'his' Bantu!

1975

February—Two hitchhikers travelling through Zimbabwe near the Mozambique border contracted the *Marburg* virus. One subsequently dies in Johannesburg. This is the first outbreak of *Marburg* disease on record in Africa. The case is well documented.

18 March—Herbert Chitepo, Southern Rhodesia's first African barrister and the National Chairman of ZANU, is killed by car bomb in Lusaka. The Rhodesians deny any involvement.

1976

June—Student uprising in South Africa. In Soweto pupils take to the street in protest against the inferior educational system for Blacks. Over 600 children are killed and hundreds of youths leave to join the ANC in neighbouring countries

September—US Secretary of State, Henry Kissinger, makes an impromptu visit to South Africa; the Rhodesian Prime Minister, Ian Smith, flies twice to South Africa in one week and agrees to the terms set out by the US Secretary of State...without protest!

September—Ian Smith announces majority rule 'within two years'.

1977
23 November—Rhodesian security forces raid two ZANLA bases in Mozambique killing over 1200 people in Tembue and Chimoio camps—again, including women and children.

Several air and land strikes are launched by the Rhodesian security forces against the main 'terrorist' bases in Mozambique. The inhabitants of several other villages and camps are annihilated and the bodies buried in mass graves.

1978
March—In Salisbury a transitional government is sworn in, ending White rule in Rhodesia.

Shortly afterwards the South African Prime Minister Vorster resigns the premiership and then the presidentship.

1982
South African forces raid ANC bases in Lesotho and 42 people are killed. ANC mission in London is bombed.

1985
June—South African troops openly carry out armed raids on the ANC offices in Botswana.

10 August—Leading anti-apartheid campaigner Rev Allan Boesak is arrested as 40 die in riots.

16 August—Bishop Desmond Tutu, the Anglican bishop of Johannesburg, says the chances of peaceful change in South Africa are virtually nil.

23 August—In South Africa 500 children are detained for boycotting schools. Many simply disappear.

6 September—President Botha closes half the Coloured schools in the Western Cape. Many die in a week of clashes with the South African Defence Force.

2 October—Rock Hudson dies of AIDS.

1986
May—South Africa forces raid ANC bases in Botswana, Zimbabwe and Zambia.

June—In South Africa over 20,000 anti-apartheid activists are arrested within three months. A national State of Emergency declared.

19 October—President Samora Machel is killed when his aircraft crashes under mysterious circumstances. Returning from talks with other African leaders, his plane overshoots the Mozambique capital and flies on over the Mozambique border. It comes down deep inside South African territory some 60 kilometres from Maputo. No cause for the crash is found, although it is claimed that the South Africans used a radio beacon to disorientate the Russian flight crew.

December—BOSS raid the homes of ANC supporters in Swaziland, killing several innocent civilians and capturing others.

BOSS continue to bomb the ANC offices in neighbouring countries in its unremitting war against those it sees as enemies of the state.

Under the Emergency Regulations some 25,000 people are imprisoned in South Africa without trial—10,000 are children under the age of eighteen.

1987
July—The southern Mozambique town of Homoine is attacked by RENAMO. 424 people are massacred. South Africa is accused of complicity.

The World Health Organisation reports 51,535 cases of AIDS; it estimates that there are at least 10 million people who have been infected worldwide. By the turn of the century there could be 100 million carriers of the disease.

Glossary

abakwetha	Xhosa—meaning initiates to the tribal ritual of attaining manhood.
amagqirha	Xhosa—meaning witch-doctors.
Amandla!	Zulu—meaning 'Power is ours', adopted as a motto by those opposed to apartheid.
apartheid	Afrikaans—meaning to keep 'groups apart'.
biltong	Afrikaans—salted, sun-dried meat, favoured by whites in Southern Africa.
camarada	Portuguese—used by FRELIMO and ZANLA meaning *comrade*. Became synonymous with guerrilla and *mukoma*.
chimbwido	Shona—word to describe a young girl who helped the guerrillas with general duties or gathering intelligence.
chimurenga	Derived from Shona—meaning rebellion or revolution. Used by ZANLA to describe 'rebels' or 'fighters' of ZANLA within the Chimurenga (Army's) High Command.
china	Slang—meaning friend; used frequently by troopers of the Rhodesian Light Infantry.
chindunduma	Shona—meaning deposits dug out of a mine; mine dumps.
comrade	A word used by the Black South African ANC forces to signify a member and also used by the freedom fighters of Zimbabwe.
dambo	Short stretch of water left on an otherwise dried up river course.
dompas	Afrikaans—passbook held by every Black South African during the apartheid era.
floppies	Slang—to describe dead terrorists; used by the Rhodesian security forces.
gat	Slang—a firearm/rifle; used by the Rhodesian security forces.
hippo	A troop carrier designed by the South African Defence Force to deflect an explosion from a land-mine away from its occupants.
kaffir	Derogatory term used often by whites—same as nigger or *munt*.
kraal	Afrikaans—to describe a cluster of huts.
koppie	Afrikaans—meaning small hill.
laager	Afrikaans—meaning a defensive circular encampment.

mujiba	Shona—word developed during the Bush War; used to describe a young boy who helped the guerrillas usually as a messenger.
mukoma	Shona—meaning brother; used by Black Zimbabweans with reference to the guerrilla fighters or the 'boys' as they were sometimes called.
munts	A derogatory term used by White Rhodesians to describe Black people. The equivalent of *kaffir* in South Africa or *nigger* in the US.
pathogen	An agent that causes disease—particularly micro-organisms such as bacteria and fungi.
Pungwe Trial	A trial held by ZANLA guerrillas at night to try local informers.
shebeen	Used to descibe an unlicensed Black pub/bar in Southern Africa.
slot	Slang—a Rhodesian military term 'to kill', 'waste' or 'slay' terrorists.
stick	Slang—a Rhodesian military term to describe a small unit of, usually, four to six men.
skuz'apo	A word that developed during the war by the freedom fighters to mean the Selous Scouts, or the 'dirty tricks' unit.
sudza	Shona—meaning maize dough.
terr	Slang—an abbreviation of terrorist; reference to Black freedom fighters who went into exile to join the Zimbabwean liberation armies; used by White Rhodesians.
Umkhonto we Sizwe	Spear of the Nation—the military wing of the ANC.
vakomana	Same meaning as *mukoma*—guerrilla fighters.
verkramp(te)	Afrikaans—too restrictive; a bigoted, narrow-minded person.
verligte	Afrikaans—more enlightened person, particularly concerning the liberalisation of the apartheid laws.
volk	Afrikaans—meaning folk.
Zvimbgawa-sungata	Shona—subservient or deferential to Whites; a traitor to his own people.

Acronyms

AIDS **Acquired Immune Deficiency Syndrome**—caused by the presence of *HIV*.

AK **Automat Kalashnikov**—rifle that became the standard weapon of the Soviet Army.

ANC **African National Congress (South Africa)**—founded in 1912 as a Black political party. Banned in 1961, and unbanned in February 1990. Its leader Nelson Mandela was appointed the first Black President of South Africa in April 1995.

African National Congress (Rhodesia)—founded in 1934 as a Black political party; was nearly defunct by 1952. Under new leadership from 1957, they attracted growing Black nationalist support. In February 1959, the ANC was banned. Undeterred, its leaders simply changed its name to the National Democratic Party (NDP). Then on 10 December 1961, the Rhodesian Government banned the NDP. Again the name was changed, this time to ZAPU—see below.

ARB **Afrikaner Regte Broederbond**—fictitious right-wing organisation in South Africa.

BOSS **Bureau of State Security**—the South African secret service; equivalent of the KGB.

CDC **Centres for Disease Control**—in Atlanta, US.

CIA **Central Intelligence Agency**—US secret service.

CIO **Central Intelligence Organisation**—Rhodesian secret service.

DCI **Director of Central Intelligence**—the head of the CIA.

FRELIMO **Front for the Liberation of Mozambique**—founded in 1962, as a coalition party in exile from three separate movements. Based initially in Tanzania, and later, led by Samora Machel, in March 1968 they re-entered Mozambique and occupied Tete Province in 1970. Mozambique, under the FRELIMO Government, celebrated independence in June 1975.

HIV **Human Immunodeficiency Virus**

OAU **Organisation of African Unity.**

RENAMO **Resistencia Nacional Mocambicana**—terrorist movement formed largely by former Black soldiers from the Portuguese Army in Mozambique. Fearing reprisals from FRELIMO, 40 men crossed into Rhodesia in June 1972, to become known as the fifth column in support of the Rhodesians. Later, in the eighties RENAMO was supported by the South Africans against the FRELIMO Government. RENAMO was also known as the National Resistance Movement (NRM) or, the Mozambique National Resistance (MNR).

RLI **Rhodesian Light Infantry**—White unit based at Cranborne Barracks, Salisbury, Rhodesia.

SAP **South African Police**

SAS **Special Air Services**—based on the British SAS; White Rhodesian paratroop unit based at Cranborne Barracks, Salisbury, Rhodesia.

UDI **Unilateral Declaration of Independence**—11 November 1965, the Smith régime in Rhodesia declared UDI, opting out of the Commonwealth and breaking ties with Britain.

ZANLA **Zimbabwe African National Liberation Army**—Military wing of ZANU. Operated out of Tanzania. Moved to Mozambique officially in March 1972. Robert Mugabe took over presidency of both organisations in 1974.

ZANU **Zimbabwe African National Union**—After breaking away from ZAPU, the Rev Ndabaningi Sithole, formed a new Black political party June 1963. Its HQ was based in Dar es Salaam. Later, led by Robert Mugabe through to, and after independence in April 1980.

ZAPU **Zimbabwe African People's Union**—(formerly the NDP). A Black political party finally banned in Rhodesia in September 1962. Moved HQ to Dar es Salaam, Tanzania, then later to Zambia. See the ANC (Rhodesia) above.

ZIPRA **Zimbabwe People's Revolutionary Army**—Military wing of ZAPU initially under Rev Ndabaningi Sithole and later Joshua Nkomo. Operated out of Zambia.

Biological Sequence

Pneumocystis carinii
(rodent)
    Animal form, first described in 1912—especially common in rodents.

Pneumocystis carinii
(human)
    Human form, first described by Van der Meer and Brug in 1942.

Marburg Virus
    First described in 1967—outbreak in a laboratory, Germany. First African case reported in 1975—contracted in Rhodesia.

Ebola Virus
    First described in 1976—outbreaks in Zaire and Sudan.

HIV
    Human Immunodeficiency Virus first described in 1979, resulting in the condition AIDS—Acquired Immune Deficiency Syndrome. Possibly around since the early sixties.

A hypothetical pathway for purposes of this narrative.
The solid boxes indicate actual pathogens and viruses; while the perforated boxes indicate the fictional pathogens and viruses.

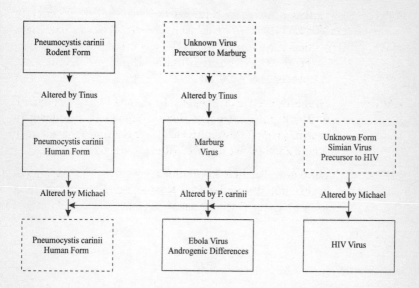